# FITZPATRICK'S
# WAR

# FITZPATRICK'S WAR

## THEODORE JUDSON

## DAW BOOKS, INC.

DONALD A. WOLLHEIM, FOUNDER

375 Hudson Street, New York, NY 10014

ELIZABETH R. WOLLHEIM

SHEILA E. GILBERT

PUBLISHERS

http://www.dawbooks.com

First Printing, August 2004

1   2   3   4   5   6   7   8   9

For my brother Tom and my nephews Brian, Zack and Jesse, all of whom are big fans of books about worlds that never were.

# FITZPATRICK'S WAR

"We would like to live as we once lived, but History will not permit it."

—President John F. Kennedy
From a speech given November 22, 1963
in Dallas, Texas

# Introduction to the Annotated Edition

*Doctor Professor Roland Modesty Van Buren*

The year of our Lord 2591 marks the fiftieth anniversary of the first publication of the manuscripts found in the private library of the celebrated antiquarian Sir Albert Makepeace McDonald. Among the books found in McDonald's collection upon his death in 2540 was *Fitzpatrick's War,* otherwise known as *The Early Life of Sir Robert Mayfair Bruce.* As was true of the other volumes in the eccentric McDonald's estate, the first edition of *Fitzpatrick's War* provoked enormous public reaction, albeit it and its brother texts did not measurably advance our knowledge of earlier periods in the Age of Steam. Millions of readers reared on Gerald's *The Age of Fitzpatrick*—still the standard text in most secondary schools—and on Miss Mary Anne Collins' epic poem *From the Atlantic to the Pacific* were shocked to read accounts of Yukon soldiers disobeying their supposedly deranged supreme commander and of other soldiers having relationships with foreign women. Bruce's portrait of the Fitzpatrick family so disturbed the Confederacy that seven members of the Senate sued (unsuccessfully) the original publisher for slander in 2543. But nothing in Bruce's book outraged right-thinking people more than the assertion that the Order of Timermen was involved in Lord Fitzpatrick the Younger's untimely death. That the noble Fitzpatrick, who set men's hearts and pagan cities aflame,[1] could have been killed by the Confederacy's most exalted

---

1. Collins, *From the Atlantic to the Pacific,* Book II, line 1437 (Downs and Sons Press, Grand Harbor City.)

order was more than the public could endure. I still remember that in my little village in Northfield there were old veterans who swore they would challenge this liar Bruce in court, only to discover that the liar in question had been dead for more than two decades. I also recall newspaper stories of angry young ladies making pilgrimages to Bruce's grave site outside Astoria, Columbus, for the sole purpose of spitting on Bruce's headstone. Even in these times Bruce's book provokes strong emotions. When it became generally known among my colleagues at St. Matthew's University that I was preparing a new edition of the liar's book, the Lord Dean of the History and Other Literatures Department took me aside one day during afternoon tea and asked me man to man, "Look here, Ro, do you really need to be blowing old cinders into new holocausts?"

Therefore, let me declare before I sojourn too far *in res* I most certainly do *not* accept the whole or any part of Bruce's account as Historic fact. Unlike real Historians, Bruce consistently strives for sensation and does not instruct his readers in virtue. Recent research has proven beyond all reasonable objection that Bruce was a disappointed, albeit brave, soldier; it can further be stated with no fear of serious contradiction that he possessed a violent temper, which can be a valuable quality in one who holds a rifle but leads to folly when that same person wields a fountain pen. Bruce was clearly one of those "worker bees jealous of the queen," as one writer has put it.[2] Worse than that, he was obviously overly infatuated with his wife, the lustful and lowborn daughter of a saloon owner, and she—as he himself admits in his book—led Bruce into his vilest mistakes. Often insubordinate and as often frustrated in his efforts to secure a higher rank, Bruce probably wrote his book as a sort of revenge against the great Fitzpatrick, a man in every way his better.

Why then, as the freshman in the famous anecdote demands, should we read this book? The answer of course is that just as Plato taught us that pleasure comes from having known pain, and as St. Augustine demonstrate that redemption arises from knowing sin, the great philosopher and Historian Murrey has shown that know-

2. From *The Liar from Arcadia* by James Rawlings Sherman, Brown Bear Press, Southfield, page 22, 2580 ed. For additional criticism of Bruce, see *Defending Honor* by Helen Johnson Smith, *Against Bruce and Satan* by Meredith Anne Stout, *His Wife's Slave* by Mary Hopeful Carter, and *Bruce's Errors* by John Evans Rogers, among many others.

ing truth comes from being familiar with lies; indeed, truth could not exist without its opposite.[3] Rest depends upon exertion, gratification upon denial, victory upon defeat, and the future upon the past. If the great Murrey (who was, as we all know, one of young Fitzpatrick's instructors, and thus appears in Bruce's fanciful story) could accept the proposition that he could grasp the truth only by knowing its opposite, then we can do no better. Even novice scholars must start with the premise that there are certain master thinkers who cannot be challenged, but only appreciated and, in rare instances, improved upon. Therefore, by confronting Bruce's outlandish exaggerations we can discern the excellence of the accepted accounts of Fitzpatrick's life.

### A Note on the Manuscript

There were two copies of the Bruce book in the McDonald collection. One, written in longhand and containing a host of misspellings and corrupt usages, is probably the older of the two and was once assumed to have been written by Bruce himself or by an amanuensis to whom Bruce dictated. The weight of evidence indicates that in fact this handwritten version is a copy created by an unknown soldier attached to the 105th Long Range Bomber Group stationed at Ft. Lewis and Clark in Columbus, which was near the village Bruce made his home during his retirement.[4] Presumably, the unknown scribe presented the copied book to McDonald, as Sir Albert was from 2510 to 2518 a squadron commander within the 105th.

The first page of the handwritten version is missing. Because the first page surely bore a dedication to the local Lord in Astoria, a Lord who had refused to print the book when Bruce presented it to him in 2490, certain people with strong romantic natures but feeble educations would have us believe Bruce ripped the dedication from the manuscript after the rejection. It is more likely the missing first page was simply lost at a later date.

The second copy is typewritten and has been edited, perhaps by McDonald or his secretary. This second version is complete and

---

3. See *On Existence*, Book I, numerous editions.

4. See "Notes on the McDonald Collection," Terrance Jane Hartman, *Literary Studies,* Vol. XCIII, Issue 2, Feb. 2588.

consequently is the version used in most printed editions, including this one.

Bruce grew up speaking the rough dialect of the rural Pacific Northwest. In spite of his education at the War College and thirty-nine years of military service in the company of well-born gentlemen, in his dotage he sometimes reverted to the corrupt tongue he learned as a boy in the logging camps and farms of his native Columbus. Wherever his language is incomprehensible to the modern reader I have substituted the contemporary equivalents. This, I hope, does not do too much violence to the original.

We can only guess at McDonald's motives when he decided to preserve Bruce's book. He was, as we used to say at school, "an odd number," and did not need a particularly good reason to save a strange manuscript. The Lord God knows Sir Albert saved dozens of other unusual works, some of which are as offensive as *Fitzpatrick's War*. It has been suggested that, like Bruce, McDonald was a lowborn soldier who, again like Bruce, became a Knight of the Field, and for that reason Sir Albert felt a certain kinship with Sir Robert, although they were men of different generations.[5] At any rate, it can be said of the eccentric collector that at least he kept his books to himself, while Bruce would have thrown his work before the entire world.

Sir Albert's nephew Donald Warrior Evens discovered the two versions, but they would not have seen publication so quickly if in 2541 had there not been another intellectual movement to further discredit the hated Shay regime. The St. George University Press made the much regretted decision to print the entire McDonald collection, some parts of which did reflect poorly upon the Shays and their cohorts, though the majority of the volumes dealt with other eras of Yukon History. Among the then newly published volumes, only *The Memoirs of Tri Ogallala*,[6] the notorious tale written by a degenerate American living in the mid-twenty-first century before the Storm Times, caused more consternation among the righteous. Would that the editors of St. George University Press had shown better judgment fifty years

---

5. Ibid.

6. St. George University Press, Midtown, 2541. The entire McDonald collection is available in nine volumes.

ago,[7] but now that the forbidden fruit has been eaten, or—more aptly—once Pandora's Box has been opened, there can be no return to blissful ignorance. We have the document before us, and we cannot ignore it; rather it is our duty to guide the uninitiated reader past Bruce's misstatements and highlight his insights, such as they are.

### The Life of Sir Robert Mayfair Bruce

We know very little of Bruce's life beyond what he tells us in his book. Records at the War College, always exquisitely accurate, tell us he entered the famed Seventh Infantry Division (then as now known as the Sparrows) of Columbus Province in June of 2411. He was then sixteen years old and the son of a forester. His father had once served in the same famed division, wherein the elder Bruce had reached the rank of sergeant major after seven years of service. After completing the standard twelve-year tour under arms, Bruce's father had chosen a position under his Liege Lord rather than a continued commission in the Confederate Army. Young Robert must have been a successful student in his village school, for he was a cadet soldier when he enlisted and was marked for higher rank when he became older. He had equaled his father's old rank of sergeant by the time he was eighteen.

Young Robert was fortunate to serve in one of the numerous wars that have and will always take place from time to time along the Mexican border. He won his Knighthood of the Field for acts of exemplary bravery at the Pass of the North in 2412, and once the Latin hordes were again driven south Bruce was allowed to attend the War College in Centralia City, as is recorded in the book. Sir Robert graduated third in his class, after only the young Fitzpatrick and Sir Jeremiah Truth Hood. Sir Robert was commissioned as a captain of the engineers in 2417 and quickly rose in rank, at first because of his valuable service as a field technician and later for his courageous performance in the Four Points War. At the age of twenty-seven, Sir Robert was a colonel during the glorious times when the Yukon Confederacy exerted a direct hegemony over the entire globe. He worked for Fitzpatrick in the Andaman

---

7. The reader should not imagine I am being condescending to St. George, which remains to this day fundamentally an engineering school. I am certain that, all in all, there are some learned scholars there. I cannot say what it was like in 2541.

Islands and elsewhere in 2423 and 2424. The years 2425 and 2426 found him stationed in a remote part of Africa. It was during this period immediately after the Four Points War that Bruce became disaffected with Fitzpatrick and came to look upon the young Consul as an Oriental tyrant. While most writers have seen Fitzpatrick as a shining star in the Yukon firmament, Bruce is not the only man to accuse the stupendously successful Consul of megalomania.[8] Still, it remains unlikely in the extreme for a hero such as Fitzpatrick to act as Mason or Bruce say he did. We do have to concede that Gerald mentions Bruce favorably;[9] the great Historian, who lived and wrote before Bruce's book appeared, went so far as to call the young Bruce "one of the unheralded heroes of the Four Points War." Bruce seems to have clashed with Fitzpatrick in 2426, yet he was readmitted to the Consul's inner circle later that same year. He was promoted to brigadier and soon was put in charge of his Consul's personal guard. In light of what soon came to pass, we may safely aver that Bruce failed miserably in this assignment. He was briefly detained by army authorities after Fitzpatrick's death, but was quickly declared not guilty of any complicity in the great man's demise. At his own request, he went to a remote post in the southwest, where he served in obscurity for another twenty-three years. Upon his retirement he returned to the Columbus countryside and lived there with his wife until he died on January 17, 2519, reportedly while asleep at the family estate in Astoria.

Bruce married Charlotte Purity Raft, a woman of even lower birth than he, when they were both the proper age of twenty-five. If we are to believe Bruce's account, they had a happy union throughout their many years together. (What is obvious from his book—and this we may indeed believe—is that Charlotte had an exceedingly strong influence upon him. It would not be going too far to state that the loyalty he felt for her displaced in his heart the

8. See, if you dare, Mason's lurid account in *My Career,* also by St. George University Press, 2541. Lord Anthony Waverly Mason was, of course, a long-time member of Fitzpatrick's inner circle. Bruce mentions him several times. Mason's depiction of Fitzpatrick and his times remains available only in the restrained version. Families having young children or impressionable young women among their members should not allow Mason's book within the household walls, as it is the product of a diseased imagination.

9. *The Age of Fitzparick,* chap. 104.

loyalty he should have felt for Fitzpatrick.) They had five daughters and a son. None of the Bruce daughters disgraced herself, which is the highest compliment anyone can pay a woman. The son became an engineer as his father had been. Some interviews conducted with elderly residents in Bruce's native Astoria cast some additional light upon his character, and I will deal with a particularly enlightening example in my afterword.

We deduce Bruce wrote his memoirs late in his life, and that someone else close to him at Ft. Lewis and Clark obtained the text directly from his hand. Then, as noted above, someone else passed the book on to McDonald.

Time has now delivered his writing to us. May God grant us the wisdom to obtain some good from reading it.

### *Acknowldgments*

I wish, of course, to thank first the University Liege Lord, Doctor Professor Henry Johnston Perriwig: may God grant him peace and prosperity, and may He give to the same to all within my Lord's family. Thank you, my Lord, for letting me toil upon your campus.

Many thanks are extended to Colonel Reginald Earnest Dodge, C.A., ret., for allowing me to use the War College's library. You, my old friend, made my work progress smoothly.

I extend my gratitude to Mr. John Bishop, graduate student, who proofread the final text nine times. I grant the same to Jim, my secretary, and to the young cleaning girl Jim found to help me translate Bruce's northwestern vulgarities into polite English. I would thank the child by name, but I seem to have forgotten what it was.

Doctor Professor Roland Modesty Van Buren
Master of the History and Other Literatures Department
St. Matthew's University, 2591 A.D.

# Original Dedication

To my Lord Luke Churchman Prim-Jones,
Liege Lord and Protector of Astoria, Columbus Province,
Yukon Confederacy, God's Earthly Kingdom:

May goodness and mercy follow you all your days,
and may the same be bestowed upon your family.
May God also allow you to accept for publication
this book written by your loyal Knight,

SIR ROBERT MAYFAIR BRUCE.

Much is written here, my Lord, I know will offend you, for this is the record of great crimes, both the crimes of others and those in which I played my shameful part. Too long the youth within our schools have learned only the vainglorious stories their elders have presented to them concerning the age of Fitzpatrick the Younger and the war he waged upon a hapless world. These stories have been told for so long and so often that those born too late to have personal memories of those times have come to believe that those who were criminals in those days were actually heroes and that those who were the real heroes failed to do their proper duties. In my ninety-second year of life I have set down this true record of everything I did and knew during those terrible years so I might begin to correct the glorious lies that have for sixty years warped our History.

I realize much of what I have written reflects horribly upon me. These events happened when I was young, and when I was a young man I was a moral coward and a fool at all I put my hand to, save at fighting and civil engineering. Some crimes committed in those days happened without my knowing of them. Much else that happened I pretended not to know. In the green times of my youth I cared only for my noble friends and the potential future I thought my actions would gain for me. My pursuit of glory made me blind to the suffering of others. There came and went several occasions in my life when had I but spoken a few brave words, I might have saved the lives of millions. I was too afraid for my own miserable life and too desperate to be a great man to say or do what I should have. Fool that I was in those years, I knew even then I had done I great wrongs. For all the years of my life I have been wounded by the failures of my youth. Now that I am an old man I know I cannot go to my grave without admitting to the world what I did.

In the six decades I have carried my guilt with me I have prayed each day to be forgiven and for the terrible burden I have carried to be lifted from my conscience. In those years I have not harmed another human being. I have striven to help those in need, and I have loved my good wife and my children as best I could. I pray that God, being infinite in His love, has forgiven me. I cannot forgive myself, not even now that I have confessed my bloody deeds in this book. I only wish, my Lord, I had told this story sooner and better than I have. If you read this and decide I should be punished for my sins, I will accept your judgment. There are dark secrets at the core of our society, and I will run any risk I must if I can now bring those secrets into the light.

# ONE

I FIRST MET Isaac Prophet Fitzpatrick in 2415 when we both were students in the same class at the War College in Centralia City. During my first two and a half years there he and I were not acquainted. As a common soldier and cadet born of common parents, I resided in the plebe barracks even after I had become an upperclassman, while Fitz and the other *Basileis*[1] lived in a private dorm atop University Heights. I had seen him in the several classes we both attended and from across the parade grounds during our morning drills. I of course had not dared to speak directly to him. It would have been extraordinarily presumptuous of me to have imposed myself upon him. Even had I been closer to his station, I still would have been too much in awe of his person to have conversed with him.

In the university mess he ate at the head table with those friends of his who would one day be famous in their own right: Valette, Hood, O'Brian, Pularski, Stein, Shelley, Mason, and Davis. The vivacious, strikingly handsome Valette was always seated to Fitz's right, the bearded Hood to his left. His entire group endlessly conversed of politics, war, and History, and each of them—save for Pularski, who remained silent unless spoken to—spoke at once, gesturing with his hands as they strove to gain young Fitzpatrick's attention. The rest of the cadets, dressed in their gray, high-collared uniforms, had to sit straight-backed at the other tables and say nothing while they ate, but from Fitz's group there al-

---

1. βασιλεις "the kings of men." The nickname of Fitzpatrick's inner circle of companions was a sly reference to Alexander's close companions.

ways arose a spring of laughter and loud exclamations that washed over the rest of the vast dining hall. The *Basileis* were permitted wine at their table at evening meal, which caused their commotion to become more animated and louder the longer they sat.

No matter how spirited the other talkers at his table became, they would shut their mouths when Fitz chose to speak. He was tall, as slender as a thoroughbred racer, and so boyishly handsome was he that his long, straight nose and fine blond hair made one think of the Highsmith painting of young King Arthur.[2] He spoke in an even, careful voice that carried through the entire mess, and for his sake the rest of the cadets would stop eating to listen. Everyone of course knew his father was Commander of all the Yukon Armies and Consul of the Senate and thus the most powerful man in the world, yet the other cadets and I showed deference to Fitz not merely because of his family; we admired Fitz for his perfect manners, for his knowledge of History, for his mastery of the Greek and Latin classics, for the courage he displayed on the training fields when the cadets were made to fight with wooden rifles,[3] but above all else we respected him because we knew even then he would one day rise to his father's position and soon thereafter would surpass that great man in stature and in glory. How each of us envied his companions and wished we too could but sit at his table and have him smile directly upon us! I was as vain as the rest of them and thought there would be nothing better in the entire world than to have the young Lord's friendship.

During my first five semesters at the War College I had to wait on tables in the great mess hall in return for my meals. The other lowborn cadets and I ate only after the young Lords had set down their trays and commenced their dinners. I did not wait upon the

---

2. Harold Early Highsmith, principal figure in the Renaissance Revival of the twenty-second century; best remembered for his mannerly, almost two-dimensional paintings that were somewhat reminiscent of Giotto. His *Young King Arthur* hangs in the Confederacy Gallery in Cumberland.

3. I should note for the sake of female readers and boys not yet old enough for military service that mock hand-to-hand fighting with wooden rifles can become quite brutal. During the year 2590, for example, no fewer than eighteen young men were beaten to death at Yukon military training camps and schools. In actual combat soldiers almost never get close enough to the enemy to use rifle butt and bayonet; the wooden rifle drill is performed to toughen the soldiers and Blue Jackets mentally and physically and not to sharpen any particular combat skill.

*Basileis* table as they were served by teams of young women from Fitz's household. On most evenings I was too far from them to catch all of what he and his friends were saying. Like everyone else I yearned to eavesdrop upon them. I may have not come from a great family, but my mother and father were respectable people and had impressed upon me a sense of propriety, and I knew it would be rude of me to linger too close to him and the other young Lords. Thus I heard only snatches of what Fitz had to say. Nor did the other waiters and I look directly at him, except when we had brought all the food out and had returned to the kitchen and from there could peek through the swinging doors at his table on the other side of the hall.

One Tuesday evening in early December, after I had taken a civil engineering exam that had lasted an hour past the normal end of the period, I had rushed to the mess hall still in my uniform. Mr. Marcello, the head cook, swore at me for being late and told me I did not have time to change into my solid white server's clothes. He tossed me a long butcher's apron and told me to clear tables instead of taking out meals.

"There is no time," he said. "Paul is taking your place. Quick, quick: get out there!"

As the exam I came from had been a final, I was wearing my cadet uniform with the horse head silhouette and the silver rose sewn on my shoulder patches.[4] The underclassmen at my customary tables had seen my decorations before; they did not so much as look up at me when I brought away their dirty dishes. I was balancing a stack of nine platters in my left hand and reaching for another with my right when a commotion erupted across the wide hall, but I did not look that way until I had all the tableware balanced in my firm grip. Upon glancing in the direction of the sudden noise I saw Lord Fitzpatrick standing from his chair above his unfinished dinner. How astonished I was to see that he was looking straight across the tables at me and was saying something to his companions. The two thousand other cadets in the hall noticed he was out of his chair and dropped

---

4. On special occasions, such as open house and exams, decorated veterans at the War College are allowed to wear their embellished tunics. Bruce is not only wearing the horse head chess piece that marks him as a Knight of the Field but likewise the Rose for Valor, which he also seems to have won on the Mexican border.

their knives and forks atop their chipped beef and toast to stand with him. In less than a half a minute one could not hear a single piece of silverware click against a single plate of china. Everyone was at attention, silently shifting their eyes from me to him and wondering what I had done to offend the normally sedate Lord Fitzpatrick.

"You!" Fitz called to me. "Come here, my friend!"

My legs felt as if they were made of porridge. With four thousand eyes following my progress, I crossed the wide hall and stood at attention an arm's length in front of him. Until that day I did not have a single demerit point on my record. Now I feared I had done something to offend the Consul's son and was about to receive a reprimand that would end my time at the college.

Fitz walked around me and examined the emblems on my shoulder.

"God bless, Val," he said to his friend Valette. "You were right! He *is* a Knight! Your name, sir?" he said to me.

"Cadet Sir Robert Mayfair Bruce, your Lordship."

"Robert the Bruce," interjected the chubby Mason.[5]

"Is that meant to be a joke?" Fitz asked him.

Fitz would tilt his head a bit when he addressed Mason, a mannerism Mason alone provoked in him.

"No disrespect intended, Fitz," said Lord Mason. "That's what he's called among the junior cadets. He's not even a White Raven.[6] He's a Nor'wester from Columbus. He had the book in Advanced Trig last spring, by the by. Not bad for a sophomore."

"You had the book in Mechanical Engineering as well, did you not, sir?" asked Hood.

Sir Jeremiah Truth Hood was the oldest cadet at the War College. He was over forty and wore a full sergeant's beard to cover the facial scars he had earned in India. Almost as tall as the six-foot-five-inch Fitzpatrick, Hood had watery eyes and a rigid mouth that did not reveal his emotions in conversation or in battle. He had not yet commanded a unit larger than a brigade, yet he was known to

---

5. Bruce's nickname at college refers to an ancient king of Scotland.

6. i.e., Bruce is not even from Scotland. The White Raven is, as most readers will know, the standard of the celebrated First Highland Division. In the colloquial terms of the day, all Scots were called such.

be the best soldier at the college and one superior in field tactics and courage even to Fitz.[7]

"None of you complained to the dons that he was cleaning tables in mess?" Fitz asked.

His companions did not reply. They knew better than to answer him when he was angry. All of his companions, including the fierce-looking Hood and Pularski, diverted their eyes rather than meet his glance.

"My friend," said Fitz to me, and actually condescended to touch my forearm, "I apologize for this outrage. I have seen you on campus and in the mess. I did not make the connection until now. I must be an absolute dullard. Please forgive me. Believe me when I tell you I never would have allowed you to be demeaned in this fashion if I had known."

To one of his serving maids he said, "Alice, tell the cook Marcello to get out here this instant."

Fitz told me to take off my apron while the maid ran to the kitchen. The other two thousand cadets were still standing as stiff as ramrods, waiting for Fitz to sit back down. I was very embarrassed to be the focus of so much attention.

Mr. Marcello charged through the swinging doors like a comet. He was a middle-aged, heavyset man, and was terrified to think young Lord Fitzpatrick was angry because of something in his mess hall. By the time he had run across the room his breathing sounded like the pant of a locomotive and his face was as red as his tongue.

"Lord Fitzpatrick, Lord Fitzpatrick," he was chanting as he ran, "if this boy has done anything . . . Bobby, what have you—"

The whole room gasped when Fitz slapped his face and Marcello staggered backward.

"He is *Sir* Robert to you!" Fitz told him. "Call him by his familiar name again, and I will set your fat backside on a stick![8] Now,

---

7. Sir Jeremiah Truth Hood, later Marshal of the Army, may not have been quite as remarkable a man as Fitzpatrick the Younger, but he certainly was among the outstanding men of the age. In 2415 he was in fact forty-six years old and an ordained minister. Other than a year in a seminary and his time in a village school, Hood had no formal education but had managed in twenty-nine years of service to rise from private to brigadier general; twice Knighted for bravery, Hood was in 2412 chosen by Fitzpatrick the Elder to attend the War College in preparation for promotion to higher rank.

8. A crude manner of saying he would have the cook impaled.

maggot, you will explain to me why you have a Knight doing a serving maid's job!"

Marcello fell to his knees and pled with folded hands as he sobbed, "Lord Fitzpatrick, dear Lord Fitzpatrick, I was doing the young gentleman a favor. I let the young gentleman eat for nothing and in return he—"

"I see," said Fitz, "you take advantage of a Knight of the Field, a war hero, because you know he is poor. You get free help, and that is a bit more of the dining budget you can pocket for your own use."

Confronted by the son of the most powerful man in the world and seeing no way to save himself, poor Marcello at that juncture disgraced himself. A yellow stain ran down the leg of his white chef's pants and onto the mess hall floor.

"You are a pig," said Fitz and turned his gaze away. "Get out of our sight."

"The lady doth piss too much," said Valette as Marcello scrambled back to his kitchen.

The younger men at Fitz's table had a good laugh at Marcello's expense, and their laughter spread to the cadets standing nearby. The underclassmen on the other side of the wide room could not hear what Valette had said or see what Marcello had done; they could see that Fitz and his friends were laughing, so they laughed just to be on the safe side. Fitz allowed himself an archaic smile[9] and sat back down in his chair. He pushed his palms downward as a signal to the other two thousand cadets, who likewise sat down and began eating again.

"Gwendolyn," Fitz called to one of the girls standing behind him, "prepare Sir Robert a place at our table. He will be dining with us from now on."

"My Lord . . . I cannot," I stammered. "I could not possibly afford—"

"Nonsense," he said and pointed to an empty space his companions had made for me. "I will take care of everything. Please sit. And we're all peers here. Therefore, I would like you to call me 'Fitz.' Should I call you 'Robert' or some other name?"

---

9. I would guess Bruce means the small, fixed smile common to the earliest Greek statues. Naturally, it would have been unseemly for a Consul's son to laugh aloud as lesser men do.

"Yes, my Lord, it is Robert," I said, still standing at attention. "Yes, 'Fitz.'"

He was amused that I was having such difficulty in enunciating that one-syllable word.

"Yes . . ." I closed my eyes and forced my mouth to shape the word. "Fitz."

"There now. You see, it didn't kill you, Robert," said Fitz. "Now, sit. Right there beside old Buck. That's a good fellow."

My heart was palpitating, and I fear my brow was slick with perspiration, yet my legs took me to the chair, and I sat. At that moment I felt I was too excited to eat anything.

"You have to realize," continued Fitz, "most of these birds of paradise you are sitting with are not here simply because of their family names.[10] We don't allow anyone into the *Basileis* unless they deserve to be here. Every chap you see here—excepting Mason—has done good service under arms. Hood and Buck are both commoners like yourself."

"Buck," as Pularski was called, was, like Hood, older than the average cadet at the War College. He was twenty-six then and already his fine light brown hair had receded a couple inches from the top of his forehead. He looked at up me when Fitz said his name, and finding nothing in me that interested him he frowned and turned his quartz-blue eyes back to his plate. This remarkable man had lost his right hand in a farming accident when he was a child; he had nonetheless joined the Army when he was two years underage,[11] and had learned to fire a rifle using his good left hand to manipulate the trigger and his mechanical right hand to hold the stock. In ten years on the western frontier of our Indian allies he

---

10. Although the Yukon Constitution of 2081 had called for the election of Lords, within decades of the Storm Times a young man born into a Lordly family could expect to inherit his father's position. District and local Liege Lords were still elected in the twenty-fifth century, much as they are today, but in Bruce's time the elections were largely *pro forma*. A prominent family or families within a given district could expect to hold the offices of Lord and Senator generation after generation. Exceptions to this corrupt custom were found in the military and the church, wherein promotion was dependent on merit; common soldiers and sailors who completed their twelve years of duty sometimes received land in the frontier districts directly from the Army or Navy. Thus they looked upon the military as a type of "Liege Lord." These abuses were not ended until the fall of the Shay regime.

11. i.e., when he was fourteen.

had killed more Moslem raiders than there were hairs remaining on his head. The battle stripes on his sleeve reached from the Knight's decoration on his shoulder to the top of his cuff. Out of Fitz's companions at college Buck was the only one not there to learn how to lead men; he did take classes, and with help he managed to graduate on time, but he really was there to protect Fitz. Up his left sleeve Buck carried a nine millimeter machine pistol loaded with ultra-high-velocity exploding bullets. With a flick of his wrist a spring mechanism would snap the weapon into his hand. Above his left shoe he wore a second pistol in a calf holster. A third was in a belt holster underneath his tunic, next to two small percussion grenades. If anyone made a threatening move toward Lord Fitzpatrick, Buck would have had the fool's soul flying out of his mouth before the would-be assassin's face hit the floor. Whenever a serving girl brought something from the kitchen, she and Buck would taste it before Fitz ate or drank from the same vessel, although Buck never drank much alcohol, as he wished to stay alert.

The serving girl Gwendolyn returned from the section of the kitchen Fitz's servants used and sat in front of me a plate of curried lamb on rice—a recipe Fitz had gathered in Asia—and a glass of bright red wine. The girls were all dressed in green velveteen dresses for the Christmas season, and when Gwen bent forward over my place setting the fullness of her breasts pushed against her outfit's deep neckline. She had long hair that she tied at the nape of her pink-white neck, and she smelled like fresh vanilla. Being a callow boy who knew nothing of women, I could not help but gawk at her. She must have noticed my errant gaze for she blushed down to the green neckline.

"The scenery is better at this table, eh, Robby?" asked Mason.

The group laughed as one at my embarrassment.

"Don't get too excited, old man," said Valette. "The young ladies are strictly off limits. Like Moses, we may glimpse the promised land, but we may not enter."

"A little tease, aren't we, Gwen?" said Mason to the girl.

"If you say so, my Lord," she said and made a shallow curtsy to him.

"That will be enough," said Fitz. "Gwen's people have been with my family for three generations. She is a good Christian girl, far too good to have to endure any nonsense from anyone."

"Thank you, my Lord Fitzpatrick," she said and bowed her head deeply to him before returning to her place among the other servants.

These young women from Fitz's household were, I would learn, a privileged group. Unlike some of those dirty-minded Lords one reads about in the gutter press, the sort of high-born men who keep young female servants to gratify their base desires, Fitz treated his girls with the greatest respect and never demanded they do anything other than wait upon himself and his companions and that they attend church on Sunday and Bible study every Wednesday night. They dressed in Nippon silk and gold brocade from Africa and were allowed the privacy of their own secluded quarters when they were not on duty. One of Fitz's greatest gifts was his ability to be at ease with everyone, be they base or noble, and he could visit his serving girls in their rooms and sit at tea with them and discuss clothes and the latest romance novels and share their small jokes with the same facility he demonstrated when he discussed world affairs with his companions. Each of those he spoke to felt as if his attentions were real. When the girls reached the age of twenty-five and could marry, Fitz saw to it that they each wed a respectable young man blessed with a steady income. Until that time came, they followed him everywhere, except when he was abroad. During the course of his short lifetime, there were men in his circle who would desert Fitz; each of us questioned his motives at one time or another, but his serving maids were always loyal. They would have died for him, had he demanded it of them. They believed that if the situation demanded it, he would do no less for them.

"You will enjoy this, Robert," said Fitz, holding his glass up to the gas light to examine the ruby purity of the wine. "It comes from my father's estate in the Meadowlands. You have had wine before, haven't you?"

"Yes, my Lord, at Communion," I said.

Fitz and his friends had another laugh at my innocence. Because I laughed with them they said I was a good fellow and drank to my health.

"Well, we drink it more often than that," said Fitz. "I take it you served under Reynolds."

"Yes, your Lordship."

"Please, please," he insisted, "you must call me 'Fitz.'"

"Yes, Fitz," I said.

"Poor brave chap," commented Stein. (Or "Banker" Stein, as they called him, alluding to his father's supposed millions.)[12] "Reynolds made more widows than heroes."

"Reynolds is an ass," agreed Fitz. "He is one of my godfathers, a friend of my father's, but then most of my father's cronies are asses. By the wounded Christ, the damned fool tried to fight set-piece battles against the bloody ragtag Mexicans! In the desert, mind you, and on a two-thousand-mile border! If it weren't for Pendleton, we would be trying to get the dagos in battle formation this very day!"[13]

Fitz, who had been the image of lighthearted good spirits a moment earlier, now was as somber as a minister. Once he started on the subject of war, Fitz could hold forth like Livy, calling out names and numbers to support his arguments, mapping geography on a table top or a dormitory floor, and retelling centuries of battles in a few terse sentences. Early in our acquaintance I thought him slightly deranged when he gave himself up to his harangues on strategy and geopolitics. After I had come to know him better, I would realize Fitz was never out of control during his early years; everything he said or did was carefully planned, and his apparent wild spontaneity had been rehearsed before a mirror long before he displayed it to us.

"Who are our allies in the world, Robert?" he asked me.

"We have only four . . . Fitz," I said. "The Slav remnant, the Ethiopians, the Philippines, and India."

---

12. Lord Peter Paul Stein's father, Lord Matthew Mark Stein, was actually a general of modest means. Peter's pet name is meant to be ironic. We may reject the notion that the nickname "Banker" is somehow an anti-Semitic slur referring to supposed Jews in Stein's family tree. The *Basileis* were young gentlemen, and gentlemen do not make vulgar slurs. Nor, for that matter, would gentlemen associate with anyone they suspected of being partly Jewish.

13. Lord Patience Virtue Reynolds (2356–2422), Marshal of the Second Army during the 2411–2412 campaign. Young Bruce, it would seem, had served under his command. Tyron Switchel Pendleton (2334–2441), considered to be a master of anti-guerilla warfare, was Reynolds's second-in-command and is generally credited with winning the victory for his commanding officer.

It is extremely doubtful that Fitzpatrick the Younger would ever have spoken so disdainfully of another Lord. Here and elsewhere we have to be suspicious of the quotes Bruce attributes to the young nobleman.

"Yes. But it was an easy question. Now: which of the four is the most important?"

"I suppose Hindustan—"

"Absolutely," he said and struck the table with his fist. "India is the key to the entire world."

"We aren't going to discuss India again, are we?" asked Valette, the one member of the inner circle who could challenge Fitz.

"I'm sounding out Robert on this," said the Consul's son. "And, yes, I want to talk about India again."

He drained his wineglass and sat it on his right, immediately at hand. He placed a pepper shaker also on his right, but at arm's length from him. He positioned his entree plate right in front of him. Near to hand on his left he placed Hood's wine glass, and farther out he sat the salt shaker.

"Imagine this shaker," he said, pointing to the shaker on his left, "represents the British Isles, the easternmost province in the Yukon Confederacy."

"I think a glass of ice water would better represent Britain," said Mason.

"Hush, Tony. The adults are speaking," continued Fitz. "Now, say this wineglass on my left is our air base in Bioko, just off the west coast of Africa and three thousand miles due south of Britain. The other wineglass on my right is Australia, the Yukon Confederacy's westernmost province, seventy-two hundred miles east of Bioko. The pepper shaker, three thousand and four hundred miles north of Australia, represents the Batan Islands."

"Pardon me, sir," I said. "I am not familiar with that place."

"You will be one day," said Fitz. "They are an obscure group north of the Philippines in the Luzon Strait. Itbayat is the largest among them; it's nearly uninhabited, and is best suited for our purposes. This big plate in the middle of my arrangement is the vast Hindu nation of India, the world's exemplar of spiritual perfection and physical degradation.

"Another question for you, Robert: Who are our two most formidable enemies? And don't mention those pathetic Latins we chase across our southern border every thirty years or so."

"That would be the Turks and the Chinese, sir," I said.

"Correct again," said Fitz, becoming more demonstrative as his monologue progressed. "A bright lad. We will get along splendidly, provided you stop calling me 'sir.'"

He took his tableware and the forks, knives and spoons of his neighbors, and using the plate as his starting point he laid out a metal web that connected the plate with the shakers and wineglasses.

"Each of these four lines of utensils represents a little more than three thousand miles," he explained. "If we had a system of air bases in each of these five places, we could cover the entire extent of both the Chinese and Turkish empires. Add the bases we already have along the Grand River and in the Falklands, and we would have coverage of the entire non-Yukon world."

"Begging your pardon . . . Fitz," I said. "What are we going to cover the world with? The only plane that has that kind of range is the Florin Bomber."[14]

"That's it!" exclaimed Fitz, pointing his finger at me. "You win the Turk's Nose!"[15]

"But, your Lordship—that is, Fitz," I said, "there are treaties—I believe your father the Consul signed some of them—forbidding production of long-range bombers like the Florin."

"True enough," he conceded, "and it is also true the Chinese are this very moment building thousands of them. My father has commenced the construction of two thousand of the same kind of behemoths for the Yukon Air Corps. Not nearly enough, and they are obsolete anyway."

"Aren't there other treaties prohibiting the building of new air bases in India and the Pacific, s—, I mean, Fitz?" I said. "Big bombers would need bigger airfields."

The second after the words left my lips I realized I was being overly bold to challenge him in this manner. He was not, however, upset with me, only a little disappointed.

"If treaties lasted forever, we would never have any more wars," he sighed. "I fear you are thinking like my father, Robert, which is

---

14. Named after the engineer who designed it, the Florin Bomber was actually a copy of a Chinese plane captured during the First Pacific War. The Florin was a lumbering giant of a plane that owed its seven thousand mile range to its gigantic—and highly vulnerable—fuel tanks. By the time of the Four Points War the Florin was considered an obsolete relic that was too slow, too difficult to control, and unable to elude enemy fighter planes.

15. A tag line from a popular child's guessing game; it means: "You have given the winning answer."

no insult; my father is a great man, or so I have been told since I was old enough to hear. Old Yukon Lords like my father want to have their farms and their little country towns; they want to go hunting Saturday morning, visit their mistresses on Saturday night, and go to church with their wives on Sunday morning. Excluding the pious ones. The pious ones among the old Lords think like farmers; they only want to go to church and to war. To little wars, of course. Defensive wars on the high seas and on the Mexican border, little wars they know they will win. They want their sons to follow after them and live the same lives they have lived and to fight the same little wars. Old Lords like my father know there are higher matters in the universe, and they are content to leave them to the church and the Timermen. Each of us at this table could inherit, if we wanted, our fathers' lives. A brilliant engineer like you, Robert, is destined to reach a station much higher than any your father knew. If you don't choose to become a Timerman—and I promise you, Robert, they will approach you—you will become, in time, a senior officer.[16] If you are sufficiently obedient and sufficiently unimaginative, you could one day become one of those juvenile legends they put in grammar school readers and so become one with Horatio and Captain Harris.[17] Then, when you are old, you could retire to your country estate and sit beneath the cottonwood trees and write your memoirs, just as Xenophon did, you will tell yourself.

"Or, my new friend, you could forget about living for your father and forget about irrelevant minutiae such as treaties and the thousand little wars that will supposedly keep us strong for three thousand years,[18] as my father is fond of saying. Or you could instead

---

16. For reasons I have never understood, the Timermen have forever recruited exclusively at the War College or at engineering schools such as Purdue and Grand Port, except in the very earliest days of the Yukon Confederacy, when they had to accept less qualified members. They have never recruited at scholarly institutions such as St. Matthew's.

17. Horatio is, of course, the celebrated Roman hero, and Captain Harris refers to Captain Julian Harris, the first man to fight his way into the American Capitol Building in 2081. Harris was better known in Bruce's time because he was the subject of the poem *The Bloody Bayonet,* which children learned in school.

18. A paraphrase of Danforth's famous proclamation in *The New Age of Chivalry* that "A thousand wars shall keep us strong for three thousand years."

dream a dream that includes the whole world rather than a small farm back home and looks to a time when there are no more wars and a universal civilization stretches from pole to pole."

As he was speaking, the cadets in charge of the great steel double doors at the front of the hall engaged the steam winch that slowly pulled away the two ton crossbar holding the ornamental doors in place. A loud *boom* sounded across the wide dining hall when the bar slipped free of one upright guard and cold air from outside flooded over us. At the same time the chapel bells on the quad began sounding, signaling to the plebes that dinner time was ended and telling the upperclassmen they had only another ten minutes. All of us now had to return to our quarters or to the library for an evening of study.

"Look at us," laughed Fitz. "I was speaking of changing the world, and the reality is we have to scurry off and push our noses in books we would rather not read while we sit in places we would rather not be. We are a sad lot, my friends."

I finished my meal and excused myself. I saluted Fitz with my hand over my heart, but he would not stand on formality; he arose and—to my amazement—took my hand as if he and I were equals. I was overjoyed beyond my capacity to tell, as he knew I would be.

"We hope to see you at breakfast," he said. "We're spoiled late risers here. We don't eat until five-thirty. Too many fresh daisies from Humbolt among us."[19]

Darkness comes early to Centralia City in winter. As I walked back to the plebe dormitory hot steam was already hissing into the street lamps, heating the metal cylinders in the center of the lamps and causing the noble gas inside to glow faintly. By the time I reached the entrance of my hall the lamps were glowing brightly. Similar steam lamps and flame lanterns shone through the windows of the city's shops and homes. From my room I could look upon the Missouri River in the distant west. Between the moonlit path of the river and my window were thousands of lights scattered like fireflies rising from the hayfields in summer. I gazed for several minutes at the vista below me and thought of the great man I was becoming. As the sky grew darker and Centralia's lights became brighter I

---

19. Fitzpatrick the Younger had collected some of his inner circle years earlier at Humbolt, an exclusive military prep school in Cumberland for boys aged twelve to sixteen. In 2588 Humbolt celebrated its 450th year of service to the Confederacy.

thought of the new universe of possibilities that had opened for me that day. As Fitz could have predicted, I was already dreaming of the glorious service I would provide the future Consul and the honors I would win from him. When my roommate Daniel Huff returned from the library, I told him all that had befallen me at the mess hall, and he congratulated me as though I had won the Tinkers' lottery.[20]

"You will have to move to a better place now that you're one of the *Basileis*," he told me.

"I can't afford to," I said.

"Lord Fitzpatrick will pay for it," said Daniel. "I knew something like this was going to happen when I heard someone was asking about that paper you wrote for civil engineering last month."

He threw off his topcoat and opened the window so he could smoke a cigarette and not leave any telltale ashes for the proctors to find.

"Whatever are you talking about?" I asked him. "He and his mates didn't know I existed until this evening."

"Believe what you wish. Stephen Harris, that drudge sitting behind us in roads and bridges class, says he saw Fitzpatrick's big scary bodyguard—"

"Buck Pularski?"

"By name," said Daniel. "He asked the instructor for your paper on low maintenance roads. Don't look surprised. They've been asking around about you for some time now. Some chap I wouldn't know from Everyman came by here last Tuesday to ask about you. He wanted to know if you had any bad habits Lord Fitzpatrick should know about."

"That is impossible."

"Perhaps I talk too much," said Daniel, flicking a quarter inch of spent ash out the window. "Anyway, I saw this coming. A bloke as sharp as you was going to end up either in the Timermen or on some leading man's staff. I should tell you this now because I don't fancy a nobody like myself will be seeing much of you after you've gone to live among the swells. I'm for the heavy artillery, just like my dad and uncles, but you, Bobby, you're going to end up working on some secret project young Fitzpatrick has got cooked up.

---

20. Also known as the numbers racket, the Tinkers' lottery, like the plague in Africa, is still with us. Two commoners like Huff and Bruce would have known the lottery as well as they knew porter beer.

I'll be able to tell the other junior officers working the 220s with me I knew you when."[21]

"Rubbish," I said and went back to working on my Greek lesson.

Time would prove Daniel correct on every point. Years later Buck Pularski would tell me that the scene with Marcello the cook was entirely a show staged to deceive me. Fitz had performed a similar routine in India with another cook, and that was why I saw Fitz and Marcello conversing together a few days after the incident in the mess hall and the two of them got along like the old friends they were. I had been deliberately held late at the exam, deliberately sent by Marcello into the hall with my decorations showing, and I took everything that happened at Fitz's table to be real because I had wished it to be real. I was a commoner from a tiny village in the northwest, and when the world's foremost young gentleman said he wished to be my friend I was so flattered I accepted everything else he said and did. Were I as wise then as I am today, I would have known that Fitz was never so impulsive as to slap someone in the heat of the moment. Certainly he would not humiliate a man who handled the very food he ate. Marcello was paid handsomely for playing his part in the charade, and he had carried a small vial of yellow dye in his pants pocket which he broke when he fell to his knees in order to simulate the flow of urine. He and Fitz had rehearsed the scene earlier that afternoon.

Young Lord Fitzpatrick was what he was. It would be as wrong to blame him for beguiling me into the *Basileis* as it would be to blame a tiger for eating deer, especially when the deer is so willing to be eaten. I blame only myself for being such easy prey for him, and I know God will judge me severely for my weakness and for the ambition that made me vulnerable to his ploys. Were I a better man back then, I would have excused myself at once from the young Lord's company. Had I done so, I would not today be plagued by nightmares of dying Chinese soldiers or of peasant farmers slowly starving on their ravaged farms. But doing what was wrong was so effortless and brought such great rewards. When the greatest crimes are committed, most of the perpetrators only have to pretend they are innocent. I was very good at doing that when I was young. I only had to deaden my conscience a bit and tell myself everything Fitz said was true and everything he did would eventually favor the side of the Angels.

---

21. He means the 220-millimeter cannons.

# TWO

THE FOLLOWING MORNING I was on the exercise grounds at the customary time of four o'clock. We ran five miles through the darkened streets of Centralia with sixty-pound packs on our backs, did twenty minutes of calisthenics, then put on body armor and fought hand to hand with wooden rifles. When it was time for us to take a swim in the icy Missouri River, the drill instructor prevented me from going with the other cadets.

"You are excused today, Sir Robert," he said. "Else you will be late for Lord Fitzpatrick's table."

The D.I. had known me from the Mexican war and regretted I would not be suffering in the forty-degree water with the other cadets.

"Young men need the river to settle their spirits," he commented wistfully to no one in particular.

At breakfast my new companions put aside world affairs and talked of the semester finals that were coming up in January as soon as we returned to the campus from Christmas vacation. As an engineering student, I particularly feared the oral exam in History and Other Literatures, for I did not have the humanities background most other cadets did. I listened to Fitz and Valette and Hood banter about Thucydides and Guicardini and envisioned only failure in my immediate future. The great Murrey himself was going to come down from his study in the university towers to observe our class take the critical test, and many peons like me feared the event would mark the end of our time at the War College.[1]

"Excuse me, Fitz," I said, his nickname no longer sticking in my throat, "but did not Doctor Murrey teach you when you were younger?"

"For the full four years I was at Humbolt," he said, and from the expression on his face I grasped that the experience had not been a pleasant one. "He taught me Latin during the day and Greek at night, as they used to say. Murrey is the most famous scholar in the Confederacy, thus in my father's mind he is the best scholar for a young boy to know."

"Is he difficult?" asked Davis (who was called "Watchcharm," for he was as small as one).

"He is hard, but fair," recalled Fitz. "He can be indulgent . . . to my father, that is, as most men are indulgent to power. I confess I owe much of my world view to his instruction. I fear, Watchcharm, he will wind you up good and proper."

We studied as one group for the next week, furiously memorizing the names of authors and books and quizzing one another on the standard questions we knew we would have to answer on the fateful day. Fitz would take command of each of these study sessions, just as we let him take command of every situation. Before the evening had progressed to the call for "lights out" he was barking at the rest of us like the class headmaster.

"Herodotus says the oldest civilization is what, Mr. Mason?" he would demand, hitting a ruler against his calf the way an instructor would hit himself with a swagger stick.

"Egypt," said Mason.

"For once correct," said Fitz. "But in truth the oldest civilization was . . . ?"

"The Chaldean?" guessed Mason.

Fitz rolled his eyes at the response.

---

1. Jonathan Nehemiah Murrey is, as most readers will know, the author of a *A History of Byzantium, The French Revolution, On Existence, Letters to my Son,* etc., etc.; the greatest Historian and philosopher of his day, he was by then excused of his teaching duties at the War College, but was still in residence. He would have been sixty-two years old in January of 2416.

It scarce needs be explained that in Bruce's time, as now, History was the most important subject a student had to master. To fail at History proves that one is not worthy to be a gentleman or a member of any honorable profession.

"Be more exact, Tony," he said. "Don't say Chaldean. That's the archaic term. Say Mesopotamian, or better still Sumerian; that is more specific. Then you might mention the cities of Ur and Erech. Now if he wants to take it back to the oldest continuously inhabited spots in the ancient Middle East, they were Catal Huyuk and. . . ."

Mason looked at him in uncomprehending wonder.

"The place where the walls came tumbling down," said Fitz, dropping a hint.[2]

"Well," said Mason, "they all came tumbling down soon or later, didn't they?"

As my old roommate Daniel had predicted, I was given new quarters in the University Heights among the other *Basileis*. Fitz paid for everything. While I was away at exercises in the morning, a pretty serving girl named Angela made my bed with fresh linen and laid out a pressed and laundered uniform for me. She polished my regulation dress shoes and my black boots and set them atop my foot locker. She swept and mopped my floor, washed the walls with soapy water and a sponge, and wiped the windows clean with ammonia. I would have liked to have paid her something for her troubles, but I was as poor as a church mouse. When she curtsied to me—something that no one had ever done before to my person—my poverty felt an especially heavy load upon me.

"You do such good work, Angela," I told her. "I am sorry I can pay you nothing."

"Lord Fitzpatrick has seen to me," she would say. "Is there anything else you would have me do, Sir Robert?"

"No, you have been too kind to me already," I would tell her, and she would curtsy again, which I should have told her not to do. I confess it pleased something base in me to have someone treat me as a Lord, so I let her bob her head to me every day before she left me.

During holiday week I remained in my room and reread works from the prescribed canon. Fitz returned to his family estate in the Meadowlands, and his other friends traveled to their various homes, leaving me alone in the old redbrick building overlooking the river on the west end of the campus. I told myself I needed the time to prepare, which was little comfort to a man who could not have afforded a train ticket home anyway.

---

2. Fitzpatrick means Jericho in the Holy Land.

For those readers of this book spared the experience of the junior midyear orals on History and Other Literatures, I should explain that it is the most unfair test the dons have devised in the long story of the Confederacy. A group of twenty-five students is packed into a classroom with their instructor, and he questions them one by one concerning a specific Historical era from the twenty-five eras deemed worthy of study. The instructor begins by drilling one student upon the History and literature of the ancient Middle East, and proceeds from there up to contemporary times. The process takes an entire day, and is obviously unfair because one pupil may be grilled upon the second or sixteenth centuries A.D., wherein there were dozens of great writers producing thousands of quotes and important ideas that have to be recalled from memory, and another student may be asked about the sixth or the twentieth and twenty-first centuries, when very little that was written has survived. The instructor's whim dictates which students get the difficult eras and which receive the easy ones. Every night that week I had nightmares in which I had to stand before my classmates and tell how Suetonius treated the twelve first century Caesars and why his treatment varied from Tacitus' book upon the same men, and of course I would have to do it in Latin.[3]

Fitz and his bodyguard Buck Pularski returned from the Meadowlands early, two days before the new year began. He tutored me for the humanities exams, and I presumed to help him for the tests in the physical sciences, although I soon perceived that he did not need anyone's assistance in any subject, for he was a master of them all. The confidence he inspired in others in every situation made me believe my upcoming performance in the orals might not be a total disaster. The oddest thing about being in Fitz's presence was that the more we became aware of his personal abilities the more we wanted to become familiar with him. I became so carried away I confided to him one evening in the dormitory's reading room that in light of my excellent grades on the written work, I might get an overall passing grade in History, provided I failed the orals by only a few points.

Fitz told me not to worry.

---

3. It is interesting to note how little academics have changed in 175 years. Bruce would have had to use Latin to speak of the Roman Historians because the worthy eras of the ancient Greeks and Romans require the worthy Greek and Latin tongues.

"You have made a commendable effort," he said. "I have never had a friend who made a real effort fail a major exam."

"Buck, Watchcharm and Lord Mason have passed every exam?" I asked, perhaps being a tad too blunt in naming the three worst scholars in our group, which amused Fitz.

"Watchcharm, like the rest of my friends, has a special talent," he told me. "Mind you, he is no wonder in the classroom. Never will be. He is the best pilot of his age I know of. He won the Desert Air Rally when he was sixteen. Besides, he is brave to the point of recklessness, and other reckless young men will follow him into Hell. Buck, on the other hand, has not ever given enough thought to danger to be called brave; he is somewhere beyond brave, wherever that is. As for Mason . . ."

He twice started to say something, and instead laughed when he thought of Lord Mason, whose youthful plump face already betrayed knowledge of more vices than an average man would know in several lifetimes.

"Ah, Tony," said Fitz, still chuckling, "Tony has mastered a workable vocabulary and often has bluffed others into thinking he is smarter than he is."

"That is *his* special talent?" I asked.

"God's wounds, no," said Fitz. "Tony, well, Tony has friends and family.[4] Anyway, as I was saying, Robert, I have found that when one is blessed in a certain capacity, Providence allows that blessing to bring favor to whatever endeavor that person attempts. You might say the one outstanding talent lifts a person to surprising levels of achievement in everything he does."

"Then you think we will all pass?"

"I am certain we will pass," he said. "Some of us by the skin of his heels, but we all will pass. I am equally certain you will pass with honors."

When school resumed and the History and Other Literatures examination at last rolled around, I entered the classroom on that much dreaded morning and saw our regular instructor Dr. Manheim pacing in the front of the students and slapping his swagger stick against the palm of his hand. Every shred of confidence Fitz had given me vanished into the stale air above the heads of the

---

4. As we shall see later, some of Lord Anthony Mason's "friends and family" were to become leading lights in the detestable Shay regime.

twenty-four other anxious cadets. Then I saw Dr. Murrey seated in a corner behind the pacing Manheim, and my heart sank into my stomach. Combat with Mexican raiders had not frightened me half as much as the confident half-smile on the face of that famous silver-haired man. He was tall and had long thin arms and legs; despite his ample gray hair, his wrinkled visage made him look older than his sixty-two years, older than the sea, as the sailors say, and far more unpleasant. Dr. Manheim in his customary corduroy jacket and bow tie looked as harmless as a house cat in comparison to the regal Murrey: Manheim was a neat little gentleman of a certain age who was so arrogant and gave such boring lectures the cadets wondered why he was not teaching at some institution that caters to rich dullards rather than at the War College.[5] Murrey, resplendent in his black silk morning jacket and white spats and bearing his duck's head walking stick, was clearly a man to be feared.

"Gentlemen Cadets," Manheim announced in his best stern voice at seven o'clock sharp, "we will now begin. Please stand when you are called upon." He glanced at the list atop his podium. "Lord Davis," he said, "please stand and be questioned regarding the History and Other Literature of the ancient Egyptians and Mesopotamians."

The lucky cur, I thought. Watchcharm had drawn the first and one of the easiest of the twenty-five eras. He had to talk a bit about *The Book of the Dead*, Gilgamesh's story, detail some king's lists, relate something about the scraps the archaeologists of earlier times had unearthed, and he was home free. Since these ancients did not speak Greek or Latin, Watchcharm's answers were all in English. He muffed one of the dynasty sequences in the Late Middle Kingdom, but he did hack a respectable path through the rest of the questions until Manheim let him be seated. Murrey did not ask him a single question.

"Next, Mr. Peasance," announced Manheim, "arise and be questioned regarding the Homeric Greeks. I am going to quote you a line from the *Iliad* and you will answer with the line that follows:

*"Zeus d'epei oun troas te kai Ektroa nian pelasse."*

---

5. Like many young students, Bruce imagined his university to be superior to all others. He certainly could not have been referring to St. Matthew's, which in Bruce's time enjoyed the same reputation it does today.

"*Tous men ea para tesi ponun texemen kai oisun,* sir," answered the cadet.

"Very good," said Manheim. "Tell me the book and line."

"Book thirteen, lines one and two, sir."

"Very good."

The process went well enough through the first three interrogations. The cadet who had to stand and be queried about the History of the Bible, however, was not as lucky as his predecessors. He was not of our group and I do not recall his name, which is for the good, as he did not have a day that should be remembered.

"What are the most important books in the New Testament?" Manheim asked him.

"The four Gospels and the Book of Acts, sir," replied the cadet.

"Why?"

"Because they are Histories, sir. The other books are merely letters and prophecy, sir."

"And why is History more important than epistles and prophecy?"

"Because History teaches us the past, sir."

"Why," interrupted Murrey, swimming head first into the questioning like a shark that has smelled blood in the water, "is it important we know the past?"

"Otherwise," responded the cadet, "we will commit the errors of those coming before us, sir."

"True enough," shrugged Murrey. "What I am asking is why it is important for us, the Yukons, to avoid the errors of the past."

The cadet wobbled a bit where he stood. He sensed he had forgotten something basic and could not recall what it was.

"Because errors could destroy our civilization, sir," he said, making a wild stab at the matter.

"And . . . ?" said Manheim, leaping upon the wound Murrey had opened.

"Come on!" I thought. "Say it! It is right in Severson."[6]

"Sir," said the cadet, his voice cracking under the strain, "we do not wish to be destroyed."

---

6. Sir James Swifthelp Severson's *The Meaning of History,* Perpetual Press, Great Mesa City, latest edition, 2570; then, as now, the standard first text in elementary school History classes.

"Because . . . ?" asked Manheim, giving the poor sod one more shot at blurting out the right answer.

"Sir . . ." said the cadet, fidgeting slightly and quickly licking his lips, "it is the nature of civilizations to wish to survive, sir."

"Oh!" said Manheim, now making his final, fatal move for the jugular. "Are you saying we Yukons simply want to survive as other nations have always wanted? You consider our nation no greater than, let us say, the Hittites? Or do you recall a grammar school lesson from your woolgathering youth? Something to the effect of our being God's last earthly bastion, the last holy redoubt? Were you not taught that if *we* commit errors as other peoples have, *we* will extinguish God's light in the world, therefore *we* must understand History and survive until Christ comes again and we are called home? Is that not what you wanted to say?"

Manheim was spitting saliva as he spewed out these sentences. The unfortunate cadet had no option but to stand at attention and endure the professor's assault.

"Sir," he feebly protested, "I was about to—"

"Enough!" screamed Manheim and struck the podium with his stick. "You may sit! If I had shown such ignorance at your age, my instructor would have had me flogged. But you may sit. Just sit. Sit and tomorrow you will return to your tractor and bother us no more!"

The beaten man's britches had no sooner touched his chair when Manheim called out, "Sir Jeremiah Truth Hood, arise and be questioned regarding the History and Other Literatures of the times between the death of Marcus Aurelius and the ascension of Theodoric the Ostrogoth."

So it went hour after hour. We marched through the centuries until twenty-two hours had passed and there were but three of us left to be questioned: Fitz, Pularski, and myself.

"Sir Robert Mayfair Bruce," called out Manheim, "arise and be questioned regarding the twentieth and twenty-first centuries."

I could not believe my good fortune: I had been given the easiest period of the twenty-five! I had to caution myself not to give a shout of joy as I stood upright.

"Sir Robert," said Manheim, "there is a vulgar name for the twentieth and twenty-first centuries. I am certain you have both read and heard it. Would you please state that vulgar name for us now?"

"Sir," I said, "do you think that would be proper, sir?"

"There are no ladies or children present," he said. "We are in a military college. You have all heard dirty language before. Please say the name."

"This time is called the Age of Shit, sir."[7]

"Correct," he said, and he smashed his stick onto the podium when someone behind me snickered. "The Age of Shit," he repeated, as though saying the phrase again would silence any sophomoric laughter. "The prevalent culture of that era is called the Culture of Shit. Now, what is the polite name for that era?"

"The Age of Electricity, sir," I said.

"Correct. Now, what Histories do we have that were written during the Age of Electricity?"

"Only one, *Vomiting out the Past* by Mrs. Agnes Sternwill House, sir, though it was written during the Storm Times, at the end of the Electrical Age."

"Why no others, Sir Robert?"

"Because nothing survived the Storm Times, save a few fragments, sir."

"And?"

"And all other Histories of that era were perverted by the strange ideologies of the day, sir. Those that still exist are on the proscribed list. Only certified scholars are allowed to read them."

"And?"

"The writers of the Electrical Age did not produce real Histories, sir. Their so-called Histories were interpretations of the past deeply influenced by the writers' twisted worldviews and had to be destroyed."

"Correct," he said. "Before I ask you about Mrs. House's book in greater detail, tell us, Sir Robert, who was the prose master of the twentieth century, of those few things that survived?"

"Pelham Grenville Wodehouse, sir," I said.

"Were there any others worth reading?"

"A few, sir. A couple of Irishmen: Yeats and O'Connor. Then there are the early comic novels of Evelyn Waugh, sir."

"Anything else?"

"Some minor poets from the British Isles, sir. America pro-

---

7. At St. Matthew's it is referred to as the Age of Excrement.

duced the journalist H.L. Mencken and the novel *Pictures from an Institution* by Randall Jarrell, sir."[8]

"Correct; now let us get back to the History recounted in *Vomiting out the Past*. What, Sir Robert, were the original Yukons called?"

"They were at first called 'the New Agrarians,' which was an organization founded in 2018 by a North American farmer named Harold Barr, sir."

"Why were they called 'Yukons,' and what else can you tell us of the early Yukons?"

"The name was originally an insult, sir. There were professional joke tellers," (I momentarily struggled to recall the ancient word) "*comedians* they were called; they said the New Agrarians were so rural they were from the Yukon, which was a remote territory in the far northwestern portion of the ancient nation of Canada, sir. The first Yukons were mostly farmers, as the recent census shows a majority of us still are.[9] They lived in isolated communities and produced food and other basic materials for themselves—subsistence farming, it was. Eventually, as other food sources in North America disappeared, the Yukons sold food to the cities. The economy of the twenty-first century was locked into a cycle of collapse, renewal, and collapse again. The financial institutions would not loan money to new farmers, foreign producers proved unreliable because of international unrest, and those individuals with money—"

"The most important group with large pools of capital was what?" asked Manheim.

"The Yellowjackets," I said.[10]

"Correct. Now continue your narrative about the early Yukons."

"As I was saying, sir," I said, "no one other than the Yukons was interested in investing in agriculture as there was little money

---

8. This book makes light of the Byzantine workings of an American university. True academicians do not find it overly amusing.

9. In 2591 only two-thirds of the Yukon population remain on the farm.

10. Formed as an immigrant criminal gang in 2008, the Yellowjackets grew and grew until they became at mid-twenty-first century a political and economic force unequaled by any other group. Composed of every one of the ethnic groups then residing in North America, their common members were identified by the black silk jacket that bore the golden image of a wasp on its back.

in it. Furthermore, the countryside was unsafe due to the presence of roving gangs—"

"The most infamous of these roving gangs was a group of motorcycle riders called . . . ?" asked Manheim.

"The Land Pirates, sir."[11]

"Go on," he said.

"The first Yukons occupied a niche in the economy, sir. As the decades went by they became the dominant suppliers of foodstuffs, textiles, wood, coal, metals and most other basic commodities on the entire continent. By the 2040s they had international communities in Australia, New Zealand, and the British Isles. Then came the PPWs, sir."

"Which were what?" asked the professor.

"Personal Pulse Weapons, sir. They were invented by Doctor Jessup at Purdue University in 2047," I said. "They were electromagnetic devices that could knock out electrical currents at a distance of six miles. The havoc they wreaked upon the American society and economy cannot be underestimated, sir."

"Yes, go on."

"By the 2060s the Yukons had become the primary agricultural force in all the English-speaking world. They became small manufacturers, first to supply their own communities' needs, and later to create exports to the cities. In return for being left alone by an increasingly powerless government, the Yukons performed certain technical tasks for the state, such as rebuilding damaged power lines and making and launching communication satellites."

"Who among the Yukons performed these technical tasks?"

"The Timermen, sir," I said.

"Who are . . . ?"

"A secret society founded at Purdue University by Doctor Jessup and others in the Engineering Department, sir. They were—rather, they are—a society of scientists and engineers. Their name comes from their use of mechanical watches instead of electronic timers. There was an anecdote of the day which had it that only the Timermen knew what the time really was."

"And why would they choose to use mechanical watches?"

---

11. The Land Pirates numbered somewhere between two and three million in the 2050s, but they were all in all, subservient to the Yellowjackets.

"Because, sir, electronic devices of all sorts were becoming increasingly unreliable. Rogue elements within the government, the Yellowjackets, the Land Pirates, and many, many other groups were using PPWs and damper units, that is, powerful generators that emitted positive ion fields which disrupted the flow of electricity in metal circuits. The early Yukons used such devices themselves for self-defense against raiders driving vehicles powered by either electronic or internal combustion engines. For this same reason the Yukon farmers and their communities adopted their machinery to steam power. They grew their biomass fuel, primarily using the raspweed, the guayule, and jojoba plants, as well as kelp and algae from the sea, animal and lumber waste, and the leaves of the eucalyptus tree. Steam heat warmed their houses in winter; steam engines driving compression pumps cooled the same homes in summer and kept their food refrigerated year round. Gas lamps using steam-heated neon and boron provided them with light."

"How did they communicate over large distances without electricity?"

Someone in the class complained to his neighbor. This was much too simple. Why was Manheim going so easy on me?

"The Timermen launched hundreds of satellites, sir, creating the Blinking Star System. Using directed ultraviolet light that can penetrate any atmospheric disturbance, they communicate with us using a simple code similar to the old Morse code. The satellites circle the earth in synchronous orbit, thus each remains over a specific spot on the earth below. We capture the dots and dashes given to us on ammonia-treated paper strips constantly rotating beneath the glass domes we can see atop every town hall, on ship decks, on the backs of many airships, and on the command vehicle of every military unit. We communicate back to the satellites using the large flat ultraviolet lamps we see in almost as many places as we find paper domes. The Timerman maintain the system and regularly change the code so only the Yukons know it and only they can use the Blinking Star network. Since the Blinking Stars are also optical satellites that have carbon filament cables that hang thousands of miles into the earth's atmosphere, they can detect the movement of individual objects and can help us navigate over oceans and wastelands, provide us the exact location of our enemies, and allow near instantaneous contact between any two Yukons who have a flat ultraviolet lamp and a paper dome, sir."

"Only Yukons have these devices?"

"Of course, sir."

"Tell us about the rise of the Yellowjackets, Sir Robert."

"During the Urban Wars of the 2050s and 2060s the Yellow-jackets and Yukons destroyed the Brain Lords—"[12]

"Who were?" demanded Manheim.

"The Brain Lords were a small sect of self-proclaimed superior humans who controlled the large corporations and the government through the use of the thinking machines called computers. We know very little about them. The one objective fact we can today state about them is that their enemies used dampers to cripple their computers and then annihilated every last one of them, sir."

"Correct; now go back to the rise of the Yellowjackets."

"At the end of the Urban Wars, sir, the Yellowjackets became the most powerful of the city gangs. There were thousands of other groups: the Accountants, the Fez, the Bloods, the Taranto-las, the Shahshahs, the Indigenous Killers, the Urbs, and many more. The Yellowjackets in time co-opted them all; they were the strongest because they controlled the illegal narcotics trade and also had a share of most legitimate industries. During the reign of Bartholomew Iz[13] the American government allotted approximately half the national budget to the Yellowjackets."

"Why would the government do that, Sir Robert?"

"By 2054 the Yellowjackets had become the nation's domestic army, sir. In 2080 they absorbed all of the overseas armed forces. In 2081 the Yellowjackets went to war on the Yukons, the last organized group outside their control, sir."

---

12. Recent archaeological excavations under Cities of the Plains Park have located five separate Brain Lord chambers (see Abernathy and Crombs, *Archaeological Journal*, pp. 128–43, vol. CCXII, issue 3). We do not know today exactly how they did what they did, but the computing machines they controlled somehow dominated the world's communications networks. We do know they were malevolent, arrogant, and fixated on protecting their power.

13. Often called "the Enemy of God," some contemporaries identified Iz with the Antichrist. He ruled North America and much of the Western world from 2074 to 2081. Born Stanley Osmond James and originally trained to be an elementary school teacher, Iz later became a lawyer, and took his new name after the Great Name Change when leading Yellowjackets took new names (see House, pp 419–46). *Gratis* the truly odd *The Diary of Tri Ogallala*—another weird tome from the McDonald collection—we now have an intimate but brief portrait of him.

"Had not the early Yukons once been allies of the Yellow-jackets? Even of Iz himself?"

"Yes, sir. As I said, during the Urban Wars the Yukons had helped the Yellowjackets destroy the Brain Lords. When Bartholomew Iz came to power, the alliance ended. But, as we know, the Yukons defeated the armed bands he sent against them, as they had defeated the Land Pirates when the Rauf regime[14] sent them against the rural areas in the 2060s. On October 1, 2081, Iz launched nuclear weapons.[15] The next day the Timermen turned on the Storm Machines, sir."

"Which are?" asked Manheim.

Again there was murmuring among the other cadets. These were matters we had learned as children. As naive as I was then, I was aware that something here was amiss.

"The Storm Machines are giant satellites fixed in orbits that are just below those of the Blinking Stars, sir. They contain nuclear generators that power enormous damper units that emit positive particles—positrons, if you will, sir—which interrupt the flow of negative charges that constitute electrical current in metal circuits. The Storm Machines send these positrons through long cables similar to those attached to the Blinking Stars downward onto the earth's surface in the form of microwaves, which are not repelled by the ionosphere as radio waves would be. When the Storm Machines were turned on October 2, 2081, electricity on the earth and up to a height of three hundred and eighty miles in the atmosphere could not be used for human purposes, three hundred and eighty miles above us being where their cables end. Currents produced by man-made generators and batteries sputtered in uncontrollable fits and starts on that day, because the Storm Machines discharge their energy in irregular pulses. Magnetic compasses do not point due north when the Storm Machines are running, a phenomenon not unlike the natural occurrence observed in 1733 by Doctor Celsius[16] during

---

14. Mohammed Rauf ruled North America from 2055 to 2074. His reign was cut short, literally, when the Yellowjackets beheaded him and installed Iz as the nation's supreme leader. Rauf had made the mistake of forgetting Iz had total power within the government. Despite his name, Rauf was never a Moslem.

15. Powerful electronic weapons. Several of the uninhabited, contaminated areas are the results of these weapons' impact.

16. Anders Celsius, Swedish Scientist, 1701–1744.

an observation of the aurora borealis. Some physicists have remarked that the effects of the Storm Machines are much like those generated by a very strong event of the northern lights; that is, both will cause electricity to fail. Unlike the aurora borealis, the Storm Machines caused a marked increase in static electricity on the earth's surface, and thus every day there were violent thunderstorms, sir."

"Which is why 2081 to 2108 is known as the 'Storm Times,'" commented Manheim. "And why are there not violent Storm Times today?"

"In some parts of the world there are, sir," I said. "After 2108 the Timermen turned the Storm Machines off. Since that time they project the system only onto those places where they detect an artificial electronic field."

"Could we say the Storm Times mark a backward step in technology, Sir Robert? You are, I am told, studying to be an engineer. You would surely know about these matters, wouldn't you?"

"We have hardly stepped backward, sir," I said. "Our modern day plastics, carbon filaments, and medicines are far more advanced than their counterparts were in the twenty-first century. Our advanced metallurgy has given us materials unknown to the Electronic Age. Our agricultural sciences have created plants and animals resistant to disease and insects. We live in a world that is cleaner, safer, and less crowded than the world of three hundred years ago. We have controlled our population growth, extended the average life span past one hundred and ten years, and made famine and epidemics Historical notions. To the Yukons, that is, sir."

"And we have ingenious ways of killing our enemies," said Murrey.

He had not spoken for hours until he made that strange remark. Even Manheim seemed taken aback when he heard him.

"Yes, sir," I said. "We have Fire Sticks, a descendant of napalm which burns for a full five seconds longer than earlier combustible jellies, even on nonflammable surfaces. We have both impact and chemical fuse bombs that—"

"I was making a comment, young man," interrupted Murrey. "I was not asking a question. I am a veteran, as you are. I am fully cognizant of how deadly we Yukons can be. Please continue, Doctor Manheim."

"Ah, yes," said the junior professor, and tugged at his starched collar. "Now, Sir Robert, a couple more questions about the early Yukons, and then we will move on. How, tell us, did the Timermen maintain the Blinking Stars and the Storm Machines? I mean to ask: how did they get into outer space without electronic equipment?"

"They perhaps do have some electronic equipment, sir," I said. "Their rocket base in the Sandwich Islands[17] is said to have some machines that do not run by steam. It is said the Storm Machines do not strike those lands. To launch their rockets into space they use chemical propellants, specifically liquid hydrogen and liquid oxygen, which the rocket's engine inject together to create an upward thrust. The Timermen seal their cabins before taking off, and the men they send up breathe oxygen kept in storage tanks until they reach an orbit above the end of the Storm Machines' cables. At that point, the space voyagers transport themselves to electrical machines the order has built in deep space. The Timermen keep the satellites fueled and in regular orbits. They naturally keep all other nations out of space. . . . There is little more I can tell you, sir. The Timermen are, after all, a secret society, sir."

"Now," said Manheim, "there is one more major factor in the latter portion of the Age of Electricity we have not mentioned."

"You are referring, sir, to the viral epidemics that ravaged North America, Europe, and the industrial nations of the far east: Ebola, malaria, AIDS, cholera, the airborne bubonic plague, Sumatran fever, red syphilis, super tuberculosis—"

"Yes, yes, and so on," said Manheim. "It would take too long to name them all. Why did these epidemics damage the advanced countries more than the poorer nations of the world?"

"The poorer countries did suffer, sir. The advanced nations had the transportation systems to spread the diseases more rapidly, and then too the central government in America was deliberately spreading the viruses. The Yukons survived because they would not allow city folk to enter their communities; that was the specific reason Bartholomew Iz declared war on them. Europe was reduced to the Slavic Remnant living in the Ural Mountains; the rest of the continent was by 2110 overrun by Moslems from the south. Japan and

---

17. Then, as now, the Timermen in charge of the satellites own the largest and southernmost of the Sandwich Islands, namely Jessup Island, where only members of their order are allowed to tread.

Korea, which were rich states at the time, became provinces of China. The population of all the English-speaking lands fell to approximately fifteen million, roughly half of what the Yukon Confederacy holds today, sir."

"Of course," said Murrey, interrupting my exam a second time, "those in the industrial nations who did not die of disease starved to death in the famine brought on by the Storm Times—except for a handful of survivors the Yukons rounded up and transported to the underdeveloped world."

"Yes, sir," I said. "Was that a question or another comment, sir?"

"Only a comment, Sir Robert," he said, and smiled and leaned his chin onto the top of his duck's head cane.

Dr. Manheim said he had asked me enough about History. He asked several easy questions regarding Wodehouse, and then said I could sit down.

"Wait," said Murrey. "I would like to quiz the young gentleman a bit further."

I stood back up. Dr. Manheim's eyes were swinging back and forth from Murrey in his chair at the front of the examination hall to someone in the cluster of cadets. The instructor's eyes had to move several times before I caught on that he was glancing at Fitz.

"Sir Robert," asked Dr. Murrey, "what primary Historical sources from the Age of Electricity have you read?"

"There are none for me to read but Mrs. House's book, sir. As I said, those that do exist are forbidden to a mere student."

"Then when you speak of this time in History, you are merely repeating what your teachers have told you?'

"Yes . . . I mean to say, sir, do we not have to believe our teachers?"

"Sir Robert," said Murrey, spinning his brass and walnut cane and watching his hands as he did, "are you familiar with the concept of shame?"

Manheim opened his mouth to protest, but after some consideration he remained silent.

"Shame, sir?" I said.

"It says in the Bible, Sir Robert, 'I shall bring on you everlasting disgrace and everlasting shame which will never be forgotten.'"

"That would be from Jeremiah, chapter twenty-two, sir," I said.

"Very good. Young gentlemen cadets should read the Bible," he said. "Tell me, do you believe there is such a thing as everlasting shame?"

"If God wills there be," I said and swallowed, "then there is, sir."

"Apparently," he said, looking at me with that superior manner of his I profoundly disliked, "He so wills it. What I want to ask you, Sir Robert, is this: do you think the Yukons of the Storm Times brought on themselves an everlasting shame?"[18]

Dr. Manheim suddenly inhaled several cubic centimeters of air. He grabbed his throat and nearly tripped over backward. The famous Dr. Murrey had not only stepped outside the accepted twenty-five categories, he had insulted the founding fathers of the Yukon Confederacy! The cadets could almost hear the words that were sounding inside Manheim's brain, "What if the university Lords hear what happened in *my* classroom?"

"What are you implying, sir?" I said to Murrey.

I was young and had not yet learned to mask my emotions as well as I would in a few years' time of observing Fitz.

"Do not be angry with me, Sir Robert," smiled Dr. Murrey. "I was implying nothing. I was stating that the early Yukons starved millions of people to death when they activated the Storm Machines. They killed millions more when they moved the surviving non-Yukons into the poorer regions of the globe."

"Most of the non-Yukons in Australia, New Zealand, Iceland, Greenland, North America, and the British Isles died during the viral plagues, sir," I said.

"Not all of them died of disease, Sir Robert," said Murrey. "According to Miss House's book, the 2060 census, the last reliable population count she knew of, tells that there were some five hundred and eighty million people living in America alone. Disease could have killed no more than two-thirds of them."

The examination room was buzzing. Fitz started from his chair, and Valette had to pull him down to prevent him from speaking out of turn.

---

18. It is unlikely a distinguished teacher and author of Murrey's stature should have posed such a question during a junior midyear examination. Out of Bruce's many questionable passages, this is one of the most questionable. The junior midyear orals are the acme of a student's time on campus. I have personally never seen an observer pose any question during a similar exam.

"I must protest, Doctor Murrey," said Dr. Manheim, trying his best to sound authoritative. "I cannot understand why you are questioning the young gentleman in this manner."

"Sir Robert is a war hero," said Dr. Murrey, calmly shifting his weight against the back of his chair and letting his walking stick rest upon his knee. "He has endured worse experiences than my questioning."

"I want it to be known that these are your questions and not mine," stated Manheim.

"So it will be known," said the unruffled Murrey.

"Are you forgetting, sir," I said, "that the early Yukons saved millions of people? Consider those fleeing the European mainland into Britain after the Moslems surged north."

"Oh, the Yukons accepted some people," he agreed, "those who had white skin and were willing to adapt to our system. Many of those refugees they accepted died anyway when the Yukons quarantined them."

"The early Yukons were products of their times," I said. "You cannot say they were nearly as reprehensible as Iz and the Yellow-jackets! They murdered tens of millions in their very homes, they built death camps, they deliberately infected hundreds of millions worldwide with deadly viruses!"

"I would concede," laughed Murrey, "that the early Yukons were not as terrible as Bartholomew Iz. Is that to be our standard, Sir Robert? Is that enough to cleanse the early Yukons of everlasting shame?"

"Are the Tartars ashamed of Timur the Lame, sir?" I said. "Are the Mongols ashamed of Genghis Khan? More than three hundred years are between us and the early Yukons. Will not three hundred years allow us to forget?"

"So you are conceding they did shameful deeds," he said. "The point you are trying to make now is that they did them long ago and therefore we should forget about them."

This time Fitz did get to his feet.

"Sir," he declared to Manheim, "I request Doctor Murrey direct his questions to me. Clearly he is attempting to provoke—"

To pull him back into his chair required the efforts of both Pularski and Valette. Someone at the back of the room shouted, "Let Bruce sit!" The other cadets muttered and shifted about in their chairs, making it necessary for Manheim to rise and ask them please to be quiet.

"Gentlemen!" he said, sounding like a man who wished he could melt into the floor. "Need I remind you the examination continues? Please," he said to Dr. Murrey, "I am asking you as a junior colleague, sir. Please, I beg you—"

"Only a little more," said Murrey, and waved the younger instructor off with a gloved hand. "I am almost finished. I apologize to you, Sir Robert, if I have angered you."

"I am not angry, sir."

"Really?"

"Really, sir," I said between clenched teeth.

"Then I hope I never keep company with you when you are truly enraged, Sir Robert," he said. "Now, let us approach this matter from another direction. Are we first Yukon soldiers or Christian gentlemen?"

"Christian gentlemen, sir, for we must fear God's judgment before everything else."

"I agree, Sir Robert. But why did the early Yukons not fear the judgment of God?"

"They did, sir," I said. "Fate had put them in an impossible situation, sir. Either they would allow themselves and their families to be destroyed, or they could destroy their enemies. They chose the latter option . . . no, 'chose' is the wrong word. They had no choice. God gave us Grace, and He also gave us the instinct for self-preservation. The early Yukons obeyed the instinct He gave them. They perhaps fell short of God's Grace, but . . . so has everyone else, sir."

"Do you fall short of God's Grace, Sir Robert?" he asked me.

"Without doubt I do, sir."

"I do too," said Murrey. "Are you ashamed of your shortcomings, Sir Robert?"

"Again, I do not know if we are using the right word, sir," I said and paused to wipe the perspiration from my face. "I would rather say, I think . . . I think 'regret' is the word I want to use. I regret I fall short of God's Grace. I regret the early Yukons did the same."

"Regret? Well, that is a start, Sir Robert," he said and softly repeated the word to himself. "Upon reflection," he said, "I think there is a certain promise in regret. Yes, I think it will do. For now. And you will do, Sir Robert. Very well. I have no more questions."

I vow I could hear Dr. Manheim sigh in relief.

"Thank you, Sir Robert," said Manheim. "You may be seated. Gentleman Cadet Sir Winifred Righteous Pularski, will you please stand and be interrogated regarding the History and Other Literatures of the Yukon era up to the year 2400?"

My pulse was racing at over a hundred and twenty beats a minute. I know because I timed it with my wristwatch. Sounds were occurring around me that my brain could not receive as words. The only thought my mind could entertain was that I had offended the great Dr. Murrey, the most honored living Historian in the Confederacy. Because of my rashness my career as an officer would be ended before it began. Pularski's interrogation seemed to last no more than a few minutes, though it could have continued for more than an hour and in my agitated state of mind I would not have noticed. When I had calmed a bit and could again hear the questions and answers Fitz was standing and Manheim was quizzing him upon present day History and Other Literatures.

"Very well spoken, Lord Fitzpatrick," I heard Manheim say after he had grilled Fitz for a mere ten minutes. "You may be seated, my Lord."

"I would please *not* be seated, sir," said Fitz, his eyes blazing like twin lighthouse beacons. "I would rather that Doctor Professor Murrey question me."

"Doctor Professor Murrey," said Murrey, "has known you, my Lord, since you were a child of six. There is nothing about you Doctor Murrey does not already know."

"It is the connection Doctor Murrey has with my family, in particular with my father," said Fitz, "which allows him to act as he does and safeguards his behavior against any response."

"Doctor Murrey is not ungrateful to the Fitzpatrick family,"[19] said Murrey. "His love for that family is what makes him wish to guide its members in the proper direction."

"Does Doctor Murrey feel guilty because he is a Yukon?" demanded Fitz.

"So now I must take the oral test? Very well. I certainly do feel guilt, mixed with pride, every day of my life, my Lord."

---

19. Coronet Noble Fitzpatrick, General of All the Confederate Armies, Consul of the Senate, and father to Fitzpatrick the Younger, had once been Dr. Murrey's Liege Lord. Murrey had also tutored the younger Fitzpatrick in the family home, and had—as mentioned above—been an instructor at Humbolt during the young Fitzpatrick's time there.

While this dangerous conversation was proceeding, Dr. Manheim positioned himself close to the closed doorway. He had set his stick beside the podium and would have quietly slipped out the door, if that had been possible. If he could have dug into the floor like an unobtrusive little mole burrowing into garden soil, he would have done that as well.

"Doctor Murrey feels shame," said Fitz, shaping the air in front of him with his hands as an orator would, "because, contrary to his own theory of opposites, he forces his small mind to embrace the world in its most quotidian form and accepts—"

"Doctor Murrey concedes he has a small mind," interrupted Murrey, "because he, in contrast to others he could name, concedes he is merely human. Doctor Murrey's small mind recalls that Lord Fitzpatrick and he have had this argument before; he remembers it progresses along these lines: there are, according to Lord Fitzpatrick, some special souls who are above such feeble emotions as guilt, great souls who are free to do God's work on earth. These great souls embrace all things possible and impossible, and they can be blamed for nothing, as they are performing the will of God, and they, the great souls, also exist outside any human conception of shame."

"Zeus sat in Heaven and looked down upon not only Troy and the attacking Greeks but also upon the peaceful cities beyond the human horizon.[20] A man freed of provincial bigotries can see as far," said Fitz. "He can see beyond shame, beyond culture, beyond History, and into possibilities yet unknown. It was not I who deported the Hindu yogi,[21] not I who called him a barbarian. For I am not a small-minded xenophobe, which is more than can be said of some people I could name! I see the beauty and good in all men, no matter where they are from and no matter their backgrounds. I see and accept. I accept everything, including the past, and I accept everything without shame. Why should I be ashamed of matters that simply, inalterably *are?*"

"I held nothing against the Hindu—"

---

20. The image is from the *Illiad,* book two.

21. Refers to an incident mentioned in Gerald, pp. 43–44. Coronet Fitzpatrick allowed a Hindustani teacher, someone his wife knew, into his court to instruct his son. Young Isaac seems to have enjoyed the strange foreigner, but Dr. Murrey—then in residence at the Fitzpatrick home—persuaded the elder Fitzpatrick to send the man away.

"So long as he remained on his side of the world!" said Fitz.

"Yes," said Murrey, recovering the smile he had beamed upon me. "And as long as we remain on ours, Lord Fitzpatrick."

"If you would but look at the world, sir," said Fitz, "you would find it does not have 'sides.' It is a round ball with one outer shell. We living on his globe must be one race under one God and have one law, or we will have no existence other than the small, separate nations and the small separate gods of small-minded men."

He abruptly sat down.

"The examination is over," he declared.

Manheim blinked at him. Since he was our professor he had fancied he alone had the authority to proclaim the examination at an end.

"Yes . . . yes, very well," he said. "You are excused, gentlemen."

We went silently into the hallway. During the short space of time I needed to march back to University Heights I was concerned that Fitz might fail the exam as I surely had. After a few moments of more sober thought I remembered exactly whose son Fitz was, and I decided his being sent from the university was as likely an occurrence as the moon falling into the sun. I alone among the *Basileis* would be sent home. I trudged through the week under the cloud of my impending dismissal. I would not go to the kiosk outside Parkman Hall that Saturday morning to see the posted marks. Instead, I packed my belongings into two suitcases and awaited a letter from the university Lord requesting that I leave Centralia City. Watchcharm Davis stunned me when he ran into my room at five past nine and told me we had all passed.

"I received a C minus," he said, as proud as Napoleon at Austerlitz. "Not with honors like you, but good for me, huh?"

"It's cruel of you to make jokes at my expense," I told him. "I don't have a wealthy Lord for a father. When I leave here tonight it will be back to the Sparrows for me. The best I can hope for is a second lieutenant's bars. When I'm older, I'll be a foreman in my Liege Lord's woods."[22]

"Before you buy a ticket for the borderlands, I think you should come with me, Robert the Bruce," he said.

He led me to the kiosk and showed my unbelieving eyes the grade lists. Not only had I passed with honors, no one in our

---

22. As a Knight of the Field, even one dismissed from the War College, he could ask his Lord for a favored job after he had performed ten more years of army service.

twenty-five-member section had failed his orals. The unlucky fellow who had stumbled on the Bible questions had gotten a D.

"We're all lieges to the Fitzpatrick family now," joked Watchcharm. "The common soldiers get frontier land, and we get our grades!"

"Do we get a bonus?" I asked him.[23]

"Speak softly, Robert the Bruce," he said and put a finger to his lips. "It's good to be grateful and foolish to be sarcastic. Stay grateful—grateful and quiet—and Fitz will see us through to our commissions."

Watchcharm told me as we strolled back to our rooms that there was to be a party that evening in Fitz's suite. The *Basileis* were expected to attend.

"This is another of Fitz's wine and cigars get-togethers," Davis explained. "He might talk. How he might talk, huh? Maybe not tonight. We'll have Mason's movie projector."

"I have seen motion pictures before," I said. "I cannot say I care for them. The sound is always bad; it never matches the images on the screens. Watching Gypsies and prostitutes stomp about in supposedly dramatic situations is not my notion of entertainment, anyway."

"Do you expect them to get respectable people to act?"[24] he

---

23. The power of the Fitzpatrick family lay in Lord Coronet Noble Fitzpatrick's control of the Military Land Office. A military veteran would receive, upon the completion of his twelve years of service, some 640 acres of so-called frontier land; that is, they were given land that had been uncultivated since the Storm Times. As Lord Coronet decided whom was granted the best land and where the new land grants were to be made, veterans shifted their loyalty to him in return for favorable consideration. Landed retired veterans who accepted Lord Coronet as their new liege Lord paid the ten percent liege tax to Coronet Fitzpatrick, most of which he redistributed to the active duty soldiers and sailors in the form of bonuses that often exceeded both the salaries paid by the Senate and their individual Liege Lords. Consequently, a majority of the retired and active duty military personnel in 2416 had sworn at least partial loyalty to the Fitzpatrick family. Bruce and his friend Lord Davis were making disrespectful jests, perhaps suggesting that young Fitzpatrick was buying their loyalty. This entire episode is fiction, as Fitzpatrick the Younger would never have participated in such a scheme. After his clan and the military, there is nothing a Yukon respects more than education, and cheating on a test would be tantamount to overthrowing the whole of our society.

24. Ever since the Storm Times, as today, acting was not, in the strictest sense, legal, but the law in this case was more honored in the breach than in the observance. If the actors in a moving picture or stage play were not from good families or if they had criminal records, the police would allow them to perform.

said. "Mason says this will be something different tonight, something you have never seen before."

I pulled Watchcharm into an inner portion of the double rows of columns that surrounded our dormitory and looked about to make certain no one was listening to us. Then I asked him about Dr. Murrey.

"Why was he allowed to challenge Fitz as he did in the exam room?" I asked.

"Fitz's parents protect Murrey, but the situation is deeper than that," said Davis. "I'm surprised a smart chap like you hasn't guessed."

"Guessed what?"

"Come, Robert. You disappoint me," he said, and he looked around as I had seconds earlier. "Look," he whispered, "the old man has practically got Timerman written on his forehead. I would say he's no small hen in the flock, either. He has been listed on the faculty for twenty years, and yet he teaches no regular classes. Murrey goes off where he likes and teaches whatever individuals he wants. He owes no fealty to a Lord; not to the college Lord, not to a local one, not to Lord Coronet Fitzpatrick. He is away from Centralia City on his way to God knows where at any time of the year. Only a Timerman chieftain could pull off that trick."

"Then if he has the power, why didn't he see to it we got lower grades?" I asked. "We did not deserve the marks we received."

"Deserve?" said Davis and gave me a wink of his green right eye and a nudge of his bony elbow. "By the Son of God, Bobby: Fitz arranged the entire show with Manheim. That is why you and I drew the easy eras. Manheim gave us the grades. Murrey was there to observe. Why? I don't know and don't want to know. Nor do you, old man. You want to keep quiet and let good things happen to you. Don't worry. Fitz will see to everything."

For Davis—may God bless his immortal soul—resolving not to worry was as much planning as he needed to do to prepare for the future. Not overanalyzing anything came easily to him. I could not escape knowing what I had done and some of the consequences it entailed. I realized that accepting my test score bound me to Fitz as securely as if I had been his liege. I had violated university code. One word from Fitz to the War College's Dean—a whispered rumor, an anonymous note, anything—and I would be sent down. After that disgrace I might not have any position higher than becoming a regular soldier in the ranks of my old division. When I weighed that prospect against becoming Fitz's man in everything but name and the rewards serving him would bring me, it was a very simple choice for me to decide I should say nothing and pretend I deserved my grade. At age twenty my talent for pretending had only made me a cheat. Before I had reached the age of thirty it had made me a participant in the murder of millions.[25] Each of us in "the kings of men" drifted into culpability by taking small steps such as accepting the arranged test. Never as we progressed further into Fitz's schemes did we feel we were being as despicable as we in fact were. Only when the terrible journey was over did we look back and know how far from God we had traveled.

"If you think it's all right . . ." I said to Davis, and together we started down a pathway no man should ever travel.

---

25. Murder is an inappropriate word. Bruce is referring to the Four Points War, and those killed in war are not murdered; they are necessary casualties, and while casualties are, perhaps, to be mourned, we should not assign to a Yukon soldier any guilt for causing them to happen. If any guilt is to be assigned in a war the Yukons fight it should be placed upon the heads of our enemies; they know full well how formidable our military forces are, and if they do not wish to die by the millions, they should remain at peace with us.

# THREE

THE SOMETHING I had never seen before at Fitz's soiree that evening was a reel of moving film belonging to that young reprobate Lord Mason. The patched together spindle he brought us was not so much an actual movie as a collection of short clips made in the Electronic Age, some portions of which had survived accidentally, and other pieces of it some antiquarian had saved for prurient reasons. His wind-up projector played sound in addition to turning the film strip past the gas-illuminated lens, or I should say it played sound when it was running modern film with its heavy plastic strips fastened next to the series of frames. As this was a copy of ancient film, it had no strip into which a phonograph needle could fit. Consequently, the film ran that night minus the sound, and that was no great loss as movie audio-output is always of poor quality.[1]

Back in my home village I had known a boy who had owned a couple of the phonograph discs made in the Electronic Age. I had little relished listening to them at his home. What the Americans thought was music was all yah-yah and buzz-buzz made when the Yellowjackets were in power; the recordings sounded as melodious as an artillery barrage wedded to the screech of a train careening from its tracks. I expected—and my expectations proved to be correct—that any visual images from that time would reflect the same mental chaos. I was not surprised Mason would be the one among the *Basileis* most interested in the relics of that era.

---

1. Better soft plastics in recent decades have improved the raspy sound of motion pictures, although readers will recognize the projector described here as being much like our modern machines.

Fitz had told me earlier his friends each had a special talent. Watchcharm Davis was brave, Hood was smart and brave, Lord Valette could read other people and was cuttingly amusing, O'Brian was gifted with a photographic memory, Shelley was a talented journalist (as befitted the son of a press Lord) and was a solid political negotiator, I was an engineer, Pularski was a killer, but Mason's gift was well hidden. Other than the valuable family connections Fitz had told me of, none of us could guess why Fitz endured Mason's company. Hood told me he thought Fitz wanted Mason about so the younger members of the *Basileis* would have an example of everything we should not become. Mason's only obvious talent, if it can be called that, was his highly developed propensity for lusting after carnal pleasures. At lust Mason was a champion. The closet in his room was crammed with pornographic magazines from South America and India, and despite having twice been reprimanded for keeping forbidden materials he clung to his nasty pictures up to the time of his graduation. He also owned strange devices manufactured in southeast Asia a gentleman should not know of, let alone own. I had never seen such filthy objects before I made his acquaintance. Mason, who often mistook his soup spoon for a teaspoon when he was at dinner, knew the objects' uses only too well. Insipid, slow to learn, and outrageously overweight for a military school cadet, Mason was rumored to have other habits I care not to put on paper.[2] The single reel of Electronic Age film Mason possessed must have cost the price of a large farm and was a tribute to his father's indulgence, as the permission to present it that evening was a tribute to Fitz's.

"You will love this," Tony Mason told us as he clipped the filmstrip in place behind the lens and lit the projector's internal lamp, which needed a minute more to glow brightly.

"Will there be anything nasty?" asked Hood. "I will not watch any pornography."

Being older than the rest of us, Hood was often put off his course by the rowdy behavior of the youthful cadets. Pious and reserved, as one would expect of an ordained minister, he missed his

---

2. For once Bruce is embarrassed to give us all the details. Mason had no such qualms when he composed his memoirs, which is why that wretched autobiography is available to the general public only in the restrained version. As a scholar, I have seen the uncut version of Mason's book, and I can testify that if young Mason really committed the crimes he confesses to, then he never should have been allowed to reach military age.

wife and his children amid the busy din of academic life. Hood found solitude every day in church and occasionally in a bottle, for the old soldier had a weakness for drink, especially when he had been away too long from his chubby and much-loved Martha.

"You could show this to children," said Mason.

"*You* probably have shown it to children," Valette taunted him.

"You may leave if this becomes offensive, Judge," said Fitz to Hood. "We will be right behind you."

"Make fun while you can," said Mason. "You will be fascinated."

Having wound the projector's flywheel as tight as a watch spring, he flipped the release switch to "start," and images began flickering on the white bedsheet Fitz had hung across his wall. At first there were some people wearing togas and laurel wreaths lying atop some chaise lounges at some sort of banquet. The pictures were grainy and in black and white.

"Are they supposed to be Romans?" asked Valette, for once not trying to be ironic.

"They do not appear to be Gypsies," said Hood.

"They let anyone be an actor in those days," explained Fitz.[3]

Suddenly the "Roman" banqueters leaped from their sofas and did an odd dance in which they flapped their arms like geese.

"Good Lord!" swore Davis. "The men are dancing!"[4]

Hood hid his eyes lest he pollute himself.

"Was there no sense of personal dignity back then?" asked Shelley.

The scene changed and before us appeared some more dancing men and women, and this group was shown in full color. They were inside some sort of domed structure. Lights were flashing

---

3. The era was not known as the Age of Excrement for nothing. During the twentieth and twenty-first centuries Christian men having no criminal records and women who were not prostitutes or Gypsies could legally take up acting.

4. As odd as it is for us to imagine in civilized times, men, sometimes in the company of women, actually danced during the Age of Electricity. According to the scant Historical record we have of that time, some of these dancing "men" even claimed they were the sort of males who find women attractive.

Many of the other scenes in Mason's film are examples of twentieth- and twenty-first-century "sports," by which the ancient Americans did not mean field sports, such as hunting or fishing, but staged spectacles based upon adoration of the human body. As Hood states, all proper activity must have a purpose; as Yukons, our activities must be somehow be related to work, worship, or warfare. Everything else diverts us from our necessary duties.

over their heads; bright, pulsating lights that hurt the eyes if one looked into them for more than a few seconds. The men were wearing trousers that had extraordinarily wide legs yet fit about their hips as tight as women's corsets. The women wore dresses so short they were parodies of dresses and allowed the harlots to show their knickers every time they moved their bare legs. The camera singled out a particular male dancer, a dark Latin I would guess he was; he wore his hair slicked down to his skull as Latins do even today. His face lacked the normal human features I had seen in Mexico. His jaw was thrust forward like a baboon's, and to make himself more absurd he swung his hips and pointed his index finger into the air, an obscene gesture I confess caused everyone in Fitz's room to laugh hysterically.

"The electrical fields must have killed billions of brain cells," said Hood.

Another segment appeared on the sheet; there were now two dancers, a man and a woman gesticulating in primate fashion inside a great bowl. One of them would make a peculiar bodily movement, and the other would mimic the motion in response.

"That is the same actor as was in the previous scene," I said. "The one that was in the white suit."

"Good eye," said Fitz.

Another change came over the white sheet and we were watching a swarming mass of hundreds of young people gyrating about inside a large enclosed space. The young women wore spiked hair like ancient Celtic warriors and swayed back and forth as though in a trance. The men had shaved heads and wore silk or sateen jackets on the backs of which were yellow and black pictures of wasps. The men all at once began smashing their female dance partners in the head with short clubs they had been carrying from cords at the back of their pants belts. Blood spatters were flying everywhere, even onto the camera lens. After all the women had collapsed, the men tried to smash one another.

"Tony," said Fitz to Mason, "this is a Yellowjacket Bash Dance. Why did you imagine we would want to see this?"

"It gets better," said Mason. "I'll skip over the rest of this part."

He turned on the fast forward switch. In quick time the carnage of the Yellowjacket dance was more disturbing than it had been at regular speed. Most of us, myself included, had to look away from the screen lest we become ill. When I looked up again I saw a group of men, ten of them, dressed in white plus fours and little boys' billed caps, and standing in an open field. Nine of them stood in place for a long time, waiting while the tenth man attempted to hit a small white object with a large club. When he at last succeeded in battering the object, one of the other men caught it and tossed it to another man.

"What is this?" asked Shelley.

"I know," I said. "I saw this in Mexico City when we went down for the surrender. It is called *Bol*."

"What is the purpose of *Bol?*" asked Hood.

"I don't know," I said. "I have heard it comes from an ancient Aztec ceremony."

"No," chimed in O'Brian, "*Bol*, or 'Bat,' as it is also called, is an American form of exercise."

"What were they exercising?" asked Hood. "Their patience? How is this exercise related to work or warfare? If it is not connected to work or warfare, it cannot be called exercise."

The scene changed and we were watching ten black men, all of them obvious freaks of gigantism, running back and forth across a wooden floor as they chased a round, orange thing and attempted to place the thing into two metal rings placed at opposite ends of the floor. Thousands of mostly white people were seated around them and mocking the poor fellows in their sweaty distress.

"*This* is like the Aztec game," said O'Brian. "But the losers weren't put to death."

"Dreadful," said Fitz. "Ten move, and ten thousand do nothing."

Some scantily clad white girls waving some sort of round, paper devices ran onto the wooden floor and performed some salacious dances during certain breaks in the action. Hood explained that these were the priestesses of the *magna mater* who would preside at the sacrifices once the ritual performance was completed.

Next we saw troops of men—I guessed they were men, but from the size of them I suppose could have been Not-Men[5]— dressed in body armor and chasing each other as well as an oblong orange object I surmised was another religious fetish. They struck

---

5. Not-Men are the creatures the Chinese made to fight the Great Pacific War. The Electronic Age men Bruce and the others saw here were made large by special diets, steroid injections and selective breeding.

each other and the object in short bursts of violent activity, and the rest of the time they stood about holding hands and touching each others' backsides.

"Speed it up again, please," said Fitz.

Mason reluctantly did as he was told. When the film slowed down there were two black men, naked to their waists, standing face-to-face in a roped off area. They alternately rubbed their bare chests together and punched each other in the head with padded fists.

"The Greeks did this," said Hood. "Then again, the Greeks did a lot of things."

"Some of these exercises might be useful in training men for combat," suggested Stein.

"Other nations have used them for that reason," said Hood. "Such activities remain true to their purpose for a while, then they become corrupted by professionalism and cheating. Gambling on sports in time becomes more important than the sports themselves. That is what happened in both ancient Greece and America. We do not wish to journey down that road."

The ensuing scene showed men on motorcycles speeding around an oval race course. Each man carried a large double-headed ax in one hand and was attempting to hack at the other riders as they raced along.

"I say we skip this part, too," said Fitz.

Mason sped forward to the image of a muscular white man, naked except for a headband and a pair of skin-tight briefs; he was screaming and shooting an enormous machine gun into the air.

"More nonsense," said Hood and rose to leave.

"We've had enough," said Fitz. "Please turn that thing off, Tony."

"I want to show you this one part," said Mason.

"Another dirty part?" asked Fitz.

"A speaker," said Mason. "I want to know if you can identify him."

He sped forward to the image of a tall man addressing an audience of tens of thousands in a vast arena. Pillars of light created by searchlights danced around the arena walls and the figure of an eagle hundreds of feet tall stood behind the speaker. Half the speaker's face was dyed black and half white. His head was shaven completely bald, and because of the dyes he appeared to be split evenly in half when viewed from the back. Everyone in the room but Mason chuckled because we each recognized the demonic figure who still haunts the textbooks of Yukon school children.

"Tony, Tony, Tony," said Fitz and shook his head. "That is Bartholomew Iz. Now do you want me to identify the *Mona Lisa?*"

"Not this one! Not this one!" protested Mason. "I didn't go forward far enough."

He hit the switch again, and we were soon beholding a small man dressed in a soldier's uniform. Beneath his sharp little nose was an abbreviated moustache. A crowd as big as the one attending Iz in the previous clip was straining to catch his every word. I recognized him immediately as a political figure from the mid-twentieth century.

"Hitler," said Fitz. "Don't tell me you have not heard of Hitler? You are in college, Tony; you really should read the odd book now and then."

"I've heard of him," said Mason. "He's the Garman."

"The word is pronounced 'Ger-man,' " said Fitz.

"Maybe I did not know him well enough," said Mason.

"Hitler killed nine and a half million people in concentration camps," said O'Brian. "He started a war that killed another fifty million."

"Once people made a great commotion over Hitler and his ilk," said Fitz. "After Iz and Rauf, he seems a very small story."

"Iz and Rauf killed nine million on any given weekend," said Hood.

"I was confused," said Mason, and pointed to the bedsheet. "Look at his armband. Isn't that the Land Pirate insignia?"

"The Land Pirates stole it from him," said Fitz. "Now turn that disgusting thing off."

"There are naked girls in the next bit," said Mason.

"Hood objects to naked girls of that era on moral grounds, and I object on aesthetic ones," said Fitz.

"They were either too fat or too thin," commented Valette.

Hood blew out the projector's flame and cranked the flywheel to rewind the film. Mason meanwhile whined that we were repressing his basic sexual drives, something the rest of us agreed was a commendable thing for us to do.

"Since you didn't like the movie," said Mason, "perhaps we

could visit the Lion's Den. I told some fellows we might drop by later tonight."

Fitz was against this suggestion. Mason, Valette, Davis, and Shelly, however, thought it was a wonderful idea and put on their caps and topcoats to go. Hood made it known he thought the Lion's Den was an abomination; that aside, he allowed he could use a dram of good whiskey instead of "lady's drink," as he termed Fitz's wine. I confessed I did not know what the Lion's Den was.

"We should go to show Robert," begged Mason. "He has to experience good and bad, embrace everything that's in the world. You know; like you always tell us."

"Your concern for Robert is very touching," said Fitz. "I am certain you would not want to go in order to satisfy your own desires."

Mason and his allies persisted until Fitz relented and he too put on his coat and cap. During our student years he always made the final decision for all of us, and anything he agreed to was fine for the entire group. We caught the city bus that took us across town to Front Street, the heart of Centralia City's riverfront district and a place uniformed cadets should not have ventured. If a military policeman from the War College had seen us down there, I feared we would have earned twenty demerits apiece. (I was overreacting again, for I should have realized that as long as we were in Fitz's company we were above the law. Any policeman so unlucky as to see us on Front Street would have fled in another direction or run the risk of being reassigned to some ungodly place like the Galapagos Islands.)

The Lion's Den was a public house of ill repute fixed between a fortune-teller's parlor and the Bargemen's and Railway Workers' Breakfast Cafe. The sturdy cinderblock establishment had three floors; the Lion's Den proper was on the ground floor, overhead was an unlicensed gaming room, and above that was a *lupanar* run by an owner separate from the family operating the drinking and gambling businesses.

"Here one can satisfy one's earthly desires, in ascending order," said Fitz to me as he led us up the steps into the smoky saloon that had a ceiling only a little over eight feet high. He did not progress any farther than the bar. He, Hood, and Pularski remained there and listened to the mournful Irish music being played on the bandstand while the others in our group drifted upstairs or into the darkened booths along the saloon's rear wall. From the red hair and oval faces of the men behind the bar and of the women waiting on the tables I gathered this was a Travelers'[6] enterprise.

"This is a new one, my Lord," said a barmaid to Fitz and pointed to me. "Is he going up to see Sandy, or is he a good boy?"

"He is the best of boys, Miss Margaret," said Fitz and sat his hat atop the bar. "He isn't going anywhere near Mr. Sandy." To me he added, "You should know, Robert, that Raft—he is the fat rogue by the beer tap with his two sons—Raft and his partner Mr. Sandy specialize in photographing Sandy's customers in compromising situations, if you catch my drift. To make a dirty story short, there are blackmailers here, among other criminal types."

"That's very harsh, Lord Fitz," protested the boisterous Margaret.

"You, my friend," continued Fitz to me, "were born too low to weather blackmail, as I was born too high. Our other friends are sons of district Lords and know their papas have already paid off Raft and Sandy. You would be dismissed from the War College if they had a picture of you. I am in a worse boat. Whiskey for the four of us, Miss Margaret. My dear father would see to it every Bishop in the church had a copy of any nasty pictures they took of me. You will find your life simpler, Bobby, if you stay down here with the rest of the lone wolves."

"I do not have any money anyway," I said and found a place at the bar to the right of Hood.

"Robert?" the barmaid asked Fitz. "Is he the one they call Robert the Bruce?"

"How would you know his name, Madame?" asked Hood, who suspected everything and everyone in the place.

"That fat Lord of yours," said Margaret, "the one we had to throw out that time."

"Lord Mason?" said Fitz.

"That's him, my Lord, by my faith," she declared. "He tells us about you and your young friends."

---

6. The Travelers are ancient Ireland's equivalent of the Gypsies. Composed of extended families, these redheaded thieves once roamed the countryside in North America and their native British Isles. Long before Bruce's time, they had been forced into doing legal work on society's margins, although they still often earned their livings from exploiting the foolishness of others.

"Does he say bad things?" asked Fitz.

"He lies so much, my Lord Fitz," she said, "we don't believe anything he says."

She went to a back room and swiftly returned with a bottle of real Scotch whiskey clasped in her short, broad fingers.

"Would the young Sir Robert like to gamble upstairs with Miss Charlotte, Lord Fitz?" she asked as she poured each of us a full shot glass. "She's a good girl, and never meets any young gentlemen."

Fitz frowned at the suggestion.

"Come, your Lordship knows she is a good girl," insisted the barmaid. "She goes to church and plays the piano in the evenings like a minister's daughter would. She even knows how to read Latin, a dead tongue only the learned know."

"So I have heard," said Fitz. "Charlotte is Raft's adopted daughter," he said to me. "She works on the second floor some evenings. You know, you might enjoy her. She's a very cunning girl. Very pretty, in a Celtic way. Keep your hand on your wallet, though."

"I can't go," I said. "I told you I have no money."

Fitz laid out ten silver quid on the varnished countertop for me.[7]

"Tell Miss Charlotte my friend would like to play at some game of chance for a time," Fitz instructed the barmaid. "She is not to cheat him out of his money all at once."

"A friend of Lord Fitz is guaranteed to be very lucky in this place," said the barmaid and took my hand to take me up the metal staircase.

"Are you sure about this?" I turned to ask.

I was not reluctant to go for the sake of any physical dangers I might encounter in a gambling parlor. I had seen other gambling parlors during my two years in the Army. What I had not yet experienced was the company of young women. Until that night the only members of the other sex I had been around were my female relatives in Arcadia. As a Christian boy I had never been allowed to

---

7. Monetary changes during the time of the Shay regime and subsequent inflation make it difficult to equate the money of Bruce's day with our contemporary currency. Following the charts in the appendices of Charles Epitome Furbasus' *A History of Coinage,* North Star Press, Superior City, 2575, the ten silver pounds Fitzpatrick gave Bruce would buy approximately two pairs of men's shoes or a lady's luncheon dress in modern times.

be near girls my own age, unless of course we were together at church or at public events where adults were also present. At the same time I was anxious to play the man of the world in front of Fitz, to whom I did not wish to appear inexperienced.

"Go. Have some fun, but not too much," said Fitz, who sensed my anxiety, and thought I was being a baby; I knew because he winked at Hood.

The barmaid led me up the staircase and away from the mournful drone of the saloon to the clicks and jabber of the crowded gaming room. As Centralia City was more a transport center than the seat of a university, railway men, steam lorry drivers, and river barge pilots, all in their gray guild dungarees, and laborers from the city's grain silos and stockyards dominated the crowds around the two roulette wheels and the six blackjack tables. They gnawed on worn clay pipes and cheap Southfield cigars and cursed their bad luck as they lost another week's pay. A few elegant swells from the financial district were playing poker at a private table and complaining loudly about the sad music drifting into the room from downstairs. I was surprised to behold there a number of War College cadets, most of them drunk and losing their monthly allowances from home at the tables. No one gave me a second glance as the barmaid and I walked to a secluded corner booth where Charlotte Raft awaited me.

She had red hair like the other members of her Traveler clan; in fact enough of it was on her head for several young women. On the evening of our first encounter she had braided the majority of it in a tightened coil that fit behind the nape of her neck. Her face was also as round as that of her stepbrothers, and her nose was wider than an artist would have placed on an idealized figure. Otherwise her features were well proportioned. Her throat and arms were slender and colored a glowing shade of pink; her hands were red and bore calluses from hard work, and she had a splash of freckles across her face and neck. In the light of the candle on her table the fine small hairs at the top of her forehead and the loose strands that framed her head burned like tiny threads of gold. Her green eyes did not look up at me as I approached. Because she smiled I sensed she knew I was pleased with her appearance. Unlike the barmaids downstairs, she was not dressed as a wanton serving wench in diaphanous lace, but wore a long silk gown crowded with the flower and star pattern sequins so popular with the tearoom set of that era.

"So this is the famous Robert the Bruce," she said and looked up from the solitaire game she was playing. "Please sit and talk to a lonely girl. Thank you, Maggie," she said to the barmaid. "I can take over from here."

"You know my name, too," I said, taking my place in the booth across from her.

She did not answer right away. She finished her game, and snapped her fingers when she ran out of plays.

"Robert," she said and fixed me with her green eyes, "how old are you?"

"Twenty. And you, Miss Raft?"

"Miss Raft?" she said, and inhaled a deep breath that swelled her upper torso as she smiled broadly at me. "Oh, I like that. You are a gentleman. You may hold my hand while we converse, Bobby."

While I was still digesting what she had said she reached across the tabletop and took both my hands in hers. This unexpected arrangement felt so pleasant I neglected to pull my hands away from her as a gentleman should have done.

"I just turned twenty-one, my love. But what are a couple months between a man and woman? In five short years you will need to take a wife, Bobby. I will gladly wait for you."

"I think . . . perhaps I should go downstairs," I managed to say.

"No, you won't," she said, and tossed her head so I could see the aforementioned golden strands shimmer around her face. "You have to stay a while longer. And I am quite serious, my love. You have to be rational about this and take into account all the facts: either your Liege Lord back home will marry you to a wealthy farm girl, or perhaps—given the course you are on—Lord Fitzpatrick will arrange a marriage with some young lady in his mother's finishing school; both of them will want to bind a war hero and brilliant engineer to a lowborn but wealthy political ally, which would not exactly be a love match, Bobby. Now then, on the other hand, I'm not bad looking. Men tell me so every day, and I think there is no vanity in repeating what I'm told so often. I'm not stupid, either. You'll need a smart woman to cover your back, Bobby, given the crowd you're running with these days. If you're the sort of man who cares, you should know I'm pure, untouched by men." She nodded toward the stairs leading to the third floor. "My stepfather would never let me go up there, nor would I want to. I swear on my mother's grave. You can ask anyone. I would be good for you.

No man married to a Traveler woman ever wanted to stay up late or get out of bed early."

"I will have to leave if you keep this up," I said and made a half-hearted effort to withdraw my hands from her.

"A girl has to try," she replied and stuck out her lower lip in a mock show of disappointment. "Come on, let's win you some money."

She literally pulled me from my seat and took me to one of the roulette tables. I thought she was either insane or making sport of me. Yet I greatly enjoyed watching how the raw green silk moved upon her as she walked. A wiser man would have realized she knew I was watching and could guess at the particular feelings her graceful swaying engendered in me, which is probably why she glanced back and smiled at me.

"How much money do you have, Bobby, my love?" she asked and took the silver from my hand without asking my permission. "Ten pounds? You see, my darling, I am not in love with you because you are wealthy."

"You must not call me 'darling,' " I whispered to her. "There are people listening."

"You, Mr. Bruce, need to learn not ever to give me orders," she said aloud and playfully touched the tip of my nose with an index finger. "Just for that I will call you 'darling' all the time, darling. Have I told you you have an absolutely precious face? And such nice strong shoulders."

She purchased ten pounds of chips on the croupier and placed the entire pile on Black 31.

"That is everything I have tonight," I said and reached to take some of the chips away, but she smacked my hand.

"I have a good feeling about this, darling," she said. "Do you like my hair? Men tell me it is one of my best features." She shook her head again, and this time, since she was standing upright, parts of her wriggled more than they had when she was seated.

The roulette ball hit Black 31, and the man behind the table paid me one hundred pounds in chips. Charlotte put the new pile on Red 12, and we won again. She cashed the chips in for a thousand pounds in gold and declared we should sit down once more.

"Thrilling, isn't it?" she said, placing the hefty pile into my hands. "You're now over your limit. Come back to the booth and flirt with me, my darling pet."

"You're a strange girl," I said, stuffing coins into the pockets of my greatcoat. "Why did you do that?"

"To show how much I love you."

She turned to me before she retook her seat, for I had followed her back to the booth a step or two behind.

"So, do you think I have a shapely backside?" she asked.

She spoke as plainly as if she were engaged in a normal conversation.

"Don't talk like that," I said, and turned my eyes to the floor. "Someone might hear you."

"You were watching it so closely, I thought I should ask," she said and sat on her side of the booth. "These drunks could care less what we say."

"Ladies and gentlemen do not speak to each other in that manner," I lectured her.

"I was not born a lady," she said. "And I have sad tidings for you, Bobby, my darling; you are the son of a nor'west forester, and no matter how hard you scrub you nails and polish your boots, you will never be a gentleman. Your Lord Fitzpatrick cannot change who your parents are."

"Why do you know so much about me?" I asked, astonished she was aware of my father's calling.

She ignored my question and persisted in acting naughty. That I was trying to be severe with her only encouraged her mischievous inclinations.

"So what do you think, sweetheart?" she insisted and gave me a wink. "Would you say I have a nice bottom?"

"Please don't do this, Miss Raft," I begged, utterly mortified she would frame such words in her pretty mouth.

"Answer my question, darling," she leaned across the table to tell me, "or I will scream at the top of my lungs that you are molesting me."

"I am on scholarship!" I said. "I will be sent down and stripped of all rank!"

She took a deep breath and opened her mouth to cry out.

"Oh, God! Don't do that!" I pled. "Yes . . . I mean, it . . . that is, you are, and I am not used to saying . . . I mean talking, in this manner. I am saying . . . you are very attractive."

"You are so sweet, Bobby, my lovely boy," she said and pinched my hand. "I'm so pleased you turned out to be sweet and handsome and well mannered and shy. You will make me a lovely husband. Once I've properly trained you, of course," she said and laughed. "Think of the money as a payment for a favor you will do for me tonight."

"What kind of favor?"

"Bobby, you are going to be a man with the power to do people all manner of favors. You shouldn't begrudge your future bride a small one," she said and held her thumb and index finger an inch apart to show how tiny the favor would be. "You only have to wait here and meet a man who wants to talk to you."

Like Hood, I had mistrusted every face in the Lion's Den the moment I entered the crowded building. That a pretty stranger asked me to marry her and for some unknown reason gave me a thousand pounds had not put my suspicions to rest. While I sat with her I kept checking the busy room for eyes that might be watching us. What, I asked myself, would Fitz think of this, were he to find out?

"Who is the man I am to meet?" I asked.

"A friend of mine and a friend of yours, except that you don't know he is yet."

She took from a sleeve pocket of her dress a silver watch and gave it to me. Centuries of handling had worn away its outer shell to the point where I could no longer read the inscription on its back. Upon opening the front cover I saw the smiling face I heard the old men in my village tell stories about when they were in their cups and recounting their days under arms. The minute and hour hands were attached to the face's nose, the small second hand was fixed to its left eye, and the hand showing the days of the week was fixed to the right. At the bottom of the face, in the place where the smiling mouth would be, were the words: *Eheu, fugaces labuntur anni!* The watch's owners had repaired the timepiece many times; probably none of its original internal workings remained. The gold inlaid lettering and details on the face were the same, I am certain, as when it was fashioned in the twenty-first century.[8]

"You, Miss Raft?"

---

8. Another of Bruce's wild distortions of fact. The Timermen would never associate with a person who was both a woman and Traveler.

"Don't be too impressed, darling," she said and took the watch back. "I'm not a full member of the order. I may never be. You might say I'm undergoing training under a Timerman chieftain. I'll never be a scientist like most of them are."

"You train *here?*" I asked, again looking at the noisy gambling hall.

"Of course not here. I go visit a teacher at the university. He is the only real Timerman I know. That, incidentally, is the man you're going to meet tonight. Till he arrives, let us talk about us," she said and took my hands in hers once more.

I was beginning to entertain the dreadful notion that pretty Charlotte Raft and the teacher she spoke of were going to do me some harm that evening. For a reason I had not yet fathomed, I feared they were going to lead me into a secluded part of the building and murder me ere I could sound the alarm to my cadet companions. I could tell from looking around me this was the sort of place that would attract murderers.

"Why are you doing this to me?" I asked her. "Is this some conspiracy against Lord Fitzpatrick?"

She could shift her mood as swiftly as an International Trade schooner could shift her sails against an October wind.[9] Charlotte must have sensed that I was afraid for she placed a serious but gentle edge on her words.

"I would not for my life do anything bad to you or Lord Fitzpatrick, Robert," she said. "On my life, I swear I would allow no one to hurt you. My teacher is not that sort of man, either. He talks and talks and never harms anyone."

She ordered drinks for us, hot chocolate no less.

"I don't want you to drink, Bobby," she cautioned me. "I have seen too many drunken men in my short life. You may have a glass of wine at supper, no more than that. The cocoa will put you to sleep tonight, when you will dream of me."

"I cannot give you orders, but you can give them to me?"

"You see, darling," she exclaimed and touched me another time on the nose, "you learn very quickly. How did you get your Knighthood, Bobby?"

---

9. At the time of which Bruce is writing the International Trade guild was restricted to transporting goods on sailing ships, as it does today. Steamships for foreign trade were allowed only after Lord Fitzpatrick the Younger came to power in 2419 and were used intermittently only until the fall of the Shays in 2453.

"I saved some men from a fire blast."[10]

"You've never killed anyone?"

"No. When you are on the ground during combat, you seldom get close enough to kill anyone. Only when there is a mass charge can you even see the enemy, and only the Chinese do that sort of fighting. The fire blast was a stroke of luck for me, as it turned out. One of the men I saved was a young Lord; his family saw to it that I was decorated."

She leaned forward and kissed the top of my hand. Again, the proper reaction would have been to take my hand away. I did not. Contrary to my better instincts—in truth, contrary to all my instincts—the peculiar redheaded girl somehow pleased me more than she frightened me. The reasonable part of my being expected she was amusing herself with me, yet being teased by a comely woman did not seem so terrible right then. The unreasonable portion of me, which at that moment, was at least half my brain and all of my body from the neck down, could only think of how warm her hands were and how I thrilled to the little pleasurable shock I felt when her eyes insisted on looking into mine.

"I could see in your face you were not a killer," she said. "I know you are a soldier, darling, but I want you to promise me you will never kill anyone. Shoot over the enemies' heads if you have to. A man has to give up a part of his soul when he kills another."

Given what I was, I must have been out of my mind to give my word to her. Fitz was right downstairs and might have found out. The temporary madness she engendered in me was so powerful I heard myself say: "I promise."

"Will you mind that I'm of the old faith?"[11] she asked.

"You're not a member of the Unified Yukon Church?"

"I attend services, and will continue to, if you expect it of me," she said. "I say my rosary in private. I warn you at the beginning: I intend to convert you after we're married."

"Is your teacher Catholic?"

"Holy Mother, no. He is the staunchest old U.Y.C. man you'll

---

10. A fire blast is soldier patois for the results of an incendiary bomb. War College records reveal that Bruce rescued five men from two burning tanks.

11. i.e., she is Roman Catholic. Catholics, Jews, Evangelicals, and other religious minorities did not yet have the freedom to practice their faiths openly, although their presence was well known and generally tolerated.

meet this side of the Archbishop of Cumberland. My late mother, God bless her," (she crossed herself) "she was not like the Rafts. She saw to it I was instructed. The secret priesthood and the Pope are quite the issues with my teacher, by the way; at times I doubt a Catholic or one from any other religious minority can progress a very great distance within the Timermen."[12]

She turned my palms upright and pretended to read my fortune while we waited. She claimed to have learned this tomfoolery at the parlor next door to the Lion's Den, where a charlatan named Madame Gyor fleeced the gullible at the rate of five pounds a head.

"The Gypsies are the only people in the world who can steal from the Travelers," she said. "We admire them enormously. Look here: you have a very long life line, my darling. You will live forever, almost. Oh my," she exclaimed as she tickled my hand with her fingertip, "look how strong your love line is! This says you will marry a wonderful redheaded woman—"

"You're certain of this?" I asked.

"—or God will strike you dead with a lightning bolt," she said, continuing the reading.

Margaret, the barmaid I had met downstairs, returned to our table and whispered something into Charlotte's ear.

"My teacher is here," Charlotte told me.

She took me to the rear of the gaming room and through a beaded curtain that hid a small unlit room containing a small table and several chairs. Parlor employees could sit there behind the curtain and keep an eye upon the gamblers outside. A lone figure was already inside when we entered, his hands on the table so I would see he had no weapon. Charlotte and I sat in the chairs across from him, and he lit the oil lantern in front of him, illuminating a face I had first seen a fortnight earlier.

"Doctor Murrey?" I said.

"Some of your classmates have, I expect, long ago guessed what I am," he said. "In my old age I am no longer as careful as I should be."

He showed me his golden Timerman watch, as the rules of

---

12. The Pope in Sao Paolo (where the Vatican fled when Rome—modern Rum—fell to the Moslems in 2095) was then Pius XVII. The Timerman would well have "issues" with the Catholic priesthood and church hierarchy, as they are secret societies outside the control of Yukon institutions.

their order demand they make themselves known whenever they are about to speak of their secret society's business.

"Will I be offered one of those, sir?" I asked.

"You presume far too much, Sir Robert," he said and put the watch away. "In spite of your qualities I have my doubts about you, young man. You are a brilliant math and science student, and we are always on the lookout for young engineers. You are also too eager to please the powerful, and you cheated on your junior mid-year orals."

"I did not cheat," I said, and swallowed hard, and in the weak light inside the small room I hoped neither Charlotte or Murrey noticed my unease.

"You merely allowed young Lord Fitzpatrick to fix the exam for you," he said. "He saw to it Manheim would give you and your new friends the easy questions, and young Fitzpatrick made certain all of you would pass."

"Tut, tut, my love," said Charlotte and wagged her finger at me. "Have you been a bad boy? But look, Doctor Murrey, he can't look at me. He has shame all over his face. That's a very good sign, don't you think?"

"He prefers to call shame 'regret,' " said the professor.

"I love him anyway," said Charlotte and put her arm inside mine.

"You've asked him to marry you?" Dr. Murrey asked her.

"He seemed taken aback at my proposal," she said, "but I think I have him interested."

"Is this your idea, sir?" I asked.

"Hardly, Sir Robert," he said. "The silly child fell in love with you when she saw you out marching on the parade ground. She, as I expect she has told you, is a religious heretic. Makes me wonder how far we can trust her. That said, she would not, all in all, be a bad match for you. You are unlikely to make what you young people call a love match, not where Fitz plans to send you.[13] Your Liege Lord back in Columbus Province may select a strapping milkmaid for you. Given what a fuzzy-thinking young mugwump you are,

---

13. Then as now, although a marriage could be arranged if one reached the age of twenty-five and had no likely candidates for a mate, most young people chose their spouses, which they called "love" or "natural" matches. In practice, only young people of great importance—as Bruce is going to be on account of his connection with Lord Fitzpatrick the Younger—had arranged marriages.

you are going, I think, to pledge your fealty to Lord Isaac Prophet Fitzpatrick. Compared to one of the trained agents from his mother's school he would select for you, little Charlotte would be a great bargain."

"Listen to the man," said Charlotte, and snuggled closer to me. "He is very wise."

Dr. Murrey took from his coat pocket a black box smaller than a cigarette pack; from it he emptied onto the table a disk about the size of a policeman's brass button. The middle of this object was a soft plastic nodule containing something in liquid form. Around the outer rim of the disk was a pliable, gel-like substance I recognized as a fire-retardant polymer. Murrey used a pen knife to carefully push away a small section of this jelly polymer, revealing a hard, black edge around the rim of the disk. He placed a finger on the middle of the disk to hold it in place and moved the knife's point against the sharp outer rim, which neatly clipped off the end of the blade as if the pen knife were as soft as a boiled noodle.

"Sir Robert, my young engineer," he said, "can you guess what this is?"

"That is a pellet from a cluster bomb, sir."

"Very good."

"The outside rim is carbon filament, and the center is . . . liquid phosphate?"

"Actually it is the advanced napalm you call Fire Sticks," he said. "Liquid phosphate was a good guess. There is a chemical fuse inside the carbon rim that ignites when there is impact and the plastic sac is ruptured. Tell me, what would happen to an airplane, let us say a big bomber, if a canister missile filled with a couple thousand of these exploded next to it, Sir Robert?"

"The plane, Doctor Murrey, would be destroyed," I said. "An airplane is full of fuel tanks and pressurized lines. One of these pellets that struck the right spot would cause an immediate explosion. One of them striking the wrong place on an airplane would start a fire that would burn metal and in few seconds would consume the entire plane. Anything not dripping with polymers would be destroyed."

"If the same missile exploded next to a fleet of airplanes . . . ?" he asked.

"Depends on the missile, sir," I said, unimpressed with a device that was not new to me and more than a little distracted by Charlotte's pliable flesh pressing against my side. "A missile fired from another airplane will hit anything within a half mile of its point of eruption. A larger, surface-launched missile could cover up to two cubic miles. This is not new technology, sir. Without electricity we cannot guide our missiles. We can track enemy planes with the Blinking Star satellites, and guide fleets of fighter planes armed with canister rockets into the enemy's path. We also can wait until the enemy draws close and fire wave after wave of larger missiles into them. Mechanical timers set the warheads off at the right moment. Essentially, air attacks against the Yukons are impossible because of pellets like that one. Maybe not impossible; I should say they would be so costly that an air campaign against us is doomed to failure."

"This old technology will protect the new air bases your friend Lord Fitzpatrick plans to build," said Dr. Murrey. "Don't be startled, young man. There is little in Fitz's plans I do not know."

He slid the pellet off the edge of the table and into the safety of the little box.

"You might have added," he said, "that our bombers and our long-range ballistic missiles utilize the same incendiary pellets to attack an enemy's stationary targets. The bombers fly to a point on their charts, and release their rockets toward the city or base or whatever. The missiles only have to be timed to explode so many seconds after being launched. Munitions overpower machinery, as they say."[14]

"They overpower people, too, sir," I said. "Armies in the field are best kept small."

"Our enemies cannot match us because . . . ?" he asked, leading me to an answer that was obvious to everyone.

"Because we alone have the Blinking Star system," I said. "Our enemies are strategically and tactically blind. We, on the other hand, always know where they are. They have no rapid communications. Without a guidance system or magnetic compass, they have a hard time of it merely flying long distances. I understand the Chinese have tried launching satellites. You Timermen have orbiting weapons that can shoot their projectiles down."

"So rumor has it," said Murrey and gave the same sly smile he

---

14. "Munitions overpower machinery," a quote from Peter Paul Hendrix's *Modern Weaponry,* a standard text of that time.

had directed toward me during the junior orals. "Well, the point of this digression, Sir Robert, is that we Yukons could conquer the world if we wanted to, don't you agree?"

"We could defeat the entire world," I said. "Conquering is another matter. We Yukons are so few; thirty million or so in all the Yukon Confederacy together. There are over four billion souls in the rest of the world."

"Young Lord Fitzpatrick will try to rule them all when he takes his father's place," said Murrey, pronouncing the line as though he were Lazarus come back to tell us all.

He seemed so ridiculously pompous that for the first time since I entered the Lion's Den I felt I might laugh.

"Fitz talks," I said. "He talks of everything. I do not put much in what he says," I lied, for I already knew Fitz's plans were more than fantasy.

"You trust him too much," said Murrey. "I can understand why he wants you to be on his general staff. Impressionable as you are, you are equally loyal to those you have given your trust to."

That remark pushed me over the edge; I laughed aloud at the preposterous suggestion.

"General staff?" I said. "General staff of what? Hadn't we ought to become lieutenants first? Fitz is my age, sir. Twenty. We are going to conquer the world at twenty?"

"Alexander the Great was two years older when he crossed the Hellespont," said Dr. Murrey, suddenly out of sorts and scowling at me. "That is the Historic golden boy young Fitzpatrick chases after in his dreams. You and your friends, whether you wish to acknowledge the truth or not, are in training to aid him to make his triumphant progress in History. I know, I know: there are thousands of more talented, more intelligent men than your self-titled *Basileis*. You and your friends will do well enough. General Hood will more than do. That one would rise to the top without Fitz's assistance. As it is, Lord Shelley will do to keep matters humming in the Senate. Young Davis will make a dangerously courageous flight commander. Lord Valette—frankly, I mistrust a boy that handsome—will do for a chief of staff. O'Brian will take care of logistics. Lord Stein will assist Hood when Hood is field commander. The terrifying Mr. Pularski will command Fitz's bodyguards. You, Sir Robert, will build his critical air bases in India. Mason, your friend Lord Mason, he would not make a decent doorstop if he were stuffed with lead and mounted on a coaster."

"Forgive me, sir," I said. "I know you are a great man, but this is madness."

"Madness runs in the Fitzpatrick family, young man," said Murrey. "I blame myself for not doing more about young Fitz. When you meet his parents you will understand why I failed."

Whatever Murrey's intentions had been when he sojourned from his cozy faculty manor to visit me on this cold January night, he was not succeeding in making me like him. His wild rantings about Fitz frightened me, in part because I recognized the shadow of truth in what he said. After months of hearing only flattery I was upset he did not disguise his low opinions of myself and my friends.

"Of what concern is it to the Timermen if Lord Fitzpatrick rises to the Consulship and destroys the Turks and Chinese?" I asked the professor. "Are not our foreign enemies your enemies too?"

"We in the Timermen are Yukons and enjoy a good war as much as the rest of the Confederacy," said Murrey, reverting to the condescending tones he had used in the examination room. "The Yukon people are bad at poetry, worse at painting and other plastic arts. We don't even write particularly good Histories, though God knows we spend oceans of ink trying.[15] We are the Shakespeares and Rembrandts of warfare. We bedazzle the entire world with our mastery of that field of endeavor. No, the Timermen aren't against war. War is what we Timerman exist for. I might add, war is why the Yukons produce top drawer engineers such as yourself. We are opposed to the war young Lord Fitzpatrick intends to fight. We have reasons you cannot yet understand."

I recalled the first informal oration I had heard Fitz give the *Basileis,* and I believed I knew how small the aspirations of this Timerman chieftain really were. Little Bobby Bruce the forester's son could already dream bigger dreams than Dr. Murrey did while sitting in his university towers.

"You are what Fitz calls an old Lord, sir," I said. "You never want the world to change."

---

15. A scholar of Murrey's stature would never slander Historical writing, the glory of learned endeavor. St. Matthew's University Press alone has, in a mere four and a half centuries, produced more than one hundred and eighty thousand separate Historical works, some two billion pages of sturdy prose, not counting footnotes, and all of these works are of a similar literary value.

"You, Sir Robert, are what we in the Timermen call a very young man," he said. "You do not understand the game that is afoot."

With that final disparaging remark he stood and found his walking cane. He went to the bead curtain and before leaving the small chamber told me, "We will be in touch, Sir Robert."

"I am confused, sir," I said. "What did you wish to accomplish when you came here?"

"I said we would be in touch," he said. "We will have an eye out for you and Miss Charlotte. Oh, young lady, please give that watch back to me for the time being," he added, and she returned to him the timepiece she had shown to me. "Keep up your studies, young lady. You, Sir Robert, need to work on your regrets. Regrets suit you as they do none of the young Lords you know."

He exited into the noisy gambling room and was soon lost in the milling crowd. Charlotte and I lingered in the hidden observation post for a few minutes longer.

"You have to go back downstairs, darling," she told me. "Before you go, I want you to listen to me: on your way to classes from your dormitory you pass Venture Park. There is a low brick wall flush to the sidewalk you take. Inside the wall on its far end, the second brick from the bottom pulls loose. I will leave a letter for you every Thursday morning for you to pick up at eight, and you will leave one for me."

"Why should I?"

"Because you love me, and I would thank you to please stop fighting against your feelings for me," she said. "You must burn my letters to you. Fitz will find out about us if you do not."

"What is there to find out?"

"I will give you a picture of myself," she went on, paying my question no heed. "You will not destroy it. Keep it on your person and look at it to see the face that will likewise dream of you. How romantic. Before you go, you may kiss me. The world being as it is, who knows when we will meet again?"

She puckered her lips and closed her eyes.

There were countless reasons not to kiss the strange girl. I could think of no honorable reason why I should. What would Fitz think if he found out? In spite of all that, I did lean toward her, and as quick as I could I bumped my mouth against hers.

"I am not your sister, Bobby," she said.

She put her arms around my neck so I might not escape her and pressed her lips on mine in an aggressive fashion I did not expect from one of her sex. I was thankful that no one of my acquaintance could see us do this. I was more grateful that none but God knew how much I enjoyed the moment.

"The idea is not to wrestle me," she said. "Put your arms around me and kiss back."

I did as she demanded, and felt still greater shame to think that God would know the thoughts she was putting in my mind.

"You see," she said and cleaned her lipstick from my face with her handkerchief.

"I'm sorry, Miss Raft," I said. "I really should go."

"Every Thursday morning at eight," she whispered to me as I went to the curtain.

I turned to look at her; probably I paused too long. My slowness pleased her, and she blew me a kiss from her hand as I left her.

In the barroom downstairs Fitz, Hood, and Pularski were playing at darts with Mr. Raft and his two sons. As should be expected, Fitz had taken command of the saloon during the time I had been gone. The customers and the members of the Irish band had ceased their singular pursuits to listen to Fitz's anecdotes and to cheer for him when he stepped to the line to take his turn. The Consul's son had mastered the minor arts as completely as he had the major categories, and to the delight of the onlookers he tossed bull's-eyes and double nineteens whenever he wished. In contrast to our radiant Lord Fitz, grizzled old Hood had never had the leisure time to waste on diversions and could not throw a dart well enough to hit the board itself three out of four times. The Raft brothers and their father barked like circus seals when our bearded Judge took his turn at the line.

"Damn silly game," Hood growled as he sent another errant dart flying off the board's metal rim.

"The old man's throwing!" one of the Raft boys shouted as Hood attempted to take aim with a second dart. "Everybody better duck!"

"Tin snips," swore Hood, and in his anger he nearly hit the elder Mr. Raft who had rashly put himself within ten feet of the board.

"Here's Robert," exclaimed Fitz. "How did you like Charlotte? A talkative child, eh?"

"I won some money, Fitz," I said, taking care not to mention Charlotte or how much I had won.

"Daft bitch," said Harry Raft of his own adopted daughter. "She was my sister's child. Gives herself airs, she does. The Queen of Front Street is what she is."

"She doesn't act like a normal woman," chimed in one of the Raft sons.

The lad speaking was named Harry Jr. His brother's name was George, but Harry Sr. and everyone else called the rough and tumble pair Ham and Eggs. I cringed at the thought of someday having such people as my in-laws.

Buck Pularski took his turn at tossing a dart and hit the zero space outside the portions of the target marked for points.

"Too light," he complained.

"Were you aiming for the board, Goliath?" asked Ham. "Or maybe the house next door?"

"Gypsies," said Buck.

"Travelers," said Harry Sr. "Big difference between the two."

"Yes," said Fitz. "Gypsies have darker skin and play better music."

"We are the kings of the sportsmen," asserted Eggs.

"Is that so? How sporting are you, gentlemen?" asked Fitz.

He emptied every coin in his pockets upon the bar top.

"I have five hundred and twenty-three pounds here," he said. "I will wager every halfpenny of it that my man Buck Pularski over there can stand on the other end of the room, his back against the wall, and hit the bull's-eye, with a knife."

"Go on, Lord Fitz," said Harry Raft Sr. "I would not take your money. You know you are the gem among our regulars."

"If he wants to give it to us . . ." said Ham out of the corner of his mouth.

"That's the spirit," said Fitz. "Easy money. Do you wish to disappoint the generation upon generation of back door creepers and cutpurses in your family tree by passing up this opportunity to grab some easy gain? Ten thousand Rafts are looking up from Hell this very moment, chanting: 'Take the wager, Harry. Take the wager.'"

"You say he would be against the wall?" asked Harry, fingering the red beard on his chin.

"Heels touching. He needs only enough room to swing his arm back," said Fitz.

The Raft men looked at each other.

"Take the bet," said Ham.

"The freak scares me," warned Eggs. "He's possessed, I think."

"What can he do?" said their father. He opened the register and counted out the five hundred and twenty-three pounds. "It's forty, forty-two feet across the room. Will you think well of us, Lord Fitz? I mean, after we have your money?"

"I will think no less of you than I do right now," said Fitz and nodded to Buck.

"Now the rules of this are—" began Harry Raft.

He did not finish because Pularski had stepped to the far wall, placed his heel to the wall, and without pausing to aim, threw the knife he kept hidden at the nape of his neck. I heard a whistling sound and saw something silver sparkle in the air at about eye level. The blade smashed into the center of the bull's-eye, disappearing up to its hilt, pinning the board to the wall. Raft and his sons jumped a couple inches off the floor when the loud *thunk* sounded in their ears. In the immediate aftermath to the toss the entire barroom stood in silence; every one of them was staring at the knife vibrating at the dead center of the target.

"No hard feelings at all, good sirs," said Fitz as he pushed the money on the bar top into the pockets of his greatcoat. He left a hundred and fifty pounds on the bar as a gratuity for Mr. Raft.

"Please see to it that my friends upstairs get home safely," he told the Raft men. "Get them a cab if they need one. Oh, Buck would want his knife returned."

The beefy Ham strained with both hands to pull the blade free. Despite his best efforts, he and his brother had to pull the entire board off the wall, then Eggs held the board while his brother yanked the weapon loose.

"You would be a bad man to have for an enemy, Lord Fitz," said Harry Raft.

"I would not know," said Fitz. "Everywhere I go, I have naught but friends. Come," he said to the rest of us, "let us leave our amorous comrades to their fleshy vices. I have some music worthy of the Angels I wish you to hear back in my dorm room."

We four—Fitz, Hood, Buck, and I—took the bus back to University Heights and there listened to a recording of Brahms' *German Requiem* on Fitz's wind-up phonograph. We listened in complete silence for Fitz insisted on hearing every perfect note, and we would not disappoint him for any reason. He went into a rapture when-ever he was enjoying beautiful music. So great was his concentra-tion he could not stand to be disturbed by sounds the composer had not written. That evening he lay on his sofa, shut his eyes, and turned off every sense other than his hearing.

"You never got around to telling us, Robert," he said when the music ended and he returned to the world. "What were your im-pressions of Charlotte Raft?"

"An unusual girl," I said. "She asked me to marry her."

Fitz and Hood thought that was a good joke. Even the somber Buck smiled.

"She was not serious," I said, when in my heart I did not know what she had intended.

"Yes," agreed Fitz, "she was pulling your nose. As pretty and as clever she might be, marrying a girl of her station could be disas-trous to your future. You will be needing a wife of an entirely dif-ferent sort. Trust me on that."

I retired to my quarters that night unaware I had that evening met the two other major actors in my young life. Only one of these new players wished me well, while the other wanted to manipulate me to accomplish other ends. Another five years would pass before I would know how beneficent the good one really was, and twelve years in total would go by before I would know I had that evening in the Lion's Den been face-to-face with one who could make the whole world sing the tune he had composed.

# FOUR

AFTER OUR JUNIOR midyears our academic careers at the War College were on a fixed course. While the majority of us continued to toil diligently with our books and slide rules, the *Basileis* knew that none of us worked under the same threat of failure that hung over the other cadets, and we ceased to fret over our grades. We knew we were going to do well as long as we remained in Fitz's circle of friends. If any of us tried a bit more than was necessary, we passed our classes with the highest honors. I feel guilty when I look back from my retirement years upon our favored positions at college. When I looked down from my room in University Heights upon the ordinary cadets being made to fight hand-to-hand with wooden rifles at five in the morning, not an atom of my body felt guilty. I rather felt I had at last discovered the proper order of things and that it was only right that some men be made to fight with wooden rifles and others sit in their quarters and watch them as they struggled.

I should mention that during our senior year there occurred an unfortunate incident which would mar our Halcyon days in Centralia City. Lords Stein and O'Brian, an unlikely pair of troublemakers as ever God created on this troubled earth—for neither was an aggressive or violent young man when left to his own inclinations—became embroiled in a heated argument over something I recall as being quite trivial. As nearly as I am able to remember, the trouble started when Stein refused to share his notes for a class on a day when O'Brian had been ill.[1] From this tiny acorn grew a

---

1. Mason's scandalous autobiography relates a similar reason for Stein and O'Brian's falling out.

mighty oak of ill feeling. Their feud progressed until the day came when they could not speak to each other without exchanging insults. Jean Valette, who fancied other people were placed on earth to keep him entertained, found the dispute between the two bookish cadets absolutely hilarious, and he made a practice of nudging the both of them toward a final confrontation.

"Hey, Jacko," Valette asked O'Brian one evening, "what did you make of Banker's presentation on Hesiod?"

"I don't listen to the bastard any longer," Jacko said.

Stein, who Valette made certain would hear everything, retorted, "O'Brian only listens to his hidden priest."[2]

The spat boiled over one evening at dinner. I remember we were eating curried ham, and Valette could not resist using something as harmless as our food as a spur to arouse the two combatants.

"I do believe Gwen has given Banker a double serving," said Jean.

"A great waste," said O'Brian. "Jews cannot eat pork."[3]

Stein exploded from his chair. He threw his plate at O'Brian and demanded satisfaction.[4] The entire dining hall of cadets stopped eating to watch the scene unfold.

"Holy Jesus Christ knows I am as good a Christian as any man here!" screamed Stein. "Meet me on the field of honor, or admit you are a damned liar!"

"Tomorrow morning at six, beyond the river, opposite the parade grounds!" said O'Brian, also standing upright. "I will take your Jew hand on it!"

"Enough of this!" said Fitz, and slapped his hands upon the table. "You, sir," he said to Stein, "sit down. You, sir," he said to O'Brian, "come with me."

Jacko reluctantly followed Fitz toward the kitchen. Stein remained standing, defiantly flexing his fists and striking an aggressive stance with his legs spread at shoulder width.

---

2. Stein implies that O'Brian is a secret Roman Catholic, as O'Brian's family had been four generations earlier.

3. Stein's grandfather had converted to Christianity when he became a Lord.

4. Demanding a duel would have been an extraordinary occurrence in the early twenty-fifth century as it would be today. The Military Code strictly forbids anyone, even a Lord, from challenging another man.

Fitz turned to him and asked, "Do you need Buck to help you sit down, sir?"

Stein looked once at Pularski and wisely found his seat again. Fitz and O'Brian entered the kitchen's swinging doors and were absent from the deathly silent mess hall for ten minutes. When they returned O'Brian marched to Stein's place at the table and made a swift bow to him. Tears were running down his cheeks as he apologized to his rival.

"I wish to tell you, sir, I have made a mistake," he said. "I misspoke—"

"That will not do," interrupted Fitz, who stood at the head of the table, his arms folded across his chest.

"I lied," said O'Brian. "I insulted my brother in Christ and ask to be forgiven."

"Shake hands in sign of friendship," commanded Fitz.

Matthew Mark Stein did not respond. O'Brian made a halting gesture with his right hand, but otherwise the two of them remained in place. A cloud came over Fitz's visage while we waited for the two men to relent. For the first time I witnessed the difference between his playacting and the occasions he showed us a real flame of his anger.

"Buck can assist you gentlemen if you are too feeble to do as I ask," he said.

They did as they were told. O'Brian returned to his place and covered his face to hide his disgraceful weeping. The rest of us had already lost our appetites and were waiting quietly for the great door to be opened so we might flee the room and the ill feelings it contained.

"You must apologize to both of them," said Fitz to Valette.

"What for?" said Jean, pretending—not very well—not to understand Fitz.

"For being at the root of this nonsense," said Fitz. "At the moment you are not funny. I indulge you too much, sir. I blame myself for letting you goad Stein and O'Brian on for so long. I apologize for that. If you, sir, wish to remain in our good graces you will do as we ask."

Valette made a flat smile. He apologized to the two young Lords, and the humiliation he accrued by doing so did not seem to discontent him. He was deeper than the other two. One could not tell what, if anything, he felt in his heart.

"We will not mention this again," said Fitz. "We will henceforth be friends once more."

He and rest of us knew in our hearts the apologies would not be the end of the dispute. From that evening forward O'Brian was a wounded soul. He would keep his wound open and unhealed until it festered and sent poison throughout his entire being and infected those around him. On the following morning he appeared to be his old self from the skin out; if one could have penetrated his outward appearances one would find that not a second passed when O'Brian did not dream of the vengeance he would take upon Banker Stein. Yet more harmful to the group than O'Brian's wound was the damage Fitz had done to his friendship with Valette. Hood alone in our group perceived the trouble this rift might cause; he took me into his quarters after one late night of study and warned me to be on the lookout.

"Fitz and Fitz's father are the only two men in the Confederacy powerful enough to humble Valette," the Judge told me in a whisper. "That pretty boy will not forget the wrong done to him, Robert. You and I would be less hurt if the Turks branded us on the forehead and sold us as slaves on the Algerian coast than Jean is harmed by the slight Fitz gave him. He was always a dangerous boy, being as close to Fitz as he is. Fitz will someday learn how dangerous he can be. You must keep your ears open, Robert. Should Valette attempt to draw you into some plot, you must not keep that information to yourself."

I pretended for my old friend's sake to be as concerned about the situation as Hood was. In reality, I had another issue that troubled me more than Valette's injured pride. Good to her word, Charlotte Raft left a letter behind the park wall for me every Thursday morning, and I stayed awake nights dreading what might happen to me if Fitz discovered the connection between the young woman and myself. He might then discover her relationship with Murrey and conclude I was plotting with the old Timerman against him. I did not write her back during the first week in hopes that she would tire of the game and make my life less complicated.

Her notes to me were silly compositions that usually began with a recapitulation of everything she had done that week and ended with a peroration concerning her undying love for me. Rather than the one photograph she promised me, she sent me two. One was a studio portrait of Charlotte in her Sunday white dress, posing as the muse of epic poetry, lyre in hand and smirking as she turned her eyes upward toward higher matters. The second was a risqué photograph of her at the beach in a tiny two-piece swimsuit; she had one hand behind her head and one on her hip and was rising on her toes the way she had seen girls pose in *The Railwayman's Gazette.*[5] Her skin was quite pale in the full light of the outdoors, as redheads' skin tends to be, but the general effect of the second picture was, I confess, appealing to me. I burned the letters, as she requested; the pictures I kept in my tunic pocket underneath a photograph of my mother. When I took out the second picture to look upon her I more than once gave myself up to thoughts a gentleman cadet should not have entertained.

In the second week of our correspondence I summoned up the courage to write her the following:

Dear Miss Raft,

I am, though I know it is wrong of me, moved by your attentions. You are, Miss Raft, a handsome and intelligent young woman, and you would, I expect, make someone a fine wife. Allow me to say I do not regret having made your acquaintance.

But you must realize the danger into which you are placing both of us. Please, please, I beg you on my knees, please do not write me any more letters. If F. discovers us, I cannot tell you what might happen. Please stop this.

Robert

She wrote me back the following Thursday.

My dearest Bobby, my precious darling,

So you think I am handsome and intelligent! I knew when we met you had immediately fallen hopelessly in

---

5. *The Railwayman's Gazette* was and is a lowbrow publication began in 2301. It features true crime stories, salacious accounts of the wealthy and famous and adventure fiction such as the well-known "Adventures of Locomotive Pete" and "Ranchland Roddy's Tales." On the inside page of the magazine for most of its years of publication could be found the photograph of a lower class girl wearing an abbreviated outfit. I know this through the testimonies of others. I have never read the magazine myself.

love with me. Upon some extensive reflection, I find I am starting to have reciprocal feelings for you. Therefore, I accept your proposal of marriage. I know we will be happy together.

Yet, my sweet poppet, I detect some slight reticence in your feelings for me. I notice I wrote twice (that is *two* times, if you are having trouble counting, my sweet engineer) before you wrote me back. Can you imagine the heartache your failure to write me caused me that first week? Then in your recent letter to me there was some nonsense about breaking off our correspondence altogether. This reluctance on your part makes me so angry I could do anything, such as run naked through your campus with your name written in lipstick all over my body. (That would be worse for you than getting caught writing to me, would it not? If you think I lack the courage to perform such a stunt, I suggest you start planning what you will say to the Cadets' Board of Inquiry.) I think it would be better if you wrote me *every* Thursday, and that you please write no more foolish things to me.

Yours forever, your fiancée
Charlotte

P.S. I have left home and am living in a flat in Chesterton.[6] Our mutual friend M. has secured me a job in a bookbinder's shop. In the evenings I am attending Mrs. Haggerty's Finishing School, where I am learning to drink tea as though it tasted good and how to keep my skirt over my undergarments on a windy day. I am becoming such a lady you could stick me with a needle and I would not say "Goddamn."

What could I do with her? I wrote her a letter detailing my most recent physics lesson, and she replied with a note in which she said she thought physics was so very romantic.

"Why do you not send me flowers once a week?" she wrote. "Now that we are engaged, flowers would be a thoughtful gesture from you. There is a shop on Corn Street that would deliver a bou-

---

6. A suburb of Centralia City.

quet to me for only two pounds fifty. My love, I know you have at least a thousand pounds to spend."

I felt trapped. I sent her letters, I sent her roses by the dozen, and at night I prayed she would become bored with me and cease this risky game. After my prayers I would take out her pictures and wish she would continue to bother me. Fate was kind to me. Another woman might have quickly lost interest in the coward I was then; I am eternally grateful Charlotte did not.

I saw her in person twice on Sundays. In the morning, when the cadet corps were marching on the parade grounds, she would be standing far away on the east side of the field, usually partially hidden behind a cluster of onlookers. She would be dressed in the same white dress she had worn in one of the photographs and would wear a straw hat and carry a parasol as the other young women did, as she did not wish to stand out from the general throng. She made no sign to me and took care not to go near the cadet corps lest someone see her approach me. Later, at noon services in the city's East Side U.Y.C. Cathedral, she would sit seventeen pews behind the second-row pew I shared with Hood and his family. Fitz and the other young Lords sat in the very front and could not see me when we were at prayers and all of us were kneeling. Then I would turn my head to the side and see Charlotte turn her head a little toward me and smile.

This dangerous situation was weighing upon me when Fitz came to visit me in my room the week before the Easter of our senior year. He rarely went anywhere without a bodyguard. When I saw it was just he standing in my doorway I thought something was terribly amiss. Perhaps he had found me out.

"Do you have a minute, Robert?" he asked as he shut the door behind him. "Is this your work?" he asked, referring to an elevation drawing of a suspension bridge on my drafting board.

"Yes, it is a copy of a pen and ink original I did last semester."

"Very good," he said, knowing his praise would please me. "May I sit?"

I pulled out a chair for him. He instead sat on the bed.

"I have a problem," he said, and made me panic for a moment. "It's Buck," he said, and I relaxed. "Do you ever angle, Robert?"

"Pardon, Fitz?"

"Angle, you know, for fish? You come from the Northwest, up

in Columbus. I assumed you might have done it some time or the other."

"I've fly fished for trout," I said.

"That is a lovely diversion," said Fitz; he made a pantomime cast with his right hand as if he were imagining himself in a silvery stream. "I enjoy fly fishing myself. Fishing for Pularski is nothing so elegant. He enjoys angling for catfish, here on the river. Have you ever done that sort of thing?"

"I have seen the commercial fishermen do it."

"What Buck does is much the same," said Fitz. "He puts some rotten meat on some hooks and runs them along the bottom of the river. Yes, I know: nasty business. Let me explain, Robert."

He left the bed and sat backward in the chair I had tried to give him in the first place.

"My father the Consul is coming to the War College to take part in our Easter ceremonies. My father is difficult to please, Robert. I will tell you that straight. He does not care for Pularski one bit; he says poor old Buck's homely face destroys his 'equilibrium.' I'm sure he means something else, but that is the word he uses. When I go home to the Meadowlands, I have to park Buck in the servants' house. Father won't let him in the mansion. When the Consul arrives this Sunday with his entourage, the dandies in the *Basileis* will want to meet him. Then Hood, well, Father has heard of Hood's exploits in India, and Father wants to meet him. So I was wondering if you would take Buck fishing, get him out of the way for the seven hours my father will be here? If you would rather stay in University Heights and be presented to the Consul, I would understand."

"I would be only too happy to go with Buck," I said, much relieved this conversation had nothing to do with Charlotte Raft. In the flush of my relief I would have done anything he asked of me. "But I don't have any gear," I added.

"That will be taken care of," said Fitz as he rose. "Be at pier number five on Front Street at eight Sunday morning. Pularski will have a boat and everything you need. Well then, I knew I could count on you. Would that the young Lords in our circle were solid, loyal chaps like you and Hood, Bobby," he said, knowing I would be delighted to be mentioned in the same phrase as the heroic Judge. "You are not disappointed you won't be meeting the Consul?"

"I did not know he was coming," I said, "so I cannot be disappointed."

"You'll have a better time on the river. He is my father, but, you know, really. Oh," he said at the door, "one more thing: if Buck does anything, let us say, untoward, I would like to hear of it. Work hard, my friend."

On Easter morning Buck, all six-feet-seven-inches of him, was waiting for me at the marina pier when I arrived at eight. He had procured a slender flat boat powered by a small steam engine that made a *putt-putt* racket when he placed it in gear. He said we would have to shut the contraption off when we ran out the fishing lines or else the noise would frighten the fish. He said almost nothing else for the first hour we were out.

We pushed upstream past the point the river divides. The city quickly vanished behind us, and newly green farms and stands of trees appeared along the river's swelling shores. The big man's silence made me nervous, and I consequently spoke too much.

"North and east of the river," I said, "was called Missouri in ancient times, as the river still is. Now it is part of Centralia Province. West and south of the river, where Northfield is today, was called Kansas, after the tributary we just passed. Kansas City, Missouri, was back there; Centralia City is built on its ruins. North of the Missouri River was North Kansas City, Missouri. On the Northfield side was Kansas City, Kansas. It's flood plains and tree farms now. You can still see bits of the old ruins among the walnuts there."

"Yes," said Buck.

Two miles past the fork in the river Buck steered the boat close to the west shore. As we swept into the reed beds, he disengaged the engine and turned down the flame so that only the pilot light was left burning. I took a long pole and held the boat in place while Buck baited the hooks and ran them out on a line. He used no fishing rod, only weights, big hooks, and a red and white bobber that floated on the surface of the brown water.

"The river is high this time of year," I said. "All that snow in Northfield and Mountain Provinces is melting."

"High water is good for catfish," he commented.

This was a complete sentence and a good omen, or so I thought. Buck watched the bobber riding the water with the undisturbable attention of an owl surveying a snowy field below him.

"I've never fished for catfish before," I said. "For trout, for salmon, once for bass; I've fished for all of them."

"Fitz says he's going to take me trout fishing someday," he said.

The bobber dipped below the surface, and Buck at once began hauling in the line. To keep his gear from snarling he pulled the line in with his good left hand and coiled the slack into a neat pile with his right, the mechanical hand he kept protected with a tight-fitting rubber glove. He seemed to enjoy the slow pace of bringing in a catch without rod or reel and halted three times to feel the fish struggle against him. Around a minute and a half went by before we saw the fish's streamlined silhouette emerge from the muddy water. Buck worked the catfish parallel to the boat and scooped it from the river with his metal hand.

"They have horns on their sides and back fins," he said, "and they bite."

A transformation occurred in Buck as soon as he had the fish inside the boat. He laid the ugly creature on its back and gently ran his good hand along its slick, green side. He repeated the gesture twice, making his strokes longer each time. I avow it appeared as though he were petting the thing. Buck's long, bony face bore an expression of tenderness that softened the hard edges of his features each time he touched the fish.

"Animals have a beauty people don't," he said.

He took the hook out of the fish's mouth and laid the monster back into the water. He held the channel cat until it became vigorous once more and slowly swam from his grip.

"You release your fish?" I asked.

"Always," he said and looked shocked that I would ask. "I never keep any fish. Do you?"

"No," I said, which was not a truthful answer. At the time I thought it was the correct one to give him.

"Do you think they feel any pain?" he asked. "Hood told me they don't."

"Scientists have proven that fish cannot feel the hook," I said, which again was not exactly the truth.

Buck seemed pleased to hear this. He put out the lines once more and became more talkative.

"I like Hood," he allowed. "I don't give a damn for the rest of them. Hood is nice to me. He's preachy for certain, but he is nice. We pray together, sometimes."

"Don't you like Fitz?" I said.

He looked at me and smiled a terrible smile that revealed his long front teeth.

"You don't know Fitz," he said. "You don't know him because you don't have any darkness here or here." He pointed to my heart and my head. "You are a good fellow. Hood thinks he understands Fitz. He has some darkness in him. Not near enough to understand Fitz. The other ones, the young Lords, they've known him forever. They do understand him, and they don't care. They think he is going to make them emperors of the world.

"When we get to India to fight the big war Fitz talks about," he asked, "would you take me fishing?"

"Certainly," I said, "if we ever go there."

"They have beautiful fish there," he said. "I've seen them. Tigers, too. They also have these tiny musk deer that have tusks like boars. The Ganges has thousands of inlets along its shore, all of them full of lily pads. You can pole a boat into one of those, and it's like a wonderland. Lotus flowers are all around and the birds and frogs sing."

As the day wore on Buck became more loquacious still. He told me the names of the birds and the trees we spotted on the riverbank. I was amazed to learn how much he knew of the natural world. He warmed to me so much he told me I should call him by his real name of Winifred, which had been the name of his favorite uncle, a man killed in the Great Pacific War. When he was not displaying his knowledge of flora and fauna he asked me questions, many, many questions.

"Hood is married, did you know?" he said.

"He is a lot older than us. He has two young sons."

"How big is Centralia City?" he asked, though I suspected he already knew.

"One hundred and twenty-one thousand people," I said, "by the 2410 census."

"There are towns in India and China with millions in them," he said.

"There are a billion people in China," I said. "Three quarters of a billion in India. I suppose they have to live somewhere."

"Why so many? The Yukon Confederacy is a lot bigger than both those countries put together. What do we have? Thirty, thirty-one million?"

"Foreign people don't marry late or have taxes and penalties on third children like we do," I said.[7] "We are a country of small farms and small businesses. There isn't a factory or mine in the Confederacy employing more than a couple hundred men. Our system of inheritance encourages families to have few children. The first son in a Yukon family gets the father's property and sometimes the father's profession. The second son gets into the military, or goes into a profession, should he be smart enough to win a scholarship. The girls get married. Additional sons in a poor family can, if the Army won't take them, become unattached drifters. In a rich family, additional sons bring on lawsuits over inheritances. China, India, the Moslems, the Latin Americans: they aren't feudal. They are big empires and have big central governments, big government corporations, big institutions. The more the merrier is what they believe."

Upon releasing another fish into the water he asked, "Do you know about Fitz's mother?"

"She is a Consul's wife," I said. "She seems to perform all her ceremonial duties with great grace. The papers say that, anyway."

Buck laughed so hard at me the huge muscles in his back twitched.

"I hope you never meet her," he said. "There is one with darkness enough to understand Fitz."

"Why do you say that?" I said. "I understand she runs a school for girls."

"She is one of those people other people think is remarkable," said Buck. "She's closer to Fitz than his father is. Or she thinks she is. Fitz gets his looks and his brains from her. Like the young Lords, she thinks Fitz is going to make her a ruler of the world.

---

7. Upon the birth of third children, Yukon parents of Bruce's time gave ten percent of their earnings to their Liege Lord and surrendered a yearly tax of ten percent on their income to the Senate until the child married at age twenty-five. The law, however, never was (and still is not) strictly enforced. Spinsters, old bachelors, and barren couples in the extended family have always adopted third children, and any children born thereafter, thus allowing the parents to sidestep half the taxes and penalties, albeit the additional children are reared in the same households as the first and second children, for the adoptions were (and are) a legal fiction. Only very prolific and careless parents have ever paid for their third children. The real reasons for our low birth rate are the widespread use of birth control pills and—as Bruce mentions—our system of inheritance and the fact that we marry later than foreigners do.

"Do you know the story of Jonah and the whale?"

"Yes."

"It wasn't really a whale," he said. "It was a big fish that swallowed him."

"I know."

"You know what Fitz says about Jonah? He says the water the fish swims in represents the ocean of consciousness. The fish is a particular type of consciousness. Jonah is an adventurer who enters this particular type of consciousness and comes back to other people to tell them what he learned.[8] What does he mean by 'consciousness?'"

"He means a way of understanding," I said.

"Oh."

I obviously had not enlightened him.

"Fitz says," said Pularski, "the Jonah story shows us we should each be heroes pursuing our own ecstasy. That's his slogan: pursue your ecstasy. He doesn't say that to you, and he made Hood angry when he said it to him. Hood says it's not Christian. What does it mean?"

"You've got me," I said. "I only know how to build things."

For the second time in our acquaintance Pularski laughed.

"I don't either," he said and slapped me on the knee. He immediately wished he had not done it, and the poor man apologized profusely.

"Winifred," I told him, "you have done nothing wrong. I'm lowborn, not a Lord; you can't violate my person by touching me."

He was so happy I was not angry with him he sat smiling at the rolling brown water for several minutes.

"Robert," he finally said, "can I ask you something personal?"

"That depends," I said.

"Will you marry?" he said. "When you're twenty-five, I mean?"

"I intend to. If any woman will have me."

"Fitz will choose your wife?"

"I'm not his liege. I'm pledged to a Lord Prim-Jones back in Columbus."

"You're lucky not to be Fitz's man," said Pularski. "Fitz told me I'm not to have a wife. He got me one of those women once. You know the kind. She told Fitz afterward I would be no good

---

8. A bit of quasi-Hindu tripe probably invented by Bruce.

as a husband, so he told me I should put marriage out of my mind."

"My grandfather told me," I said, "that being with one woman one time doesn't mean anything."

"It doesn't?"

"Absolutely not," I said.

My grandfather was a lay reader in church, and he and I certainly never had any conversation regarding sex. His wife, my grandmother, did once tell me that a pleasing lie is often a better reply than the truth.

"Fitz says many things he doesn't literally mean," I added. "When he is older and has a wife of his own, he will see to it you have one. You'll see. She will be kind to you, too. I'm certain he'll pick a kind woman."

"Thank you for saying that," he said.

He looked across the river to the cottonwood forests on the opposite shore.

"You don't lie very well, but it's good of you to try," he said. "You will have to do better if you ever lie to Fitz. He can always tell."

We fished through the morning and the early afternoon, pausing only to eat the salami sandwiches Buck had packed for us. At about two-thirty Pularski landed the boat on the north shore and showed me the ruins there. He had been in the area before with Hood and knew where many of the most interesting remains of North Kansas City lay on the flood plain. Salvage crews from Centralia City had been mining the ruins for three hundred years. What had been in past times a medium-sized city was by then mostly carted away a lorry load at a time to the other side of the Missouri. Trees were growing everywhere the concrete had been removed, which is to say the majority of North Kansas City had gone back to broadleaf forest.

Unlike the Greek and Roman ruins made of great stone blocks, which the passage of several millennia has made more evocative than when they housed people, these American ruins had eroded away into lumps of masonry and metal. The glass windows that had been extraordinarily abundant in buildings of that era laid shattered in a transparent grit that was strewn everywhere on the ground. The bricks, the ones that could be salvaged, had long since been carried away to be reground and made into new bricks. Only the rusting steel skeletons of some of the larger buildings gave one a clue that the wasteland we were walking through had once been the business district of a vibrant river town. When the salvage crews found a use for the girders, they too would vanish into the living city on the south shore. At least tens of thousands of human beings must have lived where we walked, and not one of them had left behind anything to touch later generations. The ruins told us everything we wanted to learn about decay; they spoke not a syllable of hope, beauty, or tragedy.

Pularski showed me a metal sign he and Hood had found when they came to this desolate spot on an earlier occasion. The words on it read: **DEALING DAN WILL NEVER STEER YOU WRONG.**

"A funny name," said Pularski. "What do you think it means?"

"I couldn't say," I said. "Perhaps he was some kind of political leader. One sees artists' conceptions in books of Americans putting up signs everywhere during their political campaigns."

"At school they taught us our language hasn't changed much since then."

"Yes, because of printing," I said. "Written English has been standardized for centuries."

"Then why don't we know what this means?"

"I don't know. The words haven't changed. I suppose we have."

He showed me another sign, this one etched on glass. Part of it had been broken off, leaving a remainder that read, ". . . is Lambda, Psychologist."

"Is that a Greek name?" he asked.

"Lambda is a Greek letter, and *Psychologist* must come from *psyche,* meaning mind, and *logos,* meaning word or knowledge, so it must mean something like 'one who has knowledge of the mind.'"

"He was a brain surgeon?" asked Pularski.

"Maybe," I said. "Or maybe he referred patients to surgeons."

Directly across from the spot we had looked at the signs he took me to see the stone foundations of a large building.

"It had one big room, no interior walls," said Pularski, and together we paced one hundred and twenty steps from where the front door had been to the foundation's far end.

"There were two side wings," he said and showed me how the building branched out. "Sixty paces across the way. The whole thing makes the shape of a cross."

"This was a church!" I said.

He went to the nexus of the ruined church and faced the back wall.

"I'm standing in the nave, right in front of the altar," he said. "The priest or minister or whatever he was would serve Holy Communion right here. Do you believe God's presence lasts forever, Robert?"

"Yes."

"They tore down the walls, but God is still here in front of me. Despite the whole city being gone, He's here. Hood says that's so. He is a minister, you know."

"I would not argue the question with him," I said.

"Hood and I prayed here," said Pularski. "Would you pray with me now, Robert?"

We knelt together and prayed before the vanished altar. For nearly an hour we continued in that position. My knees went numb and then became wracked with pain. The sky darkened while the birds in the ragged forest around us became quiet. To take some of the pressure off my aching knees I worked myself into the awkward position of resting on the balls of my feet. I thought Pularski must be confessing to the Lord everything evil mankind had done since we left the garden and was waiting on a written reply. When I glanced at him I saw on his long homely face the serene expression only the small, lost boy he had once been could have made, and I upbraided myself for not wanting to indulge him in something that obviously brought him great comfort. In his mind Winifred Pularski was in a safe place for as long as he remained in the ruined church. Lightning could have struck him in that moment, and I believe his soul would have flown straight up to Heaven, regardless of the many men he had killed.

"Winifred," I whispered when my legs could take no more, "I'm sorry, but it looks like rain."

"You should have said something," he said as he stood upright. "Robert, do you believe God will forgive anything we have done?"

"God will forgive whatever we repent of with a sincere heart," I said.

He smiled at me and did not at all look as terrible as he had when he smiled at me the first time. We returned to the boat and pushed southward toward Centralia City.

"Could I ask *you* something personal?" I asked him as he steered the steam engine.

"Sure."

"Why are you letting yourself go bald? A little shot of Falacil and your hair would come back in no time."[9]

"Fitz won't allow that," he said. "He says I could get to thinking I'm good looking if I had hair. It's a burden, and he says burdens build character.

"Robert?" he asked.

"Yes?"

"Are we friends?" he said, and looked at the river, as if he dreaded having his eyes on me when I gave my answer.

"Forever," I told him.

His lips quivered, and for a few seconds I feared the deadly bodyguard might cry.

"Does your family live together?" he asked when he returned to his normal self. "Your father, mother, brothers, aunts, sisters, grandparents, uncles: all together in a big family compound?"

"Certainly," I said. "We're a typical family. We're not a rich family, as you might have guessed. We only have three automobiles on the whole place. I have an uncle who's a captain in the Navy. My older brother has recently become a minister. Other than that, we're farmers and factory artisans. Oh, and two great-aunts of mine were schoolteachers. There are only thirty-seven of us in the eleven houses of our compound. That is counting the men in military service. We aren't a big family."

"Farmland?" he asked.

"We are not a village family. We have twelve hundred acres. The land is in two uncles' names," I said. "They grow blueberries, strawberries, and boysenberries. Then there are the apple and cherry orchards. Our Liege Lord has a cannery, you see. My father works in our Lord Prim-Jones' forests in the hills around our farms."

"Spinster aunts I bet," he said.

"To be sure. There are always in every family a lot more old women than men. We men get killed in the wars, so there aren't enough husbands to go around. The spinster aunts keep the families running. They teach in the village schools, adopt the third and

---

9. Falacil was the brand name of the anti-baldness drug manufactured by the now defunct Falacil Company of Grand Harbor. The drug appears to be similar to our modern day HairGrow, Locks Gel, etc.

fourth children, take charge of social events, and pick wives or husbands for those in the family who reach twenty-five and don't have anyone to marry."

"Hood's family is bigger than yours," said Pularski. "They're in Virginia. You probably knew that. Hood says when we are old and Fitz and the Army don't want us anymore I can come to his family compound and marry one of his single aunts, provided Fitz ever lets me go."

"Would you want that? Wouldn't you rather marry young and take your wife back to your family?"

"Fitz is my family," he said. "Listen, Robert, you and Hood are my friends. If something happens to Hood, should he be killed in the war Fitz is planning, would you let me stay with your family, marry one of your aunts when I get old? She wouldn't have to live with me. Our marriage would be in name only. I could work on your family's land, and your people would get my Army pension when I can't work any longer."

"You would be welcome, Winifred," I told him.

I could not imagine how I would explain Buck Pularski to my family if the need arose. I did notice, however, I was getting better at lying to him.

"The women in our family are fiercer than you," I said. "You'll be the one wanting to live apart."

"It's good to be on the water with friends," said Pularski, running his good hand along the surface of the river. "A lot better than listening to Fitz run on and on."

At the pier Pularski paid the marina keeper for the boat, and we carried our gear back toward University Heights. As we strolled to the end of Center Street and were about to emerge from between the rows of shops and enter the open spaces of the university campus, Pularski put his mechanical hand in front of me and brought me to a stop.

"About the red-haired girl," he said.

My face must have told him everything I was feeling, for he quickly tried to ease my fears.

"Don't worry," he said. "Fitz doesn't know. He had me follow you, and I saw you leave the letter for the girl, and I saw her come and get it. I haven't told Fitz, and I never will. I told him you were like a retired churchman, that you never look at women. I'm telling you this because you have to be more careful. Fitz has spies everywhere. Do you attend Bible study Wednesday nights at St. Albans?"

"Sometimes," I said.

"The gardener who takes care of the church and rectory grounds, he was in my company when I was in the Punjab and owes me a favor. He will sit next to you in your pew. You will give him your letters, and he will give you the girl's. Make the exchange when everyone kneels for the Benediction. You'll have to pay him ten pounds a month for his services. Stay away from the flower shops, Robert. You're very lucky I was the one to see you go in that place on Corn Street. Fitz's people have been told to watch florists, jewelry stores, dress shops; any place a man might buy gifts for a woman. He wants you to be in love with him, not with any secret girl. If the redhead cares for you, she'll have to live without flowers."

"Thank you, Winifred," I said.

"It's nothing."

We walked around the last corner of Center Street. As soon as we were beyond the city buildings we had a clear view across the university parks and parade grounds to the posh dormitories on the Heights. A squadron of Blue Jackets were on guard in front of our residence hall. Other groups of Navy and Army officers were loitering in the cobblestone lanes running between the other dormitories. From a half mile away we could see the sunlight glittering off their chest and shoulder decorations.

"Fitz's father is still here," said Pularski. "Those are their cars," he noted and pointed to a line of metallic Düsseldorf sedans parked above the parade grounds.[10] "Coronet Fitzpatrick never goes anywhere without his Blue Jacket houseguards and a couple of squadrons of senior officers."

"He should be gone," I said. "It's past five."

"The Consul keeps his own schedule; he says it's the rest of the world that is either late or early," said Pularski. "You go ahead. I'll stay on Center and have a cup of coffee till he's gone. The Consul doesn't care for me."

He took the fishing tackle I had been carrying and returned to town while I proceeded to my quarters. At the front door I

---

10. The luxurious Düsseldorf was then a fairly new model and only during the first decades of the twenty-fifth century was it acquiring its reputation as the exemplar of fine touring automobiles.

found the Blue Jackets would not let me enter the dormitory. They frisked me for weapons and informed me that although I was a cadet I would have to wait outside with them until the Consul left the building. The sergeant of the guard examining my papers saw that I was a Knight of the Field, a fact he could not have told from my uniform, since Pularski and I had been wearing fatigues.

"I'm terribly sorry, Sir . . . Sir Robert, is it?" he said and handed my wallet back to me. "There's nothing we can do. You know how these grandees are."

They let me sit on the steps while we waited. Hours went by. The rains came with the setting of the sun. The guards and I stood next to the wall underneath the eaves in a futile effort to keep dry. At seven they took a collection, and I went back to Center Street and purchased us sandwiches and tea. While we ate the Blue Jackets told me they were a select group picked from other Marine units. Each of them were the sons of families to whom the Fitzpatricks had allotted farm land or positions. In light of who they were, I would have thought they would be grateful to the Consul, yet there was not one among them who confessed to caring for him.

"Spend a two-year hitch as one of his houseguards, and you'll fall out of love with him yourself, Sir Robert," the sergeant told me. "There's no pleasing old Cory."

Their disdain for Coronet Fitzpatrick the Consul was matched and much exceeded by the love they showed Isaac Fitzpatrick, whom they called "the boy." A fool such as I was then might have believed these commoners would not have known much about young Isaac Fitzpatrick, Fitz being an only and much protected child. The Blue Jackets told me "the boy" and his mother had made an annual tour of the Fitzpatrick lieges' lands every summer since Fitz turned twelve. He had given speeches to the farmers and factory hands, and had walked among them, shaking hands as though he were a candidate for the Senate.

"His mother takes him about the country," a lance corporal told me. "A fine, beautiful woman she, as tall as a trooper. She and the boy got my dad his discharge and his full pension when he was sick."

Another man told me Fitz and Fitz's mother had sent his

young brother to college to become a doctor. A third Marine said he had written to Fitz and obtained a leave to attend his father's funeral.

"If you are a friend of the boy's," said the sergeant, "then you're ours, too. I met the boy when I was in hospital mending my leg from a bad meeting I'd had with some shrapnel. He has a kind and natural grace in him what made me feel as like I'd known him since the womb. Sit the boy next to his father, and you see what a pot of rubbish this genetics nonsense is—from his father's side of the tree, at least. It's his mother, God bless her, that the boy favors."

At a quarter to nine the rain turned to freezing sleet. We remained standing in the downpour.

"Old Cory's giving the boy and his chums Hell about something," said the lance corporal. "You should have seen him ragging the kids" (he meant the cadet corps) "while they was marching for him this morning. Nothing they did sufficed for him and his pothy generals and admirals and such. He had the kids marching and remarching their routines a dozen times. Missed Easter church. Good thing, too. Cory would've chewed on the minister for not giving the right sort of sermon."

The Blue Jackets had posted a lookout at the top of the first flight of stairs inside the dormitory. This man could peek through the frosted glass doors partitioning the floors from the stairwell; thus he could warn his mates when Consul was leaving. The instant he saw the golden epaulets of the lead general in the Consul's entourage on the other side of the doorway this sentry gave a low, short whistle.

"Cory's out," announced the sergeant.

The Blue Jackets tossed their cigarettes away and snapped into attention on both sides of the walkway leading to the front exit. I likewise straightened my spine beside them, despite looking out of place standing next to the line of smartly uniformed Marines.

Out the dormitory's front doors came a collection of beribboned and gold-plated senior staff members straight from a *Lazy Willy* novel. In the middle of the throng strolled the most gilded and perfumed of them all. The Consul carried a swagger stick, wore riding jodhpurs and glistening knee-high boots, and had a waxed moustache that turned up at its ends like miniature cow

horns. He could have passed for Colonel Plant himself.[11] As soon
as he reached the walkway he at once fixed upon me.

"Ah ha!" he said to the sergeant. "I see you've caught an assassin, Donaldson! Shoot the scoundrel first thing tomorrow! Let
him spend the night sweating it out!"

"My Lord and Consul," said the sergeant, his hand over his
heart. "The young gentleman is a Knight and a cadet. He was but
waiting out here while your Lordship was inside, my Lord."

"Why is out of his dress grays then?" asked the Consul and
struck me on the side with his swagger stick.

"My Lord and Consul," I said, remaining at attention despite
the stinging welt he had raised, "I have a day pass from the university, Lord. I am on leave until midnight, my Lord."

"On leave? On leave?" said the Consul, his voice rising from an
already thunderous level. "On leave while your Consul was visiting?
In my day at the War College we would have had a fellow shot for
that! Who said you could address me anyway?"

"Father," said Fitz, for he had followed the Consul to the main
doorway, "Sir Robert was doing me a favor. He kept Pularski out
of your way today."

"Can't the filthy Slav keep himself out of the way?" asked the
elder Fitzpatrick. "Can't the bugger get to some corner or other
and bloody stay there? In my day a chap could damn well keep to
himself without any damned help, sir!"

"In your day you did everything so much better than we do
now, sir," said Fitz.

"*You forget whom you address, good sir!*" bellowed the Consul.

He pointed his stick at Fitz's face as a fencer aims a sword at an
opponent.

"You are *not* yet Consul in your own stead, good sir!" he yelled.
"By God, you do not deceive me! I am not blind! I see what that
damned bitch your mother and you are about! You watch your
mouth, my boy, or you will repent your impudence on the
gallows!"

---

11. John Stewart McDuff (2311–2412) wrote the *Lazy Willy* novels (*Lazy Willy, Lazy
Willy and the Colonel's Wife, Lazy Willy Strikes It Rich,* etc. etc.), which, in spite of the
critics' scorn and the military's repeated attempts to suppress them, remain popular
even now. The books tell the story of a cunning private who again and again outwits his
superiors, particularly his nemesis, one Colonel Pother Edward Plant (or "Colonel Pot
Ted Plant," as Lazy Willy calls him).

With that threat he turned on his high black heels and strode into the still falling rain. The officers on his staff, looking as bored as they were well-fed, followed nonchalantly in his train. A comely young blonde woman was the last of his group to pass by the Blue Jackets. As she went past me, I bowed to her from the waist, since I supposed she was the Consul's niece or some other close relative. The Blue Jackets beside me bit their lips and struggled not to laugh. Fitz covered his mouth to hide a smile. This was to be the only occasion on which I met the Consul and his people; I did not know that when I watched them stride away from us in the direction of the parade grounds. I had seen and heard enough in those few seconds to be thankful I did not know him better.

"Terribly sorry about that, old man," Fitz said to me as soon as his father's group were out of earshot. "This shouldn't have happened. Are you hurt?"

"I'm fine," I said. "What did I do wrong just now? Why did you and the guards laugh when I bowed to the young lady?"

"That was Meg Sweeton, my father's favorite whore," he said without emotion. "You are perhaps the only living soul to refer to her as a lady."[12]

"Now I should apologize to you, Fitz," I said. "If I had known—"

"Don't mention it," he said. "How could you have known? Where is Buck?"

I told him Pularski was drinking what must have been his second gallon of coffee in Center Street restaurant.

"We didn't get back until past five," I said. "We could have stayed on the river till dark if we had known the Consul was still here."

"You did well, Robert," said Fitz. "No one can predict what Father will do. How do you like his mustache?" he asked and grinned slyly.

From the darkened parade grounds we could hear voices coming from the direction the Consul's men had gone. Someone was counting out a cadence in the manner of a drill instructor.

---

12. Like the scene that proceeds it, this declaration is a product of Bruce's impoverished imagination. Lord Coronet Fitzpatrick was a man of the highest moral character. True, he kept Miss Sweeton and other young women in his company, but scholars agree he did so only because he was concerned with their development and wished the young women to see something of the world before they married.

"Father is teaching the War College Lord how to march," said Fitz. "He has the poor chap going through his paces so we won't make a muck of it next time. Not that we were out of step this morning, mind you. The problem was we were three seconds too long getting across the field. He timed us. He also wanted us to wear a blue ribbon to commemorate his victory in the Pacific War. We were not informed beforehand. After the parade he made an impromptu white-glove inspection of the rooms and found dust on Mason's windowsill. If Miss Meg hadn't gotten tired of his performance he would have been lecturing us all night.

"Would you be the good soul you are and run and fetch Buck for me?" he asked. "I need to speak to him."

I went to the cafe and brought Pularski back to the dorms. By the time the two of us walked by the parade grounds the Consul and his people had climbed into their steam cars and driven away. In their absence the waterlogged university Lord had at long last been allowed to walk home through the darkened campus to his wife and a dry bed.

# FIVE

WE EXPECTED TO see the Elder Fitzpatrick again two months later on the day of our graduation, when we not only were given our diplomas from the War College but were also to be given our commissions as officers and told to report to our first postings in the military. As was to be expected—and I mean both on account of Fitz's brilliance and because of the privileges attached to his station—Fitz ended up first in our class. Hood, who had the disadvantage of not being the Consul's son, was a close second. By the end of my senior year I had won the book in six engineering and math courses during my time on campus and was third in our class despite my weaknesses in the humanities. The others among "the kings of men" also finished well within the higher third of our class, except for Buck, who did finish with a solid C-plus average without any additional skullduggery on Fitz's part, and Lord Mason, who did eventually earn a degree but was told before our expected ceremony he would not be allowed to stand on the parade grounds when the great day came. (There had been another scandal in his private life I know nothing of. Fitz and the elder Lord Mason had been impelled to petition the university on Mason's behalf or the young man would have been sent down without either degree or commission. I know only that I once heard Fitz haranguing Mason one night when I walked past the door of the latter man's room. "I am appalled I know a man of your nature, sir!" Fitz told him. Whatever he had done, the War College relented and gave Mason his diploma later that summer. As I will relate more fully below, the Army did not grant him a commission.)

At last the wet June day came round when we put on our cadet uniforms for the last time and stood in formation on the parade grounds in anticipation of the grand ceremony the Consul was going to give his only son and those of us who had the great good fortune to attend college with that young man. We polished our boots till they reflected the storm clouds above us and shined the brass on our gray tunics to the point that they glistened like the stars in Heaven. The university deans decked themselves in their tight-fitting old uniforms and took their positions along the side of the field and also waited for the Consul and his party to arrive and for the great man to speak to us and distribute the diplomas. The chapel bells sounded out nine o'clock when we first took the field. We stood at attention until ten forty-six, when the rain began to fall. Those parents and family members able to make the trip to Centralia City for the ceremony put up umbrellas or scrambled for cover under the wooden reviewing stand erected for the Consul and his party. We stood through the noon hour, though the water had by then soaked all of us through to the skin. The deans did not dare leave their places after the fit the Consul had thrown the last time he was in town. A few curses were muttered through the downpour, yet everyone stayed put. By four in the afternoon the rain became a torrent, and the wind arose from the west, making the young cadets shiver and the middle-aged university men aware of every aching joint they had ever had. At six thirty-two a man from the university's Blinking Star dome ran onto the field and informed the deans the Consul and his gang of cronies had decided to fly to Virginia Province that day rather than attend the War College's graduation; there was a new wild turkey season there that summer, and the Elder Fitzpatrick and his friends wished to arrive on the scene first and get the best blinds. If anyone in Centralia City had been inconvenienced by this decision, the Consul sent his most sincere regrets.

Upon hearing this news Fitz broke formation, went straight to the reviewing stand, and began passing out the packets containing our commissions. The deans were by then too exhausted to protest his actions.

"My friends," Fitz told our little circle of friends before we departed the university forever, "we today take the first step of our great journey. As ignominious as this beginning has been, I promise you the destination will be as correspondingly grand."

He shook hands with each of us and wished us God's speed. Fitz could always make everyone he spoke to fancy he was there only to speak to that person alone. He made me feel that when he shook my hand and told me he was proud of me. Then he did the same to the next man he addressed.

He told me then I would spend the next three years building roads and runways in India. The Second Engineering Corps[1] had given me three days to visit my family and another two to make the train ride to Grand Harbor to catch my ship. I was on the train bound for Columbus, fresh from our less than lavish commencement ceremony before I opened my letter of commission from the Senate; inside I found the official congratulatory notice, a short note from Fitz, and—to my amazement—a captain's twin bars rather than the single lieutenant's bars I was expecting. Nothing in the official notice indicated the Senate had granted me a higher rank. I knew there was no mistake when I read Fitz's words.

"To my friend and comrade, Captain Sir Robert Mayfair Bruce," he wrote.

> You have been given an assignment of the greatest importance. I have every confidence you will perform your given tasks as well as any man in the Yukon Army could. Sustain my confidence in you, and you will be one of History's heroes and will win a hero's reward.
>
> Out of my friends at college, only you and Hood did not once disappoint me. So much for blood telling. Among your many qualities, I admire your discretion above all. That is why I know I will not need to remind you that you must not discuss your new assignment with anyone. You will take especial pains not to speak of what you are doing in India with any senior officer my father might send your way. If any person, either Indian or Yukon, should visit you in the field, you are to refer him to either Mr. Sudhin Puri in the Indian Foreign Office or to Mr. Gerald Avery Tangle in the Yukon Office of International Trade.

---

1. Military designations should not be confused with their modern equivalents. The Second Engineer Corps of the early twenty-fifth century was the whole of the Australian engineers, not the specific Army corps it is today. What Bruce was doing in an Australian unit remains something of a mystery.

Colonel Robin McConnell, your new commanding officer, is a fine Aussie war dog I have known since I was a boy. Like you, Robin is a commoner and a personal friend of mine. He owes his current position to my mother. You will design, and Robin will see to it that whatever you create on your drafting board will be built. Whenever the two of you are together, I will be there in spirit.

God's Speed,<br>Fitz

The notion of sailing across the Pacific to Calcutta on a big four-masted bark did not frighten me at the time. The only thing I could think of was those gold bars. (How easily I gave myself to Fitz! Christ would not sell himself for all the world when Satan tempted him in the desert; all Fitz needed to buy my soul were a set of shiny decorations and a few words of praise. Like any young man who has met with some early success, I thought myself worthy of everything I had been given.) I was ignorant of what hardship a trip across the Pacific would entail. I had been upon the ocean only once before and on that occasion I had been aboard a steamer that took myself and twenty-four other fourth form boys on a day trip off the Columbus coast. Six hours out of Grand Harbor on *The Mother of Jesus* sailing ship I was stuck over the railing and vomiting my insides into the deep green sea. I then had a better idea of what the journey would be like. The crew was a pack of experienced if not particularly effective salts. They thought it great fun to be on a three-hundred-foot ship that was being tossed across ten thousand miles of water while they watched a young landlubber like me suffer. A Special Affairs[2] officer named Zimmerman was on the same ship; since he was as unused to the sea as I was, either he or I and occasionally both of us could be seen at the railing beside the jigger mast having "a talk with Neptune" any time of the day or night. He and I came to be as familiar a sight on the ship as the flights of gulls trailing after us and the sixty thousand square feet of plastic fiber canvas spread above us.

"Beans, salt pork, and green tea again tonight, gentlemen," the

---

2. Disbanded in 2419 upon the ascension of Fitzpatrick the Younger, the S.A. was a military police force that upheld the authority of the Senate and Consul. The regular Army and Navy despised the S.A. and frequently clashed with them.

cook would call out if he spied the S.A. man or me heading for the railing. "They'll rest easy on your stomach."

In the nine decades of my life I have been granted the time and opportunity to meet people from each of the six inhabited continents, and I can aver I never came across any social group less apt to belong anywhere in the world than the International Traders were in the times before the Treaty of Neapolis.[3] Many land-dwelling Yukons presumed in those days that, like the Navy and the seamen operating the mighty steamships that carried cargo between Yukon Provinces, the I.T. was composed of Yukon sailors when actually only the officers in that benighted organization were exclusively of Yukon stock. The common crewmen were the refugees of many nations; the tars from our Yukon Confederacy were merely the largest ethnic group among them. *The Mother of Jesus'* crew contained expatriate Chinamen, blacks from the Cape Verde Islands, Mexicans from the Baja, and Polynesians who when asked where they came from simply pointed to the ocean. Among the Yukon I.T. seamen were disinherited third and fourth sons, disgraced former soldiers, atheists banned from civil society, ex-convicts, and moral deviants sentenced to a life on the waves. The officers were either young men who had purchased their positions or Navy veterans seeking their fortunes before retirement. A curious aspect of their sordid lives was that a goodly number of these misfit adventurers in the I.T. would sometimes stumble onto the treasures they sought.

The captain, one William Moore, told me he estimated that any officer serving five years in the I.T. without being killed could retire with enough money to become a shop owner on land. Ten years in the I.T., said Captain Moore, would make an officer a millionaire. Under the standard contract, a ship's owners received two-thirds of the profits of each voyage, and the other third was divided among the thirty-man crew according to their positions. The captain got eight percent, the first mate and the ship's doctor took four percent each, two percent went to the three junior officers, the pilot as well as the sail maker and carpenter each took one percent, and the common sailors got anywhere from two-thirds to one-

---

3. Bruce's description of the International Traders of the twenty-fifth century is essentially accurate. Recent reforms have made the I.T. more congenial to other segments of Yukon society, but the I.T. will never be a fit place for gentlemen.

fourth of a percent of the total profits. The owners and other investors could be generous because the I.T. brought better returns on capital invested than any other business enterprise in the Confederacy.

In the chart room Captain Moore showed me the routes the I.T. dared to sail; they set out with Yukon grain, plastics, medicines, lumber, wool, cotton, steel, paper, ceramics, and biomass fuel and brought back gold, diamonds, and chromium from Africa, coffee, gum, and rubber from Brazil, vanilla from Madagascar, tea and silk from India, chocolate and rum from the Caribbean, platinum from the Slavs, nitrates and copper from Chile, and the sundry spices of the Malays. Since we Yukons dominate the world's production of vaccines and other drugs that are the only defense against the diseases that oppress the tropics, and as India has little fuel of its own, the medicine trade with tropical nations and the biomass export to Hindustan were particularly profitable. A pound in 2419 would purchase two gallons of biomass at a Southfield filling station. That same two gallons would sell for fifteen to twenty pounds in Delhi. A five ounce vial of Ebola vaccine sold for four times its weight in gold along the Senegal River. The average windjammer of the day held a thousand tons of precious cargo in its carbon composite hold, and while Captain Moore said it generally took ten years at sea to become wealthy, there were stories of officers who had bought their seaside mansions after one lucky voyage when the markets and the cargo were exactly right.

The dangers of the International Trade, I should point out, were as great as the possible gains. As everyone knows, by order of the Senate, the I.T. were limited to the use of sail, so that the corrupting influence of foreign contact would be restricted within the Confederacy. The barks were at the mercy of the winds and tides and of the pirates dwelling on the coastlines of many lands. The inland seas about Europe and western Asia—the Red, the Black, the Mediterranean, the Baltic, and the Persian Gulf—were infested with Moslem brigands, and I.T. ships no longer ventured there. Worse yet were the Malaccan, Moro, and Malay pirates roaming the oceans from Siam to the Philippines. Rather than chance a southeast Asia passage, I.T. ships, *The Mother of Jesus* included, sailed south of Australia and straight into the gale winds of the Roaring Forties. The Chinese government subsidized the buccaneers on its eastern coast and in the Nippon Islands. International

Trade sailors going to that portion of the globe could expect to sell their cargo on the mainland and then to be robbed as soon as they left port. In 2419 there were only three safe places on the globe for the I.T. to go: all of Latin America, across the Atlantic to western Africa, and south of Australia to India. Some greedy captains still ventured outside the safe areas in hopes of reaping huge profits; some of them came home rich, and many more never were seen again in Yukon lands.

Even when in a supposed "safe" port, an I.T. crew had to deal with the syndicates that controlled trade in other lands. Some of these syndicates were little more than criminal gangs intent on robbing both their countrymen and the I.T. Captain Moore's own brother, the captain of another ship, had been murdered by such a group in Calcutta seven years earlier when the unlucky man had hired some longshoremen who were members of a rival guild.

Any sailor partaking of the sordid pleasures one found for sale in distant ports could expect eventually to contract a disease the strongest antibiotics in the Confederacy could not kill. Unclean practices aboard ship would spread these diseases to other crew members, and thus a single case of, say, Bangkok Fever could fell a dozen men. The shipmates of a stricken man oft times would not tend to him as his death would increase their shares of the profits. Even a healthy man had to watch himself at all times on an I.T. vessel, for, given the nature of his companions, he could awaken one morning with a "second mouth" slit across his throat.

Those sailors able to escape pirates, disease, and their fellow crew members too often used drink and narcotics to destroy themselves. On *The Mother of Jesus* I witnessed men staggering on deck every day we were out; the stench of alcohol would come reeking from every filthy pore on the intoxicated men's bodies when they were under the blazing sun. The men preferred black Queensland rum they could mix with salt water to make grog, but they would drink any liquid that had a denatured aroma. When they had no rum they stole the officers' aftershave lotions, the doctor's antiseptic solutions, and the cook's food colorings. They fashioned long straws to steal sips of the biomass stored in the hold, and—if they had any sense—they stayed away from fire for several hours afterward. The drunken tars took a strange pride in how much they consumed. A chap who got wobbly legs after downing only a fifth of whiskey was deemed a woman and a coward by the master drunkards on board. The few sober men on board were held to be traitors to the service. The worst drinkers on the ship looked with utter contempt upon the Chinamen, who smoked opium behind the bulkhead in the forward hold and had no use for alcohol.

The S.A. officer Zimmerman once complained to Captain Moore after a drunken sailor fell off the rigging and nearly landed on Zimmerman's head.

"Don't you give your men proper training?" asked the pinch-faced S.A. man.

"Proper training?" said Captain Moore. "Hell, man, we don't train them, period. We have an opening, they show up, and they're in the I.T."

The one thing the common I.T. sailor did more than drink or fight was to gamble. The men bet on endless poker games played with short-carded decks. They bet on how many seconds after eleven hundred hours the captain would come on deck to make his rounds. They bet on who would next fall over the side and what the cook would serve for dinner. Some unlucky tars were so far in debt to their mates they would sail for years before seeing another payday. The losers took consolation in knowing that the winners would often blow everything they had won during one wild night in Madras or Bombay.

To an I.T. officer who made it through ten years of service, retirement meant a gingerbread mansion in Grand Harbor, Atlantis, or South Port. They would there become the financial backers of other I.T. ships and enjoy a prosperous old age married to a woman from a good family. For the rest of the old hands in the I.T., their last years would be spent as charity cases living in the United Church's poorhouses, institutions located, ironically, in the same great port cities wherein their former officers would make their homes. The non-Yukon sailors got off the boat wherever was convenient when they became too old to work. Captain Moore told me he knew of a few common seamen who had saved enough money to purchase officers' commissions for themselves and had become wealthy in their own right. Those were the exceptions. The great majority of the men on *The Mother of Jesus* and similar ships were destined to die old and alone on land or poor and young at sea. The men knew their fate, knew it above everything else, and never put aside their resentment of the officers for even a moment.

Other than the gregarious and blunt Captain Moore, I did not make friends among the ship's crew during the first portion of my long voyage. The officers on board had learned to fear everyone, as everyone on the ship hated them. The seamen knew I was too poor to rob, and because I was from the Army and had no authority over them they had no interest in anything I had to say. As soon as I had gained my sea legs and had gotten over my illness, I tried, to no avail, to make myself useful to the crew. The men had allowed the fire fighting equipment on deck to fall into disrepair and had misplaced the extinguisher tanks. I located the missing tanks in the hold and refilled each of them with baking soda. I picked up the phosphorous shells for the two three-inch Mitz guns that had been left to slide around the top deck,[4] and put them back into their caisson boxes. I had imagined that putting these incendiary shells away and restoring the fire extinguishers to working order would be doing the crew a favor, but the men said the tanks were an annoyance, something to trip over as they hustled about the slippery deck, and they soon stacked them against the midship bridge to get them out of their way.

"You have to understand," Captain Moore told me, "these lads don't care what happens. Not to them or the ship. If one shell explodes, then there's a jolly fire and maybe somebody gets killed. That makes everyone else's share that much larger. If a whole magazine goes, then there's not enough soda ash in the world to put out the fire. I appreciate the idea, lad," he said, "but couldn't you and Zimmerman find something else to do that doesn't involve us?"

The skinny chap Zimmerman was a cold fish, as was suitable to his position in the S.A. He could not speak upon any subject for more than a few seconds, and to manage that he had to space his words with inappropriate pauses.

"These men," he told me of the crew members, "they come from the cities . . . They are without education . . . Have no sense of History . . . They are not fit for regular service in the Army or Navy . . . How do you think thirty-two men like these would do

---

4. Mitz guns were powerful but difficult to move small cannons. Said to be effective in the hands of trained gunners—which I.T. crewmen seldom were—the History of the I.T. is replete with anecdotes in which I.T. sailors used the Mitz guns with disastrous effect on their own ships.

against a fast steamer that has a hundred pirates on board? Don't you think it odd they have no women here?"[5]

He was an East Port ruffian promoted beyond anyone's expectations and not hesitant to disparage others having a similar lowly background. He hated all the Yukon sailors on *The Mother of Jesus* upon learning that they, like he, were men without families. As much as he disturbed me, I could also tell he was a man who could hear grass grow, and I came to understand why a superior officer had given Zimmerman his commission. Six days out of Grand Harbor he knew the ship's doctor was an abortionist who fled to the I.T. one step ahead of the police and could disembark from the ship only in foreign ports. Zimmerman learned that the sail maker and carpenter—both of them older men and surprisingly competent at their jobs—had campaigned together on the Mexican border and were saving money to buy an excursion boat in West Port. Zimmerman had further observed that any man stationed beside the glass dome on the bridge[6] usually fell asleep before his two-hour watch was over.

"The Blinking Stars put the military messages in seven-plus code," he told me. "The weather reports and pirate warnings are in straight Morse dots and dashes . . . You might keep an eye on it . . . They're not."

He and I stayed near the aft railing during the daylight hours. I had gathered up some line and tackle from the hold and entertained myself by running baited hooks in the ship's wake. While I fished I thought of Pularski and of how I would prefer his awkward company to Zimmerman's icy presence. I likewise thought

---

5. As all readers will know, I.T. crews are exclusively male, for there are levels to which no woman, no matter how lowly in her origins or defective her character, will ever sink. Zimmerman is undoubtedly contrasting this situation with the steamers carrying out the domestic trade, wherein married women have always lived on the ships with their husbands and children. On a typical steamship—or on a zeppelin or in a train or lorry station—the women are the nurses, doctors and teachers, and the ship is much like a floating Yukon village. The peculiar all-male condition of the I.T., a situation known in greater Yukon society only in the Army and Navy, would perhaps have weighed more heavily on a more experienced adult like Zimmerman than it would upon a callow, newly commissioned officer like Bruce.

6. Bruce is referring to the dome containing the continually circulated ammonia-treated paper on which any signal from the Blinking Star system would be recorded. (See footnote 7 below.)

of Buck's warnings about Fitz's agents being everywhere. We were sitting by the railing one afternoon, and while I was fishing I had a sudden, unpleasant insight into the ship and the young man beside me.

"Do all I.T. ships have a Blinking Stars dome?" I asked. "I recall reading something somewhere . . . I think they don't."[7]

"You aren't supposed to ask that," said Zimmerman.

"This ship belongs to the Fitzpatrick family," I said, at last putting two and two together.

"You aren't supposed to know that, either," said the S.A. man.

"And you're young Lord Fitzpatrick's boy, aren't you, Lieutenant Zimmerman?"

"You're smarter than you look . . ."

Zimmerman lacked the ability to feign embarrassment when he was found out. He could feel fear and animosity. A greater range of human emotions were beyond him. He reacted to my discoveries with a flat, ambivalent stretching of his mouth, and bobbed his head.

"I'm not here to watch you . . . I'm watching the Second Engineers as a whole," he said.

"You will be with me in India?"

"Not exactly with you," he said. "More like with your unit . . . around, you might say."

Some men make one think better of them as one's knowledge of them grows. Pularski was one such man. The more I knew Zimmerman, the more the inner person he revealed to me resembled the outer man I had met on our first day out. He sat beside me in the hot sun, day after day; his face turned red and his skin peeled, but he did not complain. He did not change from his billed cap to something that would shade him.[8] The cap, he told me, was what he had been ordered to wear; he intended to wear it until his orders changed. He was suspicious of men who did not follow orders. I had to command him, as a superior officer, to put on sunscreen oil or he would have blistered himself down to the bone.

---

7. International Trade ships were allowed to have Blinking Star domes only during the time of the Shay regime. Obviously Bruce is lying when he asserts that *The Mother of Jesus* had one.

8. Unlike other branches of the Yukon military, the Special Affairs wore a black cap with a shiny plastic bill rather than the familiar gray slouch hat made of felt or waterproof canvas.

"The cook won't be wanting your fish," he said of my angling. "He boils everything . . . Fish are hard to boil."

"I release everything I catch," I told him. "A friend of mine told me both the man and the fish should live to remember the experience."

"Your friend is a sap . . ." said Zimmerman. "He would never cut it in the S.A. . . ."

He was, I realized, speaking more truth than he knew. Winifred Pularski may have done some evil deeds in his lifetime. He was still too good a man to be in the S.A. Zimmerman would in time prove he was serving exactly where he belonged.

*The Mother of Jesus* cut through the south seas to Australia in fourteen days. Many steamships could not have moved over the waves as speedily as the tall, lightweight beauty carried her carbon black hull over the Pacific. Once a man has his sea legs under him, a journey on a fast sailing ship can be a pleasure to be savored, if one forgets about the crew serving around him. The same trade winds that carried us west cooled the bright days on the glistening sea. The nights were serene times when I could sleep on deck or watch the dolphins swimming along the side of the ship in the moonlight. These were safe waters, for the Polynesians living there make war only on each other and do not extend hostilities to strangers. We did not stop at the Sandwich Islands or in New Zealand, those both being Yukon provinces wherein I.T. ships are not welcome.[9] At Melbourne we took on fresh water and twenty tons of ten-inch plastic pipe we had to tie down atop the deck. A mountain of this pinkish-gray pipe was lying stacked outside a warehouse near the end of that twisting, deep harbor. The yardmaster was disappointed we took so little of the stock he had on hand. He compensated for his disappointment by seeing to it that a steam tug took us in and out of the long harbor on the same day as we arrived.

"They don't like I.T. men in Melbourne," said Captain Moore to me when we were back at sea. "When I think upon it, I would say they don't like us anywhere but Meredith Hall."[10]

---

9. International Trade and foreign ships only dock in a few large ports.

10. Meredith Hall was then the Grand Harbor headquarters of the Universal Insurance Company, which insured ships and cargo and also handled many investments in individual I.T. voyages. The U.I.C.'s central office is currently in Oakland, across the bay from Grand Harbor.

For as long as our ship was south of Down Under, Captain Moore strained to keep the brown Australian coast to starboard and in sight until we passed Cape Leeuwin at the desert continent's southwestern corner. Late June is early winter in the southern hemisphere. We thus had to progress against icy headwinds till we could turn north toward India. To make any progress against the weather Captain Moore had to tack the ship in a zigzag pattern, and that made sailing close to the rocky south Australian shore impossible. To avoid running aground we swung hard to port, straight into the dangerous fortieth parallel and whatever storms might be lurking beyond it.

Four days from Melbourne there arose upon us a strong, cold wind straight from the frozen heart of Antarctica, a wind, declared Captain Moore, sent by an angry Almighty to drive his ship backward to the Australian coastline. He stood atop the bridge and swore an unholy streak of invectives against God and all the Saints, who were out there in the Roaring Forties, he claimed, conspiring against him. God did not relent for the sake of his tantrums, forcing Captain Moore to head *The Mother of Jesus* still farther south. He ordered the topsails furled and for a half day took the ship deeper into the raging seas ere turning west once more.

"If the sea wants us," he proclaimed to his frightened men, "it'll have to knock my ship to pieces with wind and wave. I'll be damned if I'll die on the rocks like a damned beached fish."

We continued inching along the fortieth parallel, fighting winds that became stronger the farther we crawled west. The sky turned completely overcast on the morning of our fifth day out of Melbourne. The captain could no longer take an accurate reading with his sextant[11] and had to depend upon the Blinking Stars to keep track of where we were. To utilize his lateral sail and make progress against the headwind our Captain Moore had to make a wider tacking pattern, and our progress toward Cape Leeuwin became slower and slower.

The violent seas turned Zimmerman and myself back into the seasick novices we had been upon departing Grand Harbor. On the first day of rough weather, we took refuge belowdecks. I soon found the darkened galley more of an unbearable sleigh ride than being topside had been. At least in the open air I could see the

---

11. A sextant needs a visible sun to take an accurate reading.

monstrous waves that were battering us; up there I still suffered from an unsettled stomach but not from the claustrophobia I had below. As God would have it, I was making the right choice when I put on a yellow slicker and returned to the storm.

The sky grew blacker as we sailed on. The ship's prow bounced out of the water at every wave we met. At sixteen hundred hours on the fifth day the captain ordered every canvas except the storm sails—the lowest tier of sails in the rigging—to be furled and taken down. At that point, when the heavens had become a howling eruption of sinister masses that seemed to be swelling downward toward us and the wind was screaming as it pushed through the rigging, the Yukon crew members refused to climb the masts.

"I'll have you hanged when we get to port!" yelled the captain through the stinging downpour from his post at the bridge. "You cowards! You slimy yellow cowards!"

"All by yourself, captain?" a big deckhand asked him.

They turned their backs on Captain Moore's threats and went below to drink tea and get dry. The Latins in the crew refused to climb if the Yukon hands would not; it was a matter of pride, they declared. The other officers were terrified of the storm and decided their place was with their mutinous men. The four Chinese sailors on *The Mother of Jesus* had already gone below without anyone noticing.

"Do you think we aren't all going to die when she goes down?" Captain Moore called to the mutineers.[12]

The response of his rebellious crewmen was to barricade themselves behind the galley portholes. There were only eleven men left on deck: the carpenter and the sail maker—the two old campaigners Zimmerman had spoken of—three bare-chested Polynesians, four Cape Verde Islanders, Captain Moore, and myself. The seven dark men scaled the rigging, while the two old men and I worked the winch at the base of the masts to give them enough slack to take in the sails and toss them to the deck. I am ashamed to say the foreign chaps were the best men on the ship during that crisis.

---

12. Bruce is incorrect to call the disobedient sailors "mutineers." Had these deserters been members of the Army or Navy, they would indeed be guilty of mutiny. Within the I.T. the laws are considerably murkier. In that service a man guilty of disobeying his commanding officer might—should the ship's investors insist upon the point—be hanged, flogged or merely fined. In some cases disobedient men are not punished at all, if no harm has been caused by the rebellious men's actions.

When they were in the rigging the wind pushed them away from the spars until their bodies were stretched out like streamers on a kite tail. Only a single foot of rope held them in place as they undid the wet, gray sails; from below we could see them laughing and making jests to each other in their strange language amid the lightning flashes. They moved slowly, one hand on the rope and one on the spar. Their expressions remained unexcited as Captain Moore and the storm grew more furious. When two of the large mizzen sails began to tear, the captain shouted to the men to cut them loose and let them blow freely in the gale.

"I have a store of good sail," he said to the wind. "I'm short of good men."

Though the carpenter had caulked every seam on the deck before we left North America, the ship somehow took water. Perhaps the hard rain simply riveted its way through the badly sealed side portals the slackers below us were not watching. We had to work the bilge pumps, which were powered by upright metal wheels that needed two men to keep in motion. We three Yukon men took turns at the pumps while the seven islanders slipped about the rocking deck securing everything that came loose, which in time was everything the wind could reach. The captain stayed at the helm most of the time, swearing unrepeatable oaths at the storm, at Fate, and at his dark-skinned swabbies, who in turn laughed at the sputtering, red-faced man as carelessly as they had laughed at the wind that had flayed them in the rigging. Early in the morning dark a lifeboat came free of its berth and smashed about the foredeck; the islanders and I attempted to trap it against the railing. The moment we crowded about it the ship leaped over a giant wave and tossed the boat over the side as if it were as weightless as a piece of crumpled paper.

"To blazes with you then!" bellowed Captain Moore after the lost boat. "If it won't do as it should, let the sea have it, the damned traitor!"

The carpenter and the sail maker spelled the captain at the wheel when he absolutely had to rest. We were fortunate in that the captain's cabin had an outside entrance and no doorways to the galley below. We could go there to sleep and to warm our hands when that was possible. Inside his rolltop desk Captain Moore kept some good India tea, two very nasty bottles of Australian brandy, and some tinned biscuits; for the next three days these sparse victuals would be our entire larder. The mutinous sailors below tossed Zimmerman outside to us, but he was too sick and too frightened by the storm to do any work. Captain Moore gave him a canteen full of brandy, and stuck the shivering lieutenant into a lifeboat and covered him with canvas.

"I'll allow the engineering lad and the darkies in my quarters," the captain told the sail maker. "I'll be damned to a fiery eternity before I let in an S.A. spy."

Among the other duties I performed during the storm I read the Blinking Stars dome and endeavored to use the captain's compass and sextant to verify our position.[13] As I said above, doing the latter was impossible during most of the day because of the cloud cover. I had to wait until the sun rose or set, when I could fix Sol at a specific point on the horizon before I could take a sure reading. That I could do it at all amazed Captain Moore.

"Our tax money isn't completely wasted, Charlie," he told the carpenter. "The boy learned something at that college besides where the cafeteria is."

On the third day of our troubles, God decided to perform another act of kindness, as He did on the third day after His son's death, and He broke the storm. In the soft breezes that succeeded the gale we cranked the capstan and heaved aloft the main topsails. As we picked up speed in the more placid waters, we cranked up additional canvas. The midday sun found *The Mother of Jesus* again running like a swan across a park pond, even though we had not replaced the mizzen sails, as the extra canvas was below with the mutineers. Captain Moore posted French the sailmaker at the helm and ordered the other men on deck to gather around him.

"I suppose you know how to use a gun," he said to me.

He unlocked the armory case on the wall of the bridge and gave a rifle to each of us, save for Zimmerman, whom he mistrusted. A big Polynesian took a fire ax and smashed in the main galley portal, into which Charlie the carpenter tossed a tear gas grenade. The choking, coughing, drunken crewmen came stumbling into the sunlight, rubbing their eyes with one hand and the other hand held

---

13. The Blinking Stars would give, in nonmilitary situations, a ship's latitude and longitude in degrees and minutes. If a navigator wanted the reading in seconds, he would have to use a sextant. The whole section is spurious, however, because an I.T. ship would not have had a Blinking Star dome. (See footnote 7.)

above their heads as a sign of surrender. We had them lie facedown on the deck while the islanders frisked them for knives and firearms which we threw into a sack. Captain Moore walked among the prostrate men, kicking them—the officers included—in the flanks as he berated them as criminals, traitors, and the offspring of apes and sheep. He threatened to shoot each of them in the back of the head.

"You are not proud now, are you, my dear ones?" he asked as he savaged them.

After he had kicked each of the twenty guilty men, he turned about and kicked them another time. He called them names never heard on dry land, names concerning the unnatural unions of fish and dead goats. Then, his rage spent, Captain Moore took a deep breath and told the men to get back to work.

"We've seen worse," shrugged Charlie the carpenter in summation.

Captain Moore explained to me later that he was not inclined to punish the men further because, "Punishment affects only certain men. Not the sort of men I have. If I were to flog some of that subhuman filth, they would resent it. They would get even. Maybe murder me in my sleep. If I hanged the bunch of them, I'd just have to get new ones made of the same cloth and have to waste more time breaking them in. Better I get them back into the routine and hope they forget the whole affair. Wish they hadn't drunk up the rum. They'll be in a terrible sour mood till we reach port."

The galley reeked with the stench of vomit and burned opium. The beds, the chests, the chairs: every piece of furniture therein had been broken into splinters. Only the laws of physics had prevented the rebellious drunks from busting the pieces into dust and the dust into atoms. The sleeping quarters were uninhabitable for the remainder of the journey; everyone had to sleep topside and pray for clear skies until we reached Calcutta. God undoubtedly heard our pleas for good weather. He nonetheless rained on us and rained often enough to make the worst sinners among the men regret their behavior.

I slept in a lifeboat with Charlie the carpenter and French the sailmaker. As loyal crewmen, we and the islanders had the pick of these choice quarters. The mutineers, including the officers who had fled below during the storm, had to sleep in the open, or atop the cargo in the hold when the rains came. We loyalists had as a bonus a waterproof sail we could throw over us to keep us dry in our crowded berths. During the daylight hours I helped French mend the plastic sails damaged by the storm. He had a roll of polythene tape to fix the parts together, then used a hot iron to melt the transparent tape and make a bond that was stronger than the original untorn fabric. Because of his nickname, I asked him while he worked if he knew any of the ancient French language.

"*Je swee fransais,*" he said.[14] "'I am French.' That's all I know. I had a great-aunt could speak it. Suppose you learned it at college."

"I have studied Latin, Greek and Hebrew since grammar school," I said. "At my university there were specialists teaching the other dead languages: French, German, the Norse and Celtic tongues, Egyptian, Coptic, Assyrian, Akkadian. Engineers don't need to know any of them, God be praised."

The two old artisans loved to look at my illustrated *Book of Common Prayer*, a fine leather-bound tome I had gotten from Fitz as a Christmas present. Gazing upon it and running their callused fingers over the colored pictures reminded them of attending United Yukon services when they were young and had lived with their families. They assured me the country churches they had frequented had not held any book as lovely as my gold embossed volume.

"Isn't this Ivy League," said Charlie. "If you took every four-book collection in my family and sold 'em, you wouldn't have the price of this."[15]

The old sailors showed the loyal Cape Verde men the last section in my prayer book, the portion entitled "Forms of Prayer to be Used at Sea." The black seamen could not read the words. They did see beside the text the medieval painting of Christ preaching to the fishermen, and the Cape Verde men, who were as Christian as we,[16] crossed themselves to show reverence to what they knew was a Holy text.

---

14. Esau Taylor De Klerk, Professor of Dead Tongues at St. Matthew's University, tells us that the correct spelling of the phrase is *Je suis français.*

15. "Ivy League" in Bruce's time meant "high class." The origins of the term go back to the Electrical Age. "The four-book collections" are the Bible, *The Book of Common Prayer, The Pilgrim's Progress,* and *Shakespeare's Collected Works,* the basic elements in every lowborn family library.

16. Another of Bruce's lies; no foreigners, especially darkie foreigners, could be as Christian as the Yukons.

When French and Charlie came upon the dedication Fitz had written on the front page, their estimation of me skyrocketed. Young Lord Fitzpatrick had written:

To my beloved friend and martial comrade, Sir Robert Mayfair Bruce. May this book go with you and be your guide
Lord Isaac Prophet Fitzpatrick
Christmas 2416

The two old men had to read the sentences several times before they could believe what they were seeing. Their lips moved as they consumed every word. Charlie carefully closed the book and handed it back to me.

"We knew you were a Knight, sir," he said. "We had no clue you was a personal friend of the young Lord, sir."

"No, sir," interjected French, as he too wanted to call me "sir."

"He and I went to college together," I said. "The young Fitzpatrick gave me my Knighthood for saving his life," I lied, and the lie came so easily I did not have to consider how I would say it to them.

The awe Fitz's name evoked in these simple men, to whom the Fitzpatricks were a bit higher than the Angels and only slightly lower than God, caused me to realize what wonders my connection to him could work in the greater world. At the moment Charlie handed the book back to me I knew the rest of my journey would be made smooth. Being the vain young pup I was, I thought I could do no ill when I exaggerated upon the subject of my connection to Fitz. What, thought I, would the harm be when measured against the good I was doing for myself?

"We did not know, sir," said French and touched his forehead to me.

"We'd like you to have the boat to yourself tonight, sir," said Charlie.

"We'll sleep on the deck, sir," added French.

"I'll stay awake the night and keep watch, sir," said Charlie, making his bid to best his friend's efforts to please me.

"No need for that," I said, feeling magnanimous toward the awestruck men. "Our present sleeping arrangements are satisfactory."

They took pains thereafter to see I had a pillow beneath my head and a blanket over me while I slept. Charlie and French must have whispered something to their shipmates for I was soon the most revered man on *The Mother of Jesus*. Men to whom I had never before spoken came to me to ask if I would intercede on their behalf before the young Lord Fitzpatrick.

"I have nine months left on my sentence," one young sailor told me. "My father is ill, Sir Robert, and he's the last one left in the family shop. I've not had another arrest since my last conviction, sir. I'm all right now, sir, you see. I don't look at young girls no more. Please tell your friend Lord Fitzpatrick the same when you see him. God bless him, Sir Robert. He is the people's protector. We commoners all know that. I know he will ask the provincial judge for clemency. I know it, sir."

I told the sailor and the others begging to me I would do what I could. I did not know if Fitz would accept their petitions. I did know I would not be seeing any of them ever again after we reached India and if pretending to carry their petitions to Fitz made me the most respected man on board, I was willing to pretend to do precisely that.

The previously sanguine Captain Moore, who had been referring to me as "the engineering boy," invited me into his cabin for three o'clock tea every day for the remainder of the voyage. He too insisted on calling me "Sir Robert."

"Sir Robert," he said one afternoon when we were alone in his cabin, "we'll be parting company in a few days time. You might be telling your good friend Lord Fitzpatrick—not that I want to put words in your mouth—about what happened on this here ship. I mean about the storm and the rest of it. I hope you will recall how greatly I appreciated you helping me during that bit of trouble, sir. I do appreciate your help so very much, sir."

He shook my hand as a demonstration of his strong feelings of gratitude.

"I could kill the S.A. man for you," he said. "Not me personally. One of the scummy traitors I have on board could knock him on the head, and over the side he would go. Lost at sea, we'd tell the authorities. Nobody would be the wiser. Zimmerman's been sent to snoop on you and your people in India, you know."

"They would send another to take his place," I said.

"You're right, Sir Robert," he agreed. "But do they have any more exactly like Zimmerman? I'm tempted to kill the slimy bastard to please myself."

"Lord Fitzpatrick would not like it," I said.

"I suppose not, sir," he reluctantly conceded.

One of the Cape Verde men left a votive offering of dried fruit and coffee on the deck outside my lifeboat one night while I slept. The man could not have comprehended what it was that made me special. Yukon politics were as distant from him as we are from Heaven. He had heard the others talking in hushed voices about me and did not wish to miss this opportunity to placate the divine.

During the final days of the trip the cook, a former mutineer, saw to it I had the best food *The Mother of Jesus* had to offer, which was better than the other men's daily fare, though not necessarily fine cuisine. A Chinese sailor gave me a pair of canvas deck shoes he had fashioned for me by hand; "for the friend of Lord Fitzpatrick," he said and bowed to me like I was the Consul. When a sailor on the deck began snoring during the night, his mates would immediately rouse him. "Sir Robert is trying to sleep," someone would tell him, and the noise would stop.

I so enjoyed being the focus of their attentions I would have looked upon the rest of the journey as almost a pleasure cruise if there had not occurred a striking event that reminded me of who we on the ship were and of the small roles we were each performing in the grand drama Fitz was directing. Two and a half days from port a Blinking Star flashed out a warning to the effect that two pirate steamers from the Andaman Islands were at about 18 degrees north and 89 degrees east and were headed in a northeasterly direction toward us. The man keeping watch at the glass dome was alert and quickly relayed the message to Captain Moore, who at once veered his ship to the east and out of the pirate vessels' path. At half past fourteen hundred hours the Blinking Star had changed its warning; the pirates had also turned more sharply to the east and were drawing nearer. Twenty minutes later we heard engines approaching rapidly from the northwest; the sound was not the slow, heavy *chug-chug* created in the large valves of a steamship engine, and instead was the high frequency *hummm* of a high compression airplane turbine. From over the horizon two aircraft materialized, flying low and straight for us. The men on our deck dove for cover and braced for an explosion. They were amazed when the planes passed directly over us. I saw Yukon Union Jacks painted on their fuselages and recognized the long, cigar-shape profiles that marked them as

P-18s.[17] Minutes after they disappeared over the southeastern horizon we heard the crackle of gunfire followed by two separate, louder explosions. A few minutes later the planes flew back over us, and one of them did a victory roll as he passed. As he showed us the topside of his wings, I could discern the white winged horse decals he bore beside his Union Jacks.

"There they are!" shouted Captain Moore, pointing to two columns of black smoke that arose in the place the two planes had just been. "Roasted pirates! Enjoy Hell, you bastards!" he yelled in the general direction of the burning ships.

"What is happening here, sir?" I asked him. "There should be no Yukon warplanes here."

"A lot of things in this world shouldn't be, and yet they are, Sir Robert," he said. "Look here: in the Army, who pays for the regiments?"

"The Senate pays for some with our taxes. The rest are the personal troops of the individual Lords."

"That's how it is with warships, too," said Captain Moore. "Those airplanes come from a carrier in a Lord's pay." He tugged his ear. "I reckon you can guess whose pay."

"The winged horse is the Fitzpatrick family seal."

"So it is, Sir Robert. So I have heard it is."

I did not press him further. No Lord, no matter how powerful, could legally deploy armed forces for his own use. Nor should there have been any Yukon presence other than the I.T. in this part of the Indian Ocean. Both international agreements and Yukon law forbade it. I learned later the facts Captain Moore knew then: the Fitzpatrick family dominated the I.T. routes with their majority interest in more than two hundred sailing ships and the Fitzpatricks provided safe passage to their I.T. ships by using the Navy warships they financed.[18]

---

17. A two man, propeller driven attack plane of the early twenty-fifth century. Considered slow but reliable, the P-18 was used primarily in maritime operations. The white Pegasus symbol Bruce claims to have seen on the planes marked them as the property of the Fitzpatrick family.

18. Another outrageous smear. Although Mason and a number of retired Navy men made similar charges (see *Forty Years at Sea,* Albert Jacob Yeats, New Britain Press, 2457), Gerald assures us the Fitzpatricks did not abuse their maritime prowess. Gerald points out that the Senate investigated similar charges against the Fitzpatricks in 2410 and found them innocent on all counts, and Gerald is the authoritative text.

These abuses had allowed the Fitzpatricks to amass a fortune many billions of pounds larger than anyone outside the family suspected. The Timermen had via their satellites observed everything the family did at sea, but the Timermen's attempts to have the family's actions investigated before the Senate had been suppressed by the Consul and his political cronies. At the time I watched the P-18s attack the pirate vessels, I resolved for my own sake to forget what I had seen. I put the event into the same inaccessible place I stored the other information about Fitz that I could not reconcile with my love for him or, as I should say, with my lusting after power.

Calcutta was an anthill of humanity the day we arrived; an enchanting anthill that told me I was entering a land wherein I could not guess what I would see a mile down any road I took. My father had told me I would detest the place. He could not have been more wrong. Every good spot in the world, be it Astoria in Columbus or Srinagar in Kashmir, is a place that has created itself and could exist nowhere other than where it does. India is made up entirely of places that have made themselves. The one exception was the commercial city of Diamond Harbor, where the bits and pieces of a hundred nations were gathered to connive against each other. As is always the case in artificial cities, the bits and pieces there were the worst random parts the various nations could produce. As the crewmen of *The Mother of Jesus* made their ship secure to her pier, two hundred meters away were a thousand merchants screaming at each other in a hundred mutually incomprehensible tongues about the price of a bushel of soybeans. The sailors each shook my hand, the hand of Lord Fitzpatrick's special friend, and I walked away from them and into that Babel of pickpockets, beggars, and millionaires, my duffle bag clutched to my side.

I took the train from Haura Station, or rather, I should say, Zimmerman and I took the train, for the S.A. man traveled behind me like a second shadow. A small city of people crowded on the railway platform and the adjacent derailing yard, not an extraordinary sight in India, where there are many small cities crowded into compact places. Dark Bihari and Bengali women dressed in long, red sarongs conversed in the shade of the depot, a red dot on each of their foreheads, and a golden ring in each of their noses. Frightened children dressed as miniature adults clasped tight to their mothers' legs amid the splendid chaos. Husky Sikh soldiers, the cream of the Indian Army, dressed in blue tunics and spotless white turbans stood cross-armed on the brickyard and watched over the tumult; to look at them one almost believed they were directing everyone present through mental suggestion. The largest group in the swarm were Hindi-speaking men from up the Ganges River Valley; they wore open collared rayon suits that were almost identical to the suits men wear in the commercial districts of a Yukon city, and they all seemed to be working for the government in some capacity and each had a packet of papers he needed to deliver to an important person he could not locate in the crowd. They were loud and animated, waving their papers in the air and attempting to make their deliveries by outshouting the other gentlemen in the yard. As everything in India has its opposite close at hand, interspersed among the anxious government workers were serene white-robed Brahmin, who calmly looked past the crowd and the present moment to those hidden things only initiates into their select group are permitted to see.

"How do they feed them all?" asked Zimmerman, pressing his face against the window of our railroad car as he and I looked down onto the sea of people

The train pulled out of the city and at once entered a wide, flat countryside where we could see how India fed itself. Every square foot that did not hold a house, the railway, or a road was turned to growing millet and rice. The stooped men and women toiling in the wet fields had terraced even the elevated ground the train was riding upon and were planting fresh shoots of grain right up to the steel tracks.

On the narrow road visible from our car's window we could see that most of the people walking there were carrying tattered umbrellas or bundles over their heads. The cloudy sky was close, but I could not see any falling rain. While our private car had a steam-driven overhead fan, the air around us felt sticky, and Zimmerman and I perspired freely in our gray cotton uniforms.

"What is the date?" I asked him.

"July second," he said, checking his watch.

"When is the monsoon season?"

"The what?" he asked.

"They have a rainy season over here. The monsoon. I can't remember when it happens."

In minutes we were to learn the land was deep into the wet time of year. I was glued to the car window, watching the parade of men in strange baggy white pantaloons and women dressed in long paisley skirts on the road running parallel to the railway; back in North America, when I was paying close attention as I was then, I could have seen the weather rolling in from the west. In India the storm clouds seem to rise from the ground. At two o'clock we were traveling along in sunshine. At two-twenty the sky was black and water was coming down in curtains as wide as the field of view. The people on the road covered their heads as best they could and went about their business.

"We will have great fun building roads in this," I said.

"Every clod that's arable is farmed," said Zimmerman, who was, in spite of himself, as fascinated with the ever-changing vista as I was. "They have a little coal . . . The biomass we sell them is everything they have to get along . . . That's why they love us."

He was overstating the relationship that existed between India and the Yukon Confederacy. They did not trust us and certainly did not love us. The Indians needed the Yukons to provide fuel for the occasional lorry we saw rolling past our window, and they needed some place in the world to sell their tea and silk. Above any economic consideration, they needed us for protection, because at that time the Hindus of the Asian subcontinent lived among enemies. To their northwest were the Pakistani and Afghan Moslems, the easternmost subjects of the vast (though enfeebled) Turkish Empire that stretched from the Straits of Gibraltar to Kashmir. To their north and east were Tibet and Burma, the westernmost provinces of the Chinese Empire, the most populous empire on earth and a nation surpassed in technological development only by the Yukons. South of India was a vast ocean patrolled by Islamic pirates from Malay and the East Indies. The internal and external are blurred in that part of the world, and more dangerous than her external foes were the religious and ethnic minorities Mother India held within her borders. The Turkish government in Tashkent each year budgeted money for the Moslem factions fighting an endless guerilla war against Hindu rule in Ragastan and the Punjab. The atheist Chinese financed every other manner of rebel in India: Tamil nationalists in the Decca, Christian Khasi in the east, Jains, Buddhists, Zoroastrians, Sihks, and B'hais everywhere Chinese funds and smuggled arms could reach. To fight against this sea of foes reluctant Mother India had been forced to take an alien consort in the form of our Confederacy.

One of the great oddities of India's condition in the early twenty-fifth century was the fact that her many enemies came to her to trade, and often to trade for Yukon goods brought by the I.T. Some of the rural traffic Zimmerman and I were watching outside our train window was bound over the Pangsau Pass into Burma and thence to China. There was cargo on that very train that was headed for Lahore, whence it would travel on to Baghdad, Istanbul, Morocco, or all the way west to El-Paris. This unusual situation was enormously profitable to both India and the Yukons, and to protect this one market that connected our trade to most of the old world the Confederacy had been sending mercenary troops into India for more than a century. Starting with the Mogul War[19] official Yukon Army units had been helping the Indians defend themselves (and our handsome trade income) during times of crisis. Nonetheless, it behooved Yukon soldiers operating there to keep a low profile. We were not outright colonial rulers there, yet our relationship was not one forged between two equals, and the Yukon troops operating there obeyed Yukon authority and paid little heed to the wishes of the Indians.[20] Because we were necessary, our dark-skinned clients tolerated us. They did not tolerate us so much I could not detect their resentment of us every time my foreign eyes met one of their angry glances. As any visitor to India can relate, our English language and our Union Jack flag especially aggrieved the natives, as they awoke Historical memories of another much resented time.

Zimmerman and I had orders not to leave our private car during the entire course of our train journey. A waiter brought us our meals, and we slept in wall bunks and had a water closet to ourselves. When we arrived in Delhi on the morning of our second day in India, the Mr. Puri Fitz had mentioned in his letter to me came onto the train to meet with us. He was a loquacious Avadhi Hindu of middle years; his white linen suit from Webb Row in Grand Harbor was impeccably cleaned and pressed, and he had a peach-brown head so perfectly round he was almost beautiful. Mr.

---

19. The Mogul War (2374–2379) occurred when central Asian forces proclaiming a new Mogul Empire invaded India from the northwest; they were forced to withdraw beyond the Hindu Kush Mountains after the Battle of Jind, where on June 8, 2379, McClean's Third Army annihilated the forces of the Iman Reza.

20. Bruce seems to have disapproved of this natural arrangement.

Puri carried with him a tall stack of building plans and drawings for me and a small rectangular envelope for both of us to open and read. That Zimmerman and I were still dressed in uniforms greatly distressed him.

"Why are you young gentlemen not in indigenous garments?" he asked. "Are you gentlemen not aware there are spies of the Chinese in every locality through which you are passing?"

He had a shrill, some would say effeminate, manner of speaking that Zimmerman felt obligated to mock.

"We young gentlemen have not been outside, governor," he said in a falsetto.

"That will be enough, lieutenant," I told him. "Sir," I said to Puri, "we were not given any native clothes when we left the ship. No one told us we should be dressed other than as we are."

"The Captain Moore should have acted with more discretion," said Puri. "You gentlemen will please remain here, and I will be back. The train will not advance before my return."

Forty minutes later he re-entered our car, a bundle of clothing under each arm. I put on the loose fitting jacket and trousers he gave me. The turban he provided baffled my Yukon notions of dressing. I could not get the end of the long strip of cloth tucked into the rest of its mass on the top of my head. In the mirror the thing resembled a loose bandage on a monstrous tumor.

"Perhaps, sir," I said to Mr. Puri, "we could wear those double-pointed hats I see some of the men wearing."

"You have light hair color!" Mr. Puri complained. "You must cover the light hair. You will not otherwise look native."

"Look, mate," said Zimmerman, who refused to put on any of the new clothing, "we're Yukons. We don't want any wog monkey suits."

"You are very disrespectful!" Mr. Puri responded in his fluty voice. "Lord Fitzpatrick will hear of this remark. You should be well behaved as this gentleman here is," he said as he arranged my turban. "Do you not realize you are under orders?"

"I will see he changes clothes, sir," I said.

Mr. Puri huffed at Zimmerman and stood on his tiptoes to make himself look taller, an action that did not impress the S.A. man, who regarded the officious little man with a mixture of amusement and reptilian indifference. Puri asked me to check the contents of the small envelope, and in the meantime he did not take his eyes off Zimmerman. Inside the envelope was a series of similar rectangular papers; on one side of each slip was the portrait of Gandhi[21] and on the other was a elephant. The number ten was printed in the corner of each paper, and across the center of each piece was Hindi writing I could not read.

"What are these, sir?" I asked.

"Money. Have you never seen money?"

Puri was incredulous at my ignorance.

"Ah, paper money," I said. "I have heard of it, sir. I have never actually seen any before. Yukon money has to contain silver or gold. One can buy things with these?"

"Certainly."

"You have an amazing country, sir," I allowed.

I complimented him on his natty suit, thanked him for the native garb, held the door for him, and did everything possible to make Mr. Puri feel better about us.

"You are a very respectful gentleman and officer, just as Lord Fitzpatrick said you would be," he told me as he was leaving. "Your lieutenant will have to be explained to your Lord Fitzpatrick and quite promptly."

As the reader will have noticed, I had a weakness for pleasing other people when I was young, particularly for pleasing those people who might have Fitz's ear. I apologized for Zimmerman's insults to get Puri out the door. Once we were alone Zimmerman and I had a good laugh at how I looked in the mirror.

"You wouldn't fool the Slavs' President," said Zimmerman as he looked over my shoulder.[22]

"Definitely the double-pointed cap for me," I said and took off the ridiculous turban. "You will have to change when we get to . . ." I looked at a map from my duffle bag. "To Luni. Wherever that is."

Another two days to the southwest of Delhi and we arrived at that same small city on the eastern edge of the Thar Desert, the natural barrier separating India from Pakistan and the Turkish Empire. To confuse anyone who might have noted our arrival in Diamond Harbor we had traveled from one side of Hindustan to the

---

21. Mohandas Gandhi (1869–1948), leader of the Indian independence movement.

22. A colloquialism of the day. The Slavs have no president.

other. The land west of Luni had once been irrigated and had supported a sizable population in past times. When we arrived there only a few nomad bands grazed some starving goats on the tiny patches of grass growing among the area's sand dunes. The place's destitution was stark evidence of what three hundred years of nigh continuous warfare will do to fertile land.

One of the parcels Mr. Puri had given me at Delhi contained topographic maps of the desert around Luni where the Second Engineers were to build a hundred-and-twenty-mile loop of highway connecting twenty-four air bases. Building supplies would enter India through the port of Surat to our south, and would reach Luni via existing highways. Standing on the empty railway platform and looking west across the wasteland and at the preliminary plans I had been given, I concluded the airfields were going to be too short and not thick enough to support the mighty Florin Bombers Fitz had spoken of during our time at the War College.

"These look like fighter bases to me," I explained to Zimmerman, who was examining the maps with me. "They could support tactical bombers. Under our treaties with the Chinese and Turks tactical planes are classified as defensive, so the bases are legal. All these security precautions of Fitz's really aren't necessary."

"You can't be sure of Fitz," said Zimmerman, punctuating his remark with one of his characteristic sneers.

"I don't know that I like your tone, Lieutenant Zimmerman," I said.

"I mean, Captain, Fitz always has a hidden surprise," he said. "You think he would have lived this long, playing the games he does and having the old man he does, if he didn't think a few steps ahead of everybody else?"

A dust speck appeared on the flat, sandy horizon while we were speaking. In a minute's time it grew into a small cloud that had a black dot in its middle. After two minutes it came into focus as an open Ranger driven by a square-headed bulldog of a man who was the same color as his vehicle,[23] for both were covered with a layer of brown powder. He was wearing the worst wrapped turban in all of Asia cocked to the back of his skull like a tam o'shanter, and because of his suede driving gloves, Wellington

---

23. A four-wheel drive vehicle manufactured by the Old Reliable Automobile Company of Great Lakes. It looked rather like the modern Haul Everything or the GeePee.

boots and handlebar mustache he looked about as native as butterscotch ice cream.

"Colonel Robin McConnell here, lads," he said by way of introduction, and knocked the dust off himself so we could have a look at his sunburned Aussie pate. "I've come to gather you in."

He was the most informal Yukon officer I have ever met—until I met the other Aussie officers, anyway—and too guileless a veteran from the ranks to mask his inner emotions. He and I hit it off immediately. The entire drive from the station to the construction base we were discussing soil composition in the area and the advantages of cement over tarmac. Just as quickly, Colonel Robin, as he asked me to call him, took a dislike to Zimmerman when he discovered the latter was an S.A. man.

"Why in blazes are they sending S.A. spooks out here?" Colonel Robin demanded. "I need engineers, not bloody killers!"

"Sir, I have orders—" began Zimmerman.

Colonel Robin stopped the Ranger in the middle of the dirt track and turned on Zimmerman.

"I don't want to hear it, sonny," he said, jabbing a finger at the lieutenant. "I don't care if your orders come from Lord Fitzpatrick himself. We have our orders from him, too. I'll tell you this now, mate: my people in the Second Engineers all have families, all have Liege Lords. They are good people, I'm telling you, and I don't want you prying around them the way you rats do when you're about I.T. scum and foreigners. Don't make faces at me! We know you S.A. trash are trained assassins, but we have families, bucko; you harm one of us, and we'll see you buried out in the desert and tell HQ the local bandits took you. Now, you can file your nasty little reports to whomever you answer to; in the meanwhile you stay out of my pathway and out of my shadows, or I'll kill you myself. Right now, you will shut up, Lieutenant; I am talking to Captain Bruce."

Zimmerman accepted the abuse as a part of his job. The S.A. operative did as he was told, and hid whatever he felt behind his pale and unexpressive face.

Twenty minutes later we were among the scattered mobile housing units the Second Engineers had erected in the wasteland west of Luni. Colonel McConnell had brought a select group of eight hundred men, most of them older, married veterans, and all of them Western Australians like himself. The wives and children had naturally accompanied the men, and they had created a secluded Yukon village next door to the tents of the native work crews. The Second Engineers were wearing native clothing—or approximations thereof—and were posing as white Goans building roads for the Indian government. Nowhere on the base were there any flags or military decals that would give the Yukons away. None of the Second Engineers went about armed. All our weapons were kept in the base armory. Regular Indian soldiers guarded the roads into the construction area, which we shared with six thousand Indian navvies, most of who were either Hindi-speaking Rajastanis from cities in northern India or a curious nomadic people called the Rabari, of whom I will say more later.

Beside these, there were several hundred real white Goans in the camp. These peculiar people are descendants of North American and European eccentrics who settled near the east Indian Goa during the Age of Electricity. The other Indians call them Hypees.[24] These people had lost the languages and mores of their ancestors and lived on the charity of their countrymen. When the construction west of Luni began, the original plan had been to hire two thousand Hypees as laborers, but they had proven to be too problematic for our purposes. During my time in India I rarely saw them do anything besides sit in whatever shade they could find and smoke hashish. Colonel Robin kept a contingent of them about to mislead anyone who might stumble onto our camp; a stranger would see them and presume that all the people of European descent in our group were of the Goan tribe.

Around the necks of many of the real Hypees hung a flat, rectangular device about the size of an open book. I recognized them from a photograph I had seen in a History of technology class as portable computers manufactured in the Electronic Age. Needless to say, these devices had not functioned for more than three hundred years. Even if there had been electricity to power them, constant handling had turned the computers into broken sheets of plastic that had some stray wires jutting from them. Twice a day the white Goans would get on their knees and pray in the direction of

---

24. Isolated colonies of ancient American and European people are still existent in various places throughout the world. Isaiah Roberts Bayon, in his last book, *The Lost Tribes* (Smithers and Sons, Atlantis, 2590) mentions the Hypees, whom he classifies as a type of nature cult.

ancient America.[25] At the climax of their prayers they would pound their foreheads against the silent mechanisms dangling from their necks. Colonel Robin said they were ritually jumping into a mythical place inside the computers known as Cyberspace,[26] an alternative paradise where they believe one can go while still alive. The poor hairy fools beat themselves bloody against the shabby bits of plastic and metal, and God did not let them go to any place other than where they were.

The informality of the Australian Yukons was difficult for me to accept during my first months at Luni. There the officers called the enlisted men by their Christian names. The enlisted men often forgot to salute us when we met them on the work site. Worse than that, both groups of them were incurable practical jokers. As South Sea Islanders do not make war on strangers, the Aussies did not play pranks on anyone they disliked. Zimmerman sat undisturbed and unattended each long day in a corner of the design hut where Colonel Robin had ordered him to sit. They thought me a good and useful fellow and did not leave me unmolested for a week at a time. They short-sheeted my bed, put live mice inside the pencil box I kept on my drafting table, mixed my salt and sugar together when I was at dinner, and put a toad in my boots while I slept. Their favorite stunt was to stamp a kangaroo stencil pattern on my personal items and on my engineering drawings. I soon had kangaroos on my undergarments, on the silly felt cap they had given me to wear in place of the turban, on the furniture in my quarters, and on the bar of soap I used in the bath.

"You certainly must love Australia, Bobby," said Major Staples, the director of heavy equipment. "You put a 'roo on everything you have."

"I understand it is the smartest creature on your continent, sir," I said.

"He's asking for it, he is," said Major Staples to Sergeant Stevenson, my chief draftsman. "He best sleep with his boots on tonight if he doesn't want the soles of his feet to have 'roos on them in the morning."

---

25. A distortion of several earlier religious practices.

26. Mentioned in *Tri Ogallala,* cyberspace was in fact the name of a sort of electronic forum wherein thousands could communicate at one time.

The officers' wives had less mercy on me than their husbands did. If the officers tormented me because they liked me, then their wives positively loved me. They sensed straightaway I had not been about women much and that I could be easily perplexed when they teased me. They made a practice of doing exactly that when they invited me to three o'clock tea five times a week in one of the large mobile huts that served as officers' homes. Zimmerman—whom they scorned more than their husbands did—and I were the only bachelors among the officers. The women's spouses could beg off attending these daily soirees, and the women would not invite the wretched Zimmerman to associate with them. Thus each weekday at three o'clock I was usually the only male in the den of these bemused lionesses.

"Now Captain Bobby," Kit Allison, another captain's wife, would coo to me, "you must sit next to me this time."

"No, no," would protest Mary McConnell, the colonel's wife, "he promised he would sit next to me."

"He is *my* boyfriend," Barbara Carter, the wife of the major in charge of native crews, would chime in. "My husband is madly jealous. This is the only time I get to flirt with my Bobby."

They would compromise, and the nineteen senior officers' wives would sit in a close circle around me as they sipped their tea. Unlike their husbands, the officers' wives had adapted well to native dress and made a quaint picture in their long braided hair and wraparound saris, drinking from their blue China cups and winking at each other because they knew that in that configuration I could not get away from them.

A fat zeppelin carried mail and other supplies to our base in Luni directly from Perth in Western Australia. (I would have used that conveyance for the last leg of my journey out, had its existence been known to the I.T.) A favorite trick of the officers' wives was to write letters to their single female relatives and friends back home and tell them they had a bachelor in their unit named Sir Robert Mayfair Bruce, a good friend of the young Lord Fitzpatrick. When the replies poured into camp via the airship the women would read them aloud at tea while I was trapped inside their circle.

"I have a letter from my cousin Lilly," announced Barbara Carter at one such session. "She writes: 'Dear Babs, your young man sounds promising. Please tell me more. Does he smoke? Does he snore?'"

"How would our Bobby know if he snores?" asked Kate Manfred, wife of Captain Manfred. "He isn't awake to hear himself. The Lord knows there has never been anyone in bed with him to inform him upon the matter."

I thought they would never stop laughing at me when she said that.

"Relax, Bobby," Mary McConnell told me. "All that blood rushing to your face; you'll have none left for your heart."

"Aren't they fun when they're young and ignorant?" commented Joan Van Koch, Lieutenant Van Koch's wife.

"What shall we write to Lilly on behalf of our Captain Bobby?" asked Kate.

She had pen and paper at the ready.

"Write: 'Dearest Lilly, I am overcome with love,'" narrated Kate Allison. "'My life is useless if I cannot taste the full sweetness of your tender person.'"

"Please, please, don't write that, Mrs. Manfred," I begged.

I was so confounded by them my head felt dizzy.

"Add this," said Mary McConnell, "'I cannot wait to press my yearning lips against yours. I count the days, the hours, the *nights*—'"

"Oh my, yes!" agreed the other ladies.

"'—the nights that stand between this moment and the time our two hearts shall beat as one and our two bodies will write a new chapter in the torrid annals of passion.'"

"Please, ladies, if you send that, she will have me arrested," I said.

"Don't fuss, Bobby," said Kate. "We won't send it until we've spiced it up some."

When they were not having a jolly time harassing me, the women discussed how they should manage the social life of the base. In this Luni was akin to wherever the Yukon military goes: the wives run a base as spinster aunts and older wives run family compounds. The officers' wives with whom I had tea were of course as well educated as their husbands; ten of them had some nurse's training, six were licensed teachers, one had conducted a symphony orchestra in Australia, and two of them—Kit and Mary—were physicians. Every one of them had attended a conservatory and had studied music, art, and literature. I came to India expecting the ladies to run the base hospital, the school, the mess halls, the food distribution center, and the community orchestra; those are women's institutions everywhere among the Yukons. In my innocence I did not foresee the influence the officers' wives would exert upon the day-to-day operations of the regiment. At the teas they openly discussed whom among the enlisted men should be promoted and who was not suitable for higher rank. They spoke of bonus pay, decorations, demerits, and punishments with similar frankness. The Special Assignment of the Second Engineers was an extremely well disciplined group and needed but a modicum of control to keep it humming along. I soon discerned that when a light touch was given by one of the superior officers their orders usually were identical to the decisions their wives had made the day before over Earl Grey and scones.

My ignorance knew no bounds in 2417. In that period of my life I regarded my married brother officers with something very like pity. To be warriors in the Yukon Army, the most powerful force on earth, and at the same time to be under the thumb of the woman to whom one happened to be married seemed to me to a ridiculous state of affairs. Part of my admiration for Fitz was based upon his seeming independence from other people in general and from scheming women in particular. (Remember, at this time I had not yet met his mother.) No tender soul in a skirt was ruling Fitz; he stood alone, as I imagined all true heroes stood. In imitation of him I aspired to be similarly independent, even after I married. I did not then know how marriage works, nor did I know husbands influence wives as strongly as vice versa. Had I been more knowledgeable of the world I would have realized the women at tea were oft times acting as their husbands' agents rather than upon their own whims. My mature judgment is that in our Yukon civilization only during wartime campaigns and inside peculiar institutions such as prisons, military schools, the I.T., and the Timermen, do men function apart from women. In all other situations the two sexes operate either together or against each other. I should admit also that war and our peculiar institutions are the worst aspects of Yukon society. I do not believe this is so because women are kinder or more moral than men and exert a consistently beneficent power over us, for in some ways they are crueler and less moral than we. The officers' wives I knew in India, to cite the example at hand, referred to the native workers on our base as "wogs" and refused them the extra medicine in our hospital whenever any native came begging for aid. Their husbands in contrast generally got on well with the Hindis and Rafanis and would smuggle the workers food and medical supplies when they could. Worse than their disdain for other peoples is the love our Yukon women have for warfare. To them war is red, white, and blue Union Jack bunting and brave lads in gray marching off to fight the heathens. Our wives, mothers, and sisters believe combat is glorious and that the only hardship war brings is the occasional (and heroic) death of a male relative. Taking those flaws in Yukon women into account, we are still much better men for having them about. The world today regrets that Fitz would in time become the lone figure I thought him to be, and while he would accept the formality of marriage he would never submit himself to a wife's subtle rule.

The officers' wives at Luni were fierce partisans of the Fitzpatrick family. They knew their husbands owed their positions and their generous salaries to the Fitzpatricks as surely as they knew Fitz was destined to become Consul after his father. The women of the Second Engineers wished Fitz would please them further and take an Australian to be his bride, namely the Lady Georgette Faith Woodward, the daughter of New South Wales' leading family.[27] When discussing every other real or possible marriage besides Fitz's, the officers' wives held a decidedly romantic view. They proudly told me they had wed for love when they were twenty-five and that they would have rejected any man not of their personal choosing. Only an idiot, they told me, gave a second thought to position or money in affairs of the heart. In Fitz's case they put aside their romantic sentiments and opined he should enter into a marriage that would benefit Australia.

"We are one of the three great strains in the original Yukons,"[28] asserted Susan Statsen, a lieutenant's young wife. "For once, we deserve a voice at the top!"

"Historians point out," I dared to say, "that almost half of the

---

27. Lady Georgette Faith Woodward (2398–2511), later Lady Georgette Mullens, was the daughter of Lord George Patience Woodward and a famous concert pianist and a celebrated beauty. Her father was a Senator for forty-six years and was once one of the young Fitzpatrick's leading supporters. He broke with the Fitzpatrick family after Isaac Fitzpatrick rejected his daughter's suit.

28. Refers to the fact that nearly all of the original twenty-first century Yukon settlements were located in the rural districts of ancient America, the prairie provinces of ancient Canada, or the Australian hinterlands.

original Australian Yukons were refugees of the general infection.[29] Besides, we are a confederacy of people, not of any geographic locations."

"Piffle, Bobby," said Mary McConnell. "The elder Lord Fitzpatrick married an English woman. To this day the English are crowing about that coup."

"England and the British Isles as a whole: that is our cultural homeland," I said. "They have plenty to crow about."

"Britain is a sheep pasture!" said Kate Manfred. "We were stationed there. There's nothing left but a few soggy farms and the odd military base."[30]

"There are some decent ruins," added Kit Allison. "I'll grant the place has some value as a museum."

"Look here," said Mary McConnell, taking command of the room, as she was wont to do, "saline-eating microbes have taken the salts from the soil in the Western Desert. We have made the entire continent of Australia arable. Similar microbes allow us to turn salt water into fresh. Presto chango, we can irrigate millions and millions of once useless land. We can make Australia into a garden to feed the entire world. An Australian wife would open Lord Fitzpatrick's eyes to the possibilities. We only need the water treatment plants. Think of it, Bobby: there will be frontier land for generations of future soldiers and sailors."

"I have seen Lady Woodward play," said Barbara Carter, who was our community's orchestra conductor. "She has beauty and charm enough for any man. Your precious Lord Fitzpatrick will be swept away the first time he lays eyes on her."

"I see you have everything planned for him," I said. "You have to remember that in the end he will marry whom he wishes."

---

29. Bruce is referring to the Great Pandemic of 2078, when Bartholomew Iz spread a slow-acting variety of Zaire Fever in the guise of influenza vaccines. This was the infamous "People's Program" in which Iz gave a billion humans fatal injections.

30. As Bruce pointed out above, the epidemics of the twenty-first century hit hardest those small, densely populated, industrialized island nations from which the residents could not escape, especially after the beginning of the Storm Times. Britain, like ancient Nippon, Iceland, New Zealand, and ancient Hawaii (now the Sandwich Islands), was essentially depopulated. The great majority of Britain's current residents are the descendents of Yukon colonists who wrested the British Isles from Moslem invaders in 2214. Lady Bathsheba Ruth Douglas Fitzpatrick, the mother of the younger Fitzpatrick, was one of those descendents.

"Bobby, you don't have any idea what you're talking about," said Mary McConnell. "A woman of even average intelligence and looks can make a man love her."

"Especially a man lacking experience," said Joan Van Koch. "I think we can presume his mother has up till now kept young Fitzpatrick away from young women."

"She has if she has any sense," said Kate.

"There is no way to keep young people apart, ladies," I said.

I had let myself get momentarily irritated by their snide remarks about Fitz and his mother, both of whom I felt I was obligated to defend, and I was not as careful in what I said as I should have been.

"The law says," I went on, "Lord Fitzpatrick has to marry when he turns twenty-five. All men have to marry at twenty-five, if they wish to inherit property. He does not have to marry whomever his family or anyone else selects. He could marry someone he has already met. Every last one of you has told me you married men you had fallen in love with long before your were twenty-five. The same is true of the women in my family. Young people get together in spite of what their parents want."

I did not think of what I was revealing. I took a sip of tea, and upon glancing up from my cup I beheld each of the nineteen women seated around me grinning at me as a wolf grins at a fat rabbit who is about to become supper. Mary McConnell, the most senior in age and—because of her husband—in rank, took away my cup and saucer and moved her chair closer to me so that her knees were nearly touching mine.

"You speak with such authority on the subject, Bobby," she said. "You must now tell us all about her."

"I don't know anything about Fitz's—Lord Fitzpatrick—his lady friends," I said.

I blushed. I stammered. I gazed at my feet. My actions told them everything. Their desire to learn more was such they gallantly suppressed their separate urges to laugh at me.

"Sweet Bobby," said Mary, taking my hands into hers, "you know we are not discussing Lord Fitzpatrick any longer. We are speaking of the young woman *you* love."

I had kept my correspondence with Charlotte from other men for nearly two years. Four weeks into my station in India, and the officers' wives had guessed everything from a few rash words.

"Do you have any pictures of her?" asked Peggy Means, another lieutenant's wife. "Young men are always impressed with pictures."

"Run and fetch her picture, darling," said Mary. "You need us to have a look at her."

"Please," I said, "you have misunderstood—"

"Come, come, Bobby," said Kate, shaking her finger at me. "We won't give you a moment's peace until you give in."

I must have been out of my mind from the embarrassment they were causing me. To end their pestering I took from my breast pocket the picture of Charlotte, the decent one of her in her church clothes, and showed it to them.

"She's very pretty," said Kit. "This, I would say, is the picture she gave you to show your mother. We want to see the other photographs."

"What other photos?" I said, affecting my most believable voice.

Kit leaned forward and pretended to rap my head; each time she softly touched me with her knuckles she clicked her tongue so that it seemed she was knocking on hollow wood.

"Is there nothing in there, Bobby, honey?" she asked. "There is *always* at least one other picture."

While my attention was diverted toward Kit, Mary boldly stole the second picture, the one of Charlotte in a swimsuit, from my tunic pocket. They passed it around, and it brought a mixed reaction from the officers' wives.

"I don't know," said Kit. "She is definitely a stunner . . . she may be too forward for our Bobby."

"The child is very nearly naked," said Mrs. Van Koch. "Perhaps she has loose morals."

"No, look at the silly pose and that little smile of hers," said Mary. "She's having fun."

"I love her hair," said Barbara Carter, whose hair was also red. "She has a nice, trim . . . What does a gentleman call this, Bobby?"

I was too taken aback to name the body part she was pointing at. The women enjoyed another round of raucous laughter when they saw my red-faced consternation.

"Run and get her letters," said Mary. "Don't fuss. You've been found out, and there are always letters, so you *must* do as we say. Now hurry."

She snapped her fingers at me. I should have resented her ordering me about. In my defeated condition I went to my mobile unit and brought back the most recent letter Charlotte had written me, the only one that had thus far reached me in India and the only one I had not yet destroyed. The wives passed the letter about as they had the photograph, and they formed a better opinion of Charlotte from this new document.

"She makes fun of you!" said Kit Allison with undisguised delight. "She calls you 'General Robert' and teases you in regard to your ignorance of women."

"Don't you enjoy how she demands him to write back at once?" said Barbara.

The letter had a magical effect upon the gathering. After each had read Charlotte's mocking, lighthearted epistle, they agreed unanimously I would have to marry her.

"Do you think so little of me," I said, "you would want me to marry a woman who makes sport of me?"

"Bobby, darling," said Mary and patted me on the wrist, "we think she would do you infinite good. You must know we love you dearly, and we would not hurt your feelings for all the world, but—how shall I put this?—you are, well, rather full of yourself. Don't look sad. It is a common fault in young men. Not endearing, but common, and therefore forgivable—provided you rectify the defect. You need someone like our redheaded friend to help you realize you are not the center of Creation. We appreciate that you were third in your class at the War College, a Knight and a war hero, and we know you are a close friend of the young Fitzpatrick, and we will one day tell our grandchildren we knew when you were only a wee boy, but, really, Bobby, you could stand to be taken out of yourself and to be taught—and again I'm putting this as gently as I can—you could stand to learn some humility. You are already wonderfully well-mannered and even-tempered and bashful in the bargain. You would be perfect if you weren't quite so sure you are the butter on everyone's roll, if you follow me."

"Besides," said Kate, "you obviously are in love with the girl." They all nodded in agreement.

"I have never intimated anything of the sort," I said.

"You did not have to say anything," said Mary. "You might not even know you are, yet. Again, I don't wish to upset you—and my husband says you are a brilliant engineer, and we know you have read the great books and all of that—but the plain truth is this: you are twenty-two years old and don't know your elbow from—shall we say—your knee."

"She is Catholic," I said.

"No one cares about that in the Army," said Mary. "Barbara and Kit over there are Catholic. Joan," she indicated Mrs. Van Koch, "is a Jew. Like other regiments, we have a priest and a rabbi among the enlisted men. The payroll lists them as navvies. Everyone knows they are not required to do manual work and are there to see to the men's spiritual needs. Surely the regiment you served in and your village back home were no different?'

"No," I said.

"Then why do you care if she's Catholic?" asked Kit. "Only the Lords care if one is not United Yukon Church."

"Is that it?" asked Mary McConnell, and suddenly the atmosphere in the mobile unit became chillier. "Do you think your friend Lord Fitzpatrick is going to make you a nobleman someday, and you do not want a wife who would hold you back? Does ambition rule you to that extent?"

"No, no. Nothing like that," I said.

I quickly looked about at the nineteen faces; all of them were watching me intently. On some of them I could read traces of a growing anger, and not the playful anger they normally tormented me with, but the sharp, genuine article. My lying may have fooled some sailors on an I.T. ship. I was not nearly talented enough to deceive the officers' wives.

"Is that so?" said Mary. "Can you look me in the eye while you think of your dear mother and swear to me you do not desire a marriage that will keep you in line for a Lordship?"

I made my best effort. I lifted my head and looked directly into Mrs. McConnell's face. When I tried to breathe out the words I could hear my mother and my aunts, my grandparents and all the elders in my village whispering in my ear that I was a liar.

"No," I said to the floor.

Before I spoke I had been sitting among the Graces; that answer had tossed me before the Furies. Several of the ladies hissed at me. Others made uncomplimentary remarks filled with vocabulary I had never heard the women in my village use. I distinctly heard the words "silly ass" and "overreaching little fool." Someone behind me, probably Kit Allison, slapped the back of my head so hard I spilled my tea on my lap.

"You don't deserve her!" said Barbara.

"Why don't you join the I.T.?" asked Kit. "That's where they put men who can't love women!"

Tears flowed from Mrs. Van Koch's eyes. She stood and told me, "I don't believe I can sit with you, Sir Robert. You are a vile young man."

"Ladies! Ladies, please sit!" called out Mary McConnell. She rang her spoon against her teacup until the mobile unit quieted. "Sir Robert," she said coldly to me, "I am going to speak to you now as your mother would if she were here and had heard you make that disgraceful confession: you are not merely too full of yourself, you are either so consumed by a desire for position or such an ignoramus you are blind to the obvious reality that a stupid boy like you would not remain alive a week after your precious Lord Fitzpatrick made you a Lord. You have been moving in fast company and have forgotten just who you are.

"Get him some paper and a pen," she ordered Kate Manfred. "Sir Robert, if you desire to save your life and to gain a measure of happiness in the bargain, you will this very minute write a letter to your Charlotte and tell her you love her. Promise her you will convert to her religion when you two are married."

The other ladies gathered around me and supervised me while I wrote. They added they thought I should tell Charlotte in my letter how wonderful she was and what a disgusting reprobate she had for a fiancé. They suggested the terms "buffoon," "heartless pig," and "clueless ape" to describe that latter person. When they had proofread the eight pages I wrote, they commanded me to insult myself some more and to throw some additional bouquets to Charlotte. Twelve hours after the letter was sealed, a zeppelin had taken it and the rest of the base mail to Australia. With the airship went any hopes I entertained of ever becoming a Lord. If Fitz had been there, I might have acted differently. In that portion of my life I was overly influenced by whoever I happened to be with, whether they wished me good or ill. I thought later that perhaps in his presence I would have found a way to disobey the officers' wives. But he was not, and I didn't.

Three weeks later I received another letter from Charlotte. She wrote she agreed with everything I had said about her and that she would make me a fine wife. I was disappointed she did not deny any of the ape, pig, and buffoon remarks the ladies had made me write. The officers' wives insisted on reading her reply aloud at tea. In my subsequent letter to her I told Charlotte everything that had transpired at Luni, and when she wrote back there were two letters in her envelope: one for me and one addressed to Mary McConnell and the other ladies. The officers' wives again read her letter to me aloud at tea, but set aside her letter to them for later, when I would not be present to learn its contents.

"You read mine," I protested. "Shouldn't I get to read the one she sent to you?"

They rolled their eyes at me and said I had so very much to learn.

"You are a man, Sir Robert," said Kit Allison. "You need us to be your interpreters and to tell you what our little sister Charlotte is saying to you. We know perfectly well what she is saying to us, thank you very much."

The ladies at Luni and Charlotte came to write each other as often as she and I did. I never knew what transpired between the officers' wives and the Traveler girl. I was only made to know that everything I said or did would get back to the "little sister," so I had better behave.

"Women put us through a tough process," Colonel Robin told me at work one day. (He had heard something from his wife and suspected more.) "You have to put up with them, son. Eventually they take mercy on us, or they get bored and find something else to amuse them. By the time that happens, they've got us married off anyway."

# SIX

THE FAIRY-TALE land Zimmerman and I had observed from our train window during our first days in India might as well have been ten thousand miles from our base at Luni. Although we Yukons wore sloppy versions of native clothing, we acted and worked as we would back in the Confederacy. On the construction sites we were in the midst of a sterile desert and apart in every way from the dazzling energy of the subcontinent's northern plain. Regular soldiers, most of them Sikhs, kept watch on our perimeter and shooed away the herders who wandered out of the wastelands beyond our work sites. Teamsters recruited in the big cities brought supplies by lorry or railroad car from Bombay in the east and Surat to our south. The Yukons could not leave the sites for any reason. We ground our own gravel and bought our cement from a plant forty miles away in Jodhpur. The teamsters and the Hindi laborers were subject to the wishes of the mysterious Mr. Puri I had met in Delhi; he had chosen them for their silent, obedient natures, and because the round-headed Mr. Puri had some measure of control over the workers' families back home. Colonel Robin told me I could not keep a good conscience if I inquired too deeply into the nature of this control; he did not know much about it, either, and did not desire to be enlightened. "Indian affairs for the Indians," was his motto. "The less we know, the happier we'll be." The glum Hindi men did as they were told and did not associate with us in our camp. The irrepressible Rabari tribesmen working for us provided the small spark of local color we had on the base.

A thousand years ago these nomadic camel and goat herders had made the entire frontier region their pasture. During the Electronic Age farmers and city dwellers from the east had taken the Rabari's land, and the free roaming desert dwellers had become low-caste servants of their traditional pastures' new owners. Three centuries of religious warfare between India and her Islamic neighbors had destroyed the modern economy of the region. The Rabari were fortunate in that they needed no conventional economic order to thrive, and in 2417 they were once more masters of the desert. The Indian Government in Delhi paid them a yearly stipend in return for which the Rabari patrolled the borderlands when they were not tending to their flocks. We knew these same tribesmen oft times performed reconnaissance for the Turks whenever that side paid more; therefore we paid them more than we paid the other Indian navvies. (No one in the Second Engineers spoke of where the payroll came from. We suspected in our hearts Fitz was paying for everything. The payroll and other monies came to us through Mr. Puri. We spoke as if the Indian government was our quartermaster, even though the money Mr. Puri brought us was usually in Yukon coin and not paper money like that he had given Zimmerman and myself.)[1] We paid the Rabari in malaria vaccine—a portion of which they sold to other Indians at a huge profit—and in golden twenty quid pieces stamped with the images of Lady Fitzpatrick and the Meadowlands Bank.[2]

The Rabari did not spend all their coins on goods from the local markets as the other workers did. They set aside a goodly share of their wages, punched holes in the soft golden coins and strung cords through them so they could wear them as jewelry. They had already made a display of themselves in their red turbans, purple and yellow balloon trousers, and motley jackets; with gold coins dangling from their earlobes, necks, and noses they were as gaudy as ocean sunsets. The first time we paid them in vaccine they tore open the packets and swallowed every pill we gave them; foreigners' medicine is strong magic to them, they explained through

---

1. Another slander against Fitzpatrick's memory. Building the military bases in India would have been against the elder Fitzpatrick's wishes, and thus the son could not have done it. Scholars today agree the Indians must have built the air bases themselves, although a few Yukons were there as observers during the bases' construction. See Gerald pp. 236–39.

2. The Meadowlands Bank of East Port had been given to Isaac Fitzpatrick by his uncle, Lord Dreadnought Venture Watson, in 2410.

their interpreters, and they believed the more they took the better the magic. Dozens of them were sick for weeks afterward. Our chief surgeon had to explain to them that one capsule was good for one person for half a year. After their next payday the Rabari began selling the vaccine to the local population. Before the bases in western India were completed each of the Rabari was laden with gold coin. Even their small children had so much coin dangling from them they jingled like sleigh bells as they played about the work sites.

"Here comes the banker carrying his bank," Colonel Robin would joke when he saw one of the gilded nomads clanking along beneath the weight of his fortune. "We pay them much more, and they won't be able to move."

In the long, dry evenings after the monsoon season had passed, I would sit on the steps of my mobile unit and watch the sun set over the desert. Often a score of the Rabari children would settle round me, squatting on their heels in the dust in the same posture their mothers and fathers used whenever they rested. They sounded like cats meowing when they tried to talk to me in their language. I must have sounded as odd to them, for they laughed when I addressed them in English. They watched intently as I carved a recorder from a block of scrap lumber as my father had taught me to do back in Columbus. The boldest of their group, a jingling scamp in turned-up satin slippers, took it from my hand and played a disjointed tune the other children must have recognized, seeing as how they applauded in approval of his performance. The boy held the instrument out to me, but I gestured that he should keep it. He put his finger on his chest and said his name. I made the children laugh when I tried to repeat what he said. They butchered the pronunciation of "Robert" just as badly. During these quiet evenings I would cut an apple into sections and give the parts out to them. Time would teach me their favorite treats were dried apricots, which are a delicacy all desert people treasure as though they were bits of edible gold. They so loved the pieces of dried fruit I gave them I had to slice the portions up equally before I distributed it to them or they would fight each other for them like feral dogs contesting soup bones.

Mary McConnell, the Colonel's wife, saw me feeding the children one evening and called me aside after the little ones had returned to their family tents.

"Bobby," she said, sitting down beside me, "I shan't fault you for having a tender heart. Our little sister Charlotte will be blessed to have a husband of your gentle nature. But you must not feed the native children, dear. I know you mean well; nonetheless, the results can be most cruel. The children will become dependent upon you. You will become attached to them. A war is coming, Bobby. I know we are not supposed to discuss it. Discretion and the rest of that. I know you have seen war in Mexico. You have never seen children suffer as they do in this part of the world during wartime. No one alive today has seen a war such as this one will be. We aren't supposed to say that, either, but there it is. There will be no extra food for the children then. You will have to watch children die. For your own sake, Bobby, you must keep your distance from them." She patted me on the cheek as mothers do. "Think instead of your Charlotte. Your happiness lies in that direction."

Subsequent to that discussion I no longer openly gave apricots to the children outside my housing unit. Instead I went into their encampment under the pretense of speaking to the Rabari headsmen and distributed the food and extra medicine to the little ones there. As cold as her advice was, Mrs. McConnell was quite right about the wisdom of keeping my distance. I did become too attached to the children. I spent two pounds silver every month on food, wooden toys, and bright cotton cloth for them. Every night I remembered the children in my prayers and beseeched God to protect them from the impending disaster. From the distance of sixty years I still see their dirty, smiling faces, and in the terrible hours of the night when I awake and cannot return to sleep I seem to understand as I lie looking at the ceiling what the children were saying to me then. Every word was an indictment, a curse upon my head and on the heads of the other Yukons for what was soon to happen to them and to the millions like them.

The Second Engineering Corps' Special Detachment completed the first hundred-mile loop fifteen months after my arrival. Our narrow roads had a base layer of large stones, a second and third of progressively smaller gravel, and a three-inch surface of concrete. We made the airfield runways in a similar fashion, laying each layer slightly thicker in order to handle the greater stress. Since each of the two dozen airports was built in a triangle formation that consisted of three runways at each site, a pilot could approach every port from any direction and be able to land his plane.

Each of the seventy-two airstrips was two miles long, not nearly long enough (or heavy enough) to handle the monstrous Florin or any other long-range bomber I knew of. In the center of every triangle of three runways was a square mile of leveled taxi surface. We laid the foundations of hangers, barracks, and beacon towers in the core of these taxi regions. The metal buildings themselves were being preassembled in North America and would be erected only after other fields in eastern India were completed. We dug pits for storage tanks and connected the twenty-four bases with plastic pipe (such as that we had picked up in Melbourne) to the Luni River, from which the airmen would draw water for steam. Lorries working in continuous convoys were to bring in the biomass fuel for the planes and the fresh water the airmen would drink and bathe in. Nothing was built to last for very long. We did not even lay sewage lines or dig wells; we dug simple pits for privies and bulldozed some trenches in the desert west of the bases where soldiers could dig out a more substantial defensive line when the need arose.

To protect our workers from the weather I designed a long, mobile awning made of plastic and mounted on aluminum stakes. Moisture and sunlight were thus kept off the concrete until it had time to set. Then the awning could be moved forward to new ground that was ready to be paved. In the dry, relatively flat ground of the desert each of the three teams into which Colonel Robin divided the workers averaged eight tenths of a mile of road a day. Once the work had shifted to east India we would have to build on land that was wetter and far more uneven. There we would need more men and more funds if we were going to move through the new country with anything close to the speed we had demonstrated in the west. Colonel Robin resolved we would have to ask Fitz for more money and asked me to help write the letter to my friend. Officially, we were on touchy ground if we brought the subject up to Fitz directly, since the Indian government, as noted above, was the supposed source of our monies.

"You know him better than I do," the colonel told me as we sweated over what to commit to paper. "Eschew the flowery stuff. He likes a fellow to be direct, doesn't he? Beg if you have to."

I was up until four in the morning composing that note to Fitz. I put Buck Pularski's name and address on the envelope because I feared Fitz's father the Consul might read any messages that went directly to his son. No one had breached the matter to me, yet I assumed the Consul was ignorant of our presence in India. To request more funds was to ask Fitz to spend millions of pounds on a project no one in the capital city of Cumberland could admit existed. If the letter were intercepted, I would have placed Fitz in the gravest jeopardy.

"I would not write you, Fitz," I wrote, "unless I feared falling behind schedule. You told me when you sent me to the east this would be a task of the utmost importance. I ask you not to forget your purposes. Be assured they are our purposes also."

I wrote six pages of on-bended-knee prose, and I did it without knowing what Fitz's purposes were. He had us building air bases. Beyond that, nothing was certain. We in the Second Engineers suspected these bases were not just for use by the Indians and that there was some importance attached to them we had not yet learned. My writing the letter to Fitz was akin to driving headlong into a fog. How could I not fail to make a mess of the endeavor? I contemplated the arrival of the next zeppelin with a foreboding of doom. That next airship would be carrying the reply from Fitz or an arrest warrant from his father, and neither could be good news.

I cannot overstate my jubilation when the zeppelin returned carrying an enhanced payroll and a note from Fitz that read:

Dear Colonel McConnell and Sir Captain Bruce,
    Bravos for finishing the Luni phase ahead of time. Here is the gold and vaccine you will need to pay for the new workers. Three hundred Yukon technicians and heavy equipment operators will arrive in a fortnight. Mr. Puri will meet you on the way east and will have two thousand additional native workers for you to take to Bihar.

God's Speed,<br>Fitz

"This may be Zimmerman's doing," I said to Colonel Robin while he and I read the astonishing reply. "I'm certain he's been in contact with Fitz's people all the time he's been here."

"Does this mean I have to like the bastard?" asked Robin.

"We could treat him better than we do," I said. "Give him a new desk to sit at. Say 'hello' to him in he morning. He has sat in his corner since he arrived, just watching us work."

"That's what vultures and S.A. men do, Bobby; they watch us. I'll be damned if I'll be nicer to either one of them."

We loaded our equipment, machines, and mobile houses onto the train at Luni and shipped everything nine hundred miles due east to Bihar. Only a company of Sikh warriors remained behind in Ragastan to guard the work we had completed. Minus any metal buildings, our runways and roads were scarcely visible from a couple of miles distant. A spy would have to sneak through the thorn bush thickets and sand dunes till he stood directly atop the airfields before he could see what we had built there, and the two hundred Sikhs we left behind were a caution against anyone getting that close.

Our second set of bases were to be in the Rajmahal Hills south of the Ganges River, built snug in the bend where the river turns south toward the ocean.[3] The ground out west had been dry, flat and uninhabited; the Rajmahal Hills were densely forested, broken by rolling hills, heavily populated, and for half the year the rainfall is measured not in inches but in tens of feet. The people indigenous to this region were mostly Santals, a very dark, tribal folk who have their own language and an animist religion akin to no other system of belief in India. They are unique because they have resisted integration into greater Hindustan since before recorded History began. The Santals fear and hate the outside world, which has given them naught but war, disease, and poverty, and they did not willingly cooperate with our construction schemes.

We did not make the pretense of negotiating with these primitive hill people. We fell upon the Santals like an invading army, the Indian government in our vanguard. Fitz's agent Mr. Puri led our attack into this wilderness, wielding papers of condemnation against the peasants in his path like a field hand taking a scythe against a patch of sunflowers. Any farmer who agreed to sell his land to us got one fistful of papers and another bearing a few bills of paper money. Anyone refusing to sell got whole reams of legal paper thrown at him and a rifle butt in the face from a government soldier. In our first two weeks in the area we drove three thousand Santals from their homes and let them find what protection from the elements the forest could provide them. Our bulldozers plowed

---

3. This circle of bases is, as most readers will already know, known to us as "Hood's Island."

over the sacred trees they had worshiped since Akbar reigned.[4] We pushed their tiny garden patches, their wooden huts, the Histories they had carved in their tree trunks, and everything they had once been into the gummy hill mud. With giant rollers we packed into the mud everything we had pushed aside. Up to that point in my life, this was the most shameful thing I had ever had a hand in. Of course, I had not yet lived as long as I would.

The Rajmahal Hills were a natural fortress against a Chinese invasion. They are the northernmost high ground below the Ganges, the mighty river that protects the hills to the east and north. One hundred and forty miles to the west of the point where the Ganges bends south, the Son River, a tributary of the Ganges, shields the hills from that direction. The bases we constructed atop the hills were too high to be flooded and so could be kept open during the monsoon season. Any fighter planes taking off from there could easily reach into Burma or up to the Himalayan Mountains to the north. The importance of the site and its unique qualities gave our crimes against the Santals a patina of necessity. We told ourselves we had to ruin the thousands of lives in the hills in order to protect the eight hundred million other souls living in the rest of India. We in the Second Engineers repeated that argument to each other whenever we espied a cluster of the homeless natives standing in the distance while they watched us pave over their ancestral lands. In time, a few of us perhaps came to believe the argument was just. To keep my moral senses numb to what I was doing, I concentrated on how much the completed project would please Fitz. By focusing on that goal, I could keep going straight ahead and did not allow the misery we were causing to distract me.

Twenty-two times the Indian Army had surveyed our route through the Rajmahal Hills before we began construction. On every one of these twenty-two occasions they had failed to garner any information we could use. The project in Bihar Province was necessarily a day-to-day operation. Captain Allison and I had to survey the ground a mile ahead of the work crews every morning. In the afternoon I would be in the planning unit making drawings of the projected roadway on the ground I had surveyed a few hours

---

4. Akbar (1542–1605) was Mogul ruler of north India and Afghanistan from 1556 until his death. Known for his religious tolerance, which some of his contemporaries considered a virtue.

earlier. Just as Colonel Robin had divided up the navvies into four separate crews, I had to create separate drafting teams to create detailed elevations of the sketches I made in haste.

Except for Sunday afternoons, there was no longer time for teas with the officers' wives. The ladies brought our meals to us in the drafting huts or under the mobile awning. We ate over our work, taking care not to drip food on any of our drawings. I individually completed six drawings a day, six days a week, not counting the sketches my NCO draftsmen fleshed out. My only time away from the transit or my drafting table came when one of the senior officers' wives came into the hut and ordered me to take a couple hours off to write to Charlotte or to rest. On Sunday everyone was permitted to sleep until eight and was given an additional hour to attend church in the afternoon. On the other days everyone had to work seventeen hours. Commanders of the work squadrons slept in the field as they would on campaign. We brought cots into the planning office to save us the ten-minute walk we took every night back and forth from the mobile units. In spite of our efforts, eight months into the Bihar project, we found we needed more money, especially to pay for the endless lawsuits Mr. Puri was conducting against landowners. (On this occasion Colonel McConnell and I merely spoke of the matter in front of Zimmerman, and the needed gold coins arrived on the next airship.) The Yukon women called our chaotic base "the beehive," which was too apt a name to make any of our exhausted workers smile.

Constructing triangle-shaped air bases of three runways each was impossible in the hill country. We had to fit single two-mile-long strips into the landscape where we could. A narrow valley might hold a solitary runway, a ridgetop would be crowned with another, and in any place the land opened into meadows we packed the airstrips in like zebra stripes. The taxi areas and the foundations for the prefabricated metal buildings were crammed in wherever there was room. According to our construction scheme, the Blinking Stars would guide a pilot back to the one-hundred-and-twenty-mile loop running through the hills, and the plane would follow the highway until it came to a base where a beacon light was signaling that there was room to land. To give the future users of the airfields the room they would need, we laid out eighty-four runways, as compared to the seventy-two we had built in the west.

Out of everyone connected to the Second Engineers, Zimmerman was the sole individual who did not exert himself beyond his customary efforts. As always, he stayed in his corner of the planning office and watched the rest of us. I expect he missed very little that happened.

He approached me after we had completed a particularly long day on which my group had designed three new bridges.

"I can see why Fitz chose you . . . for this job, I mean," he said. "You can work faster than anybody else . . . Fitz says only you could look at new ground and make plans to put roads over it as fast as you do."

It felt unnatural to be complimented by this man I looked down upon. In my old age I understand it was only normal for an evil man to compliment another evildoer. We were both toiling for Fitz, and both yearning for the things he alone could give us. He had every right to look down on me, for he merely murdered one person at a time while I was knowingly abetting in the preparation of one of the most unjust and senseless wars humanity has ever waged.

"Who is this girl the women have you writing?" he asked.

He did not change his expression between the compliment and the question. Zimmerman's face remained blank whatever words were escaping his mouth.

"She is Mrs. Allison's cousin in Australia," I lied. "The ladies are playing matchmaker. You know how they can be."

What made this such a good lie was the hard fact that Zimmerman did not know how women are. He was a man without a family and had been denied even the contact of female relatives I had known as a boy. He shrugged at my reply, and said it was not important.

"Look, Bruce," he said. "Captain Bruce . . . I know you've put a good word in for me with McConnell . . . that he should treat me better . . . so I'll give you a good word: there are two kinds of trouble coming . . . One is among Fitz's friends, and the other is Fitz himself . . . You want to just do your job and keep your nose out of whatever you hear happens."

He went back to his desk, making as little sound when he moved as a lizard would when slipping back into its lair. Days might pass before he again spoke to anyone else. He never revealed to us what he might be thinking or that he had any internal life whatsoever. Zimmerman simply watched and listened. And everything he saw or heard went into the letters he sent to Fitz.

Nine months after our move eastward I received a letter from Buck Pularski. He had been promoted to lieutenant and was assigned to protecting Fitz, the same job he had performed before he had his commission. Fitz was in Ohio Province and staying with his mother on a family estate Fitz had renamed Boeotia because he considered it a dull place.[5] Fitz's father and his father's cronies were out of the capital at Cumberland and staying in the Meadowlands, on the largest family holding, a seven-thousand-acre farm overlooking the Atlantic Ocean. The Consul at that time had not deigned to visit the Senate for more than a year. He had left his ally Lord Dade[6] in Cumberland to look after the affairs of state while he and his bemedaled generals hunted foxes in the green woods along the Jersey shore.

Pularski wrote that Fitz called his father's staff "men who were boys when he was a boy, growing old along with him." Meg Sweeton, the blonde mistress, was the only person under the age of fifty then within a ten-mile radius of the Consul.

In his letter Buck brought me up to date on the rest of the *Basileis*. Valette was a colonel and learning the ins and outs of command at Western Regional Headquarters in Grand Harbor. Hood, our magnificent Hood, was a lieutenant general,[7] and was training a special task force in Desert Province. Shelley was a captain on inactive half-pay and had assumed his elderly father's seat in the Senate. Davis had completed pilot's training and was flying a prototype plane about which Buck said he could not tell me much at that date. Stein was a colonel and Hood's chief aide. Stein's college rival O'Brian was in the General Quartermaster's Office in Cumberland. Mason had

---

5. The Greek province of Boeotia was in classical times considered by her neighbors to be a backwater where uncouth yokels dwelled.

6. Lord Henry Heywood Dade (2342–2419), Senator from Centralia Province from 2380 to 2419, was Fitzpatrick the Elder's champion in the Senate.

7. Both Fitzpatricks had sponsored the commission. As noted above, Hood was already a brigadier general when he was sent to the War College. In the years before the Four Points War, he was the most decorated living soldier in the Yukon Army. Gerald recounts (pp. 418–20) that Hood had already been given brevet command of the newly formed Sixth Army.

asked to become a captain, but because of his unseemly conduct, at the date of Buck's letter he was on inactive half-pay and living at his parents' home.

Pularski wrote that Fitz had not once gone to the capital to sit in the Senate seat to which Ohio Province had elected him. The young Lord remained in Boeotia where he daily entertained visitors and dispatched bags full of letters. Much was happening, wrote Buck. Although he was constantly close to Fitz, Pularski did not know half of the schemes then unfolding. A foreign-born scientist, one Richtaslav Aranov, was a frequent visitor to Fitz's country home. He was an aviation engineer, and was building the type of plane Davis had been flying. I recognized the scientist's name because he was a renegade Timerman whom the secretive order had tried before the Senate on the charge of stealing technology.[8] Fitz had given this disgraced man land in Ohio adjoining Boeotia, and he and Fitz had become so friendly Buck thought the Slav might one day be the first foreign-born Lord in Yukon History.

"You will be hearing of Fitz and myself soon," Pularski concluded his letter. "Remember, I do what I am told to do. As a soldier you must understand about orders. You are my friend forever. Someday, when things are better, you and I will go fishing again. Burn this letter after you have read it."

Two days after Christmas 2418, our planning office at Bihar had an unexpected and highly unwanted visitor from Army headquarters in Cumberland. Brigadier General Roland McArthur Strijdom[9] and his batman arrived in a Ranger from Calcutta, both of them in full Yukon uniform and looking as conspicuous as ice in Hell among the Australian engineers clad in indigenous garb. Splattered with mud from his campaign hat to his knee-high boots

---

8. Technically not true. Fitzpatrick the Younger, working through Lord Shelley, had the Senate investigation of Aranov suppressed in the Senate's Supreme Law Committee before charges could be formally made. The Timerman suit against him never reached the floor, although in 2417 Aranov was dismissed from the order. Aranov, a refugee from the Slavic Remnant beyond the Ural Mountains, never became a Lord.

9. Probably the grandson of Charles Strijdom, Admiral of the Navy. Gerald does not mention any Roland Strijdom, although such a man is listed in the War College archives and Mason makes a typically vulgar remark about a man of this name being "the first casualty of the coup."

from the long journey on bad roads, but still glittering with old-style gold medals,[10] the general burst into the main drafting unit with the fury of a typhoon and made it known straightaway he was not pleased with what he saw about him.

"What the raging Hell is going on here?" Strijdom bellowed at Colonel McConnell. "Who initiated this project? Who is paying for it? Why are you dressed up like a bunch of Woolywoolies?"

He stormed about the office, smiting everything in his path with his swagger stick as he hurled questions at us. He sent papers flying off drafting boards and kicked wastebaskets across the floor and against the wall.

"Adventurers!" the general shouted and pointed a finger at one man after another. *"Traitors!"* (That was a word that made the Yukon engineers wince.) "I know what your game is! I know who has sent you schemers here!"

Like the rest of us, Robin McConnell was standing at attention while the brigadier vented his rage upon our drawings. The general turned about and bored in on our colonel, coming so close his mouth was almost chewing upon Robin's nose.

"I have been to the Philippines, sir!" said the general. "To the stinking Babuyan and Batan Islands. You know what I found there? *Traitors* like you! They were building goddamned air bases. Just like here, sir. Just like here."

He stepped away from Robin and once more paced about the room.

"Well, sir," continued the general, now no longer shouting, "they would not let me use their ultraviolet light. They wouldn't let me communicate with the Capital through the goddamned Blinking Stars. But I am returning to the Capital, sir. When I get there, the Consul will goddamn hear of this! He shall hear what his damned, grasping son is up to!"

Zimmerman came forward from his corner, not making a sound as he stepped across the wooden floorboards.

"May I speak to you outside, General?" he said. "I have orders from Supreme Army Headquarters."

"What's this?" blustered the general as he eyed Zimmerman, who alone among us was wearing his military uniform. "An S.A.

---

10. After the ascension of Fitzpatrick the Younger in 2419, senior officers no longer wore all of their decorations, except on formal occasions.

chap? At least he knows he's supposed to be wearing a damned soldier's uniform. What's this about?"

"I have orders," repeated Zimmerman. "May I speak to you outside, sir?"

"More nonsense," said General Strijdom, yet he and his batman went out the door with Zimmerman.

They walked some twenty feet away from the building and stopped beneath the shade of a tree outside the planning unit's front yard. The general muttered profanities with every step he took. We could yet hear him swearing through the office's open front door. He turned to Zimmerman when the S.A. man halted.

"What are these orders?" we heard the general ask.

Zimmerman took an automatic pistol from a rear pocket hidden beneath his coattails and shot the batman between the eyes. The general had time to say "He—" before Zimmerman shot him the face. The S.A. agent must have been using exploding bullets, for the back of both men's heads splattered in a broad swatch across the tree trunk and the surrounding ground. Zimmerman stepped over both corpses and shot them each another time in the chest. When he was done he took the time to reload his gun before putting it away.

"I'll need somebody to help bury them," he said to those of us who had rushed from the planning office.

Like the entire planning command, Colonel McConnell was too shocked to speak immediately. He stood staring at the gory scene, his mouth as wide open as that of a child who has just seen his first lion at the zoo.

"You've murdered a goddamned general!" he said when he reclaimed the use of his tongue. "A general!"

"I had no choice," said Zimmerman.

"I have no choice but to have you hanged, sir," said Robin.

"No . . . you won't do that," said the calm, unhurried Zimmerman, and he presented the colonel with a paper he had kept in his tunic. "You'll see here I have orders . . . from 'Fitz,' as you call him, to kill anyone snooping about . . . If Fitz doesn't hear from me every two weeks, it'll be bad for you . . . I don't think you want to have me court-martialed . . . Too many questions would be raised, don't you think? Besides, there are going to be a lot of dead generals, real soon . . ."

Colonel McConnell was not a man to do anything contrary to Fitz's desires. None of us standing at the compound yard and gawking at the murder scene was the man to do that. We buried the dead general and his aide below a deep strip of pavement in one of the runways. Mr. Puri in Delhi put it about that Thugee outlaws had killed an unidentified Yukon officer and his companion on the road somewhere east of Calcutta. The false rumor eventually would get back to certain interested parties in North America. The news did not travel fast enough to make any changes in our building plans.

Only thirteen days later a newspaper from Australia arrived on our base via the airship mail; on the front page in three-inch letters the headline read: **"CONSUL SLAIN."**[11]

The story below the headline told how, while on a visit to his son and wife in Ohio Province, Lord Coronet Fitzpatrick and all fifteen members of his senior staff were in conference in a dining room when two assassins armed with hand grenades and assault rifles dashed into the meeting and opened fire. For inexplicable reasons, no bodyguards were present in that portion of the manor. The assassins were using bullets filled with cyanide. The Consul, all his staff, and Miss Meg Sweeton (whom the newspaper described as the Consul's secretary) were killed as soon as they were struck. Blue Jackets posted outside the house and Lieutenant Winifred Pularski, the younger Fitzpatrick's personal bodyguard, had killed the two murderers as they attempted to flee through the estate's formal gardens. The two killers were identified as Gregory and Alex Gyor, brothers in their early thirties and members of an obscure Gypsy criminal organization. Their weapons were Chinese made, and inside their apartment in Centralia City were found Chinese money and written orders from their Chinese spymasters. The investigating officers postulated that the two men had entered the manor via an underground passage they had discovered after stalking the area for many weeks. A local farmer told reporters he had seen two men matching the assassins' descriptions prowling the countryside only days before the attack. The newspaper did not explain why two Yukon Gypsies would be keeping orders written in Chinese or why the security at the country estate had been so lax.

---

11. Bruce learns of the terrible events of January 6, 2419, on January 9.

"I've heard the name Gyor somewhere," I said as I read the story with Colonel McConnell's draughtsmen.

Colonel Robin had spread the newspaper atop a drafting table in the planning room, and all of us posted there were trying to read the front-page item as a group. Zimmerman looked at me when I spoke. Something told me as my eyes met his I should not say I remembered that Gyor was the name of the fortune-teller on Front Street in Centralia City. Madame Gyor was the woman Charlotte said had taught her to read palms.

"No, wait," I said. "The man I'm thinking of was named Gydar. He ran a laundry in Astoria."

Zimmerman looked away from me.

The next zeppelin brought another newspaper which proclaimed that Isaac Prophet Fitzpatrick, our beloved Fitz, was the new Consul. The vote in the Senate had been unanimous.

The paper said Fitz and his mother had taken the late Consul's body to the Capital on a special train draped in black crepe from locomotive to caboose. They had stopped in twenty-six places along the route between Boeotia and Cumberland. Every time they halted Fitz had climbed atop the car carrying his father's body and had addressed the crowds of mourners.

"Citizens," he had said to the assembled people, "God has chosen this to be a day of mourning. In this terrible time I am standing above the body of my father. When I stand atop this car, I am standing on a sacred shrine, and no one in our great Confederacy knows better than I that the Isaac Prophet Fitzpatrick so many of you have known—burdened as he was with his many fears, his self-doubts, his countless shortcomings—would be unworthy to stand here. I today tell you, my friends, that everything that was ignoble in Isaac Fitzpatrick does not tread upon this hallowed place. I, like raw ore in a blast furnace, have been through the fire these recent days, my friends. The dross that was in me has been taken away. All that remains of me is the pure, refined metal my father instilled in my undeserving being. Everything that is left of me is my father.

"The man lying in this railway car was as much your parent as he was mine. He loved you no less than he loved me. Now he is passing through his children's land on his final journey, this father of ours is. His body will be laid to rest in Verkempt Park alongside the Confederacy's most celebrated heroes, thinkers, and creators. His soul will join the Angel chorus that watches over us, lamenting our daily failures, and rejoicing in our triumphs. His death has made every one of us orphans until the day God calls us to join Lord Coronet Fitzpatrick in that land that knows no death.

"But, citizens, let us not mourn too long.

"The Chinese murderers who killed our father do not understand the Yukons and our Confederacy. They do not understand that the Yukon Confederacy is a single, immortal entity. The ground you are standing upon, this train you see before you, the patriots on your left and right, the free sky above you, our splendid mountains, our rich farms, our inviolable shores, and everything else that is Yukon is one being and cannot be killed by the Chinese or by any other enemies Hell may set against us. To kill one Yukon man—even to kill one who stood as tall as my father did—is to do no more than to chop down one of our giant sequoias or to plow under a single wheat field. A new tree will grow to take the old one's place, a new stand of wheat will bloom forth in the fertile ground, and younger Yukons will lead us as my father did. To destroy us, a foreign power would have to cut our lands free from their moorings, push every grain of Yukon dirt beneath the ocean, and rain down Heaven on those Yukon sailors left riding upon the flood. Citizens, only God could destroy us so completely, and He will not lift His hand against us so long as we continue to do His earthly work, as our father here did while he lived. It is the Chinese and their cowardly, God-hating allies whom the Lord has made mortal. It is they who should fear His judgment.

"So shed your tears today. Dry your eyes in the morning. For you will awake tomorrow knowing the foreign murderers of our father have injured us but for a very short time. Be glad, my friends, to know that a hundred years from today our descendants will look back upon this day as the prelude to our greatest victories. It is the great-grandchildren of our enemies—should there be any left alive—who will then mourn this tragedy."

The people gathered at the railway, the newspaper said, wept long after the funeral train had moved on toward the next stop.

Upon arriving in Cumberland, Fitz learned of the Senate's vote to make him Consul. As his deep sense of humility demanded, he at first refused to accept the position. His father's body was not yet cold, he said, and it would be wrong to be thinking of politics at that sad moment. The Senate respectfully asked him a second time to lead them. Only because Fitz wished the best for the Confederacy, he reluctantly bowed to the Senate's wishes and became Consul of all the Confederacy.

He must have made a powerful impression upon the Confederacy's leaders when he entered the Capitol Building. The Senators, the Law Lords, and the commanders of the Army and Navy were dressed in their long robes and military uniforms and sparkled with medals and civil decorations. Fitz walked onto the well of the Senate and positioned himself atop the famous mosaic of the map of the Yukon lands, wearing the simple dark blue uniform of a Blue Jacket. Save for the stars on his shoulders, he was as unadorned as a newly enlisted private. The tall, handsome man of twenty-four waited for the great men who had stood for him to be seated again. He waited another ninety seconds beyond that point and made the anxious Senators fidget in their seats.

"My friends," he said, startling the old men seated around him who had begun to believe he might not speak that day, "may I present my mother?"

Some present gasped when Lady Bathsheba Fitzpatrick swept across the floor and seated herself in a folding chair close to her son.[12] There were more than a few who remarked that she had an air of proprietorship about her. A majority of the old men there whispered that she was about the comeliest fifty-one-year-old widow they had ever seen. The assembly dutifully stood and applauded her.

"My friends," Fitz continued, "I accept the office of Consul, which you have so graciously offered me."

Again there was a standing ovation.

"You have given me the mightiest sword in the world," Fitz said when they were all seated again. "I promise you I will use it."

With that he left the floor with his mother on his arm. The Senators looked at one another and wished someone among them would explain what had happened. They were accustomed to speakers holding the floor for hours at a time. This young fellow had not even taken the time to flatter them.

In the excitement of Fitz's first day in the Capital, the newspapers gave little note to another tragedy that had taken place in the city. Lord Senator Dade, the long-time supporter of the Elder Fitzpatrick and the only other man any of the Senators had considered

---

12. Lady Bathsheba Ruth Fitzpatrick was only the third woman ever to enter the Senate floor.

for Consul, had fallen down a long stairway in the Capitol Building and snapped his neck. A Lieutenant Pularski, the same Lieutenant Pularski who had helped kill the Elder Fitzpatrick's assassins, had discovered the old man's body at the foot of the long, marble flight.

A writer on the newspaper's editorial page predicted the new Consul would face little opposition in the Senate. Now that Fitz's childhood friend Lord Shelley had been elected Senate Leader, an entirely new generation was in charge of the Confederacy.

"We're in a different age," said Colonel McConnell as we finished the newspaper story. "We shan't be in these baggy clothes much longer."

The same zeppelin that had brought the newspaper had carried a letter from Charlotte. She wrote:

> My dearest Bobby, this will be the last letter I can write for some time. Now is a dangerous time for us, my love. Dr. M. is moving me to a safer place. Do not write me again until you hear from me. Your letters will not reach me at this address.
>
> I know I tweak you at times, but I do in truth love you. Protect yourself and wait for me. I promise I will meet you again when you least expect it.
>
> Your love, Charlotte

I took this development badly. The officers' wives took it worse than that. Mrs. McConnell reacted to the letter as though her "little sister" had died. She and the other ladies felt so badly they almost forgot to hold an ice cream and cake celebration of Fitz's assumption of the Consulship—almost, but not quite.

# SEVEN

FITZ'S FIRST REFORM after taking office was to disband the Office of Special Affairs. Two thousand S.A. men, including Zimmerman, were dismissed from the ranks with a few strokes of the Consul's pen. In the Rajmahal Hills, Colonel Robin McConnell turned our unwanted guest out the day we learned of the new edict.

"Hale and farewell to you, you murdering thug," said Robin as he drummed Zimmerman out. "There's a zeppelin coming in two days. That's not soon enough. I want you gone within the hour. We will drive you to the railway. Go to Calcutta, and catch the next I.T. ship back to where you came from. You are nothing any more. Ta ta. Please don't write. And don't let the door slam behind you."

The colonel and a host of armed Sikhs escorted Zimmerman straight from the planning office to a waiting automobile. At the last moment I ran from the office door and poked my head inside an open window of the vehicle for a final word with the taciturn man with whom I had sailed to India. I was not concerned for him; I instead suspected I could benefit in the future if I made a positive final gesture to him. After all, he was a direct line to the new Consul.

"I have some money," I said, and pressed some coin into Zimmerman's hand. "Do you have enough for passage back to North America?"

He put the money in his pocket. Robin's insults seemingly had made no impression on him. He wore the same uncommitted expression he always presented to the world.

"Thanks . . ." he said. "I have people to get me home . . . You know, Captain, you really are smarter than I first thought . . ." And he put on his disturbing grin for me as the auto pulled down the roadway, leaving me to understand he knew why I had offered him this final gift.

"You're too good to some people, Bobby," Colonel Robin said to me as we watched the automobile vanish among the dense trees.

Kindness had nothing to do with my actions. Ambition's voice was again whispering in my ear. I knew anyone with Zimmerman's connections could be expected to land on his feet and maybe in time rise to a position of considerable authority. When I gave him money I was protecting myself and my career against the day when he and I would meet again.

During his first month in power Fitz would push through the Senate a mass of legislation that would change the Confederacy for years to come. He lifted the restrictions on the I.T.; they were allowed to use as many sailing ships as they could construct to transport goods to foreign lands and to rent protection from military warships, no matter to what dangerous spots they sailed. Fitz granted war veterans two million acres of frontier land in western North America and central Australia, and he initiated projects to bring irrigation water to the thousands of new farms. David Shelley, the new Consul's main proponent in the Senate, initiated a wartime income tax of twenty percent on the rich Lords and Ladies, and of five percent on everyone else. This was done under the legal fiction that the Confederacy had entered a state of emergency that might lead to war when foreign agents killed Fitz's father.[1] He cut the sales tax on food and clothing to eight percent and increased the rate on luxury items to twelve percent. The I.T. itself had to pay an additional ten percent import fee, which was a magnanimous deed on Fitz's part, as he was in that instance taxing his own family above most other Yukons, since the Fitzpatricks then owned the largest portion of the I.T. He stopped short of formally ending the third child tax, but let it be known in speeches he would not actively enforce the law as long as the Confederacy was in crisis. Fitz immediately removed the sitting Law Lords and replaced them with nine men loyal to him alone.[2] The new Law Lords saw to it that nothing Fitz did

---

1. The Constitution forbids peacetime taxes other than the ten percent sales tax, the ten percent tariff tax, and the ten percent third child tax. Fitzpatrick the Younger was able to pass his tax reforms by suspending the Constitution due to the unprecedented state the Confederacy found herself in upon his ascension. See Gerald, pp. 532–98.

2. Gerald (footnote 124, page 541) states that the Law Lords stepped aside voluntarily.

was declared unconstitutional. Later, on August 3, 2419, the Senate adopted three new constitutional amendments guaranteeing freedom of speech, freedom of assembly, and—as no one could have predicted—freedom of religion.[3]

Even an inept observer of Yukon politics such as I was recognized there had never been a phenomenon in Yukon History akin to Fitzpatrick the Younger. In the village of my youth everyone had always observed the goings on in Cumberland as a game played among the Lords. The veterans and landowners had dutifully voted for their patrons and paid their taxes and fees.[4] The balance of power in the Senate never shifted too decidedly to one faction, and the entire Senate did little more than maintain a portion of the military, deliver the mail, and issue the war tax in times of trouble. The real work of government, maintaining the peace, the roads—and the local universities—was left to the local Lords. As long as the local Lord was fair and undemanding, no one spoke of politics. Ideology was still further removed from our daily lives than politics had been. In the months after Fitz's rise to power, there was little talk of anything else but those two subjects, including within the temporary Yukon community we had made in the Rajmahal Hills.

Mrs. McConnell hung Fitz's portrait on the planning office wall, right beside a picture of Christ in Gethsemane. The children in our school wrote poems and composed songs in honor of the bright new day the young Lord Fitzpatrick was bringing to us. There was open conversation among the enlisted men about Fitz's reforms. Some rash men said aloud they wished Fitz would abolish the Senate and rule by edict alone. Had anyone on our base been so bold as to question Fitz's power or the speed with which he moved, one of the officers' or NCOs' wives would have slapped his face. During a celebration of his reforms the base orchestra presented a special performance of Beethoven's *Ninth Symphony,* "The Ode to Joy," and I remarked to Mrs. McConnell, who was seated next to me in

---

3. These amendments (numbers 21 and 22) allow only *legitimate* speech and assembly. No sane Yukon would want his fellow citizens to assemble in order to foment rebellion or to commit other immoral acts.

4. As noted in Chapter One, the Constitution of 2081 allowed voters to elect any adult male of good community standing to the Senate. In practice, voters almost always elected the local Lord or his brother or his adult son.

the audience, that this was rather too grand for the occasion. That careless remark brought on a series of angry lectures from all the officers' wives upon the subject of familiarity breeding contempt.

"Just because he is your friend from college," Kit Allison told me, "does not mean you cannot show him the respect he merits."

A more definitive indication of the new Consul's power was how little opposition his innovations aroused. The ladies at tea had been half correct about the United Yukon Church: no one other than the Lords cared if citizens were private dissenters. The ladies had not foreseen how little the Lords themselves cared. When the Bishop of Atlantic Province issued a bull of excommunication against Fitz, the Archbishop and the Apostolic Council promptly readmitted the Consul back onto the U.Y.C.'s rolls and dismissed the Atlantic Bishop from the clergy the following day.[5] The defrocked cleric sat in front of the Archbishop's cathedral in Cumberland and there held a hunger strike to protest what he termed "this new Antichrist."[6] This lonely man of God sat on the cement steps for sixteen days, fell ill, and eventually his family had to come to Cumberland and collect him. The last I read of him, he was on the family estate in Virginia and was occupied in writing an autobiography. Other than that solitary protestor I could not detect a single voice against Fitz in the entire population. Fitz rolled the U.Y.C. on the question of religious freedom as he had rolled the Lords on the matter of taxes. Either the powerful men in Yukon society were not nearly as powerful as we had believed or in Fitz had been born a force that exceeded anything the Yukon Confederacy had previously produced. (Of course it mattered that one-third of the military had sworn at least partial fealty to the Fitzpatricks because of land grants, and it mattered more that Fitz had spies positioned everywhere.) Whatever the reasons for the Lords' timidness, the undeniable fact of the age was that they kept silent. Fitz enjoyed such a smooth, unopposed administration in his early years as Consul that there were moments when I wondered if we had ceased to be a Confederacy and had become an

5. Lord Paul Harriman De Klerk, a former Senator who had left public life for the church. Gerald describes this unfortunate episode in greater detail (pp. 649–53). De Klerk was obviously mentally unstable.

6. The new Antichrist because Bartholomew Iz was the old one.

empire.[7] Like some of the Lords in the Senate, I wondered where we were headed, and I too kept silent.

I have mentioned already the Catholic priest and Jewish rabbi who had practiced their vocations with the ranks of the Second Engineers. After Fitz amended the Constitution, they became official chaplains within our special consignment. Robin gave both of them a mobile unit as a place of worship, and what I would estimate was one in ten of our Aussie soldiers attended their services rather than the U.Y.C.'s. These new chaplains were to be merely the first of the spiritual changes we would witness on the base. Sergeant Michael Stone, a rock-ribbed bulldozer operator blessed with lungs that could have operated a mine pump, began a charismatic Protestant church in our midst. The self-anointed "Reverend" Stone followed the examples of St. Paul and John the Baptist and made a tabernacle of the open air and preached to any willing to listen, including unto the native workers, for he declared all men and women brothers and sisters in Christ. Members of his group talked in tongues, proclaimed visions, and said God had chosen to walk with them. A Lieutenant Statsen, who had been a seminary student before he joined the Army, started an "apostolic community," which he declared a high church counterpart of Sergeant Stone's proletarian congregation. Lieutenant Statsen's religious group partook of the Communion every Sunday, recited the appropriate calendar readings from *The Book of Common Prayer,* and practiced New Testament rituals they said were true to the traditional rites from which the U.Y.C. had strayed. Before we completed paving the Rajmahal Hills project no fewer than seven different religious groups were practicing on the base, leaving the U.Y.C.'s congregation much depleted. Those of us continuing to attend the once dominant church had to ask in our hearts if the U.Y.C. had any future in the Age of Fitzpatrick. Every week our members grew fewer as the parishioners drifted into the more dynamic alternatives. In the rest of the Yukon world there were soon dozens of new religious orders, a large number of them founded by dissenting U.Y.C. clerics suddenly free to give vent to their spiritual inclinations.

---

7. Another example of Bruce's complete lack of shame. Empire is a word no serious student of Yukon would ever use. When speaking of the Confederacy's benign reach throughout the world, *imperium* is as strong a name as any reasonable person would offer.

A small intellect such as I possess might have predicted that the dissolution of the U.Y.C.'s hold upon the Confederacy's spiritual life could have led to a political dissolution in the greater nation, thereby undermining Fitz's power. We small intellects could not have been more wrong. The Catholics, the Jews, and the new Protestant churches upheld Fitz as their liberator, a righteous man and a living Saint. The remnants of the U.Y.C. were meanwhile too weak to oppose him. The U.Y.C. clergy in many provinces had held sway over the local Lords; now local arrangements mattered very little, for the Consul held sway over everyone.

The final months of pouring cement in the Rajmahal Hills was an orgy of work. When we had surveyed the final twenty miles of road and had drawn the last runway elevations, the planning office workers put on coveralls and worked the night shift with the regular heavy equipment operators. The stretches of roadway sprang into existence like mushrooms coming up after a rainstorm. Every mile we finished was an opportunity for my Aussie comrades to praise Fitz, whom they credited for our new speed, albeit the Consul was half the world away. Sergeant Stone's congregation, ever a shade different from everyone else, did give some of the credit for our success to God.

While we were on our sprint to completion, our Sikh guards captured two Chinese agents lurking in the forest a few miles north of our mobile base. Forty-six hours passed before Colonel Robin learned the native soldiers had made the arrests. During that time the Sikhs tortured and interrogated their prisoners, as their customs demanded.

"Yukon soldiers do not mistreat prisoners," Colonel McConnell told the Sikh squadron that brought him the news.

The tall, ferocious men from the Western Frontier in their heavy blue tunics and black, bushy beards were astonished to hear Robin say that.

"Then what, colonel," asked a Sikh sergeant, "is the purpose of taking prisoners?"

"Soldiers take prisoners because it is dishonorable to kill other men simply because one can," said Robin.

The sergeant translated what Robin had said to his mates gathered outside the portable awning. I expect they commented to each other in their language that they knew of Yukon soldiers not so honorable as this engineering colonel.

"I want the two prisoners brought here to me at once," ordered Colonel McConnell.

Twenty-five minutes later the Sikhs brought the two Chinese to the cleared ground beside the awning, in pieces. Robin was beside himself with rage. The Indian soldiers acted as though a pile of limbs and bloody body parts was a sight the Yukons might want to see. They showed Robin the black silk uniforms the Chinese had been carrying in their backpacks.[8] Colonel McConnell's furious response was to tell them to get the disgusting mess off his road and give the parts a proper burial in the forest.

The Chinese had not given the Sikhs any useful information during their interrogation. Had they been broken there was little they could have said we did not already know. We had long assumed the People's Friend[9] and his court in Peking were aware something was happening in northeastern India. They might have also guessed that Yukons were involved in the construction of new airstrips. We had twice seen reconnaissance planes high overhead. Probably the People's Friend had seen pictures of the new roads and airstrips. The Chinese ambassador in Delhi had made a formal protest concerning new construction projects he said were "not in keeping with our nations' feelings of mutual friendship." The ambassador stopped short of demanding the airfields be destroyed, for the new runways in India did not violate any treaties and were not much different than dozens of airfields the Chinese themselves had built north of the Himalayan Mountains.

On Good Friday morning of 2420 we poured our last section of concrete, completing the Rajmahal Hills project two and a half months ahead of schedule. The Second Engineers' staff photographer took pictures of the entire loop and dispatched them on the next zeppelin headed to Australia. After four years of frenzied activity, our special detachment found it had nothing to do until the prefabricated buildings began arriving.

During the idle time, the officers' and NCOs' wives organized a formal party to be held underneath the mobile awning that had

---

8. The uniform of the notorious Revolutionary Guardians.

9. In 2420, the People's Friend, as the absolute dictator of China called himself, was the ill-fated Lao Ping, who had assumed the post in 2416, the year he overthrew his predecessor Feng-tse in a bloody coup.

been our protector in the rain-soaked hills. We were to wear Yukon clothes again on that one special night. As anyone knowing something of those times might guess, this was to be a "Roman" occasion. For those who might not know, I should explain that in the years following Fitz's ascension, the Confederacy was in the grip of a Roman Republic craze. Several new biographies of early Roman heroes had become quite popular, the most celebrated of them written by one of Fitz's lieges.[10] Literature clubs had special discussions upon Livy and Machiavelli's *Discourses on Livy*. Educated Yukons affected a simple, austere demeanor in imitation of the early Romans, which was not difficult for most Yukons to do, as we are by nature a simple and austere people. Fashion struck a daring and highly visible Roman pose. Married men took to wearing collarless white shirts and white linen jackets and trousers in imitation of the long, white Roman toga. Young men paid seamstresses to embroider snakes and star patterns onto their shirts so that the clothing resembled the breastplates centurions once wore. Women wore long white cotton dresses that, unlike the men's shirts, had no sleeves and had daring décolletage such as Yukons had never before seen; these garments more resembled the gowns chic European women favored during the Napoleonic Era—another time of Romanophilia—than any garments of actual Roman times. Like the Napoleonic outfits, these new and daring dresses were worn without petticoats and—I blush to say it—sometimes without any undergarments whatsoever. This complete lack of underclothes made the thin and nearly transparent cotton material more revealing than any fashion trend the usually reserved Yukons had ever experienced. In my youth, as today, only girls under the age of twelve wore short skirts, and tiny bathing suits were allowed only on segregated beaches. We were not used to seeing the female form revealed. I, like my contemporaries, had grown up seeing women wrapped in yard upon yard of cloth that covered them from throat to ankle. I never did know how to react to this startling new development. Whenever a shapely young woman wearing a Roman dress, women such as Kit Allison or Joan Van Koch, stood between myself and a

---

10. Refers to *Cincinatius, Coriolanus, and Scipio Africanus* by James Dawson Valmer, a professor at St. Anne's and, as Bruce states, a liege of Lord Fitzpatrick. Valmer and many others saw a similarity between Cincinatius and Fitzpatrick, both of whom had left the rustic plow when their countrymen needed them.

bright light at the party, I quickly discovered the only gentlemanly course of action was to look at a spot above her head and never to lower my gaze. In further imitation of Roman "simplicity," the ladies gave themselves elaborate coifs in which their hair was curled into hundreds of ringlets and worn off the shoulders in either a high bun or a ponytail that was held in place with shiny brass combs. At our soiree the husbands in attendance pretended not to be moved by these new manifestations of female artifice. I will only note that nine months after of our night of dress-up, five of the eight younger officers' wives gave birth within the same week. Colonel Robin told me in confidence the day after the party he was glad to get the ladies back into native saris or we might have started a local population explosion.

"Think of if, Bobby," he told me. "They're said to be dressing like that all the time back home. Either they will have to start wearing more, or we will soon outnumber the Chinese and Hindus put together."

To my knowledge there was only a small increase in the general birth rate in 2420, although women did not start wearing more until the war came. In my provincial village one could every day see girls wearing dresses in public their grandmothers would not have worn as half-slips. I mention these developments because I suspect there was a connection between the new style and the political and spiritual revolutions of our time. There is not the wordsmith in me to explain this subject as well as I should. I can but relate that it had become a common occurrence for a young woman to dress herself in a gown as insubstantial as a spider's web and then attend church or a political rally where she would work herself into a state of excited frenzy among a crowd of similarly clad young ladies. It was equally as common to see young men, including the sort of young men who would never before willingly attend church meetings or political rallies, flock en masse to those same gatherings in order to be near the excited young women, and while the young men observed the delights of the new age they would hear a minister or a politician speak upon the glories of the new Consul. The other bit of information in regard to this phenomenon I can relate to the reader is that the creator of the Roman fashion, Andre Mullins,[11]

---

11. Sir Andre Farnsworth Mullins, the President of the Grand Harbor School of Design from 2416 to 2453.

was another liege of Fitz's, and *The Lady's Companion*,[12] the bible of the Roman style, was a Fitzpatrick property.

I left India on a four-week pass on April 20, 2420, two days before my twenty-fifth birthday. Lord Fitzpatrick had asked me to visit him at his Ohio estate as soon as possible to discuss my construction projects. The officers' wives baked me a birthday cake before I left. On the loading dock leading into the zeppelin that would carry me back to North America they gave me a silk suit they said I could wear to my wedding.

"Don't marry the girl Lord Fitzpatrick picks for you unless you believe you can love her," Kit Allison advised me.

"You've forgotten your little sister Charlotte so quickly?" I asked her.

"You see we—" began Kit, but she did not finish the sentence as Mrs. McConnell had put a hand over Kit's mouth.

"Let us not vex you, Bobby," said the colonel's wife. "I know your heart is still broken."

With that they herded me onto the aircraft before I could ask what Kit had wanted to say.

I was six days in transit across the Pacific and relished every moment of the splendid trip. A sage once said the three things the Yukons do better than anyone else are farm, fight, and never forget History.[13] I would add a fourth: we travel well. Some of the happiest times in my life have passed gliding along on railroad trains, in giant dirigibles, and on tall steamships. In what other nation can one find the comfortable atmosphere of a family-operated contrivance? On my zeppelin the two fathers and a grandfather were the pilots, the wives ran the kitchen and the onboard school, and the teenage children—in their resplendent white uniforms—waited on the half-dozen passengers on the observation deck and tidied the cabins. The other travelers and I could idle at the tall bay windows and watch the wispy clouds drift eastward across the deep blue swells of the peaceful ocean below us. One of the older daughters in the families operating the airship had studied music; she played Chopin and Debussy études on the grand piano at the far end of the common room, while I had time to sip iced coffees and read old news-

---

12. Printed in Grand Harbor 2304 to 2490.

13. A paraphrase of Robert Holmes Smuts' famous phrase.

papers from North America whenever I was not conversing with the other passengers and crew. The wife running the kitchen told me her entire family had served for five years on this craft their Lord owned.

"We have a fine and easy life," she told me. "Sometimes too easy, sir. We ofttimes don't school the children as we should. The husband and I have a girl in boarding school at present. Miss her terrible. We can but teach her to read and write and her numbers and such onboard here. Our Lord is building a giant sailing ship to take advantage of the new trade laws, sir. On his ship we could keep our darlings with us permanent then."

While I was traveling I read in an old newspaper that Fitz had married. The *Grand Harbor Chronicle* had a cover photograph of him and his new bride, a dark, heavy-browed, handsome but reserved looking young woman, who was not in the least like the glamorous Lady Georgette Woodward the Australian officers' wives had desired him to wed.

"Lord Isaac Prophet Fitzpatrick, Consul of the Yukon Confederacy," read the paper, "was united in Holy Matrimony this Saturday with Lady Joan Helen DeShay,[14] daughter of Lord Malcolm Van Gleck DeShay and Lady Janet Ruth DeShay, in a private ceremony at Lord Fitzpatrick's Pallas estate in Ohio Province.[15] The lovely bride was radiant in a white taffeta gown from The House of Karl, accented by inlaid pearls and a corsage of yellow roses etc., etc."

The article noted in its final paragraph that the Fitzpatrick and DeShay families together controlled 74.4 percent of the total I.T., making the combined family by far the wealthiest people in the Confederacy.

I had difficulty imagining Fitz in love, with a woman, I mean. He had been, for as long I knew him, courteous to the other sex and considerate of their wishes. He kept his passion for them in check at all times, and I could not envision Fitz giving himself up

---

14. The Shay family did not drop the De from their name until 2424. At this time they were not yet active in politics and were the largest investors in the I.T. after the Fitzpatricks.

15. In 2024, Lord Fitzpatrick had changed the name of his Boeotia Estate to Pallas, which was the name of Alexander the Great's Macedonian capital.

to the anarchy of the mind that is love. Nor was this the sort of bride I thought he would take. The former Miss DeShay was not an unattractive woman. After studying her picture for some time I could see the intelligence in her eyes and the gentleness of her smile; she was otherwise not much different from the thousands of other upright young ladies one sees at noble social gatherings. She seemed an earnest girl, one a man would not regret knowing. I could not help thinking she was not the goddess I supposed Fitz would have chosen to be a Consul's wife.

When I arrived at Grand Harbor I caught a train that two days later brought me to Ohio. A bus took me from the depot to the Pallas manor house, where I found Fitz living alone on the vast estate. Only a handful of bodyguards—Buck Pularski among them—and several enlisted men from the Blue Jackets were at the great house to keep him company. A steady flow of official visitors were coming and going from the private library where the young Consul was holding court.

Buck was overjoyed to see me when we met in the big house's deserted living room. I feared for several seconds he might never let go when he took my right hand in his left.

"Robert, you've come back to us!" he proclaimed.

He did not release me until nearly a minute had passed.

"We can go fishing again, should Fitz ever give us the time off."

"Where is Mrs. Fitzpatrick?" I asked. "This place looks like a hunting camp."

I looked in vain for any bright, feminine touches in the enormous old house. Someone had put sheets over the furniture in the living room to keep the dust from settling. That seemed to be the extent of the housekeeping. The kitchens in the basement and servants' quarters upstairs were silent and, I surmised, empty. No one had bothered for many days to clean the carpet of the mud that had been left behind by the stream of visitors.

"She's at the Meadowlands place," said Buck. "Didn't Fitz ever tell you she owns a conservatory for young ladies there? She likes to be there at least half the school year."

"Fitz's wife owns a school in the Meadowlands?" I said.

Two other guards who had been lounging on a covered sofa in the room turned to me. Buck grabbed me above the elbow and led me a few more paces away from them.

"You must not talk about Lady Joan," he whispered. "Fitz's

*mother* has the school. Had one for decades. Lady Joan is at home with her family in Atlantis."

"Why?" I asked.

Pularski glanced at the other bodyguards. They had not taken their eyes off us since I had mentioned Fitz's new wife. I felt Buck's grip on my arm tighten.

"You must not speak of Lady Joan right now," he whispered. "Promise me. Not to anyone. Especially not to Fitz. She and Fitz live apart at this time. When she's here, they have separate quarters."

"I don't under—"

"Promise me, Robert," said Pularski.

"Agreed," I said.[16]

He released his iron grip and patted me on the shoulder.

"He's ready to see you," said Buck. "Act carefree, Robert. He's very pleased with your work. Brags about you all the time. You have nothing to worry about, so long as you say nothing that will upset him. I'm sorry; I have to frisk you. I have to check everyone who sees him."

After he had searched my person for concealed weapons, Pularski led me through a darkened hallway and into the manor's library. This was a high but narrow room, about twenty feet wide and about four times that in length. Leather bound books lined the chamber's side walls, and a high window at the far end brightened the entire space. A long wooden table filled with a jumble of opened books, unfurled maps, and mechanical drawings took up most of the floor space. Fitz was standing, his back to the window, and speaking to a colonel from the Twenty-third Engineers, who was standing at attention before the Consul. An older man in civilian clothes was seated to one side and studying a map. A male stenographer on the side of the table opposite the civilian was recording every word that Fitz and the soldier were saying. Such, I told myself, was the nerve center of the entire western world.

Fitz nodded to me and smiled as Buck and I entered. He was wearing the same unimposing Blue Jacket's uniform he had worn

---

16. Mason, in his smutty memoirs, writes that the new Lady Fitzpatrick had fled to her family estate two weeks after her marriage because her new husband was—and I apologize to all the young ladies reading this—sexually unusual. According to Mason, Lady Joan agreed to return to Lord Fitzpatrick only when he promised to control certain odd habits. As always, Gerald offers a sane explanation; Fitzpatrick, writes Gerald, from time to time sent his bride south to handle family business.

upon entering the well of the Senate. By this time he had removed the general's stars from his shoulders and was now as unadorned as a green recruit. I cannot say the weight of total command was weighing upon him; he looked to be the vigorous, confident race-horse of a man I had always known.

"See this fellow," he said to the colonel of me. "He has in the past three years been the chief design engineer in two major projects in northern India. Believe me, sir, both jobs would dwarf your one assignment. He has completed them two months ahead of schedule while working under the strictest security. You, on the other hand, Von Sundry, cannot finish one little air base on one tiny island in the space of two years."

"My Consul," the officer tried to explain, "our supplies have been stolen. Food, concrete, machines; it is impossible—"

"Not impossible, sir," said Fitz. "Yes, I am aware someone stole your supplies last August. Yours is the third theft in the past year. The Chief Quartermaster is investigating everything. The point is, Von Sundry, other commanders have had supplies stolen from them, and they did not fall sixty days behind schedule."

Fitz sat himself at the head of the table and wrote a check for the colonel from a ledger book. Reading upside down, I made out that it was for two and a half million pounds.

"Here," said Fitz, handing the slip to the colonel. "Take this to the Exchequer in Cumberland. It will pay for your little job on little Bioko Island. You have two months to get the cement down, sir."

"My Consul," said the officer, "I will need three."

"You will be done in two, sir," said Fitz and snapped the book shut. "You will be inspired. Your men, in turn, will be inspired by you."

Once the colonel had saluted and left, Fitz came around the table and embraced me.

"So, Robert," he said, "you have proven to be as trustworthy as I knew you would be. I have seen the Rajmahal and Thar photographs. Well done and ahead of time. I told mother you were the man to send."

"My Consul," I said, "when we met at college I asked you how I should call you. I have to ask you again, my Lord."

Fitz laughed at my reluctance to call him by his pet name.

"You will call me Fitz and I will call you Robert. Nothing has changed between us. Your men, however, will have to call you Major Bruce."

He gave me a small metal box containing two silver disks.[17] I have heard reports that panderers in the seedier sections of our large cities often give their whores similar trinkets to keep the unfortunate women content. Unlike me, those women do not delude themselves in regard to their masters' designs.

"The Senate will approve," he said as he looked for something else on the table. "When they catch their collective breath. Doctor, where did I put the prefabricated building plans?" he asked the civilian.

The man quickly located a stapled pamphlet. Fitz transported them into my hands. They were blueprints for five different types of structures that could be erected on the foundations we had laid in India.

"I've wondered, Fitz," I said, "why none of these buildings have any plumbing."

"We can't risk contamination from outside water," said Fitz. "You will have to seal everything. The Chinese are great ones for chemical warfare."

He ruffled the sea of papers on the table and fished out a letter of introduction.

"You will need to study those on the train ride east," he told me. "They are very simple compared to what you've been doing. Cookbook stuff, you engineers call that sort of thing. You will need the letter to get yourself a conference with mother."

"Mother?"

"You won't be able to call her that," he chuckled. "She will have to remain 'Lady Fitzpatrick' to you and the rest of the world. I assume you have your military railroad pass. Yes. Anyway, you will have to go to Meadowlands at once. Mother wishes to talk to you. We will have a long conversation when you return. I have the Turkish ambassador coming in at the top of the hour. I have to prepare for him. Seems he has heard rumors about new air bases in India. You haven't heard those rumors, have you, Robert?"

The civilian laughed. He had a long, gaunt, agonized face. To my eye, only a thin layer of skin covered the sharp angles of his skull.

---

17. The insignia of a Yukon major.

When he laughed he put me in mind of one of those glowing skele-tons children put in windows for Halloween.

"I haven't heard anything," I said.

"I will relate the same to the Turkish ambassador," said Fitz. "We will meet again in four days, on the second."

He shook my hand, and Buck and I left the library. Back in the living room I asked Pularski about the civilian.

"Strange one that," he said. "He's Doctor Aranov. I wrote you concerning him."

"The aviation expert?"

"I told you he claims to be from Panslavia—from the Slavic Remnant, I mean. He doesn't have much of an accent," said Pu-larski. "His parents must have brought him over here while he was still very young. He's made an air base west of here. He's got some strange-looking planes out there. You might like Aranov, Robert. I can't judge him myself. He operates on a higher level than I do.

"We have twenty minutes till the Turks get here," he said, checking his watch. "Would you care to see my garden?"

He led me into the formal gardens behind the house and thence to a walled area that had recently been partitioned from the rest of the grounds. The flagstone walkway we were stepping upon was the very place the Gyor brothers, the assassins of Fitz's father, had been killed. No one had tended to most of the grounds since that terrible incident; the hedges had grown out of their carefully man-icured shapes and the flower beds were sprouting weeds. As Buck unlocked the plate iron gate into the walled enclosure, two more of Fitz's bodyguards strolled past us and entered the house. One of them sent a flat, familiar smile in my direction.

"That's Zimmerman!" I said to Buck.

"He served with you in India," said Pularski and pushed open the heavy gate.

"He's a killer," I said.

Buck turned to me. His long, sad face had learned during the past four years to manage an ironic expression.

"So are we all," he said.

"Don't say that," I said. "Yukon officers cannot talk that way." (I almost said, "We can't talk that way. Someone will hear us!")

"Maybe. Let's look at the garden," he said.

We entered and he closed the gate behind us. The small cor-ner of Ohio Buck had nurtured inside the walls of the enclosure was beautiful beyond any expectations. A fringe of gold and purple flowers made a rectangular frame around a rough stone walk that itself surrounded a miniature forest of blooming trees and shrubs of a myriad variety. Raked gravel and moss-covered granite boulders fashioned to resemble a frozen seascape made a bed for the small trees Buck had so carefully pruned I could not find on them a single dead leaf. A lily pond containing several decorative koi was tucked into the angle of the outside wall farthest from the gate. A young dogwood tree, ablaze with white and pink spring blossoms, was next to the pond, balancing the water's dark blues and greens with its colors from the other end of the light spectrum.

"Daffodils, crocus, violets: my early bloomers," Buck said of the gold and purple flowers. "My bulbs are still coming up. We had a tough winter. I won't have any hollyhocks all the way out until late June. You should see the hummingbirds I have then."

"Very beautiful," I told him. "Winifred, is it true someone is stealing supplies designated for the foreign air bases?"

"Yes," he said and shook his head. "And Fitz calls *me* stupid. The thefts have to be an inside job, Robert. Which means we'll catch them, in time. Can you imagine how dumb a person would have to be to be a part of government, to know something about Fitz, and to steal from him anyway? God help the poor fools when their time comes."

He showed me the far side of the miniature forest, where there was a concrete bench sitting in the shade of the garden's only mature tree, a giant ancient oak.

"When the two families were negotiating the marriage," said Buck, "Lady Joan used to come here to read."

"I thought we weren't to speak of her," I said.

"You're right, Robert. I can't follow my own advice."

I tossed some food pellets Buck gave me to the koi in the pond. The big, slow fish rose to the surface and moved their round mouths around the floating scraps. One rose and took a pellet right from Buck's good hand. I asked him what the small ash pit beside the water was for.

"I have toads in here," he said. "I make a fire in the afternoon. Put it out before dusk. They sleep in the ashes. Keeps them warm throughout the night."

The lilac bushes in his miniature forest were in bloom, a circumstance that brought Buck great delight. He cut a sprig of them and put it in my lapel.

"Did you see a tiger?" he asked. "A man shouldn't go to India and not see a tiger. I saw one in Bengal. A long way off, he was. He looked like fire on four legs."

"No, there weren't any out west," I said. "Or in the hills. The natives say there are still some in the north, on a game preserve. I did see lots of snakes and birds."

"Then we'll have to go north together," he said. "When the war is over," he added.

"Are you certain there will be a war?"

"Certain as rain," he said. "Remember Mason? Hard to forget, isn't he? He's taken to hanging around here, trying to get an audience with Fitz. Fitz won't see him, of course. If you meet him, don't let him take you to dinner. He's worse than ever. If someone were to see you with him, it could ruin you."

"What has he done this time?"

"He's been so nasty I can't even say what he's done," said Pulaski and made a face as if he had something foul in his mouth. "A commoner would have been hanged for it."[18]

"I have to travel east," I said. "Fitz's mother wants to speak to me. You told me once you know her."

Buck nodded.

"She's a very smart woman," he said. "As smart as Fitz, probably. Too smart for me to know what she's about. Fitz loves her, and he competes with her. Now that Fitz is Consul, he has shut her out of his affairs, much to her disapproval. I would take the lilacs from my lapel when I met her. She doesn't like frivolous things. The first time you meet her you won't like her."

"Then on the second occasion one warms to her?"

"No," said Buck. "On the second time you like her even less. Your opinion of her deteriorates from that point."

"Did you know Fitz was going to make me a major?" I said.

I took out the box containing the new decorations.

"Fitz promotes everyone who does their job," said Pularski. "He wanted to make me a captain after his father was killed, and

---

18. Mason, in his filthy autobiography, admits he had a tendency to relate to small boys in a manner similar to the way Socrates related to his male students. Unlike the great Athenian, Mason never discussed philosophy with the boys he imported from Mexico.

after Senator Dade . . . had an accident. I told him I would rather have a garden."

"You aren't . . . ? Perhaps that's another subject we shouldn't discuss," I said, and as when I beheld the homeless hill people in India I felt ashamed of myself; I had accepted a promotion for my bloody work, and my humble friend Buck had wanted no vainglorious reward for what he had done.

"Yes, you will be better off if you don't know," he agreed.

He showed me the dogwood, a plant he particularly loved. He said the roots would one day reach five feet into the earth.

"For as small as it is, it takes forever to grow," he said. "She will be here a hundred years after we are gone. People then will look at this and will know we loved beautiful things."

He caressed the knotted tree trunk with his good hand as a person might stroke a pet, exactly as he had petted the catfish on the river. I could see the small space of greenery brought him great pleasure. His scarred face was as happy as it had been when we fished together on the muddy and serene Missouri.

"I would ask you to pray with me, Robert. There isn't time. I have to go inside and call a Turk a *domuz*."

"What does that mean?" I asked.

"In Turkish it means 'pig,' a big insult to a Moslem. The Turkish ambassador's bodyguards know a few English words, things like 'asshole' and 'son of a bitch.' They call us that. We call them *domuz*. While Fitz and their bosses are inside the library talking war and peace we insult each other. It's foolish, I know. It's what Fitz wants. Are you still writing the redheaded girl?"

"She hasn't written for over a year," I said. "I don't know what became of her."

"I'm sorry," he said. "She was very pretty. She had green eyes. Green eyes are supposed to be good. Or is it blue eyes?"

Buck opened the gate for us.

"You're a romantic at heart, Winifred," I said as he relocked the iron doors.

"I can't be," he said. "I lack the credentials."[19]

"You're getting clever in your old age," I told him.

---

19. An ageless Yukon gag still told today. Soldiers from the ranks who have reached high rank or office speak slyly of themselves as "lacking the credentials." The lowborn Bruce and Pularski would have heard the jest many times and in many forms.

We shook hands and asked God's blessings on one another as we parted. I was walking through the front gate and turning in the direction of the bus stop when a grotesquely fat young man in a white suit accosted me. Somehow he knew my name. I had to look hard at his pudgy face before I recognized Mason's face swimming atop that ball of lard.

"Don't you remember me, Robert the Bruce?" he said.

"Tony, you look—"

"I've gained weight," he said. "Nearly five stone. Worrying did it to me, you see. I've had nothing to do but worry since they booted me out of the Army."

I recalled what Buck had told me of Mason. I kept walking at a brisk pace toward the bus stop while I spoke to him. He was badly out of physical condition and was soon panting like a dog as he tried to keep up with me.

"How are you, other than, you know, other than . . ."

"Fine," he said. "My whole life is ruined. Other than that, I'm wonderful. Listen, Robert—my, but you are looking good—what is the name of your Lord?"

Looking at him and at the same time knowing what he was capable of doing unsettled my stomach. He was the only Yukon I ever knew who had such extraordinary inclinations and yet had not landed on the gallows or in the I.T.

"Lord Prim-Jones of Astoria," I said.

"Does he have any daughters?" asked Mason with an unpleasant giggle. "I need a wife, you see. Father tried to find a wife for me. None of the eligible girls he knows of will have me. They've heard stories. Filthy lies are what they are. Fitz says I have to get married to a noble lady and lose weight or he won't let me back in the Army. Father says if I don't get back in the Army, I'll disgrace the family, and there goes my inheritance. The old boy's put his foot down."

"My Lord Prim-Jones has two sons," I said.

Mason followed after me right up to the bus stop bench.

"The bugger!" he exclaimed. "Does he have any widowed sisters? Aunts? Cousins? Grandmothers? I'm not particular. Tell him she doesn't have to live with me. Tell him I'll pay handsomely."[20]

---

20. Offering to buy a bride in this manner has always been illegal in the Confederacy. Lord Mason would have been committing a major felony if he offered money to any noble family.

"I'm sorry," I said. "My Lord has a small family."

"Don't you know of any single young noble ladies?" he asked.

"Doesn't Watchcharm Davis have a twin sister?"

"Oh, her," he said and looked at the sky. "That little bitch said she would rather be staked to an anthill than marry me."

"Here's my bus," I said.

In truth the bus that had stopped in front of us was not the bus I wanted; it was not headed toward the railway station but to a farming town in the opposite direction. At that moment I did not care.

"Good luck," I said as I climbed the bus steps.

"Won't you stay and join me for dinner—" Mason began to say.

The bus driver had closed his doors and driven away before the young Lord had finished speaking.

# EIGHT

LADY FITZPATRICK WAS not at the Meadowlands estate when I arrived. Her servants and bodyguards said she was at a nature camp with some of her conservatory students in the City of the Plains Park. So I rented a steam auto and drove to the mouth of the Hudson River where she and her girls had pitched some large tents outside the woods on the sandy Jersey shore. I gave the Blue Jackets on post the letter of introduction Fitz had sent with me. They told me Lady Fitzpatrick could not receive me right away. The guards said she and some of her young protégées had canoed across the river and were hiking in the thick forest on Manhattan Island.

As the park's name indicates, the area had been in American times the site of a vast metropolis. After the Storm Times, the early Yukons had burned everything in the region with Fire Sticks, leaving only a layer of black obsidian glass, which had been broken down into a thick, black soil by genetically altered lichen. A luxuriant forest of maple, birch, walnut, and oak had grown on the unholy ground during the past three hundred years. Only the broken statue of the Mother of Liberty,[1] lying on her side atop a small bay island, remains to remind the visitor of the generations who once lived there. Under other circumstances I would not have minded lazing in this unspoiled wilderness for a few days, perhaps doing some fly fishing in the pristine river and staying up nights to listen to the howling of the wolves that still run wild in that uninhabited

---

1. Refers to the badly damaged copper statue that can still be seen on an island near the Hudson estuary. Christened "The Statue of Liberty" in 1884, Bruce misremembers the proper name.

region. At the time I had only three days before I had to start back to Ohio and keep my appointment with Fitz. Each morning I spoke to the guards and asked if I could proceed into the campgrounds, and they would shake their heads and say they knew no more of the Lady's plans than I did.

"The Lady Fitzpatrick may see you today, sir. Or she may not," the sergeant of the guards told me. "She keeps her own time, major. She kept a field marshal waiting for a week, sir."

I slept in the automobile at night, and in the daytime I sat beneath a tree and read my copy of Euclid and made notes in the margins of the mechanical drawings Fitz had given me. Every three hours I walked to the guard post and looked down the footpath leading to the big tents in which Lady Fitzpatrick and her charges were staying. The guards would shake their heads from side to side each time I came into sight. Two days went by before the two men on duty came to me and said I could go down in half an hour. They let me shave and check my tie and hair in their small guards' tent before I walked down the path to my conference with her. Lest they be blamed for sending a derelict into the Lady's presence, the sergeant and his corporal looked me over to be certain I was acceptable for her company.

"Let me check your hands, sir," said the stout sergeant.

He and his corporal looked at one hand apiece and were gravely disappointed with what they beheld.

"You have—what is this?—ink? You have ink stains, sir," said the sergeant, sounding as glum as if he were declaring I had incurable cancer.

"I'm an engineer," I said. "I get ink on my hands every day."

"You might stand with your hands held behind you, sir," suggested the youthful corporal.

"A very good suggestion by the lad, sir," said the sergeant. "Don't look directly at her, neither. The Lady doesn't take to anybody looking directly at her, sir."

"Don't turn up your nose at any nasty food she offers you, sir," advised the corporal. "The Lady is a *vetetarian*. She don't eat so much as a boiled egg."

"A vegetarian," I said.

"To be sure, sir," said the sergeant. "Eats like a coney, bites like a crocodile, sir."

"You two do wonders for a man's confidence," I said, making a final check of myself in their little tent mirror.

"Take nothing she does personally, sir," said the sergeant, whose manner was more familiar than I probably should have allowed. "She's humbled more important men than you and us and the rest of the military put together."

I walked down the trail and into the group of tents. I stopped outside the largest one, as the guards had told me to do, and to the partially opened flap I announced:

"Major Sir Robert Mayfair Bruce, Knight of the Field, to see Lady Fitzpatrick."

No one answered. I cleared my throat and said in a somewhat louder voice:

"Major Sir Robert Mayfair Bru—"

"For God's sake!" a loud, sharp voice inside the tent said. "I heard you the first time! Get in here!"

I went through the flap and found Lady Fitzpatrick seated on a folding chair at a portable desk. Two of her students, girls of fifteen or so dressed in schoolgirl sailor outfits, were sitting on a cot before her. Lady Fitzpatrick was a tall, thin woman; her aquiline nose bore a strong resemblance to that of her famous son. In spite of the springtime heat she was wearing a heavy black velveteen suit that covered her six-foot frame in the old, non-Romanesque fashion. Her straight black hair fell to the small of her back, and through it ran a distinctive white streak that went from her forehead to a place behind her chair I could not see from my vantage point. Harriman's *A Visit to the Capitol,* the original oil in its full bloody glory,[2] was propped against the front of the desk, directly in front of the place I was standing. The two girls on the cot had been reciting verse from memory when I had interrupted.

"Finish the line, Jane," Lady Fitzpatrick instructed one of the girls.

---

2. Jared Harriman (2072–2151), the first Yukon painter of note. His panoramic *A Visit to the Capitol* depicts the Yukon First Infantry Division entering the American Capitol Building on July 7, 2086, and the slaughter of the remaining American politicians among the members' benches and on the floor in front of the speaker's podium. Copies of *A Visit to the Capitol* were for many years posted in Yukon classrooms and homes as a visual moral lesson to the young.

" 'Thus forth he called his daughter faire,' " said the girl. " 'The fairest one his only—' "[3]

"Fairest *un!*" said Lady Fitzpatrick. "Un. Spencer was from England. His homeland, you ignorant twit. *My* homeland. You should bear that in mind when you butcher his verse. He spoke and wrote in a sixteenth-century English accent."

"Yes, Lady," said Jane. " '—his only daughter faire—' "

"Enough of your whiny little mouthing! Leave me," said Lady Fitzpatrick. "I need to speak to this gentleman."

The girls rose in unison and backed out the side of the tent opposite me. They bowed repeatedly as they went.

"And study!" Lady Fitzpatrick called after them. "Next time you will recite the succeeding twenty cantos or you will be confessing your sorrows to the Turk's stoop,[4] you addle-headed bitches!"

"Yes, Lady," said the girls.

"Stop gawking at the major, you ignorant, oversexed sluts!" demanded Lady Fitzpatrick. "You think he is a strapping fine fellow, don't you? I expect you are having nasty little thoughts about him in your nasty little brains even as I speak. Let me tell you this, you baggage, no man will ever want a couple of filthy little whores like you two! You're as stupid as you are dirty!"

"Yes, Lady," they said and disappeared out the flap.

I bowed to the Lady and waited for her to address me. She instead penned a note on her desk note pad.

"Do speak, Sir Robert," she said. "I do trust you came here to speak?"

"Yes, my Lady, I—"

"Unless you are prepared to swear personal fealty to me, I am not *your* Lady, sir," she said. "I loathe that *my* Lady business. People think they are flattering me with one tiny word. You may address me as 'Lady.' Do you enjoy that picture?"

She had noticed I was looking at the Harriman. I was merely trying not to look straight at her and had no special interest in

---

3. *The Faerie Queen,* canto XII.

4. A Turk's stoop in girl's schools is the three-foot high hobby horse over which a reprobate student drapes herself so the headmistress may cane the unlucky child upon her most vulnerable part. In boys' schools it is known by the more vulgar name the Greeks' helper.

studying Harriman's depictions of Yukon infantrymen bayoneting American legislators.

"Yes, Lady," I said. "It is a wonderful painting."

"Ha!" she guffawed. "That rubbish? That is my late husband's notion of art. I keep it about as a memento of him. The other trash he favored were all pictures of horses and fox hunting rot. Each time I look at that monstrosity I think of him. Let me see your hands."

I had been holding my hands behind my back as the corporal guardsman had suggested. When I held them out to her I had to command myself to be steady.

"Ink," she said, and made another note in her pad.

"I am sorry, Lady," I said.

"For what?" she asked. "Engineers should have ink on their hands. Calluses?" she asked, and studied the thick skin on the sides of my hands before she made another note.

"If you were a manicured dandy," she said, "I would not trust you. My son, by the way, thinks you are the best there is at what you do. He says you did a superb job in India."

"Thank you, Lady."

"Don't thank me. Thank him when you see him next. I wouldn't know if you can draw a straight line," she said. "Tell me, Sir Robert," she asked without altering her tone, "do you think Isaac is mad?"

"No, Lady," I said, much startled by the question. "Your son the Consul is a genius. Genius often resembles madness to those of us who do not possess it, Lady."

"They resemble each other because they go about in the same hat and coat," she said. "But I am not disappointed with your answer. You and that other commoner friend of his, that General Hood, you are both a good deal sharper than the young Lords he keeps close to him. My personal theory is that three hundred years of inbreeding among the upper classes have produced far too many noble idiots. Look at my late husband, for instance."

She wrote again. A small, hairy Pekingese was curled in a wicker basket underneath her desk. I did not see the homely creature until she paused to pet it.

"Do you want to marry?" she asked. "Oh, of course you do. I can see it in you. You want to have your breeding whore. Like my son. Ha! Look how that turned out! I know you men."

I could not guess how I should respond to that.

"Admit it, Sir Robert," she said, "you have a strong sensual nature."

"Yes, Lady," I said, which seemed a better answer than arguing with her.

She wrote a final note on her desk pad.

"Tell me, Sir Robert," she said, "you have recently been to my son's place in Ohio?"

"Yes, Lady."

"How is Isaac doing with that pallid brood mare he married?" she asked, as if that were the way a great Lady should speak to a man she had just met.

Rather than answer her directly, I said, "Lady Joan seems to be a young woman gifted with both great beauty and intelligence—"

"Don't give me that rubbish," interrupted Lady Fitzpatrick. "I want to know if he is inflicting upon her that bestial grunt in the night you men love so much. You may keep the beauty and intelligence fluff to yourself."

She had unnerved me before; now she terrified me. There seemed to be no escape for me but to relate to her the things Buck Pularski had told me.

"Lady Joan and your noble son seem to be living separately at the moment," I said. "She is currently visiting family members in the south."

"Ha!" declared Lady Fitzpatrick, much pleased with my answer. She clapped her hands in front of her a single time and beamed at me a smile that was far more hideous than the scowl she had been giving me since I entered the tent. "I told him he shouldn't marry until he had more experience with women. Even his idiot father knew that about the boy. Then too, he shouldn't have chosen a dewy-eyed cow like the one he did. Does he listen to me? No. The one person he can trust is me, and he now knows better than to speak to me. My advice is no longer wanted. Have you seen the papers today, Sir Robert?"

She shoved the Cumberland newspaper in front of me on her desk. The headlines were of appointments Fitz had made in the government.

"He's named a new cabinet," said Lady Fitzpatrick. "Half of them are his little friends and half are his wife's relatives. Oh, yes: he has gone and made appointments without saying a single word to me. The same is true of his imperial schemes. Now I don't care if he goes and kills a couple million Chinese. That gives the boys with the guns something to do; keeps them from getting underfoot at home. Killing in great numbers is something you men can actually do well. But Isaac should not be forming a government on his own. Governments matter to real people. I don't know why I'm telling this to you. You are not making command decisions, are you?"

"No, Lady," I said.

"You are, all in all, his friend," she said and stroked the dog some more while she paused to think. "You will see him. To tell him about your building projects and whatever? When you do meet with him, tell him I am not content to sit on the Jersey shore and train wives for his officers. I have a letter I want you to give him."

"Yes, Lady," I said.

She rose from her desk and came about with a sealed envelope.

"Since you are doing this for me, Sir Robert," she said, "I am going to do something for you. I am going to give you some advice about men. There are only four types of them in the world. There are first the fat, lazy layabouts, a type I know too well." She smirked for a second at her late husband's painting. "They are the drones of humanity. I expect you are too smart, in spite of your low birth, to let yourself be one of them. Then there are the faceless peasants. Who cares what they are like? I certainly don't. After them come the ambitious, which is, in part, what you are. Though you would do well to curb your ambitions, or else you will not get far. You lack the connections and the money, so you had best do whatever my son demands of you. That should be your road to happiness. The fourth and last type are the girly-men, those wan little boys blessed with such teensy-tiny brains they go and fall in love with their wives. You see that sort of weakling every time you go into a public place. They're the ones walking hand in hand with some beribboned cow in the city parks, whispering filthy little words in her ear. These so-called men go to church and the public concerts and pretend to enjoy the experiences for her sake. This sort reads his wife poetry and buys her flowers. He learns to do the filthy things in bed his wife wants to do and loves her babies when those filthy buggers arrive on the scene. Their sort, sir, disgusts me more than all the others put together. By God, they ought to make them wear lipstick and perfume and leave them to stay under their mommies' skirts and let those with some grit in their makeups take their place in battle. At my age I could still take the place of ten such lollipops in a real fight."

"Yes, Lady," I said.

"You have a little of this fourth type in you, Sir Robert," she said, coldly, but then she said everything with at least some coldness in her words. "Don't deny it. I see it in your eyes. That is a very dangerous way for a soldier to be. When you marry, your wife will see this in you as clearly as I, and she will attempt to control you. Don't you let her do it, Sir Robert. Give your wife that filthy thing God gave you men. That's all that's demanded of you. Should she try to influence you with her crafty, loving ways, you will give her the back of your hand. You are to be my son's man, not your wife's, Sir Robert. Do not ever forget that."

"Yes, Lady," I said.

"You may go, Sir Robert," she said and returned to her chair behind the desk.

She waved me away with a flick of her hand. I backed out the tent flap as the girls had done, bowing as they had. The fresh air outside had never felt more soothing against my damp skin. The sergeant and his corporal greeted me with salutes and broad smiles as I came back up the path to their post.

"You see, sir," said the sergeant, giving me the once-over. "Still alive. No open wounds or broken bones."

"Is she always like that?" I asked.

The corporal handed me a flask of brandy from which I took a long, soothing drink. He kept the flask handy because it seems many people needed a drink after a conference with the Lady.

"She's usually worse, sir," said the sergeant. "We couldn't hear her yelling at you this time. You should be here when she gets to beating on those poor girls. It's like to break your heart, it is."

The corporal made a gesture to his mate.

"Sir," said the sergeant, "Johnny here wants to know if your unit could use another man in the fighting. I'm too old for overseas service, but he's willing to go anywheres."

"You could stick me in the front lines, sir," said the corporal. "After a year of guarding the Lady, anything would seem easy duty."[5]

---

5. Gerald recounts that Lady Fitzpatrick was a gentle lady of refined tastes who contributed generously to the Artists' and Musicians' Guild. Bruce's depiction of her is another of his spiteful slanders.

# NINE

UPON MY RETURN to Pallas, Buck Pularski drove me to the nearby airfield he had spoken of during my earlier visit.

"Fitz is feeling better since you saw him," Buck told me as we drove through the fields of corn and soybeans. "Lady Joan has returned. She has a good influence upon him."

"He seemed fine when I was here before," I said.

"He puts up a front when you or Hood are around, Robert," said Buck. "He values your good opinion of him above everybody else's. He considers Hood and you superior men because you're both lowborn and have earned your positions. Fitz believes if Hood and you think well of him, then he's probably making an even better impression on the millions of other commoners."

"Now that we can speak of her, what is Lady Joan like?" I asked.

"She is very lovely," he said with unguarded feeling. "She knows everything about books, and she's very gentle. The most gentle person I've met. You will like her."

"As much as you do?"

"No," said Pularski, being very free about his feelings for the Consul's wife. "The more one sees her, the more one cares for her. I get to see her every day."

We drove through two checkpoints where the guards looked over our papers and then sent us onto a city of windowless, metal warehouses. I had never seen an industrial park this large on Yukon soil. The grid blocks of single-story structures went on for several miles in all directions in the flat Ohio countryside.

"They're building planes here?" I asked. "I wouldn't think the law would allow this."[1]

"These are government buildings," said Buck. "They're full of bugs."

"Bugs? Several square miles of bugs? That makes no sense."

"Locusts," said Buck. "You're looking at another of Aranov's projects. He has a brother who's a bug expert."

"An entomologist," I suggested.

"No, he is an Aranov, too," said Buck, and grinned.

"There goes a man who runs the risk of being amusing," I said, surprised to see Buck was developing a sense of humor.

"Doctor Aranov's brother is researching diseases that will kill locusts," said Buck. "The idea is to protect the new farms in Australia. Every one of these buildings has billions of them. They feed them tons of grain. The adult insects lay larvae in the sand that can stay alive for up to three years."

"Locusts can do that?"

"These can. They're genetically altered. Here we are," said Buck.

Our car emerged from the rows of nondescript buildings and onto the edge of a small airfield. A single large hangar was on the north side of the concrete runway, and beside it was a beacon tower and two fueling tanks, one for water and one for biomass. The site could have been any small military airfield except that in front of the hangar were three of the oddest looking airplanes I had seen up to that time.

Each of these planes was no larger than a normal fighter craft and each had an unpainted white outer shell made of a plastic-carbon filament composite. All were laden with ordnance for a test flight. The strangest of the three planes resembled an Australian boomerang; it was a single wing and had no tail or nose, only a rudder attached to the rear of the craft's aerodynamic structure. Two propeller engines were mounted on the back of the wing to push the plane forward. Two clear bubble canopies protected the pilot and navigator in a cockpit positioned at the boomerang's crest, and on its underside hung three large missiles, each capable of covering a square mile of land with incendiary Fire Sticks pellets.[2]

---

1. The law in 2420 limited factory size to 120 workers per plant, as opposed to the 200 limit of today.

2. See McVick's *Warplanes of the Four Points* for a fuller description of these three airplanes.

The other two airplanes looked alike in most of their aspects, although one was larger and carried more weapons on its undercarriage. They each had a torpedo-shaped fuselage and a transparent canopy over their cockpits. Both of these similar planes had a large rear wing that was bent upward seven feet from the tip. A second canard wing was attached to the front of both planes just beyond the cockpit. Like the flying wing, both of these aircraft were driven by two rear mounted and forward pushing engines. The larger of the similar planes carried a full rack of phosphorus bombs, antipersonnel canister rockets, and air-to-ground missiles, while the smallest airplane bore only four air-burst rockets. Both of these double-winged planes had fifty caliber machine guns in their wings and twenty-five millimeter cannons in their nose cones.

Buck and I left his automobile and examined the peculiar machines at close range. When I rapped my knuckles against their outside shells I heard the hollow echo of the interior fuel tanks resonate inside them. I could rock the smallest plane slightly on its shock absorbers by merely pushing against its side with my shoulder.

"They're flying fuel and water tanks," I told Pularski. "As light as dandelion seeds. They could almost fly forever when they're full."

"Not forever, Robert," said Fitz, who, with Dr. Aranov behind him, had emerged from the open hangar. "In the case of the B-110, 'the Bat Wing,' as the men call it," he pointed to the boomerang plane, "the range is ten thousand miles."

I again rapped against the outer shell of the smallest plane.

"The armor isn't too light for combat?" I asked.

"It is a woven carbon fiber," said Aranov, whom I was hearing speak for the first time. "It is fire resistant—to a degree, of course—and will deflect any small arms fire."

"The Chinese have steam jets," I said. "These cannot outrun jets."

"The planes we see here have a top speed of over six hundred and fifty m.p.h.," said Fitz. "Slower than jets, to be sure. You must bear in mind the Chinese have no early warning system. The long-range bombers will hit their targets and be gone before the Chinese can get their jets off the ground. The enemy jets have a range of only a couple hundred miles; they can't pursue us, and they can't escort their own big bombers. Our attack and fighter planes will stay close to home base and will never face Chinese or Turkish fighters."

Fitz explained how the three exotic new planes would move too quickly to be shot down by human-operated firepower. The fighters, the smallest of the canard planes, would attack the enemies' lumbering Florin class bombers long before they reached our airfields; the bigger and much slower foreign airplanes would go down by the thousands. The attack planes would strike at road and rail transport and at the other side's armies while they were on the move. The Bat Wing bombers would have at the strategic targets deep in foreign territory.

"We will bludgeon the other side into the ground," said Fitz, rather too gleefully.

At that instant I realized fully what the new bases in India and the rest of the world were for. Seconds later I found myself wishing I still did not know. Most of us learn any truth a piece at time and seldom have the opportunity to have it revealed to us all at once. The step-by-step process allows us to prepare for the truth when it is too horrible or we are too cowardly. Looking at the three new planes I had a sudden vision of countless thousands screaming in the infernos these monsters would create, but I remained too afraid to express my thoughts outright.

"None of these planes would need long, heavy runways," I said, getting at the matter indirectly and feeling my insides turn. "That is why we have been building fighter bases."

"We can cover the world," announced Aranov. "No one will dare to stand against us."

"Sir," I said, feeling such a rage for the bony man I felt I had to make some manner of objection to his exclamation, "airplanes have been a weapon for five hundred years. In that long stretch of time, aerial bombing alone has never won a single war. Conquering the whole world with airplanes would be a large task indeed."

Dr. Aranov did not take criticism well. He huffed and retreated behind Fitz to shield himself from any other comments I might make.

"You are correct, Robert," said Fitz. "Bombing alone never beat anyone. We have other ideas, other weapons."

"Weapons beyond the major's understanding," said Dr. Aranov.

"You underestimate him," said Fitz to the scientist. "He would understand quite well. You are too temperamental, Richi. He was only stating the obvious. Come on, let us return to the house. Robert has seen the aircraft. He knows everything he needs to know, for now."

Fitz rode back to Pallas in the automobile with Buck and my-self. During the ride I studied his manner for the positive influence Buck said Lady Joan had on him. I could see nothing out of the ordinary. Fitz was his usual effervescent self. As always, he said things that would have been outrageous if they had come from anyone else's lips, and he said them as carelessly as other men might speak of what they planned to have for supper.

"I apologize for Mother," he said. "I imagine she was a ripper. I could have warned you, but I have learned it is better to send people to her unprepared. Saves on worry, and how would one prepare for her?"

"She was very pleasant," I said.

Fitz laughed and punched Buck on the arm.

"Quick, Buck!" he said. "When we get home, send a message on the Blinking Stars! Someone has kidnapped Mother and put an imposter in her place!"

He clapped his hands he was so amused with my obvious false-hood. This was, I realized, the same gesture Lady Fitzpatrick had used when I visited her.

"Mother is never pleasant to anyone, Robert," he said. "This is, you know, why I love you, my friend: I always know your true feelings whatever you say. Tell me, whom did she pick for you?"

"I don't follow you," I said.

"You poor ninny," he said. "Don't you realize she was picking you a wife?"

"She didn't send one with me."

"She must have sent the lucky girl ahead to your family," said Fitz. "I told her to find you a lass with a strong frame, able to bear lots of children. The Confederacy needs more young engineers."

"She gave me a letter for you, Fitz," I said and gave him the sealed envelope I had carried from the Atlantic coast.

"She doesn't give up," said Fitz and at once tore the letter into small pieces and tossed them out the car's window. "Mother cannot accept that she is my ally and not my co-Consul. These days her usefulness to me lies primarily in the past. She should be happy in her work at that school of hers and leave the world to those of us born to wear pants."

At the manor house Fitz took me into his library and had his stenographer record our conversation for a quarter of an hour. He went over the prefabricated building plans and explained to me the parts would enter India through Serat and Calcutta, as the other supplies had. Out of the blue he asked me for my opinion on the feasibility of building a north-south railway across Africa, a subject I had not expected to discuss with him. I said construction in the desert north of that continent or in its temperate south would be a simple matter. The problem lay in central Africa, where the heavy rainfall and dense foliage of the Congo Basin and the Ethiopian Highlands would make the laying of railroad tracks tremendously difficult. He nodded at my answer, then dismissed the stenographer and gave Buck orders to wait outside the library door.

"Now," he said and sat himself down in the chair at the head of the table, "I want to talk to you about David."

"From what I read in the newspapers," I said, "he is doing well in the Senate."

"Not David Shelley," said Fitz. "Yes, he does well there. Shelley has been around politicians since he was a boy. Besides, everyone knows he speaks for me, so they listen to him. No, I want to talk to you about *the* David."

I did not reply immediately. The only other David I knew of was the shepherd who slew Goliath and grew to become the King of Israel.

"Do you mean David in the Bible?" I asked tentatively. "The one who wrote the Psalms?"

"Yes, *the* David," said Fitz. "He didn't write the Psalms, however. Not all of them, anyway. That is an ancient myth. Come and sit by me."

He pulled another chair close to him. When I sat down we were inches apart. Fitz leaned sideways so that our faces were almost touching.

"Tell me, Robert," he said, "do you believe David was a good man?"

"He was God's beloved," I said.

"Yes, yes, he was," said Fitz and slapped his palms on the table top. "That is the truth. Exactly. That is also beside the point. I am asking if he was good."

My mind scanned Sunday School lessons I had not revisited for many years.

"God left the building of the Temple to Solomon, David's son and successor," I said, "because David had Uriah the Hittite killed in battle and he marriedy Uriah's widow Bathsheba."[3]

---

3. As is told in Second Samuel, chapters 11 and 12.

"He did far, far worse than that, Robert," said Fitz.

He spoke with a curious intensity. His blue eyes blinked at times, yet their pupils did not shift. I became afraid and had to look at anything else in the room other than him.

"First of all, he was a fraud," said Fitz. "He didn't kill Goliath. Twice in the Bible it is stated that Elhanan slew Goliath.[4] In the second place, he killed King Saul—"

"Excuse me," I said; "wasn't Saul killed at Mount Gilboa by the Philistines?"[5]

"The death of Saul, like the rest of History, was written by History's winners," said Fitz. "I have read a book on the subject,[6] and the author points out that, like Hamlet's mother, the whole of First and Second Samuel protests too much. David's complicity in Saul's death is proven by the emphasis of his denial. And Saul, my friend, was as a father to young David. Now, as you have said, David committed adultery with Bathsheba and killed her husband. In his old age, he had his henchman Joab kill his son and heir Absalom. Hacked him to death as the boy dangled from a tree branch.[7] David commanded his armies to destroy all the Canaanites between Israel and the sea.[8] He was awash in a sea of blood, Robert. So, I ask you again: was he a good man?"

He sat back in the chair and waited for me to respond. The next words I spoke had to be carefully chosen or I would be letting down the most important man alive. I was no longer thinking of the thousands the planes I had seen at the airport were about to kill. I was again thinking of myself and of how much I wanted to please my all-important friend.

"No," I said, "and God loved him nonetheless."

"*Yes!*" exclaimed Fitz. "That is what Hood told me! Tell me: why did God love David?"

---

4. Second Samuel, chapter 21, verse 19, and First Chronicles, chapter 20, verse 5.

5. First Samuel, chapter 31.

6. Probably Randolph Mosbey Redman's *Old Testament Historiography,* which was then a popular text.

7. Second Samuel, chapter 18, verse 9.

8. Second Samuel, chapter 8; chapter 10, verses 15–19; chapter 12, verses 26–31.

"We cannot comprehend God," I said. "His reasoning is beyond ours."

He nodded in agreement. He began to say something, and instead he rose from his chair and walked once around the long table.

"Do you remember," he said as he again sat down, "when Doctor Murrey asked you during our oral exam if you felt shame because of what the early Yukons had done to the Americans? The question offended me at the time. He never posed a similar question when I had him as a tutor. Back then the only lesson he tried to give me was how wonderful our ancestors were. I think differently about it now. Were the early Yukons good people, Robert? They didn't, you know, just kill a few thousand Canaanites. They killed millions. Think of the agony of the last, starving remnants in the doomed American cities. Think of the poor children."

He rubbed his hands over his face as if he were wiping away something unclean from his skin.

"The Americans were a degenerate people," I said. "They brought on their own destruction."

"So our Historians say," said Fitz. "Our Historians are like the authors of the books of Samuel; they deny too much. Again, winners write History. Winners write all of History. We have no trustworthy record of what the Americans were really like."[9]

He inhaled and gripped the table's edge with both hands. Tears, real glistening tears, began to stream down his face.

"God looked away from our ancestors' crimes," he said. "He should have struck the early Yukons dead and buried them under a thousand strata of rock to hide them from the future. We know he didn't. He watched from Heaven and did nothing. He did nothing to David, other than not letting him build the temple. Nor did he do anything to Alexander when that ambitious young man put all the world under his heel. I think Alexander killed his father, too."

He looked directly at me, and despite the tears he smiled.

"As David killed his almost-father Saul, I mean," he said.

The comment made my stomach churn, for we both knew what he meant.

"God watched Caesar and Napoleon," he said. "Caesar made a desert of Gaul, and Bonaparte the Gaul tried to make a desert of

---

9. To slander History in this fashion is to slander God. Bruce compounds his blasphemy by putting these words in Fitzpatrick's mouth.

the rest of Europe. God didn't stop Genghis Khan. He didn't stop Attila. And on and on and on."

He paused. He sat in his chair and stared down at the tabletop, while I wished that Providence would put me anywhere in the universe other than that room, somewhere I would not have to answer the question I knew he was about to ask.

"Robert," he murmured, "do you believe God will love me as he loved David?"

I would today give up my soul if I could go back to that moment and tell Fitz he could still turn back from his awful destiny. I grant he had at this date already committed murder. It was equally true that he had not yet made his oceans of blood. A life spent in repentance and good deeds could still have brought him redemption. The world could have still been saved from his wrath. I could have spoken the truth to him in that moment, and my career and even my life might have been ended by my words. There was also the unexplored possibility that Fitz might have grabbed onto the truth as a drowning man grasps for a lifeline. The loss of my life would have been the loss of one man. What could that matter when placed against the entire nations Fitz was preparing to rain fire upon? I might have saved hundreds of millions of lives with those few honest words. My courage would have blessed generations that will now be left unborn and souls that are today ignorant of my existence. I might have as well saved myself a life filled with regrets. Ambition and cowardice—which in my early life were two names for the same hole in my character—made the truth stick to the roof of my mouth, and into the open air slipped the comforting lie he wished to hear.

"God loves you," I said.

"That isn't enough," he said and pawed at the tears falling as heavy as rain. "God loves earthworms. He loves the mold in a bathtub."

"There are a few special men," I said, "who, like David, walk through History as Angels walk through thunderstorms. Those about them become wet with sin, while they remain untouched. They may seem to be bad men, these special ones. If we judge them by the standards we hold ordinary men to, they are the worst of men. Ordinary standards do not apply to them. They are doing God's work here on earth, and as we do not know God's motives or His ends we cannot judge His servants. The special ones themselves do not understand His motives or discern His handiwork in their lives. Often . . . often only History, History written hundreds of years later can show the part God played in these men's actions. You, my Consul, will be remembered in ages hence as one of the special ones. You will be said to be God's beloved."

He came to me and, taking my face in his hands, he lovingly kissed me on the forehead. I could feel his warm tears dropping over my eyes and down my cheeks, tears that were soon blended with my own. Together our four eyes could not have wept enough tears to douse any of the fires that were soon to consume the world. Fitz thought I was weeping out of concern for him. In fact I was weeping because I knew I had let pass my last good chance to save my friend and his future victims. From then on there would be nothing honorable in my service to him, and I would never again be able not to know what I was doing.

"You know what Valette used to call you when you weren't about?" Fitz asked as he held me. "Sir Galahad. For your heart is pure. That is why I love you more than the others, Robert. You are innocent of everything, Sir Galahad. I feel at times I could kill the whole world: Mother, my friends, everybody, but never you. I would that you live forever."

He let go of me, and went to the window. He dried his eyes with his handkerchief as he looked outside at the untended garden, which outside of Buck's enclosure was sprouting a fresh crop of weeds. For a few troubling seconds his whole frame shook. Moments later he turned about and was the smiling, gregarious Fitz I had always known.

"I have a letter from Stein," he said matter-of-factly of an entirely different subject. "He is now Colonel Stein, God help the Confederacy. He wants you to visit him at Sixth Army headquarters in Salt Lake City. The trip is quite unnecessary. He says your Indian bases present certain logistical problems. I told him he is mistaken. He is such a fretting old woman. You may stop and see him, if you wish, on your way back to Columbus. I leave the decision to you. At home you will have some business of a personal nature."

He smiled broadly and touched his heart.

"I am aware you have a four-week pass, Robert," he continued. "I regret to tell you I need you back in India as soon as possible. You may stay at home for another week, then return to your base. Give me your hand, my friend. And your blessing."

I did as he bade me. I smiled for him, and returned outside. Buck was waiting for me and took me into his garden to introduce me to Lady Joan, the new Mrs. Fitzpatrick, who along with her elderly maid was sitting on Buck's cement bench at the back of his miniature forest. She was a pleasant, shy young woman I was not in the right frame of mind to appreciate as she deserved.

Much has been written and spoken against her family in the years since the time of Fitz's glory. History has it that the Shays (or DeShays, as they were then known) were a flock of vultures feeding upon the Fitzpatrick legacy. Speaking as one who knew the flesh and blood Lady Joan rather than the caricature her family's enemies created, I can aver she was a kind, literate lady who was writing a History book[10] and wanted nothing for herself other than a normal home life with a normal husband. As Buck had intimated during my previous visit to Pallas, she lived apart from her husband the Consul. Her rooms were on the mansion's third floor, where also lived her elderly attendant, who had been Lady Joan's nursemaid twenty-five years earlier. Whenever weather permitted, the two of them found refuge in Buck's walled garden. There she found an island of peace and beauty amid the military bustle that dominated the rest of the Pallas estate. Unlike many others, Lady Joan could look past Buck's terrifying exterior and recognize the goodness in the enormous bodyguard who stood over the two little ladies like a bear standing watch over two delicate ceramic figurines. The tall, powerful Buck was so overwhelmed by the small, sweet noblewoman, he had no inkling of how he should behave in her company. He stuttered each time he began addressing her, and stole glances at her when she was not conversing with him. Every day before she rose, Buck took a basket of fresh cut flowers to her door on the third floor and left them for her to find.

"The flowers are part of my duties," Buck told me.

I told him his lying was now much inferior to mine.

When Buck introduced me to her, Lady Joan brightened upon hearing my name.

"Winifred tells me you are a very good man, Sir Robert," she said.

"Winifred" (Buck had blushed deeply when she used his real name) "overpraises his friends, my Lady," I said.

---

10. Lady Joan Fitzpatrick in fact wrote two History books—*The Last Byzantine Emperors* and *Persia in the Seventh Century*—but both are long out of print.

"I understand you are a man my husband listens to," she said.

"Someone is flattering me."

"Be that as it may," she said, and signaled me to be seated beside her on the concrete bench, "if you are a portion of the good man Winifred says you are, might I convince you to speak to my husband upon a private matter? I am sorry I am so forward with you, Sir Robert. I do not know whom I may trust in this place, and I must go against my nature and speak frankly to anyone I think might help me."

"That depends," I said. "Fitz—I mean the Consul—"

"I know you call him Fitz," she said. "I envy the familiarity you have with him. I would that I knew him that well. My husband gives too much of himself to his public life. Winifred said I might be blunt with you, Sir Robert, and here it is: do you believe my husband might be convinced to take a vacation?"

"You wish that I suggest it to him, my Lady?" I said.

"Could you, sir?" she asked and the possibility so pleased her she sighed. "He needs to rest, Sir Robert. If you are his friend, you will have to agree with me."

When Lady Joan came to know her husband better, she would realize no one could propose to him he leave his work for any diversion as trivial as a vacation.

"I will mention it to him," I said, telling a second major lie in the space of half an hour. "You must expect nothing, my Lady. He may be cold to such a proposal."

"I pray he will listen to you, Sir Robert," she said. "God bless you, sir. You *are* a good man! Tell him also I wish to know him better. Tell him that beginnings are always difficult. That he has done nothing I will not forgive him for. That . . . tell him that many young men . . . they have failures of his sort, and he should not be ashamed. We could travel to Southfield and be alone, the two of us. There is, Sir Robert, a brain doctor I know of in Atlantis. Don't tell him that; he would bolt if he knew. I could introduce him to this doctor, and they could talk. Eventually, this doctor and I might persuade my husband to be treated . . . for his problems. You are his true friend; you know, Sir Robert, he has problems."

I bowed my head. Lady Joan thought I did so because I was feeling anguish for Fitz's sake; she did not realize I was ashamed I was misleading her. To hear this gentle lady call me a good man was somehow more painful than my time of awareness had been when I spoke to Fitz. I could not bring myself to look at her anxious face.

"Then you will do it?" she asked.

"I will," I said, and she believed me, for once one has mastered the art of dissimilation the practice of the same becomes nearly automatic.

We talked of her book and of the pretty garden. I excused myself after a few more minutes of conversation and walked with Buck to the iron gate. For one time that day I found the strength to speak the truth to someone.

"Winifred, my friend," I said, "she is the wife of the Consul of the Yukon Confederacy. Looking at her as you do is very dangerous."

"Fitz doesn't care," said Buck. "She is here, and he knows she cares for him. That is all he wants of her. I want nothing. I enjoy being about her, and that's enough. She and the maid are almost like having a family."

We parted in contrasting moods. Buck was elated to have Lady Joan at Pallas. I was despairing on account of my interview with the Consul. During my long train trip west I had to force myself to think of something else or I feared I would go mad. To take my mind elsewhere, I recited to myself all the sine and cosine tables for regular whole numbers until I went to sleep in my seat. Among the forest of lifeless mathematical figures I did not have to recall Fitz weeping or Lady Joan pleading me to help her husband or the three deadly airplanes on the Pallas runway.

After my meetings with Fitz and his mother, my stopover in Salt Lake to visit Stein seemed nothing to me at the time. I would not mention it here but that the occasion would have an effect on future events.

Banker Stein did not wish to talk to me about logistics problems in northern India. After letting me into his office at the Sixth Army Regional HQ, he talked for an hour of his new bride, whose picture he kept on his desktop.

"She kicked me out of the house last Thursday," he said, and apparently was happy to announce the incident. "For smoking. I had to spend a night in a hotel. Everything is forgiven now."

"I didn't know you smoked," I said.

"I don't," said Stein. "I'm conducting a scientific experiment. I smoked a cigar at home every night for the past two weeks, progressively using a larger and smellier brand each time. Margaret en-

dured the El Perfecto. La Bamba was the limit. Now I know precisely what she will tolerate."

"Do you test her in everything?"

"Certainly. I wear muddy boots in the house, have over old
friends from college. I would have you over, but we had Mason in
for tea, and she's told me she'll leave me if I have another one of
you in any time soon."

"You could write a book on the subject," I said. "Call it *What
a Wife Will Take*."

"If I only had the time," agreed Stein. "I would save some
other young fellows some suffering. Margaret is a great girl."

I had an eleven-fifty train to catch and wished him to get to the
point.

"What is it you want to talk to me about?" I asked.

Stein closed the door to his office. He checked the windows of
his office and drew the blinds.

"You've heard of the thefts the Quartermaster is investigating?"
he asked in a low voice.

I had. I told him I knew of three major thefts of supplies that
had been destined for overseas locations.

"What you don't know, Robert," he said, "is all three shipments were sent—or so the official documents say—through Sixth
Army depots. Most of the stolen stuff is for construction: cement,
rebar, earth-moving equipment. All of this probably was sold on
the black market. The Quartermaster's investigator has found a
bank account at the Marshal Bank here in Salt Lake, under a phony
name; there were two million pounds in it."

"So the thief is here," I said.

"Listen to me," he said, becoming more excited. "My signature somehow—maybe I signed, I don't remember—is on the daily
transport records when the stolen shipments came through here.
The bank belongs to a family friend.[11] The investigators have been
in here twice to talk to me. They think I did it! I know it!"

"You're being silly, Banker," I said.

"O'Brian is behind this," said Stein. "He is setting me up!"

"We have been in a state of emergency since Fitz's father's death,"

---

11. Andrew McPherson Lloyd was president of the Marshal Bank in 2420. He was married to Lord Stein's first cousin.

I said. "We aren't at war, although in the eyes of the law we are on account of the state of emergency. You and O'Brian had some inane dispute back in school. You should be past that. This is stealing from the military in time of war. They will hang whoever did this. O'Brian wouldn't do that to an old college chum."

"He is in the Quartermaster's office," insisted Stein. "I don't know how he's doing it. I do know this: he's fudging the monthly statements. When the Quartermaster sends out the final monthly assessments they don't match the preliminary estimates as calculated by the Memory Men."[12]

He took from his desk drawer a stack of three stapled booklets. They were the May, June, and July preliminary shipment estimates for the Second Engineers.

"Banker, you aren't supposed to have those," I told him.

"They're not what they appear to be. They're not official. I never see the official statements. A Memory Man at the Quartermaster's made them for me. I have two copies of every preliminary statement for every one of the eleven overseas bases that will be receiving shipments sent through here this summer. When the Quartermaster himself sends out the final statements, the ones that show the thefts, I and all the overseas commanders and I will have these to show that the stolen goods were never sent, or that something else happened between here and the Quartermaster's central depot."

"What if nothing is stolen this summer?"

"Then my Memory Men will send you new preliminary statements for the fall," he said. "Please sign these and date them on the outside. Fitz will trust your signature."

I had a train to catch. I expected that someone unknown to either O'Brian and Stein was stealing the construction goods, and

---

12. I had the great good fortune to research and write an article on the Memory Men ("The Memory Guild," *The Antiquarian's Notebook,* June 2584, pp. 1321–39). Their organization was formed in 2081 to make up for the loss of electronic computers. As most Memory Men are employed in government endeavors, many ordinary citizens have never had the opportunity to witness their work. I myself did not believe one man could memorize three thousand pages of text until I witnessed a Memory Man transcribe that amount of complicated data onto typed pages. Some masters of the guild are said to be able to hold ten thousand pages in their heads, and others, many of them idiot savants, can recall hundreds of columns of numbers from ancient accounts in a few seconds.

this preliminary statement ruse would succeed only in making Banker more ridiculous. The other ten planning officers receiving packets from him no doubt already judged him a fool. Had there been more time, I would have told Stein that. I would also have reminded him he was spending a fortune bribing Memory Men to transcribe shipment statements and that his new wife could find better uses for the wasted money. There was no time. I signed the booklets and put my copies in my briefcase. By the time I was again on board the train I had put them in that dark portion of my mind I used to store other matters I had chosen not to dwell upon.

# TEN

MY ENTIRE IMMEDIATE family was at the farm compound awaiting my arrival. My older brother Michael had traveled from Grand Harbor with his wife Deirdre and their two young children for the occasion. The men living on the family holdings had put on their white shirts, and every one of them had tied a cravat of some manner about his sunburned throat to give himself a touch of propriety. The women had on their Sunday dresses, which in my family still meant print cotton skirts and not the Roman styles that had conquered the rest of the Confederacy. My mother and my Aunt Nancy broke into tears as soon as my taxi pulled into the front yard. My father greeted me at the car door with a pint of the bitters Uncle Silas had brewed last October.

"My God," proclaimed Father, "the boy's a damned major!"

He hugged me and polished the shiny emblems of my rank with his shirt cuff.

"This is the closest I've been to an officer," he said.

The thirty-four members of my family who had been waiting in the yard pulled me into the main hall and made me sit at the long table in the dining room. The men put whiskey and beer in front of me and slapped me on the back. The women fussed over how thin they said I was and pushed plates overfilled with steaming food in my direction. Every living female relative I had, from the toddlers in their lace dresses to one-hundred-and-eleven-year-old Aunt Silvia, came about the table and kissed me; the older ones added a pinch on the cheek and recalled how small I used to be. My Uncle Merle brought his fiddle into the room and began to play a lively tune while I ate. My mother and Aunt Nancy remained standing at the doorway, their arms about each other, and continued to weep.

"Don't they feed you in the Army?" several aunts and grandmothers asked me as they attempted to put food into my mouth.

That particular comment was one of the few things spoken to me I could clearly comprehend. They were all speaking to me at once and laughing as they talked. To my ears they sounded as coherent as a flock of starlings.

Into this tumult strode my Great-Aunt Jessie, who at eighty-three was the most formidable woman in the household. She banged her fist on the dinner table to gain the mob's attention, and told them to be quiet. Uncle Merle foolishly played on a half a minute after she had given her order and everyone else had fallen silent; she took the instrument from his hands and told him he had been born an idiot and had gotten increasingly stupid every day he had been alive.

"You must all leave us," she commanded. "Deirdre," she said to my brother's wife, "you stay. I have need of you. Don't be drinking, boy," she said to me and took away my food and spirits. "I would that you be sober."

"Will we be having dinner later?" I said.

"Right after a young lady upstairs has a bite out of you," said Deirdre, which provoked a roar of laughter from the gathered family.

Great-Aunt Jessie chased the other thirty-two family members from the room. She had Deirdre sit on one side of me and placed herself next to me on the other side. To escape them, I would have had to have jumped over the table.

"The Consul has sent a lovely young woman to be your wife," said Great-Aunt Jessie. "She is in your parents' bedroom upstairs."

"Aunt Jessie, don't you mean the Consul's mother has sent a wife for me?" I said.

"That makes no difference to me," she sniffed.

"Should I go—" Deirdre began to say.

"I am speaking," said Great-Aunt Jessie and put her finger to her lips. "I will talk true to you," she said to me. "There is a problem. The fine lady upstairs has learned through an unnamed acquaintance that you have been in communication with another young woman."

"I used to correspond with someone," I confessed.

Once upon a time my brother's wife had been a local school-girl a few years older than I. When she had corresponded with my brother Michael while he was away in the Army, my grammar school chums and I had stolen a packet of the flowery letters Deirdre had written him. We had read these letters aloud to our elders one Sunday afternoon after church, and that was only one of the tribulations we horrid little boys had put the young couple through during the difficult times of their courtship. The beaming smile on Deirdre's face indicated she well remembered those days and was enjoying having my personal life aired before my dour great-aunt.

"That was stupid of you, boy," said Great-Aunt Jessie. "Very stupid. Is that how a gentleman acts toward a lady? Didn't you realize you could have destroyed both you and her?"

"The matter is very complicated, ma'am," I said.

"The lady's informant tells her you have told the other young woman you love her," said Great-Aunt Jessie. "Is this true?"

"More or less," I said.

"Deirdre," commanded Great-Aunt Jessie, "go up and tell our visitor Robert is 'more or less' in love with the other woman."

My sister-in-law was upstairs and back in less than a minute. The few moments she was absent created a long space of time to sit beneath Great-Aunt Jessie's unflinching glare.

"What does she say?" asked Jessie when Deirdre came bounding down the stairs.

"She says 'more or less' will not do," said Deirdre. "He has to answer yes or no."

"She says you have to answer yes or no," said Great-Aunt Jessie.

"I heard her," I said. "What is the lady's name?"

"We cannot tell you her name or describe her," asserted Great-Aunt Jessie.

"Those are the rules?"

"Yes or no?" said Great-Aunt Jessie.

When I considered that the lady upstairs had been sent from Lady Fitzpatrick I presumed she would either be an abused wretch from the conservatory or, worse still, a young disciple of Fitz's mother. Whichever of the two she was, I knew I would detest giving my life to either type. Great-Aunt Jessie's imperious demeanor increased my pique at the situation. I was a major in the Second

Engineers, a confidant to the Consul and chief planner on important secret construction projects in distant lands, and my great-aunt was treating me as if I were a naughty child. I was far beyond the time in my life I would cooperate with her in any small domestic drama. A terrifying creature I may have become, yet I was an important creature, and I did not feel I had to be careful with what I said to an old woman.

"Yes. So what of it?" I said.

"Go and tell her the answer is yes," Great-Aunt Jessie ordered Deirdre.

When Deirdre returned she said the lady upstairs wanted to hear me say I loved someone else to her face.

"Let's get this over with," I said, and rose from the table chair.

My sister-in-law went up the stairs with me to the door of my parents' room.

"It's a pity you will have to send this one away," she said to me. "She would have been good for you."

She slowly undid the door latch. She seemed beside herself with glee when she glanced back at me.

"I am pleased you find this amusing," I said.

"Sorry, Bobby," she chuckled. "You look so put out. The lady's name, by the way," she said in a whisper, "is Miss Charlotte Raft."

She gave me a shove to put me over the threshold. I heard Great-Aunt Jessie laughing at the foot of the stairs. A few seconds later Deirdre was at her side and forming a mirthful duet.

Charlotte was sitting on the end of my parents' bed, scanning through one of my mother's photograph albums. She had changed a little since I had seen her four years previously. She was thinner than I remembered, and had recently spent more time outdoors than she had done while living in Centralia City. Sunlight had lightened her hair and reddened the pale skin on her face. Unlike my family members, Charlotte was wearing the long "Roman" dress fashion prescribed. Out of modesty, and to make a good impression on my relatives, she had on a long petticoat that rendered the garment opaque. Her hair was clasped behind her head by two large brass combs.

"God bless mothers for saving these pictures," she said and showed me a picture of a naked baby boy.

"That is my brother," I said and sat beside her.

"I expect your body parts are much the same," she said. "You haven't kissed me yet," she added and pursed her lips.

I wanted to be angry with her for playing games with me. I wanted besides to learn how she came to be here. She looked inordinately pleased with herself, her eyes closed and her lips stuck out, certain in her heart that I would kiss her. She was quite correct in thinking so. She smelled like the flowers in Buck's garden, and I lingered on her mouth for longer than decorum allowed in order to taste as much of her as I could.

"You haven't gotten any better at it," she said when I moved back from her. "You do seem to enjoy it, though. You've been drinking," she said, tasting the ale my father had given me. "That will have to stop."

"I have missed you," I said.

That was not what I expected to say. I should have made a cutting remark to take the smug expression off her face.

"I have missed you too, Bobby," she said and kissed me again; then she leaned her forehead against mine and closed her eyes.

"How did you trick Lady Fitzpatrick into sending you?"

"Trickery wasn't involved," she said, rubbing her head against mine and kissing my ear. "I was in her infernal conservatory this past year, learning how to bow and to manage a crudité and to say 'how interesting, sir,' when the conversation is unbearably dull."

"How interesting."

"Don't try to be funny, Bobby," she said and kissed my mouth another time. "Doctor Murrey arranged everything."

She explained between more kissing that when Fitz's father was assassinated, Doctor Murrey—and presumably the whole Timerman hierarchy—decided Charlotte and her family should leave Centralia City for someplace safer. The Rafts had known the Gyors and knew the connection between the Gyor brothers and Fitz, a circumstance that Dr. Murrey said would make the Rafts inconvenient to the new Consul. Mr. Raft and his sons Ham and Eggs went to Northfield and worked in a cheese factory. According to Charlotte, the honest work nearly killed her stepfather and stepbrothers. Murrey had sent her into Lady Fitzpatrick's school for young Ladies in the Meadowlands.

"Fitz didn't object to you being in his mother's school?" I asked.

Charlotte had her arms around my neck and was caressing me so enthusiastically I could barely think clearly enough to form that simple sentence. As she repeatedly kissed my face, she softly moaned in a manner I confess I found alluring beyond anything I had previously experienced. I had to wonder as I held her how she could exist in the same world as Fitz and the approaching war.

"He never knew," she said. "He doesn't know I'm here now."

"Murrey was once a liege of the Fitzpatricks," I said. "Lady Fitzpatrick no doubt owed him a favor. That is how you came to be sent to be my wife."

"I'm not your wife yet," she said and climbed atop my lap. "You have to propose to me first," she said, and playfully rubbed my nose with hers.

"How do you suppose Fitz will react to our marriage?" I said.

The kissing ceased at that point. Out of the billions of possible sentences I might have uttered right then, I had selected the absolute worst. Charlotte got off my lap and backed away from me to the other side of the small bedroom. One of her green eyes closed, much as a marksman's eye does when he is sighting his target. She did not tarry long before she opened fire.

"That is the important question, isn't it?" she said. "What *Fitz* will think?" She pronounced his name as though she were expectorating something foul from her mouth. "Will your years of sucking up to him now go to waste? He's made Bobby a pretty little major while Bobby is still a virgin boy of twenty-five. Will Fitz make Bobby a colonel and someday a general and a bloody Lord when he hears Bobby has married a bar owner's Catholic stepdaughter, a Traveler lass who happens to know Fitz had *his* noble father murdered?"

"You mustn't say that!" I exclaimed. "My family is right downstairs! Do you realize how thin these walls are?"

"Oh, your family might hear!" she said and made a mock shudder of fear. "Aunt Jessie, darling," she called to the door, "are you there?"

"Er, yes, my love," said an abashed voice from the other side of the door.

Great-Aunt Jessie and Deirdre had crept up the stairs and were listening, their ears to the wood, not ten feet from us.

"Aunt Jessie," said Charlotte, "did you know the present Consul murdered his father?"

"No . . ." said Great-Aunt Jessie, "that's news to me. I have a friend in the village, Mrs. Jenny Von Krosick, by name. She did say she didn't for one second believe the Chinese had done it. She said—"

"Thank you, love," said Charlotte. "The next time you have your friend in for tea you can tell her she was right."

"I think we had better see about my pot roast," said Great-Aunt Jessie, and we could hear her and Deirdre retreating down the steps to the ground floor.

Charlotte turned her palms up and extended her arms from her sides.

"To think," she said, "your family now knows, and yet the earth continues to turn. The rivers still flow. The birds still sing."

"You needn't be self-righteous," I said, becoming nigh as enraged as she was. "You and your Timerman Guild kowtow to Fitz no less than I do!"

"What is that crack supposed to mean?" she said.

"It means that when I was sailing to India I saw Blinking Star satellites guide Fitzpatrick airplanes to pirate ships in international waters. What were your Timermen friends doing that for? Protecting I.T. ships is as illegal as murder."

I cut her off before she could make a reply.

"What's more," I went on, "the bases in India used the Timermen's Blinking Star network to send and receive messages to and from this side of the world, this while the elder Fitzpatrick didn't even know we were there. We are building air bases all over the world. Bases for the coming war, my dear, bases the satellites can see as plainly as we see the sky, and what do the Timermen do? Do they alert the Senate? Do they make a single leak to the press? I know a foreigner, a man named Puri, and he has gotten messages from Fitz over the Blinking Star system. That also is illegal. The obvious fact is, Charlotte, your guild is on Fitz's side.[1] They always have been. Or maybe Fitz is on their side. Your Doctor Murrey seems to me to be especially culpable, seeing how he has been connected to the Fitzpatrick family for much of his adult life. For that matter, how do I know you are not part of some guild conspiracy? Why does Murrey want you to marry me? Tell me that, and I will tell you this: thousands of other engineers could do what I am doing for Fitz. Only the Timermen, your guild, could serve him as they do."

---

1. Although Mason and several more recent writers have reached the same conclusion (see especially the anonymous pamphlet, "What Do the Timermen Do?," 2470, preserved in the War College Library), Gerald and other reliable sources assure us the Timermen are strictly an apolitical scientific society.

That put her back on her heels for the moment. She sat down on the bed beside me once more and digested my words.

"I will concede everything you say about the Timermen," she said. "You should know they are not my guild. I never was or will ever be a member. Really, beyond knowing Doctor Murrey, I don't know any more of their organization than you do. I doubt they would ever accept a woman, anyway. I was never an engineer, which one has to be to be one of them. They never took me upstairs[2] or to their islands. Pity. I would have enjoyed seeing the solar system. Seeing electricity work. Doctor Murrey once offered to get me the proper training. I told him I would rather marry a man with whom I could fall in love. I can't believe he is Fitz's man, though. If you knew Doctor Murrey better, you would know he could never give his loyalty to anything or anyone other than the Timermen."

She took my hand. I could not help softening to her as she was to me.

"Another thing you're wrong about," she said. "Murrey didn't choose you to marry me. I did. He wanted someone he knew planted among your *Basileis*. I knew Fitz's other friends from my stepfather's place. The young Lords were out of the question. Hood was too old and already married. The big scary one, Fitz's bodyguard—"

"Pularski," I said.

"I didn't want him," she said. "Perhaps I should've thought better of him. I understand he has played Cupid for us."

"He arranged for the gardener to handle our correspondence while we were in Centralia City. His looks aside—and in spite of what he does for Fitz—he is a good fellow. Placed in other circumstances, he would have been much more than he is."

"I saw you on the parade ground a week before we met," said Charlotte. "That's when I picked you. I had read your record. Doctor Murrey told me you were the only choice I could make. I thought you might be a nice boy, one open to improvements."

"What sort of improvements?" I asked.

She stroked my hair and adjusted my shirt collar, which had gone slightly askew after my thirty-four relatives embraced me.

"To begin with," she said, "you should be honest with yourself.

---

2. i.e., she was never in outer space.

And with me. You could confess you know your Fitz has blood on his hands. Confess it in your heart if you can't say it."

She again laid her head against mine. In other cultures, a man of twenty-five might be a jaded rogue to whom a woman's touch is a sensation as unextraordinary as sunlight. To me, feeling Charlotte's skin on mine was as impressive as my first memories of my mother's face or as the first time I looked at the stars and knew there was more in the universe than my mind could encompass. I was fortunate it was Charlotte touching me. Another woman might not have touched me as she did and held in her heart Charlotte's kind intentions.

"I am sorry," I said. "I've long known how Fitz is. You must realize how intoxicating it is for a forester's son to become the close advisor of a Consul."

"As intoxicating as the opportunity for a poor girl to marry above her station," she said. "If we do marry, I have to warn you you might not be above my station for long. You may have no career, and I may be married to a common soldier. I cannot say what Fitz might do. Doctor Murrey assures me he would not harm us; that would be destroying one of the few people he trusts. For myself, Bobby, I would not care if I were wed to a soldier in the ranks so long as he were a good man."

She waited for my response. The seaman's clock at the head of my parents' bed chimed two o'clock in the afternoon. Despite the family members gathering downstairs and in the front yard, the house was quite quiet.

"I do not deserve you, Charlotte," I said. "I have done terrible things. Things you would not tolerate."

"You have killed someone?" she asked and slid a short distance from me.

"I built those bases for Fitz. He is going to use them to attack the Chinese and the Turks."

"Did you know the purposes of the bases?" she asked me.

"Not until three days ago," I said. "I thought they were to be fighter bases. I *did* realize they were illegal. And I knew Fitz has long desired a world war."

"Would Fitz harm you if you do not complete these bases?" asked Charlotte.

"They essentially are completed. Yes, he would probably do something to me were I to disobey him. At this point matters have progressed too far to be amended. Three days ago I reassured Fitz he was God's beloved and was doing God's work."

"Oh, Bobby."

"I know," I said. "Nothing you could say would make my crime weigh upon me more than it already does."

We were both silent again for a long time.

"Fitz would not be on the verge of attacking the rest of the world," she said when she resumed the conversation, "were not each of us in the Confederacy willing to aid him. All of us, not only you, must share the blame for what he is going to do. I myself have taken instruction from a Timerman when, as you say, I know that organization has an agenda that could not withstand the light of public disclosure. I will make a deal with you, Bobby: I will have nothing more to do with the Timermen, and you will not do anything more you will regret in the future. You should do your duty and no more. I don't care if you never become a general or a Lord. I only want you to be alive. We will be our own country, we and our family, and henceforth strive to harm no one else."

"Will you marry me, Charlotte?" I said, feeling much as Fitz must have when he was like a drowning man seeking a lifeline from me.

"I will," she said, "provided you ask me properly."

She pointed to the floor, and I got down one knee and asked her a second time.

"Yes," she told me and put her hands on my shoulders. "Since you are down there, Bobby, could you promise me you won't drink? After the wedding, I mean. Taking a glass or three will be inevitable when we go down. My stepfather drank, you know, and I never cared for it."

"Not even a small glass of porter at dinner?" I asked.

"You are a forester's son, aren't you?" she said and kissed me. "A small glass would be allowable, on formal occasions. Not every day, more on the order of once a month."

Drink had never pleased me, at least not as much as I knew being with her would. I promised her I would not drink after the wedding. I would have stood up then, had she not pushed me back down.

"One more thing, darling," she said. "You promised me in your letters you would convert to my religion."

"I intend to."

"When we get to India," she said, "you can begin instruction from the regimental priest. You'll be pleased to know that after we gained the right to practice openly the church has created a new, fast course for converts. You can complete your instruction and be baptized in two months."

"Yes?" I said, not sure where she was headed.

"After you are baptized, the priest can give us a Catholic wedding."

"That's not a problem," I said. "I will be pleased to repeat my vows to you."

"Well, there is a problem, my love," she said, and added another kiss. "I promised my mother when I was a girl I would enter into a Catholic marriage. I will be wed to you tomorrow in a U.Y.C. ceremony, and I will be like a wife to you, except I was hoping you might respect the promise I made my mother and not consummate our union until we have the second ceremony. You do love me, don't you?"

"I've waited twenty-five years," I said. "I suppose I can wait another two months."

"Then you promise?"

"I promise," I said.

"Oh, another thing," she said and pushed me down yet another time. "Promise me you will let me help you. Not in your engineering chores. I mean in the more important matters you will encounter. I am not the wisest woman in the world. I can, should you let me, nonetheless help you more than you may think."

"I promise that as well," I said.

"Come up here and kiss your wife, then," she said.

I resumed my position on the bed, and Charlotte climbed back onto my lap and kissed me more passionately than an inexperienced man had reason to expect. She startled me when she pushed the slick, warm energy of her tongue into my mouth. My response amused her and made her beat a laughing retreat.

"Oh, Bobby," she declared, "once the priest has instructed you, I have much to instruct you in myself."

We went down hand in hand to the dining room. My family met us on the bottom landing and cheered as though we two were heroes returning from a war. They put us on their shoulders and carried us into the yard, and there set us at a banquet table they had filled with platters of food and bouquets of flowers while we were upstairs negotiating the match.

The fifty-three Mathiases and the sixty-seven Wallaces, the two family groups of my clan living in the Astoria area,[3] had arrived at my family's compound. Every adult among the new arrivals was armed with a tankard of ale and drank to our health when they saw us together. Our Lord Prim-Jones[4] had taken off his bedroom slippers and smoking jacket and made his obligatory appearance to offer his blessings. All the men doffed their hats when he came into our courtyard. Charlotte bowed to him and kissed the palm of his hand.[5]

"Absolutely exquisite," he pronounced upon my betrothed. "Sir Robert, you could not have selected a more beautiful bride."

Our Lord Prim-Jones dared to drink a sip of our family whiskey, wished us health and happiness, then returned in his steam car to his estate, his towering Morris chair, and his dog-eared volume of Catullus. As soon as he was out of earshot, the adult members of my clan pronounced our Lord a dilettante. They also conceded he never bothered anyone and, more importantly, he had a nice wife.

My uncle Merle resumed his fiddle playing, this time free of interference from Great-Aunt Jessie. Amy Mathias, a teenage girl with a thin, beautiful voice, stood atop a chair and sang everyday songs[6] to the old man's accompaniment. The women, even the elderly ones, danced the slow, sensuous Shanty,[7] and later Charlotte

---

3. Bruce was member of the Redadine Clan; their tartan is a simple dark blue field intersected by a horizontal gray stripe and thin, vertical, red lines.

4. Dover Stevens Prim-Jones, the grandfather of the present Lord of Astoria.

5. This, it seems, was all rustic folk of Bruce's time did to acknowledge fealty to a new Lord.

6. "Everyday songs," a Nor'western coinage meaning folk songs; they are not suitable for professional performers or for recordings but merely for everyday use.

7. A dance distinguished by short, rhythmic steps, and slow, suggestive movements of the hips. Despite the approbation of the defenders of good morals, this somewhat bawdy dance had proven indestructible, and to this day can be seen at any party wherein the female guests drink too much. I have witnessed the dance performed at faculty get-togethers when the professors' wives have had too much sherry.

danced atop the one of the long tables when the drunken mob demanded it of her. As is the custom, the guests tried to toss coins into the folds of her skirt. To catch their money, Charlotte had to lift her long, narrow dress above her knees, a move that could have scandalized the women in my family, were they still sober, and one that greatly pleased my male relatives, who threw coins for as long as they could get a good look at Charlotte's bare legs. Because my mother and Aunt Nancy were still sitting, arms about each other and weeping, my bride-to-be went to them and promised she would take good care of me.

"Bobby went to war when he was sixteen," my mother explained through her sobs. "This is different. Marriage is so final."

My female relatives kissed me again. This time the Wallaces and Mathiases took their turns. A couple of them felt my bicep muscles and called to Charlotte:

"He's too small for you, love!"

"I will exercise him every day till he gets bigger!" Charlotte called back.

Uncle Bernard recited the humorous poem he wrote about the time my father and he were lost in the woods. As usually happened when he recited, he forget several verses, and family members had to prompt him at various places to get him to the end. This was Charlotte's first exposure to Bernard's masterpiece. Great-Aunt Jessie announced in her loudest voice that she had heard "that silly prattle" seventy-two times before. Another family tradition was observed when Arthur Wallace and Henry Mathias, cousins by marriage, resumed their long standing feud and threatened to kill each other several times over. The two would-be combatants got nose to nose and called each other every name two drunken men might recall under stress. At the penultimate moment, they remembered—as they always did—their military vows and withdrew,[8] sullenly, to opposite sides of the courtyard.

I did not get to bed until three in the morning. Great-Aunt

---

8. Bruce here does not mean the vows every able-bodied Yukon man makes when he enters military service at the age of sixteen. He is referring to the vows every boy makes at age twelve, when each child begins military training as part of his secondary school education and he swears he will never use violence except to uphold the law and to fight the Confederacy's enemies.

Jessie woke me at eight and shoved me toward the shower. Her steady hands shaved me and dressed me in a fresh shirt and tie. By nine I was standing in my family's chapel. There my brother, the newly ordained U.Y.C. minister, married me to Charlotte. Thereafter, the family drank some more.

# ELEVEN

WE LEFT FOR India on a zeppelin out of West Port two days after the wedding. Charlotte and I shared the same cabin, and at night slept in separate berths. She was otherwise an affectionate bride to me. We sat long hours in the airship's gallery, taking in the misty blue ocean rolling by below us. I discovered on the trip that my wife's gregarious and flirtatious behavior was not an act she used when around me; she was as she seemed to be, though she could mask her core self when the situation required her to do so. I recall she sat for long, blissful stretches, her head resting on my heart, while she composed two lists of names, one for the boys we might have and another for the potential daughters.

"Your Aunt Jessie told me she would formally adopt our third child," she said and worked her eyebrows up and down. "Your Uncle Merle has only one child, and his wife is dead. Perhaps you could persuade him to adopt our fourth."

"You will explode the population," I told her.

"I think it would be pleasant work," she said. "Much superior to trying to depopulate the world, as some people I could mention are bent upon. Besides, it will do your kidneys good."

Every morning of the journey the grandfather of the family running the vessel left chocolates for Charlotte outside our door along with the covered pot of hot coffee. She would not eat the bonbons or let me have them, because she had announced she was putting us both on the Discipline Diet[1] for the next two months.

---

1. The Discipline Diet, a twenty-fifth century counterpart of our Modern Course in Self-Denial. Then, as now, lovers often heightened the spiritual pleasures of romance by denying themselves certain bodily pleasures such as rich food, alcohol, and sexual intercourse.

She instead used the candies to lure the zeppelin family's two youngest children from their hiding places in the galley's side doorways. These two small girls had been watching us from afar, afraid to approach us because of my uniform and because they thought Charlotte was a noble lady. Charlotte left the chocolates on the dining tables. The girls would dart from their cubbyholes and snatch the foil-wrapped treats before scurrying back into hiding. Each time she rebaited her trap, Charlotte would place the candies closer and closer to us, until the girls had to take the chocolates from her hand. After two days out of West Port Charlotte was holding the girls on her lap, reading them stories, playing peek-a-boo with them, and letting them show her their dolls.

Watching her interact with children was rather frightening for me back then. She did not simply beguile them; she could be beguiling to anyone. Charlotte loved children with an ardor most Yukons reserve for God and warfare. The little ones responded to her in a similar fashion. The two young zeppelin girls were soon calling her "Auntie Charlotte." They insisted she sit by them at supper and kiss them good night before they went to bed. She suffered them to remove the brass combs from her hair and to brush her long, auburn locks as they would do to a large doll. I could foresee in her actions a future time when Charlotte would collide head-on with the rules governing the proper conduct of a Yukon officer's wife. I attempted, none too successfully, to make some adjustments in her course.

"Do you think, my love," I said to her as she was holding the girls, "and this is only a suggestion, that you should make such a fuss over children as you do?"

"Yes, my love," she said and touched me on the nose as she often did when she was preparing to defy me, "I think I should. I think, my love, *you* do not make a fuss over children as much as *you* should."

She handed both of the giggling children to me along with their Mr. Bunny storybook. I had to read to them for the next two hours about afternoon games of hide-and-seek played by the famous Mr. Bunny and Miss Hare, his beloved special friend. If one of the girls wriggled away from me, Charlotte quickly scooped her up and handed her back to me.

"That wasn't quite what I intended," I said to Charlotte while we were in our room and preparing to retire for the night.

"I know *exactly* what you intended," she said, "and I forgive you anyway. Would you please brush my hair? The girls put more knots in than they took out."

She was in her nightgown and had her hair over her shoulders.

"Husbands do that?"

"The good ones do," she said.

She was sitting on my berth, the lower one in our quarters. For lack of knowing how to respond to her I ran her tortoiseshell brush through her thick, red mane. Charlotte had told an untruth concerning the little girls; they had combed her hair till it was a silky cascade beneath the brush. There was not a snag left for the brush to straighten.

"Are you enjoying this?" she asked.

"You have lovely hair," I told her. "When I first saw you in my parents' room I wanted to tell you your hair smells like Buck Pularski's lilacs."

"Are you sniffing at it? What an odd husband I have. At the conservatory they graded us on parts of our appearances: hands, facial makeup, teeth, feet. I was over the Turk's Stoop for everything but my hair."

"I'm sorry," I said. "I can't imagine you in that place, under that lady."

"I have scars for it. I'll show you after we become intimate."[2]

She went to the wind-up phonograph and put on a recording of a Strauss waltz. As the music began to play she twirled about two times and stopped on her tiptoes in front of me. Charlotte held out her arms for me to take.

"Dance with me, Bobby," she said.

"What?"

"My poor husband is deaf?" she said and made a wry, lopsided smile. "Come, stand up and dance with me. My stepfather used to do it with his wife."

"Your stepfather ran a saloon," I said. "I am a Yukon officer."

"I'm not," she said. "I haven't even taken a military vow. That

---

2. The following obscene passage was expurgated from the 2541 edition. I have left it in to show the reader to what depths Bruce allowed his wife to drag him. The reader must also keep in mind that Bruce himself admits that his wife was the main reason he drifted away from the glorious Fitzpatrick.

means I can cuff your ears if you don't get off your pompous back-side and dance with me."

She must have cast a spell on me. No one else could have made me do something my elders, teachers, and ministers had taught me was nearly as loathsome as bestiality or pederasty. I stood, un-steadily. Charlotte put one hand on my shoulder and another in my left hand, and we sidled about the tiny cabin, moving as gracelessly as two crabs locked claw to claw.

"Step to the right, step, step," said Charlotte. "Now to the left."

The perspiration came rolling off my face. I kept glancing at the cabin door while we moved together. I was terrified that some-one would enter at any moment and catch me, a Yukon major, dancing like a woman.

"What if we are seen?" I said, and in my excitement the words came out sounding whinier than I intended.

"The Consul probably has a spy hidden under our beds," said Charlotte. "He will know you dance with you wife. We'll be ar-rested, and then, alas, that will be the end of us. Nipped in the bud. Hoisted on our own petard. Up the stream without a paddle. Or a boat. Is that someone at the door?"

I jumped back from her. Charlotte laughed at me so hard she had to sit for a minute while the waltz finished playing.

"I'll be good now," she promised when she had recovered.

She reset the phonograph needle at the beginning of the record and had me dance with her all the way through the piece. This time she laid her head on my shoulder and did not tease me.

"One, two, three. One, two, three," she softly counted. "You see: you can do it. You have to relax, darling. You're not going to be able to do the rest of your husbandly duties if you are this nerv-ous. We will have to do this every night: you can brush my hair and dance with me. I wish we could make love tonight. You are a dear for waiting."

[3]She stayed up another half an hour, kissing me and telling me how pleased she was to be married to me, and went to bed beside herself with satisfaction. True to her word, she made me brush her hair and do the other thing each night before we went to our

---

3. The expurgated text resumes here.

separate beds. I thought myself a weakling for giving in to her as readily as I did. As an old man I think differently of those early months we were together. Giving into her has brought me the greater portion of joy I have experienced in my lifetime. I do not refer only to the obvious pleasures I found in being with her, but to a peculiar satisfaction I found whenever I could please her. Because I was yet a callow young man, Charlotte's behavior seemed dangerous to my standing within the Army and potentially fatal to our future. As I had once feared she might be working for the Timermen, I now suspected she had ulterior motives in making me do things my own inclinations would never have impelled me to do. Looking backward from the prominence of old age, I regret nothing I did for her and rue only that I did not do more that would have been to her liking.[4]

The officers' wives of the Second Engineers had long known that Charlotte was waiting in North America to be my bride. They welcomed her to the Rajmahal Hills as though she were indeed their little sister. They hugged her as she stepped off the zeppelin and feted her with wedding gifts and unanimously declared she was much prettier than she appeared in my photographs of her. They at once spirited Charlotte into the McConnells' mobile housing unit where they had a grand reception prepared for her. I was left alone on the landing dock, the luggage I would have to carry to our mobile unit piled around me.

"You look to be a married man, Major," said Colonel McConnell, who watched me lug the suitcases and trunks across the paved ground in the direction of our new home. "Nothing to be done for it," he lamented. "Right now they're telling jokes touching upon how stupid their husbands are. They may be right, son."

Father Drake began my religious instruction the evening of our arrival. Charlotte attended the classes, as did a sergeant from Perth engaged to a Catholic girl back home. Much to my wife's delight, I first learned the Catechism and how to say the Rosary. After class she would insist I dance with her when we returned home; afterward she would put on her night clothes and have me brush her hair.[5] She took my place at the afternoon teas, for the officer's wives

---

4. Can the reader require any further proof of what sort of man Bruce was?

5. This sentence is missing from the 2541 edition.

quite forgot about yours truly when they could have the witty and lovely Charlotte for company. They thought my wife was simply too charming for words, and Charlotte was indeed charming, except on certain occasions when she was alone with her husband. As she had told me when I proposed to her, she believed I needed improvement, and she was not slow to mock and tease and even to humble me if she thought that would assist my betterment.

She thankfully made a distinction between public and private behavior. Among my brother officers and their wives Charlotte affected the character the situation demanded. With Colonel McConnell (whom she called Colonel Robin from their first meeting) she was the amiable, slightly naughty girl, and artfully tickled the old warrior's fine opinion of himself. To Mrs. McConnell she was a respectful daughter, and to the other wives she was an intimate to whom they could entrust their most guarded secrets. At regimental parties she was a proper lady. When she was at the base hospital and working as a practical nurse she would swap jokes with her male patients as she changed their bedpans. I realized I was not the only man who married a woman far smarter than he, yet the ease with which Charlotte won the hearts of everyone on the base intimidated me. The only other person I had ever met as ingratiating to others as my new bride was had been Fitz. I feared in those early days of our marriage—my God forgive me—motives akin to his might lie behind her pleasing manner.

Charlotte did not differentiate between Yukon and native as markedly as the others on base did. That distressed me more than anything else she did. The Rabari children I had previously given medicine and dried fruit to quickly took a liking to her, and she to them. They flocked about her like chicks gathering about a mother hen whenever they spied her walking across the road leading from our mobile unit to the base's principal buildings. While I had been unable to learn one word of the Rabari language, she at once picked up bunches of their vocabulary. Through gestures and her rapid mastery of some of their grammar she was communicating with the nomadic people in a couple of weeks.

The inevitable result of her attentions to the Rabari children occurred six weeks after our arrival in India. I returned home one Tuesday and found eight naked little Rabaris queued up in a line inside our kitchen. Charlotte was washing them one by one in our sink and rubbing delousing salve into their scalps.

"When you took them from their homelands in the west," she explained as she busily scrubbed a girl so small she fit in the sink basin, "they didn't know how to keep free of parasites in the new environment. Look at this," she said and poured a few ounces of kerosene on the child's head, which caused a cluster of white larvae to erupt from the child's scalp. "Absolutely disgusting!" said Charlotte. "It seems the Yukon officers were too preoccupied with their damned air bases to notice suffering children."

I was speechless. She was handling the girl with the tenderness a Yukon woman would extend to a Yukon child. When the girl whimpered, Charlotte caressed her and murmured some tender words in the child's tongue.

"My dear," I said, "these are native children."

She made her peculiar, lopsided smile at me.

"Thank you for telling me, dear heart," she said. "I never would have guessed."

I gave her the same lecture Mrs. McConnell had given to me when that august woman had seen me befriending the Rabari. The coming war was going to kill millions of these people, I explained to Charlotte. We therefore should not become attached to them. That would be unfair to them and to us.

"Look at a map of northern India and southern China," I told her. "Where the Brahmputra River drops down from China you'll find the town of Wei. The Chinese are going to amass two hundred divisions[6] at Wei and march them down the Brahmaputra, to the Ganges, and eventually to these hills—or so they hope. When they come this way, they are going to destroy everything in their path, including these little ones."

"Then we will have to get these people back to their true home before that happens, won't we?" she said and turned her back on me.

"If we cannot?"

"Then," she said, "we will do what we can. Right now I am ridding these children of lice."

"You are a Yukon officer's wife!" I told her, for I was becoming as riled as she was.

"A divorce court can remedy that!" she shot back.

---

6. Chinese divisions are larger than the ten thousand man divisions the Yukons utilize. By our standards, the Chinese would in fact amass close to two thousand divisions around Wei.

"I forbid you to bathe these children!" I commanded.

That did the trick. She turned to me and contorted her face into the one-eyed expression she had given me in my parents' bedroom. The child she was washing drew away from her arms. I confess I took a half step backward.

"You 'forbid' me?" she said. "Come closer, my love. Obviously your mother did not slap your silly face often enough when you were a boy or you would not have grown to be the arrogant ass you are today!"

She said something in the Rabari language to a boy waiting to be washed. The child quickly donned his britches and ran from the mobile unit.

"Back off, dar-ling," she said to me. "If I were you, I would not speak any more nonsense before that child returns. I think he will come back with something of interest to you."

"I don't care if he comes back with Colonel McConnell himself," I said, more afraid of what my superiors might do to us if they discovered her kindness than I was of the daggers she was shooting at me. "I tell you again: I forbid you to bathe these children!"

"You repeat yourself a great deal when you want to save yourself the expense of thinking," she said and defiantly continued to clean the girl. "Soon you will be reminding me you are a close friend of the Consul. But perhaps you first wish to tell me again I am a Yukon officer's wife?"

The boy Charlotte had spoken to a few moments earlier ran back into our house carrying a long, rectangular box he handed to my wife. I at once saw it as one of the canisters containing malaria vaccine I had given to the children some months before.

"Do you see this, dar-ling?" said Charlotte and waved the empty box in my face. "It looks to have been a medicine container, don't you think, sweetheart? Containing what? Malaria vaccine perhaps? Why is your face red, Major Bruce? Look me in the eye. Have you ever seen anything like it before, my love?"

"Yes," I said in a whisper.

"Now this is very important, Major Bruce, you husband of a Yukon officer's wife," she said. "Some officer on this base has been giving vaccine and food to the Rabari children. Imagine that, sir. He probably wasn't thinking of the coming war. He had some idiotic concern for sick and hungry children. I ask you, Major Bruce: if an officer can be so recklessly compassionate, how can I, a mere officer's wife, not be corrupted by his bad example? Doesn't he know your beloved Fitz is preparing to slaughter half the world? Doesn't he know he is being unfair to them and to himself—well, you know the rest of that fatuous nonsense you only now said to me."

She threw the canister on the counter top next to the sink, making a loud *bang* and startling the children.

"I suggest you hunt down this reprobate officer and arrest him, sir," she said. "That is your duty. Then, when you have done that, sir, you may come to your wife and 'forbid' her to tend to these babies!"

She finished cleaning the girl's hair and toweled her dry. I wondered if there were anything about me she did not know or could not guess.

"I gave the children the vaccine," I said.

"Only this canister?" she asked.

"No, many like it."

She turned to me and struck a pose of feigned surprise: her mouth was wide open and both hands were held to her cheeks.

"I am *so* ashamed of you!" she said, and ran clean water into the sink. "Here I was hoping you were the brainless jackass you were pretending to be; then I learn you care for others, even non-Yukons! What a disgrace! You may apologize to me now, sir."

"For giving them medicine?" I asked.

"No, you dunce," she snapped, and her lower lip started trembling. "I love you for giving them the vaccine. You did more good here than you thought you had. You should apologize for being a hypocrite to your wife. And for that 'I forbid you' business! You cannot tell me you talked that way to the women in your home."

"No," I said, "I didn't. Charlotte, I am an officer now—"

I stopped when I heard her grinding her teeth. She closed her eyes and counted to ten on her fingers, then inhaled deeply before she spoke again.

"At the conservatory they taught us to do that lest we say something we later regret," she said. "Yes, I know you are an officer and a Knight of the Field and a personal friend of the Consul. I am so honored to know you." She made a mock bow. "I would kiss the hem of your skirt, if you wore a skirt. Of course, if your precious Fitz had asked you to wear one, you no doubt would have."

"I am sorry I made you angry," I said.

"And . . ."

"And what?"

"Tell me you are sorry for being an ass to your wife," she said, plainly beginning to shed tears.

"I am sorry I, as you say, did that . . ."

"Take a deep breath," said Charlotte. "Push the air over your tongue and lips. I know you can do it."

"I am sorry I was an ass to you," I said.

"I am sorry I lost my temper," she said. "I have many faults; my temper is my worst. I want to apologize for that crack about the skirt, too. That was uncalled for."

By that time her eyes were dripping. Charlotte was not one to cry at the drop of a hat, and hated for me to see her in that condition. She turned away and placed another child in the sink.

"Would you mind if I helped you?" I asked.

"That would get the job done sooner," she allowed.

I rolled up my sleeves and took my place beside her.

"You've splashed some water on your face," I said and wiped away her tears with a paper towel. "Is it safe to kiss you?"

"You are a Yukon officer," she said. "Surely you are brave enough to find out."

The naked Rabari children laughed at our open display of affection. To witness adult foreigners acting in such outrageous ways was to them more delightful than getting clean. Their amusement encouraged Charlotte's mischievous nature, and she kissed me each time we had washed and treated one of the eight children. I knew before this I had lost my faith in Fitz. Without being aware of the change, I was now moving into a new camp, one far different than the *Basileis* had been. From that time forward I made no more futile attempts at suppressing Charlotte's inclinations. She did as she wanted and was clever enough to avoid upsetting my superiors on the base, the same superiors whose good opinions I continued to pursue out of force of habit, but whose opinions of me had come to matter less than hers.

After dinner and my religion class on the night of the sink incident, she had me dance two waltzes with her.[7] As I brushed her hair she said once more she wished she had not lost her temper that afternoon.

---

7. The 2541 edition reads, "she made me some tea."

"There are only fourteen days left before we are truly married and you won't have to go to your little cot any more," she said. "Let's not fight. Not ever again."

"What if we disagree in the future?" I asked.

"We needn't disagree on anything," she said. "I am nearly always in the right. When I am not, I will tell you so."

Like the other Yukons on base, Charlotte wore native dress, or, I should say, she wore her unique rendition of native dress. In a sari, Charlotte, distinguished by her red hair and freckles, looked about as native as a slab of Stilton cheese sprinkled with curry would resemble Indian cuisine. Her extraordinary appearance did not stop her from enjoying the costumes she had to wear in our extended dress-up party. She let the native women bedeck her in bright scarves and jingling costume jewelry she wore with the discretion of a traveling circus parading down a provincial Main Street. This was hardly the way the other Yukon women behaved, for they abhorred the gaudy native clothes, yet Mrs. McConnell and the others forgave Charlotte's excesses for the sake of the love they bore her. Charlotte pushed the barriers of good taste so far that she wore the enormous hoop earrings the Indian women favored, and said—hoping it would provoke me—she was considering having her nose pierced.

"I would look rather rakish, wouldn't I?" she said as I brushed her hair seven days before our second wedding.

"Like the pig in *The Owl and the Pussycat*," I said.

"So you wouldn't like it?" she said. "Do you think I would embarrass you in front of the other officers? Perhaps get my Bobby a reprimand?"

"I fear you would mar your natural beauty," I said.

"Will you *forbid* me?" she asked, emphasizing the important word.

"I would ask you please not to do it. You may chose to do it anyway," I said. "I would not love you less."

"You would ask me *please?*" she said. "You would not presume to *forbid* me?"

"Yes."

She laid back against me and stroked my cheek with the palm of her hand.

"Since you asked me *please*," she said, "I won't do it."

"You mean you're going to let me have my way for once?" I asked.

"I am a little mouse," she said. "You see how you rule me."

On the Tuesday night of my final class Father Drake baptized me in the name of the Father, the Son, and Holy Spirit, and heard my first confession. Thereafter Charlotte and I repeated our vows in a small ceremony at which Captain Allison and his wife Kit were our witnesses. At home we danced,[8] and I brushed her hair. When it came time to retire I saw that Charlotte had folded my cot and put it away in a closet.

"Do you wish to talk of this?" I asked.

"Talk of what?" she laughed and pushed me onto the bed as she slipped off her nightgown. "You're a clever lad; I think you'll pick this up right away."

I was several minutes late getting to the planning office on Wednesday morning. Charlotte accompanied me to my work station and coyly explained to Colonel McConnell, "My husband was fixing the roof for me, Colonel Robin."

She twirled the end of his long mustache as she alone could do and not earn a reprimand.

"Fixing the roof! That's what you young people call it these days," he said.

"I expect you mended some roofs in your day, Colonel Robin," she said, putting her arm inside his and striking exactly the note that would please the middle-aged warrior.

"Oh, I suppose," he said. "Pardon me for saying so, Mrs. Bruce; taking in account how pretty you are, I'm surprised your young man isn't mending the roof all the blessed time."

"Oh, my Bobby is just getting used to going up the ladder, sir," she said and smiled at me. "I fear he will be injured if I demand too much of him."

The colonel made no mention of my tardiness. Forever after that day roof repair became a standing joke he and Charlotte shared. Each morning they met at the planning office door, and she would wink at him and say I had been mending the roof again. If I took too long for lunch break, Charlotte would come with me to the planning office and tell Robin I had made a noontide roof repair.

"You will kill the boy, having him up there so often," said Colonel McConnell, chuckling at his own daring.

---

8. The 2541 edition reads, "we prayed."

"My husband is a Yukon officer, sir," replied Charlotte and tossed her head so that her flame red hair showed its highlights and her costume jewelry rattled. "He will do whatever his duty requires."

Performing my conjugal duties for Charlotte was decidedly more pleasurable and more interesting than any of the other work we were doing at the base. The portions of the prefabricated buildings had been arriving via lorry from Calcutta since the time of my return to India. Putting the pieces together required the engineering mastery of a child playing with a Build-a-City set.[9] A crew of a dozen navvies could snap together a hangar or any other large structure in two hours and in another two hours have the unit securely bolted. A second group of workers carrying epoxy guns would seal every joint airtight in half that time. Working at a relaxed pace of nine in the morning until five in the afternoon, the Second Engineers had completed the entire Rajmahal Hills project in the space of three months, and that was with the weekends off. If the lorries had gotten the parts to us all at once, we could have done the work in three weeks.

The final step was to spray everything—runways, roads, and buildings—with Starshine Polymer,[10] the miraculous chemical compound that would be about us in India and on the other new air bases for the course of the war. The first shipments of Starshine we received were in the form of a gray, paintlike liquid that dried as hard as enamel on the various surfaces to which we applied it. A petrol fire will blaze for a fraction of a second without other fuel to sustain its flame. White phosphorous will burn for two and a half to four seconds, and in that space of time will ignite steel. Fire Sticks burn up to ten seconds, and it will burn dirt into a glazed crater three or four feet deep. Starshine Polymer will resist each of

---

9. For those adults denied the opportunity of playing with a Build-a-City set when they were children I will explain that they are collections of various standardized plastic pieces that one can fit together to make miniature buildings. The Junior Builder and Mr. Construction sets are modern variations of the same toy.

10. First created in the late twentieth century under another name, Starshine Polymer—which is also sold under the brand names Starlight and Sunshine Polymer—is derived from waste plastic. The material has been "polymerized"; i.e., its molecules have been rendered heavier. As Bruce explains, Starshine is produced in various liquid and solid forms and is resistant to flame.

these and every other pyrotechnic known to man. We and the Chinese had for decades used the compound to treat uniforms, tanks and other military vehicles. Never before had anyone produced Starshine in the quantities the Second Engineers were then handling. We filled tanker trailers normally used for biomass and slowly moved them down the roadways, spraying a gray, sticky coat in our wake. There was so much polymer on hand the men got to wasting some of it in odd experiments. Some of the men from the planning office set a mess of Fire Sticks ablaze atop one of the airstrips and watched the fire burn itself out, leaving behind only a small, discolored patch of black on the concrete. One daring young navvy coated the exterior of an empty barrel with Starshine, climbed inside, and let his mates light a patch of Fire Sticks on the barrel's outside hull. Not only was the barrel not damaged, the brave lad swore he did not feel any heat whatsoever. (I myself felt the barrel's interior after the worker climbed out, and I can avow that it was cool to the touch.) Once we had the ghostly surface sprayed upon everything we had made we were invulnerable to anything the Chinese might drop on us. Knowing that did not make the drying polymer smell any better. Every Yukon family in the hills moved their mobile unit away from the treated areas to escape the unnatural aroma. At night the pale surfaces reflected the moonlight and gave off an eerie glow that frightened the native workers, who moved their tents farther up the hillsides beyond our mobile units.

On September 7, 2420, the zeppelins carrying the beacon lights and the first surface to air batteries arrived in the Rajmahal Hills. Using the improved topographical charts I had made when I redid the area's surveys, I helped the new men position their air-burst rockets on the highest places to give them the widest fields of view. The new arrivals—they were, I recall, North Americans from the Seventeenth and Forty-first Anti-Aircraft Divisions—dug circular trenches around their positions and lined their excavations with sacks a layman might have mistaken for ordinary sandbags but were really sacks of woven Starlight Polymer full of a powdered variety of the same chemical. History recounts that these were the first of the polymer trenches that were to be the primary positions of the Yukon Army throughout the course of the war.

On the heels of the batteries came the F-101 fighter planes and their crews. These were the smallest of the three prototypes I had seen in Ohio on Fitz's test field. To support the new arrivals, the flow of lorries from the southeast became a constant bumper-to-bumper line of vehicles that would not cease until the Battle of Northern India began. The attack planes and long-range bombers came a few days later, but by the time they started arriving I had gone west to our construction sites near Luni to complete construction there. Younger, newly recruited men from Australia swelled the ranks of the Second Engineers I took west with me; they were not as experienced as the veterans I had been working with previously and were markedly less disciplined. Headquarters did not believe we needed select men to put up the prefabricated buildings and spray the polymer paint; at that time Central Command cared only if the job was done posthaste.

This short stint in the desert was to be my first time in the position of commander. Colonel McConnell stayed in the east to supervise, he claimed, the digging of defense works around the antiaircraft missiles. Everyone knew the antiaircraft men did not need his or any other engineer's assistance. Mrs. McConnell and the other officers' wives were becoming anxious to leave India before the fighting started, and Colonel Robin wanted—or, more likely, he was commanded—to assist his wife in getting their household in order for the trip back to Australia. The Indian Army had seen Chinese spies on the Ganges plains, and the Blinking Star satellites told us the enemy continued to mass a gigantic ground force in Sichuan and Tibet. Central Command in Cumberland had told the colonel years ago that all but a few of the Second Engineers were going home for the duration. Given my special position,[11] he correctly assumed Central Command would keep me in India and in the heart of the action, and he saw no reason not to shift some of the onus of leadership onto me while he made his exit.

Before heading to Luni, I told Charlotte she should leave for North America. She naturally ignored me and went west with me on the transport train. Living in a tent city, in the desert, among a thousand lonely young men and two thousand foreigners was a trial that would have wilted some flowers more delicate than she. My Charlotte enjoyed every minute during our sojourn in the wilderness. The lads in my command soon discovered that if they whistled at her or made improper remarks to her as she strutted through the camp in her bright orange sari she would answer,

---

11. Bruce is referring to his connection to the Consul.

"Does your mother know you're out late?" Or, "Yes, I remember the foolish things one does during puberty." Or, "Keep taking your vitamins, sonny, and one day you will be able to do more than whistle at the girls." They respected her courage. They respected her the more when they saw how she, the commander's wife, would condescend to nurse anyone, Yukon or native, at the base medical clinic. The most irreverent of the men learned to take his hat off to her when she passed on the way to a soldier's tent with her first aid kit under her arm. I overheard the same lads whisper as they looked after her impressive figure that Major Bruce was a very lucky man.

She and I lived in a double tent for the first week of our stay in Luni. Soon after that, the men, whom she took to calling "her boys," pitched a larger tent for us a hundred yards away from the general encampment. I posted guards at a discreet distance from our temporary home so we could have some privacy during the evening and night. I was exceedingly grateful for our remote position as Charlotte believed newlyweds should spend twelve hours a night in bed. I was grateful beyond my power to say that she held such beliefs, for I was taken aback by how aggressive and—for lack of a better word—how noisy Charlotte could be and was thankful the men could not hear her when she became passionate.

During a lull in one of our twelve-hour sessions Charlotte told me to what use she thought I should put the empty railroad cars arriving from the east. (I was sending our extra equipment and enlisted men to the Rajhahals, and every seven days forty-four empty cars returned to us to take back anything else I might have on hand.)

"The west will be safer when the war comes?" she asked me.

"Yes," I said, knowing she never asked questions to which there were obvious answers unless she was leading me into something larger.

"Then I think the Rabari and the rest of the native workers left in the hill country should come here," she said, and kissed my bare chest. "If we could get them out west and send them south into the Decca, they would be out of harm's way entirely."

I was most vulnerable to her suggestions when we were lying together in bed. She knew I would agree to jump off the edge of the world for her when I was in that situation.

"As I have told you, millions will be in danger no matter what we do," I said, putting up the best struggle I could. "When measured against those doomed to be lost, wouldn't our efforts to save a few hundred souls be preposterous?"

"As *I* have told *you*, we will do what we can," said Charlotte.

"Thank you, my love. God will bless you for this."

"Aren't you the confident one?" I said. "I haven't told you I will do it, yet."

"You will see to matters tomorrow," she said and kissed me.

"Are you ever ashamed of how you manage me?"

"I have no idea what you mean," she said. "Please also send the idle cars you have at Luni Station. There must be food and fresh water for the long trip west. Three pounds of rice and a pound of dehydrated vegetables per person will suffice. I've read your inventory, and you have an excess of supplies, so it will do no good to claim you cannot spare the provisions. The way you sigh is most endearing, Bobby."

During these warm nights, when we were not otherwise preoccupied, Charlotte told me some of the secrets of the Electronic Age Dr. Murrey had told her. She knew I was interested in the peculiar engineering and technological wonders of that time. She lacked the scientific background to explain everything she had been told; still she could feed me some intriguing tidbits. She told me one night there had been a highway during that era that ran from the end of the Florida peninsula to the Caribbean islands known as the Keys.

"For what purpose?" I asked her. "Such a road would present no special technological difficulties. That aside, it would be very expensive and service little traffic. I can't see the reason for building it. Were the Keys some kind of religious shrine? Americans went there on pilgrimage perhaps?"

"They wanted a road to the sea," she said.

"You're a resourceful woman," I told her. "You can tell a better fib than that. The Americans could have gotten to the sea anywhere along the Atlantic or Gulf Coasts. The Keys do not even have a good port."

"I'm not telling stories," she said. "Do you know where ancient Colorado was?"

"Half in present-day Northfield and half in Desert Province," I said. "It straddled the Rocky Mountains."

"The Americans built a four-lane highway east to west right

through Colorado to get to the mountains," she said. "The natural east-west passages are to the north and south of there. Heavy lorries could not use the highway in the winter. The Americans built it just to reach places they could ski."

"They spent a tremendous amount of money and labor to have a place to train arctic troops?"

"No," she said, "they seemed to have ski-ed—and this is what Doctor Murrey himself told me—because they enjoyed it," she said.

"They thought being outdoors, during the winter, in the mountains, slats strapped to their feet as they hurtled down a slope to a broken leg was enjoyable?" I said. "God above. Why didn't they just jump off bridges or climb high mountains for the sport of it?"

"They did, my love," said Charlotte. "And you know those rectangular tubes farmers are forever plowing up? The ones that make a little explosion when broken?"

"Television tubes. They were electronic broadcast monitors."

"I love you when you talk like an engineer," she said and touched me in a particular place. "Anyway, there was one in every home back in the Electronic Age. Some homes had two or more. People would watch actors, sports,[12] wars, crimes; everything right in their family rooms."

"I don't want to argue with you," I said.

"You're such a good boy," she laughed.

"My point is, darling," I said, "I've heard this story before. I might believe the Americans would have these devices in some places, in bars and so forth. Not in normal family homes. All civilizations we know of held the family to be sacred. The Americans could have been no different. They would not have allowed a device carrying such a powerful influence right into their homes. For one thing, the device would undermine the elders' authority. Children would come to admire the transmitter more than their parents; it could show them anything, amuse them all the time, expose

---

12. Mrs. Bruce is not here speaking of hunting or fishing or any of the other field sports. She means the spectacles Americans, like the ancient Greeks and Romans, held in enormous arenas. Americans did not attach any religious meaning, however, to the events they staged. Yukons rightly see such activities as leading to an unhealthy fascination with the body and as a waste of energy and rage more profitably given to warfare, work or worship. Several of the recorded events Lord Mason presented to the other *Basileis* above in Chapter Two are snippets of these "sports" events.

them to more information than their parents could possibly know. Youngsters would soon believe it rather than their elders."

"Doctor Murrey said—" she began to say.

"I don't believe it," I said. "People have told too many lies about the Electronic Age. You have to remember, Charlotte, these stories about the Americans were written by people who hated them and everyone else living back then. We have no real notion of what people then were truly like."

I realized a second later I had repeated what Fitz had said to me during our last meeting in Ohio. I did not share that realization with Charlotte, who in the year 2420 was the only Yukon woman I knew who disliked the young Consul.

"Go to sleep," I said to her. "You tell tall tales better than any-one, yet, my love, there is a limit."

"I wasn't letting you rest so you could go to sleep," she laughed and slipped on top of me. "Besides, I have a little nap pen-ciled in for you tomorrow evening."

The work at the Luni site went swiftly during the two months and four days we were on task. The buildings went up, the Starlight was sprayed on everything we had made, the Rabari and their countrymen were smuggled west and before the last patches of gray were dry the antaircraft crews and the first fighter planes had ar-rived ready for duty. I was anticipating returning east perhaps to learn I had earned a ticket out of India when an ugly incident among the men threatened to mar everything in the report I would have to send to headquarters. As distressing as it was for me to face at that time, a young private in my command had a carnal tryst with a native woman. His sergeant had caught the two of them in the act. In the best tradition of military service, the sergeant had passed the matter onto his lieutenant, who in turn threw the mess into my lap. For lack of a superior officer to whom I could send the case, I held a flying court-martial that found the lad guilty of frat-ernization. Army law dictated that the boy be flogged thirty-five times with a knotted whip.[13] Never before had I faced the possibil-ity of administering physical punishment to one of my men. I hated having to scourge the unlucky private; the beating was likely to kill him and certainly would cripple him if he survived. I likewise was

---

13. In our more enlightened times the punishment for fraternization has been lessened. Military law today demands convicted perpetrators be flogged only thirty times.

terrified I might endanger myself and my new wife were I to do nothing. If Charlotte heard of my predicament, I knew how she would react. I prayed to God she would not learn of the court-martial before we left the area. Upon arriving at our tent on the evening after we had tried the culprit, I saw God had chosen not to answer my prayer. Charlotte was seated on a field chair when I entered, tapping her foot and glaring at me.

"This will not do, sir," she said. "You promised me you would attempt to do better than this."

"Of what are you speaking, dear?" I said.

I did not look directly at her. Experience had taught me that once she made eye contact with me I was finished.

"You are well aware of what I am speaking!" she said. "You should get down on your knees this instant and beg God to forgive you! The thought of it! Beating a poor boy to ribbons!"

"He is not a boy. He is a Yukon soldier and should have known better."

"He is nineteen years old!" she said, getting up from her chair. "Look at me, sir!"

She took me by the chin and turned my face toward hers.

"If you flog that boy," she said, "I will put myself between him and the executioner, and the blows can fall on the commander's wife. I will cut my hand on it."[14]

"Darling, it is the law," I said.

"Have you ever had a man beaten?" she asked.

"No."

"Do you love me?"

"How can you ask?" I said.

"Then swear by the love you bear me," she said, taking my hand, "that you will never beat this boy or any other man. Of course, if you don't love me . . ."

I looked at the tent ceiling, at my boots, at the wildflowers Charlotte had put on the folding table.

"Swear," said Charlotte.

"What do you want me to do?" I said in desperation. "Let the private and his girlfriend run away into the wilderness?"

"Don't be foolish," she said. "The Indians would kill them

---

14. Unlike the early Yukons, the citizens of Bruce's time no longer cut their palms to make a blood oath. In the twenty-fifth century this was a mere figure of speech.

both. Would you only swear as I ask you, your wife would help you escape this dilemma."

"I swear I won't have this boy beaten," I said.

"Swear you will never have anyone beaten," she said.

"How can I do that? I don't know what circumstances I may face in the future. I can't—"

*"Not ever,"* she said.

I sighed, and she smiled for the first time since I entered the tent, since she knew a sigh proceeded a complete surrender. I felt at the heart of this small incident another shift in the loyalties I had held since the day I met Fitz in the college mess or even since the day I took the Military Oath. Charlotte had bit by bit loaded up the balance pan on her side of the scales until I realized I now loved her more, and more intently wished to do as she wanted, than I feared the consequences of not obeying the law.

"I swear I will not, not ever, have a man beaten," I said.

"You swear it before God?" she said.

"Before God I swear it."

She bade me sit down and sat on my lap.

"You are a good man, Bobby," she said and kissed me twice. "Now listen: rather than have the boy's punishment administered here at Luni, send him back to Australia with your written orders."

"That is your plan?" I said, disappointed she had not thought of anything better.

"He won't be carrying back orders stating he is to be beaten for being with a native girl," said Charlotte. "He will be carrying these."

She produced a letter from a fold in her sari.

"It says here Private Barnaby was caught playing cards after lights out," she said. "He will get a reprimand and a month in the brig without pay. No one here will know of his punishment, and no one in Australia will know of what he was originally convicted."

"You happened to have this letter already typed?" I said.

"I know I am married to a good man," she said. "The missive but needs your signature. As for the girl, the men could take a collection for her, each man could give her a couple pounds. She would have enough to go to her relatives in the south. She would be safe from rumors there,[15] and if, God help her, she is with child,

---

15. Her neighbors in the south would not know she had lain with a Yukon soldier.

she will have enough to make a good life for her baby. Two thousand pounds will buy her a princess' life in the Decca."

"The natives around here aren't fools," I said. "As soon as they learn she has Yukon money they will stone her as a whore."

"That is why," said Charlotte, "I took the liberty of collecting the money this morning. Some of my boys have already got her on a train headed south. She is hundreds of miles away by this hour. You see, sir, your wife is not a fool, either."

"If you asked the men for money," I said, "you will have told them Private Barnaby will not be beaten."

"I suppose I exaggerated when I told you no one here will know," she confessed. "Only the rank and file know. Your brother officers still believe you are a murderous sadist and will continue to respect you as such."

"The men will think I am weak," I said.

"They will think you are a kind man," she said and stroked my cheek with the back of her hand. "As I do. Doctor Murrey told me an old Roman once said there are but two things in the world: love and power, and no man can have both.[16] Don't feel badly because you have chosen the former and other men won't fear you. Your choice pleases God."

"My choice pleases my wife," I said and signed the letter, and as when the officers' wives sent off their first letter to her, I felt another portion of my once glorious career slipping away from me, except that on this occasion the sensation felt surprisingly pleasant.

"Yes, but unlike God, your wife needs your help fixing dinner," she said.

We were on combat rations at Luni, a sad precursor of our immediate future. Everything we ate was either boiled or devoured without preparation. We had dried beans, hard bread, beef jerky, goat jerky, dried preaches and apricots, dried rice, hardtack, dehydrated vegetables, powdered milk, a tasteless tinned vegetable paste called "Vegamix," coffee, tea, sugar, and heavy black sorghum. Charlotte threw the beans, rice, jerky, and vegetables together in a pot and added a dash of the extra powerful sorghum to give the brown confection some taste. The longer she kept it boiling, the better it tasted, but it never tasted good. She kept a kettle of this pseudo-food simmering all day.

---

16. This paraphrase is from a Roman marker in North Africa.

When she spoke of preparations she meant she wanted to see me set the table, a small chore that pleased my wife's contrary nature.

"Other men, I believe, have wives who do this sort of task themselves," I told her as I put out the plates and silverware.

"Other men's wives would bore you," she said and performed her strange ritual of touching me on the nose. "Nor would they let you on the roof as often as I do."

Private Barnaby went to Australia and to his one month in the Second Engineers' central brig. Someone, I suspect the private's mates, left a bouquet for Charlotte outside our tent during the night after the convicted man was sent away. Our guards swore they had seen nothing during the night. Before the Barnaby incident, the men had respected my wife; in the incident's aftermath they treated her as they would a noble lady. She could not carry a parcel anywhere in the camp; one of "her boys" would take whatever load she had in her hands and tote it to her destination, where he would ask if she wanted anything else done. Men who had made improper remarks to her in previous days came to her and told her to her face they thought she was absolutely the best. In the nights after the flowers appeared, small gifts of fresh fruits and vegetables— I expect they were purchased on the black market—materialized near our tent, and we ate much better during our last week at Luni.

On the day we left the desert country for the east, a cluster of Rabari children gathered on the station platform wearing masses of frayed red cord on their heads as a tribute to my redheaded wife. Charlotte kissed them as she would any child and divided her gaudy costume jewelry among them, which they gaily shook and made more racket with than she had when the trinkets were hers. As our train pulled from the yard, the children ran after us, waving to Charlotte who had her head out the window of our car and was waving and blowing kisses back to them. Her long hair flowed in the wind like a red banner as we gradually left the children behind.

"They will miss you out here," I told her as she pulled her head inside the window.

"I will miss Luni," she said and fussed with her abundant, tangled mane.

"Even the tents and the bad food?"

"We saved some people here," she said. "What do a few bad meals mean when measured against that?"

"Ah," I said, "the Catholic obsession with good deeds."

"You are becoming a decent practitioner of good deeds yourself, my dear," she said and pinched me on the knee. "I forget: you are one of us now, aren't you?"

"You will have no bad memories?"

"How could I think poorly of Luni?" she said. "Our first child was conceived here."

She looked out the window and smiled her quizzical, lopsided smile. I moved from the seat opposite hers to sit beside her.

"Oh, Charlotte," I said.

I concentrated all my mental strength on what I should say to her next. Nothing more apt came to mind.

"Oh, Charlotte," I repeated.

"Don't gush," she said and leaned her head against my chest. "You will make me cry. You may hold me, sir, if you promise to speak of other concerns."

Upon our arrival in the Rajmahal Hills we had our first glimpse of Hood's army, the soon to be famous Sixth, dressed in the familiar gray uniforms and slouch canvas hats Yukon soldiers have worn to every populated continent on the globe. The day our train pulled into the hills fell in the tail end of monsoon season, yet the clouds had lifted from the hills around us, and we had a clear view of the tens of thousands of fighting men making camp on both sides of the tracks.

Charlotte and I had not left the train ere a messenger found me and pushed a single folded sheet of paper into my hand. Upon opening it I saw the letter the man had given me read in its entirety: "The Consul has learned of your marriage." This was the only communication I had gotten from Fitz since I spoke to him at Pallas and would be the last I would receive from him until after the fighting in India was completed.

# TWELVE

THE SIXTH ARMY would number two hundred thousand men at the height of its power in 2421. Sixty thousand of them provided logistical support; they were the mechanics, drivers, medical personnel, cooks, and police. Every one of these men had been selected for his outstanding service record from the entire Army for this one expedition. The remaining one hundred and forty thousand men were members of the fourteen best combat divisions the Confederacy could produce. Hood had under his command eleven infantry divisions (two of them Blue Jackets), the Seventeenth or "Tiger" armor division, an artillery division containing a thousand 220s,[1] and an auxiliary division mostly of antiaircraft batteries that also contained a brigade of demolition engineers and a brigade that manned six gigantic twenty-one-inch artillery pieces mounted on flatbed lorries. Each of the infantry divisions had its own heavy mortar brigades and a specialized regiment of communication men and firefighters. Besides the Army units there were in the Rajmahal Hills twenty thousand men of the First Army Air Corps and twenty thousand of the Third Air Corps at Luni. These airmen servicing and flying the aircraft were separate of Hood's command and had their own leader in Lieutenant General Howe,[2] although the Air

---

1. As noted in Chapter One, this particular cannon's bore is measured in millimeters. Military measurements are irregular, some in the metric system and some in the English system, for many of these measurements are direct descendants of ancient antecedents.

2. Lord Sir General Thomas Coltrane Howe (2362–2421) would command the air arm of the Army in India until he was killed in combat and was succeeded by General Arthur Courage Smith (2364–2472).

Corps was in constant contact with Cumberland HQ and, presumably, with the Consul himself.

My old university mate, the bearded "Judge" of the *Basileis*, had chosen this ferocious group of mostly veteran warriors during his first year of Sixth Army command. For two and a half years he had trained them as a single body in the Unita Basin of Desert Province. He had put them through the four prescribed exercises six days a week and kept them in church for five hours on Sunday mornings. After the first year of training he had taken away their wooden rifles and made his men run, swim, and do calisthenics, but he forbade hand-to-hand fighting.

"Save your anger for the enemy," Hood had told them. "Save it, and let it grow like a pearl growing inside an oyster. Save it, though it gnaws at your innards like a bit of jagged glass. One day your anger will come forth as a gem that will dazzle the entire world."

Hood went among the men daily and knew thousands of junior officers and NCOs by name. He led prayer services every morning at the head of the assembled troops and again on the Sabbath after church services. His text was the same each time he bowed his head: that the final days foretold in the Book of Revelation were at hand; that the Sixth was God's army, sent to do battle against Babylon, the mother of abominations,[3] and against the minions of the eastern Antichrist.[4] He told them their victory would prepare the world for Christ's return. Defeat, he constantly warned them, would cast men's hearts and minds into darkness for another thousand years. When the early Yukon generals prayed with their men, I expect they sounded much as Hood did, and the Yukon soldiers who destroyed the Americans during the Storm Times yearned for the final battle no less ardently than Hood's men did, for the Yukons have always pined for the final victory, when we shall be free of the burden of History and the Lord will come and tell us these long years of suffering—both the suffering we have endured and that we have inflicted—were necessary to His plan.

"Victory, like the Kingdom of Heaven, lies within us," Hood told his men during their last assembly in Desert Province, when

---

3. In this instance, Peking.

4. i.e., the Islamic devotees of Mohammed.

the men were preparing to depart for India. "I know this to be true, for Heaven and Victory are born together within a man's heart in the moment he learns not to fear death. Contempt for death, my lads, brings Victory, and Heaven follows in its train as surely as the sun brings the morning. The fear of death is the one poison that can destroy them both.

"There are officers, my lads, officers in this army, who fancy that our future success will lie in the strategies we use. I have overheard other men in our ranks proclaim that if only every one of you could shoot as well as a marksman[5] we could vanquish any opponent. One corporal suggested to me you men should learn the oriental exercises,[6] and that would make us a more terrible force. Many, many of you believe our strength comes from our technology, from our Blinking Stars, from our fine airplanes and our unmatched artillery.

"I say to you, my friends, that an army unafraid of dying will defeat any opponent, regardless of strategy, expertise, training, equipment, or unknowing chance. Give me men who can calmly face their own destruction, and let the infidel Turks and the godless Chinese have our weaponry, our satellites, our training, and I guarantee I will wipe them from the face of creation just as winter obliterates the last traces of summer. Yes, we have all the advantages, save numbers, in this coming battle, and we shall use them, yet if we fear losing our earthly existences, our advantages will avail us nothing. Let us bow our heads and ask God to take the fear from our hearts so we might be the instruments of His triumph here on earth. Amen."

Hood was a living model to his men. His battle-hardened heart dreaded only defeat and being apart from his stubby, much adored

---

5. Marksman here means an infantryman armed with a long range rifle; marksmen have tested at a higher grade on the firing range than riflemen, who constitute the majority of the infantry, and slightly lower than snipers, who are a special group of men equipped with long range rifles that have telescopic sights.

6. "Oriental exercises," i.e., the so-called martial arts originating in the Far East. The Chinese made great use of them during their training, albeit such foolishness has no practical use in real combat. The corporal was a brave man to suggest this to Hood, as the oriental exercises have always been illegal in the Confederacy, and Hood could have had the solider flogged.

wife. Official History today mentions little of him beyond the Battle of Northern India. The prescribed authors cheat him of his rightful place in the long gallery of Yukon military leaders. Had his soldiers written the official History, every schoolchild would know his name as well as they know that of the Fitzpatricks. His troops loved him for his courage and for the many years he had served as a common soldier. They knew he would not ask of them more than he demanded of himself, even though that meant he would demand everything. Were his men the keepers of official History, we would remember Hood as he was: the best and bravest soldier of his generation.

Upon departing from the train Charlotte and I went to our assigned tent and changed into Yukon clothes before reporting to Hood's quarters. Charlotte in her long white dress was an erotic exclamation point walking through the thousands of gray-clad troops milling about their pup tents. The Second Engineers under Colonel McConnell's command had already departed for their home down under. Mrs. Jeremiah Hood and the wives of five senior staff officers were the only other Yukon women remaining in the soggy Rajmahal Hills. None of the older women still there could have made quite the impression on the men as did the youthful and winsome Charlotte when she walked by the soldiers. These were not green, untried men as the young fellows I had at Luni had been; when my wife walked by they watched her in silence or else they glanced at her white dress before quickly looking away. The sight of pretty Charlotte in her sheer gown saddened them rather than inspiring any feelings of lust; they knew, without knowing who she was or where she was bound, that she did not belong there and was an image from the world they had left behind. I too watched Charlotte and felt the same sadness. I knew this trip to the general's tent marked the beginning of our last days together before the war came. I took her hand in mine, and for the length of our stroll through the swarming camp her and my thoughts were the same.

Hood had set a band atop the six hills within the limits of the Sixth's city of tents. As we two walked we could hear the bagpipes making a mournful skirl in the air above the somber, purposeful soldiers. I recognized the tunes "The Rough Wind That Shook the Barley" and "Arise, You Sons of Dogs, and We Shall

Give You Flesh," and our unofficial national anthem, "Black Jack Davy."[7]

We found Hood, now wearing a Field Marshal's laurels on his collar, busy with his maps inside his tent. Couriers and senior officers were entering and exiting his small quarters at irregular intervals; they would pause to take a brief oral command or a written note from the Marshal's hand, then vanish out the open flaps. As was Hood's custom when women were present, he was polite but overly formal, as he was in public when his wife accompanied him. He bowed and kissed Charlotte's hand, then made a kind remark out the side of his mouth in regard to her beauty she could barely hear. Daddy Montrose,[8] my college classmate Lord Stein, and a secretary were seated behind him. Montrose, all five feet of him and every inch bristling with energy, was studying a map of the Gandes Valley and muttering "Goddamn" whenever he found something in the terrain he did not like. Stein sat with his arms folded, looking bored and angry.

"Back among us and ready to do some real work," said Hood to me. "Very good. Everything to be done and no time to do it," he said and patted a pile of documents on his field table. "Luni is ready. It is good to have at least one objective completed. Lord Colonel Stein, would you be so kind as to show Mrs. Bruce the new helicopters that arrived yesterday?"

Stein remained seated. He did not so much as unfold his arms.

"No, I would rather not," he said. "I doubt Mrs. Bruce is interested in helicopters . . . sir."

Daddy Montrose curled his upper lip, revealing a row of even, white teeth powerful enough to have bitten Stein in half.

"That is a Field Marshal you are addressing, young Lord," he

---

7. "Black Jack Davy" became the official Yukon anthem in 2086. In 2230 the Senate decided the ballad, which tells the story of an English Lord whose wife runs away with a Gypsy named Black Jack Davy and lives in sin until the Lord tracks the two of them down and hacks them to death with his broadsword, was not a suitable national hymn. "Oh Yukon, Land Blessed by God" was made the official anthem. To this day the common people, especially soldiers and sailors, prefer the earlier, more earthy tune.

8. Lieutenant General Israel Hard Truth Montrose (2361–2479), known as "Daddy" to his men, although he was a widower and never fathered a child; he is remembered as a hard fighter and drinker and as the able commander of Hood's Second Corps.

said to Stein. "T'would be a pity if an arrogant pup such as yourself were to go against a wall for forgetting that, sir."[9]

Stein offered the lieutenant general the universally understood salute of the middle finger. Montrose responded by putting his hand on the pistol he carried on his hip.

"Enough, gentlemen!" boomed Hood. "Lord Stein, you will go show Mrs. Bruce the new helicopters. Yes, that is an order!"

Stein grumbled, but arose and went with Charlotte through the tent flap. Almost never, I suspect, did a helicopter inspection bring anyone less pleasure than this one did to the glum Banker.

"He had damn well better apologize to me!" said Montrose, the blood vessels in his forehead appearing close to bursting.

"Israel, you have to calm down," said Hood.

"What is this?" asked Montrose, pointing at me. "Another *prima donna* the Consul has sent us? Knight of the Field?" noting the decoration on my tunic. "What's this? A youngster who's earned his position? He can't be from the damned Consul."

"Sir Major Bruce built this base and the one at Luni," said Hood, exaggerating my importance in front of his brother general. "These maps we're using, that one you have in your hand, Israel, are his work. Not every friend of the Consul is like Lord Colonel Stein. Need I remind you that *I* am the Consul's friend?"

"And we know what a lousy bastard you are, Jerry," said Daddy Montrose.

He was smiling when he spoke, and Hood's serious nature notwithstanding, both men took the remark as a joke. Hood did cough, for decorum's sake, allowing himself to hide his expression.

"You will give Robert the wrong notion of how we conduct business in the Sixth Army," said Hood.

"He's not well born, is he?" asked Montrose.

"From the ranks as you and I are, sir," said Hood.

General Montrose nodded in approval. My low birth was to be an advantage in the Sixth, given that Hood had stocked his staff and his command hierarchy with officers of common origins. Stein was the solitary Lord among them, and he—as will be seen—had not won the other officers' favor during his time under Hood's command.

"Three things, Robert," said Hood and handed me a set of maps detailing where he wanted his trenches dug.

9. i.e, to be shot.

"These will be our earthworks," he said and pointed to the series of red dots on the maps. "The men are digging as we speak, and we have our own carpenters. They have been drilled and redrilled in this. I want you to organize two survey teams out of the men you brought east and go about to each of the six hundred critical sites and make certain the men have the best advantage points and that they've raked the ground clean in front of them. I want two thousand meters cleared in front of every fortification. Slit trenches in back for the communication troops and logistics and whatnot. Here at the San," he said and put a finger on the map sixty miles south of where the San River debouches into the Ganges, "is a matter we will discuss later. Now, what sort of men are the Australians you have left?"

"Young, nonselect men from the Second Engineers, sir," I said.

"Take half of them for your two teams and send the others to Calcutta," said Hood. "I need them to load bags of polymer from the ships onto lorries.

"I am promoting you to brevet-colonel, pending the approval of the Senate," he went on. "I want the men out there where you'll be working to respect you, and you deserve it more than most."

"I think perhaps you should not do that, sir," I said. "The Senate may not approve my promotion."

"Why not?"

"Because, sir," I said, "Fit—the Consul, I think he disapproves of my marriage, sir."

"Posh. He said nothing to me of that when I saw him three weeks ago," said Hood. "He did say what a fine job you've done out here, Colonel Bruce. You know how the Consul is; one day he's furious, wait a day, and he is your best friend again. Don't worry about it. General Harrison[10] will have your golden sheaves."[11]

"Thank you, sir," I said. "I won't let you down. Those were the three things, sir?"

"By my count that's only one," said Hood. "Second . . . I say this with deep regrets. In two days there will be a zeppelin leaving here, outward bound for North America. The other staff wives and my missus will be on it. Your young bride will be on board as well."

---

10. Major General Thomas Gideon Harrison, later Field Marshal Harrison (2370–2506), commanded the Eighth Infantry Division in India and was on Hood's staff.

11. Emblems of a colonel's rank.

"Sir, I would like you to know—"

"No arguments, Sir Robert," said Hood. "I realize you are a newlywed. This is most unfair and the rest of that. You have other obligations now. You will have to put everything else out of your head. You will find, Robert, that the mark of true maturity is to allow but one governing idea into your mind at one time. An immature man entertains conflicting thoughts, conflicting emotions. I will not tolerate that in you. I expect much better than that of a colonel. We are understood?"

"Yes, sir."

"You may have the next two days off to say good-bye to her. Report back here when she is gone."

"Yes, sir."

"The third item I wish to speak to you about is our mutual friend Lord Stein," said Hood and glanced at Montrose, who was frowning. "I suppose you are aware of his dispute with Lord O'Brian?"

"Yes, he had me come to him in Salt Lake this May when I was in North America, sir," I said. "He seems to be accusing O'Brian of stealing supplies from the—"

Hood shook his head.

"I know all about the alleged thefts and of O'Brian's counteraccusations," he said. "The noble gentlemen have bedeviled us with this nonsense since the Sixth Army was formed. That childish tantrum you were witness to is typical of his behavior. Stein has twice left his post—left his post, mind you—to consult with a member of the judges' guild. *Twice*, Robert."

He held up two fingers to emphasize the point.

"I would have had him shot twice," said Daddy Montrose.

"I should tell you, sir," I said, "Lord Stein gave me documents he asked me to sign. He said they were—"

"Preliminary figures as computated by some damned Memory Men he bribed," said Hood while Montrose muttered curses.

"How many bloody Memory Men has he spent money on?" asked Montrose. "He has destroyed our logistics records! Destroyed it, Jerry!"

"O'Brian is no better," said Hood. "That young idiot has bribed some Memory Men of his own. Then, while the Sixth was in the process of transferring to India, O'Brian sent the judges' guild member he had contacted among us to take depositions from every man on my staff. Can you imagine, Robert? As you may suspect, word of this mess has reached the Consul, and the Consul is not pleased, Robert."

Hood held his arms in front of him so I might see the decorations running down both sleeves of his jacket.

"Thirty-six years, Sir Robert," he said, "I have been in the Yukon Army. The first fourteen in the ranks of the enlisted men. I started as a private. I have twenty-seven battle ribbons. I am a Knight of the Field and have more commendations for bravery than any man in active duty. Never, Robert, never have I earned one letter of reprimand in my record file. Until now. Fitz gave me one because I did not report Stein's doings to him at once. I'll not be given a second black mark, Robert. I have Stein on a short leash, sir, of that you may be assured. He is here, with me, during his waking hours. He simply sits here and pouts. I cannot give him any duties, or he will alter the books, again. In theory he is my aide! He has a guard posted on his tent at night. If he approaches you and attempts to draw you into this conspiracy he is concocting against Lord O'Brian, you will tell him to leave you alone. Should he persist, you will report his conduct to me. Immediately, Robert. You and I are commoners; we are not allowed to play in these noble gentlemen's pastimes. Should one of us behave as Stein or O'Brian have, the consequences would be fatal, sir."

"I understand, sir," I said.

"Back here in two days then," he said and rose. "Young lovers and all that . . ."

Just mentioning the subject of love was enough to embarrass the spit and polish Hood. He saluted me and gave me my leave.

"Now go to her," he said. "Send Lord Stein in here. I dare not let him out of my sight. God be with you, Sir Robert."

"And with you, Sir Marshal Hood. And with you, General Montrose," I said and saluted them both.

I found Stein and Charlotte two hundred yards away beside one of the huge Mule helicopters.[12] She was feigning interest in the ungainly mechanical beast while Stein stood next to her,

---

12. The Makeworth ME-5 or Mule was a huge transport helicopter that was the ancestor of the modern day ME-17.

hands in his pockets, the picture of the wronged man in a deep funk.

"Come, Charlotte, we need to return to our tent," I said. "They want you back there, Banker," I said to Stein.

He imposed himself between us and took hold of my tunic lapels with both hands.

"What did they say?" he demanded. "You have to tell me, Robert. I know they sent me out here so they could talk about me."

"They tell me I should avoid you, Lord Stein," I said and disengaged myself from his grip. "You are becoming a bad man to know."

"The schemers! The dirty anti-Semitic schemers!" he said. "Now they are trying to turn you against me!"

"What are you saying?" I said. "You aren't a Jew. Hood would be the last to care about that if you were."

"My grandfather was a Jew. Don't laugh. These Yukon bigots never forget! That Hood, so damned outwardly righteous! I thought he could be trusted, but you're the only trustworthy man among the officers, Bobby. You still have the papers I gave you?" he asked and renewed his hold on my lapels.

"I have them in a safe place. Please let go, Banker," I told him. "You are making a scene in front of the men."

Several soldiers seated around a campfire some twenty yards away were staring at us. During their careers in the Army they certainly had never seen an officer in the emotional state Stein was. I had to break free from him again.

"I will provide the papers you gave me if this affair comes to a head," I told Stein. "Which it won't. Gather yourself together, man. Hood is not going to throw you to the wolves. Daddy Montrose can't lay a hand on you, no matter what he says. Not that I would not be giving him the finger. You are of a noble family, Lord Stein. If every one of the senior officers out here despised you, they could not punish you in any fashion," I reminded him and straightened my tunic. "Fitz is another matter. Were I in your situation, I would forget this business you and O'Brian have going between the two of you before I provoked the Consul. I don't have to tell you how he will take this."

"You're right, Bobby," he said, and pulled himself up to his full height. "Hood is nothing. O'Brian is nothing. Our Lord Fitz-patrick is everything.[13] Thank you, Robert. Fitz will listen to you," he said and made a fist. "Oh yes. I will see them all dead!"

His reference to "Our Lord Fitzpatrick" so stunned both Char-lotte and me, we did not know whether he was making a bad joke or crafting some sort of insult. We had never heard of a Lord swear-ing fealty to anything beyond the Confederacy.

"I will be a friend to you, and forget you said that, Banker," I said. "You had best go to them. We have to leave."

"What on earth was that about?" Charlotte whispered to me as soon as we were far from him.

"Stein and O'Brian have this silly argument—" I began.

"You told me about that months ago," she said. "I meant, what did he mean by calling Fitz his Lord?"

"He was angry and misspoke," I said. "Or he was being flip-pant, trying to shock us. Lords cannot belong to other Lords. That would be insane. Not to mention unconstitutional. Fitz would not demand that of him."

Back at our new quarters Charlotte made out our folding cot to give us a place to sit. I had seen her cry once before and half ex-pected she might do it again when I told her what Hood had said. I put my arm around her, and she sat on my lap and leaned back against me. We remained fixed thusly for more minutes than either of us knew, not speaking but listening to the soldiers noisily tramp-ing around us.[14]

"Will you dance with me, Madame?" I asked her.

"Our vinyl recordings and the player are still packed," she said.

"I'll sing," I said and helped her stand.

I have a terrible singing voice and a worse sense of rhythm. Whenever I played in our community orchestra the conductor placed

---

13. What is the reader to make of this? Was Lord Stein speaking carelessly as would fit his nature, is Bruce giving a false account, or had Stein sworn fealty to Lord Fitzpatrick in an unknown ceremony? Gerald (pp. 986–89) reports that Lord Fitzpatrick, in one of the few mistakes of his Consulship, did demand certain noblemen to sin against their family names and to swear personal fealty to him. Gerald also states that this was a lesser degree of fealty and not the strict oath taken by commoners to their Lords. Mason, in his disreputable memoirs, claims the Younger Fitzpatrick made many Lords take an oath of absolute fealty.

14. The following passage is missing in the 2541 edition.

me deep in the violin section where the sheer volume of sound would cover my musical shortcomings. Dancing with Charlotte in the cramped tent I sounded exceptionally bad; I hummed "dum-dum-da-da-dum" in imitation of a waltz, and we moved two steps to our left and two to our right, which was as much movement as the tent allowed. A few tears fell, and Charlotte laughed in spite of them.

[15]"Aren't you now ashamed you were ever afraid of me?" she asked.

"I was never afraid of you."

She scowled.

"Not much," I added. "You were once an associate of a Timerman, my love."

"As I have told you," she said, "you know only a little less of the Timermen than I do. Nor can I guess what Doctor Murrey's motives were in associating with me. I strongly disagree with you that your Fitz and Doctor Murrey are on the same side, regardless of whether the Timermen as a whole support Fitz or not. The Consul and his former tutor have long had a falling out."

"I knew they disagreed over some Hindu teacher in the Fitzpatrick household," I said.

"There was another man as well, one Joseph Flag,"[16] said Charlotte. "He was a teacher at Fitz's mother's school many years ago. He must be in his sixties now. The Consul and his court keep report of him from the public because he is not a Christian."

"What is he?"

"Some type of Buddhist, slash Hindu, slash Taoist, slash pagan, slash something unique," she said. "Murrey says he follows

---

15. The 2541 text resumes here.

16. Joseph Freedom Flag (2360–2427) remains a figure of considerable mystery. Even Gerald (pp. 991–95, pp. 1377–78, p. 1551, pp. 3620–42, *et alia*) has a difficult time explaining how this champion of Eastern mysticism came to be a close advisor and friend of the Younger Fitzpatrick. Mason claims Flag had the Consul in a sort of spiritual bondage, but Gerald interprets Flag's presence at court as part of the Consul's program of religious freedom. We cannot believe the peculiar Flag had any actual influence over Fitzpatrick. No one, not even Bruce—as we see here—believed that. As Bruce relates, Flag was once an instructor in Lady Fitzpatrick's girls' school. His works, the most famous being *The Universal Hero* and *Do As You Will* were extremely popular during the Shay regime, and for that reason are out of print and virtually nonexistent today. Most copies of his books were burned during the Vengeance Night pogrom of 2453.

a philosophy of his own devising. I cannot be more precise about him. Flag's books are on the proscribed list, and cannot be read. He seems to be telling Fitz and his other devotees to do as they will and that is the one path to spiritual enlightenment."

"Fitz never needed any encouragement to do whatever he wanted," I said.

"Flag believes the man most obedient to his self is closest to God, or to whatever is at the center of true wisdom," said Charlotte. "Murrey detests him. He says Flag is practically the Antichrist."

"We Yukons have found a long list of contenders to the title of Antichrist," I said. "I think your Murrey wants Fitz's ear to himself. He's probably jealous of this Flag chap, who sounds like a crank. Cranks amuse Fitz. From what I saw of Fitz the last time we met, I don't think he's taking anyone's advice beside his own. He doesn't even listen to his mother any longer."

"Let's speak no more of the Consul," she said. "God is just. He will punish the guilty one day."

We did not go to bed till morning. We sat up long after the camp had quieted and talked as only people on the verge of a great disaster can speak. She wanted to tell me not to take chances, to stay in a rear area if I could, and to let somebody else do the dying. She did not because she knew she would frighten both of us more than circumstances already had. Soldiers are superstitious, and the sentiment infects everyone in our families; we and everyone we hold dear think that to speak of death is the same as courting it. We talked instead of inconsequential subjects not related to the course our lives were soon to take. I opened the window flaps of our tent and turned out our lamps so we could gaze at the stars in the night sky.

"Do you think there are other worlds?" Charlotte asked me. "People on other planets that orbit other suns?"

I explained to her we on earth would never know as long as the Storm Machines stayed overhead and the Timermen had a monopoly on space travel. Even if we could fly beyond our solar system, I told her, the great distances of the stars from us might prevent us from traveling to them, as we might never be able to fly faster than the speed of light.

"That is twentieth-century physics," she said. "I thought all of that was disproved back then."

I said that, yes, in the latter part of the Electronic Age scientists found that electromagnetic signals sent from one point on the earth's surface travel more quickly east to west than west to east and that gravity increases as the speed of light does, and both of those observations cut the legs from underneath most of Electronic Age physics.[17] Our modern uncertainty comes from our inability to test any theories from that time. Without electricity there are no observatories that can measure light as accurately as they did then. Lacking computers, we cannot do the necessary math.

"As far as we are concerned," I told Charlotte, "we live in a Newtonian universe. The *Principia* rules everything we can make or observe.[18] The Timermen don't have the same restraints. They fly wherever they want."

"In a pig's eye," she said. "Murrey told me they have a few robot bases on the moon, and another on Mars. Timermen in times past have gone clear to Pluto and to all the other planets on the way out. Not any longer. They send out robot ships to points beyond. Or so they once did."

"What did they find out there?"

"Lots and lots of emptiness," said Charlotte. "They found a few rocks, all of them containing the same elements we have here."

"They haven't done much in the past three hundred years."

"I don't believe they care for doing much up there," said Charlotte. "Their primary concerns in space are the maintenance of the Storm Machines and the Blinking Stars. Scientific exploration is a sideline to them. The Timermen are interested in us down here, Robert. We need to remember that."

Somehow she managed to change the conversation to what had happened to the Americans during the Storm Times, a matter she knew grated on my conscience.

"You do feel guilty about what happened to the Americans, don't you?" she said.

"You and Doctor Murrey won't leave that alone," I said. "How

---

17. See Henry Gabor's *Eternity and Ether* and *Local Gravitational Fields,* both published in 2049 and reissued in 2572 by Grand Harbor Press as part of their Classical Library series. Bruce is here for once correct; Gabor's experiments can no longer be repeated or retested, and many today doubt he was correct.

18. Bruce here means Sir Isaac Newton's *Philosophiae naturalia principia mathematica,* first published in 1687.

can I personally feel guilt over something that happened before I was born? The Americans were a lost people. They destroyed themselves. God gave us their land, as He gave the Holy Land to Abraham, 'because of the wickedness of these nations.' So it says in Deuteronomy 9:4. Were I to have lived back then, what could I, one man, have done to hold back History? I have done enough in my own time I have to repent of. I don't need to add to my record of guilt events that occurred three hundred years ago."

"But by the standards you learned at home, what happened then was wrong, wasn't it?"

"By the standards I learned at home, at school, and at church," I said, "what happened then was very wrong. That does not alter the fact that *they*, our ancestors committed those crimes, not I."

"You saw some of the Americans, I believe," she said. "When you were in Mexico, I mean."

"I saw their ghettos in Guadalajara,"[19] I said. "Pathetic urchins in the dirty streets. Burned out buildings. God, the smell of the place, Charlotte. There were dirty children playing in the alleyways. The adults, you know, still tattoo themselves."

In my mind's eye I again saw the Americans watching our mechanized column move through the streets of Guadalajara as we pursued the beaten Mexican army.[20] Some of them had retained a few English words and shouted "Hello Yankee" and "Hey Joe" at our personnel carriers as we sped past. Watching them standing in their dirty hovels I felt as though phantoms from another age were calling to us. I could not sleep for days afterward.

"I did not feel any shame for what I did not do," I said. In even the bad light inside our tent I knew Charlotte could read the lack of conviction on my face.

"Would you kneel with me and ask God for His help?" she asked and lifted me by the hand.

"Dear God," she prayed, "thank you for awakening these feel-

---

19. See Ethan Hope Beachan's *Human Refuse in Mexico* (Stephan's and Co., Centralia City, 2548) for a lengthy treatment of existent American colonies in modern Mexico.

20. Bruce participated in the pursuit after the Battle of Durango in 2412, when the last of the Mexican forces were routed and forced to flee to Mexico City, where they surrendered unconditionally.

ings in my Robert's heart. He is hurting, Lord. Do not let these feelings weigh upon him too heavily—"

"I do not feel shame for the actions of the early Yukons," I said.

"Shh, we're praying," she said, and put a finger to her mouth. "Do not let him forget, either. Let him turn these feelings into kindness and let him never do anything that would further burden his conscience. Amen."

I hesitated to add my blessing to her prayer. She poked me in the side and said: "Say 'Amen,' my love."

"Amen," I said.

Since we had gone to Hood's tent Charlotte had been downcast. Upon concluding her prayer her mood became very nearly serene. She was not exactly happy; her spirits were simply light enough to let her speak of our baby and to say she would prosper at my home in Astoria while I remained in India.

"I think Aunt Jessie and I will get on well under the same roof," she said. "We are kindred spirits."

I imagined she and Great-Aunt Jessie being so kindred in spirit they would either create a joint monarchy in my family compound or start a civil war. My father and my uncles would have to suffer their benevolent rule however she and Jessie got along. Daily consumption of alcohol and chewing tobacco would skyrocket among the old men and boys of my family, and they would remain in the rainy fields and forests of Astoria, drinking and chewing and occasionally working, for as long as the hours of daylight lasted. When the baby arrived Charlotte would be elevated to the status of queen on the family farm. I could picture the other women making a fuss over her and not letting her do any work beyond nursing the child. The men would now and again sneak into her room, their felt hats removed, and look upon her and the new arrival with the same reverence they bestowed upon the holy image of the Madonna and Child in the family chapel. I was saddened to think I would not be there among Charlotte's flood of admirers.

The next day was one of those relaxed, unplanned days of which Charlotte and I had too few during the early years of our marriage. We ate a late breakfast while the rest of the army was laboring hard at its two hundred thousand separate tasks. We brewed the last of the good Sandwich Island coffee we had saved for a special occasion. Later we together read aloud from Hendrick's *The Underwater Boat*,[21] and she had a good, therapeutic laugh when we read Jules Verne's preposterous description of a journey to the moon in an artillery shell. She took the book away from me when I started reading aloud the last of Tolkien's *The Lord of the Rings* or she might have had a prolonged laughing fit.

"No more," she protested. "We need to take some air or I shall be dizzy."

We walked arm in arm under one umbrella in the pouring rain beside a roadway and watched men laying canvas tarps over the six twenty-one-inch cannons. Only my wife could have found something humorous in those gigantic machines of destruction standing erect and lethal against the overcast sky. She elbowed me and made a naughty remark upon what the cannons resembled.

"Do you ever feel jealous of those monsters?" she teased.

"They can fire a shell for sixty miles," I said. "However, my dear, in only five or six years of use we will have to turn them into scrap. They give out completely. I dare say I will be on the artillery range long after they have been recycled into iceboxes and thimbles."

"Before you get carried away with this new imagery, I must say I prefer our old metaphor of the diligent carpenter mending the roof," said Charlotte. "All artillery, as you say, gets melted down, eventually. A good carpenter, one that can do his work to order, will never be retired."

She brushed against me in a pleasant manner I was thankful the men on the guns did not see. I did not upbraid her; that would have provoked her into doing the same thing again in a more obvious fashion that the men would definitely notice.

In a supply yard a thousand yards below the mighty guns we came upon a crew of teamsters and native workers unloading forty-

---

21. Readers will at once recognize *The Underwater Boat,* assembled by George Prophet Hendricks (2301–2405), and still widely available in the Classical Library and Everyman's editions as well as in many abridged versions. This collection of so-called science fiction and fantasy fiction from the nineteenth and twentieth centuries has long been a reliable source of amusement in many Yukon households. These tales of worlds that never were and inventions that never existed give us today a useful indication of how ridiculous the Electronic Era really was. Tolkien, who was a professor of classical languages at a great university, should have known better, yet he wrote a nearly endless epic concerning wizards, talking trees, and little people who lived below the ground.

pound bags of polymer from a fleet of lorries. Two men on the site caught my eye because they were much older than their workmates and were struggling to keep pace with the young men. I realized a few seconds later I had met them on *The Mother of Jesus.*

"French! Charlie!" I called to them. "Come here, gentlemen. You need to meet my wife."

The sail maker and the ship's carpenter with whom I had endured the storm south of the Great Australian Bight were as astonished to see me as I was to see them. They told me their plans to start a shop in Grand Harbor had fallen through when they lost their positions in the I.T. Younger men were entering the International Trade ever since the Consul opened up that service to more ships. Younger men in the I.T. would work for salaries rather than a percentage of the profits, making them a cheaper bargain than the veteran sailors. The old men's skills were no longer as gravely needed on the newer lightweight ships that carried smaller crews than the older boats. On the strength of their military records, the two old sailors had gotten corporals' commissions in the Sixth's support forces, albeit they were obviously past the time when they could do the strenuous labor of military teamsters.

"We used you as a reference, Sir Robert," admitted French. "Knowing a friend of the Consul opens doors, sir."

They were breathing hard as they spoke to us. Poor Charlie could barely keep his splayed feet under him in the slick mud.

"He's not got his land legs yet," said French of his friend. "He'll be better in a week or two."

Charlie coughed and brushed the rain off his high forehead. In a week or two he might well be dead of pneumonia if he did not get dry.

"My husband sought you gentlemen out," said Charlotte, "because he wants you both to be on his surveying crew. Isn't that so, dear?"

She stood on her tiptoes and looked me squarely in the eyes so I might make a close consideration of her serious expression.

"That's correct," I lied. "I will speak to your lieutenant and have you sent to my tent tomorrow afternoon."

"My husband has misspoken, gentlemen," said Charlotte. "He has been under great stress, so you must forgive him. What Brevet Colonel Bruce meant to say was he will speak to your lieutenant *now*, this very instant, and you both can then go to the Second Engineers' tents at once and rest up for tomorrow. That is what you meant to say, am I not correct, Brevet Colonel Bruce?"

"I suppose it is," I said.

Their lieutenant had feared the old men might die on him. He readily let them go under my command. Charlotte immediately took Charlie and French to one of the large sleeping tents the Second Engineers had pitched on the outskirts of the grand encampment and saw to it they had hot baths and dry uniforms. She put Charlie to bed and fed him hot broth as a mother would do for a sick child. I expect the old mariners had not been treated so well since they had left home. French commented while he and I watched pretty Charlotte put spoonfuls into Charlie's mouth, that Army life was obviously a big improvement over eating rotten salt pork in the I.T.

"Didn't I overhear you speaking to a Hindu workman in his tongue, Mr. Martin?" Charlotte asked Charlie as she put her hand on the old man's forehead to check for fever.

"We, me and French, ma'am, have picked up a word or two of their talk over the years," said Charlie.

"I know Hindi, Tamil-talk, and a kind of Chinese like they use in Singapore," inserted French, eager to impress my handsome wife.

"You are both very learned," said Charlotte.

She touched the old men's callused hands, and they beamed at her like little boys falling in love with their first female teacher. Other than the loose women they had met in sundry ports, Charlotte's kind attention was the only feminine affection they had known since they had been in their mothers' care. At that instant the two of them would have signed away their souls for a few days more of my wife's tender attentions.

"My husband will be absolutely brilliant after sharing your company," she told them. "I regret I will not be here to see him blossoming forth."

There is no telling how Charlie and French might have blossomed if they could have luxuriated in Charlotte's presence for another hour, but she left them to tend to each other while she embarked on another mission. She went about the remnant of the Second Engineers and selected thirty of the youngest of "her boys," none of whom she wanted laboring on the piers in Calcutta, and told them they were now members of my survey crew. The activity lit a joyful fire in her as she was doing the two things that made her most happy: she was performing a good deed and at the same time manipulating her husband.

"You will saddle me with a pack of misfits," I said, making my *pro forma* objection as we walked back to our tent.

"My husband is a genius," she said. "He could survey some stupid trenches blindfolded. What does he need other than some men to carry his gear and to hold a marker? You've already told me the soldiers will do most of the digging. Or would my husband rather have those little boys sweating like animals in Calcutta?"

"When I was sixteen," I said, "I was already a combat veteran."

"If I had been there," she asserted, "I wouldn't have allowed that either."

"You would have ordered General Reynolds to send me home to my mother?"[22]

"I would have hidden you," she said and pinched me. "I know a secret place no general can go, Brevet Colonel Bruce."

She took me to our small tent and got me undressed for bed at three o'clock in the afternoon and did not let me arise to perform my morning toilet until past noon the next day. During the long night she had me promising I would let Charlie and French rest a full week before they had to report for duty and that I would never yell at "her boys" and that the men sent to Calcutta would have full rations and extra water and would have a half hour of rest for every two hours of work.

"Wouldn't you rather I wrap them in cotton and feed them caviar?" I said.

"I would like that," she admitted. "I will settle for you letting those two old darlings sit in the shade whenever the sun is out. You will let them, won't you, dear?"

She remained in good spirits up to an hour before the time we absolutely had to rise, at which time she began sobbing as I had never seen her do before. She cursed Fitz for bringing on the war. Forgetting the superstitions soldiers observe, she told me I had to survive the approaching battle.

"You have to come back to me!" she wailed. "You have to! Promise me you will ask Hood to put you in the rear when the shooting starts. I know I give you grief about Fitz. Please, this one

---

22. See Chapter One, footnote 9.

time: use your connections with him to save yourself! Say you'll do this. Do it for our baby."

"I promise," I said in a voice that would not have fooled anyone.

"You ******!"[23] she said and punched me in my bare stomach. "You could at least try to lie better than that!"

She pushed herself to the far corner of the cot and warned me she might kick me should I attempt to embrace her. She did punch at me a second time even as I managed to get my arms around her.

"I can promise you everything else," I told her. "I can't promise you I won't do my duty. This world is governed by violence, as it ever has been. We both must acknowledge that. We are up against History here, my love, the one thing we Yukons cannot defy. I'm sorry. I would rather live in our nation of two, governed by your kindness. Given a choice, I would always choose your ways. When we face the burden of History we have no choice. We can only do what we must. For as long as I know you will return to me when this is over I know I will tolerate in my heart anything I am required to do here in India."

Even my strong-willed Charlotte had to bow to History. She shook her head "yes" and wiped the tears from her face.

"I'm sorry, Bobby," she said. "I will never strike you again."

She held me close and wept some more, wailing aloud like a child who has injured her hand in a gate.

"I promise you this," I told her. "I will live through this, and be with you once more. I don't know how; I only know I will. I promise I will not do any more that would make you ashamed of me."

Ninety minutes later she had put on her brave face and was standing on the landing platform with her baggage and the other departing wives. The great zeppelin stood ready above them, full of helium and tugging at its mooring ropes.

Hood gave a short speech to the small crowd of well-wishers there to see the women off. He quoted a passage from Proverbs, then lost track of his thoughts when he started to say something about marriage. He stopped himself in midsentence, and wished everyone God's blessing and fell silent. The Marshal, never at a loss in battle or in front of his men, was nervous in the presence of the

---

23. As editor, I have decided to here delete a word no Yukon wife, even one under duress, could ever have uttered to her husband.

six women. His squat wife stepped forward and patted his arm to console him in his distress.[24]

A band played "Scotland the Brave." Why, I cannot say. The women then went up the landing steps and entered the belly of the lighter than air machine, resembling ants slipping into a fat watermelon. Charlotte hesitated while the other were going up and the flight attendants carried up her bags; she kissed me and kept kissing me for longer than Hood and the other senior officers in attendance would have wanted. The Marshal coughed and coughed again. She ignored him each time he did so.

"Take my rosary," she whispered to me. "I stole yours this morning while you were bathing. At six in the morning and at ten at night, we can pray together on opposite sides of the world."

"Sometime today, Colonel Bruce," said Hood.

Charlotte kissed me yet again and then another time.

"I dreamed the baby will be a girl," she said and laughed. "I am going to name her Mary, after my mother."

"The airship will be in Grand Harbor anon," said the Marshal.

Charlotte went to him and kissed him on his salt-and-pepper beard.

"Please take care of my Bobby, sir," she said.

The startled warrior said "Well," and added "Indeed." He stumbled backward to the edge of the landing platform and nearly fell onto the ground. He coughed into his fist and looked utterly lost. Daddy Montrose said something to the other staff officers standing below him, and they all laughed, or so they did until Hood turned about and glared at them. While the others were distracted, Charlotte went to the stairs, brushing against my body in her jolly fashion as she passed me. She winked back at me as she went in the open door. As the zeppelin left its upright moorings, she waved to me from a galley window, and smiled for me although I could tell she was crying once more. The flying machine quickly shrank to a black oval I could cover with my hand. A minute later it had become a tiny speck that disappeared into the clouds.

---

24. Martha Swiftly Kirkpatrick Hood (2372–2425) was a sheepherder's daughter and never was seen in polite company outside the Army. Gerald (pp. 1219–20) agrees with Bruce in this instance, and writes that the Hoods were an extraordinarily well-matched couple; the dour Hood was said to be happiest when she was near, and while apart from his wife he was known to become melancholy and—in spite of his strict religious piety—he often drank too much.

# THIRTEEN

THE SIX HUNDRED and seventeen fortifications the Sixth Army built south of the Ganges, east of the San, and around the Rajmahal air bases were each large enough to hold an entire regiment of one thousand men. The mainstay of the fortifications was a four-foot-wide zigzag trench bordered front and back with three-foot-high walls of polymer bags held in place by an internal structure of steel and pressed wood. The trenches themselves were lined with more polymer bags, as were the bombardment bunkers at the rear of the lines and in the center of the fortifications. A rifleman could stand upright behind the front wall and shoot at an angle through a variety of firing holes. Each trench was chest-high, and the polymer bag wall would reach above an upright man's head. The irregular front the trenches presented to enemy snipers gave them no clear shot at our men inside the bag walls. We laid barbed wire coils in front of the lines, and sprayed polymer enamel on the open ground in front of and behind the trenches, making everything near the men non-flammable. Shallow, unlined slit trenches a hundred yards behind the main trenches provided cover for the communications men who could scurry behind the lines with mirrors and flash Morse code messages to the mortar pits three hundred yards to the rear. Other men could use the slit trenches to carry ammunition and supplies to the front and to carry the wounded to hospitals in the rear. Between the outside trench and the mortar pits were two more walled trenches dug exactly like the outside one. For two thousand meters in every direction the soldiers burned off the foliage and raked the ground level. Given that most of our trenches faced major rivers that were hundreds of yards wide, at most places the infantrymen had a clear view of a mile or more of open space the enemy would have to charge across to reach our lines. The mortar operators premeasured their ranges so that a rain of their antipersonnel shells would fall in a half-mile-wide kill zone beyond the cleared ground. Our fifty caliber machine guns, which would have the highest ground in every section of the line, could see onto a bare arc of land at least two miles wide.

Hood kept the 220 howitzers and the twenty-one-inch monsters far to the rear, where he could use them to fire over the trenches at the enemy's point of attack. Like the mortar crews, the artillery men had measured a kill zone, except their area started from a mile out, and their fire was not directed by the communication men from the front but by the Blinking Stars. The 220s had an effective range of twenty-five miles, and the giant twenty-one-inchers could reach up to sixty. When the satellites told them the enemy was massing at a particular place, the artillery men would elevate and load for the given coordinates and lob thousands of antipersonnel shells on their targets. The tactical bombers (the T-10s) and the Bat Wing strategic bombers would meanwhile be dropping Fire Sticks, cluster bombs, and canister shot on the enemy army as soon as the fighting began.

Within the trenches Hood had divided the infantrymen into the three standard classes.[1] One in every ten men was a sniper and had a .223 rifle equipped with a telescopic sight.[2] This was necessarily a bolt action weapon because it fired an extra-long round that had a three-hundred-grain boost and a sharp carbon composite core that easily penetrated body armor at a distance of one mile. The ammunition inside the snipers' long rifles made a complete twist for every eight inches of barrel traveled, giving their bullets an extraordinarily rapid spin and stability in the air. Two of every ten men were designated marksmen and bore heavy .50 Minot rifles, which were also bolt action but had a standard bead and slot sight and fired a fat "heat" round that exploded on impact. When enemy soldiers passed the white stakes on the raked ground, indicating they were four hundred yards away, the marksmen would open on

1. See Chapter Twelve, footnote 4.

2. .223 of an inch in this instance, that being the measurement of the rifle's bore. The thirty and fifty caliber designations also indicate .333 and .50 of an inch.

them with ghastly effect. Four of every ten in the front lines were riflemen equipped with the standard issue Springer thirty caliber automatic assault rifle. When any enemy troops passed the blue stakes marking three hundred yards, these four riflemen and the two men in the squad[3] operating the fifty caliber air-cooled machine gun would commence fire. When (and if) enemy soldiers reached the red stakes a hundred yards from the trenches, the tenth man would shoot his canister tubes, spewing thousands of carbon filament pellets across the open ground. At the same time the demolition specialists would pull the yardarms on consecutive rows of claymore mines set outside the barbed wire. Should the enemy get so close they could toss hand grenades over the front wall, there was a polymer fabric awning our soldiers could open over their heads; the grenades would bounce off the fabric and over the slightly lower interior wall and would explode harmlessly on the bare ground. The men in the trenches wore helmets, flak jackets, and heavy trousers and overcoats, all of them treated with polymer, making the men gray figures among the gray bags and the gray painted ground. When the fighting grew hotter, the men could put on goggles and filter masks to protect their faces and lungs. Most of them wore their masks any time they were in the trenches as the vapors from the polymer could make them nauseous in the Indian heat.

Until 2420 a land battle any organized opponent waged against the Yukons had to be a matter of numerous small unit actions spread across a front that could be hundreds of miles wide. Thanks to the Blinking Stars, we always knew where an enemy might be gathering his forces, and with our air superiority we could inflict terrible casualties on our foes while we waited in ambush for their advance. Tanks, planes, and heavy artillery were useless against the Yukons because we could always destroy them long before they came close enough to do us harm. The most effective weapon any enemy could utilize against us were incendiaries they fired at us by means of small mortars or handheld rockets. The opposition's small units would advance as quickly as possible—before our aerial and artillery bombardments killed them all—and would fire on our positions as soon as they discovered where we were. Against these tac-

---

3. For the ladies reading this, I should explain that Yukon squadrons have ten men in them.

tics and weapons we had never lost a war, though we had suffered a close run on occasion, especially against the Chinese.[4] Small units and small incendiaries would not make a dent in Hood's polymer trenches. To break our lines would require the enemy to mass at the point of attack and launch waves of soldiers directly at our positions. If our foes advanced between fortifications, they would discover our entrenchments were big circles and that there were not only three rings within each circle but that there were also three tiers of forts, and each of these contained three more lines of trenches. An indirect assault on any position would put the enemy in open ground where fire would hit them from several directions. The one way to defeat us would be to charge headlong into the first line, take it, then take the two interior lines of that fort, then take the two additional rows of forts, thus breaking through nine trenches while enduring constant bombardment and fighting off counterattacks supported by our armor division. The losses such assaults would bring were sickening to contemplate. Before a shot had been fired, I could see Hood had put the Chinese in an impossible situation.

Our air bases at Luni and Rajmahal were the only two among the worldwide installations Fitz had built that were not on islands or inside Yukon territory proper. Hood presumed—correctly, as time would show—that no Turkish or Chinese fleet could challenge the Yukon Navy on the open sea. Our two complexes in India were the only places on the globe the enemy could bring the war to us. The Turks and the Chinese had no realistic chance of defeating us outright. They were equally aware that were they to capture our two bases, conquer our Indian allies, and capture the Sixth Army, they could perhaps propose a favorable armistice that would save themselves from the strategic pounding our bombers would be administering to their territories. We thus were discomfortingly aware before any fighting had taken place that we were standing on the location of the coming war's decisive battle. We did not know when the Chinese would march down the west bank of the Brahmaputra River and had to wait for the People's Friend to give the fateful order. The reader should mark that Hood had not yet in

---

4. In the Great Pacific War of 2360 to 2362, the Chinese had briefly occupied the northern two-thirds of India, but were routed at sea and in the air; attrition eventually forced them to retreat and to eventually sign the Armistice of Jakarta in 2363.

2420 shifted any of his forces, other than the Air Corps squadrons and the antiaircraft men, to protect Luni in the far west. Our intelligence told us that many months, maybe years, would pass before the Turks could muster an army able to cross the Thor Desert on account of the unending revolts taking place among the Arabs and other subject peoples within their empire. Hood's strategy necessarily rested upon defeating the Chinese before the Turks entered the field of combat.

The Sixth Army dug its earthworks in three months. My survey and special work crews went to every site, whereat our help was superfluous in all but two instances. At those two places my survey team made only some small adjustments in the placement of the heavy machine guns. The soldiers did use the topographical maps I had made, and that made me feel not entirely useless as I went from place to place along the lines and watched the troopers attack the ground with their shovels. Many a regimental colonel greeted me as "the chap who built the site," and offered me a spot of tea while the men labored under the none too gentle autumn sun. The same officers asked me what "those lads with the poles"—meaning my survey crews—were following me about for. My officer's log[5] tells me we helped fill some ravines within the two thousand meter killing zones and leveled a few mounds. French and Charlie got to sleep more than they had in four decades while Charlotte's "boys" sat about playing mumblety peg and munching on the tinned cookies their mothers had sent them.

South of Gaya, not far from where legend says Siddhartha Gautama[6] sat beneath a Bo tree and received spiritual enlightenment, I discovered a flaw in the Sixth's lines, as Hood had intimated I would. We had lightly defended the Ganges to our north and east, as that ocean river was too broad for the Chinese to cross and then attack the fortifications on the south bank. The Yukon Navy would additionally send Hood gunboats to help turn back any suicidal attempts the enemy might make against those portions of our lines. The eastern shore of the shallower and narrower San was heavily

---

5. The daily log every officer and NCO must keep; Bruce's log exists and is in agreement with his memoirs, proving that he lies only about nonmilitary affairs.

6. The Buddha (563–483 B.C.), founder of a pagan cult still adhered to in dismal parts of Asia.

defended from where it emptied into the Ganges to a point sixty miles to the south, where our lines turned sharply to the east. At this axis point was the flaw. Atop a lone hill in the San's flood plain Hood's men had placed a single thousand-man fortification that commanded the field of view for ten miles in every direction. The adjoining forts in the line, both to the north and the east, were at least a quarter mile away, making the hill fort stick out like a bump from the rest of our defenses. If the Chinese took the hill, they would be able to fire down onto the other nearby emplacements and so control that entire section. Once they had crossed the San to the south of our lines, the enemy would make a reconnaissance in force against our southern defenses; they would quickly find the irregularity, and there they would focus their assault.

I at once went to Hood with my finding. He smiled and said I was a sharp fellow.

"I knew you would spot it right off. Put a star beside Colonel Bruce's name," he joked to his secretary.

"Do you want me to correct it, sir?" I asked him. "We could level the hill, or move the other fortifications up, making the line—"

He cut me off.

"That is where the Chinese will make the battle," he said. "There I will give them a proper cappuccino."[7]

"If they don't give us one, sir," I said. "The rumor mill has it that there are close to five million Chinese mustered north of the borderline."

"Never believe rumors, Robert," said Hood. "The Blinking Stars tell us there are approximately five million Revolutionary Guardsmen about Wei. Their total army numbers closer to twenty million."

I was thankful there were no mirrors in the Marshal's tent for I probably turned white when he told me the size of the force that Peking's tyrant had sent to the Himalayas. Hood did not seem to

---

7. A cappuccino was in ancient times some sort of a hot coffee drink. In 2062, on the eve of the Land Pirate War, a wealthy Yellowjacket couple stopped at Bob's Diner, near Crowheart, Wyoming (now part of Northfield), and demanded cappuccinos. Robert Smith, the diner's proprietor and a local Yukon chieftain, told them: "I'll give you cappuccinos," dragged the couple outside, and clubbed them to death. Smith went on to become a Yukon general, and cappuccino has ever since been soldier's slang for a mortal beating.

care whether the Chinese Army was large or not. He directed my attention to the twenty-four-month calendar for 2420 and 2421 he had hanging from his central tent pole.

"They have more men in Tibet than they can feed," he said. "Their logistic capacities are stretched to the limit and beyond. Every truck in their empire is carrying food to the front, and still a thousand men a week are dying up there from disease, cold, hunger, thirst. When the bombing starts, they will lose a quarter million dead and wounded on a cloudy day, and two million or more when we have clear sky. They have forty days, maximum. Forty days to march down the Brahmaputra and the Ganges, cross the San, and defeat us utterly at the hill south of the Bo tree. They really should move before the rains come back; they can't move fast in all that muck, or else they will have to wait until the Turks get together a force in Pakistan. But the Turks are a broken reed, Robert. A broken reed that will pierce a man's hand should he lean upon it.[8] If the Chinese do wait for the Turks, we will strike them when the monsoons return."

"Twenty million?" I said.

"To win great victories, God must send us great enemies, Sir Robert," said Hood. "Our fathers chastised them with whips, and we will chastise them with scorpions.[9]

"Oh," he said and snapped his fingers as he remembered something. "I heard from the Consul last night on the Blinking Stars. He has sent Valette, the showy fop, to Mexico City for some sort of Conference of the Americas. All of the Latin countries are sending ambassadors. According to Fitz, this will tell the shape of things to come.[10] Now I have a staff meeting in three minutes. About your business, Sir Robert."

The ambassadors' conference in Mexico City was soon the major topic in the two-week-old newspapers I and the other soldiers got

8. A paraphrase of Second Kings 18:21.

9. A play upon First Kings 12:14. Hood here refers to the Yukon victory in the Great Pacific War a generation earlier; he means that this war will be worse for the Chinese than that one.

10. Bruce's account of the Conference of the Americas in 2420 is sketchy but essentially correct. For a full telling of this seminal event see Anthony Teachwell Thatcher's *Mexico, Delhi, and London* (Shirbert and Sons, Mountain View, 2476).

in the mail from home. From the letters Charlotte and other family members sent me, I saw it had also captured the attention of ordinary citizens, largely because of the outlandish demands Valette made upon the other nations' diplomats. On October 8, 2420, the stylish, rather precious Lord Jean Valette stood in the legislative hall of the Mexican capital and told the Latin nations their separate national sovereignties were at an end. He told them the Yukon Air Corps had strategic bases in the Galapagos, the Falklands, Florida, and on the Rio Grande. From these bases we could bomb every square inch of Latin America with our new airplanes. Those nations that did not agree to the Four Points the Yukons were presenting to the conference would be attacked forthwith. These Four Points, Valette told them, were:

I. The nations were to destroy their military and commercial airplanes.

II. The nations were to scuttle their warships, and the Yukon Navy assumed the right to enter all points in the ocean and to destroy any pirate vessels they found.

III. Yukon merchants could trade without restrictions or tariffs in the other nations, and while any Yukons were on foreign soil they were to be protected from the natives.

IV. Every nation would pay a yearly tribute to the Yukon Confederacy equivalent to ten percent of each nation's gross national product as computed by the Yukon Consul.

Reading of these demands in faraway India, I almost believed Fitz was playing a vast practical joke on the world. The demands Valette made in Mexico were absurd, even when put to people we had bullied for centuries. I told Charlie and French, both of whom took everything the Consul did to be as just as the Gospel and who devoured the newspapers immediately after I had read them, that this conference represented a gross overreaching on Fitz's part, and we would soon read that Valette was on another mission to amend these four demands. A Captain Meyers of the Second Infantry and I made a wager on the affair: I bet the government in Cumberland would be backing down from the Four Points within a month. The more daring Captain Meyers bet they would not make their retreat until Christmas.

In 2420 we had the Mexicans very much under our heel. On the day Valette presented the Four Points, the other delegates present left the capital in a collective huff. The government of Octavio Passado, which the Yukons had put into office in 2412,[11] signed the necessary documents that afternoon. The Caribbean Confederacy's representatives snuck back into the Capitol Building under the cover of night and likewise signed the Four Points. Their tiny nations lay too near Yukon territory, and they had no options other than to acquiesce. We in India half expected those developments. When we read in newspapers that two weeks after the conference Brazil, Peru, Venezuela, the United States of Central America, and Guyana had agreed the Four Points, we thought the journalists were mistaken. Then the Blinking Stars brought us the same unbelievable reports. Only Greater Colombia and the Argentine Empire had refused to sign.

The Yukon Confederacy declared war upon the two defiant Latin states on October 25, 2420, and Captain Myers and I had to call off our wager. The newspapers we read in the Rajmahal Hills gave accounts of bombing sorties over Buenos Ares and of enemy ships sunk in Cartagena harbor. Reporters with Admiral Semmes[12] told of riding down both coasts of South America as the Yukon dreadnoughts drove the pitiful remains of the Latin navies ahead of them. The Consul allowed these seagoing journalists to use the Blinking Stars to send their dispatches home, thus assuring the Yukon papers would be crammed with items about big warships plowing through uncontested oceans. The air bases the strategic bombers used were off limits to newsmen. Everything we learned in the papers in regard to the bombing raids came from the War Ministry in Cumberland. We read that the Argentine and Colombian air forces were destroyed on the ground, and we saw the names of the twenty-some Yukon pilots and navigators

---

11. At the end of the Seventh Mexican War.

12. Rear Admiral Michelangelo Raphael Semmes (2339–2452) commanded the Southern Fleet during the Four Points War. Fitzpatrick the Elder had given him command in 2401. Though he was in his eighties during the war, Semmes served with great skill and vigor.

killed in action.[13] From our remote perspective, this seemed a peculiar, nearly bloodless war. Armies were not on the march; our
forces had the skies and seas to themselves; our advantages were so
overwhelming there seemed no one else in the war other than the
Yukons. The photographs we saw showed sleek ships sailing in formation and young seamen resting on sunny decks. One reporter I
read took to writing items on the species of fish he had sighted off
his ship's bow, as there was nothing else happening on the ship that
interested him.

Charlie and French became my unofficial batmen in my quarters; in plain talk that meant the two old sailors cooked and cleaned
for me. Most of the other daylight hours they followed me about
like two cocker spaniels after their master. The two old men hung
on everything I said, and I told them this strange conflict in and
around South America was bound to have a messy ending. We
Yukons, I explained to them, could destroy the enemy's ships and
planes, blow up their factories, and disrupt the Argentine and Colombian infrastructures; none of this would bring a final victory to us.
The Colombian and Argentine population would retreat to the
countryside and live on their farms and in their villages, unable to
retaliate against us but entirely unconquered.

"Strategic bombing does not win wars," I told them one day
while we were poring over the newspapers from home. "The Consul is on the verge of relearning that ancient lesson."

"Then when Lord Fitzpatrick sees it don't work over there,"
suggested French, "he may call off the show over here."

"A pleasant thought," I said. "No, I doubt that is an option."

Charlie resisted any suggestion of the Consul's fallibility. He
believed Fitz had some magic up his sleeve that would negate History's lessons.

"Lord Fitzpatrick knows things we don't," he said. "Napoleoni
might not have won with bomber planes. He wasn't Lord Fitzpatrick, was he?"

Napoleoni (Napoleon to the rest of the world) did not have
bombers at his disposal. I could have disabused Charlie of that notion and I would not have diminished his faith in the Consul. The

13. Twenty-two Yukon aviators died in the Latin portion of the Four Points War. Two
sailors died in a boiler explosion aboard the battleship *Majesty,* and four others were
killed when a powder bag exploded prematurely inside a turret on the cruiser *Mississippi.*

majority of the Sixth Army shared his high regard for Fitz. In 2420 the cult of Fitzpatrick the Younger remained in ascension both in the Confederacy and among the military men the Consul had sent abroad. His portrait was everywhere within the Sixth's encampment; on duffle bags and footlockers and—may God forgive them— next to the altars in the tent chapels the soldiers had pitched throughout the fortifications. Anything less than unconditional victory over the Colombians and Argentines would be proving the Consul was merely human, and our gung ho troopers would never admit he was anything as lowly as that.

On November 24th the soldiers' faith completely bested my pessimism. Only thirty-five days after hostilities had commenced, the Colombian president agreed to the Four Points. Four days later the Argentines did likewise. In a bit more than a month, we had conquered the entire western hemisphere.

The Sixth held a grand parade in celebration of this triumph on the other side of the globe. The bagpipe bands played "Black Jack Davy" and "Cam Ye O'er Frae France," and four hundred thousand boots tramped through the muddy grounds. Hood led the men, ten thousand at a time, in mass prayer services of thanksgiving. He read to each assembly from Deuteronomy:

"Know therefore this day that he who goes before you as a devouring fire is the Lord your God; He will destroy them and enslave them before you; so you shall drive them out, and make them perish quickly, as the Lord God has promised you."[14]

I was in the command tent the night of the celebration and overheard Daddy Montrose asking Hood if the Marshal had not perhaps laid the Lord God on a bit thick.

"For all we know of it," said Montrose, "the Air Corps burned the poor Latins into cinders. My guess is this Aranov has created some diabolical incendiary that ended everything over there this quickly. I'm not a religious man, Jerry. That said, I know natural justice, and I know plain murder. If there is a Lord God, I will lay you a year's wages He isn't showering His blessings on Yukon souls right now."

"The men need to hear it, Israel," said Hood. "God is on the men's side. He does not hold them accountable for the Four Points."

---

14. Deuteronomy, 9:3.

"Will your God be as forgiving of those in command?" said Montrose.

"Why, Daddy!" said Stein, for that young Lord was lounging on a cot at the tent's rear. "I am disappointed in you! Did you know there are those around the Consul who would take what you just now said for treason?"

Hood had ordered Montrose to ignore Stein. The general accordingly excused himself from the tent while his famous temper was still in check.

"Will you weep for the chinks you're going to kill as you do over this handful of dead dagos, old chap?" Stein called after Daddy as the corps commander passed through the tent flaps. "Buckets of blood now, rivers full then, *comilitome!*"

"Must you, Peter?" asked Hood.

"I prefer Lord Colonel Stein," said Stein. "Yes, I must. Did you hear Watchcharm Davis was over here, Robert?" he said to me.

"In the Third Air Corps?" I said.

"A fighter pilot. He has a squadron under him. I gather he's in command only when airborne. Watchcharm is the opposite of Antaeus; he is at his best when he does not touch the earth. I'm sure he wants to see you, Robert, and take you for a ride up in the hazy sky."

"I would advise against that, Sir Robert," said Hood. "Lord Davis is a very brave pilot, too brave, perhaps, for we land dwellers."

"There I have to agree with you, Judge," chimed in Stein, and he took a drink from his pocket flask. "Davis is terrifying in the air. His mates say he's scared off two navigators already."

"Drunk again," said Hood. "Lord Colonel Stein, can you not see what you are doing to yourself?"

"Whatever I'm doing, I will look better doing it than you ever could, dear sir," he replied.

"I should go, gentlemen," I said and rose.

"I'm just getting interesting," said Stein and took another swig.

"I expect another report tomorrow, Sir Robert," said Hood, saluting me. "Meanwhile, stay out of Lord Davis' fighter plane. You are no good to me dead."

I surveyed the last of the fortifications before I visited Davis. Among the *Baseileis*, he was the one least changed since our time at the War College. Lord Gawain Davis had stayed boyish, daring, and assured of his personal immortality. Like other brave men, he projected an energy that less courageous men, such as myself, enjoyed basking in, almost making us forget that being close to Davis could be hazardous. Hood knew the risks a man ran in combat, and he was brave in spite of what he knew; Davis did not realize there were dangers one should fear, and men who could be frightened baffled him.

Having married two years earlier, he was already the father of a baby boy. As one could have predicted, his young wife was a female version of himself.[15] Davis proudly told me of how while she was four months pregnant she had cleared a rail fence on horseback and slew a two-hundred-and-sixty-pound wild boar with a twelve-foot lance. As he told it, when he left for India he promised her he would shoot down forty Chinese bombers.

"Plus twenty for the baby," she had demanded.

"She's a damned pistol that one," he told me. "I love her to death, Bobby. Any child of hers is going to be a warrior. Our little Jack can already walk like a trooper. Angelica's going to teach him to say 'Enjoy Hell' first thing."[16]

While we sat in his tent we partook of the good red bourbon Davis' father made in the family distillery. I was breaking a promise I had made to Charlotte. (Like any other man, I too could pretend to be a brave man when my wife was not there to see through my pretensions, and I did not want to appear to be a teetotaler in front of Davis.) There was a collection of various beer steins sitting against the canvas wall above Davis' icebox; these, he explained when I remarked upon them, were trophies he had won from other pilots in aerial contests.

"What sort of contests?" I asked, though looking back on the conversation, I admit I should not have posed the question.

"Putting out on low fuel. Gliding back the farthest without

15. Lady Angelica Constancy Williams Davis (2394–2475), born to a family of wealthy horse breeders, was part of a fashionable hunting set in Desert Province.

16. "Enjoy Hell" is, of course, the traditional Yukon battle cry. Lord John Isaac Davis, the only child of Lord and Lady Gawain Davis, was killed in a glider accident when he was fifteen.

power. Flying under bridges. Flying the highest, above the oxygen. You know: pilot stuff."[17]

"The Chinese shouldn't bother attacking us," I said. "They should wait for you daredevils to kill yourselves."

"We're not that bad," said Davis. "Go up with me. You'll see."

"Hood ordered me not to. He seems to think you might kill me."

"I wouldn't kill you. Not on purpose, anyhow. That is, in an airplane, when one dies, everybody dies, don't they?"

"Your navigators must love you."

"Can't seem to keep a permanent one," he confessed. "This last man I had in the back seat transferred to the infantry. Said he'd rather be in the damned trenches than fly another five minutes with me. You're an engineering johnny, Bobby; you understand the *geomathatics* of the rangefinder—"

"The word is geometry, Watchcharm," I said. "We took the class together."

"I remember. I sat behind you, old man. You understood it, and I had a pilot's eyesight to rely on when test time came. So, any old how, you want to come up with me today?"

"Hood forbade it."

"Judge Jerry will never know."

"I gave him my word," I said.

"Well, if you're afraid, then . . ."

I realized Watchcharm Davis may not have passed a math exam on his own nor had he mused upon his life long enough to have ever known a moment of self-doubt. I also realized he knew how to provoke another Yukon man. Among us, slander against one's family is endurable when the slanderer smiles, denying God is acceptable in an academic setting, and after a few drinks one can make a disparaging remark about another man's wife. Never, never, never, not until the sun explodes, will we let anyone doubt our courage. When we are young our fathers tell us the story of the brave soldier boy[18] and teach us that a brave man dies in God's favor while a coward is a stranger to Heaven and to his family. Davis

17. Steam engines need both an outlet for vapor and an intake for oxygen. To fly at a height above 20,000 feet creates the possibility of extinguishing the boiler fire.

18. Bruce means the story of Peter Neely, the young private who at Tucson in 2098 attacked the Mexican line alone and was killed rather than let himself be taken prisoner.

had challenged my manhood, therefore the promises I had made to Charlotte and Hood suddenly meant nothing. Not for the first time—and sadly, not for the last—I did as I had been trained to do and not what Charlotte would have desired.

"A short trip would be fine," I said.

The ground crew needed half an hour to fire up the F-101's twin boilers. Davis and I put on flight suits and helmets lined with wool and secured ourselves beneath the canopy bubble. The foam-filled navigator's seat at the rear of the cockpit slowly adjusted to the weight of my body, and the ring at the base of the canopy hissed as a mechanic with an air pump sealed the bubble top shut. For the first three-quarters of an hour after takeoff Davis gave me an uneventful ride. I used the solar compass and the maps in the flight kit to direct him north over the wide Ganges and the thousands of green patches of the separate farm fields. Below us our gray trenches cut through this beautiful land like the outline of an infected wound, another visual reminder that we were intruders in that once fertile country. While Davis followed the river I used the rangefinder to calculate we were cruising at two thousand feet above the milky brown water. We were not on a combat mission so the Blinking Stars in our quadrant of the globe were not flashing out our latitude and longitude to the slowly rotating and ultraviolet-sensitive ammonia paper in the glass dome beside the navigator's seat. We necessarily flew by following the landmarks and by my calculations. Davis laughed at me when I took a whole half a minute to take a reading with the handheld rangefinder.

"You wouldn't have that long to measure the distance to a Chinese bomber," he yelled to me above the shrill whine of the two high-compression engines.

We turned in a wide, slow circle over the long bridge at Bhagalpur to put ourselves on the span's east side. Davis suddenly flipped the plane upside down and made it fall wing over wing like a leaf fluttering down from a dying tree. My stomach bounced off my diaphragm and onto my intestines each time he made the plane roll.

"The F-101 is fast," narrated Davis, who remained outwardly calm while gradually arousing himself from somewhere deep inside. "She's not the most maneuverable heap of bolts there is. Hard to handle. You ready to shoot the bridge?"

"What does that entail?" I stammered.

"An easy run under a wide section," he said.

He leveled off a few feet above the river and sped straight for the suspension bridge. I had time to think of my wife and to close my eyes. "Oh, Charlotte," I thought, "I am so sorry I am dying like an idiot." In the darkness I heard a scream sound in front of me. We were past the bridge and flying straight upward when I opened my eyes again and realized the scream had come from my excited pilot.

"Nice and wide under there!" shouted Davis. "The second span from the north bank is around six feet wider than my wings. You have to hit your nose right on the black mark Charlie Smithers painted or you'll take off a wing, and it's in the drink with you. Not that you would know. Hit the water at six hundred m.p.h., and you might as well crash into steel."

"Charlie Smithers?" I said.

Davis looped back to the east side of the bridge and was making a second run, this time at the aforementioned narrow second span. I could not see any damned black mark. Davis, the brainless maniac, again screamed with delight as the rusting girders of the bridge's underside came right at us.

"Oh, Charlotte, I am so far from you!" I thought and closed my eyes once more. "Forgive me for not protecting myself!"

"Whoa, that was close!" shouted Watchcharm.

"Thank you, Lord, thank you!" I thought. "Life is good. I love my wife. I love living."

"You and Charlie Smithers," I said.

"Smithers?" said Davis. "Charlie only painted the mark. He didn't live long enough to shoot the bridge. We in the 55th Squadron had to bury what was left of him outside the camp. You know, I think that mark of his is off to the right."

He flipped and tumbled until I blacked out for a spell. Davis whooped and screamed and laughed and had a wonderful time as he repeatedly abused my nervous system. He was not torturing me intentionally. To administer torture one must know that others can suffer. He dove at the ground to practice his strafing runs, and drove my eyeballs against their sockets and my internal organs against my spine. Davis whooped and yelled like a rambunctious boy riding a diversion at a country fair. I expect he thought I was enjoying the ride as much as he was.

"If I survive this," I thought, "I will never get on another airplane here in India. I will never visit Davis, or his lunatic, boar-slaying wife! God above must hide His face from what those two must do together for recreation!"

"We left with an eighth of a tank! Think of that!" I heard Davis say somewhere beyond my fog of disorientation. "We have to be getting back."

"Too bad," I said.

When we landed I was out of the cockpit and taking off my flight suit before Davis had turned off his propellers. Even on *terra firma* the center of balance inside my skull was whirling about like a carousel that had stripped its gears. I saluted Davis and pointed to my watch and said something about pressing matters in the trenches. I added I would be very busy for the next few months and could not tell when I might get another opportunity to fly with him again. My legs quickly carried me out of Davis' sight. Then I vomited everything that was in my stomach.

"Oh, Charlotte," I thought. "It is Heaven to be alive and to able to think of you! I will not be that foolish again. I will do better. You'll see."

I had to exercise my imagination to be busy the rest of that dry season, for the entire Sixth Army was soon idle. We had completed the trenches and the lorries had brought more ammunition rounds than the infantrymen could carry and more ordnance than the hangars could safely hold. Throughout that same season the Chinese stayed put on their side of the border.

From the newspapers we learned there had been a brief and inconclusive conference in Lagos City whereat Lord Valette presented the Four Points to a cadre of sub-Saharan African leaders, most of whom were not in a position to negotiate over anything.[19] The Africans put off signing because, they rightfully argued, they were unable to take independent action. (In the twenty-fourth and early twenty-fifth centuries, the Unorganized African States—as the Yukons labeled the region—were the site of constant proxy wars waged by the three great powers. The Yukons gave supplies and training to anyone in Africa claiming to be Christian, the Turks gave similar aid to the region's Moslem factions, and the Chinese backed any and every revolutionary movement. The true object of the great powers was control over the fabulous mineral wealth found largely in the continent's eastern and southern rift valleys. Decades

---

19. See Gerald, pp. 1921–24, for an account of the failed Lagos Conference.

of continuous warfare had obliterated the area's economic and political structures and had left everything from Cape Horn to Senegal under the control of local warlords and their armed thugs, a few of whom traded with the I.T. at Lagos. They were the so-called leaders Valette had addressed.)[20] The delegates returned home bearing news of the Four Points to the various groups within Africa. That broadcasting of the Yukon intentions was, I suspect, the result Valette and Fitz had hoped the conference would have.

A third Four Points conference was convened at Delhi during January of 2421 for the nations of Europe and Asia. The Chinese refused to attend. The Turks did, and they would not sign the accord.[21] Except for our allies the Slavs, all the foreign ambassadors left this meeting in a belligerent state of mind, and bestowed ample abuse upon the Yukons for attempting to place their nations in bondage. Yet the war in the Old World did not begin. The Sixth Army sat behind their earthworks week after week and waited for the Chinese to start marching south down the narrow Brahmaputra Valley. They waited until many of them doubted there would ever be a Chinese advance. To keep his men from becoming soft, Hood had to order his men from the earthworks for two hours of exercise every day. To counter their boredom he allowed them six hours a day to wander beside the river or to read the books the Literary Societies sent them through the mail.

Lord Valette passed through our peaceful camp before he made his return trip from Delhi to Grand Harbor. Hood served him dinner in the Marshal's tent, and both Hood and the young Foreign Minister regretted the occasion. The delicate Valette could not lower himself to eat bully beef and boiled cabbage. For his part, Hood had never before beheld the genteel young Lord unrestrained by Fitz's control or the rules of the War College. Upon becoming Foreign Minister and garnering considerable power in addition to the family power he had inherited, the faults in Valette's character,

---

20. Bruce is again showing his disloyalty to the Confederacy. Foreign interference—at least not Yukon interference—cannot be blamed for Africa's sorry condition. Authorities on the matter agree that the genetic inferiority of the continent's inhabitants is the reason why Africa lacked (and still lacks) political coherence.

21. See Gerald, pp. 2063–78. The Turks were by this time resigned to following the lead of the far more powerful Chinese in diplomatic and military dealings with the Yukons.

which we had only suspected when we knew him as a college student, had grown to their adult stature. As members of the *Basileis,* Davis, Stein, and myself were invited to Hood's tent to dine and to witness Valette and his entourage of five pretty young women and four even prettier young men break bread on military tinware while they sat across a campaign table from Marshal Hood, Daddy Montrose, George "Woodenhead" Santeen,[22] and William "Blue Light" Van Fleet.[23] The young aristocrats in their velvet topcoats, perfumes, and pearls and the famed fighting generals of the Sixth in their gray fatigues and untrimmed beards were as unlikely a group as Fate could have gathered together in one small place.

The English writer Oscar Wilde once traveled the nineteenth-century American west and read poetry and lectured on aesthetics in an affected lisp to gun-toting cowboys. He could have looked upon the scene that night and would have recognized the dynamic presiding over Hood's dinner party for Valette. Mr. Wilde was not shot dead during his visits to old Dodge City and Cheyenne, and, happily, the Foreign Minister and his people escaped Hood's tent unharmed that night; I did fear how Woodenhead Santeen fingered his sidearm—the makeup the young men were wearing distressed him greatly—but the dinner passed without a major incident. Taking a pause from picking at his food, the Ambassador told a ribald story in *koine,* knowing full well the straitlaced generals were college graduates and would understand him and would be offended he should say such things in the presence of ladies. The one young lady there who did know Greek threw her head back in a most unlady-like fashion and laughed aloud. (The amused young woman was, incidentally, none other than Lady Chelsea Virtue DeShay, the future Chrysanthemum Woman, then a slender eighteen-year-old with large black eyes and not yet married to Lord Newsome, the future Consul. At the time I knew only that she was a first cousin of Fitz's wife Lady Joan. How she came to be so well educated and

---

22. General George Sixpence Santeen (2370–2495), commanded the Fourth Corps of the Sixth Army. Called "Woodenhead" by his men for his complete lack of tactical skill, he was a brave man who excelled under the guidance of Hood's superior intellect.

23. William Holyname Van Fleet (2368–2421), commanded the First Corps, the elite "Northfield" units that were the cutting edge of the Sixth Army. Bruce describes him in more detail below. Among active soldiers of that era, only Hood had more combat decorations than Van Fleet.

to be an associate of Valette at such an immature age are mysteries to this soldier. It is eerie to think back upon that girlish laughing face on that night and to know that she would grow to become the most despised individual in the Confederacy's History.[24]) One of Valette's men made a biting comment upon the faded gray uniforms everyone at the encampment was wearing; I suppose he thought we could wear whatever we wanted. Daddy Montrose asked why young men of their age and good health were not serving in the armed forces when the Consul had declared a time of crisis. Lady Chelsea fired back that these were noblemen. She said Lords have privileges commoners do not.

"Since when are they excused from serving, Lady?" asked Van Fleet. "The military code applies to Lords and lowborn alike."

"Our Lord Fitzpatrick issued an edict in April," said one of the young men. "We are excused after graduation from college, if we so desire."[25]

That revelation ended what little conversation the group made that evening. I had grown up in an isolated region and for the sake of my Knighthood I had been given a privileged man's education at college. Until I served in India I did not appreciate the resentment most lowborn military men feel for the nobles. The generals in Hood's tent had heard rumors of young Lords calling Fitz "our Lord" and were less shocked by the casual usage of that phrase than they were when they learned of the new edict. From their perspective, the Consul had removed the one obligation the wealthy no-

---

24. Lady Newsome, the Chrysanthemum Woman or "the Empress," as her many enemies would call her, made her debut upon the public stage as an "aide" to Lord Valette. The evil young creature, the future dominant power in the Shay regime, had been a student in Lady Fitzpatrick's school for young ladies, and, as the whole Confederacy would come to regret, Lady Fitzpatrick had seen to it that her young charge was put on the Foreign Minister's staff, probably as a favor to the DeShay family, who were by then bound to the Fitzpatricks by marriage.

25. Refers to Consular Edict 23, which allowed a Lord "of delicate physiology" to end his military obligations at age twenty-two. Lord Fitzpatrick made the proclamation in letters he sent to noble families rather than making a public announcement. The edict was exceedingly unpopular among the commoners, and became more so during the Shay regime when a majority of young noblemen declared themselves too delicate for service. When the Shays fell in 2453, Edict 23 was at once repealed. Most Historians believe Lord Fitzpatrick was badly advised on this issue and blame the Shay family for the edict, despite what Bruce asserts below.

bility had to all the Confederacy. Hereafter the Consul and the Senate could send the armed forces into battle knowing no one of standing would be killed. To the young nobles on Valette's side of the table, paying higher taxes than the commoners satisfied their civic duty; risking combat would, to them, be asking too much, and the arrogance they wore on their lace cuffs did not improve the generals' opinion of them. Stein whispered to me at the side table where we were seated that he wished Fitz had issued the edict before he had accepted a twelve-year commission. Hood sensed the tension in the group, and decided the time had come to adjourn the unhappy party.

"Let us drink a toast to the Consul," he said and stood upright with his glass in his hand. "It is time we old men were in bed and you young people were off."

Lord Valette gathered Davis, Stein, and myself to his side after we had downed a glass of port to Fitz's health and were outside Hood's tent and strolling toward the waiting zeppelin. He gave Davis a word of encouragement, told him everyone back home was proud of him, et cetera. Valette did not mean any of it. He told Stein the Consul was probing the matter of the alleged thefts and that Stein should attend to his duties until the investigation was complete.

"Why can't I go home and have a position in the government?" asked Stein. "I don't do anything here. Why wasn't I told Fitz was changing the code? You're traveling the world with these tarts, while I'm stuck here in a mud hole, twiddling my thumbs and waiting for the Chinese to come and stick a bayonet down my throat."

"This one has a big mouth," said Lady Chelsea.

"Be quiet, C.," Valette told her. "You will have to do as Hood tells you for the time being," he said to Stein, and put his arm around Banker's shoulders. "At this time next year, you will be back in Fitz's inner circle and have tarts—as you call them—up to your elbows. This is politics. Fitz had to ameliorate the higher taxes he put on the Lords, so he let some of these stunning specimens," he pointed to his male companions, "go home to mama. Make the noble hearth and home right happy. How is the wife?"

"How is anyone's wife after a couple years?" said Stein. "She wants to shop and have babies."

"Those are healthier interests than some women have, don't you agree, Lady Chelsea?" he said and chucked the young woman under the chin. "In one short year," he said to Stein, "you will be out of gray denim and into silks—and do a little shopping of your own on the side."

"I am not a boy you can buy with a nod and a promise, Jeanie," said Stein. "I want to wear the purple like you."[26]

"Doesn't everyone? Sweet C. here would dress the entire DeShay family in purple, if she could," said Valette and patted Stein on the back. "I would love to talk to you some more, Banker. I have to get out of here, *etque* I really need to have a word with Bobby before I go. Privately. We need but a few seconds. Stay here and get acquainted with C. You will not find her like in a thousand years on a million worlds, I assure you."

Valette transferred his arm to my shoulders and led me out of the others' hearing range.

"Bobby, Bobby, Bobby," he said in a low voice and shook his head. "What were you thinking?"

"To what are you referring, Mr. Ambassador?" I asked him.

" 'Mr. Ambassador.' I like that title," he mused. "I am not speaking to you of how you comb your hair, old boy, although that could stand some improvement. I mean, How could you marry that saloon keeper's Catholic daughter?"

"The Consul's mother chose her for me," I said.

"You could have rejected her. You're a smart chap. You knew she was inappropriate," said Valette. "Fitz's mother sent you the girl to spite the Consul. Lady Fitzpatrick is fully aware the girl has some connection to Doctor Murrey, who is not exactly a favorite of Fitz's. You, on the other hand, are a particular pet of the Consul's. You could have become the chief engineer in the entire Confederacy, provided you had chosen your wife with your brain and not with some other body part. After the war, Fitz would have had you building that absurd worldwide railroad he wants. Now how can the Consul bring you and your wife into his exclusive company? You've badly hurt yourself, old man."

"I did not realize Fitz was so concerned about the social stature of his officers' wives," I said, disliking Valette more every second we were together. "The lowborn have always been welcome in his company."

---

26. In imitation of the Roman nobility, Lord Fitzpatrick's closest associates wore at least one small article of purple clothing. During the Shay regime, the ruling inner circle wore purple and the golden chrysanthemum seal to show loyalty to Lady Chelsea.

"Social stature is not the issue," said Valette. "Security is. We don't know what this wife of yours is. She has no family, unless you want to call a drunken stepfather and his two loutish sons a family. Who knows who else she might know among the criminal classes? As I say, Fitz's agents say she knew Doctor Murrey from the War College. Look, in case you haven't figured it out, he is a Timerman, Bobby. He got her into Fitz's mother's school. Probably got the old girl to pick Charlotte to be your bride. How are we to know she is not a Timerman agent herself?"

"What you mean to say," I said, enraged to hear the fop speak of Charlotte so carelessly, "is how are you to know whether she is aware that Fitz was on familiar terms with the Gyor brothers?"

He took his arm off me and took a long stride away from my side. Valette was the most cunning of men, save for our friend the Consul. Like Fitz, he never made a gesture he had not rehearsed in his mind hours earlier. A second earlier he had been my concerned friend in every cell of his pampered body; after I had said the magic name "Gyor" he assumed the role of an offended political insider.

"Why not say that louder so we can both be impaled?" he asked. "I suppose you think divorce is out of the question?"

"I care for her, Lord Valette," I said. "I don't want any future without her."

"I blame commoners' morality," said Valette and made a superfluous wave toward the firmament. "I don't blame you personally, Bobby. Hopefully, Fitz won't either. You lowborn fellows have to keep it in your pants until you marry. Then the first time you sample the goods you don't know any better than to go crazy over your new wives. If you had been given a better life, you would have run your plow through a few fields already and would know there is more to life than growing corn, as the old story goes.[27] On another subject: our friend Banker over there has given you a bundle of papers, something to do with thefts in the Quartermaster's office?"

"Yes?"

"Hang onto them. Should you survive this to-do you're about to have with the tea and bamboo crowd, you will be a witness against O'Brian for setting Stein up."

---

27. The reference here is to a coarse and seemingly deathless old joke, one too crude to quote in print. Any gentleman who has ever traveled in a smoking car will have already heard it, and lady readers will not wish to.

"You're kidding. O'Brian really did it?"

"Fitz's agents have the goods on him. The Consul will await the proper time to deal with him."

"What do you think Fitz will do?" I asked.

Valette and Fitz were, as I say, both master actors. Yet when Fitz adopted a persona, he really believed he had become that person, and could wear that new skin as his own, and could say any words he deemed necessary with a certain degree of conviction. With Valette, everything was obviously pretend. Behind each mask he wore there was always the old Valette. In a careless moment—and he had many—his real personality would inevitably make a fleeting appearance. My naive question provided him one of those moments. He showed his grinning teeth to me like a wolf leering at a lamb, and something evil illuminated his eyes.

"You really can't guess, Bobby?" he said. "Come," he said, putting his mask back on, "I have to be getting along."

We returned to the others, and Valette said in a louder voice everyone present could hear, "Fitz appreciates the work you're doing out here, Bobby. He says the India bases will be the centerpieces of this campaign. Oh, did you all know Mason is married? Here, Tabby."

He went to a voluptuous, one might say downright chubby, young lady in his group and kissed her on her bare décolletage. The lewd act embarrassed Davis and me. His entourage thought it a good jest and giggled in approval.

"May I introduce you gentlemen to Lady Tabitha Celestial DeShay Mason,"[28] said Valette, and gave a flourish of his right hand. "She is on her honeymoon."

"Where is Mason?" asked Davis.

"It's eight twenty-seven here in India," said Valette, checking his watch. "It is tomorrow morning in Cumberland, and Mason is at least three felonies ahead of us."

The smart set tumbled off to Valette's readied zeppelin, and none too soon in my opinion. When the aircraft left its mooring dock, I ran back to my tent and wrote the following to Charlotte:

> My darling, you must go at once to my Lord Prim-Jones and ask him in the name of my father and my father's father

---

28. The older sister of Lady Chelsea, Lady Tabitha (2398–2440) lived at court until she fell from favor with her sibling and was strangled in her bed.

for protection. He is an obtuse, distant man, but he will not forget my family's loyalty to him. Tell him to take you and my Great-Aunt Jessie across the Columbia River and east into the Toutle Mountains. There you will stay with Bailey Pressler, a forester like my father, and his wife Margaret. Mr. Pressler is man without family who served with my father in the Sparrows[29] and is a sworn liege of my Lord Prim-Jones. He knows the mountains better than anyone. His neighbors and his dogs will keep out any intruder. Send any letters you write me to my Lord. He will forward them to India, as he will forward my letters to you. My Lord will send a doctor every month to check on you and to care for you when you have your lying-in. If strangers appear in the mountains—in particular a towheaded young man with sleepy eyelids whose Christian name is Zimmerman—Mr. Pressler and his neighbors must kill these strangers on sight and hide the bodies.

I beg you by God's wounds to do as I ask. You must remain hidden until I can speak directly to the Consul. I do not have time to write more. Burn this letter after both you and Great-Aunt Jessie have read it.

I wrote a second note to Buck Pularski in Pallas, Ohio:

Winifred, Fitz is going to send someone to Columbus to murder my wife. I ask you as my friend to help me.

I took both letters to the pilot of the mail plane that flew from the Rajmahal base every night at midnight. I knew Valette would not forward any private note to Fitz concerning Charlotte on the Blinking Stars, since that would alert the Timermen to their designs. I asked the mail plane's pilot if he would arrive in North America before Valette's zeppelin reached Cumberland.

"They are going through Australia, sir," he said and slipped my letters into a leather bag. "Your letters will arrive home days before they do."

Two weeks later I received a letter from Pularski. He wrote that Pallas was calm. The Chinese Ambassador came every day. Fitz

---

29. The Seventh Infantry Division. See Introduction.

every day refused to see him. The Chinese, it seemed, had suddenly become very eager to talk. Valette had convened another international conference, this one in London, the English farming village that had once been a great city of the ancient world.[30] Buck asked twice if I had seen a tiger. He was upset I had not traveled north to a game preserve above Bihar he had read of in *Confederacy Geographic;* all the experts, he wrote, agreed there might still be Bengal tigers there. It was winter in Ohio, and Buck's garden was in hibernation, save for the dogwood and his solitary Scotch pine. In the afternoon, when the sun was warm, Lady Joan and her nurse would come out of the house and sit in the sunshine on Buck's concrete bench. The three of them read aloud to each other in that secluded corner of the same estate wherein Fitz was planning his gruesome world conquest. Buck said they were reading *Emma* at the moment, which was Lady Joan's favorite book and one, Buck wrote, she read with the most beautiful voice he had ever heard. At the end of his letter he wrote:

"Do not worry about that other thing. If F. does anything, I will prevent it."

---

30. Readers of History and of literature will recognize the name London as surely as they recognize that of Rome or of Babylon. Gourmets will know the modern village for the famous cheese produced there. Fitzpatrick the Younger chose the site to remind the world of the roots of our culture. The argumentative and largely pointless conference held there in 2421 lasted until the war in Asia began.

# FOURTEEN

ON THE SEVENTH of April, 2421, rain began falling on the Raj-mahal Hills at about seven o'clock in the morning. The downpour increased in the afternoon, and soon the hillsides were streaked with rivulets of running water. The Ganges to our north rose and turned from a milky tan to a deep, thick chocolate brown. The monsoons had returned to India. The Chinese had waited too long.

On the eighth, the soldiers of the Sixth Army heard the ground crews on the air bases fire up the boilers on every operative airplane the Air Corps had on site. By midmorning of that day the aircraft began to queue up along the sides of the painted runways. We could see the ground crews in their black rain gear climbing about the planes throughout the day as they filled the undercarriages and checked the sleek composite bodies one last time.

At eleven o'clock that night Hood sent word to the men to write their families letters that would leave on the midnight mail plane, for the zeppelins would not land in the encampment again until the fighting had ceased. For a few of the pilots these would be the final letters of their young lives.

At one o'clock on the morning of the ninth, Hood called a torchlight meeting for officers and NCOs in the Army and Army Air Corps. Fifteen thousand of us stood under umbrellas in the pouring rain and listened to the Marshal read from the Book of Joel:

"Proclaim this among the nations:
    Prepare for war,
        And stir up the mighty men.

Let the men of war draw near,
> Let them come up.
Beat your plowshares into swords,
> And your pruning hooks into spears;
> Let the weak say, 'I am a warrior.' "[1]

He solemnly turned next to the Psalms, and read:

"In the Lord I take refuge,
> How can you say to me,
'Flee like a bird to the mountains;
for lo, the wicked bend the bow,
they have fitted their arrow to the string,
to shoot in the dark the upright
> in the heart;
if the foundations are destroyed,
> what can the righteous do?'
The Lord in His holy temple,
> The Lord's throne is in Heaven.
> His eyes behold, His eyelids test,
> The children of men.
The Lord tests the righteous and
> The wicked,
And His soul hates him that loves
> Violence.
On the wicked he will rain coals of
> Fire and brimstone;
A scorching wind shall be the
> Portion of their cup.
For the Lord is righteous, He loves
> Righteous deeds;
The upright shall behold His
> Face."

Hood put his Bible into the pocket of his raincoat and from his speaker's podium looked down upon the expectant faces of his officers. The Marshal seemed to me to have aged forty years in the

---

1. Joel 3:9–10.

past four. His rain-streaked visage shining above the torches was drawn and carried the mark of an unspeakable sorrow.

"Thus God long ago spoke to Israel," he said. "Israel would lose her battles against the Assyrians and the Babylonians; the Persians would, in the fullness of time, rule over Abraham's children, as would the Greeks, the Romans, the Arabs, the Turks, the British, and finally, today, the Turks again. Yet Israel lives, if not as a nation then as a light unto the world that cannot be extinguished. For God set Israel free from the burden of History. That is why, in spite of four thousand years of military defeats, a man may travel to every nation and encounter Jews. For God made Israel's soul immortal, and the armies of men cannot destroy what God has made.

"The secret of the Yukons is that although we have God's word and carry his banner, we, unlike the chosen people, cannot endure a single defeat. Never let a foreigner's soft words deceive you: we are the most hated of nations. Rome at her acme was beloved compared to us. Nazi Germany and ancient America each had a warmer place in their enemies' hearts than we do in ours. Should any foe conquer us, they would not suffer one among us to live. Our conquerors would hunt down every Yukon child, every grandchild, every white-haired mother, and would kill them as cats kill vermin. They would overturn every brick we have placed atop brick and toss every word we have written into the flames. The name Yukon would be remembered only as a curse, a word to frighten children.

"God therefore has given us no option other than never to lose. We must win today and a thousand years from today and ten thousand years from now, or everything we are is lost. This is the burden of History we must carry, my friends. That is what weighs upon us from the day we are born. The burden robs us of our youth, of our personal aspirations, and ofttimes of life itself. But cast off the burden, and History will destroy us. Cast off the burden, and the future will not know you and yours ever existed."

He was silent while he summoned up the courage to finish his speech.

"My friends, our enemies are as numerous as the blades of grass. We have no choice but to be scythes in their meadow . . . Each of you have wives, children, and you love them. Your loved ones have taught you mercy. In the months to come there will come times when you will want to show that same mercy to the Chinese and to the Turks. Do not do it, my friends. Think instead of how our enemies would act if Fate had put you in their stead. Think of how much mercy they would show you and your families. There will be a day when we may spare our foes, a day when this war will be done. Until then, do not allow yourselves to feel anything beyond your hatred. Hate your enemies when the flames fall upon them. Hate them when you shoot them down. Kill them when they attack. Kill them when they retreat. Kill them when they try to burrow themselves into the ground. Kill them in the midst of their doomed cities. Kill them when they flee to the wilderness. Kill them all. Kill so many that future Historians will speak in an appalled whisper of the work we have done . . ."

Hood had let himself become too excited as he spoke. I could tell he was ashamed of his emotions and of the dreadful words he was speaking. He paused again and hung his head.

"My friends," he began anew in a calmer tone, "at home our dear ones are presently coming home from work. Some have already sat down for supper. It is a peaceful spring day. Tomorrow, or the day after, they will read in their morning papers of the events unfolding on this side of the globe, and they will think of us. We will think of them tonight . . . God's speed."

He stepped from the podium and went to his tent. The pilots and navigators ran in double-time formation to their airplanes. The steam lights along the edges of the runways came on in the misty darkness while the bagpipe bands atop the hills played "Sir Patrick Spens" and "Black Jack Davy." The infantrymen in the trenches fired parachute flares as a salute to the departing airplanes. Their flickering points of light made a halo two hundred miles in circumference around the busy runways. The vibration of the engines sounded a bass hum below the soprano screams of the bagpipes as the reflections of our handheld lanterns and torches danced in the puddles beneath our feet. By two-twenty in the morning the last of the planes was gone to the north, and the camp was silent.

The first long-range bombers, the ones that had struck at the Chinese amassing around Wei, began returning at about five in the predawn twilight. The newly blooded[2] airmen in the bubble canopies flashed the thumbs-up sign to the crewmen running onto the tarmac to rearm and refuel their planes.

---

2. "Blooded," I should inform the lady readers, is soldier's slang for "having gone into combat."

As the sun came up we saw the first of the Chinese incendiary rockets burst forth in mountains of flame upon the farmlands north of the Ganges.

*       *       *

I now must tell of the Four Points War in the eastern hemisphere, a story that every Yukon reader already knows the outlines of full well.[3] For the next thirty-eight months the world would not know peace, yet the conflict was decided in only fifty-one days. The war would be fought on the earth's three great oceans, in the air above five continents, and in the green hills of northern India. I beheld a small portion of the air war and none of the naval conflict. In India I was in the eye of the storm. Therefore I will deal with what befell at sea and in the air in a cursory fashion and tell my story of the India campaign last.

On the first day of the war, our Bat Wing bombers based in the Rajmahal Hills hit strategic targets in southern and central China. On the same day planes from Alaska struck at Chinese positions in Siberia and the Nippon Islands. Planes stationed on the Babuyan Islands hit eastern China from Manchuria to Canton, and bombers from Australia struck southeastern Asia. In the western theater bombers from England, Bioko, the Comoros, the Madeiras, and Luni flew to where they desired within the entire Turkish Empire. The original plan was to destroy the enemy air forces on the ground, and that is what happened when we attacked the Turks. The Chinese had hidden their military planes in underground hangars. Dropping incendiaries on them was ineffective. Our bombers found the Achilles' heel in the Chinese infrastructure lay in the way that a highly centralized and totalitarian nation produced and stored fuel. Unable to set aside crops to grow biomass, since everything grown in China had to be used to feed her one billion citizens, the Chinese had to extract petroleum in Siberia and bring it via pipelines to a mere fourteen giant refineries inside China proper. They operated an additional seven coal gasification plants and had two enormous petrol reserves, all of them under the direct control of the government in Peking. In the first six hours of the war the Yukon Air Corps destroyed the refineries, the gasification plants, and the pipelines' pumping stations. The Yukon airmen then started on

---

3. Bruce's account of the fighting is accurate, but lacks detail. For a fuller account, see Gerald, pp. 2018–2985.

China's bridges, irrigation dams, factory districts, and railway terminals. In the India theater our planes also struck at the ground
forces in southern China. I will tell more concerning these bombing operations below.

The Chinese had stationed jet airplanes—or, more correctly,
rocket planes—about some of their air bases and refineries. Our pilots called them "Flying Beetles," as they were fat, one-man planes
as wide as they were long. These Flying Beetles contained a large
liquid hydrogen tank on their port sides and a liquid oxygen tank on
their starboard sides; a small steam engine behind the pilot's seat at-
omized and blended the two volatile fuels together; the resulting
controlled explosion created the craft's forward thrust and produced a long red flame out the ungainly looking plane's rear exhaust
port. The two fuels required refrigerated storage and two separate
crews to fuel each jet, as a tiny drop of one fuel in the other's tank
would blast crew, craft, and fueling lorries to smithereens. The Flying Beetle was a marvelous, if complicated, piece of engineering;
most Yukon engineers considered it the height of Chinese technology, and it would be of utterly no consequence in the war. Our
heavy bombers would sight their targets from a distance of five
miles, fire their three large rockets that would break open over the
target, and release thousands of small cylinders containing Fire Sticks
incendiaries. Our airmen did not have to be accurate. The Fire
Sticks devoured land by the square mile, and left in the aftermath of
their fires black basaltic glass and cinders where people, buildings,
and machines had been. During the Four Points War we would lose
a single Bat Wing bomber to the Flying Beetles. Long before the
jets could be prepped and launched, our planes would turn and vanish over the horizon. The Chinese pilots had no means of tracking
the escaping Yukon bombers. Our airmen constantly received coded
messages from the Blinking Stars overhead and knew where the
enemy fighters were and easily avoided them.

The rockets I had seen landing beyond the Ganges were buzz
bombs the Chinese had launched from firing pads hundreds and
even thousands of miles to the north. Neither we nor they could

---

4. Ballistic missiles would travel in an arced path similar to that of an artillery shell.
Any ballistic device fired at a great distance would have to leave and then reenter the
earth's atmosphere, and if it did so at even a slightly acute or flattened angle, the rocket
would either burn up or skip off the atmosphere and enter outer space

make long-range ballistic rockets,[4] as such a rocket would need electronic guidance systems to reenter the atmosphere, a delicate maneuver that clockwork or other timer systems could not perform. For that reason the Chinese rockets cruised a few thousand feet above the earth until their fuel was exhausted; at that point the rockets would crash in a mighty ball of fire. Chinese engineers had measured the fuel as precisely as they could. During monsoon season the buzz bombs had to fly against a headwind coming off the ocean and into the rain. Only a handful of rockets landed anywhere close to their intended destinations. Our antiaircraft air burst missiles destroyed the few that approached the Rajmahal Hills. The Blinking Stars would signal that the Chinese rockets were traveling at a such and such a speed and nearing such and such a position, and we would launch a round of our missiles into the rockets' path; our projectiles would explode and fill the sky with millions of tiny pellets that would incinerate or disable the incoming weapons. The exploding buzz bombs resembled ball lightning when they went off and illuminated our northern skyline. The soldiers in the trenches counted "one thousand one, one thousand two" between the time they saw the flash and when they heard the blast to measure the distance, much as farmers on the Great Plains do to measure the time between a lightning flash and thunder.

The Chinese also set loose a flock of unmanned balloons they hoped would ride the air currents to distant places. These balloons carried in their tiny gondolas packets of anthrax or swarms of mosquitoes infected with a new strain of malaria. The winds that frustrated the buzz bombs sent the balloons back into the Chinese Empire and wrought terrible damage upon the Chinese themselves. We in India would see the effects of the malaria strain later. During the actual fighting the balloons had no bearing on the course of the war.

The mainstay of the Chinese air offensive was the massive Florin class bomber.[5] These four-engine monsters had a crew of eleven and a wingspan of at least two hundred and fifty feet. The newest E-type in the Chinese Air Force had a sky-consuming span of nearly a hundred yards. Along the cigar-shaped central frame of the Florin were nine bubble turrets for machine guns: three on the top, two on the belly, and two on each side. The big planes could hit

---

5. See Chapter One, footnote 10.

their ground targets either by shooting rockets from their under-carriages or, as was more common, by passing directly over a site and dropping bombs from an open bomb-bay door. The Chinese navigators, who doubled as copilots in the airplane's nose cone, had to rely on maps to guide them over land. Over sea they had only a solar compass, a sextant, and a chronometer—the same instruments a ship's navigator would use. There was not a fighter in their arsenal that could escort the Florins far outside China, so for mutual protection the Chinese bombers flew in tight box formations that could contain hundreds of planes within their individual grids.

Five years before the war the Florin class had been the principal offensive weapon in the Yukon Air Corps; the Chinese jets mentioned above were designed to fight the lumbering beasts that were then the terror of the Heavens. In April of 2421 the Florin was a flying anachronism, a death trap that turned hundreds of young Yukon fighter pilots into aces. The giant bomber's top speed was two hundred and ninety miles an hour; the F-101 fighter the elder Aranov brother had designed could cruise at over six hundred. The Blinking Stars told our airmen where the Chinese Florins were, their direction, and their speed. The bomber's long contrails from its four huge steam engines gave its position away long before its crews could see our fighters coming at them. The F-101s would spring upon the bombers as if from thin air and quickly fire their canister rockets into the box formations. Like every steam plane, the Florin had an interior stuffed with fuel and water tanks. A single phosphorus pellet or shell in one of the fuel tanks would start a conflagration that could not be extinguished in time to save the aircraft. Flames would race from tank to tank and into the payload. In an instant fiery pieces of the exploding bomber would be falling onto other planes in the box formation. A single air-burst canister from an F-101 might shoot pellets into two score Chinese Florins. The wounded planes could collide with dozens more of their kind on their way down.

Our fighters hunted in two groupings of thirty each. When dissecting a box, one group would move atop the Chinese Florins, and the other thirty would simultaneously hit the enemy from a flank. After both squadrons had fired all their canister rockets, the navigator in the command plane of each group would signal by means of a hand mirror for his men to commence direct assaults using their machine guns and twenty-two millimeter cannons. If our airman in both groupings ran out of ammunition before all the Florins were downed, the men would break off the attack and return to home base. Central Air Command, always in contact with the Blinking Stars, would dispatch sixty more planes to finish the job. Any Florins that somehow survived and drew near our bases would be pelted with the same sort of rocket barrage our anti-aircraft crews unleashed against the buzz bombs. Of the approximately twelve thousand bombers the Chinese got airborne, I know of five that survived to release their bombs over the Rajmahal Hills during the entire course of the war. Hundreds of Chinese Florins broke formation and returned home to fly one more day. Not one of them ever struck at our positions and made it back to base safely.

I was in charge of making repairs to the runways and roads after the air raids. Hood had given me command of the Eighty-third Teamsters, a regiment from Centralia and Southfield composed of older men who had once been combat infantrymen and of newly enlisted lads young enough to be their companions' grandsons. Added to the five hundred Aussies I still had from the Second Engineers, I had plenty of muscle to fill and pack any holes the Chinese bombs made in the pavement. There was nothing we could do about the flames on the ground untreated with polymer. We had to let those fires burn the soil down to black glass. The Florins hit four biomass storage tanks, seven hangars, and thirty-five planes on the ground; all of these enflamed structures and pieces of equipment had to be let burn till the flames hit treated ground and were extinguished. My men and I could only don polymer-treated clothing and push the smoking scraps out of the way. Two of the seventy-two runways had to be shut down completely and stripped of whatever undamaged gear we could salvage from them. Hood would rather have lost nothing to the Florins. When set against the five thousand planes we had in the Rajmahal Hills that kept on working, the handful of hits we took were certainly acceptable losses.

I expect the reader will have seen some of the famous moving pictures our fighters made while slaughtering the Chinese Florins. I was one of the first Yukons to see the rough versions of this footage, for Hood showed some of his officers several sections of film made by the spring cameras in the nose of the Yukon planes. The silent film show the fat Chinese bombers huddling together like a flock of frightened sheep while the quick, split-tailed F-101s darted about them, spitting destruction onto the big planes that seemed nearly stationary compared to the swift Yukon fighters. A few frames showed a Florin's machine gunners spinning in circles inside their canopy bubbles, unable to hit the F-101s because six hundred m.p.h. is faster than human muscles can follow. Other footage showed a Yukon pilot's gunfights moving effortlessly from dying plane to dying plane. Our airmen could have thrown rocks at the slow-as-a-tortoise Florins and would have hit them.

"How do they ever miss?" asked Daddy Montrose, who was also watching the film and was sickened by what he saw.

"No mercy, Israel," Hood cautioned him. "You will see worse before this is over."

My old friend Watchcharm Davis proved to be the champion of fighter pilots during our massacre of the Chinese Air Force. In seven days his nose camera recorded Davis killing an astonishing two hundred and sixty-seven bombers, far surpassing the forty he had promised his wife. His method was to dive close to the enemy's box formation and release his canister rockets into the heart of the grid so that the pellets did maximum damage. When using his cannon he would close until he could see the enemy tail gunner's face, then pepper the Florin from the stern to the pilot's cabin. He was slicing his two hundred and sixty-eighth victim in half when the crippled bomber's port wing exploded and sent metal fragments into the belly of Davis' fighter. In a flash the eleven Chinese crewmen and the five-foot-seven-inch Yukon ace and his navigator went down to their deaths in the same ball of flame. My courageous friend died as bravely as he had lived, happily giving his brief life to a cause that did not merit his sacrifice or those of the twelve men who perished with him.

Our strategic bombing quickly caused the Chinese Empire to run low on fuel. The enemy ceased to fly their jets on the third day of combat; they made this decision not because they lacked liquid hydrogen and nitrogen, but rather because their ground crews suddenly lacked the fuel to keep the other volatile fuels in refrigerated storage. Within eighteen days only their remaining Florins were airborne. On the twenty-seventh day, the fifth of May, the last two operative Chinese bombers left Chunking for points south. Sixty of our fighters met them over the Tibetan Plateau. Moments later the Yukons shared the sky with the birds but not with any other men for the remainder of the war.

\* \* \*

The war at sea lasted longer, yet was more one-sided than the air war.

Since the Storm Times our Navy has fought its opponents at a distance with long-range guns mounted on huge battleships. The standard naval strategy has always been to approach the enemy fleet to a distance of about forty miles and to open fire while still unseen and undetected, using the twenty-one inch guns of our battleships. The Blinking Stars would give the Yukon gunnery masters posted onboard ship glass domes the positions and headings of the enemy vessels; the masters had but to do the math and to yell the coordinates to the gunnery mates, who would elevate the guns and measure the powder packed behind the three-quarters of a ton shells. If our men ever missed, the Blinking Stars would direct volley after volley until the fleet of Yukon dreadnoughts, all of them firing in unison, found their targets. First the Yukon gunners would kill the enemy battlewagons, next move to the carriers, and finally they would destroy the smaller vessels. After damaging or sinking every target, the Yukons would send tactical bombers to drop steam-powered torpedoes into the doomed enemy ships that remained afloat. On rare occasions, the Yukon fleet would close to line of sight and blast any flaming hulks left above the water.

In the Four Points War the Yukon admirals could afford to send the T-10 tactical bombers into the fray a little sooner than they had launched other planes in the past. Otherwise they followed the classic plan with as few innovations as an experienced cook makes when following an old and proven recipe.

In the far east, the Chinese fleets at Shanghai, Cam Ron Bay, and Tokyo had to sortie at once or be destroyed in port by our Bat Wing bombers. On the tenth of April the ships at Shanghai and Cam Ron attempted to converge north of Formosa, from where they hoped to sail south through the Sakishamas and attack our air bases on the Babuyan Islands. They were fated to meet disaster the moment they went to sea. Our Admiral Semmes, now promoted to commander of our Pacific Fleet, directed a strike force of thirty-two ships that trailed the Cam Ron vessels at a discreet distance until the Chinese reached their rendezvous point above Formosa Island. On the night of the twenty-first, the Yukon ships steamed to a point thirty miles west of the unsuspecting Chinese and began firing in the early morning darkness of the twenty-second. From the brig of his flagship, *The Prince of Light*, Admiral Semmes watched the Blinking Stars as they relayed the positions of the enemy capital ships, starting with that of *The East Is Red,* the largest warship in the Chinese fleet. The gunnery mates on the eleven Yukon battleships directed the twelve big guns on each ship to fire at that one unlucky target. The Yukon gunners fired two salvos every nine seconds, sending one hundred and thirty fifteen-hundred-pound shells at every target the Blinking Stars gave them. Our crews were given a leisurely fifteen seconds to adjust their guns to the coordinates of a new target when a ship they were pounding disappeared from the Blinking Stars' optic sensors. In three minutes off the Formosa coast the Yukon gunners destroyed all eight of the Chinese battleships. Five minutes later they had sunk or set aflame the twelve enemy carriers. In another eight minutes they had dealt with the twenty Chinese cruisers. The motley—and, one expects, much terrified—collection of Chinese troop transports and destroyers that remained after this opening attack turned east and ran toward the mainland at full steam. So confused were they, they did not realize they were charging straight toward our position. By four A.M. there were seven enemy ships left that could move under their own power. At the dawn's first light our carrier planes fell upon them. Two fast Chinese destroyers came within twenty nautical miles of the port of Fuzhou before they sank. One other enemy ship, one that turned away from us, ran aground on the northeastern corner of the Formosan shoreline. There the battleship *Chosen of God* closed and blasted it to small pieces. Much of the enemy crew had by then jumped ship and swam ashore. Admiral Semmes' sailors closed to point-blank range with the few blazing wrecks that were still afloat at midday, and sent the pathetic remnants of the combined Cam Ron and Shanghai fleets to the bottom of the sea.

For the next two days tankers and supply freighters from the Babuyan Islands brought ammunition and fuel to Semmes' strike force. Once he felt he had sufficiently regathered himself, he directed his ships due north to await the death ride of the Tokyo fleet. The eighty-three ships of that Chinese formation had been creeping down the Nippon and Ryuku archipelagos toward the rendezvous point for two weeks. The Chinese had long been aware our satellites could detect them. Our opponents were not aware how obvious their movements were to us in every environment. The Tokyo fleet must have believed the small islands they lurked above were screening them to some degree.

On the twenty-ninth, the eighty-three Chinese ships made a run toward Formosa from Okinawa. Our Pacific Fleet lay in ambush. This time our vessels were again between the Chinese and the Asian mainland. When Semmes ordered the shelling to commence at 2005 hours, the panicked enemy once more made a dash for home and yet once more ran into the Yukon fleet. We do not know what the Chinese sailors did when the bombardment worsened and their steel ships splintered and burned like kindling in a bonfire. They probably called encouragement to each other and said aloud the heroic words they had learned when they were young and could believe men in extremis would say such things. The newspapers reported there was a beautiful, starlit sky that night. The fish in the water and the gulls and kites in the sky passed by the tragic scene on the surface as though nothing untoward was happening in their world. The entire catastrophe was over in thirty-four minutes. In the morning light the Yukons sent out planes to search for any survivors and found only open water in the expanse to their west. In two days time they did locate some life jackets and a few melted shards of debris. The enemy ships had gone done so quickly they had pulled their crews and equipment down with their ruined hulls beneath the peaceful sea. Thus was the end of the Chinese Navy.

In the western theater the Turks would not leave their sanctuaries in the Mediterranean and the Persian Gulf for six weeks. That vast but ramshackle empire was as ill prepared for the battle at sea as they were on land and in the air. Their largely obsolete ships were slower than ours and those of the Chinese, and the Turks had no fire retardant inside their ships' superstructures. A single Yukon bomb or shell could penetrate the hull of a Turkish ship and burn the entire vessel to the waterline. In their hopeless situation the despairing Turks allowed our airmen to destroy most of their navy in port.

Their ships in the Persian Gulf never sailed. Their battered Mediterranean fleet, what there was of it at the end of six weeks of indecision, limped through the Straits of Gibraltar and into the Atlantic on May the twenty-third. Admiral Neuhauser[6] and his Atlantic

---

6. Admiral Toynbee Grace Neuhauser (2346–2480), another of the "old sea dogs" of Fitzpatrick's era, was seven years Admiral Semmes' junior.

7. The British Navy under Admiral Nelson in 1804 defeated the French and Spanish navies at Trafalgar.

Fleet met them near the Historic location of Trafalgar[7] a day later. Neuhauser could have sent his airplanes to sink the Turkish ships long before they reached the open sea. He chose instead to give his gunners some combat practice. His men needed the experience, too. They used up an entire twenty-two minutes in sinking the forty-one Turkish ships that had blundered to within forty miles of our fleet. So died the Turkish Navy.

For the fourteen months following the Second Battle of Trafalgar, the Yukon Navy swept the pirates from the oceans of the Old World as they had already done in the New. Admiral Semmes sailed to the Bering Sea and thence down the Siberian and Chinese coasts, destroying everything that could float. Neuhauser went to the coast of Scandinavia[8] and steamed south, making detours into the Baltic, Mediterranean, and Black seas. Admiral Sandman,[9] the commander of the Indian Ocean Fleet, which had not seen action against the Turks or the Chinese, attacked the pirate stronghold in the East Indies, and from there moved west. The three Yukon fleets would converge on June second, 2422, off Madagascar.

Nearly all the pirate vessels were wooden sailing ships converted to steam; a typical vessel carried a couple cannon fore and aft and was used to assault unarmed merchant ships. Against Yukon warships made of titanium and chromium steel the pirates had no chance. The most daring of the buccaneers fled to the open sea when the Yukon Navy drew near to their hiding places. In the open water they made excellent targets for our tactical bombers. The wisest pirates abandoned their ships and fled inland to live as outlaws on terra firma. The ones who fled to the open sea lived to see how quickly wood can burn.

The convergence of the Yukon fleets marked the end of the pirates' time upon History's stage. From that day to this[10] the Yukons have held absolute sway over air and sea, and we have never allowed anyone to challenge us.

*   *   *

---

8. Bruce uses the ancient name for the region. He means the coast of El-Nord.

9. Admiral Trustworthy True Blood Sandman (2339–2440), came to be Admiral of the entire Yukon Navy. He was killed during one of the Crysanthemum Woman's many purges.

10. And into the present time.

The war in northern India is the last and the grimmest chapter in the war I must relate. It is the story of a human tide breaking upon an immobile rock and of obscene human suffering that was for naught.

The Chinese moved down the narrow valley of the Brahmaputra and into India as soon as our bombing raids began. A mass of twenty million would have had difficulties advancing across any terrain in good weather; in the Brahmaputra Valley the elevation falls twenty thousand feet in two hundred miles, and the one-lane road on the west side of the swollen river is bordered by sheer cliffs thousands of feet high. To make the way more difficult for them, our demolition men had blown away the roadway in dozens of places and had blasted every bridge across the Brahmaputra, the Ganges, and the Son. Chinese repair units had to proceed ahead of their long column inside the canyon and fix the road before the huge army could advance. Our planes hit the road every hour. Each glassy pit the Fire Sticks created in their path made their advance more difficult. As the repair crews struggled to level the road, other Yukon bombers inflicted horrible losses upon the stalled men and vehicles trapped in the slim defile. Fire Sticks canisters could fill the entire width of the river canyon with flame. T-10s sprayed cannon shells on the Chinese trucks and tanks, setting them off like strings of firecrackers. Detachments of the Indian Army meanwhile fired down on the Chinese from the safety of the high ground east of the river.

Within two days of fighting it was obvious to the ideologues directing the Chinese that they could not advance intact. They had sent cavalry on Super Steppe horses[11] into the Ganges' flood plain and had learned that our demolition men had blown up the hundreds of small dikes holding the area's tributary streams in check during the monsoon season. Most of northern India was under several feet of water. Upon digesting this information, any other opponent with whom the Yukons have ever shared the field of battle would have retreated into their home territory and sent ambassadors to make peace. Not the fanatical, hateful, courageous Chinese.

---

11. The Super Steppe Horse is, like our Ultra Arabians, a product of selective breeding and genetic enhancement. Though smaller than the Ultra Arabian, a Supeer Steppe can run at a top speed of thirty-three m.p.h. for up to twenty hours, at which time the animal, unfortunately, falls dead.

They abandoned their trucks, their tanks, their heavy artillery, and everything else that could not be carried on a man's back, and advanced toward us on foot. Infantrymen do not need a road to walk on, but they must have supplies; in their mad rush to defeat us the Chinese forgot that basic fact of warfare. When they exhausted their food and ammunition they scavenged what they could from their dead and kept going. If they did not breach our lines quickly, their cause would be hopelessly lost. Even the brave Chinese could not live long on air and dirt.

The Chinese soldiers each carried a folding screen of split bamboo that they kept moist as they marched toward the Rajmahal Hills. When incendiaries fell on them they would lie underneath the bamboo screens and cover their faces with a wet silk cloth. This procedure may have worked against flammable jelly or napalm; against Fire Sticks the screen was a psychological comfort to men about to be burned into ashes. Some of the Chinese, the elite Revolutionary Guard especially, wore polymer jackets and pants, giving them some protection against Fire Sticks, although our incendiaries often asphyxiated those individuals not set afire. The Revolutionary Guards wore body armor made of carbon composites underneath their outer clothing. This offered protection against a canister pellet that had traveled more than a quarter mile and had lost considerable energy. Heavy munitions and canister pellets fired at close range readily cut through everything they had. The majority of the Chinese swarm were only peasants recruited right from their farms. They were dressed in simple black trousers and tunics. For protection they had to call upon their gods, who did not choose to protect them very well in those terrible days. Our Bat Wing and tactical bombers feasted upon those peasants in the canyon and in the muddy fields beyond the Ganges in such numbers their blood would fertilize the Indians' crops for three decades thereafter.

The Chinese human avalanche soon overwhelmed a small blocking force the Indians had placed across the Brahmaputra Valley the day before. By the twenty-ninth of April, the Chinese vanguard had reached the Ganges opposite Bhagalpur, where the Third Corps under Daddy Montrose was stationed. The enemy made a brief reconnaissance of our positions on the southern side of the river. Contrary to reason and reality, they there attacked across a mile and a half of high water. A handful of them had canvas boats they had carried from Tibet, the others cut down trees

314 · THEODORE JUDSON

and made small rafts to paddle across, and a smattering of the Not-Men[12] threw themselves directly into the current and swam. Those Chinese having handheld rockets fired over the water at our trenches in lieu of a real artillery barrage. The Yukons remained in their bunkers until the fires died out, then went to the trenches and waited till the Chinese were almost to the south shore. Our men shouted ironic encouragement to the soon to be dead men in the river. "Closer, my boys!" and "Put your shoulders into it!" they called. For the last time the Yukon soldiers let themselves laugh. Our men threw rocks toward the water and shouted insults the on-coming Chinese could not understand. Someone, History does not record who it was, tired of the fun and could wait no longer; he shot and killed a Revolutionary Guardsman in the bow of a canvas boat and suddenly the entire front opened up on the floundering men in the brown water. No one laughed after that. At close range individual bullets went through several ranks of Chinese, killing them before their bodies could react to swift-winged death. The mortally wounded men did not have time to groan or scream a final protest against the injustice of everything. Moments before they might have been thinking of their wives and of sunsets and of the crops they would plant next spring; after the first volley they were thoughtless bunches of lost possibilities floating in a river that was quickly turning red.

A couple of the witless Not-Men reached the shallow water near the south shore and became entangled in the barbed wire we had laid immediately below the surface. They struggled in inarticulate rage for an instant before we killed them. The Chinese on the north shore regrouped and attacked again, straight into the same positions they had failed to take minutes earlier. Our communications specialists signaled with hand mirrors for our mortars and the 220 howitzers to begin firing. The incoming shells fell on the second wave as it entered the water, making the Chinese vanish behind a wall of white foam. The Yukon snipers picked off the handful who reached midstream ere they had gone a quarter mile toward us.

Hit a mule twice with an ax handle and even he will learn.[13] The

---

12. See Chapter Three, footnote 3. These were the last of their freakish kind.

13. Probably a folksy Nor'west saying. I could find no mention of the phrase in the library at St. Matthew's.

Chinese moved farther west rather than attempt a third assault across the water at Bhagalpur. Seeking vulnerable spots in our lines, they made a third assault six miles farther east at Monghyr on the night of May first. I suppose they thought the darkness would give them some cover. The Yukons fired parachute flares that illuminated the river as brightly as the sunlight had, and the results of that ill-advised attack over the Ganges were as horrifying as those of the first two.

My composite teamster regiment carried supplies to the men in the front lines after each assault. I had the additional task of overseeing repairs to the battlements while I was up there. The Chinese had left snipers along the opposite shore of the river. To avoid getting shot my men and I had to move through the slit trenches on all fours. The infantrymen had to exit and enter the lines in the same way whenever a new regiment was rotated into a fort. The medics had to transport the wounded to the hospital via the same slit trenches, as inconvenient as that route could be while dragging laden stretchers.

Charlie and French accompanied me on my trips to the front in spite of my orders to them to stay behind. They respectfully reminded me of the Military Code, and said they had to disobey me.[14] The Code is the excuse Yukon soldiers always use, even old men whose fighting days are past, to get into the fray when they feel they must. I could not refuse them. The Military Oath was the same excuse I used to perform the duties I knew were morally wrong. The two loyal sailors were never more than a few steps behind me as I scurried along amid the singing sniper bullets.

The Chinese meanwhile kept sweeping west in thousands of disorganized groups. Communication between the disparate parts of their army depended upon a network of couriers relaying messages from group to group, creating a network that deteriorated as casualties in the Chinese ranks mounted. Their communications were still functioning on May tenth, the day they reached Hajipur, opposite Patna, the capital of Bihar Province. East of Hajipur is the smaller city of Sonpur and between them flows the Grandok River into the Ganges; a million-man Indian army was lying in wait inside Sonpur for the Chinese to attempt to cross the mighty Grandok. Then the Indians would counterattack and turn the enemy eastward.

---

14. The Military Code demands a solider take the same risks his commander does.

The Yukon positions south of the Ganges were usually dug right up to the shoreline; in that sector they were on the high ground south of Patna city. We had blown up the bridges across the Ganges and would have been content to let the Chinese row across and become trapped in the burning provincial capital below us. That is, as the reader knows, not what happened. Our defensive tactics had enraged our Indian allies, who had seen the northeastern corner of their nation laid waste by the enemy. Our allies were not willing to watch the same happen to Hajipur and especially not to Patna, which had been Akbar's[15] city and is a holy place to Buddhists, Sikhs, Jains, and the majority of Hindus. Despite being much inferior in numbers to the Chinese, the Indian Second Army ignored Hood's command to destroy the bridges over the Gandok and instead moved into Hajipur and prepared to fight. Hood watched their advance from the hills above Patna and shook his head at their folly.

"The Chinese will have a victory tomorrow," he told his staff.

On the morning of the eleventh, Chinese hand rockets rained upon Hajipur from the flooded fields east of the city. By midday a human torrent made up of Indian soldiers and a million civilian refugees was flowing westward over the solitary span left standing across the Gandok. Wave upon wave of black-clad Chinese raced after them, charging right into the heart of the fleeing mob and driving untold thousands into the river. The Chinese rolled over the bridge and simultaneously sped across the Gandok on the same sort of canvas boats and makeshift rafts they had unsuccessfully used against the Yukon positions upstream. The Indians positioned in Sonpur held fire. They feared killing their own people and in the confusion and the heavy rain they could not readily tell whether those running toward them were friends or foes. When they did finally let loose their first volley into the Chinese onslaught it was too late. Seeing that the battle north of the Ganges was lost, Hood ordered the Yukon artillery to demolish both Hajipur and Sonpur. Soon thereafter our view of the north bank was hidden under the dust and smoke caused by the shelling. By nightfall the Blinking Stars were telling us the Chinese had secured a bridgehead west of the Gankok. By midnight millions of them were hurrying farther west over the bodies of our late Indian allies.

---

15. See Chapter Six, footnote 4.

A branch of the enemy throng made a southern thrust the next day at Patna in an attempt to provoke another wild civilian stampede. This time they ran straight into the Yukon embattlements on the heights south of that city. Patna was set ablaze as Hajipur had been and an assault was made across the Ganges on the now familiar rafts and canvas boats. We shelled the frail crafts for hours and our planes strafed them as well. Some eventually made it to the southern shore and entered the city. In Patna the Chinese found the civilian population had already evacuated behind the Yukon lines and that their bridgehead was only six miles long and two miles deep, not enough room for them to mass a force large enough to break the Yukon lines. The ground did offer more than sufficient space for a mass grave. What seemed to be a direct path to the Rajmahal Hills was actually a trap Hood had laid for them months earlier. A small portion of each Chinese amphibious wave could endure the trip over the water and through the bombardment, and our riflemen had no trouble gunning down this shard of the enemy army when it tried to charge our lines in the heights above the city. Those few Chinese who dug in at Patna became additional fuel for the fires that consumed the city's buildings and turned the once holy site into a black plain of hot, sticky glass.

Hood had stationed my old Columbus division, the Seventh; a New Zealand division, the Fourteenth; and the Lucky Seventeenth, an English outfit, to hold the Patna pocket. The twenty thousand Yukon riflemen along the six-mile front were packed close together, some shoulder to shoulder, making their rifle fire extremely dense. Any Chinese coming anywhere near our barbed wire met a wall of bullets as they attacked positions too far removed from the north shore to be hit by any of the enemy's handheld rockets.

My old comrades in the Sparrows were astonished that I appeared among them as a teamster colonel there to bring them fresh ammunition.

"Well done, Bobby!" exclaimed Tom Cromwell, an old mate from my squadron who had been a lance corporal when I last saw him—and still was. "I mean, sir," he added and gave me a salute.

Captain Reynard, my old lieutenant when I was a cadet soldier, invited me to have tea with him. The Chinese attacked us as the water began to boil.

"If it's not one thing it's another," said Captain Reynard. "I don't know what's worse: these bloody crazy chinks or these bloody darkies."

He pointed to the clusters of half-naked, weeping Indians wandering about pointlessly to our rear. Women with babies, old wrinkled men, barefoot children: they slipped and staggered in the heavy rain like novice skaters on ice; none among them had eaten in four days. No one could say when they might eat again. They were staring at us, their blank eyes expressing nothing. They were too exhausted, too hungry to feel anything, not even anger, for those who had driven them from their homes. When I looked at the ragged children clinging to their mothers' legs I thought of Charlotte washing other little ones at our kitchen sink. I then wished I too was past the point of feeling and would no longer have to know in my heart we in the Army had destroyed those hopeless people. In less time than it took to look the homeless refugees over, Captain Reynard and the other Sparrows went to the front wall and gave the Chinese fifteen seconds of fire, sending them back into Patna or into that land from whence none return.

"I'm sorry, old man," said Reynard as he returned to his bunker to pour the tea. "We are bang out of sugar. We'll have to drink it straight."

The Chinese north of the Ganges refused to accept Patna as a lost cause; they showered the wasted area that used to be a living city with rockets and burned away whatever was left there that was still combustible. The ground between the Yukon lines and the river bubbled and ran like molten lava. Our men had to put on gas masks to spare themselves from inhaling the black, noxious smoke rising off the basaltic glass. As soon as the glass cooled and could support a man's weight, thousands more of the Chinese charged into the river and into our lines. From the high ground we could see them before they reached the water. Our snipers could have shot them then. Being game lads, they tarried until the Chinese were on the slick, uneven ground. There the enemy went down like targets in a shooting gallery. Our mortar shells bit into the brittle surface and sent flying shards of glass that were as deadly as the shrapnel. After three more days of this pointless assaults across the ocean river only four Chinese achieved the honor of dying within fifty feet of our lines. After each slaughter the enemy's response was to send yet more men over the river to perish in the nightmare landscape. I could not bear to look at the scene for long. When I closed my eyes I found I saw in my mind images of my wife, and dreamed I was lying in bed with her on a quiet summer morning. "I will awake from this," I thought, "and be beside you." The next moment I would look again and instead of her smiling face I would see the smoke rising off the holocaust I had helped create.

At 0806 hours on the fifteenth my regiment and I were again in the trenches respelling the Sparrows when Charlie shouted something to me about the Navy coming to save the day. I could not hear him clearly over the shelling. He had to get next to me and shout into my ear before I could discern his words.

"I said, sir," he said, "the Navy is on the river. Come see."

I peered out a firing hole in the polymer bag wall and saw five Melville gunboats[16] on the Ganges headed west. Could they reach the Gandok estuary in time, they would cut off the Chinese remaining in Hajipur and the Patna pocket from the main body of their army, which had already pushed west into Uttar Pradesh Province. The swarm around Hajipur immediately raced to the Gandok when they espied the Yukon boats. The Chinese no longer had a supreme commander at this point in the battle.[17] They operated under a general plan their platoon leaders had memorized rather than under orders given each day by commanding officers. This plan did not include the possibility of being cut in half at the Gandok. They had jerry-rigged three footbridges over that tributary river into the ruins of Sonpur, two of them pontoon spans and one a cable suspension span hanging from the skeleton of the destroyed railroad bridge. Onto these three fragile structures ran millions of men; millions of others on rafts and boats plowed directly into the water. Flailing and screaming and beating the river into a white froth, they made a startling scene the Yukons on the heights stood atop their battlements to watch. Our company commanders had to hustle along the trench lines to remind the soldiers they should get behind the battlements and open fire.

The roar of our guns was more than my ears could hear. The slaughter in the two rivers was more than one man's mind could

---

16. A 140-foot heavily armored river gunboat having eight six-inch cannons, two rocket launchers, and twelve machine gun turrets.

17. General Wu, the political operative in charge of the Chinese task force, had in fact been killed on April 13, the third day of the Asian war.

absorb. Every artillery shell killed a hundred men. A rifleman could point his weapon in the general direction of the river and be assured he would hit something. Our mortars found the range of the three bridges and toppled the rows of Chinese from them like peas being scooped from a ripened pod. A sort of madness overcame us; we had an infinity of bullets and an infinity of Chinese before us. Every one of our men felt he was killing thousands. Our infantry fired every round the teamsters could carry to them; they fired until the raindrops sizzled on the rifle barrels. Death ran wild. How terrible it is, I thought, that the Yukons should be so good at this. There were millions of tiny black men in the water below us, millions of bodies. Whenever I closed my eyes I thought of Charlotte and our unborn child and wondered how I would ever justify this to them.

Later in the day fourteen more of the Melvilles arrived at Patna from downriver. They kept in formation with the other gunboats in the high water between Patna and Hajipur and did not attempt to sail into the bloody Gandok. They remained at midcurrent and fired their cannon point-blank into the enemy. The Chinese bridge-head south of the Ganges collapsed after sunset; those few of them who were not so badly wounded they could not walk—perhaps a hundred of them—retreated into the river and crossed into Uttar Pradesh in the darkness. Hood sent his armor into combat for the first time, and backed by the Sparrows and the Lucky Seventeenth, the Tiger Division retook the ground where Patna had stood after midnight on the fifteenth. The wounded Chinese caught in the path of this counterblow killed themselves rather than be taken prisoner. Out of the hundreds of thousands who had crossed the Ganges and entered the six-mile by two-mile pocket we captured twenty-two of them alive. These few were either so badly mangled and burned or so weak from hunger they could not put a gun to their heads. The Chinese completed their crossing of the Gandok the next day. Only then did the Yukon gunboats have the opportunity to blast away the remnants of the ruined bridges and to sail into that tributary, thus cutting off the enemy's line of retreat as the Chinese moved west on the trail of the beaten Indian Second Army.

At the War College the instructors taught us that no land force can endure more than forty percent casualties. The military science dons believe that the hierarchy of command and communications break down when that many men are dead or wounded, and the individual units cannot function. The Chinese had taken fifty percent casualties by the time they reached the Gandok and had lost another four million during their mass crossings. They continued as an effective fighting force because the Revolutionary Guardsmen were distributed throughout their ranks to keep the common soldiers moving ever forward. Each squadron had a minimum of two of these Guardsmen; one was the commanding sergeant, and the other was the squadron's political enforcer. Either of these two men would kill anyone in the unit refusing to follow orders. As I have said, the Guardsmen were better armed and better trained than their peasant comrades. They maintained the plan of attack during the campaign, and somehow their fanaticism sustained them. The peasants they served with had Veritas,[18] of which the Guardsmen gave each of them two tablets every day. For as long as the Guardsmen's will and their supply of drugs lasted, the Chinese kept attacking.

The enemy overtook the Indians ten miles east of Charpa and gave them another beating on the seventeenth. They reached Chapra itself on the eighteenth, and burned that beautiful city down to the bottom of the tree roots. On the night of the eighteenth, Chinese made a crossing of the Ganges east of the Son, miles beyond the point our fortifications extended. Our planes strafed and bombed them every step of the journey. Once the entire enemy army was across, a squadron of our gunboats sailed into the Ganges behind them. Now the Chinese line of retreat was cut off both at the main river and at its tributary.

On the nineteenth Hood ordered Montrose's Third Corps to build pontoon bridges and cross over the Ganges to fortify the Gandok's east bank. For the next seven days the Eighty-third Teamsters and I and my five hundred Second Engineers assisted the infantrymen in that task. We did not have the time or the equipment to build the complicated earthworks we had constructed around the Rajmahal Hills; we blasted craters into the razed ground to make mortar pits and sprayed polymer enamel over thousands of smaller holes to make cover for riflemen. We staked barbed wire under the

---

18. Veritas was a variety of the so-called "Insanity Drugs" developed during the Electronic Era. The user of the drug is put into a frenzy and loses his sense of place and time, or so the experts on the matter aver.

water near our shore and brought over some polymer bags to place around our positions. The entire Tiger Division crossed the Ganges to buttress the Third Corps, which could now prevent the Chinese from leaving the subcontinent. Our infantry dug zigzag trenches next to the river; we sprayed these and piled bags in front of them for additional protection. Hood sent a battalion of the Tigers and the Old Dominion[19] east along the northern shore of the Ganges to flush out and kill any Chinese snipers and stragglers lingering there. A regiment of the Sparrows was deployed by helicopter to seal off the mountain passes into Nepal, severing a possible line of retreat Nature had already made incredibly difficult.

While I was up north the Chinese moved south down the west bank of the Son River, probing as they went for weak places in our defenses. This seventy-mile stretch of fortifications in our lines was heavily defended by Woodenhead Santeen's Second Corps. Our trenches there were dug close to the Son. Under the water beyond our emplacements we had laid fifty yards of barbed wire. Four times the Chinese fired their rockets and charged across the Son. Four times they became entangled in the submerged wire and were cut down by the metal hail coming from our lines. Four times they failed to gain an inch east of the river and left more carnage upon the path of their failed charges. On May twenty-third they at last found the place where our lines turned sharply east and they could cross the Son and assail the flaw in our lines. On that day every Chinese soldier still sensate massed into one group and headed toward that single strategic point.

The Chinese Florins were gone by then. Our Air Corps could dedicate every active fighter plane and every tactical bomber, as well as half the Bat Wing bombers, to striking at the Chinese Army. The 101 fighters shot eight canister tubes and all the cannon shells they could carry into the enemy infantry and then returned to base to reload; every plane made a sortie every two hours, seven times a day. Our artillery fired till they smoked in the falling rain. To prevent the barrels of the big guns from melting Hood had to order the gunnery crews to fire only half the 220s and twenty-one-inch monsters at one time for an hour. Still the Chinese came on.

At the critical point in our lines, where the Chinese were gath-

---

19. The Twenty-fifth Infantry Division from Virginia Province.

ering in mass on the twenty-third, was Blue Light Van Fleet's First Corps, which contained the three storied Northfield divisions. On the interior line was the Third Division, the Northfield Shepherds, whose battle flag bore the image of the running wolf and the motto *homo homini lupus*. The men in the Third were from the prairie and were as lean and as hard as the spears of winter wheat their families grew back home. In the last three centuries every inhabited continent had felt the weight of their boot heels. The second line was held by the Second Division, the Northfield Farm Boys. Their battle flag was a plain white field holding a banana and the words **REMEMBER AMERICA**.[20] The Farm Boys had taken the bridge at the Cam[21] and had captured Alejandro Suarez.[22] Three hundred and forty Knights of the Field had served in the Second Northfield, enough silver to dazzle the Angels[23]—Angels being the only souls to meet some of the Second's Knights after they had been decorated. The front lines at the critical hill in the Son's flood plain and in the vulnerable forts around it were held by the First Northfield Division, the Old Contemptibles, the best fighting unit in the world. Like all Yukon divisions, the First kept its beginners' positions open only to hereditary succession; sons served in the same platoons as their fathers, and younger brother privates took orders from their older brother sergeants. What made the First different from other divisions was that her soldiers never took promotions outside their unit. "Better to dig latrines in the First than to command the rest of the Army" was their byword. The Old Contemptibles had captured Bartholomew Iz and had massacred the American Congress during the Storm Times. Their battle flag showed the famous picture of the dead lawyer[24] above the words **HERE THERE ARE**

---

20. As nearly as scholars can tell, the Second Division's flag constitutes something of an insult.

21. In 2142 during the Second Anglican War.

22. In 2301 during the Sixth Mexican War.

23. i.e., from the silver rose decorations.

24. Since the twenty-first century the impaled figure on the First flag has been none other than Bartholomew Iz, the former lawyer the First sat upon a pointed stake.

LIONS. The men of the First wore their death clothes[25] to the front lines and vowed before God they would not take them off until they met the Lord face-to-face or the Chinese turned tail.

General Blue Light Van Fleet placed himself in the key fort atop the hill History remembers by his name. The general was a peculiar man, as extravagantly courageous men tend to be. He stood on his left foot during battle to keep, he claimed, the blood flowing into his heart. He habitually sucked lemons to keep his senses alive. Soldiers who served under him avow he roared out passages from the Book of Joshua whenever the fighting grew particularly hot. During the Battle of Van Fleet's Hill the general rotated a fresh regiment of the First Division into the hill fort every day or, if that were not possible, whenever a break in the Chinese assaults allowed the move to be made. Not one time did Van Fleet take himself from the hill during the battle. He put his face to the polymer wall for the duration and refused to be moved. His men, those of them who lived to tell the story, say the light in his eyes had never burned brighter than it did then.

Hood sent my Eighty-third Teamsters and Second Engineers composite unit straight to the critical hill when we returned from north of the Ganges.

"Keep the First provisioned, Sir Robert," Hood told me. "Better men than you or I give fifty years to the Army and never have the opportunity to win the glory that I am giving here to you. I know you will not fail me, Bobby. When . . . that is, if you lose over a third of your men, ask Van Fleet for men from the Second to help you. Tell your officers your mission. In case you are killed, Sir Robert, they will need to know what they are about. God's speed."

When we arrived on the hill with food, water, and ammunition, the Chinese had already attacked four times. The first time they came upon it was on the twenty-third, when they were making their first reconnaissance in force. The second attack had been a classic small unit assault. They had halted three hundred yards short of our lines, fired their rockets, and proceeded from there into the flames. Our men had sent them rolling down the slope seconds later. A third attack came seven hours later; a fourth attempt

---

25. For the children and ladies who might not be familiar with the military, I should explain that death clothes are the uniforms handmade by a soldier's mother or wife. They are worn on dress occasions or when the soldiers have sworn to fight to the death.

two hours after that. My men were provisioning the First Division when the fifth attempt came. We had to jump into the crowded bunkers with the infantrymen as the incendiary rockets hit above our heads. We heard the crisp *hsst, hsst* as the projectiles split open and quickly flared out upon the polymer bags. The sergeants blew their whistles to mark the end of the bombardment and to signal the troops to sprint from the bunkers to their gun holes in the front wall. I found an unoccupied portal and peered out at the smoldering hillside below us. I saw the flags before anything else. They floated above the gray dust cloud rising from the mortar bursts. At three hundred yards the flags looked as featureless as the smoke and dust. At two hundred yards all but one of the flags had disappeared, and it had turned to bright, fluttering red. A heartbeat later men wearing clothes resembling black pajamas ran screaming from the smoke. There were perhaps thirty of them arrayed in a ragged line. They were shooting their rifles as they ran, hitting nothing specific: like the screaming and the flags, the sound of their guns bore up the men's spirits during the final moments of their lives. A roar sounded from the Yukon firing holes, and the running men each took a quick step backward and vanished from sight.

"All clear!" the sergeants called down the line.

My men and I had left the hill when a seventh Chinese assault took place less than an hour after the sixth. Three more charges came during the next two hours. The enemy regrouped, and when they came upon Van Fleet's Hill a tenth time they fired thousands of fire rockets into the slope in front of our trenches before they were knocked back again. The grass on the hillside and the bodies and finally the untreated earth itself caught fire. A portion of the slope melted away, leaving a glass wall about four feet high along the southern face of our earthworks.

The Chinese thereafter came against the hill at least once every hour. They charged in the night. Ran into each other in the rainy darkness. Shot one another by mistake. They charged against the glass wall they had made and died directly under our guns. On the twenty-fourth they attempted to climb over the top of the black barrier the fires had created. Our planes dropped Fire Sticks onto the area beyond the ledge and burned away the enemy's pole ladders. The Chinese launched their rockets into the glass cliff at close range and melted away the earth three feet farther under our barbed wire. Any Chinese soldier who got that far in front of our lines could linger for a few seconds before hand grenades thrown from the trenches or the blast of our flamethrowers killed them. To destroy a few more inches of the ground we held, the enemy were all too willing to pay the ultimate price. They came in wave upon wave, and slowly the ground eroded away much as a dirt embankment will gradually retreat from the current at the bend of a river. After thirty-one attacks the men of the First Division had to abandon their front trench on the hill because the polymer bags in their forward wall were beginning to fall over the ever receding cliff. The teamsters and I collapsed the remaining portions of the outside walls into the trench while the infantrymen retreated to the fort's second line. The Chinese then adopted the strategy of halting hundreds of yards away and firing their rifles into the air so that their bullets fell upon us in a random pattern. Our mortars and airplanes quickly slaughtered them. Before they died the Chinese riflemen would hit a few of the Yukons on the hill, including some of my men, if we happened to be working when the attack took place.

After sixty-five assaults the second line of trenches also collapsed on the south side of the hill. My teamsters and engineers destroyed the remainder of the second trench's walls as we had those of the first, the mortar men had to haul their weapons to the neighboring forts, and the infantry on Van Fleet's Hill withdrew to the third and final ring, the citadel at the crest of the hill. Support fire from then on had to come from the surrounding areas. Hood pushed all his artillery into that section of his lines and chastened the Chinese swarm relentlessly. By the end of the enemy's seventy-second attack on the twenty-seventh the Chinese had used the last of their incendiary rockets. At that time we did not know they had exhausted the last of their Veritas two days previously. On the twenty-eighth they could throw only two weak assaults on the hill during the entire twenty-four-hour period. On the following day the Chinese did not move against us even once. The Blinking Stars informed us that the enemy were massing ten miles to the south to form one great charge that would contain all of the four hundred thousand Chinese still able to walk. Hood told his staff that evening the morrow would bring the battle's climax.

# FIFTEEN

MAY 30, 2421, was another overcast, misty day on Van Fleet's Hill. We were shelling the southern horizon at sunrise. The rounds landed closer and closer to our positions as the enemy advanced toward us in the ground fog. On the hill with General Van Fleet was the First Division's Sixth Regiment, a fresh contingent at full strength. At 0731 hours Hood, watching the fighting from the fort immediately to Van Fleet's east, sent a message to his First Corps commander that he could abandon the hill should the final assaults grow too fierce.

"You have done more than I can rightly demand of you," Hood told him in his note.

Blue Light Van Fleet sent back a missive that read:

I have lived my entire life in preparation for this day, Jerry. Write my wife for me. Last year she and I celebrated twenty-five years together. I told the lads up here they could fall back if they wanted. Not one of them so chose. Good boys, Jerry. By this evening they will be immortal.

At approximately eight o'clock the uneven fragments of the first Chinese wave emerged from the mortar smoke. They did not last long under fire from the hill and its two flanking entrenchments. At four minutes after eight two hundred thousand Chinese came running from the smoke, or, I should say, they tried to run. Many were too weak to move quickly and had to be prodded forward at bayonet point by the remaining Revolutionary Guardsmen. All three forts opened on them with everything they had. The black wave convulsed in response to the ninety seconds of continuous fire, then contracted into a narrow, dense column in front of the hill fort. The riflemen and machine gunners peeled away layer upon layer of this solid mass. The mortar bursts took bites out of the Chinese as though an invisible monster were gobbling them up piece by piece. The column spread outward as it neared the hill and flowed around the glass wall and the entire base of the hill. The Chinese tried to steal into the fort via the slit trenches at the rear of the entrenchment, and found those excavations had long since been blasted away in the fighting, so they charged across the two abandoned lines and against the interior wall of the citadel where they met canister shot and murderous rifle fire headlong. I was standing near Hood's staff and could see puffs of smoke coming from the wall and could see the dead Chinese rolling backward. The black-uniformed infantry charged up the hill three more times, and three times they were mowed down till the slopes of the hill fort became cluttered with piles of dead Chinese. The scattered leavings of the two hundred thousand then retreated beyond the smoke to regroup. During the lull Hood brought every able-bodied man left in the First Division into the two forts flanking the hill and ordered them to stand in the trenches shoulder to shoulder; when the Chinese came at the hill once more the crossfire from the east and west knocked down their ranks so quickly the men in the Chinese rear became stalled behind the bodies in front of them. They again bunched into a narrow column and pressed on to the front of the hill. They carried pole ladders to the glass cliff. The men at the forefront of their lines attempted to scramble over the black glass; they kept trying to do so until the ladders were reduced to splinters or were lost to the flames and molten earth. Our mortars meanwhile devastated the backed-up column behind these shock troops. Within twenty minutes of emerging from the smoke the Chinese had to retreat in the direction they had come.

Earlier in the battle the Chinese would have sent more rockets into the slope and burned a pathway for themselves on the hill. Having used all their incendiaries, they resorted to smothering the fort with indirect rifle fire. A steady stream of enemy soldiers kept approaching the front of the hill to draw the Yukons from their bunkers and make themselves targets for the cascade of enemy bullets. The Chinese lost a couple hundred men for every Yukon soldier they struck, and for the first time in the battle the Blinking

Stars told us their soldiers were deserting their formations and re-crossing the Son River. Yet their attacks continued.

At 1439 hours another mass assault hit Van Fleet's Hill. Nearly all the one hundred and twenty thousand Chinese who could move trod toward the citadel and died in spectacular numbers. At the rear, where the slit trenches had once been, some attackers actually climbed over the dead and leaped into the inner trench. From my vantage point I could not see any of the fighting within the polymer walls; I did see two of our position flags fall as the Chinese fought through our line. I heard hand grenades exploding as the Sixth Regiment counterattacked. Minutes later I saw a few dozen Chinese racing from the south side of the citadel, where they were cut down by riflemen in the two flanking entrenchments. The main enemy swarm soon thereafter had to retreat for a third time that day.

Blue Light Van Fleet and Hood had been wrong about that morning. Evening came and still the issue was not resolved. Chinese rifle fire pecked at the hill until after sunset, inflicting casualties Hood could not access. The Marshal wanted to air drop supplies into the fort. If the Chinese began another fusillade while the helicopters were overhead we would lose the expensive airships, their crews, and the men in the trenches could be trapped in the resulting inferno should the helicopters crash upon them. Risking my composite group would be less dangerous.

"Sir Robert," Hood said to me, "you are going to have to carry supplies to them. I'm sorry, Bobby."

He studied his hands while he spoke.

I wanted to tell him I had a pregnant wife and that I wanted to live for her and our unborn child. I could not. I was a Yukon soldier and had to obey my superior and the Military Code and the years of training that lay behind his orders.

"How much do you want me to take, sir?" I asked.

"Three million rounds, two thousand ration kits, two thousand gallons of water," he said, still interested in his hands.

"I have four hundred men under twenty in my group, sir," I said. "I would, with your permission, send them on fire patrol on the air bases. The older men and I will suffice, sir."

"Yes," Hood nodded in agreement. "Send the boys back. Very commendable, Sir Robert. Very commendable. I'm sorry," he said a second time. "You have to understand . . . When one is in charge . . . May I have your hand before you go, Bobby?"

I gave it to him, and he went away slapping his palm against his thigh.

My old hands in the Eighty-third Teamsters and Second Engineers agreed it was right to send the younger men from harm's way. They told me I was a good fellow to die under and loaded themselves up like mules with water jugs, ration packets, and boxes of ammunition. I organized a vanguard of thirty who moved the carnage from our path, permitting the rest of the five hundred men I had left to follow in double file through the horrific landscape. Not all the Chinese lying before us were entirely dead. The bodies under our feet sometimes moved or groaned when we stepped on them. At the base of the hill on the fort's north side one corpse stood upright and killed three of my men with his automatic rifle. Working on reflexes, I shot him with my pistol and blew his lungs out his back. I did not pause to consider him. He was first man I had ever killed. In a thoughtless moment I had broken my promise to Charlotte. I did not have time to contemplate that or ask forgiveness. We peppered the corpses in the area with machine gun fire to make certain they were quite dead and we could proceed. The Yukons inside the fort would not come to help us carry the supplies. We called to them, and they called back we could jolly well get stuffed. They were not leaving the safety of their trenches. It took us thirty minutes to get up the slope and into the citadel. The repeated shelling around the hill had smashed the fort's drainage system, leaving the bottom of the interior trench knee deep in water and muck. Body parts and human waste were floating in the filthy mire we had to wade through. A bed of spent cartridges crunched under our boot soles when we stepped into the hideous slop. Most of the men in the Sixth Regiment had suffered fragment wounds from the exploding bullets; four hundred and sixty of them were severely wounded or dead. The regiment's colonel and both his majors were among those lost. Van Fleet was alone at his post on the south wall. After seventy-seven attacks on his fort he was covered in blood, most of it his own, and was entirely spent in mind and spirit.

"Willard, is that you?" he said to me when I approached him. "Come to take me home, have you?[1] 'As I was with Moses, so shall I be with thee: I will not fail them, nor forsake thee.'"[2]

---

1. War College records tell us that Willard Honesty Van Fleet was General Van Fleet's younger brother. He had been killed in a training accident ten years earlier.

2. Joshua, 1:5.

He carried in his right hand a sword he had taken from a dead Chinese soldier. His left arm was torn open to the shoulder and hung limp at his side. Whenever he fired his rifle he had to prop it between the firing hole and his shoulder and pull the trigger with his one good hand.

" 'And the other issued out of the city against them; so they were in the midst of Israel, some on this side, and some on that: and they smote them, so that they let none of them remain or escape,' "[3] said the general, his head thrown back so that his eyes were directed over my head and toward the cloudy heavens.

"Right you are, sir," I said. "Marshal Hood had ordered me to carry the wounded to the rear, sir."

Charlie and French, always at my heels, looked at each other. They knew Hood had ordered no such thing.

"They shall not be here when the Lord comes," said General Van Fleet, and made some weary swipes at the air with his captured sword. " 'Alas, O Lord God, wherefore hast thou at all brought these people over the Jordan?'[4] Take them, Willard, take them over the river."

"Would the General consider coming with us?" I asked. "You are badly wounded, sir."

He gazed out his firing hole at the demonic landscape. His forehead eased onto the filthy polymer wall as he closed his eyes.

"The Lord comes for me today," he whispered.

My men distributed the supplies among the infantrymen in the fort. I ordered them to gather up the wounded and to head back to the other fort, two teamsters carrying every stricken man. While I was overseeing my men's exit a young lieutenant came to me and told me how bad matters were in the citadel.

"The senior officers are dead, sir," he said. "Captain Stewart lives, but he's taken a fragment in the head. General Van Fleet . . . you have seen the general, sir. My father is . . . he was a sergeant in the Sixth, sir. He is dead too. The men look upon me as my father's son. You know how that works, sir. Sir, there is no leadership here."

"Why are you telling me this, lieutenant?" I said.

"You are a Knight of the Field, sir. A colonel," he said, pleading

3. Joshua, 8:22.

4. Joshua, 7:7.

with me. "You didn't get that silver rose for building bridges, sir. The men would respect a man like you, sir."

He put his hand on my decoration. I pitied him in that moment. Because he was a Yukon soldier like I, he knew I did not pity him nearly as much as I feared being thought a coward. Like all of my kind, I could not back down from another chance to prove my courage in spite of everything I had said to Charlotte and in spite of everything she wanted me to be.

"I will stay with fifty men," I said. "You need to have some repairs done."

The teamsters I kept on the hill with me were each over fifty-five years of age. They hugged their friends good-bye and went about moving polymer bags and clearing ditches without a murmur of complaint. We constructed twenty-six one-man bunkers on the outside wall using bags from the abandoned trenches; in these the snipers had a full range of vision around the perimeter of the fort and would be safe from indirect rifle fire. I had the men loot the body armor vests from the dead Revolutionary Guardsmen around us; these vests were too small for us to wear, so we unlaced them and hung their flaps over our backs. I told the First Division men that when the Chinese attacked we should keep our bodies pressed to the front wall and in that position only a bullet coming from directly above us and penetrating a helmet could kill a Yukon. During the rifle barrages I kept the men inside the bombardment bunkers, excepting the snipers, who stayed in their one-man posts and from there picked off anyone trying to penetrate our positions. I unfurled what was left of the ragged canopy, and my teamsters spliced together links of plastic tubes from the water jugs in order to siphon drain the trenches. I knew the Chinese would attempt to move up the pathway my men had made at the rear of the fort so I ordered that a hundred of the one hundred and thirty canister tubes we had left be sent to the bunker commanding that position; the other thirty I split among two flying squads I told to run to wherever they were needed. The proud men of the Sixth Regiment were not pleased to be taking orders from an officer outside the First Division. (I still wore the insignia of the Second Engineers.) I lied to them to quiet their misgivings and said I had been sent directly from Marshal Hood, which, to a certain extent, was true.

At 2330 hours the Chinese commenced shooting at us again. We stayed in our bunkers and did not take a single casualty while our mortars in the nearby forts ravaged the enemy riflemen. At 0214 hours on the thirty-first the weary Chinese resumed the fusillade, again to no effect other than the loss of thousands on their side of the field. Fifty minutes after three o'clock they launched another mass charge against the hill. My men had to fire parachute flares and run to their firing holes along the trench wall. The enemy bunched at the south side of the fort and at once found that approach was still impassible; the steep slope and our constant rifle fire again kept them trapped at the base of the black cliff. From inside the fort we could see the white phosphorous bursts the Chinese grenades made and could feel the explosions in the soles of our feet. We could not hear anything. Some grenades the Chinese threw at us bounced over the canopy; a very few landed in the trench and killed anyone close to their white hot bursts. One landed near me, and Charlie snatched it up and tossed it back. He said something to me I could not hear. Minutes later another grenade landed in the trench to our right. Poor Charlie stooped to pick it up just as it exploded, and I felt his warm blood splash against my face.

"He was to marry my sister," said French.

That was the only sentence I heard during the attack. French meant Charlie had been promised to his sister when they were young. French's sister had refused Charlie, so the two friends had gone to the Army together. The old sailor remembered this in the moment of his companion's death.

"We don't have time for that," I said, though in the uproar he could not understand me.

I grabbed his tunic and pulled French toward the rear of the fort, to the bunker above the open pathway. Two young infantrymen, both of whom would become Knights of the Field for the bravery they displayed on Van Fleet's Hill,[5] were already sitting at the mouth of the bunker and were firing canister tubes in turns, each man waiting for the black figures to appear on the open ground below them before letting fly. The soldier behind the bunker who was firing parachute flares to keep the open pathway illuminated took a bullet in his helmet and fell dead, his mouth open to sound a scream that never escaped his lips. I

---

5. Sir John Aaron Bowditch and Sir Edmond Freedom Marks. Bowditch would in later life become a major in the Sixth Regiment.

had to fish his flare gun from the trench water and shoot the flares in his place. When one of the lads manning the canister tubes tumbled from the rear of the bunker holding his bleeding eyes,[6] I handed the flare gun to French and took the fallen man's place at the firing hole. The enemy clambering up the pathway looked like black spiders dancing inside a golden bowl. The canister packets flew twenty feet from the tubes and opened onto the writhing figures like fire Angels spreading their wings over fields of the damned. The doomed men on the receiving end of my fire opened their arms to the storm of pellets and accepted death. I shouted at them, called them names, begged them to turn back. In answer to my pleas they spread their arms and filled up the pathway with their bodies. I had seven tubes left when the black mass ebbed and started back for the south. Within ten minutes the only sounds we could hear in the fort were dying men weeping inside and outside the walls of our wretched fortress.

I returned to the south side and found General Van Fleet lying in the water. An exploding bullet had hit him atop his left shoulder and had blown away that portion of his body. I helped him lean against the wall where he clung to the dregs of his life.

"Willard," he said to me, "the Lord says it's time. Hood's orders. Fire the purple flare, Willard. Fire this gun. It's time."

I took a snub-nosed flare gun from his waist belt.

"Fire, Willard," he whispered, "light my way to Heaven."

I shot the flare into the sky. A purple trail of sparks sped upward and burst into three lavender flowers in the starless sky.

"The farce is ended," said General Blue Light Van Fleet. " 'No man had been able to stand before us unto this day.'[7] Willard, we have to go back over the river."

He took my hand and died. We had no place for this three-star general and hero of the Confederacy to lie other than in a foot of slimy rainwater where hundreds of other broken men already lay.

The young lieutenant found me again. He said we had lost another sixty killed and seriously wounded in the attack. He was informing me the last captain on site was dead when he seemed to

---

6. This would be Marks, who was, regrettably, blind the rest of his life.

7. Joshua, 23:9.

slow down like a motion picture set on the wrong speed. He and I rose several inches off the ground along with the dirty water and the spent shell casings underneath our feet. We heard the roar of an explosion only after we had landed and a wave of dirt and water had swept over us.

"They're blowing up the world!" shouted French and pointed to the south, to where a chain of blasts was ripping open the dark plain.

We in the fort did not know until after daybreak what had happened. While my composite group and I had been north of the Ganges, Hood had ordered his demolition men to mine the land a mile in front of the hill and plant thousands of tons of dynamite one hundred and twenty feet in the earth in sixteen different places and to connect the explosives with chemical fuses. The purple flare had been the signal to blast the sixteen craters that made a two-mile-long ditch across the front shared by the three adjoining forts. Tactical bombers swooped down and dropped Fire Sticks into the ditch after the dust had settled and burned the excavation even deeper into the ground.

At 0456 the Chinese attacked the hill en masse for the seventy-ninth and final time. In the predawn darkness they charged straight from the mortar cloud and into the enormous ditch. Our artillery men knew the exact range of the crater from their positions. I could write that what transpired in the manmade ravine when the waves of men and the 220 shells arrived at the same moment was beyond my capacity to witness. After having beheld the rest of the Battle of Northern India I would say the slaughter there was no worse than what I had already seen. From the hill fort I could not see the thousands of frantic Chinese trying to crawl up the melted walls of the ditch as bits of shrapnel and basaltic glass did their dirty work. I was thankful I was spared that sight. A couple score of the enemy did somehow manage to emerge on our side of the long crater; the Yukon infantry shouted "Enjoy Hell!" to those brave few and shot them down.

At sunup the Seventh Regiment of the First Division reinforced those of us on the hill. They struggled for nigh two hours fighting their way through the dead to get to our trench. From our vantage point we could see that the entire Second Corps under Wooden-head Santeen had moved onto the open ground east of us. The Second and Third Divisions of the First Corps and the unscathed

Fourth Corps under General Early had moved into position west of us.[8] The confused leavings of the Chinese Army made an abortive assault west of the craters, head-on into the fresh Second Division. In response Hood attacked with the Second Corps in the east. The remaining Chinese force folded before them like a paper lantern. The Blinking Stars told us their reserve troops, whatever were left of them, were fleeing into the Son; their disorganized front line troops retreated from the Second Division and made a last stand on the south side of the long crater as the Fourth Corps and the Second and Third Divisions swept behind them from the east and the Second Corps performed a similar flanking movement from the west. The last of the Chinese were forced into the glass ditch. Unable to defend themselves and unable to move, they threw up their arms and surrendered. The time was 1017, on the fifty-first day of the campaign.

We on the hill needed another hour to get to the north rim of the crater. I, like the other survivors from Van Fleet's Hill, was covered with the vilest gore imaginable when I arrived at the ditch's edge. Below us we saw thousands of starved and half naked Chinese standing with raised hands atop more piles of dead men. The Yukons on the south side were forcing the prisoners to strip to their skivvies and to climb single file up that side of the ravine where other Yukons were binding the enemy soldiers' hands behind their backs. A band had appeared on the side opposite us and began playing "The Dog in the Bush" and "Black Jack Davy."

At the bottom of the crater a group of diminutive Chinese refused to remove their black tunics as the others had. A tall, burly sergeant from the Second Division slid down the glassy slope and ordered them in gestures to undress. He grabbed the Chinese soldier nearest him and ripped off the soldier's blouse. The entire Yukon contingency in the vicinity gasped at what they saw.

"They're women!" the Yukons exclaimed. "Women! They used women in the place of men!"

"Kill them!" someone on the south side yelled. "Kill the whores!"

The sergeant ripped the clothes off two more of the frightened women. His squad slid into the ditch after him and hit the women with their rifle butts. The sergeant took one by her hair and raised

---

8. General Hazard Hopefilled Early (2347–2439), "the Fighting Band Leader," had risen from a position in an Army band to command the Fourth Corps. He was seventy-four and in ill health in 2421 and would soon retire.

his bayonet to her throat. The woman was on her knees, crying as she tried to hide her nakedness. I had hated her as keenly as the other Yukons when I saw she was female; upon hearing her weep I thought of my wife on the day she left India. The memory made me feel something I could not name for this woman I did not know. Contrary to my years of training, I at once resolved to save her and her companions.

"Leave them be!" I shouted to the men below.

I slid into the ditch from the north side; the young lieutenant from the hill and French came behind me. The Second Division soldiers stood frozen in place at the bottom of the glassy depression, probably taken aback by our strange, muck-splattered appearances.

"Who are you?" the sergeant asked.

I wiped the filth from my silver rose and my colonel's sheaves. The Second Division soldiers could not see the cloth engineer's insignia on my shoulder for that decal remained covered with blood and dirt.

"I am Colonel Sir Robert Bruce," I said.

"He's the last commander on the hill," the lieutenant chimed in.

"I am acting under the direct orders of Marshal Hood," I said in the loudest voice I could summon so the men on the ledge above us could hear. "No one is to harm these prisoners. The women here are comfort ladies the Chinese forced into India. They gave them guns only for the final assault. Yukon soldiers are Christian gentlemen above all else. They do not harm prisoners of war, neither male or female."

"The fact is, sir," the lieutenant whispered to me, "in the First Division we usually don't take prisoners."

"You do today," I said. To the stunned men above me I said in my loudest voice, "Get some food and water for these people. Marshal Hood does not want anyone dying while in our custody."

They did not move at once. They thought the command over, then whispered some angry remarks to each other and did as I had ordered them. I was not acting there under orders from Hood. For everything I knew the women were soldiers of the line. I did know Hood would have the prisoners treated humanely, which he did, despite Fitz's orders on the Blinking Stars to kill everyone.[9]

---

9. Hood's refusal to follow the Consul's command marks the beginning of his decline. See Gerald pp. 3186–204.

"Sir, they'd kill us if they could," said the big sergeant.

"You may be correct, sergeant," I said, "but are you saying we should be no better than the Chinese?"

"No, sir," he and his comrades agreed.

"And since when did we ever give the Chinese a chance to take one of us prisoner?" I said, appealing to their sense of superiority.

"Right you are, sir," the sergeant chuckled, and he let go of the poor woman and went with his mates up the southern slope.

French the sailor was of great help in communicating with the Chinese. Like all officers, I spoke Latin, ancient Greek, and Hebrew. The enlisted men knew only Latin in addition to their own English tongue. The old mariner was probably the only man in our camp who knew a word of Mandarin. The Chinese were as startled as the Yukons had been when he told them they were to go up the slope and be fed. One of the women kissed my hand as she went by me, which was not much of a salve upon my feelings; her simple act of gratitude instead made me think of how I could never justify to my wife the terrible things we had done here.[10]

The forty thousand Chinese who had fled over the Son would blunder into the Indian Third and Fifth Armies at Kochas. The Chinese were out of ammunition, and the Indians were in no mood to show them mercy. Two hundred Chinese would flee that massacre to reach the Ganges, where our gunboats would kill most of them. Perhaps two dozen reached the Gandok, where the Third Corps would shoot all but a handful. On the June 27, four sick and exhausted Chinese Guardsmen climbed up Biriganj Pass toward Nepal. Snipers from the Sparrows shot them dead in one volley and built a rock monument over their bodies. Of the thirty-one thousand Chinese who surrendered to us below Van Fleet's Hill, twelve thousand died of malnutrition and cholera while in our custody. Such was the end of the Chinese army.

The Turkish army died far more quickly.

On September 19, five months after the war had begun, a force of around one hundred thousand Turkish regulars at last advanced

---

10. What does Bruce mean in this passage? Does he imply that he is ashamed he saved the Chinese women or—as is more likely, given his perverse manner of thinking—is he for some reason ashamed of something that happened in the battle? Gerald himself (pp. 2943–47) mentions Bruce's heroism on Van Fleet's Hill, and Bruce was given golden petals for his silver rose and made a double Knight by his superiors. Why would he be ashamed of any of that?

into the Thar Desert and headed toward our base at Luni. Hood had transferred the Third Corps to the west on helicopters and zeppelins, and I had overseen the building of a small system of earthworks between Luni and the desert. Our men on the ground never fired a shot in the western fighting, for our bombers annihilated the Turks from the air two hundred miles west of our base. A few of the enemy lived to retreat into Persia. We found only abandoned equipment and burned sand when we reconnoitered the site of the Turkish disaster several days later. So ended the Turkish army and the war on the ground.

The five and a half thousand Yukons who perished on Van Fleet's Hill were given a bronze plaque in the National Cathedral in Cumberland.[11] We buried whatever we could find of our fallen comrades on high ground, out of the reach of the monsoon's floods. The enemy dead were bulldozed pell-mell into ditches. The seasonal rains soon washed their decaying remains into the rivers, and we in the Sixth Army could not escape seeing and smelling the fruits of our labors long after the dry season returned to the once beautiful hills.

---

11. It is a very large plaque and prominently displayed inside the hallway leading to the rectory gardens. I located it after only a quarter-hour search.

# SIXTEEN

EIGHT MONTHS LATER the Yukon troops left in India were still burying the bodies of the enemy soldiers we had killed the previous year. After Hood commissioned the obsequious Mr. Puri to dispose of the Chinese dead, that efficient gentleman sent two hundred thousand Indian laborers to help us dig proper graves for the twenty million fallen. Under more favorable conditions Mr. Puri's men might have completed the gruesome project in a month's time. In the India of 2422 the numbers of dead kept growing after the fighting had ended. While alive the Chinese had brought famine to the Ganges Valley by razing the land they invaded, in death they brought cholera. Worse catastrophes soon followed. The packets of mosquitoes carrying the new strain of malaria that the Chinese had dropped in Burma and Canton created an epidemic that eventually would spread as far east as the Philippines and as far west as the Indus River. There were cases as far south as the Darwin region of Australia, and the Yukons had to be evacuated from that portion of the island continent for two years. Not since the Great Plague had Death triumphed over so many.[1] All of east Asia became rotten with the dead and the soon to be dead. Mr. Puri's army of grave diggers could not keep up with the ever growing number of new bodies that kept appearing in our small portion of the river valley. When the cholera and malaria spread into their ranks his men had to retreat back to the relative safety of cool, dry Delhi, and let Nature do to the corpses what she would.

---

1. Bruce means the manmade plague of the twenty-first century, not the Black Death of the fourteenth.

On the bases at Luni and in the Rajmahal Hills the Yukons had vaccine against the cholera. Only insect repellant and mosquito netting kept the new malaria in check. None of us went outside without slathering our exposed faces and hands with the pungent cream. Never did anyone of us go near the riverbank, where the clouds of bugs were the worst. Our numbers in India had thankfully dwindled since the end of the land war due to transfers back to the Confederacy. Hood had been sending infantrymen home since the fighting ceased around Van Fleet's Hill. In the summer of 2422 he also began to dismiss the airmen. There were no longer any strategic targets in the world for our Bat Wing bombers to strike. Beyond the daily reconnaissance flights, we no longer launched more than a single sortie a week. Antiaircraft gunners, teamsters, engineers, aircraft mechanics: the entire victorious Army company by company caught zeppelin flights back to the Confederacy. Weeds grew through the cracks in the unused runways and roads, while the Santals and other rightful inhabitants of the Rajmahal began to return, a family at a time, to their erstwhile farmland.

On June 14, 2422, the Turks surrendered and agreed to accept the Four Points. Like the surrenders of the South Americans, the news came to us as a lightning bolt from a cloudless sky. I had been dining out in my fellow officers' tents for a year on the well documented argument that wars cannot be won by air power alone. We did not occupy a square inch of the Turkish Empire during the entire course of the conflict. They had given up their independence anyway. My brother officers called me "Robert of very little faith" and teased me ad nauseam when we heard of the capitulation.

"Do you have any more insights to share with us, Sir Robert?" another colonel chided me over a supper of smoked fish and fried chips.

"Tell us the Chinese will never surrender, Sir Robert," a captain added. "Then it will be a certainty they will give up in another week."

They may have teased me; that did not mean the other officers were not also as at a loss for answers. No one could understand why the Turks had given up so quickly and so totally. Granted, the Turks were "the Sick Man of Eurasia," holding—just barely—an empire fractured among Uzbekis, Iranians, Berbers, Arabs, and European Moslems. Some of us in India rationalized their acceptance of the Four Points as a consequence of their empire's internal divisions rather than as a product of the military defeat the Yukons inflicted upon them. Those holding this point of view noted that North Africa and Mesopotamia bolted from the empire when the Turks surrendered, which, they said, showed the weakness of the Turkish government in Tashkent. These know-it-alls were as confused as the rest of us when the rebellious Arab states separately agreed to the Four Points in October of 2422.[2]

The unorganized African factions south of the Sahara Desert followed the Arabs' lead in November. The Turks and the Chinese had been unable to supply their proxies in that portion of the globe while those groups the Yukons supported had more guns than they had soldiers to carry them. Disturbing photographs of highly armed African boys of ten and younger became a staple of Yukon newspapers during the war years. Our journalists entered the ports of Monrovia and Lagos City to take the lurid pictures, of which both the readers back home and the rifle-toting children themselves did not seem to tire, despite the Archbishop of the United Yukon Church deemed the journalists immoral. (No Yukon was so rash as to denounce the arming of little boys and the resulting slaughters as immoral, for that would be tantamount to denouncing the Consul. I was no better than the rest of my countrymen. I knew Fitz was doing something horrible, and I dared not confess that to my brother officers.) The Turkish and Chinese proxies had to join our side and sign the Four Points. Our man in southern Africa, the bloodthirsty Joseph Jones,[3] was appointed "President" of that beleaguered region; he promptly killed his leading rivals and stole the land and gold of anyone in Africa who had any of either. The Yukon newspapers called Jones "our gift to Africa," and I suppose he was.

Clearly an unknown force was influencing world events. Speculation as to what that force might be dominated every conversa-

---

2. See Gerald pp. 3122–234 for the story of the Turkish dissolution.

3. Joseph Jones (2372–2430) was the leader of the Yukon-supported Freedom and Peace Party since 2410. True, Jones was a mass murderer and a thief, but he did bring order, of a sort, to a troubled region. Gerald (pp. 3297–98) recounts that Jones had good manners and a pleasing nature. St. Matthew's University thought so highly of him that institution granted him an honorary doctorate of letters in 2425.

tion I heard in the Rajmahal Hills. Hood told us the Blinking Stars were broadcasting latitude and longitude coordinates several times an hour, whether our planes were flying or not. Our bomber pilots had seen Yukon zeppelins over China, presumably navigating their way by using the information the Blinking Stars were giving.

At a November dinner in the staff tent Hood told his most senior officers he thought Fitz was dropping something on the Chinese.

"A rigid frame zeppelin, a big one, can carry a thousand tons of cargo around the world," said Hood over our boiled beef and potatoes. "These are H-class numbers.[4] They must have dropped the same substance on the Argentines and the Turks."

I was hesitant to speak at these staff dinners. I was a mere colonel and a brevet one at that. The other men at Hood's table were—other than Stein—his lieutenant and major generals. They tolerated me at these get-togethers because I was Hood's college chum and—after Van Fleet's Hill—a Double Knight, and because unlike Stein I kept my mouth shut.

"What could they be dropping?" Daddy Montrose thought aloud. "Some sort of poison gas?"

"Unlikely," said Hood. "The elements would quickly disperse any chemical agent. When dropped over these vast areas, a gas of any sort would be ineffective."

General Horowitz[5] suggested the Consul might be releasing a bacteria or virus on enemy land.

"Why would he need a big zeppelin to do that, Josh?" said Hood.

"Perhaps, Jerry, they are dropping mosquitoes, as the Chinese did," said General Horowitz.

"Bugs!" said Woodenhead Santeen in disgust. "The young Consul wouldn't do it!"

Stein made choking noises into his napkin, sounding like a pig that has too much corn in its mouth. The generals winced, because they knew the awful young man was about to say something.

---

4. The H-class was introduced before the war in 2415; made by the Howlet-Gunderson Company in Grand Harbor, they flew for thirty years until replaced by the improved Roget's Streamliner.

5. General Joshua Israel Horowitz (2360–2435) was then the commander of the Fourth Division. He later became a lieutenant general and led the entire Second Corps. He was murdered in 2435 during the Chrysanthemum Woman's second purge.

"I'm sorry, gentlemen," said Lord Stein upon regaining his breath. "It went down the wrong tube."

"You were laughing! What did I say that delighted the young Lord?" thundered General Santeen, squinting his eyes at Stein.

"Don't you find it humorous, gentlemen," said Stein, "that General Santeen believes that a man who murdered his father would hesitate to kill those he has never met?"

No one there was going to respond to that.

"You bearded old warriors are a curious lot," Stein went on. "You have each of you been in the service for—what?—three decades at least, and you've just polished off twenty million Chinamen, and still the thought that the Consul is perhaps killing a few million more offends you!"

Generals Montrose, Santeen, Early, and Horowitz jumped to their feet. Santeen had drawn his pistol and I believe he would have shot Stein if Hood had not jumped in front of the young Lord.

"Sit down, my friends, sit down," said the Marshal. "There will be no violence here! We will sit and eat!"

"You would have us sit with him because he is a damned Lord!" boomed Santeen.

"I would sit with him because Lord Stein is correct," said Hood.

The generals were amazed. Santeen sat down as heavily on his canvas chair as if Hood had felled him with a punch. The others settled down a moment later.

"You men are not responsible for what happened here—" Hood began.

"No, they were in India by chance and, as Fate would have it, twenty million Chinese soldiers happened to come here to commit suicide," sneered Stein.

"When set against the dead civilians here in India and the rest of the world, the twenty million are less than you imagine, sir," said Hood, still standing at the head of the table. "Now, please be quiet for a minute, Lord Stein. The point I was making is that my generals are not to blame. They are good soldiers who did as the Military Code demanded they do. I cannot excuse myself so easily. My good and loyal generals, like my men in the field, believed they were fighting for a better world, an end to oriental tyranny, for a just Consul. I knew differently. I know the Consul and know he . . . I know he is as he is. The Military Code binds no one to follow such a man. I kept that from you, my friends. I am responsible for everything."

"I don't want to hear this!" said Woodenhead Santeen, and put his hands over his ears. "The Consul is a righteous leader of men! God would not allow him to be otherwise!"

The poor man did not seem ridiculous to me. I too wished I could cover my ears and not know what we had done in India.

"That won't do, Judge Jerry," said Stein, calmly munching at his beef. "You aren't Jesus Christ. You can't assume the sins of the world. These darlings here knew what they were about. Did a bang up job of it, too. Since when did any Yukon need to rationalize why he kills the enemies of the Confederacy? Why, our sweet Bobby here, as innocent a man as you'll find in this army, he was so hot to have at the Chinese he was ready to throw away his life on that stinking hill with Van Fleet. By now, even he has to know as well as anybody what the Consul is. The truth didn't matter to him."

He gave me a mocking salute as he shoveled another forkful into his mouth.

"Locusts," I said, and felt a rush of nausea at the base of my throat.

"Pardon, Sir Robert?" said Hood.

"I said, 'locusts,' sir," I said. "Begging the generals' pardon, I just now thought of it. The Consul is breeding a type of locusts near Pallas, in Ohio Province. The younger Aranov brother is in charge of the project, sir. Dumping locusts would explain the zeppelin sorties. When any nation refuses to sign the Four Points, the Consul could inundate that country's crop lands with them, sir."

Hood tugged at his beard and sat down in his chair. Stein reached across the table for more wine. The others present let the food on their plates go cold, as did I.

"The Consul could agree to give the defeated nations insecticide after they have signed the Four Points," said Hood. "Lord Fitzpatrick's family and the DeShays together own the largest zeppelin fleets . . . Did you see the locusts going onto the airships, Sir Robert?"

"No, sir," I said. "I saw the warehouses the Consul's men were keeping the bugs in. There were miles of them, sir."

"Tens of millions starved to death," said General Joshua Horowitz as he gazed into his plate.

"It cannot be true," repeated General Santeen.

"More like hundreds of millions, General Joshua Izzy," said Stein. (A peculiar tendency of Stein's was his inclination to insult anyone who really was Jewish.) "We are now the second greatest pack of mass murderers in History. If only the world population were as big as it was three hundred years ago! We could've given Bartholomew Iz's bunch a run for their money!"

"I need proof," said Hood.

"I could find out, old man," asserted Stein.

"The Consul is not going to confide in you, Lord Colonel Stein," said Hood. "To no one's surprise, you are drunk, again, and saying improper things, sir."

"I could go to Valette or Shelley," said Stein. "Shelley would be a better source. Valette plays everything too close to his vest. Shelley gives out secrets so everyone around him feels as if he were an intimate of his. He has to do it. You know he doesn't have any real friends. Shelley boy is a born legislator."

"If I let you go to Cumberland to confer with Lord Shelley, Lord Colonel Stein," said Hood, "I will not see you back here again."

"Would that break your heart?" asked Stein.

For the only time since the ground fighting began Hood allowed himself to smile. The other generals forgot, for a few seconds, the grim discussion we had been having and likewise grinned.

"I did promise the Consul to keep you here until the fighting ended, Lord Colonel Stein," said Hood. "The fighting has indeed ended. You could send us a letter."

"He could leave tonight," said Daddy Montrose, and checked his watch. "He has a full four hours to get ready for the midnight zeppelin."

"I'm halfway home as we speak, gentlemen," said Stein. "Oh, speaking of letters, Jerry, I forgot to tell you something the wife wrote. You will enjoy this too, Bobby. Mason, our sweet Mason, is Deputy Foreign Minister."

"Why not?" muttered Hood.

"Makes one proud to be a Yukon!" said Stein and stabbed at his potatoes. "Millions die so we can have the kind of nation that promotes men of Mason's stamp into positions of power."

Stein's batman threw the young Lord's belongings together into a couple of steamer lockers and got his master on the zeppelin that night. A fortnight later the young Lord sent Hood a letter. He wrote that he was resigning his officer's commission to become

Shelley's chief aide in the Senate. Stein further declared he would stand for his father's Senate seat in the next election cycle, a position for which he was singularly unsuitable. Unlike Shelley, who could ingratiate others to him in a brief period of time, Lord Stein had the opposite effect upon those he encountered. Given that the older Senators already resented "the kiddies" running the Confederacy, Hood and I could guess how the other legislators would feel about Banker after another year's passing. Stein concluded his letter with these cryptic sentences:

> Bobby was right about the locusts. Zeppelin flights leave Pallas every six hours, former S.A. men at the helm. Between the Yangtze and the Pearle rivers there is fish to eat and not much else. Unless, *comilitome,* the Chinese are eating each other. For the sake of old times, Jerry, I would ask you to burn this letter and not to speak of the secret I have told you.

Our crimes did not remain secret for long. Unknown individuals in North America distributed pamphlets describing the famine in East Asia that autumn. Yukon civilians for the first time read of locust infestations and of the remarkable events that had transpired in India. Reporters from respectable journals did not dare touch the locust story. They did investigate the rumors they were hearing about the Battle of Northern India. Scores of journalists appeared in the Rajmahal Hills via commercial airship lines. To my great surprise one man from the Centralia City *Champion* sought me out and took notes concerning my role in the fighting.

"So you were made a Double Knight, Sir Robert, for your actions on Van Fleet's Hill?" asked the aggressive young man in a white linen suit.

"Yes, I suppose I was, sir," I said. "Who, may I ask, told you of me, sir?"

"Some odd chap informed me where I could find you," he said cheerfully. "A big fellow—I think he is a bodyguard or something—he works on the Consul's estate, he told me you were a hero."

(I would learn months later that Buck Pularski had given the journalist my name because Buck knew Fitz would be reluctant to harm Charlotte were I a hero the public knew by name.)

Stories about the ground war began appearing in the Confederacy's largest newspapers a year and a half after the battle had ended. On November 28, 2422, the East Port *Frontier-Eagle* ran a front page photograph of Chinese bodies washed from their graves near the Son. There was an accompanying story that mentioned the astonishing twenty million casualty figure. On the twenty-ninth the *Frontier-Eagle* did not appear on the doorsteps of its subscribers or in the newsstands along the east coast. A week passed, and when the *Frontier-Eagle* reappeared there was an apology on page one for what the new editor called "the prank story of November 28." The paper's old editor and the reporter who wrote the "prank story" had disappeared. The *Desert News*, the largest Salt Lake City paper, normally bore on its masthead the provincial symbol of a beehive. On the December 1 readers noted that the bees had been redrawn to resemble locusts. Lord Myers, the paper's owner and publisher, was at once called to Ohio for a personal conference with the Consul. Upon returning to Salt Lake the ashen-faced Lord Myers saw to it the bees on his paper looked like bees. The Reverend Matthew Oswald, one of the last courageous churchmen in the weakened U.Y.C., gave a fiery sermon that same November to an overflow congregation in the National Cathedral. "The life of one man is too high a price for this world," orated Reverend Oswald. "Twenty million is the price of eternal damnation." The following Monday morning his housekeeper found Reverend Oswald dead in his bed, a bullet in his brain. The Cumberland police guild and the respectable newspapers declared the death a suicide, although a gun was never found.[6] His death did not stop the pamphlets nor keep vandals from painting pictures of winged horses—the Fitzpatrick family symbol—and locusts on city walls throughout the Yukon homelands.

The source for most of the rumors were the Sixth Army veterans returning home to tell their Liege Lords the full story of the Battle of Northern India. Many of the details in the pamphlets

---

6. The reader should not believe any of this passage. The *Frontier-Eagle* report was indeed a prank. The death of Reverend Oswald really was a suicide. Official Historians do not mention the *Desert News* incident. Among those who wrote of that era, only Bruce and Mason put any faith in the locust story. Modern science tells us the locusts that caused the famines in Asia and South America were indigenous to the Middle East. Peculiar weather patterns spread the insects to China and across the Atlantic to Argentina. Lord Fitzpatrick had nothing to do with any of this. (See Gerald, page 3654, footnote 231.)

were so exact I believe they had to have been leaked by none other than Marshal Hood. The Sixth Army commander was a hero to his men, a tool of the Consul to the general population, and had become a lost soul in his own troubled mind. He could not accept what had happened in northeastern India. The fairy-tale land I had encountered five years earlier had been blasted and burned into a listless black jumble of grit that made my boots dirty every time I left my tent. Scavengers, the healthier ones, sifted through the black, swirling mess, picking burned seeds from the depleted topsoil to have something to feed their families. The unhealthy scavengers—and in time everyone in the region seemed to fall into this category—lay on the wasted ground that had once held their homes and let the windblown ashes drift over them. Hood each day went into those dismal wastes beyond our encampments on errands of mercy; he carried ration kits and had a squadron follow him carrying armfuls of the same kits for the starving Indians they would find there. The food they brought these lost souls was pitifully inadequate. Hood and his men could carry at the most four hundred cartons. Every day there would be thousands of starving people in the burned fields outside our camp. The Marshal many times sat in the ashes beside some wretched soul and held the dying creature in the last moments of life. Hood's hair and beard turned gray in the months following the battle. He forgot his years of military discipline and took to drinking whenever he was alone in his tent. On several occasions I passed his quarters late at night and heard him singing hymns in his loud, reedy voice, and I could see the shadow of his profile swaying in time to the homely music, a scene that made me wish I was a brave enough Christian to come to my old friend's aid during his time of need. The nineteen thousand captured Chinese became the focal point of the Marshal's attention in those dark days and were the project that kept him sane. Hood sent false casualty reports to the quartermaster so that the Sixth Army was sent provisions for the ten thousand Yukon men who were actually dead; he gave the extra food to the prisoners, sheltered them in the tents of the fallen Yukon soldiers, and clothed them in the surplus Yukon uniforms. He went into their barbed wire compound wearing an undecorated topcoat and brought doctors to the Chinese sick and wounded. French, who spoke to the Chinese regularly, said the prisoners thought the melancholy bearded man was some sort of priest, for he helped the doctors tend to the ailing and he knelt beside their sickbeds and prayed for the stricken. Somehow Hood obtained a shipment of vegetable seeds from Australia and had the Chinese plant gardens in their compound to augment the ration kits. The prisoners ate well from their small plots. For a few hopeful weeks Hood fancied he could obtain seeds for the Indians around us so they might also grow gardens. Fate would allow him only those few weeks to think circumstances would improve. Headquarters was already furious on account of his previous requests. They refused to send him any more supplies than his shrinking army needed. The people in the hills thus continued to perish, and the Marshal could not see the end of his despair.

I observed Hood returning to camp in the evenings from the ash-filled wastes. Hatless and unkempt, he walked ahead of his men, gesturing with his right hand as though he were speaking to an invisible person beside him. I should have gone to him sooner. I rationalized my reluctance by telling myself it would be presumptive to speak of personal matters to a Field Marshal. The truth was that it was hard for me to be near him, as that reminded me of the guilt I shared with him for all we had done. During the daylight hours I could still act as though I was not overwhelmed by the dead countryside we had created. At night I was afraid to sleep, for then I would have dreams of Hood and imagine I too could lose my mind if I gave in to the feelings that had overtaken him. I had to watch my friend stroll home on seven consecutive evenings before I could make myself approach him.

"Good evening to you, sir," I said as I walked toward him.

He nodded as he stopped next to me, but kept his gaze fixed upon the wasteland to our north.

" 'Salvation is nearer to us than we first believed,' " I said. " 'The night is far gone, the day is at hand. Let us then cast off the—' "

He looked at me and put up a hand to signal me to stop.

" 'Cast off the works of darkness and put on the armor of light,' "[7] he said, completing the verse.

He took off my slouch hat and mussed my hair as an uncle might do to a favorite nephew.

---

7. Romans, 13:11–12.

"You are a good boy, Bobby," he said. "Worried about old Hood, are you? Have you written your wife today?"

"No, sir."

"Go and do so immediately. That is an order. You have to stop concerning yourself with me. A cloud is over me at the moment; it will pass. There is no evil that lasts forever."

He swept his hand along the horizon, directing my attention to the devastation around us.

"You, sir, are the finest soldier I have ever known," I said.

"Go write your wife, Bobby."

"I will always be loyal to you, sir, and will always be your friend."

"That is very nearly what I told Fitz when last I was with him," he said. "He overvalues what you and I tell him, Bobby. He thinks we are his windows into the Yukon soul. Other than Pularski, you and I are the only honest commoners he knows. He can't decide what he should make of us. What did you tell the Consul the last time you spoke to him?"

"I told him he was God's beloved," I said. "Akin to King David."

"For two honest commoners, we were none too honest in his presence, Bobby."

"What good would we have done if we had told him the truth, sir?" I said. "He would have ignored us, and might well have killed us and our families."

"True, we have no choice in matters of state," said Hood. "What is equally true is we do not desire a choice. The Senate, the Lords: they make the decisions and ride them straight to Hell. We remain innocent. Our feudal system protects us from God's wrath. Or so we hope."

He put the hat back on my head.

"Now go and write your wife, or I'll have you court-martialed, sir," he told me.

When the rainy season came again the barren land ran into the Ganges and her tributaries rose by hundreds of acres every day. The river swelled out of her banks and turned creamy black from the ash. Soon the floods had either covered or devoured everything but the high ground atop the hills. Hood ordered his last intact division, the Second, to take the Chinese prisoners over the pontoon bridges and escort them thence to the Brahmaputra Valley. We moved them in the five hundred lorries we had left to the deep canyon where our bombers had destroyed the roadway early in the battle. There we set our recent enemies free. Each Chinese soldier was given two ration kits and was allowed to walk toward the Himalayas and freedom. The Blinking Stars saw our actions. Messages from Cumberland and Pallas flashed to Hood on the glass domes at a rate of six an hour. Hood ignored all these communications. Had any other general defied the Consul's demands in a similar situation, Fitz would have had him sacked, or worse. In the public's eye Hood was the greatest hero in the Confederacy after the young Consul, and for this act of defiance he would not get a single reprimand.

I had nine fat letters from Charlotte during her exile in the Toutle Mountains. She would have written more often if she could; under the circumstances my Lord Prim-Jones' couriers got to her only when they thought it prudent. My Lord's messengers carried packets of my letters to her, and she sent back a bundle of the notes she wrote every day. She gave me a photograph of herself when she was in the last trimester of her pregnancy. She was in profile and mugging for the camera, as she was wont to do in all her portraits. The accompanying letter contained a heap of silliness about how I would not love her after she had gotten so big with child. I had to write her back to say she was still the most beautiful of all women, which is how she expected me to respond. Two months later she sent me a score of photos of herself holding a beautiful green-eyed baby named Mary Margaret (Mary for Charlotte's mother, and Margaret for Mrs. Pressler, who had delivered the baby before my Lord's doctor could arrive at the remote cabin). Nothing I know how to say could describe the happiness on Charlotte's face. I had been careless of my future with her and the baby when I risked my life on Van Fleet's Hill. The pictures did not go inside my night-stand until I vowed I would no longer be so reckless with my life.

Charlotte never asked of the war. She requested in her letters that I not tell her anything.

"I do not wish to learn of the dangers you have endured," she wrote. "My heart would break from the worry. We will wait for our reunion; you will want to tell everything to me then."

In accordance with the heightened surveillance of the war years, letters from my parents and other family members were opened before they reached me. Charlotte's letters to me and mine to her traveled in my Lord Prim-Jones' mail pouch and under his seal.[8] Our social system works when the nobility is as loyal to us as we are to them. It was my good fortune that my Lord upheld his end of this tacit contract as bravely as any soldier in the trenches. He wrote to tell me a drawling young man with half-closed eyelids had been to the Prim-Jones estate and had inquired after Charlotte. The man—surely it was Zimmerman—learned nothing. My Lord wrote that the young man wore a strange black uniform from some new military unit known as the House Karls, an outfit about which neither my Lord or I had any previous knowledge.[9] My Lord had known the stranger was coming to Astoria because a third party (I knew it was Pularski) had sent him a note. While the House Karl was speaking to my Lord a dozen armed farmers from my Lord's estate stood at hand to see that during the interview the stranger remained a civil fellow. Two more strangers from the House Karls came to Astoria soon thereafter. They too had been preceded by a letter of warning. At the village train depot twenty of my Lord's men met the men to keep them from mischief. My Lord allowed the strangers to come to him, treated them well, and saw them directly back to the station after they had eaten a bit of lunch. No more House Karls bothered to come to Astoria after that. In 2422 the war was still officially on, and Fitz dared not strike at a Lord on that Lord's estate. Such an action would have offended all the Confederacy at a time Fitz needed the people's goodwill more than he needed Charlotte out of the way. By the end of the year, thanks again to Buck, my name was in the newspapers, and killing the wife of a hero would have brought Fitz still more problems. For these reasons Fitz decided, thank God, to leave my family alone, for a time.

Daddy Montrose took the last of the Second Division from India on December 19, 2422. On the eighteenth, Hood's wife and their young son arrived in the Rajmahal Hills on the same airship Montrose was to take to North America. Montrose protested that he had not asked Mrs. Hood to come to India. He would have been more persuasive if he had not kept touching the side of his nose while he spoke to the Marshal. Whoever was responsible for summoning her, Mrs. Hood's presence and that of the boy had a

---

8. Not even security personnel can open a Lord's sealed mail pouch.

9. Lord Fitzpatrick the Younger founded the House Karls on March 18, 2421.

positive influence on Judge. She kept him from venturing into the wastelands every day while she retaught him the private intimacies families have. She threw out his store of whiskey and got him to clean up and to wear a regular uniform again. I cannot say she made him cheerful; Hood was never a cheerful man. Something in having her about made him want to continue his broken life. When I next saw him from afar he was walking on the roadway with his eight-year-old son. The Marshal was by then no longer speaking to phantoms in the air about him or making peculiar gesticulations. His hand rested softly on the boy's shoulder. The Marshal was nodding at something the child was saying to him. Perhaps, for a few seconds, in his family's presence he forgot what had happened the year before in the dead land around him.

The last teamsters and antiaircraft men left our base on Christmas Eve, 2422. Code signals from the Blinking Stars gave orders for Hood and I and a company of First Division infantry, the only Yukon troopers left in India, to proceed on zeppelin to Samarkand. Hood used the airship's ultraviolet light to reaffirm this extraordinary command. The Blinking Star in our quadrant of the globe spelled out Samarkand in code another time, so we loaded our gear onto the airship and headed east. I like to think the Santals reclaimed the entire region in the hills after we were gone. Given the damage we had done, it is more likely that for many decades the land there belonged more to the elements than to any race of men. I know the natives still living there today have never forgiven us. Nor should they. I only pray that enough of them have returned to their ancestral homes to keep their world and their unique History alive for the generations to come. If that History includes the reasons for the natives' undying hatred for the Yukons, that is no less than we deserve.

Hood and I did not know what awaited us in central Asia. While we flew over the scarred battlefield for the last time we wondered if we were going to our executions; Hood could be put to death for liberating the captured Chinese, and I for protecting my wife. I reflected upon how glorious the Battle of Northern India had seemed in the beginning, when the planes took off inside the two-hundred-mile halo of flares and how the final act of our story there saw us sneaking away in a zeppelin from that same, now silent battlefield to our possible destruction.

We did not know then that a contingent of Yukons had gone

via airship to Samarkand months before we traveled there. The newspapers we read had not mentioned this deployment, so when our
craft arrived in that high desert country we were surprised to see
there was a small Yukon base flying the Union Jack on the ridge
north of the ancient city.

"You can see forever here, sir," said the zeppelin pilot to me as
we circled the blue-and-sandstone-colored town on our first approach to the landing dock, "and see nothing, if you catch my drift.
Those salt flats out to the west of here, sir: was there a sea out there
once or what?"

Samarkand was mostly or what. The snow white fields west of
the city were the product of many years of overirrigation in the land
between the Oxus and Jaxaries rivers, the region the classic world
called Transoxia. A crusty layer of white had risen from the water-
soaked subsoil, poisoning the cotton fields and orange groves that
once grew there, leaving behind a waste more hostile to life than the
blackened one we had recently created along the Ganges. When the
wind blew from that direction, something that happened more
often than not, tiny stinging salt crystals came careening off the
flats, bound directly for any human face or eyes left unprotected.

In the waning years of the modern Turkish Empire, Samarkand
had shrunken to a village of some five thousand Uzbeki shepherds
and a smaller community of Turkish innkeepers and merchants servicing travelers bound for nearby Tashkent, the Turkish capital.
Samarkand had been a capital city itself in the sixth century B.C.,
when it had been the center of the lost kingdom of Sogkiana. Conquered by Alexander the Great in 329 B.C. and later a major city in
the Greco-Bactrian and Kushan empires, Samarkand would become,
after the Moslem conquest in the eighth century A.D., the seat of the
mighty Saminid Dynasty. Genghis Khan sacked it in 1219. Timur the
Lame rebuilt it a century and a half later to be the capital of the Mongol world, and there Timur erected his mausoleum, a pretty blue tile
dome that still stands immediately outside the city. After the Mongols came the Bhukharans and the Russians, yet the city's true legacy
was not made by its conquerors but by the tradesmen who for two
millennia came to the city from China, India, North Africa, Europe,
and the Middle East, and made Samarkand the center of the old
world. A century of Russian rule after 1888 and two centuries of
Turkish neglect after 2174 helped make the city the insignificant spot
we found it to be in late 2422. Tashkent, the Turkish capital, was two

hundred short miles to the northeast. It had not suffered a strong rival on its doorstep. The imperial government transported the educated portion of Samarkand's population to the capital; after the salt rose, most of the remaining population had drifted away to find arable lands to the south. The city was still a place where one could find some splendid old mosques and a small private museum where for the price of a gold coin of any denomination one could look at such oddities as gilded statues of Greek gods sitting in the pose of Buddha and ivory carvings of an oriental Jesus dressed in the robes of Confucius. Such was the crumbling site of past glories Fitz had chosen to make once more the center of the world.

Two regiments of Yukon engineers were in the camp north of Samarkand and had leveled some ground there to give the zeppelins a place to land. A regiment of the black-uniformed House Karls had pitched their tents a quarter mile east of the engineers at the foot of a long slope. They had hauled several mobile houses to the north shore of the Zeravshan River to make homes for their officers. Those boxy units squatting among the riverbank's willow reeds looked as squalid as old Samarkand's ruins on the other side of the river looked magnificent. The engineer regiments had staked out a patch of land near the House Karl's tents and were leveling this to make room for a building that would cover forty acres when completed. While the gray-uniformed Yukon engineers bulldozed dirt on the treeless plane, the House Karls sat in the shade of their open tents and drank some strange concoctions called wine stingers. From their choice of beverage and their pierced ears I deduced they were nearly all former S.A. men.[10] Their armbands identified them as members of the Seventy-Seventh Division, the Living Standard of Lord Isaac Fitzpatrick, the unit the rest of the Confederacy would learn to call the Praetorian Guard.[11]

---

10. Many S.A. men had been prison convicts. While incarcerated their ears had been pierced to accommodate numbered tags, for body piercing is the most humiliating abuse a man can endure and is used by jailers to break the spirit of the inmates. Wine stingers, a mixture of cheap wine and fruit juice, were then also characteristic of the criminal class.

11. The House Karls were another of the inexplicable small missteps Fitzpatrick the Younger made during his Consulship; they were indeed mostly former S.A. men and were not well loved among the Yukon population.

Hood and I had been in the engineer's camp for an hour and were busy helping the Marshal's wife set up their tent when French spied a House Karl officer walking—or, more accurately, shuffling—toward us. The man's deliberate gait and lazy smile were recognizable from a long way off.

"It's that weird gent from *The Mother of Jesus,*" declared French. "Look, sir, some blockhead has made him a colonel!"

I told French the blockhead in question was none other than the Consul. I added that French should get a rifle and stand behind Colonel Zimmerman during the time I spoke to him. Zimmerman sidled into our camp with an awkward, nearly sideways stride, his toes pointed outward and his weight shifted onto his heels. He was wearing the black kepi cap of his division at an angle and had cultivated a blond spit curl that peeked from beneath the cap's shiny plastic brim. On the crest of the cap was the golden death's head I would see too much of during the next five years.[12] He forgot to salute me.

"Hey, we're both colonels . . ." he said. "Moving up in the world."

He grinned at French as the old man appeared behind him bearing an assault rifle.

"Not very friendly . . ." said Zimmerman. " 'Course I could kill you both easy. Don't want to . . . If I did, you'd already be dead. Want to welcome you to Sam'kand. Is that the famous Marshal?"

He saw Hood approaching us and touched the bill of his cap in lieu of a salute.

"The hero of northern India . . ." said Zimmerman. "I hear you're a hero too, Bruce."

He pointed to my gilded silver rose. Hood looked at the peculiar uniform the young man was wearing and rubbed his eyes.

"Are you some manner of policeman, sir?" Hood asked him.

"This, sir," I said "is Colonel Zimmerman, of the House Karls, lately of the S.A."

"A soldier like you . . . sir," said Zimmerman and gave Hood a short bow; I guessed that was how he thought one should acknowledge a Field Marshal.

---

12. The death's head or golden skull was the symbol of the House Karls. Lord Fitzpatrick is said to have found some wry humor in the emblem.

"By God, I thought it was a damned Halloween costume," said Hood. "This is what the Consul dresses his thugs in now?"

"You're as friendly as Bobby," said Zimmerman and grinned. "Try to give you a good word . . ." Hood walked around the House Karl, examining his unusual black clothing.

"What do you want, Colonel Zimmerman?" I asked, hoping he would say his piece and leave.

"The Consul is coming," he said. "Thought you'd like to know."

"Here? Fitz is coming here?" I said.

"Don't you know?" said Zimmerman. "Seems you soldier boys have been out of the loop. This . . ." he said and swept his hand across the flat western horizon and the tall Pamir Mountains to the east. "This is going to be the new world capital . . ."

He slowly let his hand fall to his side.

"The navel of the world, the Consul says," he said. "Be here tomorrow . . . he will tell you the rest."

"Young man," said Hood. "Have you had any military schooling, sir?"

"Sure," said Zimmerman, "I know how about rifles, handguns, edged weapons—"

"Were you ever taught anything about combing your hair, wearing your hat straight, and always calling a superior officer 'sir?' " asked Hood.

Zimmerman had to think upon this.

"Yeah . . . sir," he said and walked away without being dismissed.

"Jesus and all the Saints!" swore Hood. "The world has been stood on its head, Bobby!"

Fitz did not come to Samarkand alone. Seven ridge frame zeppelins sat down on December 27 in the salt flats beyond the House Karls' encampment. Valette; Shelley; Lord and Lady Newsome; O'Brian; Stein; Lady Joan and her maid Miss Stewart; the lesser DeShay cousins; Pularski; troops of secretaries, servants; and bureaucrats; three additional regiments of House Karls; and hundreds of comely young men and women of no particular occupation stepped into the wasteland with the Consul, dragging their long skirts and tailored trouser cuffs in the noxious white powder. Hood, his young son, and I watched them from our camp on the hill through binoculars. The Marshal remarked to me that the men dressed in velvet and the slender

women in pale green silk looked like the Cherryville set stepping
into an unfinished portion of Hell.[13] From a mile away we could
see the strained expressions on the fine peoples' faces as they
looked about them and drank in the horrible place that was to
be their new home.

"What is the Consul wearing on his head, sir?" I asked and
handed the glasses to Hood so he could examine the gleaming
thing in Fitz's hair.

"I think he must have his sunglasses pushed back," said Hood.

The thing Fitz was wearing resembled something else. Neither
of us wanted to say aloud exactly what.

The engineers had put up a tent as large as a circus big top next
to the spot they were clearing. Smaller tents and mobile units were
springing into shape around this big pavilion. The Lords and Ladies
there made themselves at home two hundred miles from the nearest indoor toilet and four thousand miles from the closest gold star
restaurant.

A messenger summoned Hood and myself to attend dinner in
the Consul's big tent at six o'clock that evening. Pularski—now
Captain Pularski—met us outside the front entrance in the cold
wind when we came down to the enormous pavilion. He embraced
me and shook my left hand with his good hand for what seemed a
minute or longer.

"I would shake your hand too, Marshal Hood," he said, saluting, "were you not such an important man these days."

"I am not so important as to forget you, my friend," said Hood
and gave Buck his left hand.

Buck glanced about us to make certain no one was eavesdrop-
ping. He tugged his ear and whispered to us, "A few warnings before you go in, gentlemen. Don't speak to O'Brian. He's in
trouble, very bad trouble. And don't gawk at Fitz. He's wearing—I don't know how to say this—a sort of crown."

"A what?" said Hood, speaking more loudly than Buck would
have desired.

"Shh, sir," said Buck. "It is, well, I think you call them tiaras.

---

13. Cherryville was and is the most fashionable suburb of Cumberland. Readers everywhere will recognize it as the home of St. Matthew's University.

It fits on the back of his head and there are curly ram's horns on it. He calls them the Horns of Ammon-Horus."[14]

"There was an ancient Egyptian god called Ammon," said Hood. "This would not be related to that?"

"Actually, it would be," said Buck. "Two more things: everyone has to kneel to him when they're introduced to him or when he enters the room. Drop to your right knee and stay there till he bids you rise."

Hood was mortified. His eyes opened so wide they threatened to come out of his head. I expect my face at that moment looked not much different.

"You can't use that expression when Fitz can see you, sir," said Buck. "He's not the chap you knew in school. Or he isn't some of the time. What I'm saying is he's a different man every day, and today he's something like a king."

"I kneel to God, not to any man!" proclaimed Hood, again using a voice that was too loud for Buck. "Has he forgotten the Constitution?"

"There you go," said Pularski. "That frame of mind will get you killed, sir. I know, yes; it's terrible. You can't say it's unconstitutional to these people. You can't let the way they are here bother you. Think of your family, sir. I'll get down and kneel to you, if you but do it for Fitz. Please, sir, do as the others have to. Just this once. Tomorrow he will forget these pretensions. One last thing: don't ask after the Consul's mother. He's at odds with her. He refuses to let her come out here and says he doesn't need her help any longer. The whole thing is very nasty. We have to go in now."

The Lords and Ladies inside the pavilion were seated in rows of canvas campaign chairs and facing a platform atop which was a high-backed chair some might describe as a throne. Hood, Pularski, and I stood behind the assembled nobility next to a small group of House Karls. O'Brian was seated in front and on our right; all the chairs about him were vacant. Two big House Karls emerged from the left side of the tent wearing absurd pastel turbans on their

---

14. Lord Fitzpatrick did wear, for a brief time, the Ammon-Horus horns in imitation of Alexander the Great, who doffed the golden crown after he visited the shrine of Ammon in Egypt. Lord Fitzpatrick did this to satisfy the local peoples' expectations of how a head of state should appear and behave. (See Gerald, appendix five.) The kneeling ceremony Bruce describes was initiated for the same reason.

heads and carrying oversized scimitars in their belts. They marched to the elevated platform and positioned themselves on opposite sides of the high chair. "General" Smythe,[15] the sneak thief in charge of the House Karls, came forth and announced like a carnival barker, "Lord Isaac Fitzpatrick, Consul of the Yukon Confederacy and Emperor of Europe, Africa, and Western Asia—"

"Emperor?" said Hood aloud.

Buck put his hand over the Marshal's mouth.

"—Lady Joan Fitzpatrick," continued Smythe, "and the Honorable Doctor Joseph Flag."

"What is this 'honorable' nonsense?" whispered Hood, having removed Buck's hand from his face. "Since when do bloody girls' schoolteachers have titles?"

"Please, you have to be quiet, sir," implored Buck. "The House Karls can hear us."

Lady Joan entered from the left, blushing because she was ashamed of the ostentatious exhibition she was playing her part in. She sat at the foot of the high chair. Flag came in next, looking ridiculous in a heavy ermine robe that was fastened about his shoulders with a golden chain. He was a handsome middle-aged man, in spite of his stooped shoulders and the singular way his head stuck far in front of his chest when he stood upright. Take away the silly robe and he looked to be the girls' schoolteacher he was.[16] Someone in Valette's party giggled when Flag took his place behind the high chair, and that ignited some general laughter among Valette's entire group. Smythe cleared his throat and peered sternly at anyone who appeared the least amused, which quickly silenced the audience. Fitz made his entry last. He wore a Blue Jacket's uniform as Buck did, except that the Consul's was made of silk and was decorated with gold lace and a golden waist sash. Fitz had on a long red cape that flowed behind him. On his feet he had red Persian slippers with toes that curled toward his shins, footwear worthy of a genie in *A Thousand and One Nights*. He wore on his face the

---

15. General Tyrone Trustworthy Smythe (2381–2426), a former chief of the S.A. who had served twelve years in prison for robbery, was the leader of the House Karls. He was not a fortuitous choice. (See Gerald page 3401.)

16. Flag was rumored to have been something of a dandy and perhaps a ladies' man when he was younger. Three decades of service under Lady Fitzpatrick seems to have mellowed the young rake considerably.

stage makeup Gypsy actors wear; the greasepaint made his skin appear extremely pale, and his lips were as bright red as the cape flowing behind him. Everyone knelt to him. (Buck had to force Hood to his knees.) Fitz swept his cape aside with a grand gesture and sat on the throne.

"My friends," he said, "you may rise."

The nobles seated themselves in their chairs. We commoners in the back stood upright again. Flag and Smythe fixed themselves in their positions behind the throne. Lady Joan sat on the edge of the platform at her husband's feet.

"Like she's a damned pet dog," swore Hood under his breath.

I only then noted the silver orb shaped like the world in Fitz's left hand. On his right hand was a huge gold ring I would later learn was embossed with the winged horse, his family's symbol and seal. Valette and Shelley came forward in turn and knelt to kiss the ring. They backed away from him, heads bowed, and resumed their seats. Buck had to reach over and close my mouth, which I had left gaping open after witnessing that extraordinary ritual.

"My friends," said Fitz, "I pray you are recuperating from the long journey and the evening finds you in good health and good spirits. We will dine presently. First, I ask you to fix in your minds this day, December the twenty-seventh, 2422; this will be a day future Historians will revere as we revere the second of October.[17] On this day we are founding Neapolis, the New City. On this day we are the first to stand in the place our descendants will call the throne of the world."

The nobles applauded.

"Before we bring out the tables, my friends," said Fitz, as he turned his gaze directly upon Hood and myself, "we wish to acknowledge the presence of two war heroes. The tall bearded gentleman you see in the back is Sir Marshal Jeremiah Hood, the champion of northern India."

The nobles applauded enthusiastically. Some wags among them shouted, "Bravo."

"Useless bastards," growled Hood.

"The young gentleman next to Sir Marshal Hood is Sir Robert

---

17. October 2, 2081, was the beginning of the Storm Times. In Bruce's day it was a national holiday; in 2480 the Senate merged Storm Times Day with Thanksgiving and both days are now celebrated on the third Thursday in November.

Bruce; he is the engineer who designed the bases at Luni and Rajmahal and was the last commander on Van Fleet's Hill."

Everyone clapped a third time. Valette, Shelley, Mason, and
Stein chanted: "Bob-by, Bob-by!"

"Without our loyal warriors, we would not be here today," said
Fitz and made a dramatic twirl with his right hand.

Valette's party tittered at the Consul's pomposity as they had
at Flag. The nervous laughter rippled throughout the audience,
some of them laughing at Fitz, and some at the "heroic" commoners. For this arrogant, giggling mob of titled buffoons and
criminals, I thought, ten thousand other Yukons and twenty million foreign soldiers had died in the Indian mud. Hood tightened
his hand into a fist and beat it against his thigh. If the laughter had
continued I feared he might have done something that would endanger his person.

*"Silence!"* shouted Fitz. "You bunch of dandies put together
aren't worth a fingernail on either of those two men! You silly, ungrateful pack of conspirators! Oh, you think I don't know?" he said
and rose to pace back and forth across the front of the platform,
looking several individual Lords and Ladies in the eye and shaming
them into silence. "I know what you noble slugs would like to do
to me! Yes, I have had my men watching you!" He shook his head
in agreement with his words. "That is why I brought you to this
empty corner of the world. Here, you may scheme all you damn
well please, my friends! You may plan and plan, build your empires
in the air, but if you want to stay above this sandy soil you will sit
on your noble backsides and damned well remain loyal! Cowards!
Plotters! *Cowardly plotters!* If you drank from one cup, I would
poison it! I would do it! You aren't worthy to breathe the same air
as these brave men! You aren't worthy of Neapolis!"

He returned to his throne and sat down heavily as he whirled
his cape out of the way. Then he lifted one finger to Smythe as a
signal to bring out the food.

"Let's eat," he said.

Teams of servants carried in six long tables already set with food
and tableware. Each place setting included a linen napkin folded in
the shape of a fluttering dove and a small bowl of green curried soup
topped by a dollop of sour cream. Red lobsters posed in fighting positions were set above each placement next to a carafe of white New
Zealand wine. To bring the tables into the seated audience in this

unusual manner required the Lords and Ladies to stand and scramble forward with their canvas chairs in hand from out of the servants' paths. As the tent was quite cold, the diners had to rush into their food before it completely lost its heat. Their haste and the ensuing pell-mell chaos were insults to their dignity, and a good reason, I suppose, for Fitz to serve them in that manner. Buck had to go forward to the Consul's placement and there eat a bite of each of Fitz's servings: he did the same at Lady Joan's placement. While the crowd was shuffling about, O'Brian tried to approach the Consul. Buck swiftly put himself between the two men and pinned O'Brian's arms behind him. Zimmerman, who had been watching the proceedings from the left of the platform, drew a pistol, and the noble diners screamed and jumped from harm's way.

"That's not necessary," said Buck and steered the pinned man about so he was shielding O'Brian from the House Karl.

"Always one step too slow, Zee." said Fitz, already tasting his soup. "Put the gun away. Lord O'Brian is going to be a good lad and sit down."

O'Brian was whimpering as Pularski took him to his chair.

"Talk to him," he whispered to Buck. "You can't let him do it."

Buck told him to relax and eat his supper. O'Brian could not. He sat staring at the rampant lobster confronting him, and perspired rivers of sweat while the other nobles gnawed loudly at their food.

Hood had reached his limit with this crowd.

"We can't be with these johnnies, Sir Robert," he said. "Better to have hardtack and Crusader's bread in our tents than stay here and have lobster with the likes of them."[18]

We left without asking to be excused. I was one step outside the tent when I began reflecting upon how careless an act this was. Hood did not give it a thought. We ate with his family and French in the double tent that was the Marshal's temporary home. I know Fitz noted our absence in the pavilion, although he never mentioned it to us in the future.

We had to return to the big tent at eight o'clock the following morning for a meeting that turned out not to be a conference with

---

18. Also called strong bread, Crusader's bread is a type of chewy nut cake said to be indestructible in both the soldier's pack and his digestive system.

the Consul but a lecture given by Doctor Flag to the assembled noblemen. Contrary to what Charlotte had intimated about Flag, he was, in my estimation and in the estimation of all who had to listen to him, the least impressive famous man any of us ever had the displeasure of beholding in person. That chilly morning, when the kerosene heaters had not yet warmed the tent's interior, he gave us a three-hour talking-to upon world religions, cultures, mythologies, History, politics, and everything else that occurred to his disorganized mind. I did learn that morning he was not the mystic Charlotte had said he was. Mysticism requires some imagination. Flag could not get beyond the basic tenets he had formulated when he was an ambitious young author wanting to outrage public opinion. He postulated that the world's beliefs were at their core all the same, that the various heroes of mythology were the same hero in different cultural guises, and that since it was the heroes (he meant the great heroic thinkers) who decided what should be believed, the more like heroes we became, the more courageous in our thoughts and deeds we were, and the more we "did as we would," the closer we came to truth. By my calculation he managed to work the phrase "do as you would" into his lecture approximately every two minutes. The repetition was not a wasted effort, as that phrase was the one portion of his speech I remember. A second thing I recall about him was his manner of pronouncing "Buddha," whom he called "Booo-dah," saying the highly stressed "ooo" sound through his pursed lips. Valette was not above having some fun with this peculiar mannerism of Flag's.

"Now, Doctor Flag," asked Valette, having raised his hand, "when Prince Gautama gained enlightenment, what do you say he was then called?"

"Booo-dah," said Dr. Flag.

Fitz sat in attendance with the others and did not take offence at Valette's mockery of his spiritual advisor. The Consul had previously lavished honors upon the teacher. Now he would not defend Flag when others challenged him. Shelley snickered at Valette's drollery, and Fitz did not protest. Indeed, I saw Fitz smile at the joke along with the others. That is why today I think Fitz kept Flag in his court as a touchstone for judging others; if one dismissed Flag out of hand, Fitz knew that person had a serious mind; if one accepted Flag's opinions, Fitz knew that person was an idiot. Not once in the many times I saw the two men together did I hear Fitz ask Flag's advice on anything.

"What are the principal religions of India again?" asked Shelley.

"Jainism, Hinduism, Booo-dism . . ." said Flag.

Even kindly Lady Joan had to turn her face to hide a chuckle. Mason was less decorous; he had been munching on some wrapped chocolates and spat out a mouthful of them onto the Lord seated in front of him when he chortled. General confusion followed, and Fitz himself laughed his fill. Dr. Flag was the one man in the tent who did not get the joke. He stuck his head out farther than usual and perhaps recalled that the girls at Lady Fitzpatrick's school had never been this unruly.

None of these high jinks amused Hood. He raised his hand and asked Flag, "Sir, am I to understand you believe all major religions profess the same core beliefs? In your words, they share the same *tao*?"

"Yes, General, that is to say—" began Flag.

"Then that would mean, let us say, that the Chinese and the Arabs share the same beliefs on marriage and family?" said Hood.

"No," said Flag, "marriage and family are a secondary question, outside the *tao*."

"Can we say," asked Hood, "that Arabs and the Chinese value life to the same degree? Or is human life another secondary question?"

Flag blinked and stuck his head out farther.

"When I say *tao*," he stammered, "I mean specific, general matters. You see, such as treating others well."

The Lords were laughing at him once more.

"You say cultures are essentially the same," continued Hood. "How would you explain, sir, the different Histories of North and South America? Both continents are inhabited by Christians. The majority in both continents are of European descent."

"Geography?" said Flag with a hopeful blink.

Valette raised his hand and asked Flag to say Buddha again. At that point Hood rose and left the tent.

"I feel it is time for lunch," he announced.

The meeting dissolved at once. Everyone agreed with the Marshal that they were ready to eat lunch at the early hour of eleven o'clock. Thereafter Dr. Flag did not give any more public lectures at Samarkand. He remained behind the throne, literally, whispering to Fitz, and sometimes the Consul heeded him, but never very much. Because people saw Flag's gray visage behind Fitz whenever the Consul entertained a large group, Fitz gave him the honorific (and absurd) title of Chief Spiritual Counselor, or CSC, as Smythe called him, a ridiculous acronym that only made Flag a bigger joke among those in Fitz's court. Valette, Stein, Shelley, and the other resident wits simply called him "Doctor Booo-dah."

Hood had a private interview with Fitz in the afternoon following the speech. French and I accompanied him to the threshold of the Consul's tent and waited there with Pularski while the two men talked in the interior of the pavilion. From our position we could hear Hood railing at the Consul; the words "grasping bastard," "bloodsucker," "disgrace to your people and the Confederacy," and "no king to me" came clearly through the canvas walls. Hood alone could speak those words to the Consul and hope to survive. Fitz knew if he killed the Marshal there would be no one left in the world he could admire. Perhaps somewhere in a segmented corner of his soul Fitz also knew Hood was speaking the truth. After an hour of yelling at the young Consul, Hood burst through the tent flaps, his slouch hat jammed down to his eyebrows. We followed him back to his tent in the engineers' camp before he spoke.

"I'm leaving here tonight, Bobby," he said. "My family and the infantry company are coming with me. You are to stay."

"Does speaking straight to him do any good, sir?" I asked.

"It made me feel better, sir."

"I feared for you in there, sir," I said. "You are much braver than I would be."

"He can only kill me."

"Has . . . has he dismissed you, sir?"

"Lord no!" he laughed. "He has made me commander of the Second Army back in the old Southwest.[19] I will be among soldiers again. You are the one I fear for, Bobby. You have to stay here. Stick close to Buck. You are among the top predators here, my boy."

I waited for four despairing days to see Fitz in private. The New Year of 2423 came while I tarried in my tent and listened to the celebrations in the big tent and asked myself how anyone, including the drunks down there, could find pleasure in this cold, windswept lair. I told old French he was now my entire command. He said

---

19. In the twenty-fifth century, the Second Army guarded the Mexican border.

that since I was a colonel, he must have become an entire regiment, since that is what colonels lead.

"A regiment has majors and captains and sergeants and the like, sir," he explained. "I figure I would be all of them. That would be like having a big promotion, wouldn't it?"

"A very big one," I agreed.

"Sir, is the Consul dressing like the Queen of Sheba?" he asked me. "The engineering lads said so."

French was ironing my spare uniform when he asked me this. I had precious few belongings for him to tend to, and he needed some imagination to keep busy. The old tar had been agitated since his friend's death on the hill, but he never mentioned old Charlie, as a true Yukon soldier would never dwell upon his private sorrow. Like me, he felt that if he acknowledged his grief others would think he was too cowardly to endure everything a soldier must.

"He dresses as he does to look regal," I told him.

"We had some of those regal boys in the I.T., sir," he said. "I was right nervous about them when they first came onboard a given ship. Close quarters and all. Most of them did have good manners, I have to say, sir. They could sew right well when I needed help mending sails. Who could blame some of them, sir? I mean, it being so lonely on those ships?"

"That is not Fitz's situation," I told him. "Keep talking like that, and you will get me into more trouble."

"The Consul is angry with you, sir? I thought he was your friend."

"He is," I said. "As much as he has friends. The problem is, he does not care for my wife."

French nearly dropped the iron off the folding board.

"How could anybody not like Mrs. Bruce, sir?" he asked. "She is the best lady of them all."

"Thank you, French," I said. "I will tell her that when I write her next."

Stein came to see me in my quarters on the first day of the new year. He did not come to me for the sake of our friendship. He wanted the papers he had given to me in Salt Lake City three years earlier. I was happy to be rid of them, but not as elated as he was to have them in his hands.

"He is mine!" he proclaimed and kissed the three packets.

"Do you remember, Banker," I asked, "when you and O'Brian were close? Back when we were all friends?"

"I remember," he said. "I have a clearer memory of what has happened since then. I remember being slandered as a thief. I remember being shunted off to India to be among the bearded commoners on Hood's staff. I remember that while I was getting mildew on my tent floor in the Rajamhal Hills my classmates from the War College were in Cumberland grabbing titles and money and sleeping with the finest daughters of the gentry. My feelings for O'Brian are a faint memory compared to all of that, Bobby dear."

He took the papers downhill to the big tent and presumably straight to Fitz. I expected the Consul would glance at the columns of figures and put them aside so O'Brian and Stein would continue to fight a battle of which Fitz long ago had grown bored.

Pularski came for me when Fitz said he would speak to me on the evening of the second. Buck accompanied me into the darkened compartments at the rear of the massive pavilion where the Consul resided. At Pallas, Fitz had been constantly at work with his assistants and the everflowing stream of visitors; at Samarkand—or Neapolis, as we were supposed to call the place—he met with his small circle of advisors for an hour in the morning and for the rest of the day he sat in his dimly lit enclosures, had a few additional audiences, then was alone with his thoughts. When I came to him he was wearing a simple dressing gown and pajamas, and was seated in a canvas chair and having some tea. I knelt to him, and he gave me a nod of acknowledgement.

"Bobby," he said, "my dear old friend, I fear we have a problem."

"Lord Fitzpatrick, I do—" I said.

"Please, please," he said, "I have told you a thousand times: you are to address me as 'Fitz.' My love for you has not diminished. Your service to me and to the Confederacy has been magnificent, Robert, as I knew it would be. Would that my other officers were half the soldier you are. No, I can find no fault in you."

Buck brought me a chair. I sat, and Pularski remained standing behind me.

"Fitz," I said, "I was wondering if I could have a new assignment. I realize we are still officially at war, and there—"

He raised his hand to cut me short.

"Yes, to be sure," he said. "I was saying, Robert, I have no problem with you. The problem lies with that redheaded whore you've married."

I flinched when he referred to Charlotte in that way.

"You don't like me saying that, do you, Bobby?" he said. "You know, I tried to send someone to visit her while you were in India. Your Lord—what is his name? Prim-Jones?—he seems to be hiding her. I sent some other chaps. That time your Lord had men waiting for my agents right at the train depot. Funny, isn't it? One would think someone in my court had warned him. What do you think, Buck?"

Pularski was accustomed to his questions. He did not twinge when Fitz sent intimations in his direction.

"Very funny, my Lord," said Buck.

"You may go now, Buck," said Fitz. "I won't need you again today."

Buck exited through the flaps, and Fitz rang a small bell on his tea table.

"I forgive you for losing your head over the cunning bitch, Bobby," he said. "My mother pushed her upon you. You are ignorant about women and the evil they can do. My mother can do more than most. Believe me. Ah, Lady Susan."

Into Fitz's compartment came a tall, flaxen-haired young woman in a neo-Roman gown. Her tousled hair came to her waist, and her eyes were as pale as aquamarine crystal. In face and form, she was a fawn with skin as fine as porcelain; in sum, a creature from a dream, the image of vulnerability and unmatched beauty. I rose and gave her my chair.

"Robert, this is Lady Susan Mitchum,"[20] said Fitz. "She has position, family, money. She is a virgin, something I know is important to a green lad like yourself. You know there's no deceit in me, Bobby, so I'll give it to you neat: marry her and I will make you a major general, commander of all my engineers, chief planner for the universal railroad I intend to build. In addition to that I'll grant you an annuity of a hundred thousand pounds."

"The lady is very beautiful, Fitz," I said, my voice wavering, "but I have a wife."

"I can have that mistake corrected," he said, and tapped his ring on the arm of his chair, "like that."

My courage was greater than I knew. For four days I had fret-

---

20. Probably Lady Susan Charity Mitchem (2398–2453), the youngest daughter of Lord Franklin Peace Mitchum, a Northfield Senator.

ted over how I would face the Consul, and once I did I found my scale of loyalties was tipped so far in Charlotte's favor I did not have to think of what my answer should be. For once I was as brave as she or Hood would have been.

"I have a wife, sir," I said. "I have everything I want in her."

*"Treason! This is treason!"* he screamed at me, leaping from his chair and becoming enraged, or at least pretending to be so. "Why do you talk to me of your whore? Do you think I care? I have killed millions! Maybe billions before I'm done! Do you think I would care if a nonentity like you loves his wife?"

"My Charlotte has never been disloyal to you, sir," I said. "We would never betray—"

"That does *not* matter, you bloody simpleton!" he said. "Had I wanted loyalty I'd get a dog! I expect more of you." He became less loud at this point. "I want you to love me. I want you to love me enough to do whatever I bid you do. If I asked you to kill yourself, you should say, 'Yes, Fitz,' and put the gun to your head. With love."

He came to me and took my hand.

"You don't know what it's like, Bobby," he said, breaking into a sob. "I love the whole world, and everybody hates me. No one understands. To do good, I have to do great evil beforehand. To build up, I first have to tear everything down. Don't you see? Do this for me. It would mean everything to me."

"I cannot," I said.

He struck me in the face. I knelt to him, and he hit me with his fist on the top of my head.

"I love you, sir, and I love my wife," I said.

"No, no, no, no, *no!*" he said and kept hitting me with his right hand, the one that had the heavy ring. "You and that goddamned Hood! So damned honorable! Too damned honorable to care about *me!* After I've given you everything! But not you! Nooo! Get out! I'll kill you! You'll see! See if I don't!"

I backed out of his chamber. He slapped Lady Susan and threw the pieces of his tea set at her as she ran from him.

"If you had been prettier, he would have taken you!" he screamed at her.

My scalp was torn in five places from the beating he had given me. Buck met me outside and wiped my blood-clotted hair with his handkerchief.

"Not a good meeting," he said.

He escorted me back to my tent where he and French washed my head and put iodine on the wounds.

"He won't harm you," said Buck. "He's bluffing. You'll see. I'll keep around here in case one of the House Karls gets the notion to take the unbidden initiative. They're a stupid lot. You never know what they might do."

He sat on the long slope between my tent and the Consul's camp until late on the morning of the third. When I arose Pularski walked me down the hill to the grand encampment. A great row was taking place at that early hour beyond the big tent. Inside my injured head the noise from that direction ricocheted off the insides of my skull like a rubber ball thrown hard against the walls of a small room. A regiment of House Karls had fallen into formation on the west side of the pavilion. Their drummers were sounding a tattoo that seemed to throb on forever. Clusters of gaily dressed Lords and Ladies fresh from their beds were milling about the black-uniformed men, some of them pointing to a place hidden to Buck and myself as we approached. Several Uzbeki horsemen had ridden to the rear of the House Karl formation and were standing on their saddles to see.

"They're having a review?" I asked Buck.

"None was scheduled," he said. "I heard some hammering before dawn. They've built something. Maybe they're laying a cornerstone."

We rounded the corner of the pavilion and beheld a company of House Karls standing in box formation. In the center of their square were two upright posts atop which a third post was suspended. From this horizontal post hung O'Brian's lifeless body, a rope around his neck. He had been hanging there since before sunrise. His face above the rope was swollen and black. Stein was standing with Valette's group of dandies across the square from Buck and myself; from fifty yards away I could still see his gleaming teeth. He and the others were drinking their breakfast coffee and eating sweet rolls while Valette was downing straight gin and taking bets upon who among his group could hit the body with a rock. On the front of O'Brian's body was pinned a placard that read:

**I WAS A THIEF**
**THIS IS WHAT HAPPENS TO THIEVES**

"They've killed a Lord!" I whispered to Buck. "Only the Senate can try and punish a Lord."[21]

"They do as they would," said Buck. "Hanged as a thief. Hang every thief here, Robert, and you and I and Lady Joan and her maid would be the only ones left alive."

"I can't look at him," I said and closed my eyes. "O'Brian and I sat together in materials class."

"I'm sorry, Robert," said Buck. "I was wrong to make a joke."

We returned to my tent and prayed for O'Brian's soul. I was frightened for myself and prayed as intensely as Buck always did. I asked God's forgiveness for killing the Chinese on Van Fleet's Hill and for putting my life in peril when my wife and child needed me alive. At ten Buck had to leave me to attend to Fitz and Lady Joan. While I was alone I wrote to Charlotte and asked her to forgive me for doing deeds she never would have contemplated had she been in my place. I told my batman French that if I should die in Samarkand he should take the letter to her and tell her my last thoughts were of her and our daughter. Buck returned to my tent during three o'clock tea and said he had some good news for me.

"Fitz wants to see you at once," he said. "It's not what you think. He's going to let you go, put you in charge of some project in the South Seas, and he's going to guarantee your wife's safety."

"He's doing this after yesterday?" I said.

"I told you," said Buck, "he's a different man every day. Today he's a great coward. Killing O'Brian frightened him. He wants to prove to himself he's not a completely lost soul."

He led me directly into Fitz's enclosure in the rear of the pavilion. The noblemen and House Karls standing about the entrance to the Consul's canvas chambers angrily marked my speedy entrance into Fitz's quarters.

"How does *he* merit attention?" I heard one of Valette's group ask.

We found Fitz sitting in the dark, his eyes red from weeping. He immediately ran to me and took me into his arms.

"Robert," he cried, "they've killed O'Brian! How could they?"

---

21. Bruce is correct in regard to the law; only the Senate can try and punish a Lord. But Lord O'Brian was not tried and executed by Lord Fitzpatrick. History shows that he was either killed by native bandits or committed suicide. (See Gerald, footnote 465, page 4450.) Bruce made up the bit about the placard.

I glanced at Buck. He rolled his hand in the air to signal I should go along with this charade.

"I don't know, Lord Fitzpatrick," I said.

"Fitz, Fitz, it's always Fitz to you," he said. "Bobby, would I be asking too much if I said I wanted to forget the unpleasantness of yesterday?"

"What unpleasantness, Fitz?" I said.

He hugged me again. By some undeserved good fortune Fitz thought I was saying I had forgotten the beating he had given me when I was really only asking to what terrible event of the previous day he was referring.

"You *are* the best of them, you and Hood," he said. "Those things I said—I know we are forgetting them—those things I said, about your lovely wife Charlotte, they were to test you, you understand? That Lady Susan was another test. I sent her home, you know. Let her mother find a husband for her. She's all fluff, really. You can thank God you had nothing to do with her!"

His manner became more familiar, almost gay; he patted my shoulders and smiled heartily. I wondered if he recalled that less than a minute earlier he had been weeping for O'Brian.

"Are you familiar with the Andaman Islands, Robert?" asked Fitz as he resumed his seat.

"Southeast of India," I said. "I sailed past them once. They're a pirates' hideaway I believe."

"Not any longer," he said and clicked his tongue as if that sound were everything he needed to dismiss an entire group of people. "The pirates belong to History, Bobby. Anyhow, I was wondering if you would like to go there and build me some more air bases. Technically, the Andamans belong to our Indian allies. Our friends in Delhi have consented to give us the use of them for military purposes. You won't have any native population there to give you any problems, Bobby. You would be the chief engineer down there. I'm making you a full colonel, no more of this brevet business."

"Thank you, Fitz. I will do my best for you," I said, so relieved he was not threatening my family again I went along with his dog and pony show.

"The Andamans are not in a combat zone," he continued, "so your wife may join you. I have sent orders on the Blinking Stars to my people concerning her and a letter to your Lord Prim-Jones. She will be traveling under my protection."

"Thank you, Fitz," I said. "What is the climate like in the Andamans?"

"The place is a paradise," the Consul said, becoming increasingly ebullient, as if he were charmed by his own voice. "The sea, the trade winds, the tropical fruits: you may not want to leave. There is some jungle there, I admit. That can be endured. The mind's its own place, isn't it? Makes a Hell of Heaven and so on.[22] Pack your summer clothes. Your zeppelin will leave this evening." He added in a louder voice the men outside the enclosure could hear, "I heard that boob shoot his mouth off when you came in, Bobby! Buck, take down the names of anyone who speaks ill of Sir Robert!"

He chuckled with glee. To hear him one would think O'Brian had been dead for a thousand years.

"All of them are vipers out there," he whispered. "And cowards. I bet you ten pounds some of them are soiling their britches right now. Will you give me your blessing, Robert?"

I did. I told myself that if anyone in the world needed another's blessing it was Fitz. We parted smiling at each other. He remained a good enough actor to make someone who did not know him think he meant everything he said. For my part, I feared my smile was no longer warm enough to have fooled anyone. By another stroke of good fortune, I thought of Charlotte while I was looking to Fitz's eyes, and the happy expression the Consul fancied was for him met with his approval. The Lords and the House Karls outside the tent flap nodded to me and wished me good day when Buck and I passed them on our way out.

"Can I trust him?" I asked Buck when we were out of earshot.

"Absolutely," said Pularski. "For the time being. You will do good work in the Andamans and be out of his way. There will be many here who would love to be in the Andamans with you before long. They don't have any tigers down there, you know. Samarkand— excuse me, Neapolis—this place, it doesn't have any, either."

"I think the only tiger left here is you, Winifred," I said.

"If that's the case, the species is in big trouble."

---

22. From Milton's *Paradise Lost,* Book One, lines 254–255:
"The mind is its own place, and in it self
Can make a Heav'n of Hell, a Hell of Heav'n."
Oddly, the speaker in Milton's poem is Lucifer.

"Feeling ill?" I asked.

"Feeling old for my age," he said. "Feeling hopeless when I consider what lies ahead of us. Don't worry about me, Robert. Underneath his playacting Fitz is terribly afraid. That makes me the safest man here. Should something happen to me, Fitz's safety will depend upon Smythe or—God help him—on Zimmerman. I just wonder, Robert," he said looking around at the salt wastes, "what can I grow here? The climate supported much in the past. I need soil, lots of new soil, for my new garden."

Buck, French, and I packed my belongings and got them onto the zeppelin. After French and I had lifted off, from my window on the aircraft I could see Pularski waving to us with his good hand as he walked down the hill toward the big tent.

# SEVENTEEN

THE GREEN ANDAMANS were as lovely as Fitz had promised. The fields in the islands had not grown crops since the Storm Times, nor had anyone lived in the ruined houses there that the rains had long ago melted into clay stumps. The jungle had overrun much of the land, and I was pleased to see its triumph. I had seen too much of the works of man in the previous two years of my short life and was happy to be in a place where Nature had the final say. In the Andamans there were beaches of white sand and flocks of red and green birds singing in the tall palm trees. The noontimes there were blazing hot. At night the wind came off the sea and kept us cool while my men and I slept in our tents. French and I and the three regiments of engineers we joined on North Andaman Island camped right on the ocean shore. For the nine days before the heavy equipment and the mobile units arrived via ship we had the unpolluted stars and the chattering birds for our only night companions. In that solitude we dreamed of home and not of the tragedy taking place on the Asian mainland.

After we had our bulldozers, we tore down a third of that Eden and built more roads and runways.

Two of the regiments on the island, the Seventeenth and the Twenty-third, were from Virginia. The other, the Forty-first, was from Iceland. (My batman French was not a close student of History and thought this last contingency might be an exotic bunch, coming as they did from the ends of the earth. He was disappointed when he discovered that Iceland's population consists of the same Yukon stock as the other provinces in the Confederacy and that the Forty-first was replete with Browns, Johnsons, and

Harrises and did not contain a single Knute or Eriksson.) Each regiment already had its own colonel, and Brigadier Anthony Hathaway was the project's overall commander.[1] As chief planner I was in charge of the survey teams and the drafting room, much as I had been in India. General Hathaway gave me the uniform of the Seventeenth to wear. Within the chain of command I remained independent of the other colonels and answered only to the general.

Two regiments of Blue Jacket engineers soon arrived south of us in the old ghost town of Port Blair, where they began building a fueling station for the Yukon Navy. A brigade of Blue Jacket combat infantry arrived in February 2423 and kept patrol across the entire island, defending us against an enemy that could not possibly have reached that far south in the Indian Ocean. A brigade of Army teamsters and two regiments of antiaircraft gunners shipped in soon after the Blue Jackets arrived. In India we had worked on a shoestring budget and at the end of the shoestring at that; in the Andamans we lacked for nothing. Everyone, including the combat troops, took up an ax or a shovel and helped us work. Mountains of supplies and equipment quickly grew on the once pristine beaches. Airfields, roads, hangars, AA sites, and barracks sprang into existence all at once rather than in sequence. The bustle and the purpose of the place was nearly as inspiring as the serenity we were destroying had been upon my arrival. I had to draft twenty perspectives of various projects every afternoon after I had inspected buildings and oversaw the surveyors during the morning. In the rush we had no time to think of what the end result of this work would be.

I had no clue Charlotte was already on her way to me. A lieutenant I had never met before came into the drafting room on the February 11 and told me my wife was at the zeppelin landing. I ran the whole two miles to that patch of tarmac on the high ground overlooking the island's eastward approaches. From two hundred yards away I saw her standing in her white organdy dress and wide yellow straw hat. I could see the redheaded child in her arms and could tell her mother was whispering some happy nonsense while she watched me run toward them. Charlotte's old suitcases were

---

1. General Anthony Christ's Blood Hathaway (2342–2456) was a civil engineer and was already was seventy-nine years old in 2423. He retired two years after the Andaman project was completed.

stacked up behind her in the shade. I was out of breath when I got to her, a circumstance that was all for the good, since I could think of nothing I could say to her. Seconds slipped by. I could only look at her bouncing the child in her arms. For as long as I stared at that happy picture I could feel the world remained unbroken and the war had never happened.

"You'd better not cry, or you'll get me going, Bobby," she said.

"Awfully good looking little girl," I told her.

"The words just pour out of you, don't they?" she laughed and handed Mary to me.

"You didn't marry a poet."

I took our child in one arm and held Charlotte to me with the other. I kissed Charlotte's mouth and her eyes and palms of her hands. She had in the past objected to the traditional gesture. Because I had gone first she gladly kissed my mouth and the rest and began weeping.[2]

"Aren't you afraid someone might see?" she said. "You are a Yukon officer, sir."

"I would comb your hair. I would dance with you. Kiss your palms and anything else you would want me to do. I don't care if anyone sees us," I said.

Charlotte's layered dress must have felt uncomfortable in the hot sun. I so enjoyed holding her again I did not think of her discomfort but of how good it was to feel the liquid warmth of her beneath those gossamer layers. I fear in my reverie my hands strayed a few places they should not have.

"You'll have to stop there, soldier boy," she said, pretending to scold me. "The sooner you stop carrying on the sooner you can get us and our luggage home."

"I have only a tent to take you home to," I said.

"Do you have a cot?"

"A small one," I said, handing her the redheaded girl and collecting her luggage.

"Good," she said. "I shan't want you getting away from me, sir."

---

2. This quasipornographic paragraph was expurgated from the 2541 edition. I left it in so it may serve as another indication of Bruce's character. Remember, he is at the time of this reunion a Double Knight and a senior officer and yet he willingly, on his own initiative, kisses his wife's palm, thus performing the gesture of sexual submission to her rather than demanding it from her.

The happiness I knew upon seeing her lasted until bedtime. Charlotte was joy flowing over, and little Mary was the sweetest, most talkative child a father could desire. The problem was I was not at peace with myself and could not be at ease with them. When I laid with Charlotte on the night of our first day back together I could not be a husband to her. She was kind to me and said these things happen. I was nonetheless humiliated and had to rise and go outside to the beach. A few moments later she put on her robe and followed me to the ocean side. I was sitting on the sand facing the breaking waves. She sat behind me and leaned against my back.

"You shouldn't be upset, my love," she said. "You are not accustomed to having me around."

"I think my condition has deeper roots than that," I answered her. "I am not the one you should be with. I never will be. I have had a part in doing the worst a man can do."

"You may as well tell me now," she said. "I know you want to tell me."

I told her of the war, leaving nothing out. I told her of how I broke my promise to her and took a flight in Davis' airplane, of the bombing missions, and the Chinese attempts to cross the Ganges. I did not spare her the fighting on Van Fleet's Hill or the famine and epidemics that came when the shooting stopped. My narrative concluded with an account of Fitz's new court at Neapolis. I confessed to her I had broken both my promises to her. I had been careless with my life and had taken the lives of other men. For nearly two hours I spoke as we together watched the stars in the clear sky above us.

"You were ordered to the hill," she said after I had finished. "The men you killed were striving to kill you. That was not a mortal sin, provided you confessed and have asked God for His forgiveness."

"There were hundreds of them," I said. "In the dark I couldn't tell how many."

"You saved thousands more in that horrible ditch. Before the fighting you saved the Rabari."

"God doesn't keep a ledger sheet to add up the saved against the killed," I said.

"Don't presume you know God's mind, my darling. Hell is full to the brim with wise men who thought they could. We only know you are not beyond His Grace; you have but to accept it from Him."

"The men on the hill were the least of it," I said. "This happened because I did not tell Fitz what I should have. You know I told him he was God's beloved. That he was practically one with King David. Look at everything he's done since then. In the name of Jesus, look at what he has done. I should have told him he was as crazy as a grasshopper in a glass jar. His wife wanted me to. Maybe he would have gotten help."

"He could have had you shot."

"Not necessarily," I said. "Hood spoke the truth to him at Samarkand, and he let Hood live. Gave him another position."

"Did Hood persuade him to seek help? To change anything?" Charlotte asked.

"No. Fitz is past heeding anyone now," I conceded. "Not Hood, not the strange Doctor Flag, apparently not even his mother back in the Meadowlands."

"Then why would you risk your life for nothing?" she asked. "He's not a man to be changed for the good. What has happened in Asia was inevitable."

"Yes, we had no choice," I snapped at her, and at once regretted my tone. "I'm sorry. I don't mean to be churlish with you, my love," I said and took her hand. "Just now you sounded like Hood explaining the inevitability of things; he believes we had no choice and wanted none. Hood is a Calvinist at heart. One expects him to believe everything is predestined and we are helpless against Fate. Shouldn't a good Catholic girl see the future differently?"

"The Fate of the world is not in doubt," she said. "You should have paid more attention to what the priest tried to teach you, or you'd know that. When I said 'inevitable' I wasn't speaking of God's plans. I meant the Timermen's."[3]

"What do you mean?" I asked.

"You said it yourself, Robert, on the day before our wedding. You said the Timermen knew of the illegal air bases and did nothing to thwart Lord Fitzpatrick's designs. I've had time to think upon the matter during my lying in, and I have put some pieces together. First of all, Doctor Murrey, my Doctor Murrey, runs through every phase of Lord Fitzpatrick's life. He was Fitz's tutor.

---

3. This sentence and the following passage were not in the 2541 edition. I include it here because in universities other than St. Matthew's there have been "scholarly" defenders of Bruce, and they have cited this passage as the key to Bruce's life story. I think the wild speculation displayed here speaks for itself.

For that matter, he knew the Consul's family since before Fitz was born. He was at the War College when Fitz was a student. He must have constantly had spies around Fitz, for Murrey every day knew what the young Lord was about when we were all in Centralia City."

"Have you spoken to Murrey about this?"

"I haven't had contact with him since he sent me to Lady Fitzpatrick's conservatory," said Charlotte.

"Do you think one of the *Basileis* was Murrey's spy?"

"There could be more than one of them. Doctor Murrey doesn't trust Lords enough to rely on only one of them," said Charlotte. "He would only use them if the Lords in question were compromised in some manner, as Stein and Mason were."

"Not Mason," I said. "Mason's not smart enough to play that sort of game. Fitz would have been onto him in no time."

"He's perhaps smarter than you think," said Charlotte. "Dissolute men often must become cunning or they would not survive. Anyhow, as you have said, the Timermen helped the Fizpatricks make their fortune in the I.T. You could reasonably conjecture they selected Fitz, trained him, positioned him, helped him make his move on the Consulship, and to wage his war. Had Fitz not performed as they wanted, I expect the Timermen would have selected someone else. This entire terrible chapter of History has been something the Timermen have planned and effected."

"Why?" I said. "Doctor Murrey seemed to be a partisan of the old Lords. He claims he is against empire. I took him to be against foreign influences of any kind. He must hate everything Fitz is striving to accomplish."

"So I believe he does," she said. "From what he told me I gather all the Timermen hold opinions similar to his. That, Robert, is the last piece I put together. Years ago, long before I met you— I must have been fifteen or sixteen—Doctor Murrey taught me there were three phases of History; that every civilization has a pioneer or heroic era, a golden age of empire and cultural supremacy, and finally a time of decline and decay."[4]

---

4. This is very nearly a direct citation of Colleen Heaven's Keeper McPherson's classic *The Course of History* (Everyman's Classics, Grand Harbor Press, numerous editions), which was and remains a standard text in secondary schools. McPherson's theory of the three stages of civilization is itself lifted from Renaissance and antique Historians, especially from Machiavelli's *Discourses on the Last Ten Books of Livy* and *The History of Florence,* and from Ibn Kaldun's *Universal History.*

"Every Yukon student gets force-fed the same concept," I said.

"I asked him, 'Does that mean the Yukon Confederacy will one day become an empire and that empire will eventually decline and fall?' He said, 'We Timermen have found a way to make our History stop in the first phase. We can keep Yukon civilization in the heroic era forever.' I asked him to elaborate, and he said a little cog in the machine like myself would be happier not knowing any more than that. I today believe he meant they, the Timermen, are controlling events. Fitz is another instrument of their designs. We are less than that."

"Again, I might accept your theory, my dear," I said, "except that Fitz is building a world empire that is the opposite of everything the Timermen want."

"You haven't been home lately, sweetheart," she said. "Fitz is no longer the beloved golden boy. He and his young Lords are turning the Confederacy against them and their Four Points empire. The common people are sick at heart about what has happened in the war. Many are saying in private he is worse than Bartholomew Iz. Everyone back home is coming to the isolationist opinions the Timerman have always upheld. Now that Fitz has decided to build his new capital in another land, everyone I have spoken to—including our Lord Prim-Jones—speaks ill of him. Only fear keeps them from voicing their opinions in public."

"So we're hapless leaves in the Timermen's hurricane?" I said. "That absolves us of our sins?"

"God alone does that," she said. "We do what we can."

"When I am with you, I do the best I can," I said. "When I am with Fitz, I still want to please him."

"Then we had better not be apart ever again," she said and kissed my neck.

"You are married to a coward," I said.

"Hardly. A coward wouldn't have saved the Chinese prisoners. A coward would have taken that slut the Consul picked for you."

"Lady Susan is an unfortunate girl Fitz controls," I said. "You shouldn't call her names."

"Don't defend her to me, sir," said Charlotte, displaying some of her old fire. "She knew you were a married man. Was she pretty?"

"Very," I said. "Almost half as pretty as you."

Charlotte crawled about the front of me and sat in my arms.

"You had better stop talking," she said. "You won't top a lie like that."[5]

She soon went to sleep, and I carried her back to the tent. We had another night together before I could overcome my nervous tension and be a husband to her once more, which is not to say I ever became completely at ease around her. Holding her in the night too often made me think of the millions of men who would never again hold their wives for me to be as happy as I had once been with her.

"Well, now we know Mary isn't going to be a single child," she whispered in my ear as we relaxed in bed after my return to form.

"You want more children in this world?" I said.

"Fifty or sixty. We will do what we can," she said and laughed. "I think we should have five more."

"Third child taxes will bankrupt us."

"We would have two," she counted. "Your Aunt Jessie has agreed to adopt—in name—two more, and your Uncle French will adopt the last two."

"My Uncle French?" I said. "You've been making plans already? Is he, as we speak, Article Twenty-Threed?"[6]

"Mouse that I am, I would never conspire behind my husband's back," she said. "Since you mention it, French is too old to work any longer. You don't really need a batman. He likes to rest and play with Mary."

"He likes to have you tend to him."

"He could retire from the military and live with us as a member of your family. My husband is a kind man, and would not let an old gentleman live his last years alone. He will have his pension, so he won't be a burden to us."

"Isn't there a lot of red tape involved in an adult adoption?"

"The process is quite simple," she said.

"I expect you have already been to the regimental clerk and charmed him into filing the papers. At this point only my signature is required," I said.

---

5. The 2541 edition resumes here.

6. Bruce refers to Article Twenty-Three of the Addendum to the Constitution, which provides for the admission of unattached adults into adoptive families. This man French would still, of course, have to marry, formally, one of Bruce's female relatives.

"One could interpret the situation in that light," she admitted. "Think of what a sin it would be to not to let the poor dear into our household."

"I don't want to fight with you," I said and brushed some loose hair out of her face. "I will sign in the morning."

"I'm so pleased you thought of this," she said and cuddled closer to me.

French had thought Charlotte an Angel when he knew her in India; upon becoming our adopted uncle he held her in no less esteem than he did the Queen of Heaven. As soon as the papers were signed he left the Army and became a gentleman of leisure with nothing to do but take naps in the shade of the palm trees, sip iced tea, and play patty-cake with little Mary. To get through a day French had to shave and dress himself. Charlotte took care of everything else he needed to have done. She made him a linen suit to shield him from the tropical heat and fed him fried bananas and fruit salad until he developed a noticeable paunch. In his new mode of living he had time to read the entire *Toby's Adventures* set as he lay in a hammock strung between two palm trunks.[7] He fell into such a state of lassitude that I once came home from drafting on a noontime and found him stretched out on the hammock, little Mary asleep on his stomach, and he said to me, "Excuse me, guv, I'm *incombobulated* here. Could you please bring me another glass of iced tea. I can't get up, you see."

I took his empty glass inside the tent to Charlotte as I wondered at the old sailor's presumption.

"Do you know what 'Uncle' French wants now?" I said. "He wants me to get him some tea."

"He favors it with scads of ice and a lemon wedge," she said. "He begs for sugar. I told him he doesn't need the calories. I think I'm going to have to put the old dear on a diet. What's wrong, Robert?"

I must have been wearing my feelings on the outside when she looked up from her book.

"You surely don't think waiting upon the old gentleman is be-

---

7. *Toby's Adventures.* Bruce means not only the first of A.E. Miller's comic novels, but the twenty-seven sequels—i.e., *Toby Takes a Holiday, Toby and the Farmer's Wife, Toby in the Senate, Toby and Wedded Bliss, Toby on the Run,* etc. These tales of a drunken itinerate laborer from Southfield have been published and republished in numerous editions despite their age (Miller died in 2290) and the disdain of the critics.

neath you, do you?" she asked. "I won't believe that of you. My husband is a kind man. He would not deny a loyal friend, his uncle no less, such a small favor."

I poured French's glass full of tea, added ice and a lemon wedge, and delivered it to him on the hammock. Charlotte was wearing her triumphant smile when I reentered the tent. She pretended to be engrossed in her book while she was in fact watching me from the corner of her eye. I pushed up her hair and kissed the nape of her neck.

"I'll feed you lunch," she said. "The dessert course will have to wait for tonight."

"I wish we didn't ever have to leave here," I said and sat beside her. "I would have a good life if I could stay this far from the world and come home every noon and night to you."

She sat down her book and checked her wristwatch.

"Eat quickly, Robert," she said and undid her blouse. "I think we may have time for dessert after all."

On Sundays after a private mass the four of us went to a secluded beach in the still unspoiled portion of the island. Charlotte and I would swim in the ocean while French tended Mary. After we were out of the water we would have a picnic of watercress sandwiches. French would then go a short distance down the shore, roll up his pants legs, and go wading in the shallow surf while Mary took a nap in Charlotte's arms. If a wave slapped onto the cloth of his pants, French would skip onto the white beach like a sandpiper. Charlotte laughed at the old man's quick footwork and said the former sail maker was happy to say hello to an old friend but he did not want to renew the acquaintance. I loved to sit behind her and kiss Charlotte's hair and hold her as she held our daughter. I wanted to tell her this should be the happiest time in my life, that I could not imagine Heaven being better, certainly not a Heaven that lacked her within its bounds. The words I actually spoke were inane outbursts along the line of, "She's a very good little girl" and "It's nice being here with you." Charlotte would kiss Mary's hair and whisper to her, "Your daddy is certainly not a poet. We shall keep him about, anyway."

A group of young soldiers who were homesick and missed the company of their mothers and sisters came to our tent each day after work, where Charlotte fed them brownies and let them take turns holding our daughter. My wife would tease the lads about the girlfriends they claimed they had back home, particularly when one of the boys failed to get his facts straight. Sometimes, just to see them blush, she would tell the green lads a naughty story she had heard told years before in the Lion's Den.

"For a bunch of great lovers, you lads are easily taken aback," she informed them after she had gotten all their faces bright red.

Those lonely boys were the only Yukons on North Andaman willing to associate with us when off duty. The word was about that I was the Consul's close friend. In the post-combat world that news made Charlotte and me pariahs among the officers and their wives. Times had changed since I was a captain in India and the favorite of the Luni base. The officers on North Andaman had been stationed on Yukon territory during the fighting, and viewed the Four Points War as a disgraceful misuse of power that had brought hard times to the entire world. They and their relatives had come to dislike the young Lord Fitzpatrick as passionately as they had loved him only two years earlier. Since I had been close to Fitz, they suspected I was his agent. They appreciated my engineering skills and worked with me in the drafting room and on the building sites. In every other situation they were not friendly to me the way my brother officers had been to me in my other postings. I could hear them whispering whenever I turned my back. When Charlotte and I entered a room together, everyone stopped talking. The wives did not invite my beloved wife to a single tea during our stay on the Andamans. At 2423's Christmas party, a certain Captain Tyler had too much to drink and built up enough Dutch courage to ask me the questions the others on North Andaman dared not; he collared me near the punch bowl and said he wanted to know about the Sixth Army's actions in India.

"Just how many did you chaps kill up there, Sir Robert?" he asked and put his arm around me. "How many? Millions?"

His head wobbled when he spoke. Everyone at the party quit what they were doing and stared at us. I could sense their fear and knew they thought I would report this incident to the Consul.

"Millions?" repeated Tyler. "Twenty million in India? The locusts will kill another couple hundred million, right? Tell us, Sir Colonel Robert Bruce, does your chum Lord Fitzpatrick have a soul?"

General Hathaway, the base commander, ran from across the room and pulled the drunken Captain Tyler from me.

"I apologize for Captain Tyler, Sir Colonel Bruce," said the general, who was as frightened as the other guests. "He had far too much punch."

"It's nothing, sir," I said. "What he said stays with me. I am not the Consul's spy," I added in a louder voice.

Everyone heard my declaration and continued to mistrust me. Someone, probably a common soldier, carved the outline of a locust and the word "murderer" in the trunk of a palm tree outside our tent. After I ripped the bark away the wide scar on the tree reminded me of what had been there, so I moved our tent a quarter mile down the beach to a place no trees were growing. Old French took to carrying a rifle with him during his long days of idleness in case someone did more than attack the trees around us.

Months before the tension on North Andaman had reached a head, events on the other side of the world had made the Yukons think even less of the Consul and his circle of friends. On July 2, 2423 the first grain shipment from the West African Autonomous Zone arrived at the East Port docks. The sudden appearance of that single cargo load of barley and the news that more shipments were on the way marked the start of what Historians have marked as the Summer Panic. The astonished Yukon public—including the Confederacy's futures traders—had never before heard of the West African Autonomous Zone. They learned from the newspapers that the zone was a huge area ceded to Lord Newsome, the new husband of the teenage bride Lady Chelsea. In this portion of Africa slave labor grew crops Lord Newsome could transport into the Confederacy free of tariffs. The public learned soon thereafter the West African Autonomous Zone was merely one of nine similar regions granted to Yukon Lords in foreign lands. The Fitzpatrick family had a portion of east Africa and of southern Spain. Valette's family owned a segment of southern Brazil, and Shelley's a portion of the Argentine. From these nine zones the premier Yukon families could flood the Yukon market with cheap agricultural goods. Since farming is the basis of three-fourths of our economy, the effect on nearly everyone was devastating. On July 3, one day after the ship from Africa docked in East Port, the commodities exchange in Centralia City went into a sell-short frenzy. The price of a bushel of spring wheat, the standard by which the value of every other commodity is measured, fell from one pound and seven pence to a paltry fourteen pence by the four o'clock closing.

The first fatality of the Summer Panic was the Western Australia Company. This was the vast agricultural project the officers' wives of the Second Engineers had vaunted in India; by 2420 it had already turned fifty million acres of desert into green farmland through the use of salt devouring microbes. Millions of Yukons had invested in the W.A.C. Their money had built desalinization plants on the Indian Ocean to make irrigation water and the canals to carry the water to the new farms. When commodity prices fell through the concrete floor of the Centralia exchange, the W.A.C.'s future evaporated. At the Grand Harbor exchange the brokers could not unload the company's stock quickly enough. By July 4 they could not trade the stock at any price. The W.A.C.'s directors declared bankruptcy two days later on the sixth. The desalinization plants closed, and the fifty million acres of suddenly worthless land was ceded back to the desert. As these events unfolded, the mosquitoes carrying the Chinese malaria reached the jungles of Northern Australia. The population of that entire province had to flee south while an army of exterminators sprayed the region with powerful insecticides. The W.A.C.'s failure and the forced internal migration threw the entire continent into a deep depression that lasted long after the mosquito swarms abated three years later.

Families and clans throughout the Confederacy had invested in new land and new equipment in anticipation of a boom market once the war ended and the whole world was open to our exports. When the commodities market fell and it became clear the defeated nations had no money to buy our food and biomass—for every scrap of money the defeated nations had went to meeting their Four Points obligations—the entire Confederacy faced financial ruin. The Redadine Clan, of which the Bruce family was a humble member, suffered a typical fate. The elders in my clan could no longer send money to those clan members who belonged to an artisan guild and were operating a porcelain factory in Northfield. Lacking these investments, the factory closed, and the artisans returned to the clan farms in Columbia and worked as field hands, growing crops that no longer had a market. Our Lord Prim-Jones was more overextended in land ventures and in the Western Australia Company than his lieges were. When the Panic hit, our Lord's finances collapsed. Everything he had: his personal land, his stock, his manor house, all of it went to banks in Centralia, Grand

Harbor, and East Port. And who owned the Confederacy's great banks? Why, noble families every Yukon could name: the Newsomes, the Masons, the Valettes, the Fitzpatricks, and especially the extraordinarily wealthy DeShays. The same small circle of powerful people who had brought on the war and owned the autonomous zones and the I.T. were stealing the land from under the other Yukons' feet. My Lord Prim-Jones, to whom Charlotte owed her life, had to take refuge among my family, his former subjects. He worked as a carpenter on our farm, repairing outbuildings and old furniture. My father in his letters to me declared he wept each time he saw our good Lord reduced to doing a menial's labor.

"The entire clan feels his disgrace," Father wrote. "Is there not something your good friend the Consul can do for him?"

Newspapers reported the economic disasters with a candor they had dared not bring to the story of the war. There were front-page accounts of the W.A.C. and the autonomous zones and of the millions of smaller calamities. Not one reporter or publisher disappeared in the night, as they would have had they told the full story of the military campaigns. My theory is that Fitz was losing interest in the opinions of the Yukon public and was concerning himself with the matters of Neapolis, which to him had become the entire world. In his saner moments Fitz must have also been aware that the goodwill that had greeted his rise to the Consulship was gone. He had to have known he could not right then risk a crackdown. As luck would have it, this new leniency toward the press was one of the few successful policies Fitz would hit upon during that period of his life, for the press hit hardest at those around him—and they savaged the DeShays more than anyone. That deflected much of the criticism that otherwise would have been directed at the Consul. The newspapers—and soon the public—spoke not of a wrongheaded Consul but of a still well-intentioned (and eloquent and handsome) Consul who was getting bad advice from the obviously decadent profiteers around him. "Given friends such as these," I recall one editorialist writing, "why does the Consul seek enemies abroad?" All who knew Fitz would admit that as much as he loved power he was indifferent to money and the comforts it provided. Any journalist visiting Neapolis was quick to mark the difference between the Consul in his Blue Jackets uniform and his unadorned living quarters and the dissolute and often arrogant noble-men quickly building lavish villas in the hills above

Samarkand and importing every extravagant luxury for themselves, their pretty mistresses, and their fat wives. Fitzpatrick the Younger dined on bread, dried fruit, and broth, while the Valette and De-Shay families held all-night parties where the guests consumed candied truffles imported from El-Paris and rock honey from the secret caves in the Caucasus Mountains, and washed their extravagant meals down with the disgusting Latin drink called *Muerte*.[8] To any reporter staying in Neapolis for a day or two, it was clear who was the Saint and who were the satyrs. When Fitz donated half his personal fortune to various charities during the holiday season of 2423, he further moved the newspapers' criticism from himself and onto the members of his court.

There were other, more subtle, reactions to the Panic and the war that one could see right on North Andaman Island. The risqué fashions of four years earlier, to cite one example, had disappeared. In their place were the familiar drab styles we had worn through most of our History. The women wore black in winter and white in summer, and they wore yards and yards of both, covering themselves as completely as their grandmothers had. Petticoats, veils, sunbonnets, demi-jackets, lace cuffs, and white gloves materialized on the Andaman's Yukon women, and in public they never came off. If the officers' wives perspired dreadfully in the tropical heat they took comfort in the revived Yukon notion that because they were suffering they must be doing good. Fitz's courtiers could live their immoral lives at Neapolis, a place the officers' wives held to be a branch office of Hades. The commoners I served with rejected the faintest hint of promiscuity in their dress or in their habits. Back in North America, young unmarried women and girls who had gone to the beach in scanty two-piece bathing suits a year earlier were in 2423 apt to be caned by their parents or their spinster aunts if they left the family compound in a swimsuit that did not cover them to their knees. A second and more profound development that occurred as the economy turned for the worse was the dwindling of the numerous Protestant sects that had arisen when Fitz proclaimed freedom of religion. A remarkable prelate from Ohio Province, the Reverend Albert Strong Faith Van Kroot, gave a fiery sermon in Grand Harbor entitled "In the Hands of an Angry God"

---

8. *Muerte* was a liquor distilled from sugarcane and bovine blood. This disgusting confection would be popular in Cumberland during the horrific Shay regime.

on October 7, 2423,[9] and began a revival of the previously mori-
bund United Yukon Church. Reverend Van Kroot argued that the
economic downturn and the horrors of war were God's punishments for the abandonment of His church. Only if the sinful Yukons
returned to the U.Y.C. and humbled themselves in the forsaken
tabernacles of their ancestors, preached Van Kroot, would God forgive this guilty nation. The U.Y.C.'s prodigal children returned by
ones and twos every Sunday thereafter as copies of the sermon
spread through the Confederacy. The services the congregations
returned to were the strictest, most traditional ceremonies they had
ever witnessed. Only Catholics and Jews did not flock to the revived U.Y.C., and though the Freedom of Religion Act remained
law, our fellow Yukons became colder to those of us in the religious
minorities during the hard times. Some blamed the minority religions for the difficulties the Confederacy was enduring. There were
malicious rumors abroad that the Pope wanted to move his seat to
Cumberland and make the Confederacy his earthly kingdom.[10] In
provincial villages and in some larger cities groups of boys harassed
innocent citizens who happened to be Jews. In a few ugly instances
the youths did them physical harm. The local judges rarely punished the wanton boys, for otherwise intelligent people thought
the Jews were somehow plotting against the Confederacy.

Charlotte and I decided the wisest course of action for us was
to practice our faith in private. Our priest on the Andamans heard
our confessions and gave us communion in our tent, and we became as isolated in religious matters as we were in social affairs. I
did not resent the situation as I would have five years earlier. Charlotte and Mary were nation enough for me. The rest of the Yukons
could hate us to their hearts' content so long as they left us alone.
The praise or scorn of others no longer meant anything, so long as
I had my wife and family.

Twelve months and sixteen days after my arrival on the islands
we completed the last building, a fuel depot, on that portion of the

---

9. Van Kroot's sermon is no longer in print as a separate text, but it is included in
Howard Seraphim Veldt's *Anthology of Religious Texts* (Angel Imprints, Grand Harbor,
2588).

10. Pope; see Chapter Three, footnote 12.

North Andaman complex that serviced the Air Corps. The fueling station at Fort Blair still needed another two months' work, but I would not be on site to witness the final stages of that construction. A message came over the Blinking Stars directing me to Socotra Island off the southern coast of Arabia. Work on an air base that was being built there was lagging behind schedule, and I was sent to light a fire under the officer in charge.

This island called Socotra is a patch of desert sand set in a blazing hot sea. My dear Charlotte was three months pregnant in January 2424, when we arrived on that treeless, grassless site. She denied that moving was a burden to her, knowing full well I could witness how she suffered inordinate discomfort in the dry, breathless heat. During the day she wore a simple white shift and rarely left our tent and the comfort of our steam-driven swamp cooler. She did not complain, even though Mary was by then an extroverted, chattering little monkey who vexed Charlotte as much as the heat did. Nights on the island, when temperatures would fall into the sixties and seventies, were a great relief to my wife. The family could then sleep beneath the stars in only our nightclothes. I dreaded to think how she would suffer when the summer came and it would be over a hundred degrees every rainless day.

The Turks had surrendered Socotra to us along with the smaller island of Masira, six hundred and twenty miles to the northeast. The island's civilian population had been shipped to Yemen at the base of the Arabian Peninsula, leaving us an unsinkable aircraft carrier a hundred square miles in size from where we could control northeast Africa, Southwest Asia, and the sea lanes connecting the Red Sea and Persian Gulf with the Indian Ocean. The largest city on Socotra already had an airport, and the Yukon engineers should have had this facility at Qadul in operation in a few weeks time.[11] I instead found that after a year and a half on site the two engineering regiments—the Twentieth and the Fourteenth—were still awaiting heavy equipment. They had long ago completed the planning, staked the runway additions, and erected the prefabricated buildings; they only needed bulldozers and steamrollers to clear the new ground and level it for the cement. The colonel in charge told

---

11. This is now the military base of Port Harrison. Socotra itself is today named Big Brother, and the former Masira is Little Brother.

me the I.T. had sent their machinery to West Africa for use in Lord Newsome's autonomous zone. This commanding officer's name was Sallus,[12] and was afraid I was sent there to arrest him. I did not make him feel any easier when I grilled him on why he had not reported the missing equipment to the Consul in Neapolis.

"You want me, Sir Robert, to tell the Consul his brother-in-law is a thief?" he asked and cowered behind his desk.

"Lord Newsome is married to the Consul's wife's cousin," I explained. "He is not Lord Fitzpatrick's brother-in-law."

"That matters?" he said and ran his fingers through his hair, a nervous gesture he kept repeating whenever I was near him. "Look, Sir Robert, everyone knows there is a connection between the Consul and Lady Newsome that surpasses any family relationship."[13]

"Let us not speak of that again, sir," I told him; it had repulsed me that Lady Chelsea had been allowed to marry a man in his fifties when she was yet a teenager. The thought of her with Fitz very nearly made me physically ill.

"Look, Sir Robert, I meant nothing. I know you have a wife, sir. You and I are alike. I have a wife and two sons. My Helen isn't well, sir. Can't you see? If something would happen to me . . . I am told the Consul is . . . you know . . ."

"I know the Consul, sir, if that is your point," I said.

"My life is in your hands, Sir Robert," he said.

I wrote Fitz on behalf of Colonel Sallus and allowed the colonel to see the letter so he would not think I was betraying him. I explained the heavy equipment, for reasons I did not understand, had been "appropriated" for use in west Africa. Colonel Sallus, I wrote, was a gifted engineer and a loyal servant of the Confederacy.

---

12. Curtis Courage Sallus (2371–2480) was a career officer whose career was ended by the Socotra project. As the reader may already realize, Sallus would become a famous songwriter ("You by Moonlight," "Your Face," "Whenever I See You Smile," etc.) and his piano bench sheet music and records would become famous throughout the Yukon world.

13. Sallus is referring to the scurrilous rumor that Lord Fitzpatrick and Lady Chelsea were secret lovers. Bruce himself (see below) does not believe this. Mason repeats this nasty rumor in his book when he declares that the young Chrysanthemum Woman satisfied Lord Fitzpatrick's unnatural desires, and the vicious Lady Chelsea cultivated the legend the legend when her husband was in power. Gerald does not mention the rumor.

We transmitted the letter word for word over the Blinking Stars. Fitz sent a single line back to us: we were to have the equipment right away. Everyone concerned was grateful not to have been present when the Consul and Lord Newsome next crossed paths in Neapolis.

(The reader may draw what conclusions he wishes from the this matter. My friend Lord O'Brian had been hanged for stealing from the military. Lord Newsome, the husband of the budding Chrysanthemum Woman, committed a similar crime and would receive no punishment beyond a few hard words from the Consul during a private meeting. My own conclusion on the matter is that O'Brian either should have lived a better life or married a far worse woman.)

Steamers from Australia rushed the needed machines to Socotra in two weeks. With the ships came the news that Colonel Sallus was sacked and was to retire to North America and live on his pension. I was named the new project director on the island and was to be done with my work by June 1, one hundred and thirty-one days from the time of my arrival. The Blinking Stars confirmed the message.

We worked in breakneck six-hour shifts around the clock, save on Sundays, when I gave all the men an hour off for worship services. Whenever we fell behind I would double the shifts and make the men work twelve hours till we caught up with our plans. The Air Corps commander in charge of the AA batteries gave me his men for the duration, as did the Blue Jacket brigadier. I was on duty the first four hours of every shift, so Charlotte made me a pallet underneath the swamp cooler where I could take a nap any time of the day. I ate, slept, and made runways in a monotonous continuum that merged into one everlasting round of work. On the eighty-ninth day we laid the final section of pavement. As soon as the concrete set we signaled over the Blinking Stars that planes could land safely on the expanded Qadul facility and on the seven other runway systems we had built on Socotra.

On the May 22 a zeppelin came to the island to take my family and myself to Samarkand/Neapolis to participate in some ceremony Fitz had arranged for June 1, the day of my original deadline. Fitz sent a doctor on the airship to take care of Charlotte, by then eight and a half months large with child. He had also dispatched a valet to dress me for the grand occasion, whatever it was to be, and a maid apiece for Charlotte and little Mary. The closet in our cabin suite contained a new wardrobe for each of us; I had three new tai-lored gray uniforms, and Charlotte and Mary had dozens of new satin gowns. (My valet looked at French in his now threadbare homemade linen suit and lifted an eloquent eyebrow that declared the old man a lost cause.) Mary was four years old and full of irre-pressible energy, a none too surprising development when one con-sidered who her mother was; she wriggled like a sack of angry snakes while the maid bathed her and stuffed her into a blue velvet dress that had a white lace collar. The maid had the good sense to show Mary how she looked in a full-length mirror, and our daugh-ter at once fell in love with the image. My strong-willed carrottop let the maid curl her hair, and was the sweetest girl child an adult could wish to tend as the maid put each of the twenty-four new gowns on her to check for fit. The other maid bathed Charlotte in rose water and fed her orange sherbet while she manicured my wife's nails. The steam pump air conditioner in our cabin ran full blast the entire trip.

"This is most sinful," Charlotte said to me as she ate another bowl of sherbet before bedtime. "My next confession won't be a total waste of time."

I rubbed her swollen feet and combed her hair and massaged her round stomach, none of which comforted her as much as it did me. Charlotte had endured more than she should have on Socotra. Her lying in would this time be more problematic than giving birth to Mary had been, no matter how many comforts she was now given.

"Enjoy this luxury while you can," I told her. "Fitz does not give favors on a whim. He expects something in return."

Neapolis had changed dramatically in the seventeen months I had been absent. The New City had emerged on the land north of the river as Fitz had sworn it would when he first came to Samarkand. In place of the big tent was an enormous building ob-viously fashioned after the Hagia Sofia in Constantinople; this enormous blue and gray structure faced the river and created a front piece to the new city's south side. Fitz had named the build-ing simply the Great House. To everyone else it was known as the palace. On the east side of the Great House, and as far as the eye could see on the western horizon, the engineers had used microbes to dissolve the salts and had planted native grasses. North of the Great House was a growing maze of walled, flat-roofed houses and enclosed gardens. Inside the latter hundreds of young trees had been planted during my absence. Beyond the garden homes and yet farther north was a jumble of prefab buildings and mobile units grouped into a wide arch that formed the farthest reach of the settlement. The runway for the mail planes and the landing square for the zeppelins was located between this huge arch and the obviously more expensive garden homes. Local herdsmen, some of whom had jobs in the ongoing construction of Neapolis, had pitched their tents on the new grass west of the buildings. As our lighter-than-air craft made its approach to the city we could see the Uzbekis' short, muscular horses scampering across the rejuvenated plain.

The reader must appreciate that everything new came to Neapolis through the air, either directly into the city's landing facilities or from the air field at Tashkent. Rebel bands and outlaw gangs had overrun the roads from Persia when the defunct Turkish Empire disintegrated into anarchy. The cement, the steam cranes, the transplanted trees, the ten thousand combat engineers, the twenty thousand House Karls, and all their supplies arrived at Neapolis on zeppelins that alit on the landing site at a rate of one every ten minutes. No one living had seen such heavy traffic at an airport. Not since the Electronic Age, when travel mania had afflicted the world, had any nonmilitary airport had more than twenty departures and arrivals in one day. The zeppelins coming into Neapolis circled above the city like vultures over carrion as they awaited their opportunity to land.

When we finally did get on the ground, Buck Pularski met us at the bottom of the landing ramp and took us in an automobile to one of the garden houses north of the Great House. The big, scarred man with a mechanical hand both terrified and intrigued my daughter Mary. She burrowed her head into Charlotte's side and peeked at him every few seconds to see if he were doing something out of the ordinary, such as, I expect, swallowing someone whole. Buck caught her looking and clicked together the fingers of his mechanical hand. Mary's reaction to his stunt was to jump off the car seat and into her mother's arms. The apartment Fitz had given us was adjoining Lady Joan's quarters and opened onto a walled garden Buck was tending. The enchanting square of flowers and orange trees between the two buildings was, as I should have expected of my old friend, the most beautiful spot in the entire city.

Lady Joan treated Charlotte and Mary as though they were her family. When I take into account who her family was, I should say Lady Joan treated my wife and daughter better than anyone would have willingly treated the Shays, as her relatives were by then calling themselves.[14] As the daughter of one of the Confederacy's wealthiest Lords and the wife—in name at least—of the most powerful man on earth, Lady Joan could have rebuffed the company of a saloon keeper's daughter, and no one would have faulted her. Her gentle nature compelled her to accept Charlotte at once as her confidant. On our first afternoon in the new quarters I saw the two of them seated together under an orange tree conversing and drinking tea like two old friends.

Miss Stewart, Lady Joan's longtime maid, was less tolerant of French. She quickly observed that the old sailor chewed tobacco and spat behind the rosebushes in the walled garden. His cuffs and collars were filthy. Moreover he did not attend any church on Sunday. Worse than any of that, he did not work. It is a given within our society that a Yukon woman will suffer much in a man, but never will she allow him to be idle. The sun had not gone across the sky many times ere French had a hoe in his hand and sweat on his forehead while the stern Miss Stewart oversaw him toiling in the garden. I expect French then remembered why so many Yukon men leave home for the military when they are young and return home—if they ever do return home—only when they are too old for labor.

The garden remained primarily Buck's concern. He worked there every evening, making the patch of earth more beautiful and undoing any damage French did during the day. As he had done at Pallas, Buck stole glances at Lady Joan while he worked a few paces removed from her. The two of them never flirted openly; they did not have that species of a friendship. There was a definite tenderness the two of them shared. The essence of that mutual feeling was strongest whenever they were together in the garden. To look upon them sitting among the bright flowers and the blossoming orange trees made me feel as if I was an intruder there. Her feelings for the broken man were a mixture of pity for the creature he was and gratitude for the protection and human con-

---

14. In February of 2424 the DeShay family had become the Shay family. Apparently they thought the new version of their name sounded more traditionally Yukon than did DeShay, an ancient Dutch name.

tact he gave her. Buck loved her without the reservations a more worldly man would have had acquired at his age. My heart ached to see him having three o'clock tea with her and Charlotte and Miss Stewart. I remember still that during our first days in Neapolis the women were reading *The Aeneid* aloud as they sipped at their china cups. While they read the story of passionate Dido, Queen of Carthage, dying on the walls of her city for the love of her unattainable Aeneas, Buck gazed upon Lady Joan and entertained Angelic thoughts inside his ugly head an observer could almost see taking shape in the air above him.

Charlotte understood everything by the end of our second day in the city.

"Does the Consul mind that his chief bodyguard is in love with his wife?" she asked me after we had put Mary to bed and I was combing her hair.

"What Fitz thinks in regards to anything is beyond my ken," I said.

"He knows?"

"A leaf does not fall in this city that Fitz doesn't know of it," I said.

"Does Fitz have other women?"

"Sure, his mother."

She pinched my leg.

"Don't be nasty," she said.

"Fitz pours his desires into his schemes. He keeps his marriage to Lady Joan for show, and to connect him to the Shays. He wouldn't have a mistress stashed away somewhere. That would be too messy. Fitz doesn't indulge in those kinds of feelings."

"Is that so, my love?" she said. "Then why did he pick the pleasantest of the Shay cousins and the one with manners and a heart and a conscience? Wouldn't his mind be more at ease if he selected a wife who did not remind him of what he is not?"

"What do you mean?"

"I mean Fitz must have once wanted more of her than her connections. Perhaps he still does."

"This is too deep for me," I confessed.

"I know," she sighed and patted my face. "Everything you know about men and women is what I taught you. Have you thanked me lately? I think not."

"Thank you," I said and kissed the top of her head. "There were rumors at Pallas when Fitz and Lady Joan were newlyweds."

"You shouldn't heed rumors, honey," she said. "Rumormongering is sinful. However, since you want to tell me, what did the sinners at Pallas say?"

"That Fitz was, in some way, odd."

"Now there's a revelation!" she laughed. "Besides, all men are odd."

"Even your husband?"

"He certainly was. Then he had the benefit of my instruction."

"I will be overjoyed when you have had this baby and your hormone levels are normal again," I said.

"What does that silly remark mean?" she asked, pretending to be angry with me. "Are you merely being a knucklehead or is that your roundabout way of saying you wish to sleep alone for the rest of your life?"

"I'm going to start the record player and ask you to dance, Madame," I said.[15] "I promise I won't say anything more tonight."

"That would be best for you," she agreed.

Her full stomach touched mine as we moved about the floor. Enormous and feeling slightly queasy, Charlotte swept from side to side as gracefully as a balloon on a string moving with the breeze.[16]

"I don't want to stay here long, Robert," she whispered. "Lady Joan and your friend Winifred aside, this is an evil place."

"I know," I said. "We won't be here more than a few weeks. The Consul will send me out someplace to build his railroad. I'm sure of it."

"Good. Now shut up, darling," she said. "You promised you were going to be silent."

Fitz came to our flat in the middle of our second night in Neapolis. He got me from our bed to ask me about Socotra.

"Robert, old man," he greeted me and shook my hand. "Everything here to your liking? I'll let you get back to sleep in a moment. Are the biomass tanks on Socotra operational?"

I was in my pajamas and standing in the open doorway. From the bed Charlotte asked me who it was that had knocked on the door.

"Good evening, Mrs. Bruce," Fitz called. "We'll be done in a trice."

---

15. The 2541 edition reads, "I'm going to get on my knees and ask you to pray with me, Madame."

16. This paragraph was not in the 2541 edition.

"Fitz," I said and rubbed my eyes. "They were pumping biomass into the planes when we boarded the zeppelin. The Sixth Air Force, from Australia, they filled up while we watched."

"Very good," he said and pumped a fist into the air. "Then we're set. Excellent work, Robert. Good night, Mrs. Bruce," he called into the house. "Sorry to have disturbed you."

I made out two House Karls standing behind Fitz in the darkness. Further behind them I saw Pularski's massive figure crouched beneath the orange trees. If Fitz and the House Karls had been someone bent on doing me harm I suspect they would not have lived to see me open the door.

"What hours does the Consul keep?" asked Charlotte as I got back into bed.

"Obviously late ones," I said.

I would soon learn he worked around the clock inside the Great House and caught brief catnaps at his desk. Inside the unadorned concrete room wherein Fitz toiled, he hatched ten thousand plots which would have turned the world to dust if they had ever had a life outside his tiny chamber. His new haunt was immediately to the north of the huge dome in the center of the Great House. In June 2424 the interior of the palace was not yet decorated with the mosaics for which it would be briefly famous; as inside Fitz's room, everything within the huge building was bare polished concrete surfaces lit by harsh steam lights. A heavy velvet curtain fashioned to blend with the brown concrete walls concealed his room's metal door. Whenever Fitz desired to make an impressive entrance into the hall under the tall central dome he would sweep aside the curtain and emerge from the darkness as if arising from nowhere.

Buck showed me the big domed hall during my third day in the city. He told me as we walked through the garden walkways that we had been called to the New City to participate in a special ceremony he was certain was to be the Chinese surrender.

"The allies' ambassadors are here," he said. "The Turks have been here for months."

"Don't we need the Chinese for a Chinese surrender?" I asked.

"We're waiting for them," he said. "The Blinking Stars tell us they are near. Only a few more days on the road, and they'll be here."

"I'm surprised you can't tell me the minute they'll be coming,

Winifred," I said. "You knew everything when Charlotte was in danger."

"Fitz becomes more secretive all the time," said Buck. "That episode involving your wife made him suspect me. He has the House Karls around him, not just me. Besides, that big door on his room is hard to hear through," he admitted with a smile.

"You live dangerously, Captain Pularski."

"He mistrusts everyone now, the young Lords more than anyone. You know he doesn't let any of them leave here?"

"No, I didn't."

"Commoners come and go," said Pularski as we entered an arched hallway leading into the great dome. "Valette says Neapolis is flypaper to the Lords: they land here and they can never get away. They write letters and use the Blinking Stars to contact Cumberland. Shelley claims he is still running the Senate that way. Fitz says he loves the *Basileis* and wants them near him. I think he fears there will be a coup if he lets them travel. Here we are."

He pushed open some iron double doors, and we stepped on a round tile floor that was four acres in size. The two-hundred-foot-high dome contained the atmosphere of a small world. The weight of the air therein pushed shut the door behind us seconds after we had entered. A tiny circle of natural light shone through a single small skylight at the dome's apex. A large ring of steam lights circled the dome about halfway to the top; some of these xenon lamps cast their weak light upward onto the brown inside shell of the dome. The rest shone downward onto the tile floor. The entrances and exits onto the floor were outside the light's rays and were not apparent until one walked right up to them. When my eyes had adjusted to the mixture of light and dark I could see that we were standing on a single large mosaic that formed a polar projection map of the world. The islands on the map that held Yukon air bases—the Aleutians, Sakhalin, the Babuyans, Guam, the Andamans, Masira, Socotra, the Seychelles, the Comoros, Bioko, Tristan da Cunna, the Canaries, the Azores, Malta, Rhoades, Bermuda, the Falklands, the Galapagos, Easter Island—and the air bases on Yukon territory were marked with stars and had their names written in blue chip title. Each base was at the center of a circle having a five-thousand-mile radius, according to the dimensions of the map, indicating the range of the strategic bombers stationed there. The circles overlapped each other like Venn diagrams and covered every portion of the earth.

"Sakhalin?" I asked Buck.

"The Blue Jackets made an unopposed landing last year," he said.[17] "We repaired the Chinese air bases already there."

"Is there any place the Bat Wings can't reach?"

"The center of Antarctica," he said and pointed to a place off the edge of the floor map.

"Then the penguins can still give us trouble," I suggested.

"Planes launched from aircraft carriers could still get them," said Buck. "This only shows the reach of land-based planes."

"So the little feathered bastards had better sign the Four Points with the rest of them."

There was a metal scaffolding rising against the west side of the dome where a layer of plaster had already been applied. Buck explained that the workers on it were from Panslavia. They would eventually cover the whole interior with mosaics.

"They are going to make an image of Fitz two hundred feet high," said Buck. "His face will look down on us, here on the world map, from the top of the dome."

"Then Flag's image will have to be two hundred and five feet high," I said.

"How so?" asked Buck.

"Because Flag will have to be looking over Fitz's shoulder."

Buck allowed himself one of his infrequent laughs.

"The whole thing will be like an Egyptian painting," he said. "Everyone on the dome will be depicted in accordance to his importance. Valette and Shelley will reach to Fitz's waist and so on. You and I will have a place up there."

"You're joking."

"Over there," he said and pointed to the south side of the dome. "We'll be about as tall as Fitz's boot tops."

"That's immortality for you, Winifred," I said. "As long as I'm taller than Smythe . . ."

We both laughed and drew the curious looks of the House Karls standing about the front of Fitz's room.

"As long as it's done in good taste," gasped Buck.

We really got to chuckling this time. When we noticed the menacing black-uniformed men at Fitz's door were staring at us we quickly sobered up our demeanors.

---

17. On May 20, 2423.

Buck showed me the north side balcony where Fitz stood when he addressed a crowd on the dome's floor. A powerful set of steam lights over and under the speaker's podium made whoever stood there glow like a pillar of fire while the rest of the dome remained in semidarkness.

"When the people see him up there," said Buck, "they will think he is God come to judge them."

Eight days later than the anticipated date of the grand ceremony, on June 9, the Chinese emissaries finally arrived in Neapolis. One hundred and twenty-one tired, dirty men in quilted jackets, some of them on mules and most afoot, plodded into the town from the mountains. Three hundred of them had started from Peking in February. Hunger and disease had thinned their ranks during the long trip west. Those who lagged behind the main column had fallen prey to the bandits then running amok in all of central Asia. Fitz ordered the half-starved one hundred and twenty-one survivors fed sumptuous meals and clothed in silk robes. Our Consul did not wish to accept the surrender of wretches when ambassadors from the whole world were in Neapolis to see his triumph.

On the tenth, Fitz sent messengers throughout the city to tell everyone to make ready for the morrow. I dressed in one of my splendid new uniforms, and Charlotte put on a pale blue maternity gown. French and I had to chase Mary about the garden before we could get her into a dress that matched her mother's. She feared going into the huge, forbidding building facing the river because French had told her all manner of weird tales about that place being the home of the emperor of the world, which, Uncle French had explained, was a forty-foot-tall monster with enormous fangs. I had to bribe Mary with apple juice and graham crackers while Charlotte made light of my difficulties as I endeavored to put knickers on the angry, fighting child; Mary wiggled until she wore herself out and, thank God, went to sleep in my arms, and I could carry her to the Great Hall. She slept the entire four hours we were there. House Karls dressed in red and black outfits such as hotel doormen wear conducted Charlotte and me to seats on portable wooden bleachers set on the south side of the domed hall. The dignitaries from the allied and defeated nations stood below us on the floor's mosaic map of the world. Two ranks of House Karls in their regulation uniforms stood at attention around the edge of the map. Scores more of their comrades secured the exits.

The principal Lords and Ladies were on the north balcony with Fitz, high above the mere mortals on the floor. (Among the nobility at Neapolis there was no greater distinction between those in the Consul's good graces and those on his left-hand side than being among the chosen few in the balcony with Fitz or being one of the downcast many who had to find a place on the dome's floor.) The gossips in the bleacher crowd—and life in the cramped society of Neapolis made everyone a gossip at times—noted that Lord Stein was on the balcony with Lord Valette and Shelley and their wives and mistresses. They also remarked that Lady Chelsea Shay Newsome and her husband were seated to the Consul's immediate right. The young Chrysanthemum Woman was actually sitting as close as Lady Joan was on the Consul's left. What really set the tongues to wagging in the bleachers was that it was to Lady Chelsea the Consul made small talk during the time the crowd was gathering below them.

I saw Hood, Montrose, Santeen, and the other generals from the disbanded Sixth Army seated above us in the portable stands. I caught Daddy Montrose's eye for a second, and he nodded to me. He nudged Hood at his side, but the Marshal did not look for me or anyone else in the crowd. Hood's eyes were glazed and his face was flushed; his head was bending so far forward it rested on his chest.

"Hood looks sick," I whispered to Charlotte.

"The Marshal looks drunk, my dear," she whispered back. "I'm sorry. I've seen more drunken men than you."

When Fitz stepped to the podium the steam lights directly above his head and below his feet made him glow like an open flame, as Buck had said they would. On his head was a high crown that had seven shining points, one for each of the continents of the conquered world. On his shoulders was draped a long purple robe. We could faintly see the outline of Dr. Flag's black figure standing behind him in the shadows outside the column of light. Buck positioned himself at the left of the balcony, apart from the nobles. From there he surveyed the crowd below for any potential trouble. Fitz must have looked terrifying to the men on the floor. He was terrifying to me, and I was not there to surrender to him.

"Why purple?" Charlotte whispered.

"It goes back to the Romans," I said. "The color indicates nobility."

"Is that why your three chums up there are wearing it?" she asked.

I had not realized until my wife mentioned it that Valette, Shelley, and Stein had on purple jackets made of the same plush velvet as Fitz's robe. They in turn knelt and kissed his signet ring before he spoke.

"My friends," Fitz began, and his words echoed off the curved surfaces of the dome like a clacker hitting the sides of a bell, "and those who say they wish to be our friends, we have gathered here to forgive past transgressions and to lay the foundations of the new world government that shall rule us all."

He paused to allow the four translators standing on the floor directly beneath the balcony to speak. The first translated Fitz's words into Mandarin, the second into Turkish, the third into Arabic, and the fourth into Russian, the language of Panslavia. Those in the crowd unable to understand English or any of the other four languages—and there were many from southern Africa and Latin America who could not—had to wait in uncomprehending fear through the entire ceremony.

"When our enemies first began this war," continued Fitz, "they stood like gods upon their vast empires and beat their chests and said aloud, 'We *are* gods! Let us make the world our footstool! We shall crush the Yukons first! They alone stand in the way of our mad ambitions!'"

He paused for the translators.

"Laying it on a bit thick," whispered Charlotte.

"Especially since we made war on them," I said.[18]

"If they drag it out so," said Charlotte, "I won't be able to stay for the whole show. These wooden seats are too much for me."

Fitz was only getting warm. He accused the Chinese of killing his father. He told the story of Sadiya Bridge, a tale that was news to me and the other war veterans. (It seems the Chinese had attacked a bridge in northern India on April 8, 2421, two days before we commenced bombing. Charlotte said she remembered something in the papers about the incident.) Fitz said the Chinese and the Turks had wanted to divide the world between them. The truth, like land, belongs to the winners, so Fitz said it was the Turks

---

18. Bruce is simply, impossibly wrong. The war began at the Sadiya Bridge. (See Gerald pp. 980–89, 1622–75, and 2295–389.)

and the Chinese who had unleashed the locusts and the malaria-bearing mosquitoes. The generals seated below us shook their heads in disbelief.

"God alone kept the pestilence from Yukon territory," said Fitz.

After four hours Charlotte could not stand the wooden bleachers any longer. We had to excuse ourselves, and I helped her down the stands and back to the garden apartment. French followed behind us carrying Mary. We laid mother and daughter on the same bed, and I took off Charlotte's shoes and rubbed her poor feet.

"You'll miss the big to-do," she said.

"I know," I said. "Thank you for getting me out of there."

I learned the rest of the surrender ceremony from Buck. Fitz had punished the assembled by speaking for another two hours. Then the representatives of the defeated nations had to go to a stand on the east side of the floor and sign the Four Points. According to Buck, three old Chinese men[19] in tricked up bathrobes who were constantly brushing the tears from their eyes went to the stand and wrote their names in a language no one there but they and the translator could read. Dignitaries from the Philippines and India ran forward and struck the Chinese as the old men attempted to shuffle back into the crowd. The Yukons in the balcony cheered this disgraceful scene as the defenseless men from Peking were beaten to their knees.

"Now," said Fitz, after the House Karls had restored order to the floor, "it is time for the allies to sign."

The Indians, the Philippines, and the Panslavs stood on the tile floor as helpless as shipwrecked sailors washed upon a distant shore. From the ranks of the Indian delegation Mr. Puri, the Yukon Confederacy's man in Delhi, stepped forward and called to the balcony, "But, your Consulship, Your Excellency—"

The allied representatives tried to get to the exits and found the House Karls standing in their way. They called to the balcony and found that Fitz would not respond to them.

"The Consul cannot hear you," Fitz said.

The allied representatives argued among themselves for a quarter of an hour while the Yukon Lords in the balcony mocked them and tossed bits of food from their buffet table at those on the floor

---

19. The infamous Gang of Three; Li Ch'i-chao, Hong Kuo-fan, and Kang Hsi.

below. Several of the Indians shoved Mr. Puri away from their group when he attempted to address his congregation. One of his countrymen slapped his face when Puri persisted on speaking.

"Gentlemen," Fitz told them, "I'll have your signatures . . . or your heads."

"Your Excellency, this is not justice!" Mr. Puri called to him.

"Go weep," said Fitz.[20]

The allied delegations signed the Four Points. All the world, as the map on the floor symbolized, had fallen under Yukon control. The ceremony adjourned, and sparkling wine and cigars were passed around in the balcony. As for Mr. Puri, the Indians did not wait to return to Delhi to kill him. One of their delegation gave a few gold coins to a House Karl, and Mr. Puri's body was found the next day floating amid the other debris in the Zerayshan River.

Pularski escorted Lady Joan and Miss Stewart to their garden house. He stopped by our flat and told me I was wanted at a celebration in Valette's quarters. Though it was far below her station to do so, Lady Joan volunteered to stay with Charlotte in my absence.

"You won't have to stay long," Buck told me. "Pop in and out. Most of them will be in their cups. They won't know you've gone."

As I should have guessed, Valette had the largest and most lavishly furnished of the new homes in Neapolis. He had the most servants and hangers-on and needed the most room. On this day of our great triumph his mistresses and underlings were absent. Only the leading Lords and military commanders were allowed in his long dining hall. The Lords were well oiled by the time I arrived, excepting Fitz, who had given up drink when he became Consul. The lowborn generals were decidedly sober and sulking in a group removed as far from the loud and drunken Lords as the confines of Valette's house allowed. The Consul's treatment of the allies had appalled the military men. The intoxicated glee of the young Lords at the end of this disgraceful war was confirming everything the senior officers suspected of this unjust new order. Lord Newsome was sleeping on the floor beside a sofa in a puddle of vomit. Lady Chelsea, the only woman present, was smoking a cigar and flicking the spent ash at the dour generals and admirals on the opposite side

---

20. "Go weep" was the Scythians' reply to the Persians in Book IV of Herodotus' *Persian Wars*. What Lord Fitzpatrick really said was, "Come, let us build a better world together." (See Gerald, page 4987.)

of the room. Valette stood atop a table at the front of the room and proposed toasts to the glorious Lord Fitzpatrick.

"Alexander the Great conquered the known world in thirteen years," he proclaimed. "Lord Fitzpatrick conquered the world, the whole stinking world, in four!"

The Lords applauded and spilled their drinks on the Turkish carpet.

"Alexander was thirty-two at the moment of his triumph," said Valette. "Lord Fitzpatrick is a downy-faced lad six months from his thirtieth birthday!"

"Hurray!" observed the Lords.

"Alexander died at thirty-three," Buck whispered to me. "Do you think Fitz will last that long among this bunch?"

The Consul moved about the room congratulating and praising everyone. He had removed his crown and robe and was once more in his familiar Blue Jacket uniform.

"The war is over," he told the generals. "Better times are ahead."

He spied Buck and myself and came over to welcome me.

"Bobby, my Bobby," he said and embraced me. "Has any leader had a more loyal, more able man than you? Still wearing a colonel's sheaves, I see. I think it's high time you had a brigadier's stars, General Bruce."

"Thank you, Fitz," I said, still ruled at this late hour in my story by my overwhelming desire to please him when we met face-to-face.

"How is your lovely wife?" he asked. "Does she want for anything in her condition?"

"No, thank you. She is well taken care of," I said. "I think within a week we will need a doctor."

"I would chat some more with you," he said. "I have to circulate. You understand. Could you keep an eye on Hood? I am worried for him."

Fitz moved on to Admiral Semmes and congratulated him.

Hood looked terrible up close. His hair and beard had gone from gray to snowy white since I had served with him in India. His eyes were closed as he stood in the overdecorated dining hall. I knew he was awake, for he was leaning against Montrose and speaking into his ear. Lord Stein approached them to show off his new purple jacket, and, I suppose, to aggravate his former commanders. Hood would not open his eyes for him. Montrose, being Daddy Montrose, told Stein to "go and bugger some other purple boy." Stein replied that a commoner, not even a lieutenant general, could talk to a Lord and statesman using that sort of vocabulary. Fitz intervened at that point and told Stein to leave the generals alone. (The Consul's habit was to side with commoners in any personal dispute. He thought this pretense of evenhandedness compensated for siding with the Lords in issues of policy.) He apologized to Montrose and promised him Stein would behave.

Valette suggested we watch a motion picture a zeppelin crew had made over China. His servants set up a projector and a screen in the middle of the hall and dimmed the lights. We soon discerned that it was a silent color film taken from the belly of an airship; it showed the Yangtze River from the height of about two hundred feet and followed that muddy stream east toward the ocean. First we saw green mountain vistas from Kuming.

"This is not so bad," I heard Woodenhead Santeen say. "Reports had it that the land was bare."

The trees in the mountains had enough leaves to give the steep slopes a verdant cover. As the elevation dropped the land flanking the river turned yellow, then became a brown shade that was interrupted by patches of gray that marked where the burned cities had been. When the zeppelin's camera reached the heart of Sichuan Province we had to squint to tell the difference between the river and the bare mud flats around it. We saw some red-tiled roofs and empty sunken roads and clumps of dead trees. There were no living, moving people. The locusts had stripped the landscape clean. The raucous dining hall became quieter as the images became increasingly bleak. The images of death kept reeling past the screen, and Lord Mason wondered aloud if there going to be any naked girls in this movie. We saw skeletons, some of them human, lying on the barren flats. When the camera moved over a major city, we could see the river had left its banks and had washed away many of the buildings like the sea taking away sand castles from a beach. Not a single sandbag had been placed on the banks to hold back the water. In that part of China there were no longer human hands able to make barriers. I had helped bring this about, I told myself. There were no words in my vocabulary I could utter that could justify this abomination, no act of contrition that could ever take away what I had done. This was the price I had paid to win my stars from

Fitz. These images on the screen were something I could never explain to my Charlotte and have not attempted to explain to anyone for the past sixty years.

In the shocked silence that had overtaken the room Hood began speaking:

" 'Hear this, you aged men,[21]
    give ear, all inhabitants of the land:
Has such a thing happened in your life,
    Or in the days of your fathers?
        Tell your children of it—' "

"Who is talking?" asked Lord Shelley.

" 'And let your children tell their children,' " continued Hood,
" 'and their children another generation.
    What the cutting locust left,
    The swarming locust has eaten.' "

"Someone shut him up!" commanded Fitz.

Hood spoke louder. Montrose wrapped his arms about his friend, but he could not force him to be silent. The Marshal continued to rant:

" 'What the swarming locust left,
    the hopping locust has eaten,
and what the hopping locust left,
    the destroying locust has eaten.' "

Buck and I ran to Hood and pulled him toward the door.

" 'Awake, you drunkards and weep';" Hood screamed to the crowd in the hall. " 'And wail, all you drinkers of wine.' "

"Take him to his bed and let him sleep it off," ordered Fitz. To Valette he said, "You had to show *that* film! Turn the damned thing off!"

The group of us carried Hood outdoors. Montrose shook him

---

21. Hood is quoting the First Chapter of Joel, the same book he quoted when he addressed the officers of the Sixth Army as the Asian theater of the Four Points War began.

and begged him to come to his senses. From the depths of his delirium Hood recognized me.

"Bobby, is that you?" he asked and patted my face. "I did not know you were here. I'm sorry you had to see this. You know, Bobby, we are all going to Hell."

"Perhaps, sir," I said.

Marshal Hood began to cry and would not be consoled. Buck lifted him under his arms, and I picked up his legs. Together we carried him to the tents east of the palace where the generals were staying. We laid him on a cot and put a blanket over him. Buck set a pillow under Hood's snow-white head. General Montrose said he would stay with Hood until sunup. In the morning, at the earliest hour the Consul could arrange, the other generals towed Hood onto a zeppelin bound for North America.

The party at Valette's flat continued apace long after I left, and probably continued in some form even as the aircraft carried Hood from the city.

Fifteen days later on the twenty-fifth Charlotte gave birth to a ten-pound, seven-ounce girl she named Joan Elizabeth after Lady Joan and a late aunt. My wife had a hard twenty hours of labor. True to her stubborn nature, she would not take drugs or complain. Like all women, she would not allow her husband to be in the room with her when the baby at last arrived. Lady Joan and the Consul's doctor attended her throughout the ordeal until the moment I was permitted to go to the bed and see the red, squalling baby Charlotte was holding on her stomach.

"The heat on Socotra was too much," I said as Lady Joan washed the baby and I cooled Charlotte's face with a wet cloth. "The strain wore on you. We perhaps shouldn't have any more, Charlotte. We cannot risk losing you."

"Hush," she told me. "We'll see what the doctor says. Isn't he a worrier, Lady Joan?"

The Lady agreed I was.

"Shouldn't we give our daughter another middle name, darling?" I said. "Yukon children should have virtuous middle names."

"Lady Joan is going to chase you from the room now, dearest," she said. "I am going to sleep. When I wake up, our daughter will still be named Joan Elizabeth."

We lived another three weeks in the garden house, during which time Charlotte recovered her usual robust health and baby

Joan showed she had hearty lungs and an incredibly active digestive system. We owed much to Pularski during our stay. He daily brought us fresh produce from the base commissary. He would bring us a crate of peaches or tomatoes or fresh lettuce; good food that was precious in Neapolis, where everything had to be flown in from the outside world. Buck had become something of a chef since his War College years; he made dinner each evening for all of us living in the two adjoining homes. Lady Joan called him "her cook"; as a gesture of her gratitude she bade him sit next to her at the dining table we shared. I would have been as grateful to him as she was if Buck had not taken up vegetarianism.

"Winifred cannot stand to hurt animals," said Lady Joan in his defense while we were feasting upon something with lots of beans and tomatoes in it.

"Lady, he does not have to hurt them," I said. "We have butchers for that. He has only to exploit the cruelty of others. Denying oneself meat is unhealthy."[22]

"Nonsense," said Charlotte. "That is an old husband's tale. I think Captain Pularski is very kind—to us and to the animals. Don't you agree, Lady Joan?"

"Yes, indeed," she said. "Winifred is very kind, to us especially."

Their praise made Buck's scarred face redden. His tongue grew thick in his mouth and he could not make a reply to the women.

Our daughter Mary had also come to think well of the gigantic Buck. She had stalked him in the garden while he worked, hiding behind the flower beds and the mossy rocks while he loosened the soil and did the watering. His impressive size fascinated her, as did his mechanical right hand. With a shock of hair as red as her mother's, Mary was never exactly camouflaged while she spied on him, and certainly she was not invisible to Buck, whose life work had been to spot irregular movements about him. She became bolder around him after a time, and would come from her cover long enough for him to show her how to snap a snapdragon or how to sniff at a rose. In time, she let him lift her aloft so she could pick oranges from the trees. He allowed her to examine his won-

---

22. The best scientists agree with Bruce on this point. One of the contributory reasons for the decline of the West in the late Electronic Age was the mania for vegetarianism. John God's Will Smith's *Vegetable Rot* (Agriculturalist's Press, Centralia City, 2590) is a recent explanation of why the human system needs the amino acids found in meats.

drous metal hand, something he never would have permitted an adult to do. Mary was apt to talk and talk when she was about anyone else; when she was sitting beside Buck or following him about the garden she seldom said anything. She watched him rapt, in a constant awe for this brutish-looking giant whom she no longer feared but by whom she was endlessly intrigued.

When Fitz finally chose to see me I had only a swift three minutes with him. After the surrender ceremony, Neapolis had become a more lively place. Ambassadors from other nations, merchants seeking concessions in the I.T., and Yukon noblemen wanting offices in Fitz's government had made the long air journey and were monopolizing the Consul's attention. I was fortunate to see him for as long as I did.

"I have to be short with you, Robert," he said when I entered his undecorated chamber. "Here are the maps, the plans, and so on, for your new assignment in Africa. Somewhere in Mali. You'll have to leave tomorrow."

He was not alone in his room. Valette and Stein and several of their assistants were present and were arguing with each other about the Universal Railroad. The plans Fitz had handed me were for a six-hundred-mile section to be built in northwest Africa.

"Could I ask you a couple questions about this, Fitz?" I said.

"Certainly, Robert. I'll do my best to answer anything you might want to know."

"Do we control this area where I'm going to lay railway? I mean, are Yukon troops there?" I asked.

The group of nobles stopped and listened. The question had apparently arisen before.

"Our mission is not to control every square inch the railroad is going," said Fitz. "The signers of the Four Points will have to control the ground for us. Where you're going is Turkish land. If the Turks can't keep order there, then it's too bad for the Turks."

"Blessed Jesus Christ!" I thought. "The Turks have not exercised real, on the ground control, in Mali for two generations!"[23]

"I see," I said. "One last question: the I.T. already operates a worldwide trading network that delivers goods everywhere at low cost, in most localities at a lower cost than a railroad could. As the

---

23. Actually, the situation was worse than that. Not since the Desert War (2307–2309) had the Turks had troops in Mali.

Universal Railroad is going to be competing against the I.T., I assume the Senate is going to be subsidizing this project until the railway becomes competitive. That is what they will do, won't they?"

This question also had apparently come up previously. The nobles present rustled their papers forcefully and looked meaningfully at each other. Fitz momentarily seemed to be annoyed with me for touching upon a sensitive subject. He quickly recovered his smile.

"You have to see, Bobby," interrupted Valette, "the railway is to be an ongoing process. It will, eventually, supplement the I.T. commerce. We'll have to wait many years to see a profit—"

"It is an ongoing process," said Fitz and lifted a finger before him like a rocket soaring toward the clouds.

The Consul spoke as a man who had answered all the questions he wished to that day.

"I see," I said.

"So, off you go then, Robert," smiled Fitz. "Blessings all around. God's speed. Send in that Sultan What's-His-Face on your way out, please."

Thus Charlotte, French, our two daughters, and I said goodbye to Lady Joan and Buck and took a zeppelin bound for Africa to work on the will-o'-the-wisp known as the Universal Railroad.

# EIGHTEEN

ON PAPER THE Universal Railroad was two separate railway networks. The New World system was to reach nine thousand miles from Nome to Tierra del Fuego and would connect the existing lines between those two terminals. The Old World network was to run from Singapore to Scandinavia and from Capetown to the Arctic Ocean and likewise tie together the railroads already there. We were going to build within these grand lines fantastic passages over the Bosporus, under the English Channel, and through the Darren Gap. The newspapers said a passenger would be able to board a train in Edinburgh in the morning and wake in the same sleeping car as it hurtled across Mesopotamia. The next day the imaginary traveler could disembark in India. The Universal Railroad was to bind the diverse nations of the earth together into one economic and social system. Moslems in central Europe would dine on bananas picked the week before in Senegal. Argentinian schoolchildren would take their winter holidays in Nova Scotia. Everything on paper was to be sunshine and bright uplands.

In the three-dimensional world that exists beyond paper, the Universal Railroad was a cash cow the Lords in Fitz's circle milked dry in one year, one month, and four days after the work crews departed for forty-one separate sites across the globe. The Senate appropriated twenty billion pounds for the first—and final—stage of construction, an amount greater than the monies the Confederacy had spent on the war. Forty thousand men went to the remote bases from which the Consul's plans declared the railroad lines would grow like enormous spiderwebs. One billion pounds paid for the workers' transport, their supplies, and their temporary housing.

The other nineteen billion disappeared into the silken pockets of those in the nobility controlling the I.T. Equipment never went to the men in the field. Contracts were made with factories and lumberyards belonging to Fitz's friends, and the shipments never left the warehouses. The International Trading Company received payments for carrying phantom cargos. Private engineering companies that did not exist were paid for producing detailed plans no one ever saw and no one would have ever needed anyway. The men in the far-flung sites meanwhile sat in desolate—often dangerous—localities, and waited for the work to begin. They waited until the Senate, at Fitz's request, ended funding for the abortive project.

I, like official History, blame the court members at Neapolis for this fiasco more than I do the Consul. Fitz was yet again appeasing the nobles around him rather than gathering wealth for the Fitzpatrick family. The Universal Railroad was his method of once more paying back the powerful people he had angered with his tax increases and with the failure of the Western Australia Company. At that juncture in his career Fitz believed he was secure in his power for as long as he kept the other noble families content, or at least kept content those families powerful enough to harm him. As I have often noted, he never was interested in mere money. Whatever profits he gained from the scheme I am certain he poured into his building projects at Neapolis or gave to charity.[1]

My command, if such a purposeless enterprise may be called that, was located east of the Bandiagara Cliffs in the Sahara Desert. I had three companies, two of them engineers and one teamsters. We lived outside the village of Yougodogorou among the Dogon people, who considered us gods, for we had come to them from the sky in a long silver cloud. We had sufficient food and shelter in our desert encampment. Once a month a zeppelin from Bioko brought us more provisions. What we did not have was a stick of wood or a single steel spike, and we never would have them.

Our neighbors the Dogon were a small, famished-looking people only a foot or so taller than the Pygmies of the central African jungle. According to the Dogon legends, they had in the remote past lived in the Niger Basin to the south and had fled to the cliff

---

1. Bruce's description of the Universal Railroad Company is, unfortunately, generally correct. (See Gerald, page 5451.)

country because of other tribes' repeated attacks. In the high desert they had found security and a few fertile patches of soil wherein they grew millet, their staple crop. They were happy to be hosts to the strange white gods, provided we were respectful of their ways and gave them our extra food. Since they believed we lived in the sky, the place from which the weather came, the Dogon hoped, if they appeased us during our stay, we might make the rains come more often to their parched land.

Charlotte made the best of our odd situation in the arid country. As she had done among the natives in India, she quickly picked up much of the Dogon's difficult language simply by sitting with the women and helping them bake their unleavened bread. For the sake of what they considered her unusual appearance, the village elders accepted her as a special sort of goddess. The shaman among the Dogon foretell the future by drawing a pattern in the sand in the evening and in the morning they check the footprints the wild foxes have made across their patterns in the night. Charlotte's hair seemed to them to make her a kind of fox woman who carried magic on her head. She let one of the local medicine men cut a lock from her long tresses, and he used it as a talisman to keep away any evil spirits that might be prowling in the desert night around Yougodogorou. Charlotte's hair was so precious to them I expect I could travel to that remote spot even today and find another generation of shaman that has preserved the fox woman's talisman.

My thoughtful wife worried the skinny Dogon were not getting enough to eat and coerced me, in her pleasant but assertive fashion, into digging them a well for their crops. At the base of the high cliff overlooking their village, my men and I dug with shovels a hundred-and-twenty-foot hole before we could make a small pool of water form at the bottom of the pit. We dug a second well three miles to the north in a wadi bed, where the water was abundant and spurted from the earth after we had dug only fifteen feet. We made a ditch leading back to the village, giving the Dogon access to an abundant aquifer, for which we imagined they would be grateful. And they were grateful to us, for the first piddling well we had dug. That hole was the sort of primitive facility they would have made themselves, if they had the time and manpower. They could take a basket tied to a rope and dip in the deep pool to get a couple gallons to pour on their small millet patches, precisely as they had always done. The second well produced, in their opinion, too much water. Nor did they want to maintain the three miles of ditches, as they would have to learn a new skill to do so. The Dogon did not wish to hurt our feelings; they said they enjoyed watching the water bubble from the ground. They just could see no practical use for it.

The Dogon resisted any plan Charlotte could devise to improve them. From the zeppelin pilot she purchased packets of high yield barley and wheat and had me instruct the villagers on how to raise the new crops that would make them healthier. The village elders politely told us the Dogon grew millet, some squash, a few vegetables. Other people grew other things. Since we were gods, they had assumed we had understood this before we arrived. When Charlotte got the notion to give the children malaria vaccine, the elders told her the Dogon had their own kind of medicine. They did not want us to build them a hospital or a school, and there were no materials to make a large western-style building in the desert if they had desired us to build one. They did concede they admired the air conditioner in our tent—they called it "the cold wind box"—and a crowd of them daily came to see the magic steam-driven machine and to touch Charlotte's red hair and that of our daughters.

They trusted us, and—as far as we could tell—the Dogon had a strong affection for their strange visitors from the sky, yet they were amazed at our ignorance of certain important matters. On the other hand, we had dug that first well, so obviously we had good intentions. As a gesture of their trust they showed Charlotte and me the sacred places wherein they kept their dead. Should the study of other cultures one day be revived,[2] future scholars would find a treasure trove of material at tiny Yougodogorou and its neighboring villages, where the remains of the dead are stored inside the caves dotting the face of the sheer cliffs overhanging every Dogon community. The chieftain showing us these holy sites wanted us to climb into the caves by rappelling down the escarpments via the flimsy vine ropes the Dogon grave keepers use. We thought better of that, and let him show us the caves that opened immediately

---

2. In ancient times this study was called "anthropology," from the Greek *anthropos,* human, and *logos,* study or word. Like phrenology, astrology, and sociology, anthropology was one of the mystery sects that did not survive the Storm Times. The Yukons of course do study other cultures, namely those that existed in the past that are worthy of our attention.

onto the desert floor. The bodies inside the open caves were wrapped from head to foot in brown blankets and had slowly dried in the hot air until they were naught but brown skeletons resting on the ledges along the cave walls. The chief said that hundreds of years ago, the Dogon had carried the bones of their ancestors from the Niger Basin to the Bandiagara Cliffs. Those who had died since then were laid beside their ancestors, and thus the dead from all the past ages of the tribe could keep watch over the living in the villages beneath their unsealed graves.

I told the chief through Charlotte that it was admirable they took such thoughtful care of their dead.

He asked me if the Yukons kept our dead with us.

No, we bury our dead in the place they died, I told him. We had, I explained, a strong magic called History that kept the dead with us in spirit.

The old chief was favorably impressed. History, he declared, must be the strongest magic in the world.

"Yes, it is," I said. "We Yukons base everything we do upon it."

Each month I sent letters to Fitz in Neapolis. Every day I used our only ultraviolet light to send messages over the Blinking Stars to the Quartermaster in Cumberland. I always gave the same information they were getting from the forty-one other site commanders of the Universal Railroad: we were sitting in a wasteland unable to build anything. We had no materials. We had no equipment. The three companies of men with me were too few to build six hundred miles of rail. And so on. No one answered me. If they had sent us anything, the shipments would have had to have passed through Lord Newsome's West African Autonomous Zone, and the goods would have been stolen in transit.

The message we really hoped for as we waited in the Sahara were orders from the Consul telling us to go home. In my idle hours I had time to read all of Spinoza and French's *Toby* books. I understood the latter. I also had the opportunity to become better acquainted with my two redheaded daughters. Joan, I found, was a baby like other babies and could smile at her mother and blow saliva bubbles when she was happy, which, praise God, was most of the time. Mary had become an adventurous, curious child who never walked anywhere she could run. If I let her, she would take off her clothes and roam about naked with the Dogon children who always dressed as God had made them. To keep her from that uncivilized practice (and from sunburn), I played hide-and-seek with her among the sandstone boulders and held her on my lap and read *Piggy and I* to her a couple of hundred times.[3] As the months wore on she came to love me as wildly as she did her Uncle French and the fellow at Neapolis she referred to as "the big man," whom she dearly wanted to visit again.

In spite of her failure to improve the Dogon, Charlotte loved our tent home. She was there the wife of the commanding officer on the base. The other officers' wives *had* to have her for tea and *had* to include her in their social activities whether they wanted to or not. For the Thanksgiving holiday she organized the three companies into one massive choral group and got to conduct them herself, an act of leadership that convinced the Dogon she was the true chief of the strange white gods. Yougodogorou was the closest to a honeymoon she and I had had since we were married. I was free from the demands of work and could be more attentive to her and the children. The nights in the desert were fiercely cold and long, creating a climate that pleased us both in ways modesty prevents me from explaining. The pleasures we had known earlier in our marriage returned to us, and now we were more familiar with each other than we had been then and much wiser.

"I wouldn't mind if this were your permanent assignment," she told me one night in bed.

"That would mean my young men would grow to old bachelors," I said.

"We could fly in wives for them," she suggested.

"Why not? The Confederacy is spending fifty million pounds a day on the Universal Railroad. Three hundred young brides for our men would use, say, ten minutes of the budget."

"Ask headquarters for a featherbed while you're making requests," she said. "Three hundred featherbeds. We'll breed a new city of Yukons to rival that wicked place Fitz is building."

"Don't hate Neapolis too much," I told her. "I fear it will someday again be our home."

I thought that someday had arrived on December 2, 2424, the day a letter came from the Consul summoning me to Neapolis. I was to travel alone and at once, the letter said, to handle a matter of the greatest importance.

---

3. The library at St. Matthew's has no record of such a book.

"My peace of mind and the peace of the Confederacy depend upon you," Fitz wrote.

"What do you make of it?" asked Charlotte while I packed my suitcase.

"There's been a coup, an attempted one at least," I said. "My guess is Fitz's relatives the Shays are behind the scheme. The Consul has gotten wind of it. He knows that in a crisis he cannot trust most of the people around him. I know you despise him. But having Fitz in power is better than having one of the Shays as Consul."

She blessed me, and I took a zeppelin straight to Neapolis, where I found I was one crisis too early in my presumptions, for Fitz was in the midst of the Hood affair rather than facing an attempted rebellion.[4] Neapolis had changed again during the seven months I had been in Africa. The green grasslands to the west had become home to tens of thousands of pastoral families who had pitched their felt tents and brought their herds of horses and sheep to the rejuvenated river plain. North of the Great House the sprawl of houses with walled gardens had run against a long rectangle of low walls that were the foundations of the gigantic Universal Church. The workers on the new site were exclusively foreigners, Turks and Panslavs chief among them. Fitz had sent the Yukon engineering regiments home. The developments had pushed the jumble of mobile units and mud huts of the House Karls and various workers and other camp followers into an even larger crescent shape that constituted a lawless area on the outskirts of town the locals had named Pandemonium. I did not have time to examine much of Neapolis after my arrival for a troop of House Karls conducted me straight into Fitz's chamber as soon as I landed. Buck herded everyone else from the room when I entered, leaving me alone with the Consul.

Fitz emphatically welcomed me and called me his dear friend. He was in his sympathetic mode that day and had rubbed his eyes red before I arrived so I might think he had been weeping.

"Robert, Hood has gone mad," he said.

"The Marshal has . . . he has harmed someone?"

"Worse," said Fitz. "He resigned his commission when he returned to the Second Army. He has left the Confederacy, Robert. He and his wife."

---

4. See Gerald (pp. 5014–17) for an accurate account of this episode.

"Where has he gone?"

"To China!" barked Fitz and clenched his fists in anger.

He threw himself into the chair at his desk and struggled to regain the persona he wanted to project for me. After his many years of playacting, Fitz no longer could have been a star in a Gypsy theater troupe. He now tended to forget the role he wanted to assume, and when his blood was up he would become the man he really was. In the ninety short seconds I had been with him he had gone too swiftly from wounded victim to enraged emperor to have misled anyone.

"We put pressure on the Chinese," he continued. "They located him in a village on the Yangtze. The place is called Linli; it's near Wuhan."

"Is he—I beg you pardon, Fitz, for asking this—is he organizing an army, some kind of force against you?" I asked.

"He and his wife are . . . they're growing rice. He took his life savings and bought seed. He must have bribed a zeppelin pilot to take him there. Stein warned me Hood has had these delusions of being Jesus Christ. Now he has run off to feed the hungry, care for the sick, probably pray over the dying yellow bastards. Can you imagine what the press will write when they hear of this?"

"What do you want me to do?"

"Go to him," said Fitz, leaning onto his desk with such force he nearly pushed it over onto its side. "A gunboat will take you upriver from Wuhan. Talk to him. He is fond of you, Robert. As we all are. Tell him he must come home. If he wants to leave the Army, fine. I don't care. The war is over. Let him retire, go home to Virginia, and grow rice there. That damned General Montrose went and couldn't get him back. You *must* convince him to return, Robert. You *must!*"

"I will try, Fitz," I said. "You know Judge can be difficult when he wants to be. I cannot guarantee—"

"*Try*, Robert, *try!*" commanded Fitz and pounded on the arm of his chair. "If you fail . . . then you fail. Tell Hood I love him, Robert. That is important. Tell him I love him after everything that has transpired. Be sure you use the word 'love.' God's speed, Robert."

Buck took me to the zeppelin. I told him everything Fitz had said to me. I suspected I was being redundant because Buck always eavesdropped at Fitz's door.

"He won't come back with you," said Pularski. "He's escaped to his Fate. Hood will be content to die in China."

We gave each other our blessings at the zeppelin door, and two days later I landed at Wuhan, or rather at the blackened skeleton of the city that once was Wuhan. There I boarded a Dorkronk gunboat headed upstream.[5] A second gunboat was anchored in midcurrent and followed us after we set sail from the badly damaged dock. The crew on my boat were I.T. Chinese from Singapore. The two officers on board were the only Yukons on the craft other than myself. The captain's name was Jones, or so he claimed. He had a convict's pierced ear and told me several different versions of his past life. His first mate was a twisted brute the captain called Oscar; this second thug terrorized the Chinese sailors with a long iron bludgeon and thus kept the boat moving forward. The boat's hold was blazing hot inside and gave off a strong sour smell that betrayed what the Dorkronk's cargo usually was. Rumor had it that I.T. ships hauled raw opium grown in Ceylon and Afghanistan to southern Asia before the Four Points War. Jones' boat had plied the same trade in the months following the fighting, though he was necessarily running empty on this trip. No one in China could afford to buy his wares anymore. We were grateful for the second craft following us upstream; it twice had to pull our boat off sandbars during our short jaunt upriver. Yukons had not sailed this far up the Yangtze since before the first Pacific War,[6] and the charts the captain had of the ever changing river were more than a century out of date. Jones' haphazard method of navigating this difficult waterway was to stay in the middle of the channel and hope for the best and then panic when the best did not happen.

"Captain Jones," I asked him, "why don't you put a man with a weighted rope at the prow to measure the depth?"

"What's this?" he asked. "They teach you engineers these things? A man with a rope you say?"

"You have been a captain long, sir?" I said.

"Since last week," he admitted. "I got kicked out of the House

---

5. A forty-five-foot river and coastal ship removed from service in 2436.

6. Bruce means the Pacific War of 2297–2302 and not the Great Pacific War of 2360–2362.

Karls. A little thing about drinking. You're a pal of the Consul's. Maybe you could get me reinstated."

I told him he would certainly make a better House Karl than a boat captain, and he took my remark to be a great compliment.

We needed two days to reach Linli. I slept in the empty hold in spite of the offensive smell since sleeping on the deck was riskier given the swarms of mosquitoes rising off the river at night. Everyone on the gunboat repeatedly rubbed handfuls of insect repellant on their faces, hands, and clothing for fear of being bitten and infected with the new malaria strain. During my daytime hours on deck I kept a whisk moving about my person to prevent any bugs from landing on me. The few people we saw on the shoreline had smeared themselves with ash to protect their bodies. The sight of the gray, emaciated figures walking along the shoreline terrified the Chinese crewmen, who thought the ash people were the spirits of the recently dead.

There were no docks at Linli large enough to accommodate the gunboats, so Jones dropped anchor in the middle of the river, and a rowboat powered by four crewmen took me to the shore. The original village on the shoreline was abandoned. A newer settlement had been built above the empty buildings of the old one; this one had lines of citronella bushes running through its streets and around its houses.[7] Someone had recently crushed several of the large green leaves on every bush to release the plant's medicinal scent. The villagers had picked other leaves from the bushes to rub over their bodies and keep the bugs from landing. The newly plastered adobe houses inside the rows of plants were each big enough to hold a few dozen people.

Two small boys saw me approaching and retreated through curtains covering the doorway of one of the larger homes. Hood emerged a few seconds later, followed by the two children. He was hatless and wore a simple white shirt and tan trousers. His white beard was trimmed, and he had the clear, focused eyes of a sober man. We embraced in a dirt yard inside a ring of mosquito plants.

"So they sent you, Bobby," he said. "You are not, I hope, on a mission that will bring you dishonor."

---

7. Citronella bushes *(cymbopagen nardus),* also called the mosquito plant, are originally from southeast Asia; they are used as insect repellant in primitive societies.

I took off my Sam Browne belt and my pistol and handed them to him.

"If I do anything dishonorable, sir, you may shoot me," I said.

He handed my belt and weapon back to me.

"No need for that," he said. "What about them?" he asked, indicating the two gunboats in the river.

"The crews are Chinese. The officers are definitely S.A., sir."

"We're supposed to call them House Karls now," he laughed. "Come, take a weight off your feet."

We sat together on a stubby wooden bench outside the curtained doorway.

"Those House Karls, sir," I said; "they're waiting to hear how I do with you."

"Brigadier Bruce, is it?" he said and gave me a bemused whistle as he examined the star on my tunic collar.

"Yes, sir. For seven months," I said. "I've come to tell you the Consul loves you."

"I love him too," said Hood, "as much as I can."

"He wants you to go home, sir," I went on. "You don't have to return to your post. You can go home to Virginia, sir."

"Tell Fitz I am home. And, please, stop calling me 'sir,' Bobby. I am no longer in the Army."

"You will recall Bede and the other biographers of the Saints wrote that the early martyrs became martyrs largely because they made the Roman centurions crazy with their evasive answers," I said.

"Are you a centurion then, Bobby? If you are, you had best look after yourself. In those martyr stories the centurion always converts in the final scene and goes to the chopping block or into the arena along with the Saint. Come on, I'll show you our farm."

We walked around the rows of large adobe houses. On the side away from the river I saw perhaps two hundred acres of rice paddies cut into sections by rows of citronella. Some smaller plots had tomatoes, corn, and legumes within their boundaries, in addition to the young rice shoots. Hood explained how the area's population had fallen drastically since the war began and the locusts had come. After the Chinese surrender and long after the damage to the croplands had been done, the Yukons had dropped sterile locusts; they had mated with the others, and so reduced the ravenous swarms to a manageable level. While the malaria epidemic still raged along the river, it was a small inconvenience compared to the loss of food.

"We will have to leave the river valley someday," said Hood. "Build new houses higher in the hills. The water down here affords the mosquitoes too many places to hatch their larvae. Draining the standing water is useless. The spring floods fill the ponds right up again."

He took me into an adobe house he had set aside for malaria patients. Twenty stricken people of all ages lay on reed mats spread upon the dirt floor. Hood's wife Martha was giving the dying people water, brushing away the flies, and doing whatever she could think of that might make them more comfortable.

"We can't cure them," said Hood. "Our job is to keep the fifty-four healthy folks in our community in good shape."

"How did you get here, Judge?" I asked.

"I knew some people who could help me."

"One of them owned a zeppelin."

"Perhaps," he said. "We got ahold of some nonhybrid seed and twenty-five tons of polished rice. The people were hiding in the hills when we arrived. Eating leaves, roots, grubs, anything they could. Most of the land along the Yangtze was denuded and eroding into the river. Our bombers destroyed all the upriver dams. We built the first house on our own. Thereafter the people came down to us one by one. They had been turned into animals, Robert. Dying from malnutrition, their clothes merely rags. Some of them ate a bowl of rice and died on the spot from indigestion. But most lived. This is what we've built in seven months. Next year we will have seed to raise food for three hundred more."

Martha and he went to the cooking house to prepare lunch. Several women and their children were already there stirring a large pot of boiled rice they had flavored with a smattering of beans and carrots. Martha rang a triangle, and the rest of the fifty-four healthy Chinese in Hood's village came in from the fields to eat. None of them paused to stare at me, a stranger in a Yukon uniform, standing in the middle of their dining hall. They each took a wooden bowl and scooped a helping of rice from the full cauldron the women had been tending. Hood prepared one bowl for himself and one for me, and we sat on the benches in the dusty yard with the others. Martha took four servings to the Chinese sailors who had rowed me ashore. A small girl of about the age of my Mary scurried from the seated diners and touched Hood's white beard, then ran away giggling. I surmise this was a familiar prank among the community, for everyone laughed with her, including Hood.

"*How boo how,* Ying Chao," ("Hello, Ying Chao") said Hood.[8]

The hungry Chinese at the tables were uncouth eaters. They swept the boiled rice into their open mouths with peculiar wooden sticks like those I had seen the Chinese sailors on *The Mother of Jesus* use, and they chewed noisily with their mouths still open. It occurred to me as I observed this paucity of manners how odd it was to be eating food among these people I would have tried to kill less than a year earlier. Three children sitting on the bench with Hood were peering around him at my uniform and at the bowl of rice I could not eat with the strange wooden sticks. I went around to them and carefully divided my food into their bowls. The instant I stepped back from them they fell upon each grain of rice as though it were the last morsel of food on earth.

"They won't forget you," said Hood.

"This is an odd world," I told him. "Looking at how they accept you, one would think you had lived here a hundred years."

"Yes, Martha and I are where we should be."

"If you stay here," I said, and my throat constricted, "Fitz will send someone to kill you."

"That doesn't matter," he said. "But I am touched that you care."

"Buck loves you as much as I do," I said. "He will mourn you the rest of his life."

"Buck is a good sort," agreed Hood, "given what he does. You and I chose to become officers. Lady Fitzpatrick made poor Buck Fitz's bodyguard while Buck was yet a boy. I wish I could have seen a tiger for him. That might have compensated a little for the disappointment we people have been to him. He would, you know, have had a better life if he had been a tiger himself."

After lunch Martha and Hood showed me the house in which they lived. They owned a chair, a bed, a big wooden cross they had nailed to their bedroom wall, and a small bamboo table that looked as if it were not sturdy enough to hold a large book. We three prayed together in their quarters before Hood walked me down to my rowboat.

---

8. *How boo how.* I have not been able to locate a scholar capable of translating the phrase. I will assume the words do mean "hello" until I can locate someone who can tell me something different.

"There is nothing I can say?" I asked him.

"Tell them I am insane," said Hood. "Some of them believe madness excuses anything."

"Do you think Fitz is mad?"

"Some Historian may say that a thousand years from now. Hitler, Stalin, Caligula, Iz: someone got around to calling each of them insane at one time or another. I think they were afflicted by love of power, Robert, not madness. I have had a small taste of power myself and nearly lost my soul. Had I drank as deeply from that cup as Fitz has, I might have done everything he has."

We stood by the river and watched the gunboats rising and falling in the river. I was afraid for him but unwilling to force him into returning with me.

"Why two gunboats?" he asked.

"They pull each other off the shoals," I said. "The officers in charge give incompetence a deeper meaning. They are forever running aground."

"Would that you and I had been less competent," said Hood.

"You told the Army, Judge, that day we went to war, the Yukons could never lose. The world would show us no mercy should we ever fall. If that is true, shouldn't you return with me and help defend the Confederacy? Don't each of us have the obligation to shoulder the burden of History?"

"It is true we dare not lose," he said. "It is equally true that the old order changeth, yielding to the new.[9] Nothing can last forever, Robert. Guilt will bring the Yukons down. The process leading to our destruction may take many centuries, many wars, many atrocities. Yet there will be a time when our History will be too heavy for us to bear."

"I am afraid this will be . . ." I began and could say no more.

"Don't grieve for me, Bobby," he said. "You'll make me worry. I'm closing in on sixty, and you know how sentimental we middle-aged men can be. I am forgiven, Bobby. This village and the grain will live on when I am gone, and this, this village—not the evil I did in India—will be my legacy. A good legacy."

"Your children . . . they are safe?"

"Our oldest son is grown and married; he is a minister, as I was once. Our youngest is with Montrose. Old Daddy is a daddy in-

---

9. A paraphrase of Tennyson's *Idylls of the King,* "The Passing of the King," line 408.

deed," he chuckled. "Martha and I will send for our boy when we have moved our community to the hills. You know, local legends have it there used to be tigers up there a few hundred years ago. Tell Buck I will keep an eye open for one."

We exchanged blessings before I went to the rowboat and thence to the gunboat. Jones at once asked me if Hood was not coming.

"What is that to you, sir?" I asked. "Sir Marshal Hood is not your concern."

"I need to signal the other boat," he said.

"Why?"

"They need to know we're headed back to Wuhan," he said. "You absolutely sure the gentleman ain't coming along with us?"

"Yes," I said. "Please get on with it."

I went below deck and wrote my report for Fitz in the captain's cabin. Two hours later I returned topside to the steering deck and saw we were miles downstream from Linli and under full steam. I looked up river from that elevated platform and could not see the second gunboat.

"Where is the other boat, sir?" I asked Jones, who was at the helm.

"What?" he said.

"You heard me. The other gunboat?"

"Oh, they passed us a while back," he said.

I could see far down the river from the steering deck. There was nothing there, not so much as a puff of smoke from a steam exhaust.

"Turn this boat around," I ordered Jones.

"We've got to get you back to Wuhan," he said.

I took out my pistol and placed the end of the barrel between his eyes.

"Call your man Oscar onto the bridge," I told him.

"There's no need for that, sir, your honor," he said, quaking in his filthy britches. "We were following orders."

He summoned Oscar with the bell. When the brute came through the portal I made him lie on the deck so I could check him for weapons. I then made both him and Jones stand at the wheel where I could keep an eye on them.

"Turn this boat around, now," I demanded.

Forty minutes later we met the second boat going downstream as we went up. On the prow of the second boat I saw a figure in a black House Karls uniform; a short-billed kepi cap sat at a jaunty angle on his head. He had half-closed eyes, a blond spit curl on his forehead, and a smile that seemed to sink toward the left side of his face. Zimmerman waved at me as we passed him. He pointed a finger at our boat and cocked his thumb as though he were firing a gun.

At Linli I made Jones and Oscar row me to the shore, my gun still on them. Everyone in the village had fled into the trees beyond the rice fields, leaving their implements lying in the light green rows where they had dropped them. I found Hood and his beloved Martha lying face down in front of their house in the place Zimmerman had shot both of them twice in the head. I threw fistfuls of dirt into the air and wept over their bodies while Jones and Oscar cowered on their knees, both thinking I was about to kill them.

"We had nothing to do with this," whined Jones.

"Had he come along like he was supposed to," chimed in Oscar, "that fella wouldn't have done this to him."

I threw a handful of dirt into his fat face.

"Shut your mouths!" I told them. "Go to the fields and get two spades. I don't want to hear what you have to say about these people!"

I buried my old friend and his wife in a single grave. I had Jones and Oscar pile stones over the couple to keep away the wild dogs that roamed the river valley. The wooden cross from their bedroom wall became Hood's and Martha's marker.

All the way back to Wuhan I kept the two House Karls tied up and steered the boat myself. They swore the rope was not necessary; they had orders to do me no harm. I told them even a slow learner like myself could come to know how much he could trust former S.A. men. I did not sleep during the two days we were on the river. Only when we reached Wuhan and I had locked myself in my zeppelin cabin and the airship was under way did I allow myself some rest. At Neapolis I went to the Great House and located Buck in a hallway outside the central dome.

"I am going to kill him," I told Buck.

"No, you're not," he said.

He lifted me by the collar with his mechanical hand and shoved me against the wall. With his good hand he took my gun from my hand. I struggled to hold onto my weapon. Despite having known him for a decade, he was much stronger than I could have guessed and pulled the pistol from me as effortlessly as he would have taken a toy from a small child.

"He murdered Hood!" I yelled at him.

"I know," said Buck. "I heard this morning. Right now I'm keeping my other friend alive. Listen to stupid old Pularski: Fitz is going to send you back to Africa. Go. Your wife and children are there."

"Don't you care?" I asked. "Do you want him to get away with it?"

"I care more than you know, Robert," he said. "You have to think of this: suppose I let you go and somehow God lets you get past the House Karls and you kill him. Do you think this would be a better world if Valette becomes Consul? Or Lord Newsome? Him with his lovely wife? Are you thinking of what would happen to your wife after you are dead?"

I saw the irrefutable reasoning in what he said. I quit my futile straining against him, and Buck let me sit on the hallway floor to weep again for Hood.

"So he gets away with this," I sobbed. "Doesn't he ever pay?"

"Not yet," said Buck. "God is watching him. Let God decide when his time has come."

He took me to a room in the Great House's second floor where he kept a cot and a wardrobe and put me up for the night. In the morning a courier brought me orders to return to Africa. Before I left on the airship Fitz gave me a brief audience in his room. Valette, Shelly, and Stein were also in attendance and were wearing their purple jackets and making a great show of being busy with the affairs of state. Fitz glanced at my report on my mission to China and set it aside on his cluttered desk.

"A tragedy," he said and stroked his chin.

"Yes," I agreed and strove to keep my anger in check.

The Lords present also agreed.

"Who would have predicted Hood would be killed by Chinese river pirates?" mused Fitz.

I began to tremble. Buck had wisely kept my pistol until I was ready to board the zeppelin.

"Pirates killed Hood?" I said.

"Yes," said Fitz.[10] "Are you well, Robert?"

---

10. History records that Marshal Hood was killed by pirates on the Yangtze. (See Gerald pp. 5204–18.) Lord Fitzpatrick attempted to rescue his insane friend, but, sadly, the relief party he dispatched arrived too late.

He had noted my quivering. Buck grumbled something; I looked at him and saw him quickly shake his head from side to side.

"My report is incomplete," I said. "Marshal Hood told me something very important when I spoke to him."[11]

"Really?" said Fitz.

"He said you are in danger, Fitz," I said. "He said now that you have conquered the world, there is nothing more you can do to your enemies and nothing more you can give to your friends. He said your friends will fear you are going to turn on them."

"Did he?" said Fitz and gripped the arms of his chair.

Valette, Shelley, and Stein ceased rustling their meaningless papers and listened to us.

"Those closest to you, said Hood," I continued, "will soon try to replace you."

"Enough!" said Valette.

"If they fail," I said, "the Timermen will—"

"Tell him to be silent!" said Valette to Fitz.

"—will try next," I said. "They will try until they succeed."

"Are you through?" asked the Consul.

"Yes," I said.

Valette whispered something into Fitz's ear. The Consul pushed him away and told him to say no more.

"Go back to Africa, Brigadier Bruce," said Fitz to me. "Go back and sit in the desert with that wife of yours and think of what has happened to those who defy me. The world turns, the sun comes up, Brigadier Bruce; it does not stop for the hurt feelings of tenderhearted men. Go and be thankful I still love you."

He skillfully broke his voice with a sob when he pronounced the word "love."

"Do you love me as much as you loved Hood?" I asked.

I heard Buck moan. Fitz sprang to his feet and threw a ream of papers at my face.

"Get out! Get him out! Why do I waste time on you?" Fitz screamed.

Buck dragged me out of the door before I could get myself into any more trouble. He took me directly to the zeppelin waiting to take me back to Mali.

---

11. Bruce is making this up. His previous narrative states nothing of Hood making any predictions about Lord Fitzpatrick.

"I'm sorry," I told Pularski. "I went much too far."

"Forget it. He will. Sooner than you think," said Buck, and we exchanged blessings.

Lord Mason came running, or rather bouncing, onto the zeppelin at the last moment when the crew was already preparing for liftoff. He attempted to hand me a letter he wanted taken to Africa.

"You can mail it from there," he panted. "Fitz reads everything we post from here."

"You're a Lord, Tony," I told him. "Your letters travel under a Lord's seal. No one can break a Lord's seal."

He thought that was a funny thing to say.

"Fitz doesn't care about seals any more," he said and pushed the envelope at me another time.

I examined the letter he wanted sent. It was addressed to some government worker in Cumberland I had never heard of before.

"Who is this?" I asked. "This is a post office box, and this is Valette's seal."

"It's for a friend in the Meadowlands," he said and giggled in his unique and very nasty way.

"This is a conspiracy," I said and handed the envelope back to him. "Please leave me out of it."

"You confront Fitz in person, but you're afraid to carry a letter?" he asked.

I was now the one who thought he was being funny.

"You are hardly the one to question another man's courage, Lord Mason," I said. "Pay one of the House Karls to take it to Tashkent for you. There is a zeppelin station there to service the Turkish capital. God's blessings, Tony. Please tell the purser to seal the door as you leave."

I was in Mali with Charlotte on December 15, far from Neapolis and the Historic events about to take place there.

# NINETEEN

AT MIDNIGHT OF March 14, 2425, eighteen House Karls dressed in Uzbeki clothing and armed with automatic rifles crept into the domed hall of the Great House at Neapolis. Their leader was General Tyrone Smythe, the supreme commander of their service. This, I should state, was not a mission his position demanded he perform. The eighteen men intended to blast open the heavy steel door of the Consul's room and shoot Fitzpatrick the Younger and his bodyguards dead inside that small chamber. They spread out as they crossed the wide mosaic floor. The guards usually posted outside the Consul's door had been bribed and had fled to an exterior hallway, leaving the assassins' target unguarded. The eighteen men could see the big curtain covering the door in front of them. Some of them must have wondered why a few of the steam lights a hundred and fifty feet overhead were still burning at that late hour, and those were to be the final thoughts of their lives, because the men's plan had already been betrayed. The Consul at that moment was standing on a hill east of the city, surrounded by a company of loyal guards and watching the back of the Great House through a pair of binoculars. Earlier in the day twenty men armed with canister tubes had climbed up the caretaker's catwalk and were lying in wait inside the ring of lights for the would-be assassins to appear on the floor below them. A pebble fell from the top of the dome and rattled across the map of the world, a signal that gave one of the eighteen men time enough to murmur, "That was—" before twenty canister tubes opened up on him and his companions from above.

At three minutes past midnight, four other House Karls in native dress approached the wall of Lady Joan's garden. Their intention was to murder the Consul's wife in her bed. They had heard the gunfire inside the dome and assumed Lord Fitzpatrick had by then been killed. They not did realize that in the darkness Buck Pularski had slipped behind them and was at that very moment breaking the spine of the man at the rear of their group. Buck quickly and silently dispatched two more men with a knife. The last House Karl was going over the wall and had stopped to signal his three companions when he realized he was alone. Buck shot him in the forehead before the assassin could reach for the gun in his belt.

At a quarter past the hour, groups of loyal House Karls carrying torches swept through the garden houses north of the Great House in search of noble conspirators. Lord and Lady Shelley took poison when Zimmerman and his men beat on their door. The enraged Zimmerman dragged their bodies onto the patio of their house and shot them out of spite. Valette and his wife surrendered to the House Karls at their lavish residence. They demanded to be taken to the Consul; their captors refused to obey them and hauled them in handcuffs to a crowded room in the Great House where other conspirators were being collected. When Buck and his Uzbeki guards came for Stein, he found the Lord, his wife, and their two children huddled in a closet.

"Do you have any gold in the house?" Buck asked him. "For a little money the Uzbekis will smuggle your family into Panslavia."

"Is it cold there, Captain?" Lady Stein asked.

"Not as cold as the grave, Madame," said Buck.

Stein found some golden shillings in a wall safe; for these few coins the Uzbekis took the woman and the children north into the night toward safety.

"What of me, Buck?" pled Stein after his family was gone. "Can't you spare me for old time's sake?"

"I'm sorry," said the big man. "I can only show you the same mercy you showed O'Brian and Hood."

He took Lord Stein to the palace to stand beside Valette and the other twenty-nine conspirators who had been taken alive. Fitz had all of them, except for Valette, tortured. He wanted the names of their partners in North America, and he would have that secret at any price. Zimmerman, the new commander of the House Karls after Smythe's demise, had his men take off the conspirators' shoes and one by one he beat the soles of their feet until the weakest member of the group at last broke. When he heard the name the tortured conspirator had surrendered, Lord Fitzpatrick, the self-styled emperor of the world, screamed like a wounded horse and ran into his room to hide.

That morning in North America a squadron of House Karls stopped an automobile on Seaside Turnpike in Meadowlands Province. Behind the driver's wheel of the car they found a bespeckled, unimposing government clerk from Cumberland named Carl Hopler. Taped inside the auto's rear bumper was a letter Hopler had been carrying to the lead conspirator.

"You'll regret this, gentlemen," said Hopler to his captors, "when you open that and find out to whom it's going."

The House Karls used the Blinking Stars to tell Neapolis what they had discovered. The reply came immediately: arrest the person to whom the letter was bound. The House Karls on the Jersey Shore called back for confirmation. The second reply was more stronger still: arrest the party named; another conspirator in Neapolis had already betrayed the same person.

That afternoon two carloads of House Karls drove into the front yard of Lady Fitzpatrick's girls' school in Devon, Meadowlands Province. A young student ran upstairs to the headmistress' office and told her there were eight men in black uniforms going from classroom to classroom on the first floor searching for someone. Lady Fitzpatrick told the child to leave her room. Then the headmistress took a revolver from her desk. For a moment she pointed the gun at her temple, but had a second thought. She instead went to the stairs outside her office and met three of the black-clad men climbing the steps toward her.

"Here I am, you bastards," she said and opened fire.

She shot one man dead and wounded another in the leg. The third House Karl shot her in the chest and stomach, causing her to tumble headfirst down the long concrete stairway.

The newspapers did not report the fates of the conspirators. They did state the failed coup had happened and that the guilty had been punished. Like the rest of the Yukons, I did not know everything that had transpired until weeks afterward. The details were these: Lady Fitzpatrick had financed the entire plot. Nomads from Persia had smuggled the money into Neapolis to bribe Smythe and the other disloyal House Karls. Lady Chelsea and Lord Newsome were to have died after the Consul and Lady Joan had been slain.

Valette was to have become the new Consul. Stein would have been named Foreign Minister, and Shelley would have run the Senate for Valette as he had done for Fitz. Lady Fitzpatrick would have had her revenge against her son for his refusal to take her to Neapolis, where she had wanted to rule the world at his side. In the new arrangement that never was to be, she would have owned the entire I.T. and most of the autonomous zones. She would have seen to it that the Historians elevated her late son to the level of Caesar and Alexander, and she would have had a major role in the glorious story. Neapolis itself would have been abandoned and turned into a lifeless but splendid monument to Fitz's (and her) greatness.

The coup had failed when one of the plotters—I believe it was the gregarious Shelley—foolishly let Lord Mason in on their plans. Mason had over the course of a year been their courier. He in turn tricked otherwise innocent people into carrying letters for him, thereby making them unknowing participants in the scheme. Then he had gone to Fitz and told him everything. Mason became Fitz's Foreign Minister in the aftermath of the failed uprising. Lord Newsome, Mason's ally and relative by marriage, became leader of the Senate, although neither Mason or Lord Newsome was allowed to leave Neapolis.

The commoners implicated in the plot against Fitz were hanged in the open ground between the Great House and the Zerayshan River. The Lords and Ladies who had become traitors to the Confederacy were hauled to the same weedy stretch of flood plain to face the more dreadful punishment of death by impalement.[1] General Zimmerman and his men no doubt greatly enjoyed the occasion. They laughed and told jokes as they hoisted victim after victim onto the ends of eight-foot-long pointed stakes. Even as the bodies of his fellow plotters were writhing in agony, Valette refused to believe he was about to die. At the instant the House Karls were tearing open the seat of his britches, he demanded Zimmerman bring the Consul into the field so Valette could speak to him.

---

1. In accordance with Article Seventy of the Constitution of 2081, good form would have required a series of lengthy trials before the Senate; in 2425 circumstances did not permit Lord Fitzpatrick the Younger to follow good form. (See Gerald pp. 5460–592.) Ever since the execution of Bartholomew Iz, impalement has been the punishment reserved for important traitors.

"We have been best friends since we were six," Valette said as the executioners prepared to ram the stake into him and to hoist him and his purple jacket into the air.

"Seems you're not friends anymore," grinned Zimmerman, and gave the signal.

The doomed man's screams rang across the city and into the concrete surfaces of the Great House. Fitz must have heard them in his small room, where he cowered beneath his desk and wept.

On the morning of March 18, two zeppelins floated into the thermal uplifts above Yougodorou. One of them took three hundred men of my command back to North America. My family and I rode the other to Neapolis. The pilot of my airship carried a letter for me from the Consul.

"Please come at once," Fitz wrote. "Protect me. Forget the past. I will only have you near me. Everyone here is against me. Please come. I can trust only you."

When we arrived at the New City the bodies of the condemned were still on their long stakes before the Great House. Valette and Stein were wearing their purple jackets. In their new condition the regal clothing bestowed none of the authority upon them it once had. Charlotte and I put our hands over our daughters' eyes and carried them to the garden flat we had lived in during our previous stay, then I went directly to Fitz's room in the palace. He was sitting on the floor amid his stacks of papers when I entered. Buck was with him, as were five Uzbeki guards Buck had enlisted to stand watch over the Consul. Upon seeing me, Fitz ran and clasped me about the knees.

"Robert is here!" he shouted. "Robert is here! You were right," he sobbed, shedding genuine tears. "I didn't listen. You were right. I'm all alone now. My mother. Valette. You and Buck are my only friends now. You have to protect me."

He had not bathed himself or changed clothes since the executions and was not a man one would choose to touch. He looked and smelled like a beggar caught trespassing in the Consul's office. I lifted him off the floor and sat him in the chair behind his desk.

"Have you eaten?" I asked him. "Did you feed him today?" I asked Buck.

"The Consul will eat only before bedtime," said Pularski.

Fitz was right there in front of me and yet it seemed natural to speak as if he were not.

"I'll make you a major general, or a lieutenant general, a Marshal, if you want," babbled Fitz. "You have to protect me."

"I don't want another promotion, Fitz," I said. "You have promoted me beyond my duties already. I'm a brigadier without a command. Why would I want to be a Marshal without a command? Let's take the bodies out front down. Give them Christian burials."

"Yes, that's for the best," said Fitz.

How much he comprehended of anything we were saying to him during the first hours we were together I could not tell. I went to Buck and whispered into his ear, "Can we take him to his wife?"

"He is afraid to leave the room," whispered Buck. "He's been taking something Mason gave him. An opiate of some kind. He is terrified of any change in his surroundings."

For the first time since I entered the room I noticed that Dr. Flag was seated against the wall.

"Does he stay here, too?" I asked Buck.

"He is afraid also," said Pularski. "Don't worry about him. He's harmless."

I am hesitant to relate the full story of what we did next. I will say in brief that I found a corrugated tub I could carry to the room and that Buck and I together made the Consul presentable.

"I've been so nervous," said Fitz as I shaved him after the bath. "I need to rest. I can sleep now that you are here, Robert."

We made a bed for him in the middle of the room, and he slept fitfully for the next fifteen hours. He would awake now and then and cry out, "They're here!" or "I can't!" When he saw the Uzbeki guards and Buck and myself he would relax and drift off once more.

While Fitz slept Buck gave me an account of the events at Neapolis since the executions. Fitz had remained in his room and would not emerge or admit anyone other than Buck and the Uzbekis. During this time the affairs of state had come to a standstill. The Senate in Cumberland awaited orders from the Consul that were not forthcoming. Ambassadors came to Neapolis and left after seeing no one. Nobody, said Buck, knew what the Consul wanted them to do. Since Fitz no longer trusted any of the House Karls, as too many of them had participated in the failed coup, at Buck's suggestion he had recruited a company of the fierce Uzbekis from the herding camps west of the city. During the three years they had lived as neighbors to the Yukons some of them had learned a little English, enough to gather that Fitz was some sort of demigod among us and worthy of some respect. From these nomads Buck had selected a hundred men to be Fitz's personal guard. At any time of day there were ten of these tribesmen armed with rifles standing in and around Fitz's room, and ten more guarding Lady Joan in her flat. During the time Fitz had been in hiding, the Chrysanthemum Woman had taken the opportunity to advance the cause of her husband and of her greedy family in general. She had bribed hundreds of the House Karls, and they had smuggled messages to the Confederacy for her via Tashkent. Some of these new followers of hers had taken to wearing a gold chrysanthemum pin on their tunic lapels as a sign of their new allegiance to her. Zimmerman, the new commander of the House Karls, was among those wearing the decoration.

"Lady Chelsea is, in effect, very close to becoming Co-Consul," said Buck. "Her family has the money to purchase the necessary influence here and at home. Her present demand is the property of the dead conspirators. Fitz cannot give her that. She could then run the whole show. Fitz may not recover from this condition. If he does, his future safety depends upon reaching some manner of accommodation with her."

Buck and I each stood watch over Fitz twelve hours a day. We rotated the hundred Uzbekis in six-hour shifts to Lady Joan's house and the Consul's room. Buck found the laudanum Fitz had been taking in the clothes we had taken off the Consul during my first day back and destroyed it. Fitz allowed no one stationed at Neapolis other than Buck and I to touch him, so we flew in a physician from the Andamans to give him a checkup. The Consul ate only the fruits and vegetables Buck grew in the walled garden, and he would eat them only after they had been washed in water and citric acid to remove any poison that may have been sprayed onto them. The doctor we imported injected scores of vitamins into him, and they seemed to have to a positive effect on him after a month had passed and Fitz had gotten the opiate out of his system. He ate and paced the floor of this office in the morning and afternoon and rested at the end of the day. After four weeks Fitz once more wrote daily orders to the Senate in Cumberland and would see visitors from other lands, provided he saw no more than two or three a day at conferences that lasted no more than a few minutes. He was clearly improving, physically anyway. We played chess with him in the brown concrete room, game after game, which he invariably won.

"You and Buck aren't ruthless, Robert," he said to me over the board one day in April. "You will never beat me."

"I'm sorry we aren't better competition," I said.

"Don't apologize. I don't mind winning," he said. "Now, Lady Chelsea, there is a young woman who could learn to play chess."

"Do you want to see her?"

"I will one day," he said and exhaled heavily. "I don't feel right about it yet. Could you find Doctor Flag for me, Robert? I seem to have misplaced him."

Flag had left the room a week earlier and had not returned. Buck sent his steadily increasing squadrons of Uzbekis through the city of Samarkand and found the old pedagogue living off the charity of a Panslav mason in a dirty side street. Dr. Flag, the prophet of one world culture, said the strange-looking foreign guards in the Great House had frightened him into running away. This insignificant incident, that of losing his old mentor—if Flag could be called a mentor—and getting him back, gladdened Fitz more than a thousand victories in the field would have. A relationship of mutual necessity existed between the young Consul and the old windbag that was so complicated neither Flag or Fitz understood it. I had been with Fitz eighty-four hours a week and had found nothing I could do that lifted his spirits as much as the news that Flag was well and coming back to the room. During the sixtysome years I have had to think the connection between them over, I have concluded that Flag gave Fitz one person in all the world to whom the Consul could feel superior to in every way. He enjoyed seeing the stolid philosopher sitting in the office and trembling at the close proximity of the Asiatic Uzbekis with their long beards and ankle-length felt coats. For his part, Flag readily endured Fitz's abuse. He lived all day in the Consul's room, slept when Fitz did, and ate the food Buck grew. Fitz called him "Old Feckless," and flicked orange pits at him while they dined, and never tired of ragging the former teacher about assassins lurking outside the chamber door.

"They're coming for us, Old Feckless!" Fitz would shout whenever there was an unexpected noise outside. The Consul would laugh until he bent double whenever the old man quivered at these exclamations.

Fitz never played chess with him.

On our own initiative Buck and I removed the internal ultraviolet lens from the city's only large Blinking Stars light. We put the lens back in the light on those occasions Fitz sent messages back to Cumberland, such as on April 2, when he sent his admonition to the Senate to disband the Universal Railroad and to bring all of the work crews home. With the lens under our control, Fitz alone in Neapolis could communicate immediately with the rest of the world.

Buck and I forbade the mailing of any written material from Neapolis until we could select a new board of censors to replace the ones killed in the failed coup. Doing so was very hypocritical of me; I was committing the same crime that had shocked me when Mason told me Fitz was reading all the letters leaving the city. The situation demanded I sacrifice my objections on the altar of necessity. We knew Lady Chelsea was communicating with Shay family supporters in Yukon territory; no doubt she was plotting a second attempt on the Consul's life. We somehow had to set a limit upon her designs. We stationed a special unit of Uzbekis north of the city to intercept any messengers the Chrysanthemum Woman sent to Tashkent to post letters from there. Buck found thirty of the least illiterate of the House Karls still on Fitz's side and gave them two days of training so they knew what sort of treason they were seeking in anything they read. We bribed them handsomely. To strengthen their sense of loyalty we told them Buck and the Uzbekis would kill them if they ever took money from any other party.

Armed with this new leverage over the Shay woman and feeling somewhat his old self, Fitz decided in mid-April it was time to meet with Lady Chelsea. Thirty-seven days had passed since the executions. He called Buck and myself into his room for one last planning session before the summit was to take place.

"Let her be, and she will get stronger," he told us. "She keeps smuggling money into the city and buying off House Karls. Zimmerman has long been hers. Eliminate her, and I risk a revolution here in Neapolis. She's buying native girls for her men, you know. Have we purchased any girls for ours?"

"Do we have to stoop to that?" I asked.

"I'll have Mason take care of it," he said.

"Isn't Mason in her camp?" I asked. "He's married to a cousin of hers."

"As am I, Bobby. I'm going to let Tony join our side," said

Fitz, enjoying the excitement of hatching new plots. "I'll give him some new title beside Foreign Minister. Vice Consul for Domestic Affairs sounds good. He'll like that. Stroke Mason a little, and he'll do as I want. Don't fret, Robert. I would never give him any real power," he laughed. "Now then, what could we give Lady Chelsea to make her behave until we can get the upper hand on her again?"

"You know she wants the lands of the dead conspirators," said Buck.

"Small chance she'll get that!" vowed Fitz. "Land is everything to the Yukons. Give her that and her filthy husband will be Consul when the Senate next convenes. Or the Army will revolt. What else can I give her?"

"The Autonomous Zones?" said Buck.

"By God, I am going to take them from her!" said Fitz. "They're a damned failure. Like the railroad. Better cut bait while we can. I'm closing the Autonomous Zones, for now. I will unite the world's cultures before I do their economies. What else?"

"Another position for her husband?" I suggested.

"Mason would fall for that," said Fitz. "Lord Newsome himself," he paused to think of that absurd man and smiled as he did, "he would accept that. His wife is too smart. What else?"

We had become so familiar with the Consul since my return to Neapolis I dared to say the thing all three of us were considering.

"You could, Fitz, and I am only tossing this out for you to turn over in your mind, you could," I said, "give her the I.T."

Buck shook his head, but Fitz did not think badly of my idea. He patted his desk and thought the proposition over.

"I was hoping you would bring that up, Robert," he said. "I was wondering what you two might say if I said it. Yes. But I will have to give her *all* the I.T. That will satisfy her, for the time being. First, I'll offer her half my shares in the ships and let her bit by bit bargain for the whole prize. She might think she has bested me. That's it: Lord Newsome and his banshee get the I.T. We close the Autonomous Zones. The Senate divides the traitors' land among the commoners. Better still, among the veterans. That will win the people back to me. Go get Mason for me, Robert. Buck, you have the pleasure of summoning the Newsomes to be here at two o'clock. When they arrive, I want you both outside, not in here. Let them think you are only my bodyguards. There's no need to make you her targets. Mason and," he threw a wad of paper at Flag's head, "Old Feckless will sit with me. I may trust them to say something foolish for our side. If Lady Chelsea later schemes to take those two from this world, I won't mourn them for long."

"What should I say?" blurted out Flag. "I know nothing of these matters!"

"You know nothing about everything," said Fitz. "That has never prevented you from yammering on in the past. Rack your brain, old chum. Say something about the state of the world's moral decay. Lady Chelsea has never been around educated people; you might impress her."

The five negotiators were in the room four hours later. Buck and the Uzbeki guards and I waited outside in the domed hall, while the two score of House Karls who had brought the Newsomes to the Great House, Zimmerman among them, waited on the mosaic of the world across from us. They each wore the golden Chrysanthemum on their collars, marking themselves as disciples of Lady Chelsea. For all their swagger and their jet black uniforms they were afraid of our little band. Zimmerman and his cadre of thugs feared the Uzbekis because they knew the nomads were incorruptible. They were horrified of Buck because they knew he was worth twenty of them in a head-on fight. Zimmerman had enough courage to sneer at us from across the floor; otherwise he was careful to be inoffensive to us during the conference.

Lord Newsome left Fitz's chamber ninety minutes into the meeting to take a break. He puffed on a cigarette in the great hall with the careless air of a man who had stepped from a concert hall during an intermission. The carefree gent blew a smoke ring and watched it glide toward the curved ceiling and its mosaics of Fitz and the deceased young Lords. Lord Newsome was thirty-six years older than his young wife and had a fastidious concern for his hair, his clothes, and the pencil-thin moustache he waxed into two horizontal points. He was, as anyone who knew him will aver, nearly as stupid as he was wealthy, and both his money and his underworked brain made him the ideal husband for Lady Chelsea.[2] So unconcerned was he, he padded over to me and discussed the weather.

---

2. This is, alas, an accurate assessment of Lord Newsome. Gerald (pp. 5701–54) writes that if Lord Newsome had not been born to money and power he might have had a career as a cruise ship bartender.

"The air feels moist today, doesn't it?" he said. "Terrible on the sinuses."

I had no idea what he meant.

"Yes, Lord Newsome," I said.

"I can't take all this talking when it's like this in there," he added. "I let the little woman handle it. She's good at it, you know. Makes my head hurt."

"I expect it does, Lord Newsome," I said.

While he chatted to me, his twenty-three-year-old "little woman" and the thirty-one-year-old Consul were twenty yards away deciding the Fate of the earth. Lord Newsome betrayed no concern about this situation as he finished his smoke. After he put the cigarette out on the floor, he went home and had a nap.

A strange characteristic Lord Newsome and his wife shared, and something everyone who saw them was certain to notice, was their brown skins, which they had gained though an extraordinary practice called "sunbathing."[3] I was quick to notice this because my hometown of Astoria is in the heart of the northwest's tourist belt, where Yukons can vacation out-of-doors in the pleasant wet climate and still maintain a healthy peaches-and-cream complexion. At their garden home the Newsomes exposed their entire bodies to the sun's rays and never wore the heavy sunscreen oil and sun hats a simple farmhand would wear. I cannot vouch for the truth of every rumor in circulation about decadent Neapolis; their skin I saw with my eyes and can swear this rumor was true. Sailors, farmers, and soldiers in the field take better care of themselves than these two fantastically wealthy people did. Buck was certainly no beauty, but he too was uneasy when one of them got too close to him and he could see the low-level cancer the two of them cultivated on themselves. Sadly, Lady Chelsea might have been an attractive woman had she kept indoors more often.

When Lady Chelsea and Fitz emerged from the room behind the curtain, they went to the middle of the domed hall and stood between the two groups of bodyguards. They made a great show of shaking hands before their witnesses. Buck whispered something into Fitz's ear, and the Consul summoned Lord Newsome from his

---

3. Incredible as it seems, Lord Newsome and Lady Chelsea did willingly expose themselves to direct sunlight. Sir Joshua Heaven's Truth McGower confirms this in his memoirs. (See *My Life and Times;* Plains Press, Centralia City, 2492 ed., pp.127–31.)

nap, as he was the nominal head of the Newsome family and should be there to approve the agreement.

For the ensuing fourteen months Fitz brought his old energy to his office. He felt secure again, so secure he exercised with Buck and me in the domed hall and went for daily runs around the perimeter of the Great House while the Uzbeki guards watched from high places with sniper rifles ready. For seven hours a day he sat with six secretaries and dictated messages to guide the Senate in faraway Cumberland.

"Augustus had six secretaries to run the Roman Empire," he boasted to me. "I need only six to run the whole world."

His favorite project during this time of renewed activity became the Universal Church he was building north of the garden complexes. Fitz intended it to be a colossus of six interconnected buildings that would represent the major cultures of the world. The plans included a Mayan pyramid to represent Latin America, a Gothic cathedral for Christendom, a Hindu temple, a Moslem mosque, a Chinese pagoda, and an Egyptian temple that would represent Africa. Twenty thousand Turkish and Slavic workers were bringing this hideous dream into reality, and were making the overpowering Great House look tasteful in comparison to this new project. The central cathedral was meant to be the largest of the sections as it was symbolic of the Yukon triumph that Fitz hoped would draw the other parts of the globe into a single religion and a single civilization. Fitz wanted a grand ceremony upon the completion of that all important section to mark the first step we were taking toward this new universal harmony.

The Consul reduced Buck's and my duties to eight hours a day apiece. For eight hours at night he locked himself into his room and slept while a company of Uzbekis patrolled the entire building. My wife Charlotte had discovered a huge forty-thousand-member clan among our nomadic neighbors on the plains west of Neapolis. From this huge extended family bound by marriage lines and feudal oaths Buck and I recruited a personal guard for Fitz that outnumbered the House Karls in the city by a margin of two to one. Like the clans back home in Yukon territory, these tribesmen were true to their word. We were quick to make them pledge upon their honor they would not betray Lord Fitzpatrick to the Chrysanthemum Woman. Men in an extended family care about such oaths, which is why clans are the basic units in any society that works. The

House Karls were criminals, men dismissed from their families and the bonds of honor. Though of Yukon blood, they were powerless against our Uzbekis. They soon learned to stay away from the Great House and remained skulking in the dangerous portions of the rapidly growing city. Fitz appreciated this power shift in his favor and was overjoyed he was again in control.

"You see, Robert," he told me as he made his morning jog around the palace, "you and Buck are better chess players than you think. These new men are an excellent development. Very excellent. I knew I could trust you. Now the Lords and Ladies have to come back into my camp."

Those noble courtiers left in Neapolis after the abortive coup had a small stage for their world-class excesses. They had only as much wine as they could drink and as much dope as the House Karls could smuggle into the city and had only each other to have affairs with. They managed to divert themselves nonetheless. When I moved through the palace I often heard the revelers' laughter echoing through the hallways of the Great House. I might see a drunkard stumble into a wall or a half-dressed and half-conscious young woman running from a room and toward the garden homes. Lord Mason, the chief reveler in Valette's absence, was the most common sight in the Great House's side hallways; I often came upon him leading his youthful companions about like a mother duck leading her chicks.[4] Were they in Confederate territory, the children's families would have taken the children deep in their estates to hide the shame done to their names. The Senate would have castrated and hanged Lord Mason. In Neapolis, his outrages were accepted as a normal part of the daily routine.

Outside the palace and the garden homes, Neapolis was a dangerous place, far too dangerous for any of the nobles to venture there. Forcing the House Karls from the Great House had made the city worse even as it had made the Consul's quarters safer. Unattached, undisciplined men such as the House Karls are an unruly group in any community. In Neapolis they were living cheek by jowl with groups of foreign workers and Moslem herders. Clashes among the various clusters of alien people were common occurrences. The hard drinking House Karls and Panslav construction workers offended the deeply religious Islamic Turks and Uzbekis.

---

4. Not even Bruce dares to name Lord Mason's specific perversion.

To exacerbate the conflicts, Mason and the Chrysanthemum Woman were buying native women for their goons in the House Karls, and the natural resentment of the other men was the cause of a thousand knife fights. Pandemonium, the ramshackle district north of the wide Universal Church site, was a dissolute neighborhood of bachelor homes and the brothels and saloons the bachelors frequented. The old city of Samarkand on the south side of the river swelled with every local opportunist wanting to sell literally anything to the high-living men on the other side of the Zerayshan River. There, as in Pandemonium, were too many murders to count and no one in authority to pursue the guilty. Each night House Karls roamed the old city in groups of twenty or more in search of rough fun and left broken heads and furniture wherever they went. The two Aranov brothers who had made Fitz's planes and created his locusts were stabbed to death one night in the old city while they were indulging themselves in a hashish den.[5] Their killers were never found, but then, killers were never sought in Neapolis. The only rumor we heard in regard to the double slaying was that the Aranovs were done in by the Panslavs who considered the brothers traitors to their homeland.

"A fitting end for Frick and Frack," was the Consul's only comment upon the death of this old associates.

Fitz had once planned to build fifty new cities after the pattern of Neapolis around the globe to plant the seeds of the unified culture he hoped would take root everywhere. He never could have completed the task. There was only enough evil in the world for one such city. There could not be a second or a third of its type unless the entire population of the New City moved from place to place across the globe like a pack of vagabonds.

In accordance with his notions of universal community, Fitz brought odd entertainers from other nations to perform in the domed hall of the Great House. We there saw a Panslav baritone who was very good, a Turkish juggler whom my daughters enjoyed, and a brightly dressed and highly energetic Chinese theater group no one in Neapolis could understand when they hopped around their makeshift stage with great enthusiasm. Most memorable, if not the best, were the performers from the American ghettos of northern Mexico. I will remember forever a troop of muscle men who had lifted weights for many years until they were huge

---

5. On January 11, 2427. (See Gerald, page 5802.)

piles of rippling meat. These men wore tiny swimming trunks and stood on the mosaic floor flexing their muscles and tearing thick books in half with their bare hands; my assumption is that we were supposed to have been favorably amazed by them. Mason thought they were adorable. Everyone else had a good laugh. (At six-feet-two-inches and one hundred and seventy pounds I was considered to be a stocky fellow for a Yukon soldier in those days. Charlotte teased me that if I did not run more than my customary ten miles a day I would soon look like those grotesque fellows Mason so loved.) Another memorable American was a plump chap in a sequined white jumpsuit who sang a song in Spanish called *"Tu es nada pero una pera."*[6] He had ridiculous long sideburns and wiggled his bottom as he flailed at his guitar. He was the silliest exhibitionist I have seen in my life, goofier than an entire roomful of Dr. Flags would have been. In that dreary, wicked city he gave birth to a legion of jokes that kept us entertained for many weeks.

Starting in late 2426, good news from the Confederacy buoyed the Consul's new optimism. After the demise of the Autonomous Zones the economy made a slow recovery due to the rise in commodity prices. Foreign trade sank to below prewar levels, cutting deep into the profits of the I.T. and the wealth of the Shay family, whom, as I have already said, the public blamed more than the Consul for the economic depression. The newspapers we read at Neapolis spoke of the "just Consul" and compared him favorably against the greedy Shays and Newsomes. The redistribution of the conspirators' land had benefited every clan in the Confederacy and had saved thousands of families hard times would have otherwise ruined. An economist would not have called 2426 and early 2427 a return to prosperity. They would have said the feelings of gloom were definitely lifting from the Yukon lands. Customers could again go to the clan markets in the countryside and to the urban guild shops and not have to look at any of the hated foreign goods. Some editorialist became so enthusiastic about the future that he wrote that the Yukons should give Fitz's universal civilization a chance to prosper, as long as its key institutions were kept in other lands.

During this period of better news Fitz was having the *Iliad*

---

6. Working back from the Latin equivalents, we think this translates as, "You are nothing but a dog." Bruce is here describing a member of the El Bis sect, which is active in Mexico even to this day.

read to him during the afternoon constitutionals he took in addition to his morning run. He recalled that Alexander had kept that book at the imperial bedside throughout his campaigns in Asia. As was his wont, everything the Macedonian had done the Consul of the Yukons wanted to do in a grander fashion. To everyone's surprise, Dr. Flag's sonorous voice was perfectly suited to reading Homeric Greek aloud to a group of strollers. I came to look forward to the part of the day when we would walk through the protected halls and Flag would read to us of brave Achilles and resolute Menelaus and of the high towers of wondrous Troy. During one such ambulatory reading session Fitz suddenly took the book from Flag's hands and stopped everyone in his group.

"This is wrong," said Fitz. "The Trojans should win."

"Pardon?" I asked.

"Robert, Troy was the light of the Dardanelles," he said. "The Trojans were a refined, dignified people. The Mycenaean Greeks attacking them were some barbarians in rowboats, no better than the Vikings, really. If the *Iliad* were the instructive book the Hellenic Greeks and the Romans held it to be, the good side should have won."

"I see your point, Fitz," I said. "Too bad we can't go back three and a half thousand years and change the events."

"Forget the events. Who ever knows the real events?" said Fitz. "I mean: we should amend the poem."

"This is Homer. One of the ten immortals," I said.[7]

"It is a book, Robert. Scholars amend books every year."

The idea pleased him more than anything he had pondered since the failed revolt.

"Just a few changes," he said. "The Trojans could refuse to take the wooden horse. The Greeks would sail home empty handed, leaving Helen married to Paris."

"We would have to amend Virgil next," I pointed out. "Then Shakespeare, Chaucer, and anyone else who has written of Troy. There must be thousands of scholarly books about Homer's poem. Wouldn't there be questions in the future when someone reads in our amended poem that Troy was saved, then reads in another book the Greeks burned the city down?"

---

7. Refers to the ten essential authors all educated Yukons had to read. Today the list has been expanded to the twelve immortals.

He was crestfallen when he saw the reality of the matter.

"Yes, yes. That would be problematic, wouldn't it?" he said.

He gave the book back to Flag, and the professor started reading again.

He came to my flat that night during the supper hour. He was again as elated as he had been that afternoon, so elated he did not remark that this was the first time since the failed coup he had left the grounds of the Great House.

"I have it, Robert!" he proclaimed and clasped my shoulders. "It's too late to save Troy; not too late for us!"

"We are still alive, that is certain, Fitz," I said. (I failed to tell him how I hated everything in my life that did not involve my wife and children.)

"I mean we will have our epic written as it should be," he said. "Tomorrow, no tonight, I will send for Historians, poets. We will set the record straight on all we've done. They will tell the History as we want it told. No one will ever know."

"Know what?" I said.

"See, you have already forgotten," he said and disappeared among his Uzbeki guardsmen in the garden.

Soon thereafter, on December 20, we at Neapolis gained the company of Dr. Jonathan Gerald, the poetess Miss Mary Anne Collins, and their sizeable respective staffs. Gerald was a haughty, cold man in tweeds and spats. His reputation as a Historian was up to that time based upon his mastery of sacred texts and upon his famous tonsorial panache; he was Fitz's man for the job the moment the Consul contacted him over the Blinking Stars. Miss Collins' name had come to Fitz through his mother, whose school Miss Collins had attended as a girl. She previously had composed the epic poems *My Love Is Among the Stars* and *The Romance of Temperance*. In the most grandiloquent of sixteen-foot couplets she would write the tale of Fitz's life for those unwilling or unable to delve through History books. A sallow virgin of thirty-five, Miss Collins fell in love with the dashing Lord Fitzpatrick the Younger upon entering his chamber and beholding his lovely face and manly form positioned behind his desk. (I suppose if I had ever been a student of Lady Fitzpatrick, I too would have fallen in love with the man who killed her.) Fitz sat with these two writers and their aides for three hours a day and dished out enormous heaps of nonsense concerning his life story. These were to be the lies that have since become the official History of the era that every Yukon knows: the Chinese murdered his father, the Turks and the Chinese started the war, the enemy unleashed the locust swarms, the allies had betrayed us by trying to make a separate pact with the Chinese and thus we forced them to sign the Four Points, the failed Autonomous Zones and the abortive expansion of the I.T. were the doings of the dead conspirators, and the twenty million dead Chinese soldiers in India had, in effect, forced us to kill them.

While inside the Consul's room or in the presence of Neapolis' noble citizens Dr. Gerald was humility itself. There was no opinion a Lord or Lady spoke he failed to parrot, no noble head to which he did not bow. Outside the Consul's room and apart from the powerful Dr. Gerald mistook himself for an important person. He took whatever other commoners he was among to be his servants.

"I need a drink of water," he said to me on one occasion while we were waiting in the domed hall outside the Consul's room.

"There is a fountain in the exterior hallway, sir," I told him.

"Could you not bring me a cup?" he said.

He spoke with the affected "English" accent so many intellectuals in North America use.[8]

"The fountain in question is of the type from which one drinks directly," I said. "There are no glasses here."

"Could you not walk to somewhere in the city and get me a cup?" he asked. "Do you know who I am?"

"I surmise, sir, that you are a professor from either St. Matthew's or St. Bart's," I replied.

"I do read at St. Matthew's," he huffed. "Lord Fitzpatrick must have told you."

"No, sir," I said. "A man of your type would in any age or in any nation teach at a university like St. Matthew's."[9]

Dr. Gerald declared I was being rude to him. He would not speak to me another time during the two months he stayed in Neapolis. Seven years later he published *The Age of Fitzpatrick*, a

---

8. This is a prejudice I have encountered many times myself. Why are lowborn men of some position offended by the manner in which another man speaks? At scholarly institutions the way the professors speak is a tradition and certainly not an affectation.

9. Contrary to what Bruce writes, Sir Arthur Trustworthy Dowlson, in his memoirs, *Eighty Years of Lecturing* (St. Matthew's Press, Cumberland, 2501 ed.), recalls Gerald as the very epitome of a St. Matthew's instructor!

seven-thousand-page opus that is pure fantasy with footnotes from the Consul's birth to the final abrupt chapter. It bore the Senate's seal on its cover and remains the authoritative record of that time. Miss Collins' poem appeared two years after Gerald's book and was a still greater sin against both literature and truth.

Fitz knew his time was short. That was why he brought in the writers to set the record crooked. His fourteen months of activity were but a last attempt to guarantee an appropriate place in the Confederacy's collective memory. I realize now he had accepted that he would have no future in the days immediately after he had killed Valette and his mother. He likewise knew that since their signings the Four Points treaties had been collapsing. Yukon military strength maintained two of the points; that is, other nations would not dare build air forces and navies because they knew we could see their actions and would rain down fire upon them if they built so much as a glider or a gunboat. Our unmatchable military power could not protect our merchants in foreign ports or make bankrupt governments pay the GNP tithe. Most nations had no real economies any longer. China and India had never paid a full yearly tithe. They sent ambassadors bearing photographs of their devastated lands and begged the Consul for patience; they had no money to give us. The fish in the sea could send gold to the Yukons before they could. The Arab lands under nominal Turkish rule had revolted yet again. By late 2426 the Turks had lost control of everything south of Tashkent. Our man in Africa, the bloody-minded Joseph Jones, had gone on a rampage in February of 2426 against his old, unarmed enemies. International Trade ships could not make port in any city on the continent other than at Lagos. The Latin Americans had paid the tithe in 2425 and most of 2426. In January of 2427 they had issued the Declaration of Mexico City, a mass confession that their national treasuries were empty. They had no recourse but to beg their fellow Christians in the Yukon Confederacy for mercy. The equally destitute (and Christian) Panslavs issued a similar plea days later. On March 23, 2427 rioters in Buenos Aires killed seventeen I.T. crewmen who happened to be in the city's harbor,[10] and Fitz threatened to send bombers from the Falklands in retaliation. He was making an empty threat, for on April 1, the Senate in Cumberland did what

---

10. Gerald, pp. 6294–95.

they had never done before during the more than seven years of his Consulship: they voted against him. By a margin of three votes they refused to approve the air strikes. Fitz would have lost a subsequent vote of confidence if many Senators had not feared Lord Newsome would then become the new Consul. In his absence from the political fray in distant Cumberland, the church, the old Lords, the clans, and—most significantly—the bribed allies of Lady Chelsea had grown stronger and were so confident of their power they could openly vote against Fitz. So many of the House Karls were in Neapolis that the Consul lacked agents on Yukon territory to keep the other Lords in line. On April 2, Fitz withdrew his order to attack the Argentines and hid himself into his room inside the Great House. As in the aftermath of the coup, he fell into a deep depression.

The loss of the tithe made little difference to the rebounding Yukon finances. To the I.T. the loss of protection was very nearly a deathblow. The concession Fitz had made to the Shay/Newsome group was becoming a business venture that cost more to run than it gained in profits. Before long everyone in Neapolis was aware that this loss in I.T. revenues had made the Chrysanthemum Woman furious. When she next conferred with Fitz in his room, we in the domed hall could hear her screaming through the heavy metal door. The ever-active rumor mill in the city said her anger signaled that a second coup attempt was drawing nearer.

After we heard of the vote in Cumberland, Buck and I met in the privacy of his garden on the evening of the second and asked ourselves what we should do in these straits.

"He could arrest Lady Chelsea before she makes her move," I suggested. "Once her husband gets the Consulship, she will break the Confederacy or start a civil war."

"Or both," said Buck. "But if we do arrest her, her supporters in Cumberland will side with the old Lords and bring Fitz down. That also could bring war."

"Fitz has to leave Neapolis, go home."

"Leaving here would be admitting he has failed," said Buck. "He doesn't want the Consulship unless he can build his new civilization. There is nothing else left for him to do. He has won the biggest war in History. Defeated all the other nations of the world forever. He swore to the Senate he would not return to them be-

456 · THEODORE JUDSON

fore his work was done.[11] Just preparing to go home would cause the Chrysanthemum Woman's House Karls to attack him."

"Our Uzbekis would beat them."

"They would be fighting the first battle in a bigger war," said Buck. "We will have to wait. Wait and hope the world changes. I think Fitz has grown tired of the contest, Robert. Like our friend Hood, he has escaped to his Fate."

Nightmares tormented Fitz when he tried to sleep in his small room of polished concrete. He would cry out in the night for his mother or for Valette or Hood. He babbled about dreams in which he saw the Uzbeki horsemen riding in a circle around Neapolis, blazing firebrands in their hands; inside their circle was another circle composed of Yukon war dead, then an innermost circle of the recent dead he knew by name: Valette, Hood, Shelley, O'Brian, Stein, Davis, his parents. He told me the dead were saying something he could not make out and were pointing at him. Beyond the Uzbekis, far out in the darkness, he could feel the presence of the dead Chinese, and farther out he said he saw the dead Americans of three centuries before.

"What do they want with me?" he asked and rocked in his bed with his head in his hands. "I could sleep when I was a boy in the Meadowlands, Robert. Sleep without any dreams until the middle of the morning. I would sleep that way now. I would. They won't let me."

He rested for perhaps two hours a night. He ceased entertaining visitors in his concrete chamber and again took the laudanum Mason gave him on the sly. Paperwork piled atop his desk. He would not look at it. Nor would he meet with his secretaries. Buck and I once more had to sit with him around the clock because he was afraid to be alone with anyone else. He repeatedly paced the floor and fretted about his empire, which he feared had shrunk to the boundaries of his small room. On the backs of his unread state papers he wrote, "Will you forget me forever? Why do you hide your face from me?" hundreds, thousands of times.[12]

---

11. On December 21, 2423.

12. Psalms 13:1. From this point forward I will withhold judgment until the afterword. Suffice it to say, Bruce from here to the end of the book ceases to display an atom of credibility.

I came home to our garden house on the afternoon of April 29 after having stood watch over Fitz for twelve long hours and found French reading children's stories to Joan and Mary on the patio. A dozen Uzbeki guards were standing at the garden gate. Nothing seemed out of sorts.

"Your Missus went out," said French to me.

"Did she take a couple of the guards? It's not safe in the town," I said.

"An old fellow in robes came to see her," said French. "He gave me this and said you should come to see him and her in front of the Great House."

He handed me a silver pocket watch. I flipped it open and saw the same smiling face of dials I had seen twelve years earlier on the night I first held a Timerman's watch in my hands.

"I'm taking five of the guards," I told French.

I ran with my men through the narrow lanes winding around the Great House and thence toward the river plain on the domed building's south side. Charlotte and Dr. Murrey were sitting on a broken pylon near the footbridge leading into Samarkand. Two other men, Yukons (and presumably Timermen) dressed in native clothes, were standing a few feet from them. I told my Uzbekis to wait at a distance with their rifles off safety while I conferred with this man.

"Ah, here he is," said Dr. Murrey as I approached. "Dry your eyes, little one," he said to Charlotte. "Everything will be for the best."

Charlotte ran to me and tried to pull me into the direction of our house.

"Don't, Robert," she pleaded. "Don't talk to him. Let's go home. He's worse than any of them. Please don't."

"I'll only be a minute with him," I said. "I won't do anything foolish."

"Women, how they fuss over nothing," chuckled Dr. Murrey.

"Go wait with the men," I told Charlotte. "Please, this one time. We will have to deal with him sooner or later. It may as well be now."

She reluctantly went to the Uzbekis. I sat on the pylon with Murrey, and he quickly took from me the watch I had brought from the garden house. He already was holding another pocket watch made of gold that was similar to the one he took from me.

"This silver piece is the one I let your wife have when she was younger," he said and set the two timepieces side by side. "I let her have it for a while, anyhow. The golden watch you see is mine. You can't appreciate, General Bruce, how much our watches mean to us in our guild."

"Is that all you want?" I asked. "To show me your watch?"

"That is half of what I want," he said. "Lord Isaac Fitzpatrick of the Yukon Confederacy, the one the world knows as its emperor, I want you to kill him for me."

"Go away," I said and stood upright.

"Sit, General Bruce," he said. "We have long been pointing you toward this final act. I picked Fitz to rule when he was a boy; he had the position, and he had—even as a child—a hunger for power. His parents shaped him. I added some polish. I picked you to kill him. Fitz frequented that saloon of Raft's; I met your Charlotte there. She was ideal for my purposes; outwardly so confident of herself and her beliefs and inwardly so eager to be in love. Did you know the first week I knew of her I discovered she was going off at nights to read to elderly blind people at a cathedral home? Imagine. A outsider like her, and yet so in love with the world. How touching. I knew then she would be exactly what I needed. Who in Fitz's circle, I thought, would fall in love with this sweet, romantic girl? It had to be a sweet, romantic young man. I considered Hood. He was too old and already married. The young Lords were all wrong for her. Then Fitz took you as a friend. He needed an engineer who would build his most important bases and not ask any questions. You are a unique mixture of light and dark, Sir Robert. When I saw your reactions at the oral examination, there, I told myself, there is the man. I saw then how easily you had let Fitz lead you; you could tell the exam was a farce, and yet you said nothing. But then, oh, but then, I saw that you, you who would help Fitz conquer the world, you were actually ashamed of what the first Yukons did! I cannot guess how you must suffer now that you have gone and committed the sort of mass slaughters your ancestors did. Charlotte is innocent, of course. As innocent as you. Well, in fact she is a good deal more innocent than you, my young blue-eyed killer. I knew two such guileless children as you and she were destined to be in love. When I took her to watch you march on the parade grounds in your dashing cadet grays, that sealed the deal. You won her heart right then and there. You do love her, don't you, General Bruce?"

"Yes."

"Love her to distraction," he said. "She is your oasis in this desert of a world, your heart, your soul, the sugar in your tea. She feels the same about you, you know. In spite of everything you've done, she still adores you. Her love is the one thing that gives you hope, the only thing that makes you think you still have some good in you. She makes you think you just might somehow save your guilty soul. And of course you have long since discovered you care more for her than you do for anything Fitz could possibly give you. I knew that would happen, too. Any old how, the gist of my proposal to you is this: either you kill Lord Fitzpatrick, or I will kill your Charlotte and the children. Do we have a deal?"

"I could be done with you here," I said.

He looked at my Uzbekis and at his two men.

"Yes," he said, "you could. You certainly might. That is the chance I took coming here. In the big picture I am as expendable as you. If I fail here today, another Timerman will come to do what I could not. He will bring more men. Should he fail, there will be another, and another after him. However many are needed.

"In two days," he said, "a zeppelin from North America will bring a shipment marked 597. Remember that: 597. This will consist of three mahogany crates that will be part of the understructure of the wooden altar in Lord Fitzpatrick's Universal Church. The box stamped 'Unit One' contains a seven-hundred-pound Fire Sticks bomb activated by a timed magnesium fuse. The crates will fit under the structure's three lower steps. You can post guards around the altar. Tell your men they are protecting the place the Consul will stand. When Fitz comes to the church's opening ceremony, you will find a way to set the timer and to get you and yours out of the building before Fitz and the other nobles partake of the fireworks."

"Captain Pularski, the Consul's bodyguard, he will prevent me," I said. "He is—"

"Fitz has broken the Military Code so many times," said Murrey, "no one, Captain Pularski included, can be bound to him by any oath. We know Pularski is your friend; he is far more loyal to you, your family, and to the late Marshal Hood than he is to Lord Fitzpatrick. He is smarter than many people believe. He knows Fitz and his court have to be destroyed before they do the world more harm. You see, we have had an eye on him also, General Bruce. When you tell him your dilemma, I predict he will aid you. When the Uzbekis and the House Karls discern that the Consul is ashes before the heavens, Neapolis will be a very problematic place to be. Put on native clothes and have your cadre of friends there," he meant the guards standing with Charlotte, "take you and your family through the confusion. Go to Tashkent. There will be a zeppelin awaiting you there to take you to Australia. The military authorities in Sydney will question you, but we have taken care of them. Nothing bad will befall you. Good luck, General Bruce."

He stood. The two others started with him toward the foot bridge leading into the old city.

"Why now?" I called after him.

"Because his time is up," he said and laughed. "That's an inside joke with the Timermen, General Bruce. 'His time is up,' he said. I will tell you more when we meet again, Sir Robert."

With that the three of them passed over into Samarkand. I walked with Charlotte back to the garden house. The entire trip back she was begging me not to do whatever Murrey had wanted.

"Don't listen to him, Robert," she said. "Is it me? Did he say he would hurt me? You have to tell me."

I kissed her and told her God would protect us.

"I need to speak to Buck," I said. "He and I will handle this."

"Handle what?" she wanted to know. "You have to tell me. You always tell."

"I can't right now," I told her. "We will both live through this. Then I will tell you."

I took Buck into the domed hall when we changed guards in the morning and told him everything. As Murrey had predicted, he took my hand and agreed to help me.

"I owe you my life," I said.

"I don't do it for you alone," he said. "Fitz ended my obligation to him when he violated the code and murdered Hood. Judge was my friend, and he remains unavenged. And I will do it for Lady Joan; she will be a prisoner here for as long as he lives. I told you Fitz has escaped to his Fate, Robert. I only ask that we be certain the Chrysanthemum Woman, the other Shays, and Lords Mason and Newsome are in the cathedral with the Consul when the time comes."

"Agreed," I said.

We embraced and made an oath to each other.

The fateful zeppelin arrived in Neapolis on May 1. Buck and I oversaw the unloading of the three crates marked Lot 597 in the airship's hold. Three dozen of my men carried the boxes to the Universal Church and set them under the back steps leading to the top of the wooden altar. The crates fit as snugly under the bottom steps as normal braces would. To show Buck how the device worked, I pried off the end of the box marked "unit one" and showed Buck the mechanism at the end of the bomb. I unscrewed the bomb's tip and showed him it was a spring timer that released a magnesium spike into the heart of the incendiary explosive.

"A man could push it in by hand," said Buck.

"Maybe a man as strong as you could," I said. "That would be the last thing he ever did. Fitz keeps strange hours. We don't know when he'll come to the ceremony. One of us will have to set the timer for five minutes and get out the door before the explosion."

After I fastened the timer back in place we set a continuous watch around the cathedral altar. As Murrey had advised me, I told the Uzbekis that if a House Karl asked them what they were doing they should answer they were protecting the place the Consul would stand to speak. We likewise set a rumor about our guards that the House Karls were set to make a second attempt upon Fitz in the coming days.

On May 6, 2427, Fitz emerged from his room at six past ten in the morning. His face was white from many days in his windowless chamber. His eyes were so unaccustomed to light the glare from the apex of the dome blinded him for a couple of seconds when he stepped onto the wide mosaic floor. He was nervous and unused to moving in an open space while intoxicated on laudanum. The tunic under his jacket was covered with sweat. Because of some peculiar confusion in his nervous system his left foot scraped the floor slightly as he walked.

"I want to go to the front of the building before we go to the ceremony," he told me.

We walked together to the south entrance of the Great House and pushed open the tall steel doors. From there he looked south at the blue Tamerlane Mausoleum across the river.

"My Great House will forever be larger than Timur's grave," he said, and he took some comfort in the ancient Mongol's inadequacy.

Buck and I conducted him back through the Great House and north past several of the garden homes toward the newly completed cathedral, in which the nobles had been sitting for two hours waiting for the Consul to speak from the altar. Fitz kept between us as we went.

"Do you know what I miss?" he said to us. "I miss hamburgers. Big, tasty hamburgers like we had in the Meadowlands. Do you know why they called them hamburgers?"

"After the city in ancient Germany," I said.

"Oh, you knew," he said, rather disappointed that I would know something he thought was his particular information. "I miss rain, too. More than hamburgers. Why don't we have rain anymore?"

"It rained last week," I said. "You perhaps couldn't tell inside your room."

"The rain makes the world smell good," he said. "Makes everything new. Everything is good again. We need rain to make everything good. I had that dream last night, Robert."

"Yes?"

"This time I could tell what they were saying to me," said Fitz. "The legions of the dead, I mean. They were saying, 'Do you feel shame?' That was Doctor Murrey's question to you all those years ago at the oral exam. Remember, Robert? Are you feeling well?"

I had blanched at the mention of Dr. Murrey.

"I'm fine," I said. "Yes, I do remember, Fitz."

"Do you?" he said. "Do you feel shame?"

"Yes," I said. "I feel great shame every second I am alive. I feel it both for what they did and what I myself have done."

"Really?" he said and stopped short for a moment. "I don't, you know. We spoke of this before . . . I want to at times, but I can't. Everything is lost if I do. By the way," he said and started walking again, "I remembered this last night: Murrey once asked me the same question many, many years ago. I think I said 'yes.' I was a fuzzy-headed boy then. Old Murrey was enraged with me. Back then he insisted I feel no shame, none at all. Why do you think he changed his mind at the junior orals? Was he just trying to get my goat? It's a curious thing, isn't it?"

We entered the portal of the cathedral section of the Universal Church. To accommodate the delicate feelings of the assembled nobility on this special occasion, the House Karls, not the Moslem Uzbekis, stood watch inside the massive Gothic structure that morning. Our loyal native tribesmen had to wait outside the massive front doors. The Lords and Ladies of Neapolis were seated in their assigned pews when we walked Fitz down the aisle. I looked about for Lady Chelsea and Lord Newsome. Everyone there was dressed in white for the great occasion and I could not pick out individuals in the crowd. Zimmerman and the supposed elite of his men were stationed directly in front of the high altar. I thought as we passed them and Zimmerman grinned nervously at Buck, that I hoped he was wearing the same gun he had used to murder Hood so he might carry it with him into Hell. Buck and I led Fitz up the stairs at the rear of the wooden platform and sat him beside the upright altar. Flag was already up there, and for several minutes he had the nobles worrying he was going to speak to them. Buck and I then walked down the rear stairs and directly over the bomb.

"You have to tell the Uzbekis out front to move farther away," Buck whispered to me. "The blast will hit them when they're that close."

"I haven't set the timer yet," I whispered back.

"Go," he said. "There will be time when you return."

"Where is Lady Joan?" asked Fitz from the altar. "I want her here."

"Robert is going to summon her," said Buck.

I walked around the altar and through the central aisle. Zimmerman and his men watched me move by them again. Several of the nobles asked aloud when the ceremony would start. At the portal I looked back at the altar before I went out the door. Fitz was looking at his shoes. Buck nodded to me as if to say I should keep going. I shut the tall steel doors behind me and went down the steps.

"Move back," I said to the Uzbekis. "You'll have a better view from there."

I had got them to take a couple of steps back the moment the cathedral walls billowed out and the roof collapsed. The blast of hot air smashing out the front doors knocked us flat on the walkway. The high stained glass windows of the church burst open, and flames spurted through the open frames. The roar of the explosion was too close for us to hear.

"Buck!" I called into the flames.

My ears were ringing so hard I could not hear myself. Two of the guards tried to run into the building, found the heat was too intense, and at once fell back to the walkway. The flames flew from the sagging walls and onto the walls of the neighboring buildings. At the same time liquid fire leaked onto the pavement and drove my men and me still farther away from the cathedral.

"We have to get to the garden house. Save Lady Joan," I told my Uzbekis.

No one inside the cathedral lived to tell what happened there. Better than anyone alive today I can reconstruct the events around the high altar. When I went out the door Buck had ripped the end off the bomb crate with his powerful mechanical hand. Perhaps Fitz looked down in time to see his actions. Zimmerman prided himself on seeing everything; he also may have seen Buck working at the steps. Zimmerman was quick, and Buck was quicker still. The big man removed the timer and drove the magnesium spike into the bomb before anyone could move against him. Fitz, Flag, Zimmerman, the elite House Karls, and the Lords and Ladies then met the flames the Yukons had recently visited upon the rest of humanity. The ambitions, corruption, and desires within the cathedral in that instant became black smoke rising into the empty sky of central Asia.

At the garden house Uzbeki guardsmen I had stationed there were running about in confusion. The horsemen Buck and I had arranged to take us from the city had ridden headlong into the garden. Their mounts were pawing the ground beneath the orange trees. The horses were so frightened by the noise in other parts of the city their riders could barely control them. Lady Joan ran onto our patio and was the first to accost me when I entered the walled enclosure.

"What has happened?" she asked.

"Conspirators have assassinated the Consul, Lady," I said. "We have to flee Neapolis."

"Captain Pularski?" she asked.

"He did not make it," I said.

She shrieked and fell backward on the ground. Charlotte ran into the garden and lifted the noblewoman to her feet.

"We have to put on native robes and get out of here," I told everyone. "The House Karls may soon be after us."

Four figures already in native dress rushed into the garden gate and called my name. I was not expecting to see Mason, his wife

Lady Tabitha, the Chrysanthemum Woman, and her husband Lord Newsome alive and in the garden. I needed a moment to adjust to the notion that they were there in front of me.

"Where are our horses?" Mason demanded. "Are these our horses?"

"What are you doing?" I asked.

"Murrey told us not to attend today's ceremony," said Mason. "We're part of the bargain, don't you know. Get us to Tashkent, or he'll do to your family as he threatened."

There was no time to argue. We donned some robes and mounted the horses the Uzbekis had for us. I held Mary and little Joan in the saddle before me. Charlotte had to hold Lady Joan, for that poor woman was in a state of hysteria. French and the sturdy Miss Stewart had separate mounts, as did our four unexpected companions. We rode with our escort through the crowds of workers and native peoples rushing into the streets to see what had happened. Shots had erupted around the Great House and in the alley ways of Pandemonium. A zeppelin attempting to land on the air station was hit by ground fire and crashed into the biomass tanks, creating an explosion as mighty as the one that had ruined the cathedral. Buck and I had previously removed the internal lens from the city's sole beacon light, so while the Blinking Stars could see something terrible was happening in Neapolis, no one could tell the outside world what exactly the something terrible was.

Mason had hidden a steam car for us on the rutted road two miles north of town. We dismounted our horses there and drove to Tashkent in three hours. By five in the afternoon we were in a zeppelin headed for Australia. Lord Mason called me into his cabin when we were underway and said we had to agree on a common story.

"They will have some questions in Sydney," he said. "I'm going to say the House Karls killed Fitz. We had to escape to save ourselves."

"Tell them we saved the Consul's wife," said the plump Lady Tabitha, who was having a cocktail at the cabin bar. "We're heroes."

"Are you a Timerman?" I asked her fat husband.

Mason glanced out the cabin door to see if Lady Chelsea or Lord Newsome were listening in the hallway. He would rather not have discussed the question even in front of his wife.

"No," he grinned. "Morals charges, as you call them, kept me out. Plus you have to be an engineer or some sort of scientist. You remember how I did in school, Bobby. Fat chance that was going to happen. I did some favors for our mutual friend Doctor Murrey. That's all."

"He in return provided you with a wife," I dared to guess. "Being married got you back into your family's good graces, and into Fitz's government. You're the reason Murrey knew Buck and I would agree to kill the Consul."

"Something like that," said Mason.

"You were Murrey's spy all along. He had you betray the conspirators as well, after you had brought scores of others into the plot."

"Isn't it funny," he said and opened the door for me to leave, "how you and I are the last of the *Basileis*? The rich kid without any discernable talents and the lowborn engineer. Who would have predicted that?"

Our zeppelin steered a southeastern course far from Neapolis. Were we to have flown near that ill-conceived city on that flight we would have seen the entire settlement in flames. Before the fighting there would end the Uzbekis would swarm over the House Karl positions and leave very few of the mobile units in Pandemonium standing. The Panslavic workers would smash through the fighting surrounding them and make a remarkable overland journey to their homeland in the Urals.[13] When a Yukon rescue party reached the razed city ten days later they found some fifteen hundred House Karls barricaded into four adjoining walled gardens. The herdsmen camped west of the city had taken in their tents and vanished into the high desert. Only the old city of Samarkand south of the river was left undestroyed in what had once briefly been the capital of the world.

---

13. This epic journey is the subject of Garnet Grace Sheridan's *The Incredible Escape* (Frontier Press; Grand Harbor, 2538).

THE MILITARY POLICE in Sydney detained me after we landed in that city. I was in a Blue Jacket brig house for four short hours while two men from military intelligence questioned me about what had happened in central Asia. I told them the story Mason had invented: as nearly as I could tell, some of the House Karls had killed Fitz, and I had saved Lady Joan. The two men did not press me very hard. I recall my time in the brig's interrogation room with them as more a matter of them filling out the proper forms regulations demanded than of me being accused of anything.

When they released me, the senior of my two interrogators said there was another gentleman I had to see before I left the building. He led me into a side office in which Dr. Murrey was seated on a chaise lounge. The professor was in a dapper blue suit and high starched collar and was toying with the head of his duck's head cane, a habit of his he had displayed at the junior oral exams twelve years before. The intelligence officer shut the door and left the two of us alone.

"Here you are, General Bruce, no more worries for you," he said and extended his hand.

I chose not to take it, and sat in a straight backed chair opposite him.

"Don't pout, sir," he said. "You are too young to be disappointed. You have much to please you, young man. You have a pretty, spirited wife who is as dotty for you as you are for her. You are alive and in good health. You have a position higher than your family could have ever hoped for. To crown everything, I am about to tell you the last secret of the world."

"Hood already told me two," I said. "The first is that the Yukons can never lose a war. The second is that we will one day have to lose; our guilt will bring us down."

"What guilt?" laughed Dr. Murrey. "Way back when I asked you that question during the oral exams, I could tell you were not cut out to be a Timerman. Oh, you're smart enough, more than brave enough to make the grade. Your problem is that only a few weaklings among the Yukons feel any guilt—call it 'regrets' or 'shame' or whatever you wish. The great majority of our country-men believe the beautiful lies History tell them. None of the Timer-men regret anything.

"No, Brigadier Bruce, the last and only secret of the world, the thing that lets the Timerman keep the Yukons in the first stage of civilization and never will allow the Confederacy to pass into empire and decadence is this: rigorists always win. I do not need to adorn that truth. The great Arab Historian[1] might have said: 'The faction that maintains its solidarity of purpose always is the victor.' The Roman Republic beats mercantile and superstitious Carthage, hungry barbarians beat degenerate imperial Rome, Mongols beat decadent Sung China, Roundheads beat Cavaliers, fire-breathing abolitionists beat genteel southerners, Bolsheviks beat moderate Russian reformers, and Yukons beat Americans. Rigorists always win."

"So?" I said.

"So, keeping the Yukons rigorous is the job of the Timermen. Now, you commoners present us no problem. None at all. Your families, your clans, your guilds, your schools, your military tradi-tions, your advanced religiosity, your love of craftsmanship and of the land: all that keeps you in line and on your toes. Only electric-ity, foreign ideas, poverty, or wealth could corrupt the commoners, and we keep you from all four. The criminal class, the fallen chumps without families, they're even less of a problem. Knock 'em in the head, lock 'em up, or put them in special groups such as the I.T. and the S.A. where they can at least have the hope of life on Easy Street, and they are effectively controlled. There are never very many of the lumpen devils anyway. The upper classes and those with some outstanding talent or flaw, now, they give us all our headaches. Wealth and power ruin the best of them after a time.

---

1. Presumably Ibn Kaldun.

They have to be skimmed off every so often, like cream from milk. No. That's an inappropriate metaphor."

He fell silent for a few seconds and fingered his duck's head cane as he thought.

"Like extracting poison from a wound," he said. "Yes, that's better. Like what you have done to Fitz and his circle."

"You didn't get all the poison," I said. "Lady Chelsea and Lord Newsome have survived."

"They will complete the process Fitz began," said Murrey. "He tried to change the Confederacy into an empire. She will attempt to cause a revolution. The Chrysanthemum Woman will establish a gloriously evil court in Cumberland after her husband becomes the new Consul. Every blue-blooded thief, every well-born pervert, every thug with a grievance against the world, all the misunderstood artists and thinkers, anyone who longs for what they think is progress: they all will come to her and have a place in her court. She will drain the Treasury, kill some nobles and wealthy commoners for their property, and scandalize the churchmen until the commoners overthrow her. The Yukons will wreak a terrible vengeance upon her and her followers, and reestablish the old order by electing new Lords who follow the old ways. Life will then go on as before you and Fitz were born."[2]

"Then what?" I asked.

"Then in a few hundred years the new noble families will become as corrupt as the old ones are today. The Timermen of that age will have to deal with them. The story will repeat itself. In a few thousand years of these repeating cycles, the rest of the world will be beaten down till they are as primitive as cavemen. We may then let the Yukons have electricity again—or maybe not. But be assured, Sir Robert, the Yukon Confederacy will go on and will never change very much from what it has always been."

"Don't the deaths of all those people haunt you?" I asked. "In the end, how can the Timerman not feel any guilt?"

"People die. That's History. Some die sooner; some die later. That makes the story interesting. You should be grateful to the Timermen, General Bruce."

---

2. Bruce's defenders have pointed to this paragraph as proof of his reliability, as it correctly states the History of the Confederacy after Fitzpatrick's death. These defenders fail to note that Bruce wrote this long after the Chrysanthemum Woman's fall, and he

"Grateful?"

"Absolutely. We Timermen, the real Timermen—not spies like that odious Mason or special necessary cases like your sweet wife—we have to spend five years on an island in the Pacific during our time of early training. I won't tell you the island's name or location; I will tell you the Storm Machines over that small section of the globe are turned off. We have electricity there—"

"This is the Big Island in the Sandwich Chain, isn't it?" I asked. "You launch your spaceships and satellites from there?"

"So you've heard the stories," he laughed. "No, we have to be discreet, General Bruce: I say neither yes or no. As I was saying, on this unnamed island we have the complete archives of the Electronic Era. As you may suspect, General Bruce, those times were not quite as terrible as we paint them. Oh, there were those alive then who thought they were living in the worst portion of History. Everyone in every era thinks that. Most of the really terrible things happened only after we Timermen released the pulse weapons on the black market in 2047. That is when Bartholomew Iz and the Yellowjackets came along. Although there were unhealthy trends before 2047, Sir Robert. Trends that had to be corrected. There were machines that made some people superfluous. Other machines that could kill people on their own initiative. People were sentimental, as we are today. But back then they had become disconnected from the sources of their sentiments; I mean their traditions, their beliefs. They were losing themselves, really. The small, particular things and places were all going away, all becoming part of an homogenized whole. Every city was the same city. Every man the same man. So the Timermen first built the pulse weapons, then the Storm Machines and the Blinking Stars, and we put an end to those trends. Nor can we allow the Yukons to devolve back to a condition similar to that prevailing during electronic times. If we had let you be born into an electronic world you, Sir Robert, would be a humbled nonentity doing meaningless work in an office containing a hundred other drudges doing similarly meaningless labor. You would be pushed around in small ways by everyone in authority, married to a man-hating shrew, afraid of being attacked on the streets, and insulted by everything you saw, read, or heard. Instead, look at you: a Double Knight, a hero, the lover of a woman who adores you, an actor in an epic chapter of History. You are Sir Brigadier General Robert Mayfair Bruce, and not a frightened, harassed nobody. Be happy in the life we have given you, sir, and fare well in this heroic world."

"Don't any of you hope for anything better?" I asked him. "Do you really only want the Yukons to go on, generation after generation, abusing the rest of humanity?"

"Oh, Sir Robert," he said as he slowly pulled himself up with his walking stick, "you make the common error of thinking History is guided by an arrow pointed in only one direction. Your background in applied science has led you to think somehow the world can be improved over time in the way science builds up knowledge one age after another. History, as I say, is no more than what happens. Sometimes this occurs. Sometimes that. There are no laws that govern History. No goal toward which it proceeds. Now, we in the Timermen happen to like what has been happening for the past three hundred years. That is reason enough for us to continue carrying on as we have been. Good day to you, sir."

He left the small room, never to enter my life again. The senior intelligence officer came for me, and led me out the front door of the Blue Jacket building. Charlotte and our two daughters were waiting for me outside at the bottom of the short but wide cement steps, all three of them anxious for my safety.

\* \* \*

I would never again have an active duty promotion in the Army. I soon left the engineers and transferred to the Second Army commanded by General Montrose. There I commanded the Twenty-Ninth Mounted Infantry in the desert country bordering northern Mexico. For twenty-three years I made patrols in the jagged hills and dry canyons; I captured a few smugglers and rescued several hundred peasants who were lost in that desolate land. I never again fired a gun in anger or allowed any of my men to do so, either. Any Mexicans we found in the desert were given water and provisions and allowed to return to their home south of the Grand River. During my time in the southwest I became good friends with Daddy Montrose and his foster son, James Revenge Hood,[3] who at eighteen went to the War College and at twenty-five became Montrose's Chief of Staff. General Montrose seven times sent a recommendation for promotion on my behalf to the Senate while I was under his command. I was known in that august body only as the

---

3. Later Lord Hood (2415–2537), the future Consul of the Confederacy.

late Lord Fitzpatrick's friend, a designation that carried no weight in the new government. Seven times the Senate chose to ignore Montrose's recommendations in my favor.

In 2450, at the age of fifty-five, I resigned my position and returned to the family farm in Astoria, Columbus. There I have lived on my pension while managing six hundred acres of my family's farmland. The Senate reduced my general's pension to a sergeant major's in 2452, when they deemed it unseemly for a Roman Catholic to have ever held an officer's rank. I returned to active duty one last time in 2453 during the Campaign of Revolt. Later that same year, Lord Hood granted me a lieutenant general's pension and named me a Hero of the Confederacy and added my name to the lists kept on the bronze plates inside the National Cathedral in Cumberland.

Charlotte had her six children: Mary, Joan, Jessie, Rebecca, Sarah, and our son Winifred. She raised our daughters to be "mice" who would love and dominate their husbands as thoroughly as their mother had hers. She helped Winnie to become strong enough to endure his sisters. My wife had the pleasure of helping her daughters select their grooms, and arranged a romantic assignation for Winnie and Sarah's best friend Allison McKay, a young woman who is now our daughter-in-law. We have eighteen grandchildren and twenty-one great grandchildren, so far. At ninety-three, Charlotte is as she always was, and I am beginning to give up hope of ever changing her.

The old sailor French lived with us for thirty-nine more years as my adopted uncle. Today he is buried in the family cemetery above the Columbia River, although his name lives on as the given name of one of my grandchildren.

Lady Joan Fitzpatrick lived a quiet life after her husband's death. In 2435 a Chinese naturalist discovered a population of Siberian Tigers north of the Amur River in Manchurian territory. Lady Joan paid the government in Shenyang twenty million pounds to establish a refuge in the area and to name it the Winifred Pularski Preserve. She lived in exile on the island of Sakhelin, which was as close as a Yukon could live to the reserve. She would write another History book in the last years of her life, and died tragically young at age eighty-one.

As Dr. Murrey predicted, the Shays became the most hated government in Yukon History after Lord Newsome became Consul in 2427. Actual power belonged to his irrepressible, cunning wife,

Lady Chelsea, whom History knows as the notorious Chrysanthe-mum Woman. She formed a court that refined the arts of institu-tionalized theft and murder to near perfection. Her most famous mode of operation was to make false accusations against property owners, have her phony courts sentence the accused to death, and seize the belongings of her victims after the sentences were deliv-ered. She printed counterfeit foreign money and smuggled it abroad to buy gold to finance her lavish government spending. Her public works projects were all frauds she and her family raided to gain yet more capital for the Lady's schemes. Parents still frighten naughty children with tales of the Chrysanthemum Woman and of how she branded the corpses of her victims with the Shay family seal after she had murdered them.

Lord Mason remained Foreign Minister in the new court and grew fatter and more perverse as he aged. His wealth likewise grew and grew until his patroness Lady Chelsea likewise took close no-tice. In 2440, when he was forty-six, he and his wife Lady Tabitha were strangled while they slept and had the Chrysanthemum branded on their foreheads and their fortunes were seized by Lady Chelsea. Lord and Lady Mason were not, I scarce need to report, sleeping in the same bed at the time of their deaths.

After twenty-six years of misrule, the Confederacy revolted against the Shays. In June of 2453, the year of the Campaign of Revolt, the Second Army, led by an aged General Montrose and a young General James Hood, marched on the capital in Cumberland. The Consul's forces of former House Karls were helpless before the rebels, for the Timermen had given control of the Blinking Stars to the Army and allowed young Hood an easy victory. Lady Chelsea and Lord Newsome fled the capital at the approach of the rebels. They were soon captured in Virginia and brought back to Cum-berland to be impaled before the Senate Hall.

"I should have married Fitzpatrick," were the Lady's last cryp-tic words before the executioners drove the stake into her.

The young General Hood, soon to be Lord Hood and the Consul until 2503, sent the nobles, henchmen, and scoundrels of Lady Chelsea's court back to their various homes in the provinces. These outcasts lived in their villages and hometowns for three months and hoped they had been forgotten and forgiven for their excesses. On October 12, 2453, now forever known as Vengeance Night, their neighbors and fellow clan members took all 102,128 of the former Shay lieges and associates to village greens across the Confederacy and beneath chilly autumn skies slaughtered Lady Chelsea's followers like sheep brought to the butcher. The lands of the dead were divided equally among the nation's clans, and new nobles were elected to fill the vacancies in the Senate. In my village, the Redadine clan elected Luke Churchman Prim-Jones, the son of the Lord I had been born under, to be the new Lord of Astoria. On the day he heard this happy news, the young man set aside the carpenter's tools he had inherited from his father and went to live once more in his ancestors' mansion.

In the aftermath of the revolt the Confederacy became the country it had been when I was young. The I.T. shrank to a fleet of twenty sailing ships that carry a few luxury items and some biomass to foreign lands, and thus provide the only contact we have with other nations. Most Yukon families live on farms, as they ever have. The Lords hunt foxes and wild boar for their recreation. The women have tea at three o'clock in the afternoon and arrange musical programs for summer evenings. The United Yukon Church again dominates the nation's moral life. A few years ago, we waged another small, victorious war against a Mexican bandit, exactly as we had done in the days of my youth and many times before that.[4]

December 9, Fitz's birthday, is today a national holiday. A forty-foot bronze statue of Lord Fitzpatrick the Younger stands facing the Senate Hall in Cumberland to honor him. Fitz is there depicted as a medieval knight dressed in full armor. His figure bravely slices a fifteen-foot broadsword through the humid Cumberland air. The four continents he conquered lie symbolically at his feet: a dragon that signifies east Asia, a llama for South America, a camel for Moslem Europe and the Middle East, and a lion for Africa. The golden myth that Dr. Gerald and Miss Collins wrote for him has become the Confederacy's memory of my former friend. He is in the minds of his countrymen the good Consul followed by the evil Chrysanthemum Woman, much as Richard the Lionheart was followed by King John in the legends of another time. Fitz is the Yukon Alexander, the founder of the string of air bases that still prevent other peoples from building air forces and navies to challenge the Confederacy in any manner. When the statue was erected in 2429 the plaque on its platform read:

---

4. In 2489 the Yukon Army defeated the forces of Juan Carlos Sedonia.

LORD ISAAC PROPHET FITZPATRICK, 2394–2427
CONSUL OF THE YUKON CONFEDERACY 2419–2427
CONQUEROR OF THE WORLD AT AGE 29
TAKEN BY GOD AT AGE 32

In 2454 Lord Hood had the following added:

**EVERY ONE THAT DOETH EVIL IS GOOD IN THE SIGHT OF THE
LORD, AND HE DELIGHTS IN THEM.**[5]

\*     \*     \*

That, I must say, is not where I wish to end the story. I would rather end this narrative in those moments after I left the Blue Jacket brig in Sydney and went down the steps to Charlotte. She was worried for me and at the same time was scolding me for not telling her everything I knew while we were still in Neapolis. Our two daughters were trying to take my hand and were fighting each other as they climbed up the stairs to get to me first. I had to pick both of them up before I could hear anything Charlotte was saying to me. That is where I will end. Charlotte and her children were the better portions of my life, and I would rather give my reader that small scene of them on the steps with me than any of the terrible scenes I participated in during my early years. Perhaps the reader will look upon my family and believe I did at least one good thing in those times, and if the reader cannot forgive the rest of what I did, he will concede I was not entirely a monster, but merely an ordinary man who did horrible things.

---

5. Malachi 2:17.

# Editor's Afterword

I have withheld comment throughout most of Chapter Nineteen and the Epilogue because I wished the reader to absorb both the full extent of Bruce's lies and of his supposed self-confessed misdeeds. There hardly needs to be an explanation why Bruce's Liege Lord refused to publish his book when the old man presented it to him. Bruce here claims he murdered one of the most beloved individuals in Yukon History, an act of treason—if he had in fact did what he confesses to have done—for which he should have rightfully been impaled. Telling such an extravagant tale should have satisfied the worst of liars. But not Sir Robert. He adds to this fantasy of his by casting dispersions upon that most benign of organizations, the Timermen.

Bruce is, as the reader will have already decided, making all of this up out of whole cloth. Gerald avers there was a dispute at Neapolis between the Uzbekis and the rowdy House Karls that grew into a full-scale battle.[1] Ever the peacemaker, Fitzpatrick the Younger attempted to put an end to this dispute and was tragically killed in the melee. Dr. Gerald worked within a great university system, his work was vetted and fact-checked by other members of his faculty, and his book underwent peer review immediately before its publication, as happens to all true History texts. Bruce, on the other hand, is a disappointed man making unsubstantiated claims. To favor Bruce's account over that of Dr. Gerald is to favor fiction over

---

1. Pages 6903–78.

all of official History. Some false scholars have made much of the fact that his account agrees with Lord Mason's smutty memoirs, but then Bruce admits he and the disgusting Mason conspired to make up a story when they were fleeing from Asia. That their books agree merely means they both falsified History.

In regards to the nonsense Bruce writes about the Timermen we only need to recall that the Senate has on five separate occasions conducted investigative hearings upon that organization, and on each occasion the Senate has found that guild to be a fraternal society primarily concerned with advancing the Confederacy's understanding of science.[2] Out of patriotic zeal the Timermen operate and maintain the Blinking Star satellites and the antielectrical Storm Machines from a secret base in the Pacific Ocean. In doing these tasks, the Timermen function much as an irregular third branch of the military in coordination with the Army and the Navy. As in the regular branches of the military, "a certain level of secrecy must be maintained for the organization to function as it should."[3] It is this rightful level of security the Timermen shroud themselves within that has long caused certain irresponsible people such as Bruce to speculate about this very special group of chosen men. Few speculators have, I must say, been as irresponsible as Bruce is in his memoirs. According to him, the Timermen are some manner of sinister conspiracy that is managing the affairs of the Confederacy and through the Confederacy the entire world. We know this cannot be true, for otherwise our lives would have no meaning. Were Bruce writing the truth, our labors, our wars, and our sacrifices would take place simply to sustain the Timermen's rule.

The root of Bruce's lies can be found in the despair he must have felt on account of his aborted career. To have been a confidant of one of the greatest Consuls while he was still a young man and then to have passed the remainder of his life in relative obscurity must have been devastating to his fragile sense of self. The other factor contributing to the decay of Bruce's personality was the influence his oversexed wife had upon him. This unnatural woman, who had even less social status and formal education than her husband, turned Bruce—as he readily admits—against Fitzpatrick the

2. In 2145–46, in 2289, in 2301–2302, in 2410, and in 2580.

3. From the Senate report of 2580.

Younger and against all that is finest in Yukon culture. Any fair reader of this text will select this defiant woman to be the greatest villain in the book, and those same fair-minded readers must be angered to know she—like her husband—died of old age before she could be granted the punishment she so greatly deserved.

In the March 2575 edition of *The Confederacy Today* weekly magazine, an article by John Rafterry Cather gives us an insight into the deterioration Bruce's mind and personality suffered in the last decades of his life. Mr. Cather located a fisherman in Astoria named Edward Tolde whose family knew Sir Robert a hundred years earlier. I think I only need to quote the simple fisherman as he speaks in the article to give us an accurate picture of what sort of man Bruce was. I will conclude my commentary with what Tolde said to Cather, which speaks for itself:

Sir Robert was a peculiar sort of chap in the village, sir. I mean to say, he was more approachable and kinder to people than you would think a man of his position would be. He had his general's pension when he was old, and he and his wife always sent off a portion of what they got each month to an orphanage in Grand Harbor or else they gave to anybody in the village they thought needed some help. His family didn't starve; they just never lived like they could have. Some people in Astoria took advantage of him, to tell the truth. They begged him for money. The old boy didn't care. He helped everybody. Once a village girl had a baby out of wedlock; instead of sending the baby girl away to be raised by the church like usually happens, Sir Robert and his wife Charlotte adopted the baby as their child.[4] They weren't the girl's—I mean the young mother—they weren't her blood relatives or anything. They went so far as to let the real mother come to their house and see the child any time she wished. The Bruces were different like that.

Unlike the other old men in town, Sir Robert never told stories of the fighting he did. When he talked about the Army at all he said things that would've gotten anybody else who wasn't a general or a Double Knight in a bunch of

---

4. This probably would be Bruce's youngest daughter Sarah. There is no record, however, of her adoption, as the Bruces seem to have raised the child as their own.

trouble. He told the boys in the village they should try to avoid serving in a combat unit. If they couldn't, he said they should fire their weapons over the enemies' heads because if they ever killed anybody they'd feel haunted the rest of their lives. Unlike the other old men, he never wore his military decorations on national holidays. The one time the local Lord asked him to speak on Lord Fitzpatrick's birthday, Sir Robert told him he wouldn't do it because the world would've been better had Lord Fitzpatrick the Younger never been born.

For all the great things people in the area said Sir Robert had done, he was a sad old man. My uncle Samuel said the old man would sit on a rock down by the ocean and look out at the water for hours on end. Of course it rains practically every day in Astoria. Sir Robert would sit on his rock in the rain, looking out at the sea. He'd stay there until his wife came for him. They say she was the only one could approach him when he was in one of those blue funks of his.

A strange story I know about him: one spring we had on the beach south of town a Nipponese fishing boat wash up on shore. You see, it was a sailing ship with a crew of nine and full of salmon the yellow bastards had been catching in our waters! A bunch of local fishermen went down there to where the foreign boat was and were going to give those thieves a taste of rough justice, but Sir Robert—and he was nearly ninety then—he drove his steam car down there and put himself between the crowd of Yukons and the beached ship—I mean he got right into the surf. He told the men from the village they would have to kill him before they could get to the men in the boat. What could they do? He was a Double Knight and just about the most famous man in our little community. He paid the local fishermen— get this—for the salmon the Nipponese had taken. Then he paid to have a tug pull the boat off the shore. He even paid to give the foreign sailors fresh food and water for their trip home. My uncle said he didn't know which bunch of men was more amazed with what he did; the Yukons or the Nipponese. To top everything, after the fishing boat was gone Sir Robert told the men on the beach they were better men for letting the foreigners go unharmed and they would think well of themselves when they got to be his age.

Oh, one more thing: they say that as sad as Sir Robert sometimes got, he was that happy when he was with his wife or his kids. This is a true thing, but you probably can't print it in your story: one time he and his Mrs. were walking home from church—I mean their church; they were of the old religion, you know—and it was an Easter Sunday and all the town was dressed to the nines, and people were out on Main Street talking to each other. Right there, in the middle of town, right in front of everybody, Sir Robert—I'm telling the truth here—he takes his wife's hand and kisses her palm. Then he kisses the other palm. Right in front of the whole town. Then she kissed his hands. Well, I guess if he hadn't been a Double Knight the local Lord would have had the both of them arrested. They say everybody told stories about it for months afterward. People said he and she even danced together at night in their home. Not that anybody in my family ever peeked in their windows. That's just what people in the village said. They were strange old people."[5]

---

5. *The Confederacy Today,* "The Eccentric Knight of Astoria," March 2575, pp. 120–22.